The
Robinson Crusoe
Trilogy

The Robinson Crusoe Trilogy

Together With the Adventures of the
Real Robinson Crusoe, Alexander Selkirk

4 Books in One Special Edition

The Life and Adventures of Robinson Crusoe,
The Farther Adventures of Robinson Crusoe,
and Serious Reflections of Robinson Crusoe
Daniel Defoe

The Story of Alexander Selkirk
Samuel Griswold Goodrich

LEONAUR

The
Robinson Crusoe
Trilogy
Together With the Adventures of the Real Robinson Crusoe, Alexander Selkirk
4 Books in One Special Edition
The Life and Adventures of Robinson Crusoe, The Farther Adventures of Robinson
Crusoe, and Serious Reflections of Robinson Crusoe
by Daniel Defoe
The Story of Alexander Selkirk
by Samuel Griswold Goodrich

First published under the titles
The Life and Adventures of Robinson Crusoe, The Farther Adventures of Robinson
Crusoe, Serious Reflections of Robinson Crusoe
and
The Story of Alexander Selkirk

FIRST EDITION

Leonaur is an imprint
of Oakpast Ltd

ISBN: 978-1-78282-164-9 (hardcover)
ISBN: 978-1-78282-165-6 (softcover)

http://www.leonaur.com

Publisher's Notes

The views expressed in this book are not necessarily
those of the publisher.

Contents

The Life and Adventures of Robinson Crusoe,
The Farther Adventures of Robinson Crusoe,
and Serious Reflections of Robinson Crusoe

Contents

PART 1

Life and Adventures of Robinson Crusoe

I was born in the year 1632, in the city of York, of a good family, though not of that country, my father being a foreigner of Bremen, who settled first at Hull: he got a good estate by merchandise, and leaving off his trade, lived afterwards at York; from whence he had married my mother, whose relations were named, a very good family in that country, and from whom I was called Robinson Kreutznaer; but, by the usual corruption of words in England, we are now called— nay, we call ourselves, and write our name—Crusoe; and so my companions always called me.

I had two elder brothers, one of whom was lieutenant-colonel to an English regiment of foot in Flanders, formerly commanded by the famous Colonel Lockhart, and was killed at the battle near Dunkirk against the Spaniards. What became of my second brother I never knew, any more than my father or mother did know what was become of me.

Being the third son of the family, and not bred to any trade, my head began to be filled very early with rambling thoughts; my father, who was very ancient, had given me a competent share of learning, as far as house education and a country free-school generally go, and designed me for the law; but I would be satisfied with nothing but going to sea; and my inclination to this led me so strongly against the will, nay, the commands of my father, and against all the entreaties and persuasions of my mother and other friends, that there seemed to be something fatal in that propensity of nature, tending directly to the life of misery which was to befall me.

My father, a wise and grave man, gave me serious and excellent counsel against what he foresaw was my design. He called me one morning into his chamber, where he was confined by the gout, and expostulated very warmly with me upon this subject: he asked me what reasons, more than a mere wandering inclination, I had for leaving my father's house and my native country, where I might be well introduced, and had a prospect of raising my fortune by application and industry, with a life of ease and pleasure. He told me it was men of desperate fortunes on one hand, or of aspiring, superior fortunes on the other, who went abroad upon adventures, to rise by enterprise, and make themselves famous in undertakings of a nature out of the common road; that these things were all either too far above me, or too far below me; that mine was the middle state, or what might be called the upper station of low life, which he had found, by long experience, was the best state in the world, and the most suited to human happiness; that the middle station of life was calculated for all kind of virtues and all kind of enjoyments; that peace and plenty were the handmaids of a middle fortune; that temperance, moderation, quietness, health, society, all agreeable diversions, and all desirable pleasures, were the blessings attending the middle station of life; that this way men went silently and smoothly through the world, and comfortably out of it, not embarrassed with the labours of the hands or of the head, not sold to a life of slavery for daily bread, or harassed with perplexed circumstances, which rob the soul of peace, and the body of rest.

After this, he pressed me earnestly, and in the most affectionate manner, not to play the young man, nor to precipitate myself into miseries which nature, and the station of life I was born in, seemed to have provided against; that as he would do very kind things for me if I would stay and settle at home as he directed, so he would not have so much hand in my misfortunes, as to give me any encouragement to go away: and to close all, he told me I had an elder brother for an example, to whom he had used the same earnest persuasions to keep him from going into the Low Country wars, but could not prevail, his young desires prompting him to run into the army, where he was killed; and though he said he would not cease to pray for me, yet he would venture to say to me, that if I did take this foolish step, God would not bless me, and I should have leisure hereafter to reflect upon having neglected his counsel, when there might be none to assist in my recovery.

I observed in this last part of his discourse, which was truly prophetic, though I suppose my father did not know it to be so himself, the tears run down his face very plentifully, especially when he spoke of my brother who was killed; and that when he spoke of my having leisure to repent, and none to assist me, he was so moved that he broke off the discourse, and told me his heart was so full he could say no more to me.

I was sincerely affected with this discourse, as indeed who could be otherwise? and I resolved not to think of going abroad any more, but to settle at home according to my father's desire. But, alas! a few days wore it all off; and, in short, to prevent any of my father's further importunities, in a few weeks after, I resolved to run quite away from him. However, I did not act quite so hastily as the first heat of my resolution prompted, but I took my mother, at a time when I thought her a little pleasanter than ordinary, and told her that my thoughts were so entirely bent upon seeing the world, that I should never settle to anything with resolution enough to go through with it, and my father had better give me his consent than force me to go without it; that I was now eighteen years old, which was too late to go apprentice to a trade, or clerk to an attorney; that I was sure, if I did, I should never serve out my time, but I should certainly run away from my master before my time was out, and go to sea; and if she would speak to my father to let me go one voyage abroad, if I came home again, and did not like it, I would go no more; and I would promise, by a double diligence, to recover the time that I had lost.

This put my mother into a great passion; she told me she knew it would be to no purpose to speak to my father upon any such subject; and that, if I would ruin myself, there was no help for me; but I might depend I should never have their consent to it; and I should never have it to say that my mother was willing when my father was not.

Though my mother refused to name it to my father, yet I heard afterwards that she reported all the discourse to him, and that my father, after showing a great concern at it, said to her, with a sigh, "That boy might be happy if he would stay at home; but if he goes abroad, he will be the most miserable wretch that ever was born; I can give no consent to it."

It was not till almost a year after this that I broke loose, though, in the meantime, I continued obstinately deaf to all proposals of settling to business, and frequently expostulated with my father and mother about their being so positively determined against what they knew my inclinations prompted me to. But being one day at Hull, whither I went casually, and without any purpose of making an elopement at that time, and one of my companions going by sea to London in his father's ship, and prompting me to go with them, with the common

13

allurement of a seafaring man, that it should cost me nothing for my passage, I consulted neither father nor mother any more, nor so much as sent them word of it; but leaving them to hear of it as they might, without asking God's blessing or my father's, without any consideration of circumstances or consequences, and in an ill hour, God knows, on the 1st of September, 1651, I went on board a ship bound for London. The ship was no sooner got out of the Humber, than the wind began to blow and the sea to rise in a most frightful manner; and, as I had never been at sea before, I was most inexpressibly sick in body, and terrified in mind. I began now seriously to reflect upon what I had done, and how justly I was overtaken by the judgment of Heaven for my wicked leaving my father's house, and abandoning my duty.

All this while the storm increased, and the sea went very high, though nothing like what I have seen many times since; no, nor what I saw a few days after; but it was enough to affect me then, who was but a young sailor, and had never known anything of the matter. I expected every wave would have swallowed us up, and that every time the ship fell down, as I thought it did, in the trough or hollow of the sea, we should never rise more: in this agony of mind, I made many vows and resolutions, that if it would please God to spare my life in this one voyage, if ever I got once my foot upon dry land again, I would go directly home to my father, and never set it into a ship again while I lived.

These wise and sober thoughts continued all the while the storm lasted, and indeed some time after; but the next day the wind was abated, and the sea calmer, and I began to be a little inured to it; however, I was very grave for all that day, being also a little sea-sick still; but towards night the weather cleared up, the wind was quite over, and a charming fine evening followed; the sun went down perfectly clear, and rose so the next morning; and having little or no wind, and a smooth sea, the sun shining upon it, the sight was, as I thought, the most delightful that ever I saw.

I had slept well in the night, and was now no more seasick, but very cheerful, looking with wonder upon the sea that was so rough and terrible the day before, and could be so calm and so pleasant in so little a time after. And now, lest my good resolutions should continue, my companion, who had enticed me away, comes to me: "Well, Bob," says he, clapping me upon the shoulder, "how do you do after it? I warrant you were frighted, wer'n't you, last night, when it blew but a capful of wind ?"

"A capful, d'you call it ?" said I; "'twas a terrible storm."

"A storm, you fool you," replies he; "do you call that a storm? Why, it was nothing at all; give us but a good ship and sea-room, and we think nothing of such a squall of wind as that; but you're but a fresh-water sailor, Bob. Come, let us make a bowl of punch, and we'll forget all that; d'ye see what charming weather 'tis now?"

To make short this sad part of my story, we went the way of all sailors; the punch was made, and I was made half-drunk with it; and in that one night's wickedness I drowned all my repentance, all my reflections upon my past conduct, all my resolutions for the future. As the sea was returned to its smoothness of surface and settled calmness by the abatement of that storm, so the hurry of my thoughts being over, my fears and apprehensions of being swallowed up by the sea being forgotten, and the current of my former desires returned, I entirely forgot the vows and promises that I made in my distress; and I had, in five or six days, got as complete a victory over my conscience as any young fellow that resolved not to be troubled with it could desire. But I was to have another trial for it still.

The sixth day of our being at sea we came into Yarmouth Roads; the wind having been contrary, and the weather calm, we had made but little way since the storm. Here we were obliged to come to an anchor, and here we lay, the wind continuing contrary, *viz.*, at south-west, for seven or eight days, during which time a great many ships from Newcastle came into the same roads, as the common harbour where the ships might wait for a wind for the river.

We had not, however, rid here so long, but we should have tided it up the river, but that the wind blew too fresh, and, after we had lain four or five days, blew very hard. However, the roads being reckoned as good as a harbour, the anchorage good, and our ground-tackle very strong, our men were unconcerned, and not in the least apprehensive of danger, but spent the time in rest and mirth, after the manner of the sea; but the eighth day, in the morning, the wind increased, and we had all hands at work to strike our top-masts, and make everything snug and close, that the ship might ride as easy as possible. By noon the sea went very high indeed, and our ship rid forecastle in, shipped several seas, and we thought once or twice our anchor had come home; upon which our master ordered out the sheet-anchor, so that we rode with two anchors ahead, and the cables veered out to the better end.

By this time it blew a terrible storm indeed; and now I began to see terror and amazement in the faces even of the seamen themselves.

The master, though vigilant in the business of preserving the ship, yet, as he went in and out of his cabin by me, I could hear him softly to himself say several times, "Lord, be merciful to us! we shall be all lost; we shall be all undone!" and the like. During these first hurries I was lying still in my cabin; but when the master himself came by me, and said we should be all lost, I was dreadfully frighted. I got up out of my cabin and looked out; but such a dismal sight I never saw: the sea ran mountains high, and broke upon us every three or four minutes; when I could look about, I could see nothing but distress round us; two ships that rid near us, we found, had cut their masts by the board, being deep laden; and our men cried out, that a ship which rid about a mile ahead of us was foundered. Two more ships, being driven from their anchors, were run out of the roads to sea, at all adventures, and that not with a mast standing. The light ships fared the best, as not so much labouring in the sea; but two or three of them drove, and came close by us, running away with only their spritsail out before the wind.

Towards evening the mate and boatswain begged the master of our ship to let them cut away the fore-mast, which he was very unwilling to do; but the boatswain protesting to him, that if he did not, the ship would founder, he consented; and when they had cut away the fore-mast, the main-mast stood so loose, and shook the ship so much, they were obliged to cut that away also, and make a clear deck.

Anyone may judge what a condition I must be in at all this, who was but a young sailor, and who had been in such a fright before at but a little. But the worst was not come yet; the storm continued with such fury, that the seamen themselves acknowledged they had never seen a worse. We had a good ship, but she was deep laden, and wallowed in the sea, so that the seamen every now and then cried out she would founder. It was my advantage in one respect that I did not know what they meant by founder, till I inquired. However, the storm was so violent, that I saw, what is not often seen, the master, the boatswain, and some others more sensible than the rest, at their prayers, and expecting every moment that the ship would go to the bottom. In the middle of the night, and under all the rest of our distresses, one of the men that had been down to see, cried out we had sprung a leak; another said, there was four feet water in the hold.

Then all hands were called to the pump. At that word, my heart, as I thought, died within me; and I fell backwards upon the side of the bed where I sat, into the cabin. However, the men roused me, and told me, that I, that was able to do nothing before, was as well able to pump as another; at which I stirred up, and went to the pump, and worked very heartily. While this was doing, the master seeing some light colliers, who, not able to ride out the storm, were obliged to slip, and run away to the sea, and would come near us, ordered a gun to be fired as a signal of distress. I, who knew nothing what they meant, thought the ship had broken, or some dreadful thing happened. In a word, I was so surprised that I fell down in a swoon. As this was a time when everybody had his own life to think of, nobody minded me, or what was become of me; but another man stepped up to the pump, and thrusting me aside with his foot, let me lie, thinking I had been dead; and it was a great while before I came to myself.

We worked on; but the water increasing in the hold, it was apparent that the ship would founder; and though the storm began to abate a little, yet as it was not possible she could swim till we might run into any port, so the master continued firing guns for help; and a light ship, who had rid it out just ahead of us, ventured a boat out to help us. It was with the utmost hazard the boat came near us, but it was impossible for us to get on board, or for the boat to lie near the ship's side, till at last the men rowing very heartily, and venturing their lives to save ours, our men cast them a rope over the stern with a buoy to it, and then veered it out a great length, which they, after much labour and hazard, took hold of, and we hauled them close under our stern, and all into their boat. It was to no purpose for them or us, after we were in the boat, to think of reaching to their own ship; so all agreed to let her drive, and only to pull her in towards shore as much as we could; and our master promised them that if the boat was staved upon shore, he would make it good to their master: so partly rowing, and partly driving, our boat went away to the northward, sloping towards the shore almost as far as Winterton Ness.

We were not much more than a quarter of an hour out of our ship till we saw her sink, and then I understood for the first time what was meant by a ship foundering in the sea. I must acknowledge I had hardly eyes to look up when the seamen told me she was sinking; for from the moment that they rather put me into the boat, than that I might be said to go in, my heart was, as it were, dead within me, partly with fright, partly with horror of mind, and the thoughts of what was yet before me.

While we were in this condition—the men yet labouring at the oar to bring the boat near the shore—we could see (when, our boat mounting the waves, we were able to see the shore) a great many people running along the strand to assist us when we should come near; but we made but slow way towards the shore; nor were we able to reach the shore, till, being past the lighthouse at Winterton, the shore falls off to the westward towards Cromer, and so the land broke off a little the violence of the wind. Here we got in, and, though not without much difficulty, got all safe on shore, and walked afterwards on foot to Yarmouth, where, as unfortunate men, we were used with great humanity, as well by the magistrates of the town, who assigned us good quarters, as by particular merchants and owners of ships, and had money given us sufficient to carry us either to London or back to Hull, as we thought fit.

But my ill fate pushed me on now with an obstinacy that nothing could resist; and though I had several times loud calls from my reason, and my more composed judgment, to go home, yet I had no power to do it.

My comrade, who had helped to harden me before, and who was the master's son, was now less forward than I. The first time he spoke to me after we were at Yarmouth, which was not till two or three days, for we were separated in the town to several quarters, his tone was altered; and, looking very melancholy, and shaking his head, he asked me how I did; and, telling his father who I was, and how I had come this voyage only for a trial, in order to go farther already; his father turning to me, with a very grave and concerned tone, "Young man," says he, "you ought never to go to sea any more; you ought to take this for a plain and visible token that you are not to be a seafaring man."

"Why, sir," said I, "will you go to sea no more?"

"That is another case," said he; "it is my calling, and therefore my duty; but as you made this voyage for a trial, you see what a taste Heaven has given you of what you are to expect if you persist. Perhaps this has all befallen us on your account, like Jonah in the ship of Tarshish. Pray," continues he, "what are you; and on what account did you go to sea ?"

Upon that I told him some of my story; at the end of which he burst out into a strange kind of passion. "What had I done," says he, "that such an unhappy wretch should come into my ship? I would not set my foot in the same ship with thee again for a thousand pounds." However, he afterwards talked very gravely to me, exhorting me to go back to my father, and not tempt Providence to my ruin; telling me I might see a visible hand of Heaven against me. "And, young man," said he, "depend upon it, if you do not go back, wherever you go, you will meet with nothing but disasters and disappointments, till your father's words are fulfilled upon you."

We parted soon after; for I made him little answer, and I saw him no more; which way he went I knew not. As for me, having some money in my pocket, I travelled to London by land; and there, as well as on the road, had many struggles with myself, what course of life I should take, and whether I should go home or go to sea.

As to going home, shame opposed the best motions that offered to my thoughts; and it immediately occurred to me how I should be laughed at among the neighbours, and should be ashamed to see, not my father and mother only, but even everybody else.

In this state of life, I remained some time, uncertain what measures to take, and what course of life to lead. An irresistible reluctance continued to going home; and as I stayed awhile, the remembrance of the distress I had been in wore off; and as that abated, the little motion I had in my desires to return wore off with it, till at last I quite laid aside the thoughts of it, and looked out for a voyage.

That evil influence which carried me first away from my father's house, whatever it was, presented the most unfortunate of all enterprises to my view; and I went on board a vessel bound to the coast of Africa; or, as our sailors vulgarly called it, a voyage to Guinea.

It was my great misfortune that in all these adventures I did not ship myself as a sailor; when, though I might indeed have worked a little harder than ordinary, yet at the same time I should have learnt the duty and office of a fore-mast man; and in time might have qualified myself for a mate or lieutenant, if not for a master. But as it was always my fate to choose for the worse, so I did here; for having money in my pocket, and good clothes upon my back, I would always go on board in the habit of a gentleman; and so I neither had any business in the ship, nor learned to do any.

It was my lot first of all to fall into pretty good company in London. I first got acquainted with the master of a ship who had been on the coast of Guinea: and who, having had very good success there, was resolved to go again: this captain taking a fancy to my conversation, which was not at all disagreeable at that time, hearing me say I had a mind to see the world, told me if I would go the voyage with him I should be at no expense; I should be his messmate and his companion; and if I could carry anything with me, I should have all the advantage of it that the trade would admit; and perhaps I might meet with some encouragement.

19

I embraced the offer; and entering into a strict friendship with this captain, who was an honest, plain-dealing man, I went the voyage with him, and carried a small adventure with me, which, by the disinterested honesty of my friend the captain, I increased very considerably; for I carried about £40 in such toys and trifles as the captain directed me to buy. This £40 I had mustered together by the assistance of some of my relations whom I corresponded with; and who, I believe, got my father, or at least my mother, to contribute so much as that to my first adventure.

This was the only voyage which I may say was successful; for I brought home five pounds nine ounces of gold-dust for my adventure, which yielded me in London, at my return, almost £300, and this filled me with those aspiring thoughts which have since so completed my ruin.

I was now set up for a Guinea trader; and my friend, to my great misfortune, dying soon after his arrival, I resolved to go the same voyage again, and I embarked in the same vessel with one who was his mate in the former voyage, and had now got the command of the ship. This was the unhappiest voyage that ever man made; for though I did not carry quite £100 of my new-gained wealth, so that I had £200 left, which I had lodged with my friend's widow, who was very just to me, yet I fell into terrible misfortunes; the first was this—our ship making her course towards the Canary Islands, or rather between those Islands and the African shore, was surprised in the grey of the morning by a Turkish rover of Sallee, who gave chase to us with all the sail she could make. We crowded also as much canvas as our yards would spread, or our masts carry to get clear; but, finding the pirate gained upon us, and would certainly come up with us in a few hours, we prepared to fight; our ship having twelve guns, and the rogue eighteen.

About three in the afternoon he came up with us, and bringing to, by mistake, just athwart our quarter, instead of athwart our stern, as he intended, we brought eight of our guns to bear on that side, and poured in a broadside upon him, which made him sheer off again, after returning our fire, and pouring in also his small shot from near two hundred men which he had on board. However, we had not a man touched, all our men keeping close. He prepared to attack us again, and we to defend ourselves; but laying us on board the next time upon our other quarter, he entered sixty men upon our decks, who immediately fell to cutting and hacking the sails and rigging. We plied them with small shot, half pikes, powder chests, and such like, and cleared our deck of them twice; but our ship being disabled, and three of our men killed and eight wounded, we were obliged to yield, and were carried all prisoners into Sallee, a port belonging to the Moors.;

The usage I had there was not so dreadful as at first I apprehended; I was kept by the captain of the rover as his proper prize, and made his slave, being young and nimble, and fit for his business. At this surprising change of my circumstances, from a merchant to a miserable slave, I was perfectly overwhelmed; and now I looked back upon my father's prophetic discourse to me, that I should be miserable and have none to relieve me, which I thought was now so effectually brought to pass, that I could not be worse; but, alas! this was but a taste of the misery I was to go through, as will appear in the sequel of this story.

As my master had taken me home to his house, so I was in hopes that he would take me with him when he went to sea again, believing that it would some time or other be his fate to be taken by a Spanish or Portugal man-of-war; and that then I should be set at liberty. But this hope of mine was soon taken away; for when he went to sea, he left me on shore to look after his little garden, and do the common drudgery of slaves about his house; and when he came home again from his cruise, he ordered me to lie in the cabin to look after the ship.

Hero I meditated nothing but my escape, and what method I might take to effect it, but found no way that had the least probability in it; so that for two years, though I often pleased myself with the imagination, yet I never had the least encouraging prospect of putting it in practice.

After about two years, an odd circumstance presented itself, which put the old thought of making some attempt for my liberty again in my head. My patron lying at home longer than usual without fitting out his ship, he used, constantly, once or twice a week, sometimes oftener, if the weather was fair, to take the ship's pinnace, and go out into the road a-fishing; and, as he always took me and young Maresco with him to row the boat, we made him very merry, and I proved very dexterous in catching fish; insomuch that sometimes he would send me with a Moor, one of his kinsmen, and the youth—the Maresco, as they called him, to catch a dish of fish for him.

It happened one time, that going a-fishing in a calm morning, a fog rose so thick that, though we were not half a league from the shore, we lost sight of it; and rowing we knew not whither or which way, we laboured all day, and all the next night, and when the morning came, we found we had pulled oft' to sea instead of pulling in for the shore; and that we were at least two leagues from the shore. However, we got well in again, though with a great deal of labour and some danger.

But our patron, warned by this disaster, resolved to take more care of himself for the future; and having lying by him the long-boat of our English ship that he had taken, he resolved he would not go a-fishing any more without a compass and some provision; so he ordered the carpenter of his ship to build a little state-room, or cabin, in the middle of the long-boat, like that of a barge, with a place to stand behind it to steer, and haul home the main-sheet; and room before for a hand or two to stand and work the sails. The cabin lay very snug and low, and had in it room for him to lie, with a slave or two, and a table to eat on, with some small lockers to put in some bottles of liquor, and his bread, rice, and coffee.

We went frequently out with this boat a-fishing, and as I was most dexterous to catch fish for him, he never went without me. It happened that he had appointed to go out in this boat with two or three Moors of some distinction in that place, and for whom he had provided extraordinarily, and had therefore sent on board the boat overnight a larger store of provisions than ordinary; and had ordered me to get ready three fusees with powder and shot, which wore on board his ship, for that they designed some sport of fowling as well as fishing.

I got all things ready as he had directed, and waited the next morning; when by-and-by my patron came on board alone, and told me his guests had put off going, from some business that fell out, and ordered me, with the man and boy, as usual, to go out with the boat and catch them some fish, for that his friends were to sup at his house; and commanded that as soon as I got some fish I should bring it home to his house: all which I prepared to do.

This moment, my former notions of deliverance darted into my thoughts, for now I found I was likely to have a little ship at my command: and my master being gone, I prepared to furnish myself, not for fishing business, but for a voyage; though I knew not, neither did I so much as consider, whether I should steer—anywhere to get out of that place was my desire.

My first contrivance was to speak to this Moor, to get something for our subsistence on board; so he brought a large basket of rusk or biscuit, and three jars of fresh water, into the boat. I knew where my patron's case of bottles stood, and I conveyed them into the boat while the Moor was on shore, as if they had been there before for our master. I conveyed also a great lump of bees-wax into the boat, which weighed above half a hundredweight, with a parcel of twine or thread, a hatchet, a saw, and a hammer, all of which were of great use to us afterwards, especially the wax to make candles. Another trick I tried upon him, which he innocently came into also: his name was Ismael, which they call Muley, Or Moely; so I called to him:—"Moely," said I, "our patron's guns are on board the boat; can you not get a little powder and shot? It may be we may kill some alcamies (a fowl like our curlews) for ourselves, for I know he keeps the gunner's stores in the ship."

Accordingly he brought a great leather pouch, which held a pound and a half of powder, and another with shot, that had five or six pounds, with some bullets, and put all into the boat. At the same time, I had found some powder of my master's in the great cabin, with which I filled one of the large bottles in the case; and thus furnished with everything needful, we sailed out of the port to fish.

After we had fished some time and caught nothing, for when I had fish on my hook I would not pull them up, that he might not see them, I said to the Moor, "This will not do; our master will not be thus served; we must stand farther off." He, thinking no harm, agreed, and set the sails; and, as I had the helm, I run the boat out near a league farther, and then brought her to; when, giving the boy the helm, I stepped forward to where the Moor was, and making as if I stooped for something behind him, I took him by surprise with my arm under his waist, and tossed him clear overboard into the sea. He rose immediately, for he swam like a cork, and begging to be taken in, told me he would go all over the world with me. He swam so strong after the boat, that he would have reached me very quickly, upon which I stepped into the cabin, and fetching one of the fowling-pieces, I presented it at him, and told him I had done him no hurt, and if he would be quiet I would do him none. "But," said I, "if you come near the boat, I'll shoot you through the head, for I am resolved to have my liberty;" so he turned himself about, and swam for the shore, and I make no doubt but he reached it with ease, for he was an excellent swimmer.

When he was gone, I turned to the boy, whom they called Xury, and said to him, "Xury, if you will be faithful to me, I'll make you a great man; but if you will not stroke your face to be true to me," that is, swear by Mahomet and his father's beard, "I must throw you into the sea too." The boy smiled in my face, and spoke so innocently, that I could not distrust him, and swore to be faithful to me, and go all over the world with me.

While the Moor was swimming, I stood out directly to sea with the boat, rather stretching to windward, that they might think me gone towards the Straits' mouth (as indeed anyone that had been in their wits must have been supposed to. do); for who would have supposed we were sailed on to the southward, where whole nations of negroes were sure to surround us with their canoes, and destroy us; where we could not go on shore but we should be devoured by savage beasts, or more merciless savages of human kind?

But as soon as it grew dusk in the evening, I changed my course, and steered directly south and by east; and having a fresh gale of wind, and a smooth sea, I made such sail that I believe by the next day at three o'clock in the afternoon, when I first made the land, I could not be less than one hundred and fifty miles south of Sallee.

The wind continued fair till I had sailed in that manner five days; and then the wind shifting to the southward, I concluded also that if any of our vessels were in chase of me, they would now give over; so I ventured to make to the coast, and came to an anchor in the mouth of a little river, I knew not what, or where; I neither saw, or desired to see, any people; the principal thing I wanted was fresh water. We came into this creek in the evening, resolving to swim on shore as soon as it was dark, and discover the country; but as soon as it was quite dark, we heard such dreadful noises of the barking, roaring, and howling of wild creatures, of we knew not what kinds, that the poor boy was ready to die with fear, and begged of me not to go on shore till day.

"Well, Xury," said I, "then I won't; but it may be we may see men by day who will be as bad to us as those lions."

"Then we give them the shoot gun," says Xury, laughing, "make them run way."

I was glad to see the boy so cheerful, and I gave him a dram to cheer him up; and we dropped our little anchor, and lay still all night; I say still, for we slept none; for in two or three hours we saw vast great creatures, of many sorts, come down to the seashore and run into the water, wallowing and washing for the pleasure of cooling themselves; and they made such hideous howlings and yellings, that I never indeed heard the like.

Xury was dreadfully frighted, and indeed so was I too; but we were both more frighted when we heard one of these mighty creatures

24

come swimming towards our boat; we could not see him, but we might hear him by his blowing to be a monstrous huge and furious beast. Xury said it was a lion, and cried to me to weigh anchor and row away: "No," says I, "Xury; we can slip our cable, with the buoy to it, and go off to sea; they cannot follow us far." I had no sooner said so, but I perceived the creature within two oars' length; however, I immediately fired at him, upon which he turned about, and swam towards the shore again.

But it is impossible to describe the horrid noises, and hideous cries and howlings, that were raised upon the report of the gun. This convinced me that there was no going on shore for us in the night on that coast, and how to venture on shore in the day was another question too; for to have fallen into the hands of any of the savages had been as bad as to have fallen into the hands of lions and tigers.

Be that as it would, we were obliged to go on shore somewhere or other for water, for we had not a pint left in the boat. Xury said, if I would let him go on shore with one of the jars, he would find if there was any water, and bring some to me. I asked him why he would go? The boy answered with so much affection as made me love him ever after. "If wild mans come, they eat me, you go way."

"Well, Xury," said I, "we will both go, and if the wild mans come, we will kill them, they shall eat neither of us." So we hauled the boat in near the shore, and waded on shore, carrying nothing but our arms, and two jars for water.

I did not care to go out of sight of the boat, fearing the coming of canoes with savages down the river; but the boy seeing a low place about a mile up the country, rambled to it, and by-and-by I saw him come running towards me. I thought he was pursued by some savage, or frighted with some wild beast, and I ran forwards to help him; but when I came nearer to him, I saw something hanging over his shoulders, which was a creature that he had shot, like a hare; it was very good meat; but the great joy that poor Xury came with, was to tell me he had found good water, and seen no wild mans.

But we found afterwards that we need not take such pains for water, for a little higher up the creek we found the water fresh when the tide was out, so we filled our jars, and feasted on the hare we had killed, and prepared to go on our way, having seen no footsteps of any human creature in that part of the country.

I had no instruments to take an observation to know what latitude we were in; but my hope was, that if I stood along this coast till I came to that part where the English traded, I should find some of their vessels that would relieve and take us in.

We made on to the southward continually for ten or twelve days, living very sparingly on our provisions, which began to abate very much, and going no oftener to the shore than we were obliged for fresh water. My design in this was, to make the River Gambia or Senegal, that is to say, anywhere about the Cape de Verd, where I was in hopes to meet with some European ship.

When I had pursued this resolution about ten days longer, I began to see that the land was inhabited; and, in two or three places, as we sailed by, we saw people stand upon the shore to look at us; we could also perceive they were quite black, and naked. I was once inclined to have gone on shore to them; but Xury said to me, "No go, no go." However, I hauled in nearer the shore that I might talk to them, and I found they ran along the shore by me a good way: I observed they had no weapons in their hands, except one, who had a long slender stick, which Xury said was a lance, and that they could throw them a great way with good aim; so I kept at a distance, but talked with them by signs as well as I could; and particularly made signs for something to eat; they beckoned to me to stop my boat, and they would fetch me some meat.

Upon this, I lowered the top of my sail, and lay by, and two of them ran up into the country, and in less than half an hour came back, and brought with them two pieces of dry flesh and some corn. We were willing to accept it; but how to come at it was our next dispute, for I would not venture on shore to them, and they were as much afraid of us: but they took a safe way for us all, for they brought it to the shore and laid it down, and went and stood a great way off till we fetched it on board, and then came close to us again.

We made signs of thanks to them, for we had nothing to make them amends; but an opportunity offered that very instant to oblige them wonderfully: for while we were lying by the shore, came two mighty creatures with great fury from the mountains towards the sea. The man that had the lance or dart did not fly from them, but the rest did; however, as the two creatures ran directly into the water, they did not offer to fall upon any of the negroes, but plunged themselves into the sea, and swam about, as if they had come for their diversion: at last one of them began to come nearer our boat than at first I expected; but I lay ready for him, for I had loaded my gun with all possible expedition, and bade Xury load both the others. As soon as he came fairly within my reach, I fired, and shot him directly in the head: he immediately made to the shore, but died just before he reached it.

It is impossible to express the astonishment of these poor creatures at the noise and fire of my gun; some of them were ready to die for fear, and fell down as dead with the very terror; but when they saw the creature dead, and that I made signs to them to come to the shore, they took heart and came, and began to search for the creature. By the help of a rope, which I slung round him, and gave the negroes to haul, they dragged him on shore, and found that it was a most curious leopard, spotted, and fine to an admirable degree.

The other creature, frighted with the noise of the gun, swam on shore, and ran up directly to the mountains whence they came. I found quickly the negroes wished to eat the flesh of this creature, so I was willing to have them take it as a favour from me. They offered me some of the flesh, which I declined, pointing out that I would give it them; but made signs for the skin, which they gave me very freely, and brought me a great deal more of their provisions. I then made signs to them for some water, and held out one of my jars to them, turning it bottom upward, to show that it was empty, and that I wanted to have it filled. They called immediately to some of their friends, and there came two women, and brought a great vessel; this they set down to me, as before, and I sent Xury on shore with my jars, and filled them all three.

I was now furnished with roots, corn, and water; and leaving my friendly negroes, I made forward for about eleven days more, without offering to go near the shore. At length, doubling the point, I saw plainly land on the other side, to seaward: then I concluded that this was the Cape de Verd, and those the islands, called, from thence, Cape de Verd Islands. However, they were at a great distance, and I could not tell well what I had best to do; for if I should be taken with a fresh of wind, I might neither reach one or other.

In this dilemma, as I was very pensive, I stepped into the cabin, and sat down, Xury having the helm; when, on a sudden, the boy cried out, "Master, master, a ship with a sail!" and the foolish boy was frighted out of his wits, thinking it must be some of his master's ships sent to pursue us, but I knew we were far enough out of their reach. I jumped out of the cabin, and immediately saw that it was a Portuguese ship.

With all the sail I could make, I found I should not be able to come in their way, but that they would be gone by before I could make any signal to them; but after I had crowded to the utmost, and began to despair, they, it seems, saw, by the help of their glasses, that it was some European boat; so they shortened sail to let me come up. I was encouraged with this, and made them a signal of distress, and fired a gun, both which they saw. Upon these signals they very kindly brought to, and lay by for me and in about three hours' time I came up with them.

They asked me what I was, in Portuguese, and in Spanish, and in French, but I understood none of them; but, at last, a Scots sailor, who was on board, called to me; and I answered him, and told him I was an Englishman, that I had made my escape out of slavery from the Moors, at Sallee; they then bade me come on board, and very kindly took me in, and all my goods.

It was an inexpressible joy to me that I was thus delivered from such a miserable and almost hopeless condition; and I immediately offered all I had to the captain of the ship, as a return for my deliverance; but he generously told me he would take nothing from me, but that all I had should be delivered safe to me, when I came to the Brazils.

"No, no," says he, "*Seignor Inglese,* I will carry you thither in charity, and those things will help to buy your subsistence there, and your passage home again."

In this proposal he was just in the performance to a tittle; for he ordered the seamen, that none should touch anything that I had: then he took everything into his own possession, and gave me back an exact inventory of them.

My boat was a very good one; and he told me he would buy it. I told him, he had been so generous to me that I could not offer to make any price of the boat, but left it entirely to him: upon which he told me he would give me a note of hand to pay me eighty pieces of eight for it. He offered me also sixty pieces of eight more for my boy Xury; but I was very loath to sell the poor boy's liberty, who had assisted me so faithfully in procuring my own. However, when I let him know my reason, he owned it to be just, and offered that he would set him free in ten years, if he turned Christian: upon this, and Xury saying he was willing to go to him, I let the captain have him.

We had a very good voyage to the Brazils, and I arrived in All Saints' Bay, in about twenty-two days after. And now I was once more delivered from the most miserable of all conditions of life; and what to do next with myself I was to consider.

The generous treatment the captain gave me I can never enough remember: he would take nothing of me for my passage, gave me twenty *ducats* for the leopard's skin, and forty for the lion's skin, and caused everything I had in the ship to be punctually delivered to me; and what I was willing to sell he bought off me: in a word, I made about two hundred and twenty pieces of eight of all my cargo; and with this stock I went on shore in the Brazils.

I had not been long here before I was recommended to the house of a good honest man, who had a plantation and sugar-house. I lived with him some time, and acquainted myself with the manner of planting and making of sugar; and seeing how well the planters lived, and how they got rich suddenly, I resolved, if I could get a licence to settle there, I would turn planter: resolving, in the meantime, to find out some way to got my money, which I had left in London, remitted to me. To this purpose, getting a letter of naturalisation, I purchased as much land as my money would reach, and formed a plan for my plantation and settlement suitable to the stock which I proposed to myself to receive from England.

I had a neighbour, a Portuguese, of Lisbon, but born of English parents, whose name was Wells, and in much such circumstances as I was. My stock was low, as well as his; and we rather planted for food than anything else, for about two years. However, we began to increase, and our land began to come into order; so that the third year we planted some tobacco, and made each of us a large piece of ground ready for planting canes in the year to come: but we both wanted help; and now I found I had done wrong in parting with Xury.

But I had no remedy but to go on: I had got into an employment quite remote to my genius, and directly contrary to the life I delighted in, and for which I forsook my father's house, and broke through all his good advice.

I had nobody to converse with, but now and then this neighbour; no work to be done, but by the labour of my hands; and I used to say, I lived just like a man cast away upon some desolate island, that had nobody there but himself.

I was, in some degree, settled in my measures for carrying on the plantation, before my kind friend the captain went back; for the ship remained there nearly three months; when, telling him what little stock I had left behind me in London, he gave me this friendly and sincere advice:—"*Seignor Inglese*," says he (for so he always called me), "if you will give me letters to the person who has your money in London, to send your effects to Lisbon, to such persons as I shall direct, and in such goods as are proper for this country, I will bring you the produce of them: but I would have you give orders but for one hundred pounds sterling, which, you say, is half your stock, and let the hazard be run for the first; so that if it come safe, you may order the rest the same way; and, if it miscarry, you may have the other half to have recourse to for your supply."

This was so wholesome advice, and looked so friendly, that I could not but be convinced it was the best course I could take; so I prepared letters to the gentlewoman with whom I had left my money, and a procuration to the Portuguese captain, as he desired.

I wrote the English captain's widow a full account of all my adventures, and what condition I was now in, with all other necessary directions for my supply; and when this honest captain came to Lisbon, he found means to send over, not the order only, but a full account of my story to a merchant at London, who represented it effectually to her: whereupon she not only delivered the money, but, out of her own pocket, sent the Portugal captain a very handsome present for his humanity and charity.

The merchant in London, vesting this hundred pounds in English goods, such as the captain had written for, sent them directly to him at Lisbon, and he brought them all safe to me to the Brazils: among which he had taken care to have all sorts of tools, iron work, and utensils, necessary for my plantation, and which were of great use to me.

When this cargo arrived, I thought my fortunes made, for I was surprised with the joy of it; and my good steward, the captain, had laid out the five pounds, which my friend had sent him for a present for himself, to purchase and bring me over a servant, under bond for six years' service, and would not accept of any consideration, except a little tobacco, which I would have him accept, being of my own produce.

Neither was this all; for my goods being all English manufacture, particularly valuable in the country, I found means to sell them to a very great advantage; so that I had more than four times the value of my first cargo, and was now infinitely beyond my poor neighbour in the advancement of my plantation; for the first thing I did I bought a negro slave, and a European servant also, besides that which the captain brought me from Lisbon.

I went on the next year with great success in my plantation; I raised fifty great rolls of tobacco on my own ground, more than I had disposed of for necessaries among my neighbours , and these fifty rolls, being each of above a hundred weight, were well cured, and laid by against the return of the fleet from Lisbon; and now increasing in business and in wealth, my head began to be full of projects and undertakings beyond my reach.

To come, then, by the just degrees, to the particulars of this part of my story:—You may suppose that having now lived almost four years in the Brazils, and beginning to thrive and prosper very well upon my plantation, I had not only learned the language, but had contracted acquaintance and friendship among my fellow-planters, as well as among the merchants at St. Salvador, which was our port; and that, in my discourses among them, I had frequently given them an account of my two voyages to the coast of Guinea; the manner of trading with the negroes there, and how easy it was to purchase upon the coast for trifles—such as beads, toys, knives, scissors, hatchets, bits of glass, and the like—not only gold dust, Guinea grains, elephants' teeth, &c., but negroes, for the service of the Brazils, in great numbers.

They listened always very attentively to my discourses on these heads, but especially to that part which related to the buying negroes; which was a trade, at that time, not only not far entered into, but, as far as it was, had been carried on by the permission of the Kings of Spain and Portugal, and engrossed in the public stock; so that few negroes were bought, and those excessively dear.

It happened, being in company with some merchants and planters of my acquaintance, and talking of those things very earnestly, three of them came to me the next morning, and told me they had been musing very much upon what I had discoursed with them of the last night, and they came to make a secret proposal to me; and, after enjoining me secrecy, they told me that they had a mind to fit out a ship to Guinea; that they had all plantations as well as I, and were straitened for nothing so much as servants; that as it was a trade that could not be carried on, because they could not publicly sell the negroes when they came home, so they desired to make but one voyage, to bring the negroes on shore privately, and divide them among their own plantations; and, in a word, the question was, whether I would go their supercargo in the ship, to manage the trading part upon the coast of Guinea; and they offered me that I should have my equal share of the negroes, without providing any part of the stock.

This was a fair proposal, had it been made to anyone that had not had a settlement and a plantation of his own to look after, which was in a fair way of coming to be very considerable, and with a good stock upon it. But for me, that was thus entered and established, and had nothing to do but to go on as I had begun, for three or four years more, and to have sent for the other hundred pounds from England; and who in that time could scarce have failed of being worth three or four thousand pounds sterling, and that increasing too—for me to think of such a voyage was the most preposterous thing that ever man in such circumstances could be guilty of.

But I, that was born to be my own destroyer, could no more resist the offer than I could restrain my first rambling designs. In a word, I told them I would go with all my heart, if they would undertake to look after my plantation in my absence, and would dispose of it to such as I should direct, if I miscarried. This they all entered into covenants to do; and I made a formal will, disposing of my plantation and effects, in case of my death, making the captain of the ship that had saved my life my heir, but obliging him to dispose of my effects; one-half of the produce being to himself, and the other to be shipped in England.

In short, I took all possible caution to preserve my effects, and to keep up my plantation: had I used half as much prudence to have looked into my own interest, I had certainly never gone away from so prosperous an undertaking, upon a voyage to sea, attended with all its common hazards, to say nothing of particular misfortunes to myself.

But I was hurried on, and obeyed blindly the dictates of my fancy rather than my reason; and accordingly, the ship being fitted out, the cargo furnished, and all things done, as by agreement, by my partners in the voyage, I went on board in an evil hour, the 1st of September, 1659, being the same day eight years that I went from my father and mother at Hull.

Our ship was about one hundred and twenty tons burden, carried six guns and fourteen men, besides the master, his boy, and myself; we had on board no large cargo of goods, except of such toys as were fit for our trade with the negroes, such as beads, bits of glass, shells, and other trifles, especially little looking-glasses, knives, scissors, hatchets, and the like.

The same day I went on board we set sail, standing away to the northward upon our own coast, with a design to stretch over for the African coast. We had very good weather till we came to the height of Cape St. Augustino; whence, keeping farther off at sea, we lost sight of land, and steered as if we were bound for the isle Fernando de Noronha. In this course we passed the line in about twelve days' time, when a violent tornado, or hurricane, took us quite out of our knowledge. It blew in such a terrible manner, that for twelve days together we could do nothing but drive, and, scudding away before it, let it carry us whither ever fate and the fury of the winds directed.

In this distress we had, besides the terror of the storm, one of our men die of the calenture, and one man and the boy washed overboard. About the twelfth day, the weather abating a little, the master made an observation as well as he could, and found that he was upon the coast of Guiana, and began to consult with me what course he should take, for the ship was leaky, and very much disabled, and he was going directly back to the coast of Brazil.

I was positively against that; and looking over the charts of the sea-coast of America with him, we concluded there was no inhabited country for us to have recourse to, till we came within the circle of the Carribbee Islands, and therefore resolved to stand away for Barbadoes; which, by keeping off at sea, to avoid the in-draft of the bay or gulf of Mexico, we might easily perform, as we hoped, in about fifteen days' sail; whereas we could not possibly make our voyage to the coast of Africa without some assistance both to our ship and to ourselves.

With this design, we changed our course, in order to reach some of our English islands, where I hoped for relief; but our voyage was otherwise determined; for a second storm came upon us, which carried us away with the same impetuosity westward, and drove us so out of the way of all human commerce, that had all our lives been saved as to the sea, we were rather in danger of being devoured by savages, than ever returning to our own country.

In this distress, the wind still blowing very hard, one of our men early in the morning cried out, "Land !" and we had no sooner run out of the cabin to look out, in hopes of seeing whereabouts in the world we were, than the ship struck upon a sand, and in a moment the sea broke over in such a manner that we expected we should all have perished; and we were immediately driven into our close quarters, to shelter us from the very foam and spray of the sea.

It is not easy for anyone who has not been in the like condition to describe or conceive the consternation of men in such circumstances. We knew not where we were, or upon what land we were driven; and as the rage of the wind was still great, we could not hope to have the ship hold many minutes without breaking into pieces, unless the winds, by a kind of miracle, should turn immediately about. In a word, we sat looking upon one another, and expecting death every moment, every man preparing for another world; for there was little or nothing more for us to do in this; but, contrary to our expectation, the ship did not break yet, and the master said the wind began to abate.

Now, though we thought that the wind did a little abate, yet the ship having thus struck upon the sand, and sticking too fast for us to expect her getting off, we were in a dreadful condition indeed, and had nothing to do but to think of saving our lives as well as we could. We had a boat at our stern just before the storm, but she was first staved by dashing against the ship's rudder, and, in the next place, she broke away, and either sunk or was driven off to sea; so there was no hope from her. We had another boat on board, but how to get her off into the sea was a doubtful thing; however, there was no time to debate, for we fancied the ship would break in pieces every minute, and some told us she was actually broken already.

In this distress, the mate of our vessel laid hold of the boat, and with the help of the rest of the men, got her slung over the ship's side; and getting all into her, let go, and committed ourselves, being eleven in number, to God's mercy and the wild sea.

And now our case was very dismal indeed; for we all saw plainly, that the sea went so high, that the boat could not live, and that we should be inevitably drowned. As to making sail, we had none; so we worked at the oar towards the land, though with heavy hearts, like men going to execution; for we all knew that when the boat came nearer the shore, she would be dashed in a thousand pieces by the breach of the sea. However, we committed our souls to God in the most earnest manner; and the wind driving us towards the shore, we hastened our destruction with our own hands, pulling as well as we could towards land.

After we had rowed or rather driven about a league and a half, as we reckoned it, a raging wave, mountain-like, came rolling astern of us with such fury, that it overset the boat at once; and separating us, as well from the boat as from one another, gave us not time to say, "O God!" for we were all swallowed up in a moment.

Nothing can describe the confusion of thought which I felt, when I sank into the water: for though I swam very well, yet I could not deliver myself from the waves so as to draw breath, till that wave having driven me, or rather carried me, a vast way on towards the shore, and having spent itself, went back, and left me upon the land almost dry, but half dead with the water I took in. I had so much presence of mind, as well as breath left, that seeing myself nearer the main land than I expected, I got upon my feet, and endeavoured to make on towards the land as fast as I could, before another wave should return and take me up again: but I soon found it was impossible to avoid it; for I saw the sea come after me as high as a great hill, and as furious as an enemy, which I had no means or strength to contend with: my business was to hold my breath, and raise myself upon the water, if I could: and so, by swimming, to preserve my breathing and pilot myself towards the shore, if possible, my greatest concern now being, that the sea, as it would carry me a great way towards the shore when it came on, might not carry me back again with it when it gave back towards the sea.

The wave that came upon me again, buried me at once twenty or thirty feet deep in its own body, and I could feel myself carried with a mighty force and swiftness towards the shore a very great way; but I held my breath, and assisted myself to swim still forward with all my might. I was ready to burst with holding my breath, when, as I felt myself raising up, so, to my immediate relief, I found my head and hands shoot out above the surface of the water; and though it was not two seconds of time that I could keep myself so, yet it relieved greatly, gave me breath and new courage. I was covered again with water a good while, but not so long but I held it out; and finding the water had spent itself, and began to return, I struck forward against the return of the waves, and felt ground again with my feet. I stood still a few moments, to recover breath, and till the waters went from me, and then took to my heels and ran, with what strength I had, farther towards the shore. But neither would this deliver me from the fury of the sea, which came pouring in after me again; and twice more I was lifted up by the waves and carried forwards as before, the shore being very flat.

The last time of those two had well nigh been fatal to me; for the sea having hurried me along, as before, landed me, or rather dashed me, against a piece of a rock, and that with such force, as left me senseless, and indeed helpless, as to my own deliverance; for the blow taking my side and breast, beat the breath, as it were, quite out of my body; and had it returned again immediately, I must have been strangled in the water: but I recovered a little before the return of the waves, and seeing I should be covered again with the water, I resolved to hold fast by a piece of the rock, and so to hold my breath, if possible, till the wave went back. Now, as the waves were not so high as at first, being nearer land, I held my hold till the wave abated, and then fetched another run, which brought me so near the shore, that the next wave, though it went over me, yet did not so swallow me up as to carry me away; and the next run I took, I got to the main land; where, to my great comfort, I clambered up the cliffs of the shore, and sat me down upon the grass, free from danger, and quite out of the reach of the water.

I was now landed, and safe on shore, and began to look up and thank God that my life was saved, in a case wherein there was, some minutes before, scarce any room to hope. I believe it is impossible to express, to the life, what the ecstasies and transports of the soul are, when it is so saved, as I may say, out of the very grave.

I walked about on the shore, lifting up my hands; and my whole being, as I may say, wrapt up in a contemplation of my deliverance; making a thousand gestures and motions, which I cannot describe; reflecting upon all my comrades that were drowned, and that there should not be one soul saved but myself; for, as for them, I never saw them afterwards, or any sign of them, except three of their hats, one cap, and two shoes that were not fellows.

I cast my eyes to the stranded vessel, when, the breach and froth of the sea being so big, I could hardly see it, it lay so far off; and considered, Lord! how was it possible I could get on shore?

After I had solaced my mind with the comfortable part of my condition, I began to look round me, to see what kind of place I was in, and what was next to be done: and I soon found my comforts abate, and that I had a dreadful deliverance: for I was wet, had no clothes to shift me, nor anything either to eat or drink; neither did I see any prospect before me, but that of perishing with hunger, or being devoured by wild beasts: and that which was particularly afflicting to me was, that I had no weapon, either to hunt and kill any creature for my sustenance, or to defend myself against any other creature that might desire to kill me for theirs. In a word, I had nothing about me but a knife, a tobacco-pipe, and a little tobacco in a box. This was all my provision; and this threw me into terrible agonies of mind, that, for a while, I ran about like a madman. Night coming upon me, I began, with a heavy heart, to consider what would be my lot if there were any ravenous beasts in that country, as at night they always come abroad for their prey.

All the remedy that offered to my thoughts, at that time, was to get up into a thick bushy tree, like a fir, but thorny, which grew near me, and where I resolved to sit all night, and consider the next day what death I should die, for as yet I saw no prospect of life. I walked about a furlong from the shore, to see if I could find any fresh water to drink, which I did to my great joy; and having drunk, and put a little tobacco in my mouth to prevent hunger, I went to the tree, and getting up into it, endeavoured to place myself so as that, if I should sleep, I might not fall. And having cut a short stick, like a truncheon, for my defence, I took up my lodging; and having been excessively fatigued, I fell fast asleep, and slept as comfortably as, I believe, few could have done in my condition, and found myself more refreshed with it than I think I ever was on such an occasion.

When I waked it was broad day, the weather clear, and the storm abated, so that the sea did not rage and swell as before; but that which surprised me most was, that the ship was lifted off in the night from the sand where she lay, by the swelling of the tide, and was driven up almost as far as the rock, where I had been so bruised by the wave dashing me against it. This being within about a mile from the shore where I was, and the ship seeming to stand upright still, I wished myself on board, that at least I might save some necessary things for my use.

When I came down from the tree, I looked about me again, and the first thing I found was the boat, which lay, as the wind and sea had tossed her up, upon the land, about two miles on my right hand. I walked as far as I could upon the shore to have got to her; but found a neck, or inlet, of water between me and the boat, which was about half a mile broad; so I came back for the present, being more intent upon getting at the ship, where I hoped to find something for my present subsistence.

A little after noon I found the sea very calm, and the tide ebbed so far out, that I could come within a quarter of a mile of the ship. And here I found a fresh renewing of my grief, for I saw that if we had kept on board, we had been all safe: that is to say, we had all got safe on shore, and I had not been so miserable as to be left entirely destitute of all comfort and company, as I now was. This forced tears to my eyes again; but I resolved, if possible, to get to the ship; so I pulled off my clothes, and took the water. But when I came to the ship, my difficulty was still greater to know how to get on board; for, as she lay aground, and high out of the water, there was nothing within my reach to lay hold of. I swam round her twice, and the second time I spied a small piece of rope, which hung down by the fore-chains so low, that with great difficulty I got hold of it, and by the help of that rope I got up into the forecastle of the ship. Here I found that the ship was bulged, and had a great deal of water in her hold; but that she lay so on the side of a bank of hard sand, that her stern lay lifted up upon the bank, and her head low, almost to the water. By this means all her quarter was free, and all that was in that part was dry. First, I found that all the ship's provisions were untouched by the water. I also found some rum in the great cabin, Now I wanted nothing but a boat, to furnish myself with many things which I foresaw would be very necessary to me.

We had several spare yards, and two or three large spars of wood, and a spare top-mast or two in the ship: I resolved to fall to work with these, and I flung as many of them overboard as I could manage for their weight, tying every one with a rope, that they might not drive away. When this was done, I went down the ship's side and pulling them to me, I tied four of them together at both ends, as well as I could, in the form of a raft, and laying two or three short pieces of plank upon them, cross-ways, I found I could walk upon it very well, but that it was not able to bear any great weight, the pieces being too light. So I went to work, and with the carpenter's saw I cut a spare top-mast into three lengths, and added them to my raft, with a great deal of labour and pains. But the hope of furnishing myself with nec-essaries, encouraged me to go beyond what I should have been able to have done upon another occasion.

My raft was now strong enough to bear any reasonable weight. My next care was what to load it with, and how to preserve what I laid upon it from the surf of the sea: but I was not long considering this. I first laid all the plank or boards upon it that I could get, and having considered well what I most wanted, I got three of the seamen's chests, which I had broken open and emptied, and lowered them down upon my raft; the first of these I filled with bread, rice, three Dutch cheeses, five pieces of dried goat's flesh, and a little European corn. As for liquors, I found several cases of bottles belonging to our skipper, in which were some cordial waters; and, in all, about five or six gallons of rack. These I stowed by themselves, there being no need to put them into the chest, nor any room for them. It was after long searching that I found out the carpenter's chest, which was indeed a very useful prize to me, and much more valuable than a ship-lading of gold would have been at that time. I got it down to my raft, whole as it was, without losing time to look into it, for I knew in general what it contained.

My next care was for some ammunition and arms. There were two very good fowling-pieces in the great cabin, and two pistols. These I secured first, with some powder-horns and a small bag of shot, and two old rusty swords. There were three barrels of powder in the ship, but I knew not where our gunner had stowed them; but with much search I found two of them dry and good. Those two I got to my raft, with the arms. And now I thought myself pretty well freighted, and began to think how I should get to shore with them, having neither sail, oar, or rudder; and the least cap-full of wind would have overset all my navigation.

I had three encouragements: 1st, a smooth, calm sea; 2ndly, the tide rising and setting in to the shore; 3rdly, what little wind there was blew me towards the land. And thus, having found two or three broken oars belonging to the boat, and besides the tools which were in the chest, two saws, an axe, and a hammer; with this cargo I put to sea. For a mile, or thereabouts, my raft went very well, only that I found it drive a little distant from the place where I had landed before; by which I perceived that there was some in-draft of the water, and consequently, I hoped to find some creek or river there, which I might make use of as a port to get to land with my cargo.

As I imagined, so it was. There appeared before me a little opening of the land, and I found a strong current of the tide set into it; so I guided my raft, as well as I could, to keep in the middle of the stream.

But here I had like to have suffered a second shipwreck, which, if I had, I think, verily, would have broke my heart; for, knowing nothing of the coast, my raft ran aground at one end of it upon a shoal, and not being aground at the other end, it wanted but a little that all my cargo had slipped off towards the end that was afloat, and so fallen into the water. I did my utmost, by setting my back against the chests, to keep them in their places, but could not thrust off the raft with all my strength; neither durst I stir from the posture I was in: but holding up the chests with all my might, I stood in that manner near half an hour, in which time the rising of the water brought me a little more upon a level; and, a little after, the water still rising, my raft floated again, and I thrust her off with the oar I had into the channel, and then driving up higher, I at length found myself in the mouth of a little river, with land on both sides, and a strong current running up. I looked on both sides for a proper place to get to shore, resolved to place myself as near the coast as I could.

At length I spied a little cove on the right shore of the creek, to which, with great pain and difficulty, I guided my raft, and at last got so near, that reaching ground with my oar, I could thrust her directly in.

But here I had like to have dipped all my cargo into the sea again; for that shore lying pretty steep—there was no place to land, but where one end of my float, if it ran on shore, would lie so high, and the other sink lower, as before, that it would endanger my cargo again. All that I could do, was to wait till the tide was at the highest, keeping the raft with my oar like an anchor, to hold the side of it fast to the shore, near a flat piece of ground, which I expected the water would flow over; and so it did. As soon as I found water enough, I thrust her on upon that flat piece of ground, and there moored her, by sticking my two broken oars into the ground,—one on one side, near one end, and one on the other side, near the other end; and thus I lay till the water ebbed away, and left my raft and all my cargo safe on shore.

My next work was to view the country, and seek a proper place for my habitation, and where to stow my goods, to secure them from whatever might happen. Where I was, I yet knew not: whether on the continent or an island; whether inhabited or not inhabited; whether in danger of wild beasts or not. There was a hill not above a mile from me, which rose up very steep and high, and which seemed to overtop some other hills, which lay as in a ridge from it, northward. I took out one of the fowling-pieces, and one of the pistols, and a horn of powder; and thus armed, I travelled for discovery up to the top of that hill, where, after I had with great labour and difficulty got to the top, I saw my fate, to my great affliction, *viz.*, that I was in an island environed on every side by the sea: no land to be seen except some rocks, which lay a great way off, and two small islands, less than this, which lay about three leagues to the west.

I found also that the island I was in was barren, and uninhabited. Yet I saw abundance of fowls, but knew not their kinds, neither, when I killed them, could I tell what was fit for food, and what not. At my coming back I shot at a great bird, which I saw sitting upon a tree, on the side of a wood. I believe it was the first gun that had been fired there since, the creation of the world. I had no sooner fired, than from all parts of the wood there arose an innumerable number of fowls, of many sorts, making a confused screaming and crying, every one according to his usual note, but not one of them of any kind that I knew. As for the creature I killed, I took it to be a kind of a hawk, its colour and beak resembling it, but it had no talons or claws more than common. Its flesh was carrion, and fit for nothing.

Contented with this discovery, I came back to my raft, and fell to work to bring my cargo on shore, which took me up the rest of that day: what to do with myself at night I knew not, nor indeed where to rest, for I was afraid to lie down on the ground, not knowing but some wild beast might devour me.

However, as well as I could, I barricaded myself round with the chests and boards that I had brought on shore, and made a kind of hut for that night's lodging. As for food, I yet saw not which way to supply myself, except that I had seen two or three creatures, like hares, run out of the wood where I shot the fowl.

I now began to consider that I might yet get a great many things out of the ship, which would be useful to me, and particularly some of the rigging and sails, and such other things as might come to land; and I resolved to make another voyage on board the vessel, if possible. And as I knew that the first storm that blew must necessarily break her all in pieces, I resolved to set all other things apart, till I had got everything out of the ship that I could get.

I got on board the ship as before, and prepared a second raft; and, having had experience of the first, I neither made this so unwieldy, nor loaded it so hard, I brought away several things very useful to me; as, first, in the carpenter's stores, I found two or three bags full of nails and spikes, a great screw-jack, a dozen or two of hatchets, and, above all, that most useful thing called a grindstone. All these I secured, together with several things belonging to the gunner; particularly two or three iron crows, and two barrels of musket bullets, seven muskets, and another fowling-piece, with some small quantity of powder more; a large bagful of small shot, and a great roll of sheet-lead; but this last was so heavy I could not hoist it up to get it over the ship's side.

Besides these things, I took all the men's clothes that I could find, and a spare fore-top sail, a hammock, and some bedding; and with this I loaded my second raft, and brought them all safe on shore, to my very great comfort.

I was under some apprehension during my absence from the land, that at least my provisions might be devoured on shore: but when I came back, I found no sign of any visitor; only there sat a creature like a wild cat, upon one of the chests, which, when I came towards it, ran away a little distance, and then stood still. She sat very composed and unconcerned, and looked full in my face, as if she had a mind to be acquainted with me. I presented my gun to her, but, as she did not understand it, she was perfectly unconcerned at it, nor did she offer to stir away; upon which I tossed her a bit of biscuit, though, by the way, I was not very free of it: however, I spared her a bit, and she ate it, and looked (as if pleased) for more; but I thanked her, and could spare no more: so she marched off.

Having got my second cargo on shore—though I was obliged to open the barrels of powder, and bring them by parcels, for they were too heavy, being large casks—I went to work to make me a little tent, with the sail, and some poles which I cut for that purpose: and into this tent I brought everything that I knew would spoil either with rain or sun; and I piled all the empty chests and casks up in a circle round the tent, to fortify it from any sudden attempt, either from man or beast.

When I had done this, I blocked up the door of the tent with some boards within, and an empty chest set up on end without; and spreading one of the beds upon the ground, laying my two pistols just at my head, and my gun at length by me, I went to bed for the first time, and slept very quietly all night, for I was very weary and heavy.

I had the biggest magazine of all kinds now that ever was laid up, I believe, for one man; for while the ship sat upright, I got everything out of her that I could: so every day, at low water, I went on board, and brought away something or other; but particularly the third time I went, I brought away as much of the rigging as I could, as also all the small ropes and rope twine I could get, with a piece of spare canvas, which was to mend the sails upon occasion, and the barrel of wet gunpowder.

But that which comforted me more still, was, last of all, after I had made five or six voyages, and thought I had nothing more to expect from the ship that was worth my meddling with, I found a great hogshead of bread, three large runlets of rum, or spirits, a box of sugar, and a barrel of fine flour. I soon emptied the hogshead of the bread, and wrapped it up, parcel by parcel, in pieces of the sails, which I cut out, and got all this safe on shore also.

The next day I made another voyage, and now, having plundered the ship of what was portable and fit to hand out, I began with the cables, cutting the great cable into pieces, such as I could move, I got two cables and a hawser on shore, with all the iron-work I could get; and having cut down the spritsail-yard, and the mizen-yard, and everything I could, to make a large raft, I loaded it with all these heavy goods, and came away; but my good luck began now to leave me; for this raft was so unwieldy, and so overladen, that after I was entered the little cove, where I had landed the rest of my goods, not being able to guide it so handily as I did the other, it overset, and threw me and all

42

my cargo into the water; my cargo was a great part of it lost, especially the iron, which I expected would have been of great use to me: however, when the tide was out, I got most of the pieces of cable ashore, and some of the iron, though with infinite labour. After this, I went every day on board, and brought away what I could get.

I had been now thirteen days on shore, and had been eleven times on board the ship; but preparing the twelfth time to go on board, I found the wind began to rise: however, at low water I went on board, and though I thought I had rummaged the cabin so effectually that nothing more could be found, yet I discovered a locker with drawers in it, in one of which I found two or three razors, and one pair of large scissors, with some ten or a dozen of good knives and forks; in another I found about thirty-six pounds value in money—some European coin, some Brazil, some pieces of eight, some gold, and some silver.

I smiled to myself at the sight of this money: "O drug !" said I aloud, "what art thou good for? Thou art not worth to me—no, not the taking off the ground: one of those knives is worth all this heap: I have no manner of use for thee; e'en remain where thou art, and go to the bottom, as a creature whose life is not worth saving." However, upon second thoughts, I took it away; and wrapping all in a piece of canvas, I began to think of making another raft: but while I was preparing this, I found the sky overcast, and the wind began to rise, and in a quarter of an hour it blew a fresh gale from the shore. It presently occurred to me, that it was in vain to pretend to make a raft with the wind off shore; and that it was my business to be gone before the tide of flood began, otherwise I might not be able to reach the shore at all. Accordingly, I let myself down into the water, and swam across the channel which lay between the ship and the sands, and even that with difficulty enough, partly with the weight of the things I had about me, and partly from the roughness of the water.

But I had got home to my little tent, where I lay, with all my wealth about me very secure. It blew very hard all that night, and in the morning, when I looked out, behold no more ship was to be seen!

My thoughts were now wholly employed about securing myself against either savages, if any should appear, or wild beasts, if any were in the island; and I had many thoughts of the method how to do this, and what kind of dwelling to make—whether I should make me a cave in or a tent upon the earth; and, in short, I resolved upon both; the manner and description of which, it may not be improper to give an account of.

I soon found the place I was in was not fit for my settlement, because it was upon a low, moorish ground, near the sea, and I believed it would not be wholesome, and more particularly because there was no fresh water near it; so I resolved to find a more healthy and more convenient spot of ground.

I consulted several things in my situation: 1st, health and fresh water; 2ndly, shelter from the heat of the sun; 3rdly, security from ravenous creatures, whether men or beasts; 4thly, a view to the sea, that if God sent any ship in sight, I might not lose any advantage for my deliverance.

In search of a place proper for this, I found a little plain on the side of a rising hill, whose front towards this little plain was steep as a house-side, so that nothing could come down upon me from the top. On the side of the rock there was a hollow place, worn a little way in, like the entrance or door of a cave; but there was not really any cave, or way into the rock, at all.

On the flat of the green, just before this hollow place, I resolved to pitch my tent. This plain was not above a hundred yards broad, and about twice as long, and lay like a green before my door; and, at the end of it, descended irregularly every way down into the low ground by the seaside. It was on the N.N.W side of the hill; so that it was sheltered from the heat every day, till it came to a W and by S. sun, or thereabouts, which, in those countries, is near the setting.

Before I set up my tent, I drew a half-circle before the hollow place, which took in about ten yards in its semi-diameter, from the rock, and twenty yards in its diameter from its beginning and ending.

In this half-circle I pitched two rows of strong stakes, driving them into the ground till they stood very firm like piles, the biggest end being out of the around above five feet and a half, and sharpened on the top. The two rows did not stand above six inches from one another.

Then I took the pieces of cable which I had cut in the ship, and laid them in rows, one upon another, within the circle, between these two rows of stakes, up to the top, placing other stakes in the inside, leaning against them, about two feet and a half high, like a spur to a post; and this fence was so strong, that neither man nor beast could get into it or over it. This cost me a great deal of time and labour, especially to cut the piles in the woods, bring them to the place, and drive them into the earth.

The entrance into this place I made to be, 1 not by a door, but by a short ladder to go over the top; which ladder, when I was in, I lifted over after me; and so I was completely fenced in and fortified, as I thought, from all the world, and consequently slept secure in the night, which otherwise I could not have done; though, as it appeared afterwards, there was no need of all this caution from the enemies that I apprehended danger from.

Into this fence, or fortress, with infinite labour, I carried all my riches, all my provisions, ammunition, and stores, of which you have the account above; and I made a large tent, which, to preserve me from the rains, that in one part of the year are very violent there, I made double, one smaller tent within, and one larger tent above it; and covered the uppermost with a large tarpaulin, which I had saved among the sails.

And now I lay no more for a while in the bed which I had brought on shore, but in a hammock, which had belonged to the mate of the ship.

Into this tent I brought all my provisions, and everything that would spoil by the wet; and having thus enclosed all my goods, I made up the entrance, which till now I had left open, and so passed and repassed, as I said, by a short ladder.

When I had done this, I began to work my way into the rock, and bringing all the earth and stones that I dug down out through my tent, I laid them up within my fence, in the nature of a terrace, so that it raised the ground within about a foot and a half; and thus I made me a cave, just behind my tent, which served me like a cellar to my house.

It cost me much labour and many days before all these things were brought to perfection; and therefore I must go back to some other things which took up some of my thoughts. At the same time it happened, after I had laid my scheme for the setting up my tent, and making the cave, that a storm of rain falling from a thick, dark cloud, a sudden flash of lightning happened, and after that, a great clap of thunder, as is naturally the effect of it. I was not so much surprised with the lightning, as I was with a thought which darted into my mind as swift as the lightning itself: my powder! My very heart sank within me when I thought that, at one blast, all my powder might be destroyed; on which, not my defence only, but the providing me food, as I thought, entirely depended. I was nothing near so anxious about my own danger, though, had the powder took fire, I should never have known who had hurt me.

Such impression did this make upon me, that after the storm was over, I laid aside all my works, my building and fortifying, and applied myself to make bags and boxes, to separate the powder, and to keep it a little and a little in a parcel, in hope that whatever might come, it might not all take fire at once; and to keep it so apart, that it should not be possible to make one part fire another. I finished this work in about a fortnight; and I think my powder, which in all was about two hundred and forty pounds weight, was divided into not less than a hundred parcels. As to the barrel that had been wet, I did not apprehend any danger from that; so I placed it in my new cave, which, in my fancy, I called my kitchen; and the rest I hid up and down in holes among the rocks, so that no wet might come to it, marking very carefully where I laid it.

In the interval of time while this was doing, I went out once at least every day with my gun, as well to divert myself, as to see if I could kill anything fit for food; and as near as I could, to acquaint myself with what the island produced. The first time I went out, I presently discovered that there were goats in the island, which was a great satisfaction to me; but then it was attended with this misfortune to me, *viz.*, that they were so shy, so subtle, and so swift of foot, that it was the difficultest thing in the world to come at them; but I was not discouraged at this, not doubting but I might now and then shoot one, as it soon happened; for after I had found their haunts a little, I laid wait in this manner for them: I observed that if they saw me in the valleys, though they were upon the rocks, they would run away, as in a terrible fright; but if they were feeding in the valleys, and I was upon the rocks, they took no notice of me; from whence I concluded, that by the position of their optics, their sight was so directed downward, that they did not readily see objects that were above them; so afterwards, I took this method—I always climbed the rocks first, to get above them, and then had frequently a fair mark.

The first shot I made among these creatures, I killed a she-goat, which had a little kid by her, which she gave suck to, which grieved me heartily; for, when the old one fell, the kid stood stock still by her, till I came and took her up; and not only so, but when I carried the old one with me, upon my shoulders, the kid followed me quite to my enclosure; upon which, I laid down the dam, and took the kid in my arms, and carried it over my pale, in hopes to have bred it up tame; but it would not eat; so I was forced to kill it, and ate it myself. These two supplied me with flesh a great while, for I ate sparingly, and saved my provisions, my bread especially, as much as possibly I could.

Having now fixed my habitation, I found it absolutely necessary to provide a place to make a fire in, and fuel to burn; and what I did for that, as also how I enlarged my cave, and what conveniences I made, I shall give a full account of in its place; but I must now give some little account of myself, and of my thoughts about living, which, it may well be supposed, were not a few.

And now being about to enter into a melancholy relation of a scene of silent life, such, perhaps, as was never heard of in the world before, I shall take it from its beginning, and continue it in its order. It was, by my account, the 30th of September, when I first set foot upon this horrid island; when the sun being to us in its autumnal equinox, was almost just over my head: for I reckoned myself by observation, to be in the latitude of nine degrees twenty-two minutes north of the line.

After I had been there about ten or twelve days, it came into my thoughts that I should lose my reckoning of time for want of books, and pen and ink, and should even forget the Sabbath days; but to prevent this, I cut with my knife upon a large post, in capital letters; and making it into a great cross, I set up on the shore where I first landed, "I came on shore here on the 30th of September, 1659."

Upon the sides of this square post I cut every day a notch with my knife, and every seventh notch was as long again as the rest, and every first day of the month as long again as that long one; and thus I kept my calendar, or weekly, monthly, and yearly reckoning of time.

In the next place we are to observe that among the many things I brought out of the ship, I got several things of less value, but not at all less useful to me, which I omitted setting down before, as pens, ink, and paper; several parcels in the captain's, mate's, gunner's, and carpenter's keeping; three or four compasses, some mathematical instruments, dials, perspectives, charts, and books of navigation; all which I huddled together, whether I might want them or no; also I found three very good Bibles, which came to me in my cargo from England, and which I had packed up among my things; some Portuguese books also; and several other books, all which I carefully secured. And I must not forgot, that we had in the ship a dog, and two cats, of whose eminent history I may have occasion to say something in its place; for I carried both the cats with me; and as for the dog, he jumped out of the ship of himself, and swam on shore to me the day after I went on shore with my first cargo, and was a trusty servant to me many years; I wanted nothing that he could fetch me, nor any company that he could make

47

up to me; I only wanted to have him talk to me, but that would not do. My pens, ink, and paper I husbanded to the utmost; and while my ink lasted, I kept things very exact, but after that was gone I could not. for I could not make ink by any means that I could devise.

And this put me in mind that I wanted many things, notwithstanding all that I had amassed together; and of these, ink was one; as also a spade, pick-axe, and shovel, to dig or remove the earth; needles, pins, and thread: as for linen, I soon learned to want that without much difficulty.

This want of tools made every work I did go on heavily; and it was near a whole year before I had entirely finished my little pale, or surrounded my habitation. The piles or stakes, which were as heavy as I could well lift, were a long time in cutting and preparing in the woods, and more, by far, in bringing home; so that I spent sometimes two days in cutting and bringing home one of these posts, and a third day in driving it into the ground; for which purpose, I got a heavy piece of wood at first, but at last bethought myself of one of the iron crows; which, however, though I found it, made driving those posts or piles very laborious and tedious work. But what need I have been concerned at the tediousness of anything I had to do, seeing I had time enough to do it in? nor had I any other employment, if that had been over, at least that I could foresee, except the ranging the island to sock for food, which I did, more or less every day.

I now began to consider seriously my condition, and the circumstances I was reduced to; and I drew up the state of my affairs in writing, not so much to leave them to any that should come after me, for I was likely to have but few heirs, as to deliver my thoughts from daily poring upon them, and afflicting my mind: and as my reason began now to master my despondency, I began to comfort myself as well as I could, and to set the good against the evil, that I might have something to distinguish my case from worse; and I stated very impartially, like debtor and creditor, the comforts I enjoyed against the miseries I suffered, thus:—

EVIL.

I am cast upon a horrible, desolate island, void of all hope of
  recovery.
I am singled out and separated, as it were, from all the world,
  to be miserable.
I am divided from mankind—a solitaire; one banished from
  human society.

I have not clothes to cover me.

I am without any defence, or means to resist any violence
of man or beast.

I have no soul to speak to, or relieve me.

GOOD.

But I am alive, and not drowned, as all my ship's company
were.

But I am singled out, too, from all the ship's crew, to be spared
from death; and He that miraculously saved me from
death, can deliver me from this condition.

But I am not starved, and perishing on a barren place,
affording no sustenance.

But I am in a hot climate, where, if I had clothes, I could
hardly wear them.

But I am cast on an island where I see no wild beasts to
hurt me, as I saw on the coast of Africa; and what if I had
been shipwrecked there?

But God wonderfully sent the ship in near enough to the
shore, that I have got out as many necessary things as will
either supply my wants or enable me to supply myself,
even as long as I live.

Upon the whole, here was an undoubted testimony, that there was
scarce any condition in the world so miserable, but there was something negative or positive to be thankful for in it.

Having now brought my mind a little to relish my condition, and
given over looking out to sea, to see if I could spy a ship,—I began to
apply myself to arrange my way of living, and to make things as easy
to me as I could.

I have already described my habitation, which was a tent under the
side of a rock, surrounded with a strong pale of posts and cables; but I
might now rather call it a wall, for I raised a kind of a veil up against
it of turfs, about two feet thick on the outside: and after some time
(I think it was a year and a half) I raised rafters from it, leaning to the
rock, and thatched or covered it with boughs of trees, and such things
as I could get, to keep out the rain; which I found at some times of
the year very violent.

I have already observed how I brought all my goods into the cave
which I had made behind me. But I must observed too, that at first
this was a confused heap of goods, which as they lay in no order, so

49

they took up all my place; I had no room to turn myself; so I set myself to enlarge my cave, and work farther into the earth; and when I found I was pretty safe as to beasts of prey, I worked sideways, to the right hand into the rock; and then turning to the right again, worked quite out and made me a door to come out on the side of my pale or fortification.

This gave me not only egress and regress, as it was a backway to my tent and to my storehouse, but gave me room to store my goods.

And now I began to apply myself to make such necessary things as I found I most wanted, particularly a chair and a table; for without those I was not able to enjoy the few comforts I had in the world; I could not write, or eat, or do several things with so much pleasure, without a table: so I went to work. And here I must needs observe, that as reason is the substance and origin of the mathematics, so by stating and squaring everything by reason, and by making the most rational judgment of things, every man may be, in time, master of every mnemonic art. I had never handled a tool in my life; and yet, in time, by labour, application, and contrivance, I found, at last, that I wanted nothing but I could have made it, especially if I had had tools. However I made abundance of things, even without tools; and some with no more tools than an adze and a hatchet, which perhaps were never made that way before, and that with infinite labour.

For example, if I wanted a board, I had no other way but to cut down a tree, set it on an edge before me, and hew it flat on either side with my axe, till I had brought it to be as thin as a plank, and then dub it smooth with my adze. It is true that by this method I could make but one board out of a whole tree; but this I had no remedy for but patience, any more than I had for the prodigious deal of time and labour which it took me up to make a plank or board: but my time or labour was little worth, and so it was as well employed one way as another.

However, I made me a table and a chair, in the first place; and this I did out of the short pieces of boards that I brought on my raft from the ship, lint when I had wrought out some boards as above, I made large shelves, of the breadth of a foot and a half, one over another all along one side of my cave, to lay all my tools, nails, and iron-work on; and, to separate everything into their places, that I might come easily at them.

I knocked pieces into the wall of the rock to hang my guns and all things that would hang up: so that my cave looked like a general magazine of all necessary things; and I had everything so ready at my hand, that it was a great pleasure to me to see all my goods in such order, and especially to find my stock of all necessaries so great.

Having settled my household stuff and habitation, made me a table and a chair, and all as handsome about me as I could, I began to keep my journal; of which I shall here give you the copy (though in it will be told all these particulars over again) as long as it lasted; for having no more ink, I was forced to leave it off.

The Journal.

September 30, 1659.—I, poor, miserable Robinson Crusoe, being shipwrecked during a dreadful storm, in the offing, came on shore on this dismal, unfortunate island, which I called "The Island of Despair;" all the rest of the ship's company being drowned, and myself almost dead.

All the rest of the day I spent in afflicting myself at the dismal circumstances I was brought to, *viz.,* I had neither food, house, clothes, weapon, nor place to fly to: and, in despair of any relief, saw nothing but death before me: either that I should be devoured by wild beasts, murdered by savages, or starved to death for want of food. At the approach of night I slept in a tree for fear of wild creatures; but slept soundly, though it rained all night.

October 1.—In the morning I saw, to my great surprise, the ship had floated with the high tide, and was driven on shore again, much nearer the island; which as it was some comfort, on one hand, for seeing her sit upright, and not broken to pieces, I hoped if the wind abated, I might get on board, and get some food and necessaries out of her for my relief; so, on the other hand, it renewed my grief at the loss of my comrades, who, I imagined, if we had all stayed on board, might have saved the ship, or, at least, that they would not have been all drowned, as they were; and that, had the men been saved, we might perhaps have built us a boat, out of the ruins of the ship, to have carried us to some other part of the world. I spent great part of this day in perplexing myself on these things; but, at length, seeing the ship almost dry, I went upon the sand as near as I could, and then swam on board. This day also it continued raining, though with no wind at all.

From the 1st of October to the 24th.—All these days entirely spent in several voyages to get all I could out of the ship, which I brought on shore, every tide of flood, upon rafts. Much rain also in the days, though with some intervals of fair weather; but it seems this was the rainy season.

Oct. 20.—I overset my raft, and all the goods I had got upon it; but being in shoal water, and the things being chiefly heavy, I recovered many of them when the tide was out.

Oct. 25.—It rained all night and all day, with some gusts of wind; during which time the ship broke in pieces, the wind blowing a little harder than before, and was no more to be seen, except the wreck of her, and that only at low water. I spent this day in covering and securing the goods which I had saved, that the rain might not spoil them.

Oct. 26.—I walked about the shore almost all day, to find out a place to fix my habitation, greatly concerned to secure myself from any attack in the night, either from wild beasts or men. Towards night, I fixed upon a proper place, under a rock, and marked out my encampment; which I resolved to strengthen with a work, wall, or fortification, made of double piles, lined within with cables, and without with turf.

From the 26th to the 30th, I worked very hard in carrying all my goods to my new habitation, though some part of the time it rained exceedingly hard.

The 31st in the morning, I went out into the island with my gun, to see for some food, and discover the country; when I killed a she-goat, and her kid followed me home, which I afterwards killed also because it would not feed.

November 1.—I set up my tent under a rock, and lay there for the first night; making it as large as I could, with stakes driven in to swing my hammock upon.

Nov. 2.—I set up all my chests and boards, and the pieces of timber which made my rafts, and with them formed a fence round me, a little within the place I had marked out for my fortification.

Nov. 3.—I went out with my gun, and killed two fowls like ducks, which were very good food. In the afternoon went to work to make me a table.

Nov. 4.—This morning I began to order my times of work, of going out with my gun, time of sleep, and time of diversion; *viz.*, every morning I walked out with my gun for two or three hours, if it did not rain; then employed myself to work till about eleven o'clock; then ate what I had to live on; and from twelve till two I lay down to sleep, the weather being excessively hot; and then, in the evening to work again. The working part of this day and of the next were wholly employed in making my table, for I was yet but a very sorry workman, though time and necessity made me a complete natural mechanic soon after, as I believe they would do any one else.

Nov. 5.—This day, went abroad with my gun and my dog, and killed a wild cat; her skin pretty soft, but her flesh good for nothing; every creature that I killed I took off the skins and preserved them. Coming back by the seashore, I saw many sorts of sea-fowls, which I did not understand; but was surprised, and almost frightened, with two or three seals, which, while I was gazing at, not well knowing what they were, got into the sea, and escaped me for that time.

Nov. 6.—After my morning walk, I went to work with my table again, and finished it, though not to my liking; nor was it long before I learned to mend it.

Nov. 7.—Now it began to be settled fair weather. The 7th, 8th, 9th, 10th, and part of the 12th (for the 11th was Sunday), I took wholly up to make me a chair, and with much ado brought it to a tolerable shape, but never to please me; and even in the making I pulled it in pieces several times.

Note.—I soon neglected my keeping Sundays; for, omitting my mark for them on my post, I forgot which was which.

Nov. 13.—This day it rained, which refreshed me exceedingly, and cooled the earth; but it was accompanied with terrible thunder and lightning, which frighted me dreadfully, for fear of my powder. As soon as it was over, I resolved to separate my stock of powder into as many little parcels as possible, that it might not be in danger.

Nov. 14, 15, 16.—These three days I spent in making little square chests, or boxes, which might hold about a pound, or two pounds at most, of powder; and so, putting the powder in, I stowed it in places as secure and remote from one another as possible. On one of these three days, I killed a large bird that was good to eat, but I knew not what to call it.

Nov. 17.—This day I began to dig behind my tent into the rock, to make room for my further convenience.

Note.—Three things I wanted exceedingly for this work, *viz.*, a pickaxe, a shovel, and a wheelbarrow, or basket; so I desisted from my work, and began to consider how to supply that want, and make me some tools. As for the pickaxe, I made use of the iron crows, which were proper enough, though heavy; but the next thing was a shovel or spade; this was so absolutely necessary, that, indeed, I could do nothing effectually without it; but what kind of one to make I knew not.

Nov. 18.—The next day, in searching the woods, I found a tree of that wood, or like it, which, in the Brazils, they call the iron-tree, for its exceeding hardness; of this, with great labour, and almost spoiling my axe, I cut a piece, and brought it home, too, with difficulty enough, for it was exceeding heavy. The excessive hardness of the wood, and my having no other way, made me a long while upon this machine, for I worked it effectually, by little and little, into the form of a shovel or spade; the handle exactly shaped like ours in England, only that the board part having no iron shod upon it at bottom, it would not last me so long; however, it served well enough for the uses which I had occasion to put it to.

I was still deficient, for I wanted a basket, or a wheelbarrow. A basket I could not make by any means, having no such things as twigs that would bend to make wicker-ware—at least, none yet found out; and as to a wheelbarrow, I fancied I could make all but the wheel; but that I had no notion of; neither did I know how to go about it; besides, I had no possible way to make the iron gudgeons for the spindle or axis of the wheel to run in; so I gave it over, and so, for carrying away the earth which I dug out of the cave, I made me a thing like a hod, which the labourers carry mortar in, when they serve the bricklayers. This was not so difficult to me as the making the shovel; and yet this and the shovel, and the attempt which I made in vain to make a wheelbarrow, took me up no less than four days.

Nov. 23.—My other work having now stood still, because of my making these tools, when they were finished I went on, and working every day, as my strength and time allowed, I spent eighteen days entirely in widening and deepening my cave, that it might hold my goods commodiously.

Note.—During all this time, I worked to make this room, or cave, spacious enough to accommodate me as a warehouse, or magazine, a kitchen, a dining-room, and a cellar. As for my lodging, I kept to the tent; except that sometimes, in the wet season of the year, it rained so hard, that I could not keep myself dry, which caused me afterwards to cover all my place within my pale with long poles, in the form of rafters, leaning against the rock, and load them with flags and large leaves of trees, like a thatch.

December 10.—I began to think my cave or vault finished, when on a sudden (it seems I had made it too large) a great quantity of earth fell down from the top and one side; so much that it frighted me, and not without reason, too; for if I had been under it, I had never wanted a grave-digger. I had now a great deal of work to do over again, for I had the loose earth to carry out: and, which was of more importance, I had the ceiling to prop up, so that I might be sure no more would come down.

Dec. 11.—This day I went to work with it accordingly, and got two shores or posts pitched upright to the top, with two pieces of boards across over each post; this I finished the next day; and setting more posts up with boards, in about a week more I had the roof secured; and the posts, standing in rows, served me for partitions to part off the house.

Dec. 17.—From this day to the 20th I placed shelves, and knocked up nails on the posts, to hang everything up that could be hung up; and now I began to be in some order within doors.

Dec 20.—Now I carried everything into the cave, and began to furnish my house, and set up some pieces of boards like a dresser, to order my victuals upon, but boards began to be very scarce with me: also I made me another table.

Dec. 24.—Much rain all night and all day: no stirring out.

Dec. 25.—Rain all day.

Dec. 26.—No rain, and the earth much cooler than before, and pleasanter.

Dec. 27.—Killed a young goat, and lamed another so that I caught it, and led it home in a string; when I had it at home, I bound and splintered up its leg, which was broken.

N.B.— I took such care of it that it lived, and the leg grew well and as strong as ever: but by nursing it so long it grew tame, and fed upon the little green at my door, and would not go away. This was the first time that I entertained a thought of breeding up some tame creatures, that I might have food when my powder and shot was all spent.

Dec. 28, 29, 30, 31—Great heats, and no breeze, so that there was no stirring abroad, except in the evening, for food; this time I spent in putting all my things in order within doors.

January 1.—Very hot still; but I went abroad early and late with my gun, and lay still in the middle of the day. This evening, going farther into the valleys which lay towards the centre of the island, I found there were plenty of goats, though exceedingly shy, and hard to come at; however, I resolved to try if I could not bring my dog to hunt them down.

Jan. 2.—Accordingly, the next day I went out with my dog, and set him upon the goats; but I was mistaken, for they all faced about upon the dog, and he knew his danger too well, for he would not come near them.

Jan. 3.—I began my fence, or wall; which, being still jealous of my being attacked by somebody, I resolved to make very thick and strong.

N.B.—This wall being described before, I purposely omit what was said in the journal; it is sufficient to observe that I was no less time than from the 3rd of January to the 14th of April working, finishing, and perfecting this wall, though it was no more than about twenty-four yards in length, being a half-circle, from one place in the rock to another place, about eight yards from it, the door of the cave being in the centre behind it.

All this time I worked very hard, the rains hindering me many days, nay, sometimes weeks, together; but I thought I should never be perfectly secure till this wall was finished; and it is scarcely credible what inexpressible labour everything was done with, especially the bringing piles out of the woods, and driving them into the ground; for I made them much bigger than I needed to have done.

When this wall was finished, and the outside double-fenced, with a turf wall raised up close to it, I persuaded myself that if any people were to come on shore there they would not perceive anything like a habitation; and it was very well I did so, as may be observed hereafter, upon a very remarkable occasion.

Daring this time I made my rounds in the woods for game every day, when the rain permitted me, and made frequent discoveries in these walks of something or other to my advantage; particularly I found a kind of wild pigeons, which build, not as wood-pigeons in a tree, but rather as housepigeons, in the holes of the rocks; and taking some young ones, I endeavoured to breed them up tame, and did so; but when they grew older they flew away, which perhaps was at first for want of feeding them, for I had nothing to give them; however, I frequently found their nests, and got their young ones, which were very good meat. And now, in the managing my household affairs, I found myself wanting in many things, which I thought at first it was impossible for me to make; as, indeed, with some of them it was: for instance, I could never make a cask to be hooped. I had a small runlet or two, as I observed before, but I could never arrive at the capacity of making one by them, though I spent many weeks about it; I could neither put in the heads, or join the staves so true to one another as to make them hold water; so I gave that also over.

In the next place, I was at a great loss for candles; so that as soon as ever it was dark, which was generally by seven o'clock, I was obliged to go to bed. I remembered the lump of bees'-wax with which I made candles in my African adventure; but I had none of that now; the only remedy I had was, that when I had killed a goat I saved the tallow, and with a little dish made of clay, which I baked in the sun, to which I added a wick of some oakum, I made me a lamp; and this gave me light, though not a clear steady light like a candle. In the middle of all my labours it happened that, rummaging my things, I found a little bag, which had been filled with corn for the feeding of poultry. The little remainder of corn that had been in the bag was all devoured with the rats, and I saw nothing in the bag but husks send dust; and being willing to have the bag for some other use, I shook the husks of corn out of it on one side of my fortification, under the rock.

It was a little before the great rains just now mentioned that I threw this stuff away, taking no notice, and not so much as remembering that I had thrown anything there, when about a month after, or thereabouts, I saw some few stalks of something green shooting out of the ground, which I fancied might be some plant I had not seen; but I was surprised, and perfectly astonished, when, after a little longer time, I saw about ten or twelve ears come out, which were perfect green barley, of the same kind as our English barley.

It is impossible to express the astonishment and confusion of my thoughts on this occasion; I had hitherto acted upon no religious foundation at all; indeed, I had very few notions of religion in my head, nor had entertained any sense of anything that had befallen me, otherwise than as chance, or, as we lightly say, what pleases God, without so much as inquiring into the end of Providence in these things, or His order in governing events for the world. But after I saw barley grow there, in a climate which I knew was not proper for corn, and especially that I knew not how it came there, it startled me strangely, and I began to suggest that God had miraculously caused His grain to grow without any help of seed sown, and that it was so directed purely for my sustenance on that wild, miserable place.

This touched my heart a little, and brought tears out of my eyes, and I began to bless myself that such a prodigy of nature should happen upon my account; and this was the more strange to me, because I saw near it still, all along by the side of the rock, some other straggling stalks, which proved to be stalks of rice, and which I knew, because I had seen it grow in Africa, when I was ashore there.

I not only thought these the pure productions of Providence for my support, but not doubting that there was more in the place, I went all over that part of the island where I had been before, peering in every corner, and under every rock, to see for more of it, but I could not find any. At last it occurred to my thoughts, that I shook a bag of chickens' meat out in that place, and then the wonder began to cease; and I must confess, my religious thankfulness to God's providence began to abate, too, upon the discovering that all this was nothing but what was common; though I ought to have been as thankful for so strange and unforeseen a providence, as if it had been miraculous; for it was really the work of Providence to me, that should order or appoint that ten or twelve grains of corn should remain unspoiled, when the rats had destroyed all the rest, as if it had been dropped from heaven; as also, that I should throw it out in that particular place, where, it being in the shade of a high rock, it sprang up immediately; whereas, if I had thrown it anywhere else, at that time, it had been burnt up and destroyed.

I carefully saved the ears of this corn, you may be sure, in their season, which was about the end of June; and, laying up every corn, I resolved to sow them all again, hoping, in time, to have some quantity, sufficient to supply me with, bread. But it was not till the fourth year that I could allow myself the least grain of this corn to eat, and even then but sparingly, as I shall say afterwards, in its order; for I lost all that I sowed the first season, by not observing the proper time; for I sowed it just before the dry season, so that it never came up at all, at least not as it would have done: of which in its place.

Besides this barley, there were, as above, twenty or thirty stalks of rice, which I preserved with the same care and for the same use, to make me bread, or rather food; for I found ways to cook it without baking, though I did that also after some time.

But to return to my journal:

I worked excessively hard these three or four months, to get my wall done; and the 14th of April, I closed it up, contriving to go into it, not by a door, but over the wall, by a ladder, that there might be no sign on the outside of my habitation.

April 16.—I finished the ladder; so I went up the ladder to the top, and then pulled it up after me, and let it down in the inside: this was a complete enclosure to me; for within I had room enough, and nothing could come at me from without, unless it could first mount my wall.

The very next day after this wall was finished, I had almost had all my labour overthrown at once, and myself killed; the case was thus:— As I was busy in the inside, behind my tent, just at the entrance into my cave, I was terribly frighted with a most dreadful surprising thing indeed: for, all on a sudden, I found the earth come crumbling down from the roof of my cave, and from the edge of the hill over my head, and two of the posts I had set up in the cave cracked in a frightful manner. I was heartily scared; thinking that the top of my cave was fallen in, as some of it had done before: and for fear I should be buried in it, I ran forward to my ladder, and not thinking myself safe there neither, I got over my wall for fear of the pieces of the hill, which I expected might roll down upon me.

I had no sooner stepped down upon the firm ground, than I plainly saw it was a terrible earthquake; for the ground I stood on shook three times at about eight minutes' distance, with three such shocks as would have overturned the strongest building that could be supposed to have stood on the earth, and a great piece of the top of a rock, which stood about half a mile from me, next the sea, fell down, with such a terrible noise as I never heard in all my life. I perceived also the very sea was put into violent motion by it; and I believe the shocks were stronger under the water than on the island.

I was so much amazed with the thing itself, having never felt the like, nor discoursed with anyone that had, that I was like one dead or stupefied; and the motion of the earth made my stomach sick, like one that was tossed at sea; but the noise of the falling of the rock awaked me, as it were, and rousing me from the stupefied condition I was in, filled me with horror, and I thought of nothing then but the hill falling upon my tent and all my household goods, and burying all at once; and this sunk my very soul within me a second time.

After the third shock was over, and I felt no more for some time, I began to take courage; and yet I had not heart enough to go over my wall again, for fear of being buried alive, but sat still upon the ground greatly cast down and disconsolate, not knowing what to do. All this while, I had not the least serious religious thought, nothing but the common "*Lord have mercy upon me!*" and when it was over, that went away too.

While I sat thus, I found the air overcast, and grow cloudy, as if it would rain; soon after that, the wind arose by little and little, so that in less than half an hour it blew a most dreadful hurricane: the sea was, all on a sudden, covered over with foam and froth; the shore was covered with the breach of the water; the trees were torn up by the roots; and a terrible storm it was. This held about three hours, and then began to abate; and in two hours more it was quite calm, and began to rain very hard. All this while I sat upon the ground, very much terrified and dejected; when on a sudden it came into my thoughts, that these winds and rain being the consequences of the earthquake, the earthquake itself was spent and over, and I might venture into my cave again. With this thought, my spirits began to revive; and the rain also helping to persuade me, I went in and sat down in my tent; but the rain was so violent, that my tent was ready to be beaten down with it; and I was forced to go into my cave, though very much afraid and uneasy, for fear it should fall on my head.

This violent rain forced me to a new work, *viz.*, to cut a hole through my new fortification, like a sink, to let the water go out, which would else have flooded my cave. After I had been in my cave for some time, and found still no more shocks of the earthquake follow, I began to be more composed. And now to support my spirits, which indeed wanted it very much, I went to my little store and took a small sup of rum; which, however, I did then and always very sparingly, knowing I could have no more when that was gone. It continued raining all that night, and great part of the next day, so that I could not stir abroad; but my mind being more composed, I began to think of what I had best do: concluding, that if the island was subject to these earthquakes, there would be no living for me in a cave, but I must consider of building a little hut in an open place, which I might surround with a wall, as I had done here, and so make myself secure from wild beasts or men; for I concluded if I stayed where I was, I should certainly, one time or other, be buried alive.

With these thoughts I resolved to remove my tent from the place where it now stood, which was just under the hanging precipice of the hill; and which if it should be shaken again, would certainly fall upon my tent: and I spent the two next days, being the 19th and 20th of April, in contriving where and how to remove my habitation. The fear of being swallowed up alive made me that I never slept in quiet; and yet the apprehension of lying abroad without any fence was almost equal to it: but still, when I looked about, and saw how everything was put in order, how pleasantly concealed I was, and how safe from danger, it made me very loath to remove. In the meantime, it occurred to me that it would require a vast deal of time for me to do this, and that I must be contented to venture where I was, till I had formed a camp for myself, and had secured it so as to remove to it. So with this resolution I composed myself for a time; and resolved that I would go to work with all speed to build me a wall with piles and cables, &c, in a circle, as before, and set my tent up in it, when it was finished; but that I would venture to stay where I was till it was finished and fit to remove. This was the 21st.

April 22.—The next morning I began to consider of means to put this resolve into execution; but I was at a great loss about my tools. I had three large axes, and abundance of hatchets, but with much chopping and cutting knotty hard wood, they were all full of notches, and dull, and though I had a grindstone, I could not turn it and grind my tools too. This cost me as much thought as a statesman would have bestowed upon a grand point of politics, or a judge upon the life and death of a man. At length I contrived a wheel with a string to turn it with my foot, that I might have both my hands at liberty.

April 28, 29.—These two whole days I took up in grinding my tools, my machine for turning my grindstone performing very well.

April 30.—Having perceived my bread had been low a great while, now I took a survey of it, and reduced myself to one biscuit a day, which made my heart very heavy.

May 1.—In the morning, looking towards the sea side, the tide being low, I saw something lie on the shore bigger than ordinary, and it looked like a cask; when I came to it, I found a small barrel, and two or three pieces of the wreck of the ship, which were driven on shore by the late hurricane; and looking towards the wreck itself, I thought it seemed to lie higher out of the water than it used to do. I examined the barrel which was driven on shore, and soon found it was a barrel of gunpowder, but it had taken water, and the powder was caked as hard as a stone; however, I rolled it farther on shore for the present, and went on upon the sands, as near as I could to the wreck of the ship to look for more.

When I came down to the ship, I found it strangely removed. The forecastle, which lay before buried in sand, was heaved up at least six feet, and the stern, which was broke in pieces and parted from the rest by the force of the sea, soon after I had left rummaging her, was tossed, as it were, up, and cast on one side; and the sand was thrown so high on that side next her stern, that whereas there was a great place of water before, so that I could not come within a quarter of a mile of the wreck without swimming, I could now walk quite up to her when the tide was out. I was surprised with this at first, but soon concluded it must be done by the earthquake; and as by this violence the ship was more broke open than formerly, so many things came daily on shore, which the sea had loosened, and which the winds and water rolled by degrees to the land.

This wholly diverted my thoughts from the design of removing my habitation, and I busied myself mightily, that day especially, in searching whether I could make any way into the ship; but I found nothing was to be expected of that kind, for all the inside of the ship was choked up with sand. However, as I had learned not to despair of anything, I resolved to pull everything to pieces that I could of the ship, concluding that everything I could get from her would be of some use or other to me.

May 3.—I began with my saw, and cut a piece of a beam through, which I thought held some of the upper part or quarter deck together, and when I had cut it through, I cleared away the sand as well as I could from the side which lay highest: but the tide coming in, I was obliged to give over for that time.

May 4.—I went a fishing, but caught not one fish that I durst eat of, till I was weary of my sport; when, just going to leave off, I caught a young dolphin. I had made me a long line of some rope-yarn, but I had no hooks; yet I frequently caught fish enough, as much as I cared to eat; all which I dried in the sun, and ate them dry.

May 5.—Worked on the wreck; cut another beam asunder, and brought three great fir-planks off from the decks, which I tied together, and made to float on shore when the tide of flood came on.

May 6.—Worked on the wreck; got several iron bolts out of her, and other pieces of iron-work; worked very hard and came home very much tired, and had thoughts of giving it over.

May 7.—Went to the wreck again, not with an intent to work, but found the weight of the wreck had broke itself down, the beams being cut; that several pieces of the ship seemed to lie loose, and the inside of the hold lay so open that I could see into it, but it was almost full of water and sand.

May 8.—Went to the wreck, and carried an iron crow to wrench up the deck, which lay now quite clear of the water or sand. I wrenched open two planks, and brought them on shore also with the tide. I left the iron crow in the wreck for next day.

May 9.—Went to the wreck, and with the crow made way into the body of the wreck, and felt several casks, and loosened them with the crow, but could not break them up. I felt also a roll of English lead, and could stir it, but it was too heavy to remove.

May 10—14.—Went every day to the wreck; and got a great many pieces of timber and boards or plank, and two or three hundredweight of iron.

May 15.—I carried two hatchets, to try if I could not cut a piece off the roll of lead, by placing the edge of one hatchet, and driving it with the other; but as it lay about a foot and a half in the water, I could not make any blow to drive the hatchet.

May 16.—It had blown hard in the night, and the wreck appeared more broken by the force of the water; but I stayed so long in the woods, to get pigeons for food, that the tide prevented my going to the wreck that day.

May 17.—I saw some pieces of the wreck blown on shore, at a great distance, near two miles off me, but resolved to see what they were, and found it was a piece of the lead, but too heavy for me to bring away.

May 24.—Every day, to this day, I worked on the wreck; and with hard labour I loosened some things so much with the crow, that the first blowing tide several casks floated out, and two of the seamen's chests; but the wind blowing from the shore, nothing came to land

63

that day but pieces of timber, and a hogshead, which had some Brazil pork in it, but the salt water and the sand had spoilt it. I continued this work every day to the 15th of June, except the time necessary to get food, which I always appointed, during this part of my employment, to be when the tide was up, that I might be ready when it ebbed out; and by this time I had got timber and plank, and iron-work, enough to have built a good boat, if I had known how; and also I got at several times, and in several pieces, near one hundred-weight of the sheet-lead.

June 16.—Going down to the sea-side, I found a large tortoise, or turtle. This was the first I had seen, which, it seems, was only my misfortune, not any defect of the place, or scarcity; for had I happened to be on the other side of the island, I might have had hundreds of them every day, as I found afterwards; but perhaps had paid dear enough for them.

June 17.—I spent in cooking the turtle. I found in her three score eggs; and her flesh was to me, at that time, the most savoury and pleasant that ever I tasted in my life, having had no flesh, but of goats and fowls, since I landed in this horrid place.

June 18.—Rained all day, and I stayed within. I thought, at this time, the rain felt cold, and I was something chilly; which I knew was not usual in that latitude.

June 19.—Very ill and shivering, as if the weather had been cold.

June 20.—No rest all night; violent pains in my head, and feverish.

June 21.—Very ill; frighted almost to death with the apprehension of my sad condition—to be sick, and no help; prayed to God, for the first time since the storm off Hull, but scarce knew what I said, or why; my thoughts being all confused.

June 22.—A little better; but under dreadful apprehensions of sickness.

June 23.—Very bad again; cold and shivering, and then a violent headache.

June 24.—Much better.

June 25.—An ague very violent: the fit held me seven hours: cold fit, and hot, with faint sweats after it.

June 26.—Better; and having no victuals to eat, took my gun, but found myself very weak: however, I killed a she-goat, and with much difficulty got it home, and broiled some of it, and ate. I would fain have stewed it, and made some broth, but had no pot.

June 27.—The ague again so violent that I lay a-bed all day, and neither ate nor drank. I was ready to perish for thirst; but so weak, I had not strength to stand up, or to get myself any water to drink. Prayed to God again, but was light-headed; and when I was not, I was so ignorant that I knew not what to say; only I lay and cried, "Lord, look upon me! Lord, pity me! Lord, have mercy upon me!" I suppose I did nothing else for two or three hours; till the fit wearing off, I fell asleep, and did not wake till far in the night.

When I awoke, I found myself much refreshed, but weak and exceeding thirsty; however, as I had no water in my habitation, I was forced to lie till morning, and went to sleep again. In this second sleep, I had this terrible dream: I thought that I was sitting on the ground, on the outside of my wall, where I sat when the storm blew after the earthquake, and that I saw a man descend from a great black cloud, in a bright flame of fire, and light upon the ground: he was all over as bright as a flame, so that I could but just bear to look towards him: his countenance was most inexpressibly dreadful, impossible for words to describe; when he stepped upon the ground with his feet, I thought the earth trembled, just as it had done before in the earthquake, and all the air looked, to my apprehension, as if it had been filled with flashes of fire. He was no sooner landed upon the earth, but he moved forward towards me, with a long spear or weapon in his hand, to kill me; and when he came to a rising ground at some distance, he spoke to me—or I heard a voice so terrible that it is impossible to express the terror of it. All that I can say I understood, was this:—"*Seeing all these things have not brought thee to repentance, now thou shalt die;*" at which words, I thought he lifted up the spear that was in his hand to kill me.

No one that shall ever read this account will expect that I should be able to describe the horrors of my soul at this terrible vision. I mean, that even while it was a dream, I even dreamed of those horrors. Nor is it any more possible to describe the impression that remained upon my mind when I awaked, and found it was but a dream.

I had, alas! no divine knowledge. What I had received by the good instruction of my father was then worn out by an uninterrupted series, for eight years, of seafaring wickedness, and a constant conversation with none but such as were, like myself, wicked and profane to the last degree. I do not remember that I had, in all that time, one thought that so much as tended either to looking upwards towards God, or inwards towards a reflection upon my own ways; but a certain stupidity of soul, without desire of good, or conscience of evil, had entirely overwhelmed me; and I was all that the most hardened, unthinking, wicked creature among our common sailors can be supposed to be: not having the least sense, either of the fear of God, in danger, or of thankfulness to God, in deliverance.

It is true, when I got on shore first here, and found all my ship's crew drowned, and myself spared, I was surprised with a kind of ecstasy, and some transports of soul, which, had the grace of God assisted, might have come up to true thankfulness; but it ended where it began, in a mere common flight of joy, without the least reflection upon the distinguished goodness of the hand which had preserved me, and had singled me out to be preserved when all the rest were destroyed. Even when I was, afterwards, on duo consideration, made sensible of my condition, how I was cast on this dreadful place, out of the reach of human kind, out of all hope of relief, or prospect of redemption, as soon as I saw but a prospect of living, and that I should not starve and perish for hunger, all the sense of my affliction wore off; and I began to be very easy, applied myself to the works proper for my preservation and supply, and was far enough from being afflicted at my condition, as a judgment from Heaven, or as the hand of God against me: these were thoughts which very seldom entered my head.

But to return to my journal:—

June 28.—Having been somewhat refreshed with the sleep I had had, and the fit being entirely off, I got up; and though the fright and terror of my dream was very great, yet I considered that the fit of the ague would return again the next day, and now was my time to get something to refresh and support myself when I should be ill; and the first thing I did, I filled a large square case-bottle with water, and set it upon my table, in reach of my bed; and to take off the chill or aguish disposition of the water, I put about a quarter of a pint of rum into it, and mixed them together. Then I got me a piece of the goat's flesh, and broiled it on the coals, but could eat very little. I walked about, but was very weak, and withal very sad and heavy-hearted under a sense of my miserable condition, dreading the return of my distemper the next day. At night, I made my supper of three of the turtle's eggs, which I roasted in the ashes, and ate in the shell, and this was the first bit of meat I had ever asked God's blessing to, that I could remember, in my whole life. After I had eaten, I tried to walk, but found myself so weak, that I could hardly carry a gun, for I never went out without that, so I went but a little way, and sat down upon the ground, looking out upon the sea, which was just before me, and very calm and smooth.

Some such thoughts as these occurred to me: God knows that I am here, and am in this dreadful condition; and if nothing happens without His appointment, He has appointed all this to befall me. Nothing occurred to my thought to contradict any of these conclusions, and therefore it rested upon me with the greater force, that it must needs be that God had appointed all this to befall me; that I was brought into this miserable circumstance by His direction, He having the sole power, not of me only, but of everything that happened in the world. Immediately it followed—Why has God done this to me? What have I done to be thus used? My conscience presently checked me in that inquiry, as if I had blasphemed, and methought it spoke to me like a voice, "Wretch! dost thou ask what thou hast done? Look back upon a dreadful misspent life, and ask thyself, what thou hast not done? Ask, why is it that thou wert not long ago destroyed? Why wert thou not drowned in Yarmouth Roads; killed in the fight when the ship was taken by the Sallee man-of-war; devoured by the wild beasts on the coast of Africa; or drowned here, when all the crew perished but thyself? Dost thou ask, what have I done?"

I was struck dumb with these reflections, as one astonished, and had not a word to say—no, not to answer to myself, but rose up pensive and sad, walked back to my retreat, and went up over my wall, as if I had been going to bed; but my thoughts were sadly disturbed, and I had no inclination to sleep: so I sat down in my chair, and lighted my lamp, for it began to be dark. Now, as the apprehension of the return of my distemper terrified me very much, it occurred to my thought, that the Brazilians take no physic but their tobacco for almost all distempers, and I had a piece of a roll of tobacco in one of the chests, which was quite cured, and some also that was green, and not quite cured.

I went, directed by Heaven no doubt, for in this chest I found a cure both for soul and body. I opened the chest, and found what I looked for, the tobacco: and as the few books I had saved lay there too,

I took out one of the Bibles which I mentioned before, and which to this time I had not found leisure, or inclination, to look into. What use to make of the tobacco I knew not, in my distemper, or whether it was good for it or no; but I tried several experiments with it, as if I was resolved it should hit one way or other. I first took a piece of leaf, and chewed it in my mouth, which, indeed, at first, almost stupefied my brain, the tobacco being green and strong, and that I had not been much used to. Then I took some and steeped it an hour or two in some rum, and resolved to take a dose of it when I lay down; and, lastly, I burnt some upon a pan of coals, and held my nose close over the smoke of it as long as I could bear it, as well for the heat, as almost for suffocation.

In the interval of this operation, I took up the Bible and began to read, but my head was too much disturbed with the tobacco to bear reading, at least at that time: only, having opened the book casually, the first words that occurred to me were these, "Call on me in the day of trouble, and I will deliver thee, and thou shalt glorify me." These words were very apt to my case, and made some impression upon my thoughts at the time of reading them, though not so much as they did afterwards; for, as for being delivered, the word had no sound, as I may say, to me; the thing was so remote, so impossible in my apprehension of things, that I began to say as the children of Israel did when they were promised flesh to eat, "Can God spread a table in the wilderness?" so I began to say, "Can God Himself deliver me from this place?" And as it was not for many years that any hopes appeared, this prevailed very often upon my thoughts; but however, the words made a great impression upon me, and I mused upon them very often.

It grew now late, and the tobacco had dozed my head so much that I inclined to sleep; so I left my lamp burning in the cave, lest I should want anything in the night, and went to bed. But before I lay down, I did what I never had done in all my life; I kneeled down, and prayed to God, to fulfil the promise to me, that if I called upon Him in the day of trouble, He would deliver me. After my broken and imperfect prayer was over, I drank the rum in which I had steeped the tobacco; which was so strong and rank of the tobacco, that I could scarcely get it down; immediately upon this I went to bed. I found presently it flew up into my head violently; but I fell into a sound sleep, and waked no more till, by the sun, it must necessarily be near three o'clock in the afternoon the next day; nay, to this hour I am partly of opinion, that I slept all the next day and night, and till almost three the day after: for otherwise, I know not how I should lose a day out of my reckoning in the days of the week, as it appeared some years after I had done; for if I had lost it by crossing and recrossing the Line, I should have lost more than one day; but certainly I lost a day in my account, and never knew which way.

Be that, however, one way or the other, when I awaked I found myself exceedingly refreshed, and my spirits lively and cheerful; when I got up, I was stronger than I was the day before, and my stomach better, for I was hungry; and, in short, I had no fit the next day, but continued much altered for the better. This was the 29th.

The 30th was my well day, of course, and I went abroad with my gun, but did not care to travel too far. I killed a sea-fowl or two, something like a brand goose, and brought them home; but was not very forward to eat them; so I ate some more of the turtle's eggs, which were very good. This evening I renewed the medicine, which I had supposed did me good the day before, the tobacco steeped in rum; only I did not take so much as before, nor did I chew any of the leaf, or hold my head over the smoke; however, I was not so well the next day, which was the 1st of July, as I hoped I should have been; for I had a little spice of the cold fit, but it was not much.

July 2.—I renewed the medicine all the three ways; and dosed myself with it as at first, and doubled the quantity which I drank.

July 3.—I missed the fit for good and all, though I did not recover my full strength for some weeks after. While I was thus gathering strength, my thoughts ran exceedingly upon this scripture, "I will deliver thee;" and the impossibility of my deliverance lay much upon my mind, in bar of my ever expecting it; but as I was discouraging myself with such thoughts, it occurred to my mind that I pored so much upon my deliverance from the main affliction, that I disregarded the deliverance I had received; and I was, as it were, made to ask myself such questions as these, *viz:* Have I not been delivered, and wonderfully too, from sickness? from the most distressed condition that could be, and that was so frightful to me? and what notice had I taken of it? Had I done my part? God had delivered me, but I had not glorified Him; that is to say, I had not owned and been thankful for that as a deliverance: and how could I expect greater deliverance? This touched my heart very much; and immediately I knelt down, and gave God thanks aloud for my recovery from my sickness.

July 4.—In the morning, I took the Bible; and beginning at the

New Testament, I began seriously to read it, and imposed upon myself to read awhile every morning and every night; not tying myself to the number of chapters, but as long as my thoughts should engage me. It was not long after I set seriously to this work, till I found my heart more deeply and sincerely affected with the wickedness of my past life.

The impression of my dream revived; and the words, "*All these things have not brought thee to repentance*," ran seriously in my thoughts. I was earnestly begging of God to give me repentance, when it happened providentially, the very day that, reading the Scripture, I came to these words, "*He is exalted a Prince and a Saviour, to give repentance and to give remission.*" I threw down the book; and with my heart as well as my hands lifted up to heaven, in a kind of ecstasy of joy, I cried out aloud, "Jesus, thou son of David! Jesus, thou exalted Prince and Saviour! give me repentance!"This was the first time I could say, in the true sense of the words, that I prayed in all my life; for now I prayed with a sense of my condition, and with a true scripture view of hope, founded on the encouragement of the word of God; and from this time, I may say, I began to have hope that God would hear me.

Now I began to construe the words mentioned above, "*Call on Me, and I will deliver thee*," in a different sense from what I had ever done before; for then I had no notion of anything being called deliverance, but my being delivered from the captivity I was in: for though I was indeed at large in the place, yet the island was certainly a prison to me, and that in the worst sense in the world. But now I learned to take it in another sense: now I looked back upon my past life with such horror, and my sins appeared so dreadful, that my soul sought nothing of God but deliverance from the load of guilt that bore down all my comfort. As for my solitary life, it was nothing; I did not so much as pray to be delivered from it, or think of it; it was all of no consideration in comparison to this. And I add this part here, to hint to whoever shall read it, that whenever they come to a true sense of things, they will find deliverance from sin a, much greater blessing than deliverance from affliction.

But, leaving this part, I return to my journal:—From the 4th of July to the 14th, I was chiefly employed in walking about with my gun in my hand, a little and a little at a time, as a man that was gathering up his strength after a fit of sickness: for it is hardly to be imagined how low I was, and to what weakness I was reduced. The application which I made use of was perfectly new, and perhaps which had never cured an ague before; neither can I recommend it to anyone to practise by this experiment: and though it did carry off the fit, yet it rather contributed to weakening me; for I had frequent convulsions in my nerves and limbs for some time; I learned from it also this, in particular, that being abroad in the rainy season was the most pernicious thing to my health that could be, especially in those rains which came attended with storms and hurricanes of wind; for as the rain which came the dry season was almost always accompanied with such storms, so I found that rain was much more dangerous than the fain which fell in September and October.

I had now been in this unhappy island above ten mouths: all possibility of deliverance from this condition seemed to be entirely taken from me; and I firmly believed that no human shape had ever set foot upon that place. Having now secured my habitation, as I thought, fully to my mind, I had a great desire to make a more perfect discovery of the island, and to see what other productions I might find, which I yet knew nothing of.

It was on the 15th of July that I began to take a more particular survey of the island itself. I went up the creek first, where I brought my rafts on shore. I found, after I came about two miles up, that the tide did not flow any higher; and that it was no more than a little brook of running water, very fresh and good; but this being the dry season, there was hardly any water in some parts of it. On the banks of this brook, I found many pleasant *savannahs* or meadows, plain, smooth, and covered with grass: and on the rising parts of them, next to the higher grounds, where the water, as might be supposed, never overflowed, I found a great deal of tobacco, green, and growing to a great and very strong stalk; there were divers other plants, which I had no notion of or understanding about, that might perhaps, have virtues of their own, which I could not find out.

I searched for the cassava root, which the Indians, in all that climate, make their bread of, but I could find none. I saw large plants of aloes, but did not understand them. I saw several sugar-canes, but wild, and for want of cultivation, imperfect. I contented myself with these discoveries for this time, and came back, musing with myself what course I might take to know the virtue and goodness of any of the fruits or plants which I should discover; but could bring it to no conclusion; for, in short, I had made so little observation while I was in the Brazils, that I knew little of the plants in the field, that might serve me to any purpose now in my distress.

The next day, the 16th, I went up the same way again; and after going something farther than I had gone the day before, I found the brook and savannahs cease, and the country became more woody. In this part, I found different fruits, and particularly melons upon the ground, in great abundance, and grapes upon the trees; the vines had spread over the trees, and the clusters of grapes were just now in their prime, very ripe and rich. This was a surprising discovery, and I was exceeding glad of them; but I was warned by my experience to eat sparingly of them, remembering that when I was ashore in Barbary, the eating of grapes killed several of our Englishmen, who were slaves there, by throwing them into fluxes and fevers. But I found an excellent use for these grapes; and that was, to cure or dry them in the sun, and keep them as dried grapes or raisins are kept, which I thought would be wholesome and agreeable to eat, when no grapes could be had.

I spent all that evening there, and went not back to my habitation, which, by the way, was the first night, as I might say, I had lain from home. In the night, I took my first contrivance, and got up into a tree, where I slept well; and the next morning, proceeded upon my discovery, travelling nearly four miles, as I might judge by the length of the valley, keeping still due north, with a ridge of hills on the south and north side of me. At the end of this march, I came to an opening, where the country seemed to descend to the west; and a little spring of fresh water, which issued out of the side of the hill by me, ran the other way; and the country appeared so fresh, so green, so flourishing, everything being in a constant verdure, that it looked like a planted garden. I descended a little on the side of that delicious vale, surveying it with a kind of secret pleasure, though mixed with my other afflicting thoughts, that this was all my own; that I was king and lord of all this country indefeasibly, and had a right of possession; and, if I could convey it, I might have it in inheritance as completely as any lord of a manor in England.

I saw here abundance of cocoa trees, orange and lemon, and citron trees; but all wild, and very few bearing any fruit. However, the green limes that I gathered were not only pleasant to eat, but very wholesome; and I mixed their juice afterwards with "water, which made it very wholesome, and very cool and refreshing. I found now I had business enough, to gather and carry home; and I resolved to lay up a store, as well of grapes as limes and lemons, to furnish myself for the wet season, which I knew was approaching. In order to do this, I gathered a great heap of grapes in one place, a lesser heap in another place, and a great parcel of limes and lemons in another place; and taking a few of each with me, I travelled homewards: and resolved to come again, and bring a bag or sack, or what I could make, to carry the rest home. Accordingly, having spent three days in this journey, I came home (so I must now call my tent and my cave), but before I got thither the grapes were spoiled; the richness of the fruit, and the weight of the juice, having broken them and bruised them, they were good for little or nothing: as to the limes, they were good, but I could bring but a few.

The next day being the 19th, I went back, having made me two small bags to bring home my harvest; but I was surprised, when coming to my heap of grapes, which were so rich and fine when I gathered them, I found them all spread about, trod to pieces, and dragged about, some here, some there, and abundance eaten and devoured. By this, I concluded there were some wild creatures thereabouts, which had done this; but what they were, I knew not. However, as I found there was no laying them up on heaps, and no carrying them away in a sack, but that one way they would be destroyed, and the other way they would be crushed with their own weight, I took another course; for I gathered a large quantity of the grapes, and hung them upon the out branches of the trees, that they might cure and dry in the sun; and as for the limes and the lemons, I carried as many back as I could well stand under.

When I came home from this journey, I contemplated with great pleasure the fruitfulness of that valley, and the pleasantness of the situation; the security from storms on that side the water, and the wood: and concluded that I had pitched upon a place to fix my abode, which was by far the worst part of the country. Upon the whole, I began to consider of removing my habitation; and looking out for a place equally safe as where now I was situate, if possible, in that pleasant, fruitful part of the island.

This thought ran long in my head, and I was exceeding fond of it for some time, the pleasantness of the place tempting me; but when I came to a nearer view of it, I considered that I was now by the sea-side, where it was at least possible that something might happen to my advantage; and, by the same ill fate that brought me hither, might bring some other unhappy wretches to the same place; and though it was scarce probable that any such thing should ever happen, yet to enclose myself among the hills and woods in the centre of the island, was to anticipate my bondage, and to render such an affair not only improbable, but impossible; and that therefore I ought not by any means to remove. However, I was so enamoured of this place, that I spent much of my time there for the whole of the remaining part of the month of July, and though, upon second thoughts, I resolved not to remove, yet I built me a little kind of a bower, and surrounded it at a distance with a strong fence, being a double hedge, as high as I could reach, well staked, and filled between with brushwood; and here I lay very secure, sometimes two or three nights together; always going over it with a ladder; so that I fancied now I had my country house and my sea-coast house; and this work took me up to the beginning of August.

I had but newly finished my fence, and began to enjoy my labour, when the rains came on, and made me stick close to my first habitation; for though I had made me a tent like the other, with a piece of a sail, and spread it very well, yet I had not the shelter of a hill to keep me from storms, nor a cave behind me to retreat into when the rains were extraordinary.

About the beginning of August, as I said, I had finished my bower and began to enjoy myself. The 3rd of August, I found the grapes I had hung up perfectly dried, and indeed were excellent good raisins; so I began to take them down from the trees, and it was very happy that I did so, for the rains which followed would have spoiled them, and I had lost the best part of my winter food; for I had above two hundred large bunches of them. No sooner had I taken them all down, and carried most of them home to my cave, but it began to rain; and from hence, which was the 14th of August, it rained, more or less, every day till the middle of October; and sometimes so violently, that I could not stir out of my cave for several days.

In this season, I was much surprised with the increase of my family: I had been concerned for the loss of one of my cats, who ran away from me, or, as I thought, had been dead, and I heard no more tidings of her, till to my astonishment, she came home about the end of August, with three kittens. This was the more strange to me, because, though I had killed a wild cat, as I called it, with my gun, yet I thought it was a quite different kind from our European cats; but the young cats were the same kind of house-breed as the old one; and both my cats being females, I thought it very strange. But from these three cats, I afterwards came to be so pestered with cats, that I was forced to kill them like vermin, or wild beasts, and to drive them from my house as much as possible.

From the 14th of August to the 26th, incessant rain, so that I could not stir, and was now very careful not to be much wet. In this confinement, I began to be straitened for food: but venturing out twice, I one day killed a goat; and the last day, which was the 26th, found a very large tortoise, which was a treat to me, and my food was regulated thus:—I ate a bunch of raisins for my breakfast; a piece of the goat's flesh, or of the turtle, for my dinner, broiled, for I had no vessel to boil or stew anything; and two or three of the turtle's eggs for my supper.

During this confinement in my cover by the rain, I worked daily two or three hours at enlarging my cave, and by degrees worked it on towards one side, till I came to the outside of the hill, and made a door or way out, which came beyond my fence or wall; and so I came in and out this way. But I was not perfectly easy at lying so open; for, as I had managed myself before, I was in a perfect enclosure; whereas now, I thought I lay exposed, and open for anything to come in upon me; and yet I could not perceive that there was any living thing to fear, the biggest creature that I had yet seen upon the island being a goat.

Sept. 30.—I was now come to the unhappy anniversary of my landing. I cast up the notches on my post, and found I had been on shore three hundred and sixty-five days. I kept this day as a solemn fast, even till the going down of the sun; I then ate a biscuit-cake and a bunch of grapes, and went to bed, finishing the day as I began it, with religious exercise. I had all this time observed no Sabbath-day; for as at first I had no sense of religion upon my mind, I had, after some time, omitted to distinguish the weeks, by making a longer notch than ordinary for the Sabbath-day, and so did not really know what any of the days were; but now, having cast up the days as above, I found I had been there a year, so I divided it into weeks, and set apart every seventh day for a Sabbath; though I found at the end of my account, I had lost a day or two in my reckoning. A little after this, my ink began to fail me, and so I contented myself to use it more sparingly, and to write down only the most remarkable events of my life, without continuing a daily memorandum of other things.

The rainy season and the dry season now began to appear regular to me, and I learned to divide them so as to provide for them accordingly; but I bought all my experience before I had it, and this I am going to relate was one of the most discouraging experiments that I made.

I have mentioned that I had saved the few ears of barley and rice, which I had so surprisingly found spring up, as I thought of themselves, and I believe there were about thirty stalks of rice, and about twenty of barley; and now I thought it a proper time to sow it, after the rains, the sun being in its southern position, going from me. Accordingly, I dug up a piece of ground as well as I could with my wooden spade, and dividing it into two parts, I sowed my grain; but as I was sowing, it casually occurred to my thoughts that I would not sow it all at first, because I did not know when was the proper time for it, so I sowed about two-thirds of the seed, leaving about a handful of each. It was a great comfort to me afterwards that I did so, for not one grain of what I sowed this time came to anything; for the dry months following, the earth having had no rain after the seed was sown, it had no moisture to assist its growth, and never came up at all till the wet season had come again, and then it grew as if it had been but newly sown.

Finding my first seed did not grow, which I easily imagined was by the drought, I sought for a moister piece of ground to make another trial in, and I dug up a piece of ground near my new bower, and sowed the rest of my seed in February, a little before the vernal equinox; and this having the rainy months of March and April to water it, sprung up very pleasantly, and yielded a very good crop; but having part of the seed left only, and not daring to sow all that I had, I had but a small quantity at last, my whole crop not amounting to half a peck of each kind. But by this experiment I was made master of my business, and knew exactly when the proper season was to sow, and that I might expect two seed-times and two harvests every year.

While this corn was growing, I made a little discovery, which was of use to me afterwards. As soon as the rains were over, and the weather began to settle, which was about the month of November, I made a visit up the country to my bower, where, though I had not been some months, yet I found all things just as I left them. The circle or double hedge that I had made was not only firm and entire, but the stakes which I had cut out of some trees that grew thereabouts, were all shot out and grown with long branches, as much as a willowtree usually shoots the first year after lopping its head. I was surprised, and yet very well pleased, to see the young trees grow; and I pruned them, and led them up to grow as much alike as I could; and it is scarce credible how beautiful a figure they grew into in three years; so that though the edge made a circle of about twenty-five yards in diameter, yet the trees soon covered it, and it was a complete shade, sufficient to lodge under all the dry season. This made me resolve to cut some more stakes, and make me a hedge like this, in a semi-circle round the wall of my first dwelling, which I did; and placing the trees or stakes in a double row, at about eight yards distance from my first fence, they grew presently, and were at first a fine cover to my habitation, and afterwards served for a defence also, as I shall observe in its order.

I found now that the seasons of the year might generally be divided, not into summer and winter, as in Europe, but into the rainy seasons and the dry seasons, which were generally thus:—

The half of February, the whole of March, and the half of April—rainy, the sun being then on or near the equinox.

The half of April, the whole of May, June, and July, and the half of August—dry, the sun being then to the north of the Line.

The half of August, the whole of September, and the half of October—rainy, the sun being then come back.

The half of October, the whole of November, December, and January, and the half of February—dry, the sun being then to the south of the Line.

The rainy seasons sometimes held longer or shorter, as the winds happened to blow, but this was the general observation I made. After I had found, by experience, the ill consequences of being abroad in the rain, I took care to furnish myself with provisions beforehand, that I might not be obliged to go out, and I sat within doors as much as possible during the wet months. This time I found much employment, and very suitable also to the time, for I found great occasion for many things which I had no way to furnish myself with but by hard labour and constant application; particularly I tried many ways to make myself a basket, but all the twigs I could get for the purpose proved so brittle that they would do nothing. It proved of excellent advantage to me now, that when I was a boy, I used to take great delight in standing at a basket-maker's, in the town where my father lived, to see them make their wicker-ware; and being, as boys usually are, very officious to help, and a great observer of the manner in which they worked those things, and sometimes lending a hand, I had by these means full knowledge of the methods of it, and I wanted nothing but the materials, when it came into my mind that the twigs of that tree whence I cut my stakes that grew might possibly be as tough as the sallows, willows, and osiers in England, and I resolved to try.

Accordingly, the next day I went to my country-house, as I called it, and cutting some of the smaller twigs, I found them to my purpose as much as I could desire; whereupon I came the next time prepared with a hatchet to cut down a quantity, which I soon found, for there was great plenty of them. These I set up to dry within my circle or hedge, and when they were fit for use, I carried them to my cave; and here, during the next season, I employed myself in making, as well as I could, a great many baskets, both to carry or to lay up anything, as I had occasion; and though I did not finish them very handsomely, yet I made them sufficiently serviceable for my purpose; and thus, afterwards, I took care never to be without them; and as my wicker-ware decayed, I made more, especially strong deep baskets to place my corn in, instead of sacks, when I should come to have any quantity of it.

Having mastered this difficulty, and employed a world of time about it, I bestirred myself to see, if possible, how to supply two wants. I had no vessel to hold anything that was liquid, except two runlets, which were almost full of rum, and some glass bottles—some of the common size, and others, which were case-bottles, square, for the holding of waters, spirits, &c. I had not so much as a pot to boil anything, except a great kettle, which I saved out of the ship, and which was too big to make broth, and stew a bit of meat by itself. The second thing I fain would have had was a tobacco-pipe, but it was impossible to make one; however, I found a contrivance for that, too, at last. I employed myself in planting my second rows of stakes or piles and in this wicker-working all the summer or dry season, when another business took me up more time than it could be imagined I could spare.

I mentioned before that I had a great mind to see the whole island, and that I had travelled up the brook, and so on to where I built my bower, and where I had an opening quite to the sea, on the other side of the island. I now resolved to travel quite across to the sea-shore on that side; so, taking my gun, a hatchet, and my dog, and a larger quantity of powder and shot than usual, with two biscuit-cakes and a great bunch of raisins in my pouch for my store, I began my journey. When I had passed the vale where my bower stood, as above, I came within view of the sea to the west, and it being a very clear day, I fairly descried land, at a very great distance; by my guess, it could not be less than fifteen or twenty leagues off.

I could not tell what part of the world this might be, otherwise than that I knew it must be part of America, and, as I concluded, by all my observations, must be near the Spanish dominions.

After some thought upon this affair, I considered that if this land was the Spanish coast, I should certainty, one time or other, see some vessel pass or repass one way or other; but if not, then it was the savage coast between the Spanish country and Brazils, where are found the worst of savages.

With these considerations, I walked very leisurely forward; I found that side of the island where I now was much pleasanter than mine— the *savannah* fields sweet, adorned with flowers and grass, and full of very fine woods. I saw abundance of parrots, and fain I would have caught one, if possible, to have kept it to be tame, and taught it to speak to me. I did, after some painstaking, catch a young parrot, for I knocked it down with a stick, and having recovered it, I brought it home; but it was some years before I could make him speak; however, at last, I taught him to call me by my name very familiarly. But the accident that followed, though it be a trifle, will be very diverting in its place.

I was exceedingly diverted with this journey. I found in the low grounds hares (as I thought them to be) and foxes? but they differed greatly from all the other kinds I had met with, nor could I satisfy myself to eat them, though I killed several. But I had no need to be venturous, for I had no want of food, and of that which was very good, too, especially these three sorts, *viz.*, goats, pigeons, and turtle, or tortoise, which, added to my grapes, Leadenhall-market could not have furnished a table better than I, in proportion to the company.

I never travelled in this journey above two miles outright in a day, or thereabouts; but I took so many turns to see what discoveries I could make, that I came weary enough to the place where I resolved to sit down all night; and then I either reposed myself in a tree, or surrounded myself with a row of stakes set upright in the ground, from one tree to another, so as no wild creature could come at me without waking me.

As soon as I came to the sea-shore, I was surprised to see that I had taken up my lot on the worst side of the island, for here, indeed, the shore was covered with innumerable turtles, whereas, on the other side I had found but three in a year and a half. Here was also an infinite number of fowls of many kinds, some I had seen, and some I had not seen before, and many of them very good meat, but such as I knew not the names of, except those called penguins.

I could have shot as many as I pleased, but was very sparing of my powder and shot, and therefore had more mind to kill a she-goat, if I could, which I could better feed on; and though there were many goats here, more than on my side the island, yet it was with much more difficulty that I could come near them, the country being flat and even, and they saw me much sooner than when I was on the hill.

I confess this side of the country was much pleasanter than mine: but yet I had not the least inclination to remove, for as I was fixed in my habitation it became natural to me, and I seemed all the while I was here to be as it were upon a journey, and from home. However, I travelled along the shore of the sea towards the east, I suppose about twelve miles, and then setting up a great pole upon the shore for a mark, I concluded I would go home again, and that the next journey I took should be on the other side of the island east from my dwelling, and so round till I came to my post again.

I took another way to come back than that I went, thinking I could easily keep all the island so much in my view, that I could not miss finding my dwelling by viewing the country; but I found myself mistaken, for, being come about two or, three miles, I found myself descended into a very large valley, but so surrounded with hills, and those hills covered with wood that I could not see which was my way by any direction but that of the sun, nor even then, unless I knew very well the position of the sun at that time of the day. It happened, to my further misfortune, that the weather proved hazy for three or four days while I was in the valley, and not being able to see the sun, I wandered about very uncomfortably, and at last was obliged to find the sea-side, look for my post, and come back the same way I went; and then by easy journeys I turned homeward, the weather being exceeding hot, and my gun, ammunition, hatchet, and other things, very heavy.

In this journey my dog surprised a young kid, and seized upon it, and I, running in to take hold of it, caught it, and saved it alive from the dog. I had a great mind to bring it home if I could, for I had often been musing whether it might not be possible to get a kid or two, and so raise a breed of tame goats, which might supply me when my powder and shot should be all spent. I made a collar for this little creature, and with a string, which. I made of some rope-yarn, which I always carried about with me, I led him along, though with some difficulty, till I came to my bower, and there I enclosed him and left him, for I was very impatient to be at home, whence I had been absent above a month.

I cannot express what a satisfaction it was to me to come into my old hutch, and lie down in my hammock-bed. This little wandering journey, without settled place of abode, had been so unpleasant to me, that my own house, as I called it to myself, was a perfect settlement to me compared to that; and it rendered everything about me so comfortable, that I resolved I would never go a great way from it again, while it should be my lot to stay on the island.

I reposed myself here a week, to rest and regale myself after my long journey; during which, most of the time was taken up in the weighty affair of making a cage for my Poll, who began now to be a mere domestic, and to be well acquainted with me. Then I began to think of the poor kid which I had penned in within my little circle, and resolved to go and fetch it home, or give it some food; accordingly I went, and found it where I left it, almost starved for want of food. I went and cut boughs of trees, and branches of such shrubs as I could find, and threw it over, and having fed it, I tied it as I did before, to lead it away; but it was so tame with being hungry, that I had no need to have tied it, for it followed me like a dog; and as I continually fed it, the creature became so loving, so gentle, and so fond, that it became from that time one of my domestics also, and would never leave me afterwards.

The rainy season of the autumnal equinox was now come, and I kept the 30th of September in the same solemn manner as before, being the anniversary of my landing on the island, having now been there two years, and no more prospect of being delivered than the first day I came there.

It was now that I began sensibly to feel how much more happy this life I now led was, with all its miserable circumstances, than the wicked, cursed, abominable life I led all the past part of my days; and now I changed both my sorrows and my joys; my very desires altered, my affections changed their gusts, and my delights were perfectly new from what they were at my first coming, or, indeed, for the two years past.

I began to exercise myself with new thoughts; I daily read the word of God, and applied all the comforts of it to my present state. One morning, being very sad, I opened the Bible upon these words, "I will never, never leave thee, nor forsake thee;" immediately it occurred that these words were to me; why else should they be directed in such a manner, just at the moment when I was mourning over my condition, as one forsaken of God and man? "Well then," said I, "if God does not forsake me, of what ill consequence can it be, or what matters it, though the world should all forsake me, seeing on the other hand, if I had all the world, and should lose the favour and blessing of God, there would be no comparison in the loss."

From this moment I began to conclude in my mind, that it was possible for me to be more happy in this forsaken, solitary condition, than it was probable I should ever have been in any other particular state in the world; and with this thought I was going to give thanks to God for bringing me to this place. I know not what it was, but something shocked my mind at that thought, and I durst not speak the words. "How canst thou become such a hypocrite," said I, even audibly, "to pretend to be thankful for a condition, which, however thou mayest endeavour to be contented with, thou wouldst rather pray heartily to be delivered from?" So I stopped there, but though I could not say I thanked God for being there, yet I sincerely gave thanks to God for opening my eyes, by whatever afflicting providences, to see the former condition of my life, and to mourn for my wickedness, and repent. I never opened the Bible, or shut it, but my very soul within me blessed God for directing my friend in England, without any order of mine, to pack it up among my goods, and for assisting me afterwards to save it out of the wreck of the ship.

In this disposition of mind, I began my third year; and though I have not given the reader the trouble of so particular an account of my works this year as the first; yet in general it may be observed, that I was very seldom idle, but having regularly divided my time according to the several daily employments that were before me, such as, first, my duty to God, and the reading the Scriptures, which I constantly set apart some time for, thrice every day; secondly, the going abroad with my gun for food, which generally took me up three hours in every morning, when it did not rain: thirdly, the ordering, cutting, preserving, and cooking, what I had killed or caught for my supply: these took up great part of the day; also, it is to be considered, that in the middle of the day, when the sun was in the zenith, the violence of the heat was too great to stir out; so that about four hours in the evening was all the time I could be supposed to work in, with this exception, that sometimes I changed my hours of hunting and working, and went to work in the morning, and abroad with my gun in the afternoon.

To this short time for labour, may be added the exceeding laboriousness of my work; the many hours which for want of tools, want of help, and want of skill, everything I did took up out of my time: for example, I was full two and forty days in making a board for a long shelf, which I wanted in my cave; whereas, two sawyers, with their tools and a saw-pit, would have cut six of them out of the same tree in half a day.

My case was this: it was to be a large tree which was to be cut down, because my board was to be a broad one. This tree I was three days in cutting down, and two more cutting off the boughs, and reducing it to a log, or piece of timber. With inexpressible hacking and hewing, I reduced both the sides of it into chips till it began to be light enough to move; then I turned it, and made one side of it smooth and flat as a board from end to end; then turning that side downward, cut the other side, till I brought the plank to be about three inches thick, and smooth on both sides. Anyone may judge the labour in such a piece of work, but labour and patience carried me through that, and many other things, as will appear by what follows.

I was now, in the months of November and December, expecting my crop of barley and rice. The ground I had manured and dug up for them was not great; for, as I observed my seed of each was not above the quantity of half a peck, but now my crop promised very well, when on a sudden I found I was in danger of losing it all again by enemies of several sorts, which it was scarcely possible to keep from it; as, first the goats, and wild creatures which I called hares, who, tasting the sweetness of the blade, lay in it night and day, as soon as it came up, and ate it so close, that it could get no time to shoot up into stalk.

This I saw no remedy for, but by making an enclosure about it with a hedge; which I did with a great deal of toil, and the more, because it required speed. However, as my arable land was but small, suited to my crop, I got it totally well fenced in about three weeks' time; and shooting some of the creatures in the daytime, I set my dog to guard it in the night, tying him up to a stake at the gate, where he would stand and bark all night long; so in a little time, the enemies forsook the place, and the corn grew very strong and well, and began to ripen apace.

But as the beasts ruined me before, while my corn was in the blade, so the birds were as likely to ruin me now, when it was in the ear; for going along by the place to see how it throve, I saw my little crop surrounded with fowls, of I know not how many sorts, who stood, as it were, watching till I should be gone. I immediately let fly among them, for I always had my gun with me. I had no sooner shot, but there rose up a little cloud of fowls, which I had not seen at all, from among the corn itself.

This touched me sensibly, for I foresaw that in a few days they would devour all my hopes; that I should be starved, and never be able to raise a crop at all, and what to do I could not tell; however, I resolved not to lose my corn, if possible, though I should watch it night and day. In the first place, I went among it, to see what damage was already done, and found they had spoiled a good deal of it; but that as it was yet too green for them, the loss was not so great, but that the remainder was likely to be a good crop, if it could be saved.

I stayed by it to load my gun, and then coming away, I could easily see the thieves sitting upon all the trees about me, as if they only waited till I was gone away, and the event proved it to be so; for as I walked off, as if I was gone, I was no sooner out of their sight, than they dropped clown one by one into the corn again. I was so provoked, that I could not have patience to stay till more came on, knowing that every grain that they ate now was, as it might be said, a peck-loaf to me in the consequence; but coming up to the hedge I fired again, and killed three of them. This was what I wished for; so I took them up, and served them as we serve notorious thieves in England—hanged them in chains, for a terror to others. It is impossible to imagine that this should have such an effect as it had, for the fowls would not only not come at the corn, but, in short, they forsook all that part of the island, and I could never see a bird near the place as long as my scarecrows hung there. This I was very glad of, and about the latter end of December, which was our second harvest of the year, I reaped my corn.

I was sadly put to it for a scythe or sickle to cut it down, and all I could do was to make one, as well as I could, out of one of the broadswords, or cutlasses, which I saved among the arms out of the ship. However, as my first crop was but small, I had no great difficulty to cut it down; in short, I reaped it my way, for I cut nothing off but the ears, and carried it away in a great basket which I had made, and so rubbed it out with my hands; and at the end of my harvesting, I found that out of my half-peck of seed I had near two bushels of rice, and about two bushels and a half of barley; that is to say, by my guess, for I had no measure at that time.

However, this was a great encouragement to me, and I foresaw that, in time, it would please God to supply me with bread: and yet, here I was perplexed again, for I neither knew how to grind or make meal of my corn, or, indeed, how to clean it and part it; nor, if made into meal, how to make broad of it: and if how to make it, yet I knew not how to bake it; I resolved not to taste any of this crop, but to preserve it all for seed against the next season; and, in the meantime, to employ all my study and hours of working to accomplish this great work of providing myself with corn and bread.

It might be truly said, that now I worked for my bread. I believe few people have thought much upon the strange multitude of little things necessary in the providing, producing, curing, dressing, making, and finishing this one article of bread.

I, that was reduced to a mere state of nature, found this to my daily discouragement, and was made more sensible of it every hour.

First, I had no plough to turn up the earth; no spade or shovel to dig it. Well, this I conquered by making me a wooden spade, as I observed before, but this did my work but in a wooden manner, and though it cost me a great many days to make it, yet for want of iron, it not only wore out soon, but made my work the harder, and made it be performed much worse. However, this I bore with, and was content to work it out with patience, and bear with the badness of the performance. When the corn was sown, I had no harrow, but was forced to go over it myself, and drag a great heavy bough of a tree over it, to scratch it, as it may be called, rather than rake or harrow it. When it was growing, and grown, I have observed already how many things I wanted to fence it, secure it, mow or reap it, cure and carry it home, thrash, part it from the chaff, and save it.

Then I wanted a mill to grind it, sieves to dress it, yeast and salt to make it into bread, and an oven to bake it, but all these things I did without, as shall be observed; and yet the corn was an inestimable comfort am advantage to me, too. All this made everything laborious an tedious to me, but that there was no help for; neither was my time so much loss to me, because, as I had divided it, a certain part of it was every day appointed to these works; and as I had resolved to use none of the corn for bread till I had a greater quantity by me, I had the next six months to apply myself wholly, by labour and invention, to furnish myself with utensils proper for the performing all the operations necessary for making the corn, when I had it, fit for my use.

But first I was to prepare more land, for I had now seed enough to sow above an acre of ground. Before I did this, I had a week's work at least to make me a spade, which, when it was done, was but a sorry one indeed, and very heavy, and required double labour to work with it. However, I got through that, and sowed my seed in two large flat pieces of ground, as near my house as I could find them to my mind, and fenced them in with a good hedge, the stakes of which were all cut of that wood which I had set before, and knew it would grow; so that, in one year's time, I knew I should have a quick or living hedge, that would want but little repair. This work did not take me up less than three months, because a great part of that time was the wet season, when I could not go abroad. Within doors I found employment in the following occupations—always observing, that all the while I was at work, I diverted myself with talking to my parrot, and teaching him to speak; and I quickly taught him to know his own name, and at last to speak it out pretty loud, Poll, which was the first word I ever heard spoken in the island by any mouth but my own.

This, therefore, was not my work, but an assistance to my work, for now, as I said, I had a great employment upon my hands, as follows: I had long studied to make, by some means or other, some earthen vessels, which, indeed, I wanted sorely, but knew not where to come at them. However, considering the heat of the climate, I did not doubt but if I could find out any clay, I might make some pots that might, being dried in the sun, be hard enough and strong enough to bear handling, and to hold anything that was dry, and required to be kept so; and as this was necessary in the preparing corn, meal, &c, which was the thing I was doing, I resolved to make some as large as I could, and fit only to stand like jars, to hold what should be put into them.

It would make the reader pity me, or rather laugh at me, to tell how many awkward ways I took to raise this paste; what odd, misshapen, ugly things I made; how many of them fell in, and how many fell out, the clay not being stiff enough to bear its own weight; how many cracked by the over-violent heat of the sun, being set out too hastily; and how many fell in pieces with only removing, as well before as after they were dried; and, in a word, how, after having laboured hard to find the clay—to dig it, to temper it, to bring it home, and work it—I could not make above two large earthen ugly things (I cannot call them jars) in about two months' labour.

However, as the sun baked these two very dry and hard, I lifted them very gently up, and set them down again in two great wicker baskets, which I had made on purpose for them, that they might not break; and as between the pot and the basket there was a little room to spare, I stuffed it full of the rice and barley straw; and these two pots being to stand always dry, I thought would hold my dry corn, and perhaps, the meal, when the corn was bruised.

Though I miscarried so much in my design for large pots, yet I made several smaller things with better success; such as little round pots, flat dishes, pitchers, and pipkins, and any things my hand turned to; and the heat of the sun baked them quite hard.

But my end was to get an earthen pot to hold what was liquid, and bear the fire; which none of these could do. It happened after some time, making a pretty large fire for cooking my meat, when I went to put it out after I had done with it, I found a broken piece of one of my earthenware vessels in the fire burnt as hard as a stone, and red as a tile. I was agreeably surprised to see it, and said to myself, that certainly they might be made to burn whole, if they would burn broken.

This set me to study how to order my fire, so as to make it burn some pots. I had no notion of a kiln, such as the potters burn in, or of glazing them with lead, though I had some lead to do it with; but I placed three large pipkins, and two or three pots, in a pile, one upon another, and placed my firewood all round it with a great heap of embers under them. I plied the fire with fresh fuel round the outside, and upon the top, till I saw the pots in the inside red-hot quite through, and observed that they did not crack at all; when I saw them clear red, I let them stand in that heat about five or six hours, till I found one of them, though it did not crack, did melt or run; for the sand which was mixed with the clay melted by the violence of the heat, and would have run into glass if I had gone on; so I slacked my fire gradually till the pots began to abate of the red colour, and watching them all night, that I might not let the fire abate too fast, in the morning I had three very good (I will not say handsome) pipkins, and two other earthen pots, as hard burnt as could be desired, and one of them perfectly glazed with the running of the sand.

After this experiment, I need not say that I wanted no sort of earthenware for my use; but as to the shapes of them, they were very indifferent, as anyone may suppose.

No joy at a thing of so mean a nature was over equal to mine, when I found I had made an earthen pot that would bear the fire; and I had hardly patience to stay till they were cold, before I set one on the fire again, with some water in it, to boil me some meat, which it did admirably well; and with a piece of a kid I made some very good broth, though I wanted oatmeal, and several other ingredients requisite to make it as good as I would have had it been.

My next concern was to get me a stone mortar to stamp or beat some corn in; for as to the mill, there was no thought of arriving at that perfection of art with one pair of hands. To supply this want, I was at a great loss; for, of all the trades in the world, I was as perfectly un-qualified for a stone-cutter, as for any whatever; neither had I any tools to go about it with. I spent many a day to find out a great stone big enough to cut hollow, and make fit for a mortar, and could find none at all, except what was in the solid rock, and which I had no way to dig or cut out; nor indeed were the rocks in the island of hardness suf-ficient, but were all of a sandy crumbling stone, which neither would bear the weight of a heavy pestle, nor would break the corn, without filling it with sand; so, after a great deal of time lost in searching for a stone, I gave it over, and resolved to look out for a great block of hard wood, which I found indeed much easier; and getting one as big as I had strength to stir, I rounded it, and formed it on the outside with my axe and hatchet, and then, with the help of fire, and infinite labour, made a hollow place in it, as the Indians in Brazil make their canoes. After this, I made a great heavy pestle, or beater, of the wood called the iron-wood; and this I prepared and laid by against I had my next crop of corn, which I proposed to myself to grind, or rather pound, into meal, to make bread.

My next difficulty was to make a sieve, to dress my meal, and to part it from the bran and the husk; without which I did not see it pos-sible I could have any bread. This was a most difficult thing, even to think on, for to be sure I had nothing like the necessary thing to make it; I mean fine thin canvas, or stuff, to scarce the meal through. And here I was at a full stop for many months; nor did I really know what to do. Linen I had none left, but what was mere rags; I had goats'-hair, but neither knew how to weave it or spin it; and had I known how, here were no tools to work it with. All the remedy that I found for this was, that at last I did remember I had, among the seamen's clothes which were saved out of the ship, some neckcloths of calico or mus-lin; and with some pieces of these I made three small sieves, proper enough for the work; and thus I made shift for some years: how I did afterwards, I shall show in its place.

The baking part was the next thing to be considered, and how I should make bread when I came to have corn; for, first, I had no yeast; as to that part, there was no supplying the want, so I did not concern myself much about it. But for an oven, I was indeed in great pain. At length, I found out an experiment for that also, which was this: I made some earthen vessels very broad, but not deep, that is to say, about two feet diameter, and not above nine inches deep; these I burned in the fire, as I had done the other, and laid them by; and when I wanted to bake, I made a great fire upon my hearth, which I had paved with some square tiles, of my own baking and burning also.

When the firewood was burned pretty much into embers, I drew them forward upon this hearth, so as to cover it all over, and there I let them lie till the hearth was very hot; then sweeping away all the embers, I set down loaves, and whelming down the earthen pot upon them, drew the embers all round the outside of the pot, to keep in and add to the heat; and thus, as well as in the best oven in the world, I baked my barley loaves, and became, in a little time, a good pastry-cook into the bargain; for I made myself several cakes and puddings of the rice; but I made no pies, neither had I anything to put into them, except the flesh either of fowls or goats.

All these things took me up most part of the third year of my abode here; for, it is to be observed, that in the intervals of these things, I had my new harvest and husbandry to manage; for I reaped my corn in its season, and carried it home as well as I could, and laid it up in the ear, in my large baskets, till I had time to rub it out, for I had no floor to thrash it on, or instrument to thrash it with.

And now, my stock of corn increasing, I wanted to build my barns bigger; I wanted a place to lay it up in, for the increase of the corn now yielded me so much, that I had of the barley about twenty bush-els, and of the rice as much, or more, insomuch that now I resolved to begin to use it freely; for my bread had been quite gone a great while; also I resolved to see what quantity would be sufficient for me a whole year, and to sow but once a-year.

Upon the whole, I found that the forty bushels of barley and rice were much more than I could consume in a year; so I resolved to sow just the same quantity every year that I sowed the last, in hopes that such a quantity would fully provide me with bread, &c.

All the while these things were doing, my thoughts ran many times upon the prospect of land which I had seen from the other side of the island; and I was not without secret wishes that I were on shore there, fancying I might find some way or other to convey myself farther, and perhaps at last find some means of escape.

Now I wished for my boy Xury, and the long-boat with the shoul-der-of-mutton sail, with which I sailed above a thousand miles on the coast of Africa; but this was in vain: then I thought I would go and look at our ship's boat, which was blown up upon the shore a great way, in the storm, when we were first cast away. She lay almost where she did at first; and was turned, by the force of the waves and the winds, almost bottom upward, but no water about her. If I had had hands to have refitted her, and to have launched her into the water, the boat would have done well enough, and I might have gone back into the Brazils with her easily; but I might have foreseen that I could no more turn her and set her upright upon her bottom, than I could remove the island; however, I went to the woods, and cut levers and rollers, and brought them to the boat, resolving to try what I could do; suggesting to myself, that if I could but turn her down, I might repair the damage she had received, and she would be a very good boat, and I might go to sea in her very easily.

I spared no pains in this piece of fruitless toil, and spent three or four weeks about it; at last, finding it impossible to heave it up with my little strength, I fell to digging away the sand, to undermine it, and so to make it fall down, setting pieces of wood to thrust and guide it right in the fall.

But when I had done this, I was unable to stir it up again, or to get under it, much less to move it forward towards the water; so I was forced to give it over.

This at length put me upon thinking whether it was not possible to make myself a canoe, or *periagua*, such as the natives of those climates make, even without tools, of the trunk of a great tree. This I not only thought possible, but easy, and pleased myself extremely with the thoughts of making it, and with my having much more convenience for it than any of the negroes or Indians; but not at all considering the particular inconveniences which I lay under more than the Indians did, *viz.*, want of hands to move it, when it was made, into the water; for what was it to me, if when I had chosen a vast tree in the woods, and with much trouble cut it down, if I had been able with my tools to hew and dub the outside into the proper shape of a boat, and burn or cut out the inside to make it hollow, so as to make a boat of it—if, after all this, I must leave it just where I found it, and not be able to launch it into the water?

I went to work upon this boat the most like a fool that ever man did, who had any of his senses awake. I pleased myself with the design, without determining whether I was ever able to undertake it; not but that the difficulty of launching my boat came often into my head; but I put a stop to my inquiries into it, by this foolish answer: "Let me first make it; I warrant I will find some way or other to get it along when it is done."

I felled a cedar-tree, and I question much whether Solomon ever had such a one for the building of the Temple of Jerusalem, it was five feet ten inches diameter at the lower part next the stump, and four feet eleven inches diameter at the end of twenty-two feet. It was not without infinite labour that I felled this tree; I was twenty days hacking and hewing at it at the bottom; I was fourteen more getting the branches and limbs cut oft', which I hacked and hewed through with axe and hatchet, with inexpressible labour: after this, it cost me a month to shape it and dub it to a proportion, and to something like the bottom of a boat, that it might swim upright as it ought to do. It cost me near three months more to clear the inside, and work it out so as to make an exact boat of it; this I did, without fire, by mere mallet and chisel, and by the dint of hard labour, till I had brought it to be a very handsome *periagua*, and big enough to have carried six and twenty men, and consequently big enough to have carried me and all my cargo.

When I had gone through this work, I was extremely delighted with it. The boat was really much bigger than ever I saw a canoe or *periagua*, that was made of one tree, in my life. Many a weary stroke it had cost, you may be sure: and had I gotten it into the water I make no question but I should have begun the maddest voyage, and the most unlikely to be performed, that ever was undertaken.

But all my devices to get it into the water failed me. It lay about one hundred yards from the water; but the first inconvenience was, it was up hill towards the creek. To take away this discouragement, I resolved to dig into the surface of the earth, and so make a declivity: this I began: but when this was worked through, and this difficulty managed, it was still much the same, for I could no more stir the canoe than I could the other boat. Then I measured the distance of ground, and resolved to cut a dock or canal, to bring the water up to the canoe. Well, I began this work; and when I began to calculate how deep it was to be dug, how broad, how the stuff was to be thrown out, I found that, by the number of hands I had, being none but my own, it must have been ten or twelve years before I could have gone through with it; for the shore lay so high, that at the upper end it must have been at least twenty feet deep; so, with great reluctancy, I gave this attempt over also.

I had now been here so long that many things which I brought on shore for my help were either quite gone, or very much wasted, and near spent.

My ink had been gone some time, all but a very little, which I eked out with water, till it was so pale, it scarce left any appearance of black upon the paper. As long as it lasted, I made use of it to minute down the days of the month on which any remarkable thing happened to me: and, first, by casting up times past, I remembered that there was a strange concurrence of days in the various providences which befell me, and which, if I had been superstitiously inclined to observe days as fatal or fortunate, I might have had reason to have looked upon with a great deal of curiosity.

First, I had observed, that the same day that I broke away from my father and friends, and ran away to Hull, in order to go to sea, the same day afterwards I was taken by the Sallee man-of-war, and made a slave; the same day of the year that I escaped out of the wreck of that ship in Yarmouth Roads, that same day-year afterwards I made my escape from Sallee in a boat; the same day of the year I was born on, *viz.*, the 30th of September, that same day I had my life so miraculously saved twenty-six years after, when I was cast on shore in this island; so that my wicked life and my solitary life began both on a day.

The next thing to my ink being wasted, was the biscuit which I brought out of the ship; this I had husbanded to the last degree, allowing myself but one cake of bread a day for above a year; and yet I was quite without bread for near a year before I got any corn of my own.

My clothes, too, began to decay; as to linen, I had had none a good while, except some chequered shirts which I found in the chests of the other seamen, and which I carefully preserved; because many times I could bear no other clothes on but a shirt.

Upon these views, I began to consider about putting the few rags I had into some order; I had worn out all the waistcoats I had, and my business was now to try if I could not make jackets out of the great watch-coats which I had by me, and with such other materials as I had; so I set to work, tailoring, or rather, indeed, botching, for I made most piteous work of it. However, I made shift to make two or three new waistcoats, which I hoped would serve me a great while; as for breeches or drawers, I made but a very sorry shift indeed till afterwards.

I have mentioned that I saved the skins of all the creatures that I killed, I mean four-footed ones, and I had them hung up stretched out with sticks in the sun, by which means some of them were so dry and hard that they were fit for little, but others were very useful. The first thing I made of these was a great cap for my head, with the hair on the outside, to shoot off the rain; and this I performed so well, that after, I made me a suit of clothes wholly of these skins.

After this, I spent a great deal of time and pains to make an umbrella; I was in great want of one; I had seen them made in the Brazils, where they are very useful in the great heats there, and I felt the heats every jot as great here, and greater too, being nearer the equinox; besides, as I was obliged to be much abroad, it was a most useful thing to me, as well for the rains as the heats. I took a world of pains with it, and was a great while before I could make anything likely to hold: nay, after I thought I had hit the way, I spoiled two or three before I made one to my mind: but at last I made one that answered indifferently well; the main difficulty I found was to make it let down. I could make it spread, but if it did not let down too, and draw in, it was not portable for me any way but just over my head. However, at last, I made one to answer, and covered it with skins, the hair upwards, so that it cast off the rain like a penthouse, and kept off the sun so effectually, that I could walk out in the hottest of the weather with greater advantage than I could before in the coolest, and when I had no need of it, could close it, and carry it under my arm.

I cannot say, that after this, for five years, any extraordinary thing happened to me, but I lived on in the same course, in the same place as before; the chief things I was employed in, besides my yearly labour of planting my barley and rice, and curing my raisins, of both which I always kept up just enough to have sufficient stock of one year's provision beforehand; and my daily pursuit of going out with my gun, I had one labour, to make a canoe, which at last I finished: so that, by digging a canal to it of six feet wide and four feet deep, I brought it into the creek, almost half a mile. As for the first, which was so vastly big, I was obliged to let it lie where it was, as a memorandum to teach me to be wiser the next time; indeed, the next time, though I could not get a tree proper for it, and was in a place where I could not get the water to it at any less distance than near half a mile, yet, as I saw it was practicable at last, I never gave it over; and though I was near two years about it, yet I never grudged my labour, in hopes of having a boat to go off to sea at last.

However, though my little *periagua* was finished, yet the size of it was not at all answerable to the design which I had in view when I made the first; of venturing over to the *terra firma,* where it was above forty miles broad; accordingly the smallness of my boat assisted to put an end to that design, and now I thought no more of it. My next design was to make a cruise round the island; for as I had been on the other side in one place, crossing over the land, so the discoveries

I made in that little journey made me very eager to see other parts of the coast; and now I had a boat, I thought of nothing but sailing round the island.

For this purpose, I fitted up a little mast in my boat, and made a sail too out of some of the pieces of the ship's sails which lay in store. Having fitted my mast and sail, and tried the boat, I found she would sail very well: then I made little lockers, at each end of my boat, to put provisions, necessaries, ammunition, &c., into, to be kept dry, and a little, long, hollow place I cut in the inside of the boat, where I could lay my gun, making a flap to hang down over it, to keep it dry.

I fixed my umbrella also in a step at the stern, to stand over my head, and keep the heat of the sun off me, like an awning; and thus I every now and then took a little voyage upon the sea: but never went far out, nor far from the little creek. At last, being eager to view the circumference of my little kingdom, I resolved upon my cruise; and accordingly I victualled my ship for the voyage, putting in two dozen of loaves of barley bread, an earthen pot full of parched rice, a little bottle of rum, half a goat, and powder and shot for killing more, and two large watch coats I had saved out of the seamen's chests; these I took, one to lie upon, and the other to cover me in the night.

It was the 6th of November, in the sixth year of my reign, or captivity, which you please, that I set out on this voyage, and I found it much longer than I expected; for though the island itself was not very large, yet when I came to the east side of it, I found a great ledge of rocks lie out about two leagues into the sea, and beyond that a shoal of sand, lying dry half a league more, so that I was obliged to go a great way out to sea to double the point.

When first I discovered them, I was going to give over my enterprise, and come back again, not knowing how far it might oblige me to go out to sea; and, above all, doubting how I should get back again: so I came to an anchor; for I had made a kind of an anchor, with a piece of a broken grappling which I got out of the ship.

But the third day, in the morning, I ventured: but I am a warning to all rash and ignorant pilots; for no sooner was I come to the point, when I was not even my boat's length from the shore, but I found myself in a great depth of water, and a current like the sluice of a mill: it carried my boat along with it with such violence that all I could do could not keep her so much as on the edge of it; but I found it hurried me farther and farther out from the eddy, which was on my left hand.

There was no wind stirring to help me, and all I could do with my paddles signified nothing; and now I began to give myself over for lost; for as the current was on both sides of the island, I knew in a few leagues' distance they must join again, and then I was irrecoverably gone; so that I had no prospect before me but of perishing, not by the sea, for that was calm enough, but of starving from hunger. I had, indeed, found a tortoise on the shore, as big almost as I could lift, and had tossed it into the boat; and I had a great jar of fresh water; but what was all this to being driven into the vast ocean, where, to be sure, there was no shore, no main land or island, for a thousand leagues at least.

And now I saw how easy it was for the providence of God to make even the most miserable condition of mankind worse. Now I looked back upon my desolate, solitary island, as the most pleasant place in the world, and all the happiness my heart could wish for was to be but there again. It is scarcely possible to imagine the consternation I was now in, being driven from my beloved island into the wide ocean, almost two leagues, and in the utmost despair of ever recovering it again. However, I worked hard till my strength was almost exhausted, and kept my boat as much to the northward, that is towards the side of the current which the eddy lay on, as possibly I could; when about noon, as the sun passed the meridian, I thought I felt a little breeze of wind in my face, springing up from S.S.E. This cheered my heart a little, and especially when, in about half an hour more, it blew a pretty gentle gale.

By this time I had got at a frightful distance from the island, and had the least cloudy or hazy weather intervened, I had been undone another way, too; for I had no compass on board, and should never have known how to have steered towards the island, if I had but once lost sight of it; but the weather continuing clear, I applied myself to get up my mast again, and spread my sail, standing away to the north as much as possible, to get out of the current.

Just as I had set my mast and sail, and the boat began to stretch away, I saw by the clearness of the water some alteration of the current was near; and presently I found to the cast, at about half a mile, a breach of the sea upon some rocks: these rocks caused the current to part again, and as the main stress of it ran away more southerly, leaving the rocks to the. north-cast, so the other returned by the repulse of the rocks, and made a strong eddy, which ran back again to the north-west, with a very sharp stream.

They who know what it is to have a reprieve brought to them upon the ladder, or to be rescued from thieves just going to murder them, or who have been in such extremities, may guess what my present surprise of joy was, and how gladly I put my boat into the stream of this eddy; and the wind also freshening, how gladly I spread my sail to it, running cheerfully before the wind, and with a strong tide or eddy under foot.

This eddy carried me about, a league in my way back again, directly towards the island, but about two leagues more to the northward than the current winch carried me away at first; so that when I came near the island, I found myself open to the northern shore of it, that is to say, the other end of the island, opposite to that which I went out from.

When I had made something more than a league of way by the help of this eddy, I found it was spent, and served me no farther. However, being between two great currents in the wake of the island, I found the water at least still, and running no way; and having still a breeze of wind fair for me, I kept on steering directly for the island, and in about an hour came within about a mile of the shore, where, it being smooth water, I soon got to land.

When I was on shore, I fell on my knees, and gave God thanks for my deliverance, resolving to lay aside all thoughts of my deliverance by my boat; and refreshing myself with such things as I had, I brought my boat close to the shore, in a little cove that I had spied under some trees, and laid me down to sleep, being quite spent with the labour and fatigue of the voyage.

I was now at a great loss which way to get home with my boat; I had run so much hazard, and knew too much of the case, to think of attempting it by the way I went out; so I resolved on the next morning to make my way westward along the shore, and to see if there was no creek where I might lay up my frigate in safety, so as to have her again, if I wanted her. In about three miles, I came to a very good inlet or bay, about a mile over, which narrowed till it came to a very little rivulet or brook, where I found a very convenient harbour for my boat, and where she lay as if she had been in a little dock made on purpose for her. Here I put in, and having stowed my boat very safe, I went on shore to look about me, and see where I was.

I soon found I had but a little passed by the place where I had been before, when I travelled on foot to that shore; so taking nothing out of my boat but my gun and umbrella, for it was exceedingly hot, I began my march. The way was comfortable enough after such a voyage as I had been upon, and I reached my old bower in the evening, where I found everything standing as I had left it.

I got over the fence, and laid me down in the shade to rest my limbs, for I was very weary, and fell asleep; but judge you, if you can, that read my story, what a surprise I must be in, when I was awaked out of my sleep by a voice, calling me by my name several times, "Robin, Robin, Robin Crusoe; poor Robin Crusoe! Where are you, Robin Crusoe? Where are you? Where have you been?" I was so dead asleep at first, being fatigued with rowing the first part of the day, and with walking the latter part, that I did not wake thoroughly; but dozing between sleeping and waking, thought I dreamed that somebody spoke to me; but as the voice continued to repeat "Robin Crusoe, Robin Crusoe," at last I began to wake more perfectly, and was at first dreadfully frightened, and started up in the utmost consternation; but no sooner were my eyes open, but I saw my Poll sitting on the top of the hedge; and immediately knew that it was he that spoke to me; for just in such bemoaning language I had used to talk to him, and teach him: and he had learned it so perfectly that he would sit upon my finger, and lay his bill close to my face, and cry, "Poor Robin Crusoe! Where are you? Where have you been? How came you here?" and such things as I had taught him.

However, even though I knew it was the parrot, and that indeed it could be nobody else, it was a good while before I could compose myself. First, I was amazed how the creature got thither; and then, how he should just keep about the place, and nowhere else; but as I was well satisfied it could be nobody but honest Poll, I got over it; and holding out my hand, and calling him by his name, "Poll," the sociable creature came to me, and sat upon my thumb, as he used to do, and continued talking to me, "Poor Robin Crusoe! and how did I come here? and where had I been?" just as if he had been overjoyed to see me again; and so I carried him home along with me.

I had now had enough of rambling to sea for some time, and had enough to do for many days, to sit still, and reflect upon the danger I had been in. I would have been very glad to have had my boat again on my side of the island; but I knew not how it was practicable to get it about. I contented myself to be without any boat, though it had been the product of so many months' labour to make it, and of so many more to get it into the sea.

In this government of my temper, I remained near a year; and lived a vow sedate, retired life, as you may well suppose; and my thoughts being very much composed as to my condition, and fully comforted in resigning myself to the dispositions of Providence, I thought I lived really very happily in all things, except that of society.

I unproved myself in this time in all the mechanic exercises which my necessities put me upon applying myself to; and I believe I should, upon occasion, have made a very good carpenter, especially considering how few tools I had.

Besides this, I arrived at an unexpected perfection in my earthenware, and contrived well enough to make them with a wheel, which I found infinitely easier and better; because I made things round and shaped, which before were filthy things indeed to look on. But I think I was never more vain of my own performance, or more joyful for anything I found out, than for my being able to made a tobacco-pipe; and though it was a very ugly, clumsy thing when it was done, and only burned red, like other earthenware, yet as it was hard and firm, and would draw the smoke, I was exceedingly comforted with it, for I had been always used to smoke; and there were pipes in the ship, but I forgot them at first, not thinking that there was tobacco in the island; and afterwards, when I searched the ship again, I could not come at any pipes.

In my wicker-ware, also, I improved much, and made abundance of necessary baskets, as well as my invention showed me; though not very handsome, yet they were such as were very handy and convenient for laying things up in, or fetching things home. Also, large deep baskets were the receivers of my corn, which I always rubbed out as soon as it was dry, and cured, and kept it in great baskets.

I began now to perceive that my powder abated considerably: this was a want which it was impossible for me to supply, and I began seriously to consider what I must do when I should have no more powder; that is to say, how I should kill any goats. I had, in the third year of my being here, kept a young kid, and bred her up tame, and I was in hopes of getting a he-goat: but I could not by any means bring it to pass, till my kid grew an old goat; and as I could never find in my heart to kill her, she died at last of mere age.

But being now in the eleventh year of my residence, and my ammunition growing low, I set myself to study some art to trap and snare the goats, to see whether I could not catch some of them alive; and particularly, I wanted a she-goat great with young. For this purpose, I made snares to hamper them; but my tackle was not good, for I had no wire, and I always found them broken, and my bait devoured. At length, I resolved to try a pitfall: so I dug several large pits in the earth, in places where I had observed the goats used to feed, and over those pits I placed hurdles, of my own making too, with a great weight upon them; and several times I put ears of barley and dry rice, without setting the trap; and I could easily perceive that the goats had gone in and eaten up the corn, for I could see the marks of their feet. At length, I set three traps in one night, and going the next morning, I found them all standing, and yet the bait eaten and gone: this was very discouraging. However, I altered my traps: and, not to trouble you with particulars, going one morning to see my traps, I found in one of them a large old he-goat; and in one of the others, three kids, a male and two females.

As to the old one, I knew not what to do with him; he was so fierce, I durst not go into the pit to him, to bring him away alive, which was what I wanted; so I even let him out, and he ran away as if he had been frightened out of his wits. But I did not then know what I afterwards learned, that hunger will tame a lion. If I had let him stay there three or four clays without food, and then have carried him some water to drink, and then a little corn, he would have been as tame as one of the kids; for they are mighty sagacious, tractable creatures, where they are well used.

However, for the present I let him go, knowing no better at that time: then I went to the three kids, and, taking them one by one, I tied them with strings together, and with some difficulty brought them all home.

It was a good while before they would feed; but throwing them some sweet corn, it tempted them, and they began to be tame. And now I found that if I expected to supply myself with goats' flesh, when I had no powder or shot left, breeding some up tame was my only way, when, perhaps, I might have them about my house like a flock of sheep. But, then, it occurred to me that I must keep the tame from the wild, or else they would always run wild when they grew up; and the only way for this was to have some enclosed piece of ground, well fenced either with hedge or pale, to keep them in so effectually, that those within might not break out, or those without break in.

This was a great undertaking for one pair of hands; yet, as I saw there was an absolute necessity for doing it, my first work was to find out a proper piece of ground, where there was likely to be herbage for them to eat, water for them to drink, and cover to keep them from the sun.

Those who understand such enclosures will think I had very little contrivance, when I pitched upon a place very proper for all these, which had two or three little drills of fresh water in it, and at one end was very woody,—they will smile at my forecast, when I shall tell them I began by enclosing this piece of ground in such a manner, that my hedge or pale must have been at least two miles about. Nor was the madness of it so great as to the compass, for if it was ten miles about, I was like to have time enough to do it in; but I did not consider that my goats would be as wild in so much compass as if they had had the whole island, and I should have so much room to chase them in that I should never catch them.

My hedge was begun and carried on, I believe, about fifty yards when this thought occurred to me; so I presently stopped short, and, for the beginning, I resolved to enclose a piece of about one hundred and fifty yards in length, and one hundred yards in breadth, which, as it would maintain as many as I should have in any reasonable time, so, as my stock increased, I could add more ground to my enclosure.

This was acting with some prudence, and I went to work with courage. I was about three months hedging in the first piece; and, till I had done it, I tethered the three kids in the best part of it, and used them to feed as near me as possible, to make them familiar; and very often I would go and carry them some ears of barley and corn, or a handful of rice, and feed them out of my hand; so that, after my enclosure was finished, and I let them loose, they would follow me up and down, bleating after me for a handful of corn.

This answered my end, and in about a year and a half I had a flock of about twelve goats, kids and all; and in two years more I had three-and-forty, besides several that I took and killed for my food. After that, I enclosed five several pieces of ground to feed them in, with little pens to drive them into, to take them as I wanted, and gates out of one piece of ground into another.

But this was not all; for now I not only had goats' flesh to feed on when I pleased, but milk too, a thing which, indeed, in the beginning, I did not so much as think of, and which, when it came into my thoughts, was really an agreeable surprise, for now I set up my dairy, and had sometimes a gallon or two of milk in a day. And as Nature, who gives supplies of food to every creature, dictates even naturally how to make use of it, so I, that had never milked a cow, much less a goat, or seen butter or cheese made only when I was a boy, after a great many essays and miscarriages, made both butter and cheese at last, also salt (though I found it partly made to my hand by the heat of the sun upon some of the rocks of the sea), and never wanted it afterwards.

It would have made a stoic smile to have seen me and my little family sit down to dinner. There was my majesty, the prince and lord of the whole island; I had the lives of all my subjects at my absolute command; I could hang, draw, give liberty, and take it away, and no rebels among my subjects. Then, to see how like a king I dined, too, all alone, attended by my servants! Poll, as if he had been my favourite, was the only person permitted to talk to me. My dog, who was now grown very old and crazy, and had found no species to multiply his kind upon, sat always at my right hand, and two cats, one on one side of the table, and one on the other, expecting now and then a bit from my hand, as a mark of my special favour.

But these were not the two cats which I brought on shore at first, for they were both of them dead, and had been interred near my habitation by my own hand; but one of them having multiplied by I know not what kind of creature, these were two which I had preserved tame. With this attendance and in this plentiful manner I lived; neither could I be said to want anything but society.

I was something impatient to have the use of my boat, though very loath to run any more hazards; and therefore sometimes I sat contriving ways to get her about the island, and at other times I sat myself down contented enough without her. But I had a strange uneasiness in my mind to go down to the point of the island, where, in my last ramble, I went up the hill to see how the shore lay; this inclination increased upon me every day, and at length I resolved to travel thither by land, following the edge of the shore. I did so; but had anyone in England met such a man as I was, it must either have frightened him, or raised a great deal of laughter; and as I frequently stood still to look at myself, I could not but smile at the notion of my travelling through Yorkshire with such an equipage, and in such a dress. Be pleased to take a sketch of my figure as follows:—

I had, a high shapeless cap, made of a goat's skin, with a flap hanging down behind, as well to keep the sun from me as to shoot the rain off from running into my neck, nothing being so hurtful in these climates as the rain upon the flesh under the clothes.

I had a short jacket of goat's skin, the skirts coming down to about the middle of the thighs, and a pair of open-kneed breeches of the same; the breeches were made of the skin of an old he-goat, whose hair hung down such a length on either side, that, like pantaloons, it reached to the middle of my legs; stockings and shoes I had none, but had made me a pair of somethings, I scarce know what to call them, like buskins, to flap over my legs, and lace on either side like spatterdashes, but of a most barbarous shape, as indeed were all the rest of my clothes.

I had on a broad belt of goat's skin dried, which I drew together with two thongs of the same instead of buckles, and in a kind of a frog on either side of this, instead of a sword and dagger, hung a little saw and a hatchet, one on one side, and one on the other. I had another belt not so broad, and fastened in the same manner, which hung over my shoulder, and at the end of it, under my left arm, hung two pouches, both made of goat's skin too, in one of which hung my powder, in the other my shot. At my back I carried my basket, and on my shoulder my gun, and over my head a great clumsy, ugly, goat's skin umbrella, but which, after all, was the most necessary thing I had about me next to my gun.

As for my face, the colour of it was really not so *mulatto*-like as one might expect from a man not at all careful of it, and living within nine or ten degrees of the equinox. My beard I had once suffered to grow till it was about a quarter of a yard long; but as I had both scissors and razors sufficient, I had cut it pretty short, except what grew on my upper lip, which I had trimmed into a large pair of Mahometan whiskers, such as I had seen worn by some Turks at Sallee, for the Moors did net wear such, though the Turks did; of these *moustachios*, or whiskers, I will not say they were long enough to hang my hat upon them, but they were of a length and shape monstrous enough, and such as in England would have passed for frightful.

But all this is by the bye; for, as to my figure, I had so few to observe me, that it was of no manner of consequence, so I say no more of that. In this kind of dress I went my new journey, and was out five or six days. I travelled first along the sea-shore, directly to the place where I first brought my boat to an anchor to get upon the rocks; and having no boat now to take care of, I went over the land a nearer way to the same height that I was upon before, when, looking forward to the point of the rocks which I was obliged to double with my boat, I was surprised to find the sea all smooth and quiet—no rippling, no motion, no current, any more there than in other places.

I was at a strange loss to understand this, and resolved to spend some time in observing it, to see if nothing from the sets of the tide had occasioned it. I was presently convinced that the tide of ebb setting from the west, and joining with the waters from some great river, must be the occasion of this current; and that according as the wind blew more forcibly from the west or from the north, this current came near, or went farther from the shore of the island; for, waiting thereabouts till evening, I went up to the rock again, and then the tide of ebb being made, I plainly saw the current.

This observation convinced me that I had nothing to do but to observe the ebbing and the flowing of the tide, and I might very easily bring my boat around the island; but I had such terror upon my spirits at the remembrance of the danger I had been in, that I could not think of it.

You are to understand that now I had two plantations in the island. One was my little fortification under the rock, with the cave behind, which by this time I had enlarged into several apartments. The driest and largest apartment had a door out beyond where my wall joined to the rock and was all filled up with large earthen pots, and fourteen or fifteen great baskets, which would hold five or six bushels each. Here I laid up my stores of provisions, especially my corn. As for my wall, made with long stakes or piles, those piles grew all like trees, and were by this time so big, and spread so very much, that there was not the least appearance of any habitation behind them.

Near this dwelling of mine, but a little farther from the sea, lay two pieces of cornland, which I kept cultivated and sowed.

Besides, I had my country-seat. I kept the hedge which circled it constantly in repair to its usual height, and the ladder standing always on the inside. The trees, which at first were stakes, were now grown very firm and tall, and so cut that they might spread and grow thick and wild, and make the more agreeable shade. In the middle I had my tent, being a piece of a sail spread over poles set up for that purpose; and under this I had made a couch, with the skins of the creatures I had killed, and with other soft things, and a blanket laid on them, and a great watch-coat to cover me; and here, whenever I had occasion, I took up my habitation.

Adjoining this, I had enclosures for a part of my goats; and as I had taken an inconceivable deal of pains to fence this ground, I was anxious to see the fence kept entire, lest the goats should break through. I never left off till I had stuck the outside of the hedge so full of small stakes, that it was rather a pale than a hedge, and there was scarce room to put a hand through. Afterward when those stakes grew, as they all did in the next rainy season, they made the enclosure strong like a wall.

In this place also I had my grapes growing, which I principally depended on for my winter store of raisins, and which I never failed to preserve very carefully, as the best and most agreeable dainty of my whole diet. Indeed, they were not agreeable only, but nourishing, and refreshing to the last degree.

As this was half-way between my other habitation and the place where I had laid up my boat, I generally stopped here on my way thither. I used frequently to visit my boat; and I kept all things about, or belonging to her, in very good order. Sometimes I went out in her to divert myself, but scarcely ever above a stone's cast or two from the shore, I was apprehensive of being hurried out of my knowledge again by the currents or winds, or any other accident. But now I come to a new scene of my life.

It happened one day, about noon, going towards my boat, I was exceedingly surprised with the print of a man's naked foot on the shore, which was very plain to be seen on the sand. I stood like one thunderstruck, or as if I had seen an apparition. I listened, I looked round me, but I could hear nothing nor see anything; I went up to a rising ground, to look farther; I went up the shore, and down the shore, but it was all one: I could see no other impression but that one. I went to it again to see if there were any more, and to observe if it might not be my fancy; but there was no room for that, for there was exactly the print of a foot—toes, heel, and every part of a foot. How it came thither I knew not, nor could I in the least imagine; but after innumerable fluttering thoughts, like a man perfectly confused and out of myself, I came to my fortification, not feeling, as we say, the ground I went on, but terrified to the last degree, looking behind me at every two or three steps, mistaking every bush and tree, and fancying every stump at a distance to be a man.

When I came to my castle (for so I think I called it ever after this), I fled into it like one pursued.

I slept none that night; the farther I was from the occasion of my fright, the greater my apprehensions were. Sometimes I fancied it must be the devil, and reason joined in with me in this supposition, for how should any other thing in human shape come into the place? Where was the vessel that brought them? What marks were there of any other footstep? And how was it possible a man should come there? I considered that the devil might have found out abundance of other ways to have terrified me than this of the single print of a foot; that as I lived quite on the other side of the island, he would never have been so simple as to leave a mark in a place where it was ten thousand to one whether I should ever see it or not, and in the sand too, which the first surge of the sea, upon a high wind, would have defaced entirely. All this seemed inconsistent with the thing itself, and with all the notions we usually entertain of the subtlety of the devil.

While these reflections were rolling in my mind, I was very thankful in my thoughts, that I was so happy as not to be thereabouts at that time, or that they did not see my boat, by which they would have concluded that some inhabitants had been in the place, and perhaps have searched farther for me. Then terrible thoughts racked my imagination about their having found out my boat, and that there were people here, and that, if so, I should certainly have them come again in greater numbers, and devour me; that if it should happen that they should not find me, yet they would find my enclosure, destroy all my corn, and carry away all my flock of tame goats, and I should perish at last for mere want.

Thus my fear banished all my religious hope, all that former confidence in God, which was founded upon such wonderful experience as I had had of His goodness; as if He that had fed me by miracle hitherto could not preserve, by His power, the provision which He had made for me by His goodness. I reproached myself with my laziness, that would not sow any more corn one year than would just serve me till the next season, as if no accident could intervene to prevent my enjoying the crop that was upon the ground; and this I thought so just a reproof, that I resolved for the future to have two or three years' corn beforehand; so that, whatever might come, I might not perish for want of bread.

One morning early, lying in my bed, and filled with thoughts, about my danger from the appearances of savages, I found it discomposed me very much; upon which these words of the Scripture came into my thoughts *"Call upon me in the day of trouble, and I will deliver thee, and thou shalt glorify me."* Upon this, rising cheerfully out of my bed, my heart was not only comforted, but I was guided and encouraged to pray earnestly to God for deliverance: when I had done praying, I took up my Bible, and opening it to read, the first words that presented to me were, *"Wait on the Lord, and be of good cheer, and he shall strengthen thy heart; wait, I say, on the Lord."* It is impossible to express the comfort this gave me. In answer, I thankfully laid down the book, and was no more sad, at least on that occasion.

In the middle of these cogitations, apprehensions, and reflections, it came into my thoughts one day, that all this might be a mere chimera of my own, and that this foot might be the print of my own foot, when I came on shore from my boat; this cheered me up a little, too, and I began to persuade myself it was all a delusion; that it was nothing else but my own foot; and why might I not come that way from the boat, as well as I was going that way to the boat? Again I considered also, that I could by no means tell, for certain, where I had trod, and where I had not; and that if, at last, this was only the print of my own foot, I had played the part of those fools who try to make stories of spectres and apparitions, and then are frightened at them more than anybody.

Now I began to take courage, and to peep abroad again, for I had not stirred out of my castle for three days and nights, so that I began to starve for provisions; for I had little or nothing within doors but some barley-cakes and water: then I knew that my goats wanted to be milked too, which usually was my evening diversion; and the poor creatures were in great pain and inconvenience for want of it; and, indeed, it almost spoiled some of them, and almost dried up their milk. Encouraging myself, therefore, with the belief that this was nothing but the print of one of my own feet, and that I might be truly said to start at my own shadow, I began to go abroad again, and went to my country-house to milk my flock: but to see with what fear I went forward, how often I looked behind me, how I was ready, every now and then, to lay down my basket and run for my life, it would have made anyone have thought I was haunted with an evil conscience, or that I had been lately most terribly frightened; and so, indeed, I had.

However, I went down thus two or three days, and having seen nothing, I began to be a little bolder, and to think there was really nothing in it but my own imagination; but I could not persuade myself fully of this till I should go down to the shore again, and see this print of a foot, and measure it by my own, and see if there was any similitude or fitness, that I might be assured it was my own foot: but when I came to the place—first, it appeared evidently to me, that when I laid up my boat, I could not possibly be on shore anywhere thereabouts: secondly, when I came to measure the mark with my own foot, I found my foot not so large by a great deal. Both these things filled my head with new imaginations, and gave me the vapours again to the highest degree, so that I shook with cold like one in an ague; and I went home again, filled with the belief that some man or men, had been on shore there; or, in short, that the island was inhabited, and I might be surprised before I was aware; and what course to take for my security I knew not.

The first thing I proposed to myself was, to throw down my enclosures, and turn all my tame cattle wild into the woods, lest the enemy should find them, and then frequent the island in prospect of the same or the like booty: then the simple thing of digging up my two corn fields, lest they should find such a grain there, and still be prompted to frequent the island: then to demolish my bower and tent, that they might not see any vestiges of habitation, and be prompted to look farther, in order to find out the persons inhabiting.

These were the subjects of the first night's cogitations after I was come home again, while the apprehensions which had so overrun my mind were fresh upon me, and my head was full of vapours.

This confusion of my thoughts kept me awake all night; but in the morning I fell asleep; and having, by the amusement of my mind, been, as it were, tired, and my spirits exhausted, I slept very soundly, and waked much better composed than I had ever been before. And now I began to think sedately; and, upon debate with myself, I concluded that this island (which was so exceedingly pleasant, fruitful, and no farther from the main land than as I had seen) was not so entirely abandoned as I might imagine; that although there were no stated inhabitants who lived on the spot, yet that there might sometimes come boats off from the shore, who, either with design, or perhaps never but when they were driven by cross winds, might come to this place; that I had lived here fifteen years now, and had not met with the least shadow or figure of any people yet; and that, if at any time they should be driven here, it was probable they went away again as soon as ever they could, seeing they had never thought fit to fix here upon any occasion; that the most I could suggest any danger from was, from any casual accidental landing of straggling people from the main, who, as it was likely, if they were driven hither, were here against their wills, so they made no stay here, but went off again with all possible speed; seldom staying one night on shore, lest they should not have the help of the tides and daylight back again; and that, therefore, I had nothing to do but to consider of some safe retreat, in case I should see any savages land upon the spot.

Now I began sorely to repent that I had dug my cave so large as to bring a door through again, which door, as I said, came out beyond where my fortification joined to the rock: upon maturely considering this, therefore, I resolved to draw me a second fortification, in the same manner of a semicircle, at a distance from my wall, just where I had planted a double row of trees about twelve years before, of which I made mention: these trees having been planted so thick before, they wanted but few piles to be driven between them, that they might be thicker and stronger, and my wall would be soon finished. So that I now had a double wall; and my outer wall was thickened with pieces of timber, old cables, and everything I could think of, to make it strong; having in it seven little holes, about as big as I might put my arm out at. In the inside of this, I thickened my wall to about ten feet thick, with continually bringing earth out of my cave, and laying it at the foot of the wall, and walking upon it; and through the seven holes I contrived to plant the muskets, of which I took notice that I had got seven on shore out of the ship; these I planted like my cannon, and fitted them into frames, that held them like a carriage, so that I could fire all the seven guns in two minutes' time; this wall I was many a weary month in finishing, and yet never thought myself safe till it was done.

When this was done, I stuck all the ground without my wall, for a great length every way, as full with stakes or sticks of the osier-like wood, which I found so apt to grow, as they could well stand; insomuch, that I believe I might set in near twenty thousand of them, leaving a pretty large space between them and my wall, that I might have room to see an enemy, and they might have no shelter from the young trees, if they attempted to approach my outer wall.

Thus, in two years' time, I had a thick grove; and in five or six years' time I had a wood before my dwelling, growing so monstrously thick and strong that it was indeed perfectly impassable: and no men, of what kind soever, could ever imagine that there was anything beyond it, much less a habitation. As for the way which I proposed to myself to go in and out (for I left no avenue), it was by setting two ladders, one to apart of the rock which was low, and then broke in, and left room to place another ladder upon that; so when the two ladders were taken down, no man living could come down to me without doing himself mischief; and if they had come downs they were still on the outside of my outer wall.

Thus I took all the measures human prudence could suggest, for my own preservation; and it will he seen, at length, that they were not altogether without just reason; though I foresaw nothing at that time more than my mere fear suggested to me.

While this was doing, I was not altogether careless of my other affairs; for I had a great concern upon me for my little herd of goats: they were not only a ready supply to me on every occasion, and began to be sufficient for me, without the expense of powder and shot, but also without the fatigue of hunting after the wild ones; and I was loath to lose the advantage of them, and to have them all to nurse up over again.

For this purpose, after long consideration, I could think of but two ways to preserve them; one was, to find another convenient place to dig a cave under ground, and to drive them into it every night; and the other was to enclose two or three little bits of land, remote from one another, and as much concealed as I could, where I might keep about half a dozen young goats in each place; so that if any disaster happened to the flock in general, I might be able to raise them again with little trouble and time: and this, though it would require a good deal of time and labour, I thought was the most rational design.

Accordingly, I spent some time to find out the most retired parts of the island; and I pitched upon one, which was as private, indeed, as my heart could wish for: it was a little damp piece of ground, in the middle of the hollow and thick woods, where I almost lost myself once before, endeavouring to come back that way from the eastern part of the island. Here I found a clear piece of land, near three acres, so surrounded with woods, that it was almost an enclosure by nature; at least, it did not want near so much labour to make it so, as the other piece of ground I had worked so hard at.

I immediately went to work with this piece of ground; and, in less than a month's time, I had so fenced it round that my flock were well enough secured in it; so, without any further delay, I removed ten young she-goats, and two he-goats, to this piece; and, when they were there, I continued to perfect the fence, till I had made it as secure as the other; which, however, I did at more leisure, and it took me up more time by a great deal. All this labour I was at the expense of, purely from my apprehensions on the account of the print of a man's foot; for, as yet, I had never seen any human creature come near the island; and I had now lived two years under this uneasiness, which, indeed, made my life much less comfortable than it was before, as may be well imagined by any who know what it is to live in the constant snare of the fear of man.

After I had thus secured one part of my little living stocks I went about the whole island, searching for another private place to make such another deposit; when, wandering more to the west point of the island than I had ever done yet, and looking out to sea, I thought I saw a boat upon the sea, at a great distance. I had found a perspective glass or two in one of the seamen's chests, which I saved out of our ship, but I had it not about me; and this was so remote that I could not tell what to make of it, though I looked at it till my eyes were not able to hold to look any longer; whether it was a boat or nor, I do not know, but as I descended from the hill I could see no more of it, so I gave it over; only I resolved to go no more out without a perspective glass in my pocket.

When I was come down the hill to the end of the island, where, indeed, I had never been before, I was presently convinced that the seeing the print of a man's foot was not such a strange thing in the island as I imagined: but that it was a special providence that I was cast upon the side of the island where the savages never came, I should easily have known that nothing was more frequent than for the canoes from the main, when they happened to be a little too far out at sea, to shoot over to that side of the island for harbour: likewise, as they often met and fought in their canoes, the victors, having taken any prisoners, would bring them over to this shore, where, according to their dreadful customs, being all cannibals, they would kill and eat them.

When I was come down the hill to the shore, I was perfectly confounded and amazed; nor is it possible for me to express the horror of my mind, at seeing the shore spread with skulls, hands, feet, and other bones of human bodies; and particularly, I observed a place where there had been a fire made, and a circle dug in the earth, like a cockpit, where I supposed the savage wretches had sat down to their inhuman feastings upon the bodies of their fellow-creatures.

I was so astonished with the sight of these things, that I entertained no notions of any danger to myself from it for a long while; all my apprehensions were buried in the thoughts of such a pitch of inhuman, hellish brutality, and the horror of the degeneracy of human nature, which, though I had heard of it often, yet I never had so near a view of before; in short, I turned away my face from the horrid spectacle, and with all the speed I could, walked on towards my own habitation.

When I came a little out of that part of the island, I stood still awhile, as amazed, and then recovering myself, I looked up with the utmost affection of my soul, and, with a flood of tears in my eyes, gave God thanks, that had cast my first lot in a part of the world where

I was distinguished from such dreadful creatures as these; and that, though I had esteemed my present condition very miserable, had yet given me so many comforts in it that I had still more to give thanks for than to complain of.

In this frame of thankfulness, I went home to my castle, and began to be much easier now, as to the safety of my circumstances, than ever I was before: for I observed that these wretches never came to this island in search of what they could get; perhaps not seeking, wanting, or expecting, anything here; and having often, no doubt, been up in the covered, woody part of it, without finding anything to their purpose. I knew I had been here now almost eighteen years, and never saw the least footsteps of human creature there before; and I might be eighteen years more as entirely concealed as I was now, if I did not discover myself to them, which I had no manner of occasion to do; it being my only business to keep myself entirely concealed where I was, unless I found a better sort of creatures than cannibals to make myself known to.

Yet I entertained such an abhorrence of the savage wretches that I have been speaking of, and of the wretched, inhuman custom of their devouring and eating one another up, that I continued pensive and sad, and kept close within my own circle, for almost two years after this. I did not so much as go to look after my boat all this time, but began rather to think of making another; for I could not think of ever making any more attempts to bring the other boat round the island to me, lest I should meet with some of these creatures at sea.

Time, however, and the satisfaction I had that I was in no danger of being discovered by these people, began to wear off my uneasiness about them; and I began to live just in the same composed manner as before, only with this difference, that I used more caution, and kept my eyes more about me, lest I should happen to be seen by any of them; and particularly, I was more cautious of firing my gun, lest any of them, being on the island, should happen to hear it. It was, therefore, a very good providence to me that I had furnished myself with a tame breed of goats, and that I had no need to hunt any more about the woods, or shoot at them; and if I did catch any of them after this, it was by snares and traps, as I had done before: so that for two years after this, I believe I never fired my gun once off, though I never went out without it; and, what was more, as I had saved three pistols out of the ship, I always carried them out with me, or at least two of them, sticking them in my goatskin belt. I also furbished up one of the great cutlasses that I had out of the ship, and made me a belt to hang it on also; so that I was now a most formidable fellow to look at when I went abroad, if you add to the former description of myself, the particular of two pistols, and a great broad-sword hanging at my side in a belt, but without a scabbard.

As in my present condition there were not really many things which I wanted, so, indeed, I thought that the frights I had been in about these savage wretches, and the concern I had been in for my own preservation, had taken off the edge of my invention for my own conveniences; and I had dropped a good design, which I had once bent my thoughts too much upon, and that was to try if I could not make some of my barley into malt, and then try to brew myself some beer. This was really a whimsical thought, and I reproved myself often for the simplicity of it: for I presently saw there would be the want of several things necessary to the making my beer, that it would be impossible for me to supply; as, first, casks to preserve it in, which was a thing that, as I have observed already, I could never compass: no, though I spent not only many days, but weeks, nay months, in attempting it, but to no purpose.

In the next place, I had no hops to make it keep, no yeast to make it work, no copper or kettle to make it boil; and yet I with all these things wanting, I verily believe, had not the frights and terrors I was in about the savages intervened, I had undertaken it, and perhaps brought it to pass, too; for I seldom gave anything over without accomplishing it, when once I had it in my head to begin it. But my invention now ran quite another way; for, night and day, I could think of nothing but how I might destroy some of these monsters in their cruel, bloody entertainment; and, if possible, gave the victim they should bring hither to destroy. But what could one man do among them, when perhaps there might be twenty or thirty of them together, with their darts, or their bows and arrows, with which they could shoot as true to a mark as I could with my gun?

While my mind was thus filled with thoughts of revenge and a bloody putting twenty or thirty of them to the sword, as I may call it, the horror I had at the place, and at the signals of the barbarous wretches devouring one another, abetted my malice. Well, at length I found a place in the side of the hill, where I was satisfied I might securely wait till I saw any of their boats coming; and might then, even before they would be ready to come on shore, convey myself unseen into some thickets of trees, in one of which there was a hollow large enough to conceal me entirely; and there I might sit and observe all their bloody doings, and take my full aim at their heads, when they were so close together as that it would be next to impossible that I should miss my shot, or that I could fail wounding three or four of them at the first shot. In this place then, I resolved to fulfil my design; and accordingly, I prepared two muskets and my ordinary fowling-piece. The two muskets I loaded with a brace of slugs each, and four or five smaller bullets, about the size of pistol bullets; and the fowling-piece I loaded with near a handful of swan-shot of the largest size; I also loaded my pistols with about four bullets each; and, in this posture, well provided with ammunition for a second and third charge, I prepared myself for my expedition.

After I had thus laid the scheme of my design, I made my tour every morning to the top of the hill, to see if I could observe any boats upon the sea, coming near the island, or standing over towards it; but I began to tire of this hard duty, after I had for two or three months constantly kept my watch, but came always back without any discovery; there having not, in all that time, been the least appearance, not only on or near the shore, but on the whole ocean, so far as my eyes or glass could reach every way.

As long as I kept my daily tour to the hill to look out, so long also I kept up the vigour of my design, and my spirits seemed to be all the while in a suitable form for so outrageous an execution as the killing twenty or thirty naked savages, for an offence which I had not at all entered into any discussion of in my thoughts, any farther than my passions were at first fired by the horror I conceived at the unnatural customs of the people of that country. But now, when I began to be weary of the fruitless excursion which I had made so long and so far every morning in vain, so my opinion of the action itself began to alter; and I began, with cooler and calmer thoughts, to consider what I was going to engage in; what authority or call I had to pretend to be judge and executioner upon these men as criminals, whom Heaven had thought fit, for so many ages, to suffer to go on unpunished, and to be, as it were, the executioners of His judgments one upon another; how far these people were offenders against me, and what right I had to engage in the quarrel of that blood which they shed promiscuously upon one another.

When I considered this a little, it followed necessarily that I was certainly in the wrong; that these people were not murderers in the sense that I had before condemned them in my thoughts, any more than those Christians were murderers who often put to death the prisoners taken in battle; or more frequently, upon many occasions, put whole troops of men to the sword, without giving quarter, though they threw down their arms and submitted.

These considerations really put me to a pause, and to a kind of a full stop; and I began, by little and little, to be off my design, and to conclude I had taken wrong measures in my resolution to attack the savages; and that it was not my business to meddle with them, unless they first attacked me; and this it was my business, if possible, to prevent: but that, if I were discovered and attacked by them, I knew my duty.

In this disposition I continued for near a year after this; and so far was I from desiring an occasion for falling upon these wretches, that in all that time I never once went up the hill to see whether there were any of them in sight, or to know whether any of them had been on shore or not, that I might not be tempted to renew any of my contrivances against them, or be provoked by any advantage that might present itself, to fall upon them: only this I did; I went and removed my boat, which I had on the other side of the island, and carried it down to the east end of the whole island, where I ran it into a little cove, which I found under some high rocks, and where I knew, by reason of the currents, the savages durst not, at least would not, come with their boats on any account whatever.

With my boat I carried away everything that I had left there belonging to her, though not necessary for the bare going thither, *viz.*, a mast and sail which I had made for her, and a thing like an anchor, but which indeed could not be called either anchor or grapnel; however, it was the best I could make of its kind; all these I removed, that there might not be the least shadow for discovery, or appearance of any boat, or of any human habitation upon the island. Besides this, I kept myself more retired than ever, and seldom went from my cell except upon my constant employment, to milk my she-goats, and manage my little flock in the wood, which, as it was quite on the other part of the island, was out of danger.

I believe the reader of this will not think it strange, if I confess, that these anxieties, these constant dangers I lived in, and the concern that was now upon me, put an end to all invention, and to all the contrivances that I had laid for my future accommodations and conveniences. I had the care of my safety more now upon my hands than that of my food. I cared not to drive a nail, or chop a stick of wood now, for fear the noise I might make should be heard: much less would I fire a gun for the same reason: and, above all, I was intolerably uneasy at making any fire, lest the smoke, which is visible at a great distance in the day, should betray me. For this reason, I removed that part of my business which required fire, such as burning of pots and pipes, &c, into my new apartment in the woods; where, after I had been some time, I found to my unspeakable consolation, a mere natural cave in the earth, which went in a vast way, and where, I dare say, no savage, had he been at the mouth of it, would be so hardy as to venture in.

The mouth of this hollow was at the bottom of a great rock, where, by mere accident (I would say, if I did not see abundant reason to ascribe all such things now to Providence), I was cutting down some thick branches of trees to make charcoal; and before I go on I must observe the reason of my making this charcoal, which was thus: I was afraid of making a smoke about my habitation, as I said before: and yet I could not live there without baking my bread, cooking my meat, &c, so I contrived to burn some wood here, as I had seen done in England, under turf, till it became dark or dry coal: and then putting the fire out, I preserved the coal to carry home, and perform the other services for which fire was wanting, without danger of smoke. But this is by the bye. While I was cutting down some wood here, I perceived that, behind a very thick branch of low brushwood or underwood, there was a kind of hollow place: I was curious to look in it, and getting with difficulty into the mouth of it, I found it was sufficient for me to stand upright in it, and perhaps another with me; but I must confess to you that I made more haste out than I did in, when, looking farther into the place, and which was perfectly dark, I saw two broad shining eyes of some creature, whether devil or man I knew not, which twinkled like two stars; the dim light from the cave's mouth shining directly in, and making the reflection.

However, after some pause, I recovered myself, and began to call myself a thousand fools, and to think that he that was afraid to see the devil, was not fit to live twenty years in an island all alone; and that I might well think there was nothing in this cave that was more frightful than myself. Upon this, plucking up my courage, I took up a firebrand, and in I rushed again, with the stick flaming in my hand: I had not gone three steps in, before I was almost as much frightened as before; for I heard a very loud sigh, like that of a man in some pain, and it was followed by a broken noise, as of words half expressed, and then a deep sigh again. I stepped back, and was indeed struck with such a surprise

115

that it put me into a cold sweat, and if I had had a hat on my head, I will not answer for if that my hair might not have lifted it off.

But still plucking up my spirits as well as I could, and encouraging myself a little with considering that the power and presence of God was everywhere, and was able to protect me, I stepped forward again, and by the light of the firebrand, holding it up a little over my head, I saw lying on the ground a monstrous, frightful, old he-goat, just making his will, as we say, and gasping for life, and dying, indeed, of mere old age. I stirred him a little to see if I could get him out, and he essayed to get up, but was not able to raise himself; and I thought with myself he might even lie there,—for if he had frightened me, so he would certainly fright any of the savages, if any one of them should be so hardy as to come in there while he had any life in him.

I was now recovered from my surprise, and began to look round me, when I found the cave was but very small,—it might be about twelve feet over, but in no manner of shape, neither round nor square, no hands having ever been employed in making it but those of mere Nature. I observed also that there was a place at the farther side of it that went in further, but was so low that it required me to creep upon my hands and knees to go into it, and whither it went I know not; so, having no candle, I gave it over for that time, but resolved to come again the next day provided with candles and a tinder-box, which I had made of the lock of one of the muskets, with some wildfire in the pan.

Accordingly, the next day I came provided with six large candles of my own making (for I made very good candles now of goats' tallow, but was hard set for candle-wick, using sometimes rags or rope-yarn, and sometimes the dried rind of a weed like nettles); and going into this low place I was obliged to creep upon all fours, almost ten yards,—which, by the way, I thought was a venture bold enough, considering that I knew not how far it might go, nor what was beyond it. When I had got through the strait, I found the roof rose higher up, I believe near twenty feet; but never was such a glorious sight seen in the island, I dare say, as it was to look round the sides and roof of this vault or cave—the wall reflected a hundred thousand lights to me from my two candles. What it was in the rock,—whether diamonds or any other precious stones, or gold,—which I rather supposed it to be,—I knew not.

The place I was in was a most delightful cavity, or grotto, though perfectly dark; the floor was dry and level, and had a sort of a small loose gravel upon it, so that there was no nauseous or venomous creature to be seen, neither was there any damp or wet on the sides or roof; the only difficulty in it was the entrance,—which, however, as it was a place of security, and such a retreat as I wanted, I thought was a convenience,—so that I was really rejoiced at the discovery, and resolved, without any delay, to bring some of those things which I was most anxious about to this place; particularly, I resolved to bring hither my magazine of powder, and all my spare arms, *viz.*, two fowling-pieces—for I had three in all—and three muskets—for of them I had eight in all; so I kept in my castle only five, which stood ready mounted like pieces of cannon on my outmost fence, and were ready also to take out upon any expedition.

Upon this occasion of removing my ammunition I happened to open the barrel of powder which I took up out of the sea, and which had been wet, and I found that the water had penetrated about three or four inches into the powder on every side. which caking and growing hard, had preserved the inside like a kernel in the shell, so that I had near sixty pounds of very good powder in the centre of the cask. This was a very agreeable discovery to me at that time; so I carried all away thither, never keeping above two or three pounds of powder with me in my castle, for fear of a surprise of any kind; I also carried thither all the lead I had left for bullets.

I fancied myself now like one of the ancient giants who were said to live in caves and holes in the rocks, where none could come at them; for I persuaded myself, while I was here, that if five hundred savages were to hunt me, they could never find me out—or if they did, they would not venture to attack me here. The old goat whom I found expiring died in the mouth of the cave the next day after I made this discovery; and I found it much easier to dig a great hole there, and throw him in and cover him with earth, than to drag him out; so I interred him there.

I was now in the twenty-third year of my residence in this island, and was so naturalized to the place and the manner of living, that, could I but have enjoyed the certainty that no savages would come to the place to disturb me, I could have been content to have capitulated for spending the rest of my time there, even to the last moment, till I had laid me down and died, like the old goat in the cave. I had also arrived to some little diversions and amusement?, which made the time pass a great deal more pleasantly with me than it did before;— first, I had taught my Poll, as I named before, to speak; and he did it so familiarly, and talked so articulately and plain, that it was very pleasant to me, for I believe no bird ever spoke plainer,—and he lived with me no less than six-and-twenty years; how long he might have lived afterwards I know not, though I know they have a notion in the Brazils that they live a hundred years.

My dog was a pleasant and loving companion to me for no less than sixteen years of my time, and then died of mere old age. As for my cats, they multiplied to that degree, that I was obliged to shoot several of them at first, to keep them from devouring me and all I had; but, at length, when the two old ones I brought with me were gone, and after some time continually driving them from me, and letting them have no provision with me, they all ran wild into the woods, except two or three favourites, which I kept tame, and whose young, when they had any, I always drowned; and these were part of my family. Besides these, I also kept two or three household kids about me, whom I taught to feed out of my hand; and I had two more parrots, which talked pretty well, and would all call "Robinson Crusoe," but none like my first; nor, indeed, did I take the pains with any of them that I had done with him. I had also several tame sea-fowls, whose names I knew not, that I caught upon the shore, and cut their wings; and the little stakes which I had planted before my castle wall being now grown up to a good thick grove, these fowls all lived among these low trees, and bred there, which was very agreeable to me,—so that I began to be very well contented with the life I led, if I could have been secured from the dread of the savages. But it was otherwise directed.

It was now the month of December, in my twenty-third year; and this being the southern solstice (for winter I cannot call it), was the particular time of my harvest, and required me to be pretty much abroad in the fields, when, going out early in the morning, even before it was thorough daylight, I was surprised with seeing a light of some fire upon the shore, at a distance from me of about two miles, towards that part of the island where I had observed some savages had been, as before, and not on the other, side; but, to my great affliction, it was on my side of the island.

I was indeed terribly surprised at the sight, and stopped short within my grove, not daring to go out, lest I might be surprised; and yet I had no more peace within, from the apprehensions I had that if these savages, in rambling over the island, should find my corn standing or cut, or any of my works and improvements, they would immediately conclude that there were people in the place, and would then never rest till they had found me out. In this extremity I went back directly to my castle, pulled up the ladder after me, and made all things without look as wild and natural as I could.

Then I prepared myself within, putting myself in a posture of defence; I loaded all my muskets, which were mounted upon my new fortification, and all my pistols, and resolved to defend myself to the last gasp,—not forgetting seriously to commend myself to the divine protection, and earnestly to pray to God to deliver me out of the hands of the barbarians. I continued in this posture about two hours, and began to be impatient for intelligence abroad, for I had no spies to send out.

After sitting a while longer, and musing what I should do in this case, I was not able to bear sitting in ignorance any longer; so setting up my ladder to the side of the hill, where there was a flat place, and then pulling the ladder after me, I set it up again, and mounted the top of the hill, and pulling out my perspective-glass, which I had taken on purpose, I laid me down flat on my belly on the ground, and began to look for the place. I presently found there were no less than nine naked savages, sitting round a small, fire they had made, not to warm them, for they had no need of that, the weather being extremely hot, but, as I supposed, to dress some of their barbarous diet of human flesh which they had brought with them.

They had two canoes with them, which they had hauled up upon the shore; and it was then ebb of tide, they seemed to me to wait for the return of the flood to go away again. It is not easy to imagine what confusion this sight put me into, especially seeing them come on my side of the island, and so near to me; but when I considered their coming must be always with the current of the ebb, I began afterwards to be more sedate in my mind, being satisfied that I might go abroad with safety all the time of the flood of tide, if they were not on shore before; and having made this observation, I went abroad about my harvest work with the more composure.

As I expected, so it proved; for, as soon as the tide made to the westward, I saw them all take boat and row away. I should have observed, that for an hour or more before they went off they were dancing, and I could easily discern their postures and gestures by my glass.

As soon as I saw them shipped and gone, I took two guns upon my shoulders, and two pistols in my girdle, and my great sword by my side without a scabbard, and with all the speed I was able to make, went away to the hill where I had discovered the first appearance of all; and as soon as I got thither, I perceived there had been three canoes more of the savages at that place; and looking out farther, I saw they were all at sea together, making over for the main.

This was a dreadful sight to me, especially as, going down to the shore, I could see the marks of horror which the dismal work they had been about had left behind it, I was so filled with indignation at the sight, that I now began to premeditate the destruction of the next that I saw there, let them be whom, or how many soever. It seemed evident to me that the visits which they made thus to this island were not very frequent, for it was above fifteen months before any more of them came on shore there again—that is to say, I neither saw them nor any footsteps or signals of them in all that time; yet all this while I lived uncomfortably, by reason of the constant; apprehensions of their coming upon me by surprise.

During all this time I was in the murdering humour, and spent most of my hours, which should have been better employed, in contriving how to circumvent and fall upon them the very next time I should see them—especially if they should be divided, as they were the last time, into two parties; nor did I consider at all that if I killed one party—suppose ten or a dozen—I was still the next day or week, or month, to kill another, and so another, even *ad infinitum*, till I should be, at length, no less a murderer than they were in being man-eaters— and perhaps much more so. I spent my days now in great perplexity and anxiety of mind, expecting that I should one day or other fall into the hands of these merciless creatures; and if I did at any time venture abroad, it was not without looking round me with the greatest care and caution imaginable.

And now I found, to my great comfort, how happy it was that I had provided a tame flock or herd of goats; for I durst not upon any account fire my gun, especially near that side of the island where they usually came, lest I should alarm the savages: and if they had fled from me now, I was sure to have them come again with perhaps two or three hundred canoes with them in a few days, and then I knew what to expect. However, I wore out a year and three months more before I ever saw any more of the savages, and then I found them again, as I shall soon observe. It is true they might have been there once or twice; but either they made no stay, or at least I did not see them; but in the month of May, as near as I could calculate, and in my four-and-twentieth year, I had a very strange encounter with them; of which in its place.

It was in the middle of May, on the sixteenth day, I think, as well as my poor wooden calendar would reckon—for I marked all upon the post still—that it blew a very great storm of wind all day, with a great deal of lightning and thunder, and a very foul night it was after it. I knew not what was the particular occasion of it; but as I was reading in the Bible, and taken up with very serious thoughts about my present condition, I was surprised with the noise of a gun, as I thought, fired at sea. This was, to be sure, a surprise quite of a different nature from any I had met with before; for the notions this put into my thoughts were quite of another kind. I started up in the greatest haste imaginable; and, in a trice, clapped my ladder to the middle place of the rock, and pulled it after me; and mounting it the second time, got to the top of a hill the very moment that a flash of fire bid me listen for a second gun, which, accordingly, in about half-a-minute, I heard; and by the sound, knew that it was from that part of the sea where I was driven down the current in my boat.

I immediately considered that this must be some ship in distress, and that they had some comrade, or some other ship in company, and fired these for signals of distress, and to obtain help. I had the presence of mind, at that minute, to think, that though I could not help them, it might be they might help me; so I brought together all the dry wood I could get at hand, and, making a good pile, I set it on fire upon the hill. The wood was dry, and blazed freely; and, though the wind blew very hard, yet it burned fairly out, so that I was certain, if there was any such thing as a ship, they must needs see it, and no doubt they did; for as soon as ever my fire blazed up, I heard another gun, and after that several others, all from the same quarter. I plied my fire all night long, till daybreak: and when it was broad day, and the air cleared up, I saw something at a great distance at sea, full east of the island, whether a sail or a hull I could not distinguish—no, not with my glass; the distance was so great, and the weather still something hazy also; at least, it was so out at sea.

I looked frequently at it all that day, and soon perceived that it did not move; so I presently concluded that it was a ship at anchor; and being, eager, you may be sure, to be satisfied, I took my gun in my hand, and ran towards the south side of the island, to the rocks where I had formerly been carried away by the current; and getting up there, the weather by this time being perfectly clear, I could plainly see, to my great sorrow, the wreck of a ship, cast away in the night upon those concealed rocks which I found when I was out in my boat. Had they

121

seen the island, as I must necessarily suppose they did not, they must, as I thought, have endeavoured to have saved themselves on shore by the help of their boat; but their firing off guns for help, especially when they saw, as I imagined, my fire, filled me with many thoughts. First, I imagined that upon seeing my light, they might have put themselves into their boat, and endeavoured to make the shore; but that the sea running very high, they might have been cast away.

Other times, I imagined that they might have lost their boat before, as might be the case many ways; particularly by the breaking of the sea upon their ship, which many times obliged men to stave, or take in pieces, their boat, and sometimes to throw it overboard with their own hands. Other times, I imagined they had some other ship or ships in company, who, upon the signals of distress they made, had taken them up, and carried them off. Other times, I fancied they were all gone off to sea in their boat, and being hurried away by the current that I had been formerly in, were carried out into the great ocean, where there was nothing but misery and perishing: and that, perhaps, they might by this time think of starving, and of being in a condition to eat one another.

There are some secret moving springs in the affections, which, when they are set a-going by some object in view, or, though not in view, yet rendered present to the mind by the power of imagination, that motion carries out the soul, by its impetuosity, to such violent eager embracings of the object that the absence of it is insupportable. Such were these earnest wishings that but one man had been saved. I believe I repeated the words, "O that it had been but one!" a thousand times; and my desires were so moved by it, that when I spoke the words my hands would clinch together, and my fingers would press the palms of my hands, so that if I had had any soft thing in my hand, I would have crushed it involuntarily; and the teeth in my head would strike together; and set against one another so strong, that for some time I could not part them again.

But it was not to be; either their fate or mine, or both, forbade it, for till the last year of my being on this island, I never knew whether any were saved out of that ship or no; and had only the affliction, some days after, to see the corpse of a drowned boy come on shore at the end of the island which was next the shipwreck. He had no clothes on but a seaman's waistcoat, a pair of open-kneed linen drawers, and a blue linen shirt; but nothing to direct me so much as to guess what nation he was of. He had nothing in his pockets but two pieces-of-eight and a tobacco-pipe—the last was to me of ten times more value than the first.

It was now calm, and I had a great mind to venture out in my boat to this wreck, not doubting but I might find something on board that might be useful to me. But that did not altogether press me so much, as the possibility that there might be yet some living creature on board, whose life I might not only save, but might, by saving that life, comfort my own to the last degree; and this thought clung so to my heart that I could not be quiet night nor day, but I must venture out in my boat on board this wreck; and committing the rest to God's providence, I thought the impression was so strong upon my mind that it could not be resisted, that it must come from some invisible direction, and that I should. be wanting to myself if I did not go.

Under the power of this impression, I hastened back to my castle, prepared everything for my voyage, took a quantity of bread, a great pot of fresh water, a compass to steer by, a bottle of rum (for I had still a great deal of that left), and a basket of raisins; and thus, loading myself with everything necessary, I went down to my boat, got the water out of her, got her afloat, loaded all my cargo in her, and then went home again for more. My second cargo was a great bag of rice, the umbrella to set up over my head for a shade, another large pot of fresh water, and about two dozen of small loaves, or barley-cakes, more than before, with a bottle of goat's milk, and a cheese: all which, with great labour and sweat, I carried to my boat; and praying to God to direct my voyage, I put out, and rowing the canoe along the shore, came at last to the utmost point of the island on the north-east side, and hauled my boat into a little creek on the shore.

I resolved, the next morning, to set out with the first of the tide; and, reposing myself for the night in my canoe, under the great watch-coat I mentioned, I launched out, and having a strong steerage with my paddle, I went, at a great rate, directly for the wreck, and in less than two hours I came up to it. It was a dismal sight to look at: the ship, which, by its building, was Spanish, stuck fast, jammed in between two rocks, all the stern and quarter of her were beaten to pieces by the sea; and as her forecastle, which stuck in the rocks, had run on with great violence, her mainmast and foremast were broken short off; but her bowsprit was sound, and the head and bow appeared firm. When I came close to her, a dog appeared upon her, who seeing me coming, yelped and cried; and, as soon as I called him, jumped into the sea to come to me: I took him into the boat, but found him almost dead with hunger and thirst. I gave him a cake of my bread, and he devoured it like a ravenous wolf that had been starving a fortnight in the snow: I then gave the poor creature some fresh water, with which, if I would have let him, he would have burst himself.

After this I went on board; but the first sight I met with was two men drowned in the cook-room, or forecastle of the ship, with their arms fast about one another. I concluded, as is indeed probable, that when the ship struck, it being in a storm, the sea broke so high, and so continually over her, that the men were not able to bear it, and were strangled with the constant rushing in of the water, as much is if they had been under water. Besides the dog, there was nothing left in the ship that had life; nor any goods, that I could see, but what were spoiled by the water. There were some casks of liquor, whether wine or brandy I knew not, which lay lower in the hold, and which, the water being ebbed but, I could see; but they were too big to meddle with.

I saw several chests, which I believe belonged to some of the seamen; and I got two of them into the boat, without examining what was in them. Had the stern of the ship been fixed, and the forepart broken off, I am persuaded I might have made a good voyage; for, by what I found in these two chests, I had reason to suppose the ship had a great deal of wealth on board; and, if I may guess from the course she steered, she must have been bound from Buenos Ayres, or the Rio de la Plata, in the south part of America, beyond the Brazils to the Havannah, in the Gulf of Mexico, and so perhaps to Spain. She had, no doubt, a great treasure in her, but of no use, at that time, to anybody; but what became of the crew I then knew not.

I found, besides these chests, a little cask full of liquor, of about twenty gallons, which I got into my boat with much difficulty. There were several muskets in the cabin, and a great powder-horn, with about four pounds of powder in it: as for the muskets, I had no occasion for them, so I left them, but took the powder-horn. I took a fire-shovel and tongs, which I wanted extremely; as also two little brass kettles, a copper pot to make chocolate, and a gridiron; and with this cargo, and the, dog, I came away, the tide beginning to make home again: and the same evening, about an hour within night, I reached the island again, weary and fatigued to the last degree. I reposed that night in the boat; and in the morning I resolved to harbour what I had got in my new cave, and not carry it home to my castle.

After refreshing myself, I got all my cargo on shore, and began to examine the particulars. The cask of liquor I found to be a kind of rum, but not such as we had at the Brazils; and, in a word, not at all good; but when I came to open the chests, I found several things of great use to me: for example, I found in one a fine case of bottles, of an extraordinary kind, and filled with cordial waters, fine and very good; the bottles held about three pints each, and were tipped with silver. I found two pots of very good *succades*, or sweetmeats, so fastened also on the top that the salt water had not hurt them; and two more of the same, which the water had spoiled.

I found some very good shirts, which were very welcome to me; and about a dozen and a half of white linen handkerchiefs, and coloured neckcloths; the former were also very welcome, being exceedingly refreshing to wipe my face in a hot day. Besides this, when I came to the till in the chest, I found there three great bags of pieces-of-eight, which held about eleven hundred pieces in all; and in one of them, wrapped up in a paper, six *doubloons* of gold, and some small bars of gold; I suppose they might all weigh near a pound. In the other chest were some clothes, but of little value; but, by the circumstances, it must have belonged to the gunner's mate; though there was no powder in it except two pounds of fine glazed powder, in three small flasks, kept, I suppose, for charging their fowling pieces on occasion.

Upon the whole, I got very little by this voyage that was of any use to me; for, as to the money, I had no manner of occasion for it; it was to me as the dirt under my feet, and I would have given it all for three or four pair of English shoes and stockings, which were things I greatly wanted, but had none on my feet for many years. I had, indeed, got two pair of shoes now, which I took off the feet of the two drowned men whom I saw in the wreck, and I found two pair more in one of the chests, which were very welcome to me; but they were not like our English shoes, either for ease or service, being rather what we call pumps than shoes. I found in this seaman's chest about fifty pieces-of-eight, in *rials*, but no gold: I suppose this belonged to a poorer man than the other, which seemed to belong to some officer. Well, however, I lugged this money home to my cave, and laid it up, as I had done that before which I had brought from our own ship; but it was a great pity, as I said, that the other part of this ship had not come to my share; for I am satisfied I might have loaded my canoe several times over with money; and, thought I, if I ever escape to England, it might lie here safe enough till I come again and fetch it.

Having now brought all my things on shore, and secured them,

I went back to my boat, and rowed her along the shore to her old harbour, where I laid her up, and made the best of my way to my old habitation, where I found everything safe and quiet. I began now to repose myself, live after my old fashion, and take care of my family affairs; and for a while I lived easy enough, only that I was more vigilant than I used to be, looked out oftener, and did not go abroad so much; and if, at any time, I did stir with any freedom, it was always to the east part of the island, where I was pretty well satisfied the savages never came, and where I could go without so many precautions, and such a load of arms and ammunition as I always carried with me if I went the other way. I lived in this condition near two years more; but my unlucky head, that was always to let me know it was born to make my body miserable, was all these two years filled with projects and designs, how, if it were possible, I might get away from this island; for, sometimes I was for making another voyage to the wreck, though my reason told me that there was nothing left there worth the hazard of my voyage; sometimes, for a ramble one way, sometimes another: and I believe verily, if I had had the boat that I went from Sallee in, I should have ventured to sea, bound anywhere, I knew not whither.

I am now supposed to be retired into my castle, after my late voyage to the wreck, my frigate laid up and secured under water, as usual, and my condition restored to what it, was before: I had more wealth, indeed, than what I had before, but was not at all the richer; for I had no more use for it than the Indians of Peru had before the Spaniards came there.

It was one of the nights in the rainy season in March, the four-and-twentieth year of my first setting foot in this island of solitude, I was lying in my hammock, awake, very well in health, had no pain, no distemper, no uneasiness of body, nor any uneasiness of mind more than ordinary, but could by no means close my eyes, that is, so as to sleep; no, not a wink all night long, otherwise than as follows:—It is impossible to set down the innumerable crowd of thoughts that whirled through that great thoroughfare of the brain—the memory, in this night's time: I ran over the whole history of my life in miniature, or by abridgment, as I may call it, to my coming to this island, and also of that part of my life since I came to this island. In my reflections upon the state of my case since I came on shore on this island, I was comparing the happy posture of my affairs in the first years of my habitation here, with the life of anxiety, fear, and care, which I had lived in ever since I had seen the print of a foot in the sand; not that I did not believe the savages had frequented the island even all the while, and might have been several hundreds of them at times on shore there; but I had never known it, and was incapable of any apprehensions about it; my satisfaction was perfect, though my danger was the same, and I was as happy in not knowing my danger as if I had never really been exposed to it.

I looked upon my present condition as the most miserable that could possibly be; that I was not able to throw myself into anything but death, that could be called worse; and if I reached the shore of the main, I might perhaps meet with relief, or I might coast along, as I did on the African shore, till I came to some inhabited country, and where I might find some relief; and, after all, perhaps I might fall in with some Christian ship that might take me in; and if the worst came to the worst, I could but die, which would put an end to all these miseries at once.

When this had agitated my thoughts for two hours or more, with such violence that it set my very blood into a ferment, and my pulse beat as if I had been in a fever, merely with the extraordinary fervour of my mind about it, nature, as if I had been fatigued and exhausted with the very thoughts of it, threw me into a sound sleep. One would have thought I should have dreamed of it, but I did not, nor of anything relating to it: but I dreamed that as I was going out in the morning as usual, from my castle, I saw upon the shore two canoes and eleven savages, coming to land, and that they brought with them another savage, whom they were going to kill, in order to eat him; when, on a sudden, the savage that they were going to kill, jumped away, and ran for his life; and I thought, in my sleep, that he came running into my little thick grove before my fortification, to hide himself; and that I, seeing him alone, and not perceiving that the others sought him that way, showed myself to him, and smiling upon him, encouraged him: that he kneeled down to me, seeming to pray me to assist him; upon which I showed him my ladder, made him go up, and carried him into my cave, and he became my servant: and that as soon as I had got this man, I said to myself, "Now I may certainly venture to the main land, for this fellow will serve me as a pilot, and will tell me what to do, and whither to go for provisions, and whither not to go for fear of being devoured; what places to venture into, and what to shun."

I waked with this thought; and was under such inexpressible impressions of joy at the prospect of my escape in my dream, that the disappointments which I felt upon coming to myself, and finding that it was no more than a dream, were equally extravagant the other way, and threw me into a very great dejection of spirits.

Upon this, however, I made this conclusion—that my only way to go about to attempt an escape was, if possible, to get a savage into my possession; and, if possible, it should be one of their prisoners, whom they had condemned to be eaten, and should bring hither to kill. But these thoughts still were attended with this difficulty, that it was impossible to effect this without attacking a whole caravan of them, and killing them all; and this was not only a very desperate attempt, and might miscarry; but, on the other hand, I had greatly scrupled the lawfulness of it to myself; and my heart trembled at the thoughts of shedding so much blood, though it was for my deliverance. The eager prevailing desire of deliverance at length mastered all the rest; and I resolved, if possible, to get one of these savages into my hands, cost what it would. My next thing was to contrive how to do it, and this indeed was very difficult to resolve on; but as I could pitch upon no probable means for it, so I resolved to put myself upon the watch, to see them when they came on shore, and leave the rest to the event; taking such measures as the opportunity should present, let what would be.

With these resolutions in my thoughts, I set myself upon the scout as often as possible, and indeed so often, that I was heartily tired of it; for it was above a year and a half that I waited; and for great part of that time went out to the west end, and to the south-west corner of the island almost every day, to look for canoes, but none appeared. This was very discouraging, and began to trouble me much; but the longer it seemed to be delayed, the more eager I was for it: in a word, I was not at first so careful to shun the sight of these savages, and avoid being seen by them, as I was now eager to be upon them. Besides, I fancied myself able to manage one, nay, two or three savages, if I had them, so as to make them entirely slaves to me, to do whatever I should direct them, and to prevent their being able at any time to do me any hurt. It was a great while that I pleased myself with this affair; but nothing still presented itself; all my fancies and schemes came to nothing, for no savages came near me for a great while.

About a year and a half after I entertained these notions, I was surprised one morning by seeing no less than five canoes all on shore together on my side the island, and the people who belonged to them all landed and out of my sight. The number of them broke all my measures; for seeing so many, and knowing that they always came four or six, or sometimes more in a boat, I could not tell what to think of it, or how to take my measures, to attack twenty or thirty men single-handed; so lay still in my castle, perplexed and discomforted. However, I put myself into the same position for an attack that I had formerly provided, and was just ready for action, if anything had presented. Having waited a good while, listening to hear if they made any noise, at length, being very impatient, I set my guns at the foot of my ladder, and clambered up to the top of the hill, by my two stages, as usual; standing so, however, that my head did not appear above the hill, so that they could not perceive me by any means. Here I observed, by the help of my perspective glass, that they were no less than thirty in number; that they had a fire kindled, and that they had meat dressed. How they had cooked it I knew not, or what it was; but they were all dancing, in I know not how many barbarous gestures and figures, their own way, round the fire.

While I was thus looking on them, I perceived, by my perspective, two miserable wretches dragged from the boats, where, it seems, they were laid by, and were now brought out for the slaughter. I perceived one of them immediately fall; being knocked down, I suppose, with a club or wooden sword, for that was their way; and two or three others were at work immediately, cutting him open for their cookery, while the other victim was left standing by himself, till they should be ready for him. In that very moment, this poor wretch, seeing himself a little at liberty, and unbound, Nature inspired him with hopes of life, and he started away from them, and ran with incredible swiftness along the sands, directly towards me;.

I mean towards that part of the coast where my habitation was. I was dreadfully frightened, I must acknowledge, when I perceived him run my way; and especially when, as I thought, I saw him pursued by the whole body; and now I expected that part of my dream was coming to pass, and that he would certainly take shelter in my grove: but I could not depend, by any means, upon my dream, that the other savages would not pursue him thither, and find him there. However, I kept my station, and my spirits began to recover when I found that there was not above three men that followed him; and still more was I encouraged, when I found that he outstripped them exceedingly in running, and gained ground on them; so that, if he could but hold out for half an hour, I saw easily he would fairly get away from them all.

There was between them and my castle, the creek, which I mentioned often in the first part of my story, where I landed my cargoes out of the ship; and this I saw plainly he must necessarily swim over, or the poor wretch would be taken there; but when the savage escaping came thither, he made nothing of it, though the tide was then up; but, plunging in, swam through in about thirty strokes, or thereabouts, landed, and ran with exceeding strength and swiftness. When the three persons came to the creek, I found that two of them could swim, but the third could not, and that, standing on the other side, he looked at the others, but went no farther, and soon after went softly back again; which, as it happened, was very well for him in the end. I observed that the two who swam were yet more than twice as long swimming over the creek as the fellow was that fled from them. It came very warmly upon my thoughts, and indeed irresistibly, that now was the time to get me a servant, and perhaps a companion or assistant; and that I was plainly called by Providence to save this poor creature's life.

I immediately ran down the ladders with all possible expedition, fetched my two guns, for they were both at the foot of the ladders, as I observed before, and getting up again with the same haste to the top of the hill, I crossed towards the sea; and having a very short cut, and all down hill, placed myself in the way between the pursuers and the pursued, hallooing aloud to him that fled, who, looking back, was at first perhaps as much frightened at me as at them; but I beckoned with my hand to him to come back; and, in the meantime, I slowly advanced towards the two that followed; then rushing at once upon the foremost, I knocked him down with the stock of my piece. I was loath to fire, because I would not have the rest hear; though, at that distance, it would not have been easily heard, and being out of sight of the smoke, too, they would not have known what to make of it. Having knocked this fellow down, the other who pursued him stopped, as if he had been frightened, and I advanced towards him: but as I came nearer, I perceived presently he had a bow and arrow, and was fitting it to shoot at me: so I was then obliged to shoot at him first, which I did, and killed him at the first shot.

The poor savage who fled, but had stopped, though he saw both his enemies fallen and killed, as he thought, yet was so frightened with the fire and noise of my piece, that he stood stock still, and neither came forward, nor went backward, though he seemed rather inclined still to fly than to come on. I hallooed again to him, and made signs to come forward, which he easily understood, and came a little way; then stopped again, and then a little farther, and stopped again; and I could then perceive that he stood trembling, as if he had been taken prisoner, and had just been to be killed, as his two enemies were. I beckoned to him again to come to me, and gave him all the signs of encouragement that I could think of; and he came nearer and nearer, kneeling down every ten or twelve steps, in token of acknowledgment for saving his life. I smiled at him, and looked pleasantly, and beckoned to him to come still nearer: at length, he came close to me; and then he kneeled down again, kissed the ground, and laid his head upon the ground, and, taking me by the foot, set my foot upon his head; this, it seems, was in token of swearing to be my slave for ever. I took him up, and made much of him, and encouraged him all I could.

But there was more work to do yet; for I perceived the savage whom I had knocked down was not killed, but stunned with the blow, and began to come to himself: so I pointed to him, and showed him the savage, that he was not dead; upon this he spoke some words to me, and though I could not understand them, yet I thought they were pleasant to hear; for they were the first sound of a man's voice that I had heard, my own excepted, for above twenty-five years. But there was no time for such reflections now; the savage who was knocked down recovered himself so far as to sit up upon the ground, and I perceived that my savage began to be afraid; but when I saw that, I presented my other piece at the man, as if I would shoot him: upon this, my savage, for so I call him now, made a motion to me to lend him my sword, which hung naked in a belt by my side, which I did.

He no sooner had it, but he runs to his enemy, and at one blow, cut off his head so cleverly, no executioner in Germany could have done it sooner or better; which I thought very strange for one who, I had reason to believe, never saw a sword in his life before, except their own wooden swords: however, it seems, as I learned afterwards, they make their wooden swords so sharp, so heavy, and the wood is so hard, that they will even cut off heads with them, ay, and arms, and that at one blow too. When he had done this, he comes laughing to me in sign of triumph, and brought me the sword again, and with abundance of gestures which I did not understand, laid it down, with the head of the savage that he had killed, just before me.

But that which astonished him most, was to know how I killed the other Indian so far off; so pointing to him, he made signs to me to let him go to him; and I bade him go, as well as I could. When he came to him, he stood like one amazed, looking at him, turning him first on one side, then on the other; looked at the wound the bullet had made, which it seems was just in his breast, where it had made a hole, and no great quantity of blood had followed; but he had bled inwardly, for he was quite dead. He took up his bow and arrows, and came back; so I turned to go away, and beckoned him to follow me, making signs to him that more might come after them. Upon this, he made signs to me that he should bury them with sand, that they might not be seen by the rest, if they followed; and so I made signs to him again to do so. He fell to work, and in an instant he had scraped a hole in the sand with his hands, big enough to bury the first in, and then dragged him into it, and covered him; and did so by the other also; I believe he had buried them both in a quarter of an hour.

Then calling him away, I carried him, not to my castle, but quite away to my cave, on the farther part of the island: so I did not let my dream come to pass in that part, that he came into my grove for shelter. Here I gave him bread and a bunch of raisins to eat, and a draught of water, which I found he was indeed in great distress for, from his running: and having refreshed him, I made signs for him to go and lie down to sleep, showing him a place where I had laid some rice-straw, and a blanket upon it, which I used to sleep upon myself sometimes; so the poor creature lay down, and went to sleep.

He was a comely, handsome fellow, perfectly well made, with straight strong limbs, not too large, tall and well shaped; and, as I reckon, about twenty-six years of age. He had a very good countenance, not a fierce and surly aspect, but seemed to have something very manly in his face; and yet he had all the sweetness and softness of a European in his countenance too, especially when he smiled. His hair was long and black, not curled like wool; his forehead very high and large; and a great vivacity and sparkling sharpness in his eyes. The colour of his skin was not quite black, but very tawny: and yet not an ugly, yellow, nauseous tawny, as the Brazilians and Virginians, and other natives of America are, but of a bright kind of a dun olive-colour, that had in it something very agreeable, though not very easy to describe. His face was round and plump; his nose small, not flat like the negroes; a very good mouth, thin lips, and his fine teeth well set, and as white as ivory.

After he had slumbered about half an hour, he awoke again, and came out of the cave to me; for I had been milking my goats, which I had in the enclosure just by: when he espied me, he came running to me, laying himself down again upon the ground, with all the possible signs of an humble, thankful disposition, making a great many antic gestures to show it. At last he lays his head flat upon the ground, close to my foot, and sets my other foot upon his head, as he had done before; and after this, made all the signs to me of subjection, servitude, and submission, imaginable, to let me know how he would serve me so long as he lived. I understood him in many things, and let him know I was very well pleased with him. In a little time, I began to speak to him, and teach him to speak to me; and, first, I let him know his name should be Friday, which was the day I saved his life: I called him so for the memory of the time. I likewise taught him to say Master; and then let him know that was to be my name: I likewise taught him to say Yes or No, and to know the meaning of them. I gave him some milk in an earthen pot, and let him see me drink it before him, and sop my bread in it; and gave him a cake of bread to do the like, which he quickly complied with, and made signs that it was very good for him. I kept there with him all night; but, as soon as it was day, I beckoned to him to come with me, and let him know I would give him some clothes; at which he seemed very glad, for he was stark naked. As we went by the place where he had buried the two men, he pointed exactly to the place, and showed me the marks that he had made to find them again, making signs to me that we should dig them up again and eat them. At this, I appeared very angry, expressed my abhorrence of it, made as if I would vomit at the thoughts of it, and beckoned with my hand to him to come away, which he did immediately, with great submission. I then led him up to the top of the hill, to see if his enemies were gone; and, pulling out my glass, I looked, and saw plainly the place where they had been, but no appearance of them or their canoes; so that it was plain they were gone, and had left their two comrades behind them, without any search after them.

But I was not content with this discovery; but having now more courage, and consequently more curiosity, I took my man Friday with me, giving him the sword in his hand, with the bow and arrows at his back, which I found he could use very dexterously, making him carry one gun for me, and I two for myself; and away we marched to the place where these creatures had been; for I had a mind now to get some fuller intelligence of them. When I came to the place, my very blood ran chill in my veins, and my heart sunk within me, at the horror of the spectacle; indeed, it was a dreadful sight, at least it was so to me, though Friday made nothing of it. The place was covered with human bones, the ground dyed with their blood, and great pieces of flesh left here and there, half-eaten, mangled, and scorched; and, in short, all the tokens of the triumphant feast they had been making there, after a victory over their enemies.

I saw three skulls, five hands, and the bones of three or four legs and feet, and abundance of other parts of the bodies; and Friday, by his signs, made me understand that they brought over four prisoners to feast upon; that three of them were eaten up, and that he, pointing to himself, was the fourth; that there had been a great battle between them and their next king, of whose subjects, it seems, he had been one, and that they had taken a great number of prisoners; all of which were carried to several places, by those who had taken them in the fight, in order to feast upon them, as was done here by these wretches upon those they brought hither.

I caused Friday to gather all the skulls, bones, flesh, and whatever remained, and lay them together in a heap, and make a great fire upon it, and burn them all to ashes. I found Friday had still a hankering stomach after some of the flesh, and was still a cannibal in his nature; but I showed so much abhorrence at the very thoughts of it, that he durst not discover it: for I had, by some means, let him know that I would kill him if he offered it.

When he had done this, we came back to our castle; and there I fell to work for my man Friday; and first of all, I gave him a pair of linen drawers, which I had out of the poor gunner's chest I mentioned, which I found in the wreck, and which, with a little alteration, fitted him very well; and then I made him a jerkin of goat's skin, as well as my skill would allow (for I was now grown a tolerably good tailor); and I gave him a cap which I made of hare's skin, very convenient and fashionable enough: and thus he was clothed, for the present, tolerably well, and was mighty well pleased to see himself almost as well clothed as his master. It is true, he went awkwardly in these clothes at first: wearing the drawers was very awkward to him, and the sleeves of the waistcoat galled his shoulders and the inside of his arms; but a little easing them where he complained they hurt him, and using himself to them, he took to them at length very well.

The next day, after I came home to my hutch with him, I began to consider where I should lodge him; and, that I might do well for him and yet be perfectly easy myself, I made a little tent for him in the vacant place between my two fortifications, in the inside of the last, and in the outside of the first. As there was a door or entrance there into my cave, I made a formal framed door-case, and a door to it of boards, and set it up in the passage, a little within the entrance; and, causing the door to open in the inside, I barred it up in the night, taking in my ladders too; so that Friday could no way come at me in the inside of my innermost wall, without making so much noise in getting over that it must needs awaken me; for my first wall had now a complete roof over it of long poles, covering all my tent, and leaning up to the side of the hill, which was again laid across with smaller sticks, instead of laths, and then thatched over a great thickness with the rice-straw, which was strong, like reeds, and at the hole which was left to go in or out by the ladder, I had placed a kind of trap-door, which, if it had been attempted on the outside, would not have opened at all, but would have fallen down and made a great noise: as to weapons, I took them all into my side every night. But I needed none of all this precaution; for never man had a more faithful, loving, sincere servant than Friday was to me; without passions, sullenness, or designs, perfectly obliged and engaged; his very affections were tied to me, like those of a child to a father; and I dare say he would have sacrificed his life to save mine, upon any occasion whatsoever: the many testimonies he gave me of this, put it out of doubt, and soon convinced me that I needed to use no precautions for my safety on this account.

I was greatly delighted with him, and made it my business to teach him everything that was proper to make him useful, handy, and helpful; but especially to make him speak, and understand me when I spoke: and he was the aptest scholar that ever was; and particularly was so merry, so constantly diligent, and so pleased when he could but understand me, or make me understand him, that it was very pleasant to me to talk to him. Now my life began to be so easy that I began to say to myself, that could I but have been safe from more savages, I cared not if I was never to remove from the place where I lived.

After I had been two or three days returned to my castle, I thought that, in order to bring Friday off from his horrid way of feeding, and from the relish of a cannibal's stomach, I ought to let him taste other flesh; so I took him out with me one morning to the woods. I went, indeed, intending to kill a kid out of my own flock, and bring it home and dress it; but as I was going, I saw a she-goat lying down in the shade, and two young kids sitting by her. I catched hold of Friday— "Hold!" said I, "stand still;" and made signs to him not to stir: immediately, I presented my piece, shot, and killed one of the kids. The poor creature, who had, at a distance, indeed, seen me kill the savage, his enemy, but did not know, nor could imagine, how it was done, was sensibly surprised; trembled, and shook, and looked so amazed that I thought he would have sunk down.

He did not see the kid I shot at, or perceive I had killed it, but ripped up his waistcoat, to feel whether he was not wounded; and, as I found presently, thought I was resolved to kill him: for he came and kneeled down to me, and embracing my knees, said a great many things I did not understand; but I could easily see the meaning was, to pray me not to kill him.

I soon found a way to convince him that I would do him no harm; and taking him up by the hand, laughed at him, and pointing to the kid which I had killed, beckoned to him to run and fetch it, which he did: and while he was wondering, and looking to see how the creature was killed, I loaded my gun again. By-and-by, I saw a great fowl, like a hawk, sitting upon a tree within shot; so, to let Friday understand a little what I would do, I called him to me again, pointed at the fowl, which was indeed a parrot., though I thought it had been a hawk; I say, pointing to the parrot, and to my gun, and to the ground under the parrot, to let him see I would make it fall, I made him understand that I would shoot and kill that bird; accordingly, I fired, and bade him look, and immediately he saw the parrot fall. He stood like one frightened again, notwithstanding all I had said to him; and I found he was the more amazed, because he did not see me put anything into the gun, but thought that there must be some wonderful fund of death and destruction in that thing, able to kill man, beast, bird, or anything near or far off; and the astonishment this created in him was such as could not wear off for a long time; and, I believe, if I would have let him, he would have worshipped me and my gun.

As for the gun itself, he would not so much as touch it for several days after; but he would speak to it and talk to it, as if it had answered him, when he was by himself; which, as I afterwards learned of him, was to desire it not to kill him. Well, after his astonishment was a little over at this, I pointed to him to run and fetch the bird I had shot, which he did, but! stayed some time; for the parrot, not being quite dead, had fluttered away a good distance from the place where she fell: however, he found her, took her up, and brought her to me; and as I had perceived his ignorance about the gun before, I took this advantage to charge the gun again, and not to let him see me do it, that I might be ready for any other mark that might present; but nothing more offered at that time: so I brought home the kid, and the same evening I took the skin off, and cut it out as well as I could; and having a pot fit for that purpose, I boiled or stewed some of the flesh, and made some very good broth.

After I had begun to eat some, I gave some to my man, who seemed very glad of it, and liked it very well; but that which was strangest to him was to see me eat salt with it. He made a sign to me that the salt was not good to eat; and putting a little into his own mouth, he seemed to nauseate it, and would spit and sputter at it, washing his mouth with fresh water after it: on the other hand, I took some meat into my mouth without salt, and I pretended to spit and sputter for want of salt, as much as he had done at the salt; but it would not do; he would never care for salt with his meat or in his broth, at least not for a great while, and then but a very little.

Having thus fed him with boiled meat and broth, I was resolved to feast him the next day by roasting a piece of the kid: this I did by hanging it before the fire on a string, as I had seen many people do in England, setting two poles up, one on each side of the fire, and one across on the top, and tying the string to the cross stick, letting the meat turn continually. This Friday admired very much; but when he came to taste the flesh, he took so many ways to tell me how well he liked it, that I could not but understand him: and at last he told me, as well as he could, he would never eat man's flesh any more, which I was very glad to hear.

The next day, I set him to work to beating some corn out, and sifting it in the manner I used to do, as I observed before; and he soon understood how to do it as well as I, especially after he had seen what the meaning of it was, and that it was to make bread of; for after that, I let him see me make my bread, and bake it too; and in a little time, Friday was able to do all the work for me as well as I could do it myself.

I began now to consider, that having two mouths to feed instead of one, I must provide more ground for my harvest, and plant a larger quantity of corn than I used to do; so I marked out a larger piece of land, and began the fence in the same manner as before, in which Friday worked not only very willingly and very hard, but did it very cheerfully: and I told him what it was for—that it was for corn to make more bread, because he was now with me, and that I might have enough for him and myself too. He appeared very sensible of that part, and let me know that he thought I had much more labour upon me on his account than I had for myself; and that he would work the harder for me, if I would tell him what to do.

This was the pleasantest year of all the life I led in this place. Friday began to talk pretty well, and understand the names of almost everything I had occasion to call for, and of every place I had to send him to, and talked a great deal to me; so that, in short, I began now to have some use for my tongue again, which, indeed, I had very little occasion for before. Besides the pleasure of talking to him, I had a singular satisfaction in the fellow himself: his simple, unfeigned honesty appeared to me more and more every day, and I began really to love the creature; and on his side, I believe he loved me more than it was possible for him ever to love anything before.

I had a mind once to try if he had any inclination for his own country again; and having taught him English so well that he could answer me almost any question, I asked him whether the nation that he belonged to never conquered in battle? At which he smiled, and said, "Yes, yes, we always fight the better;" that is, he meant, always get the better in fight; and so we began the following discourse:—

Master.—You always fight the better; how come you to be taken prisoner then, Friday?

Friday.—My nation beat much for all that.

Master.—How beat? If your nation beat them, how came you to be taken?

Friday.—They more many than my nation, in the place where me was; they take one, two three, and me: my nation over-beat them in the yonder place, where me no was; there my nation take one, two, great thousand.

Master.—But why did not your side recover you from the hands of your enemies, then?

Friday.—They run, one, two, three, and me, and make go in the canoe; my nation have no canoe that time.

Master.—Well, Friday, and what does your nation do with the men they take? Do they carry them away and eat them, as these did?

Friday.—Yes, my nation eat mans too: eat all up.

Master.—Where do they carry them?

Friday.—Go to other place, where they think.

Master.—Do they come hither?

Friday.—Yes, yes, they come hither; come other else place.

Master.—Have you been here with them?

Friday.—Yes, I have been here (points to the N.W side of the island, which, it seems, was their side).

By this, I understood that my man Friday had formerly been among the savages who used to come on shore on the farther part of the island, on the same man-eating occasions he was now brought for: and, some time after, when I took the courage to carry him to that side, being the same I formerly mentioned, he presently knew the place, and told me he was there once, when they eat up twenty men, two women, and one child: he could not tell twenty in English, but he numbered them, by laying so many stones in a row, and pointing to me to tell them over.

I have told this passage, because it introduces what follows. After this discourse I had with him, I asked him how far it was from our island to the shore, and whether the canoes were not often lost. He told me there was no danger, no canoes ever lost; but that after a little way out to sea, there was a current and wind, always one way in the morning, the other in the afternoon. This I understood to be no more than the sets of the tide, as going out or coming in; but I afterwards understood it was occasioned by the great draft and reflux of the mighty River Oroonoko, in the mouth or gulph of which river, as I found afterwards, our island lay; and that this land which I perceived to the W and N.W. was the great island of Trinidad, on the north point of the mouth of the river.

I asked Friday a thousand questions about the country, the inhabitants, the sea, the coast, and what nations were near: he told me all he knew, with the greatest openness imaginable. I asked him the names of the several nations of his sort of people, but could get no other name than Caribs: from whence I easily understood that these were the Caribbees, which our maps place on the part of America which reaches from the mouth of the river Oroonoko to Guiana, and onwards to St. Martha. He told me, that up a great way beyond the moon, that was, beyond the setting of the moon, which must be west from their country, there dwelt white-bearded men, like me, and pointed to my great whiskers; and that they had killed much mans, that was his word: by all which I understood he meant the Spaniards, whose cruelties in America had been spread over the whole country, and were remembered by all the nations from father to son.

I inquired if he could tell me how I might go from this island and get among those white men: he told me, "Yes, yes, you may go in two canoe." I could not understand what he meant, or make him describe to me what he meant by two canoe, till at last, with great difficulty, I found he meant it must be in a large boat, as big as two canoes. This part of Friday's discourse I began to relish very well; and from this time I entertained some hopes that, one time or other, I might find an opportunity to make my escape from this place, and that this poor savage might be a means to help me.

During the long time that Friday had now been with me, and that he began to speak to and understand me, I was wanting to lay a foundation of religious knowledge in his mind; particularly I asked him one time, who made him. The poor creature did not understand me at all, but thought I had asked him who was his father: but I took it up by another handle, and asked him, who made the sea, the ground we walked on, and the hills and woods. He told me, "It was one Benamuckee, that lived beyond all;" he could describe nothing of this great person, but that he was very old, "much older," he said, "than the sea or the land, the moon or the stars." I asked him then, if this old person had made all things, why did not all things worship him? He looked very grave, and, with a perfect look of innocence, said, "All things say to him." I asked him, if the people who die in his country went anywhere? He said, "Yes, they all went up to Benamuckee." Then I asked him whether those they eat up went thither too? He said, "Yes."

From these things, I began to instruct him in the knowledge of the true God: I told him that the great Maker of all things lived up there, pointing up towards heaven; that He governed the world by the same power and providence by which He made it; that He was omnipotent, and could do everything for us, give everything to us—take everything from us; and thus, by degrees, I opened his eyes.

I had, God knows, more sincerity than knowledge in all the methods I took for this poor creature's instruction, and must acknowledge, what I believe all that act upon the same principle will find, that in laying things open to him, I really informed and instructed myself in many things that either I did not know, or had not fully considered before, but which occurred naturally to my mind upon searching into them, for the information of this poor savage; and I had more affection in my inquiry after things upon this occasion than ever I felt before: so that, whether this poor wild wretch was the better for me or no, I had great reason to be thankful that ever he came to me; my grief sat lighter upon me; my habitation grew comfortable to me beyond measure: and when I reflected that in this solitary life which I had been confined to, I had not only been moved to look up to heaven myself, and to seek the hand that had brought me here, but was now to be made an instrument, under Providence, to save the life, and, for aught I knew, the soul of a poor savage.

I continued in this thankful frame all the remainder of my time; and the conversation which employed the hours between Friday and me was such as made the three years which we lived there together perfectly and completely happy.

After Friday and I became more intimately acquainted, and that he could understand almost all I said to him, and speak pretty fluently, though in broken English, to me, I acquainted him with my own history, or at least so much of it as related to my coming to this place; how I had lived there, and how long: I let him into the mystery, for such it was to him, of gunpowder and bullet, and taught him how to shoot. I gave him a knife, which he was wonderfully delighted with; and I made him a belt, with a frog hanging to it; and in the frog, instead of a hanger, I gave him a hatchet, which was not only as good a weapon in some cases, but much more useful upon other occasions.

I described to him the country of Europe, particularly England, which I came from; how we lived, how we worshipped God, how we behaved to one another, and how we traded in ships to all parts of the world. I gave him an account of the wreck which I had been on board of, and showed him, as near as I could, the place where she lay: but she was all beaten in pieces before, and gone. I showed him the ruins of our boat, which we lost when we escaped, and which I could not stir with my whole strength then; but was now fallen almost all to pieces.

Upon seeing this boat, Friday stood musing a great while, and said nothing. I asked him what it was he studied upon. At last, says he, "Me see such boat like come to place at my nation." I did not understand him a good while; but, at last, when I had examined further into it, I understood by him, that a boat, such as that had been, came on shore upon the country where he lived. I presently imagined that some European ship must have been cast away upon their coast, and the boat might get loose and drive ashore; but was so dull that I never once thought of men making their escape from, a wreck thither, much less whence they might come; so I only inquired after a description of the boat.

Friday described the boat to me well enough; but brought me better to understand him when he added with some warmth, "We save the white mans from drown." Then I presently asked if there were any white mans, as he called them, in the boat. "Yes," he said; "the boat full of white mans." I asked him how many. He told upon his fingers seventeen. I asked him then what became of them? He told me, "They live, they dwell at my nation."

This put new thoughts into my head; for I presently imagined that these might be the men belonging to the ship that was cast away in the sight of my island, and who, after the ship was struck on the rock, and they saw her inevitably lost, had saved themselves in their boat, and were landed upon that wild shore among the savages. Upon this I inquired of him more critically what was become of them. He assured me they still lived there; that they had been there about four years; that the savages left them alone, and gave them victuals to live on. I asked him how it came to pass they did not kill them and eat them. He said, "No, they make brother with them;" that is, as I understood him, a truce; and then he added, "They no eat mans but when make the war fight;" that is to say, they never eat any men but such as come to fight with them, and are taken in battle.

It was after this some considerable time, that being upon the top of the hill, at the east side of the island, from whence, I had, in a clear day, discovered the continent of America, the weather being very serene, Friday looks very earnestly towards the main land, and, in a kind of surprise, falls a jumping and dancing, and calls out to me, for I was at some distance from him. I asked him what was the matter. "O joy!" says he; "O glad! there see my country, there my nation !" I observed an extraordinary sense of pleasure appeared in his face, and his eyes sparkled, and his countenance discovered a strange eagerness, as if he had a mind to be in his own country again.

This observation of mine put a great many thoughts into me, which made me, at first, not so easy about my new man Friday as I was before; and I made no doubt but that, if Friday could get back to his own nation again, he would not only forget all his religion, but all his obligation to me, and would be forward enough to give his countrymen an account of me, and come back, perhaps, with a hundred or two of them, and make a feast upon me, at which he might be as merry as he used to be with those of his enemies, when they were taken in war. But I wronged the poor, honest creature very much, for which I was very sorry afterwards. However, as my jealousy increased, and held me some weeks, I was a little more circumspect, and not so familiar and kind to him as before: in which I was certainly in the wrong too; the honest, grateful creature having no thought about it, but what consisted with the best principles, both as a religious Christian and as a grateful friend; as appeared afterwards to my full satisfaction.

While my jealousy of him lasted, you may be sure I was every day pumping him, to see if he would discover any of the new thoughts which I suspected were in him; but I found everything he said was so honest and so innocent, that I could find nothing to nourish my suspicion; and, in spite of all my uneasiness, he made me at last entirely his own again; nor did he in the least perceive that I was uneasy, and therefore I could not suspect him of deceit.

One day, walking up the same hill, but the weather being hazy at sea, so that we could not see the continent, I called to him, and said, "Friday, do not you wish yourself in your own country, your own nation?"

"Yes," he said, "I be *mucho* glad to be at my own nation."

"What would you do there?" said I: "would you turn wild again, eat men's flesh, and be a savage, as you were before?"

He looked full of concern, and shaking his head, said, "No, no, Friday tell them to live good; tell them to pray God; tell them to eat corn-bread, cattle-flesh, milk; no eat man again."

"Why, then," said I to him, "they will kill you."

He looked grave at that, and then said, "No, no, they no kill me, they willing love learn."

He meant by this, they would be willing to learn. He added, they learned much of the bearded mans that came in the boat. Then I asked him if he would go back to them. He smiled at that, and told me that he could not swim so far. I told him I would make a canoe for him. He told me he would go, if I would go with him.

"I go !" says I; "why they will eat me if I come there."

"No, no," says he, "me make they no eat you; me make they much love you." Then he told me, as well as he could, how kind they were to seventeen white men, who came on shore there in distress.

From this time, I confess, I had a mind to venture over, and see if I could possibly join with those bearded men, who, I made no doubt, were Spaniards and Portuguese; not doubting, but, if I could, we might find some method to escape from thence, being upon the continent, and a good company together, better than I could from an island forty miles off the shore, alone, and without help. So, after some days, I took Friday to work again, by way of discourse, and told him I would give him a boat to go back to his own nation; and, accordingly, I carried him to my frigate, which lay on the other side of the island, and having cleared it of water (for I always kept it sunk in water), I brought it out, showed it him, and we both went into it. I found he was a most dexterous fellow at managing it, and would make it go almost as swift again as I could. So when he was in, I said to him, "Well, now, Friday, shall we go to your nation?" He looked very dull at my saying so; which it seems was because he thought the boat too small to go so far. I then told him I had a bigger: so the next day I went to the place where the first boat lay which I had made, but which I could not get into the water. He said that was big enough: but then, as I had taken no care of it, and it had lain two or three and twenty years there, the sun had split and dried it, that it was rotten. Friday told me such a boat would do very well, and would carry "much enough vittle, drink, bread."

Upon the whole, I was by this time so fixed upon my design of going over with him to the continent, that I told him we would go and make one as big as that, and he should go home in it. He answered not one word, but looked very grave and sad. I asked him what was the matter with him. He asked me again, "Why you angry mad with Friday?—what me done?" I asked him what he meant. I told him I was not angry with him at all. "No angry!" says he, repeating the words several times, "why send Friday home away to my nation?"

"Why," says I, "Friday, did not you say you wished you were there?"

"Yes, yes," says he, "wish we both there; no wish Friday there, no master there."

In a word, he would not think of going there without me. "I go there, Friday?" says I, "what shall I do there?"

He turned very quick upon me at this. "You do great deal much good," says he; "you teach wild mans be good, sober, tame mans; you tell them know God, pray God, and live new life."

"Alas, Friday !" says I, "thou knowest not what thou sayest; I am but an ignorant man myself."

"Yes, yes," says he, "you teachee me good, you teachee them good."

"No, no, Friday," says I, "you shall go without me; leave me here to live by myself as I did before."

He looked confused again at that word; and running to one of the hatchets which he used to wear, he takes it up hastily, and gives it to me.

"What must I do with this ?" says I to him.

"You take kill Friday," says he.

"What must I kill you for ?" said I again.

He returns very quick—"What do you send Friday away for? Take kill Friday, no send Friday away." This he spoke so earnestly that I saw tears stand in his eyes. In a word, I so plainly discovered the utmost affection in him to me, and a firm resolution in him, that I told him then, and often after, that I would never send him away from me, if he was willing to stay with me.

Upon the whole, as I found by all his discourse a settled affection to me, and that nothing could part him from me, so I found all the foundation of his desire to go to his own country was laid in his ardent affection to the people, and his hopes of my doing them good; a thing which, as I had no notion of myself, so I had not the least thought or intention, or desire of undertaking it. But still I found a strong inclination to attempting my escape, founded on the supposition gathered from the discourse, that there were seventeen bearded men there; and therefore, without any more delay, I went to work with Friday to find out a great tree proper to fell, and make a large *periagua*, or canoe, to undertake the voyage.

There were trees enough in the island to have built a little fleet of good large vessels; but the main thing I looked at was, to get one so near the water that we might launch it when it was made, to avoid the mistake I committed at first. At last, Friday pitched upon a tree; for I found that he knew much better than I what kind of food was fittest for it. Friday wished to burn the hollow or cavity of this tree out, to make it for a boat, but I showed him how to cut it with tools; which, after I had showed how to use, he did very handily; and in about a month's hard labour, we finished it and made it very handsome; especially, when, with our axes, which I showed him how to handle, we cut and hewed the outside into the true shape of a boat. After this, however, it cost us near a fortnight's time to get her along, as it were, inch by inch, upon great rollers into the water: but when she was in, she would have carried twenty men with great ease.

When she was in the water, though she was so big, it amazed me to see with what dexterity, and how swift my man Friday could manage her, turn her, and paddle her along. So I asked him if he would, and if we might, venture over in her. "Yes," he said, "we venture over in her very well, though great blow wind." However, I had a farther design that he knew nothing of, and that was to make a mast and a sail, and to fit her with an anchor and a cable. As to a mast, that was easy enough to get; so I pitched upon a straight young cedar tree, which I found near the place, and which there were great plenty of in the island, and I set Friday to work to cut it down, and gave him directions how to shape and order it. But as to the sail, that was my particular care. I knew I had pieces of old sails enough; but as I had had them now six-and-twenty years by me, and had not been very careful to preserve them, not imagining that I should ever have this kind of use for them, I did not doubt but they were all rotten; and, indeed, most of them were so. However, I found two pieces, which appeared pretty good, and with these I went to work; and with a great deal of pains and awkward stitching, you may be sure, for want of needles, 'I at length made a three-cornered ugly thing, like what we call in England a shoulder of mutton sail, to go with a boom at bottom, and a little short sprit at the top, such as usually our ships' long-boats sail with, and such as I best knew how to manage, as it was such a one as I had to the boat in which I made my escape from Barbary.

I was near two months performing this last work, *viz.*, rigging and fitting my mast and sails; for I finished them very complete, making a small stay, and a sail, or foresail to it, to assist if we should turn to windward; and what was more than all, I fixed a rudder to the stern of her to steer with.

After all this was done, I had my man Friday to teach as to what belonged to the navigation of my boat; for, though he knew very well how to paddle a canoe, he knew nothing of what belonged to a sail and a rudder; and was the most amazed when he saw me work the boat to and again in the sea by the rudder, and how the sail gibbed, and filled this way or that way, as the course we sailed changed; I say, when he saw this, he stood like one astonished and amazed. However, with a little use, I made all these things familiar to him, and he became an expert sailor—except that of the compass, I could make him understand very little. On the other hand, as there was very little cloudy weather, and seldom or never any fogs in those parts, there was the less occasion for a compass, seeing the stars were always to be seen by night, and the shore by day, except in the rainy seasons, and then nobody cared to stir abroad either by land or sea.

I was now entered on the seven-and-twentieth year of my captivity in this place; though the last three years that I had this creature with me ought rather to be left out of the account, my habitation being quite of another kind than in all the rest of the time. I kept the anniversary of my landing here with the same thankfulness to God for his mercies as at first: and if I had such cause of acknowledgment at first, I had much more so now, having such additional testimonies of the care of Providence over me, and the great hopes I had of being effectually and speedily delivered; for I had an invincible impression upon my thoughts that my deliverance was at hand, and that I should not be another year in this place. I went on, however, with my husbandry; digging, planting, and fencing, as usual. I gathered and cured my grapes, and did every necessary thing as before.

The rainy season was, in the meantime, upon me, when I kept more within doors than at other times. We had stowed our new vessel as secure as we could, bringing her up into the creek, where I landed my rafts from the ship; and hauling her up to the shore at high-water mark, I made my man Friday dig a little dock, just big enough to hold her, and just deep enough to give her water to float in; and then, when the tide was out, we made a strong dam across the end of it, to keep the water out; and so she lay dry as to the tide from the sea: and to keep the rain off, we laid a great many boughs of trees, so thick that she was as well thatched as a house; and thus we waited for the months of November and December, in which I designed to make my adventure.

When the settled season began to come in, as the thought of my design returned with the fair weather, I was preparing daily for the voyage. And the first thing I did was to lay by a certain quantity of provisions, being the stores for our voyage; and intended, in a week or a fortnight's time, to open the dock, and launch out our boat. I was busy one morning upon something of this kind, when I called to Friday, and bid him to go to the sea-shore, and see if he could find a turtle or tortoise, a thing which we generally got once a-week, for the sake of the eggs as well as the flesh. Friday had not been long gone when he came running back, and flew over my outer wall or fence, like one that felt not the ground, or the steps he set his feet on; and before I had time to speak to him, he cries out to me, "O master! O master! O sorrow! O bad!"

"What's the matter, Friday?" says I.

"O yonder there," says he, "one, two, three canoes; one, two, three!"

By this way of speaking I concluded there were six; but on inquiry, I found there were but three.

"Well, Friday," says I, "do not be frightened." So I heartened him up as well as I could. However, I saw the poor fellow was most terribly scared, for nothing ran in his head but that they were come to look for him, and would cut him in pieces and eat him; and the poor fellow trembled so that I scarcely knew what to do with him. I comforted him as well as I could, and told him I was in as much danger as he, and that they would eat me as well as him. "But," says I, "Friday, we must resolve to fight them. Can you fight, Friday?"

"Me shoot," says he, "but there come many great number."

"No matter for that," said I again; "our guns will fright those that we do not kill."

So I asked him whether, if I resolved to defend him, he would defend me, and stand by me, and do just as I bid him. He said, "Me die, when you bid die, master." So I went and fetched a good dram of rum and gave him; for I had been so good a husband of my rum, that I had a great deal left. When he had drunk it, I made him take the two fowling-pieces, which we always carried, and loaded them with large swan-shot, as big as small pistol-bullets. Then I took four muskets, and loaded them with two slugs, and rive small bullets each; and my two pistols I loaded with a brace of bullets each. I hung my great sword, as usual, naked by my side, and gave Friday his hatchet.

When I had thus prepared myself, I took my perspectiveglass, and went up to the side of the hill, to see what I could discover; and I found quickly by my glass, that there were one-and-twenty savages, three prisoners, and three canoes; and that their whole business seemed to be the triumphant banquet upon these three human bodies. I observed also, that they had landed, not where they had done when Friday made his escape, but nearer to my creek, where the shore was low, and where a thick wood came almost close down to the sea. This, with the abhorrence of the inhuman errand these wretches came about, filled me with such indignation that I came down again to Friday, and told him I was resolved to go down to them, and kill them all; and asked him if he would stand by me. He had now got over his fright, and his spirits being a little raised with the dram I had given him, he was very cheerful, and told me, as before, he would die when I bid die.

In this fit of fury I divided the arms which I had charged, as before, between us; I gave Friday one pistol to stick in his girdle, and three guns upon his shoulder, and I took one pistol and the other three guns myself; and in this posture we marched out. I took a small bottle of rum in my pocket, and gave Friday a large bag with more powder and bullets; and as to orders, I charged him to keep close behind me, and not to stir, or shoot, or do anything till I bid him, and in the meantime not to speak a word. In this posture I fetched a compass to my right hand of near a mile, as well to get over the creek as to get into the wood, so that I could come within shot of them before I should be discovered, which I had seen by my glass it was easy to do.

While I was making this march, my former thoughts returning, I began to abate my resolution: I do not mean that I entertained any fear of their number, for, as they were naked, unarmed wretches, it is certain I was superior to them—nay, though I had been alone. But it occurred to my thoughts, what occasion, much less what necessity, I was in to go and dip my hands in blood, to attack people who had neither done or intended me any wrongs, who, as to me, were innocent, and whose barbarous customs were their own disaster, being in them a token, indeed, of God's having left them, with the other nations of that part of the world, to such stupidity, and to such inhuman courses, but did not call me to take upon me to be a judge of their actions, much less an executioner of His justice,—that whenever He thought fit He would take the cause into His own hands, and by national vengeance punish them as a people for national crimes, but that, in the meantime, it was none of my business,—that it was true Friday might justify it, because he was a declared enemy, and in a state of war with those very particular people, and it was lawful for him to attack them,—but I could not say the same with regard to myself. These things were so warmly pressed upon my thoughts all the way as I went, that I resolved I would only go and place myself near them that I might observe their barbarous feast, and that I would act then as God should direct; but that unless something offered that was more a call to me than yet I knew of, I would not meddle with them.

With this resolution I entered the wood, and with all possible wariness, Friday following close at my heels. I marched till I came to the skirt of the wood on the side which was next to them, only that one corner of the wood lay between me and them. Here I called softly to Friday, and showing him a great tree which was just at the corner of the wood, I bade him go to the tree, and bring me word if he could see there plainly what they were doing. He did so, and came immediately back to me, and told me they might be plainly viewed there,—that they were all about their fire eating the flesh of one of their prisoners, and that another lay bound upon the sand a little from them, whom he said they would kill next, and this fired the very soul within me. He told me it was not one of their nation, but one of the bearded men he had told me of, that came to their country in the boat. I was filled with horror at the very naming of the white-bearded man; and going to the tree, I saw plainly by my glass a white man, who lay upon the beach of the sea with his hands and his feet tied, and that he was an European, and had clothes on.

There was another tree, and a little thicket beyond it, about fifty yards nearer to them than the place where I was, which, by going a little way about, I saw I might come at undiscovered, and that then I should be within half a shot of them; so I withheld my passion, though I was indeed enraged to the highest degree: and going back about twenty paces, I got behind some bushes, which held all the way till I came to the other tree, and then came to a little rising ground, which gave me a full view of them at the distance of about eighty yards.

I had now not a moment to lose, for nineteen of the dreadful wretches sat upon the ground, all close huddled together, and had just sent the other two to butcher the poor Christian, and bring him perhaps limb by limb to their fire, and they were stooping down to untie the bands at his feet. I turned to Friday:—"Now, Friday," said I, "do as I bid thee." Friday said he would. "Then, Friday," says I, "do exactly as you see me do; fail in nothing." So I set down one of the muskets and the fowling-piece upon the ground, and Friday did the like by his, and with the other musket I took my aim at the savages, bidding him to do the like; then asking him if he was ready, he said, "Yes."

"Then fire at them," said I; and at the same moment I fired also.

Friday took his aim so much better than I, that on the side that he shot he killed two of them, and wounded three more; and on my side I killed one, and wounded two. They were, you may be sure, in a dreadful consternation; and all of them that were not hurt, jumped upon their feet, but did not immediately know which way to run, or which way to look, for they knew not from whence their destruction came. Friday kept his eyes close upon me, that, as I had bid him, he might observe what I did; so, as soon as the first shot was made, I threw down the piece, and took up the fowling-piece, and Friday did the like; he saw me cock and present; he did the same again. "Are you ready, Friday?" said I.

"Yes," says he.

"Let fly, then," says I, "in the name of God !" and with that I fired again among the amazed wretches, and so did Friday; and as our pieces were now loaded with what I call swan-shot, or small pistol-bullets, we found only two drop; but so many were wounded, that they ran about yelling and screaming like mad creatures, all bloody, and most of them miserably wounded, whereof three more fell quickly after, though not quite dead.

"Now, Friday," says I, laying down the discharged pieces, and taking up the musket which was yet loaded, "follow me," which he did with a great deal of courage; upon which I rushed out of the wood

150

and showed myself, and Friday close at my foot. As soon as I perceived they saw me, I shouted as loud as I could, and bade Friday do so too, and running as fast as possible towards the poor victim, who was lying upon the beach between the place where they sat and the sea. The two butchers, who were just going to work with him, had left at the surprise of our first fire, and fled in a terrible fright to the sea-side, and had jumped into a canoe, and three more of the rest made the same way.

I turned to Friday, and bade him step forwards and fire at them; he understood me immediately, and running about forty yards, to be nearer, he shot; and I thought he had killed them all, for I saw them all fall of a heap into the boat, though I saw two of them up again quickly; however, he killed two of them, and wounded the third so that he lay down in the bottom of the boat as if he had been dead.

While my man Friday fired at them, I pulled out my knife and cut the flags that bound the poor victim; and loosing his hands and feet, I lifted him up, and asked him in the Portuguese tongue, what he was. He answered in Latin, "*Christianus*"; but was so weak and faint that he could scarce stand or speak. I took my bottle out of my pocket, and gave it him, making signs that he should drink, which he did; and I gave him a piece of bread, which he ate. Then I asked him what countryman he was: and he said *Espagniole*; and being a little recovered, let me know, by all the signs he could possibly make, how much he was in my debt for his deliverance. "*Seignior*," said I, with as much Spanish as I could make up, "we will talk afterwards, but we must fight now: if you have any strength left, take this pistol and sword, and lay about you."

He took them very thankfully; and no sooner had he the arms in his hands, but, as if they had put new vigour into him, he flew upon his murderers like a fury, and had cut two of them in pieces in an instant; for the truth is, as the whole was a surprise to them, so the poor creatures were so much frightened with the noise of our pieces that they fell down for mere amazement and fear, and had no more power to attempt their own escape, than their flesh had to resist our shot: and that was the case of those five that Friday shot at in the boat; for as three of them fell with the hurt they received, so the other two fell with the fright.

I kept my piece in my hand still without firing, being willing to keep my charge ready, because I had given the Spaniard my pistol and sword: so I called to Friday, and bade him run up to the tree from whence we first fired, and fetch the arms which lay there that had been discharged, which he did with great swiftness: and then giving him my musket, I sat down myself to load all the rest again, and bade them come to me when they wanted.

While I was loading these pieces, there happened a fierce engagement between the Spaniard and one of the savages, who made at him with one of their great wooden swords, the weapon that was to have killed him before, if I had not prevented it. The Spaniard, who was as bold and brave as could be imagined, though weak, had fought the Indian a good while, and had cut two great wounds on his head; but the savage being a stout, lusty fellow, closing in with him, had thrown him down, being faint, and was wringing my sword out of his hand; when the Spaniard, though undermost, wisely quitting the sword, drew the pistol from his girdle, shot the savage through the body, and killed him upon the spot, before I, who was running to help him, could come near.

Friday, being now left to his liberty, pursued the flying wretches, with no weapon in his hand but his hatchet; and with that he despatched those three who, as I said before, were wounded at first, and fallen, and all the rest he could come up with: and the Spaniard coming to me for a gun, I gave him one of the fowling-pieces, with which he pursued two of the savages, and wounded them both; but, as he was not able to run, they both got from him into the wood, where Friday pursued them, and killed one of them, but the other was too nimble for him; and though he was wounded, yet had plunged himself into the sea, and swam with all his might off to those two who were left in the canoe, which three in the canoe, with one wounded, that we knew not whether he died or no, were all that escaped our hands of one-and-twenty.

The account of the whole is as follows:—three killed at our first shot from the tree; two killed at the next shot; two killed by Friday in the boat; two killed by Friday, of those at first wounded; one killed by Friday in the wood; three killed by the Spaniard; four killed, being found dropped here and there, of the wounds, or killed by Friday in his chase of them; four escaped in the boat, whereof one wounded, if not dead—twenty-one in all.

Those that were in the canoe worked hard to get out of gunshot, and though Friday made two or three shots at them, I did not find that he hit any of them. Friday would fain have had me take one of their canoes, and pursue them; and, indeed, I was very anxious about their escape, lest carrying the news home to their people, they should come back perhaps with two or three hundred of the canoes and devour us by mere multitude; so I consented to pursue them by sea, and running to one of their canoes, I jumped in, and bade Friday follow me: but when I was in the canoe, I was surprised to find another poor creature lie there, bound hand and foot, as the Spaniard was, for the slaughter, and almost dead with fear, not knowing what was the matter; for he had not been able to look up over the side of the boat, he was tied so hard neck and heels, and had been tied so long, that he had really but little life in him.

I immediately cut the twisted flags or rushes, which they had bound him with, and would have helped him up; but he could not stand or speak, but groaned most piteously, believing, it seems, still, that he was only unbound in order to be killed. When Friday came to him I bade him speak to him, and tell him of his deliverance; and pulling out my bottle, made him give the poor wretch a dram; which, with the news of his being delivered, revived him, and he sat up in the boat. But when Friday came to hear him speak, and look in his face, it would have moved anyone to tears to have seen how Friday kissed him, embraced and hugged him, cried, laughed, hallooed, jumped about, danced, sung; then cried again, wrung his hands, beat his own face and head; and then sung and jumped about again, like a distracted creature. It was a good while before I could make him speak or tell me what was the matter; but when he came a little to himself, he told me that it was his father.

It is not easy for me to express how it moved me to see what ecstasy and filial affection had worked in this poor savage at the sight of his father, and of his being delivered from death; nor, indeed, can I describe half the extravagances of his affection after this; for he went into the boat, and out of the boat, a great many times: when he went in to him, he would sit down by him, open his breast, and hold his father's head close to his bosom for many minutes together, to nourish it; then he took his arms and ankles, which were numbed and stiff with the binding, and chafed and rubbed them with his hands; and I, perceiving what the case was, gave him some rum out of my bottle to rub them with, which did them a great deal of good.

This affair put an end to our pursuit of the canoe with the other savages, who were now almost out of sight; and it was happy for us that we did not, for it blew so hard within two hours after, and before they could be got a quarter of their way, and continued blowing so hard all night, and that from the north-west, which was against

153

them, that I could not suppose their boat could live, or that they ever reached their own coast.

But to return to Friday; he was so busy about his father, that I could not find in my heart to take him off for some time; but after I thought he could leave him a little, I called him to me, and he came jumping and laughing, and pleased to the highest extreme; then I asked him if he had given his father any bread. He shook his head, and said, "None: ugly dog eat all up self." I then gave him a cake of bread, out of a little pouch I carried on purpose; I also gave him a dram for himself, but he would not taste it, but carried it to his father. I had in my pocket two or three bunches of raisins, so I gave him a handful of them for his father. He had no sooner given his father these raisins, but I saw him come out of the boat, and run away as if he had been bewitched, for he was the swiftest fellow on his feet that ever I saw: I say, he ran at such a rate that he was out of sight, as it were, in an instant; and though I called, and hallooed out too, after him, it was all one—away he went; and in a quarter of an hour I saw him come back again, though not so fast as he went; and, as he came nearer, I found his pace slacker, because he had something in his hand. When he came up to me, I found he had been quite home for an earthen jug, to bring his father some fresh water, and that he had got two more loaves of bread: the bread he gave me, but the water he carried to his father; however, as I was very thirsty too, I took a little of it. The water revived his father more than all the rum or spirits I had given him, for he was fainting with thirst.

When his father had drunk, I called to him to know if there was any water left: he said "Yes;" and I bade him give it to the poor Spaniard, who was in as much want of it as his father; and I sent one of the cakes, that Friday brought, to the Spaniard too, who was indeed very weak, and was reposing himself upon a green place under the shade of a tree; and whose limbs were also very stiff, and very much swelled with the rude bandage he had been tied with. When I saw that upon Friday's coming to him with the water, he sat up and drank, and took the bread and began to eat, I went to him and gave him a handful of raisins: he looked up in my face with all the tokens of gratitude and thankfulness that could appear in any countenance; but was so weak, notwithstanding he had so exerted himself in the fight, that he could not stand up upon his feet; he tried to do it two or three times, but was really not able, his ankles were so swelled and so painful to him; so I bade him sit still, and caused Friday to rub his ankles, and bathe them with rum, as he had done his father's.

I observed the poor affectionate creature, every two minutes, turn his head about, to see if his father, was in the same place and posture as he left him sitting; and at last he found he was not to be seen; at which he started up, and, without speaking a word, flew with that swiftness to him, that one could scarce perceive his feet to touch the ground as he went: but when he came he only found he had laid himself down to ease his limbs, so Friday came back to me presently; and then I spoke to the Spaniard to let Friday help him up, if he could, and lead him to the boat, and then he should carry him to our dwelling, where I would take care of him. But Friday, a lusty strong fellow, took the Spaniard upon his back, and carried him away to the boat, and set him down softly upon the side of the canoe, with his feet in the inside of it; and then lifting him quite in, he set him close to his father; and presently stepping out again, launched the boat off, and paddled it along the shore faster than I could walk: so he brought them both safe into our creek, and leaving them in the boat, ran away to fetch the other canoe. As he passed me I spoke to him, and asked him whither he went.

He told me, "Go fetch more boat:" so away he went like the wind; and he had the other canoe in the creek almost as soon as I got to it by land; so he wafted me over, and then went to help our new guests out of the boat, which he did; but they were neither of them able to walk, so that poor Friday knew not what to do.

To remedy this, I went to work in my thought, and calling to Friday to bid them sit down on the bank while he came to me, I soon made a kind of hand-barrow to lay them on, and Friday and I carried them both up together upon it between us.

But when we got them to the outside of our wall, we were at a worse loss than before, for it was impossible to get them over, and I was resolved not to break it down, so I set to work again: and Friday and I, in about two hours' time, made a very handsome tent, covered with old sails, and above that with boughs of trees, being in the space without our outward fence, and between that and the grove of young wood which I had planted; and here we made them two beds of such things as I had, *viz.*, of good rice-straw, with blankets laid upon it, to lie on, and another to cover them, on each bed.

My island was now peopled, and I thought myself very rich in subjects; and it was a merry reflection, which I frequently made, how like a king I looked.

As soon as I had secured my two weak, rescued prisoners, and given them shelter, and a place to rest them upon, I began to think of making some provision for them; and the first thing I did, I ordered Friday to take a yearling goat, betwixt a kid and a goat, out of my particular flock, to be killed; when I cut off the hinder-quarter, and chopping it into small pieces, I set Friday to work to boiling and stewing, and made them a very good dish, I assure you, of flesh and broth; and as I cooked it without doors, so I carried it all into the new tent, and having set a table there for them, I sat down, and ate my own dinner also with them, and, as well as I could, cheered and encouraged them.

After we had dined, I ordered Friday to take one of the canoes, and go and fetch our muskets and other firearms, which, for want of time, we had left upon the place of battle; and, the next day, I ordered him to go and bury the dead bodies of the savages. I also ordered him to bury the horrid remains of their barbarous feast: all which he punctually performed, and effaced the very appearance of the savages being there; so that when I went again, I could scarce know where it was, otherwise than by the corner of the wood pointing to the place.

I then began to enter into a little conversation with my two new subjects: and, first, I set Friday to inquire of his father what he thought of the escape of the savages in that canoe, and whether we might expect a return of them, with a power too great for us to resist. His first opinion was, that the savages in the boat never could live out the storm which blew that night they went off, but must, of necessity, be drowned, or driven south to those other shores, where they were as sure to be devoured as they were to be drowned if they were to be cast away: but, as to what they would do, if they came safe on shore, he said he knew not; but it was his opinion, that they were so dreadfully frightened with the manner of their being attacked, the noise, and the fire, that he believed they would tell the people they were all killed by thunder and lightning, not by the hand of man; and that the two which appeared, *viz.*, Friday and I, were two heavenly spirits, or furies, come down to destroy them, and not men with weapons.

This, he said, he knew; because he heard them all cry out so, in their language, one to another; for it was impossible for them to conceive that a man could dart fire, and speak thunder, and kill at a distance, without lifting up the hand, as was done now: and this old savage was in the right; for, as I understood since, by other hands, the savages never attempted to go over to the island afterwards, they were so terrified with the accounts given by those four men (for it seems they did escape the sea), that they believed whoever went to that enchanted island would be destroyed with fire from the gods. This, however, I knew not; and, therefore, was under continual apprehensions for a good while, and kept always upon my guard, with all my army; for, as there were now four of us, I would have ventured upon a hundred of them, fairly in the open field, at any time.

In a little time, however, no more canoes appearing, the fear of their coming wore off; and I began to take my former thoughts of a voyage to the main into consideration; being likewise assured, by Friday's father, that I might depend upon good usage from their nation, on his account, if I would go. But my thoughts were a little suspended when I had a serious discourse with the Spaniard, and when I understood that there were sixteen more of his countrymen and Portuguese, who having been cast away and made their escape to that side, lived there at peace, indeed, with the savages, but were very sore put to it for necessaries, and, indeed, for life. I asked him all the particulars of their voyage, and found they were a Spanish ship, bound from the Rio de la Plata to the Havanna, being directed to leave their loading there, which was chiefly hides and silver, and to bring back what European goods they could meet with there; that they had five Portuguese seamen on board, whom they took out of another wreck; that five of their own men were drowned, when first the ship was lost, and that these escaped through infinite dangers and hazards, and arrived, almost starved, on the cannibal coast, where they expected to have been devoured every moment. He told me they had some arms with them, but they were perfectly useless, for that they had neither powder nor ball, the washing of the sea having spoiled all their powder, but a little, which they used at their first landing, to provide themselves some food.

I asked him what he thought would become of them there, and if they had formed any design of making their escape. He said they had many consultations about it; but that having neither vessel, nor tools to build one, nor provisions of any kind, their councils always ended in tears and despair. I asked him how he thought they would receive a proposal from me, which might tend towards an escape; and whether, if they were all here, it might not be done. I told him, with freedom, I feared mostly their treachery and ill usage of me, if I put my life in their hands; for that gratitude was no inherent virtue in the nature of man, nor did men always square their dealings by the obligations they had received, so much as they did by the advantages they expected.

He answered, with a great deal of candour and ingenuousness, that their condition was so miserable, and that they were so sensible of it, that he believed they would abhor the thought of using any man unkindly that should contribute to their deliverance; and that, if I pleased, he would go to them, with the old man, and discourse with them about it, and return again, and bring me their answer; that he would make conditions with them upon their solemn oath, that they should be absolutely under my direction, as their commander and captain: and they should swear upon the holy sacraments and gospel to be true to me, and go to such Christian country as I should agree to, and no other; and to be directed wholly and absolutely by my orders, till they were landed safely in such country as I intended; and that he would bring a contract from them, under their hands, for that purpose.

Then he told me he would first swear to me himself, that he would never stir from me as long as he lived, till I gave him orders; and that he would take my side to the last drop of his blood, if there should happen the least breach of faith among his countrymen. He told me they were all of them very civil, honest men, and they were under the greatest distress imaginable, having neither weapons or clothes, nor any food, but at the mercy and discretion of the savages; out of all hopes of ever returning to their own country; and that he was sure, if I would undertake their relief, they would live and die by me.

Upon these assurances, I resolved to venture to relieve them, if possible, and to send the old savage and this Spaniard over to them to treat. But when we had got all things in readiness to go, the Spaniard himself started an objection, which had so much prudence in it on one hand, and so much sincerity on the other hand, that I could not but be very well satisfied in it; and, by his advice, put off the deliverance of his comrades for at least half a year. The case was thus: he had been with us now about a month, during which time I had let him see in what manner I had provided, with the assistance of Providence, for my support; and he saw evidently what stock of corn and rice I had laid up: which, though it was more than sufficient for myself, yet it was not sufficient, without good husbandry, for my family, now it was increased to four; but much less would it be sufficient if his countrymen, who were, as he said, sixteen, still alive, should come over; and, least of all, would it be sufficient to victual our vessel, if we should build one, for a voyage to any of the Christian colonies of America; so he told me he thought it would be more advisable to let him and the other two dig and cultivate some more land, as much as I could spare seed to sow, and that we should wait another harvest that we might have a supply of corn for his countrymen, when they should come; for want might be a temptation to them to disagree, or not to think themselves delivered, otherwise than out of one difficulty into another.

His caution was so seasonable, and his advice so good, that I could not but be very well pleased with his proposal, as well as I was satisfied with his fidelity; so we fell to digging, all four of us, as well as the wooden tools we were furnished with permitted; and, in about a month's time, by the end of which it was seed-time, we had got as much land cured and trimmed up, as we sowed two-and-twenty bushels of barley on, and sixteen jars of rice, which was all the seed we had to spare: indeed, we left ourselves barely sufficient for our own food, for the six months that we had to expect our crop, reckoning from the time we set our seed aside for sowing; for it is not to be supposed it is six months in the ground in that country.

Having now society enough, and our number being sufficient to put us out of fear of the savages, if they had come, unless their number had been very great, we went freely all over the island, whenever we found occasion; and as we had our escape or deliverance upon our thoughts, it was impossible, at least for me, to have the means of it out of mine. For this purpose, I marked out several trees, which I thought fit for our work, and I set Friday and his father to cut them down; and then I caused the Spaniard, to whom I imparted my thoughts on that affair, to oversee and direct their work. I showed them with what indefatigable pains I had hewed a large tree into single planks, and I caused them to do the like, till they had made about a dozen large planks of good oak, near two feet broad, thirty-five feet long, and from two inches to four inches thick: what prodigious labour it took up, anyone may imagine.

At the same time, I contrived to increase my little flock of tame goats as much as I could; and, for this purpose, I made Friday and the Spaniard go out one day, and myself with Friday the next day (for we took our turns), and by this means we got about twenty young kids to breed up with the rest; for whenever we shot the dam, we saved the kids, and added them to our flock. But, above all, the season for curing the grapes coming on, I caused such a prodigious quantity to be hung up in the sun, that I believe we could have filled sixty or eighty barrels; and these, with our bread, formed a great part of our food.

It was now harvest, and our crop in good order; it was not the most plentiful increase I had seen in the island, but, however, it was enough to answer our end; for, from twenty-two bushels of barley, we brought in and threshed out above two hundred and twenty bushels; and the like in proportion of the rice, which was store enough for our food to the next harvest, though all the sixteen Spaniards had been on shore with me; or, if we had been ready for a voyage, it would very plentifully have victualled our ship to have carried us to any part of America. When we had thus housed and secured our magazine of corn, we fell to work to make more great baskets, in which we kept it; and the Spaniard was very handy and dexterous at this.

And now, having a full supply of food for all the guests I expected, I gave the Spaniard leave to go over to the main, to see what he could do with those he had left behind him there. I gave him a strict charge not to bring any man with him who would not first swear, in the presence of himself and the old savage, that he would no way injure, fight with, or attack the person he should find in the island, who was so kind as to send for them in order to their deliverance; but that they would stand by him and defend him against all such attempts, and wherever they went, would be entirely under and subjected to his command; and that this should be put in writing, and signed in their hands. How they were to have done this when I knew they had neither pen or ink, was a question we never asked.

Under these instructions the Spaniard and the old savage went away in one of the canoes which they might be said to come in, or rather were brought in, when they came as prisoners to be devoured by the savages. I gave each of them a musket, with a firelock on it, and about eight charges of powder and ball, charging them to be very good husbands of both, and not to use either of them but upon urgent occasions.

This was a cheerful work, being the first measures used by me, in view of my deliverance, for now twenty-seven years and some days. I gave them provisions of bread, and of dried grapes, sufficient for themselves for many days, and sufficient for all the Spaniards for about eight days' time; and wishing them a good voyage, I saw them go, agreeing with them about a signal they should hang out at their return, by which I should know them again when they came back, at a distance, before they came on shore. They went away, with a fair gale, on the day that the moon was at full, by my account in the month of October.

It was no less than eight days I had waited for them, when a strange and unforeseen accident intervened, of which the like has not, perhaps, been heard of in history. I was fast asleep in my hutch one morning, when my man Friday came running in to me, and called aloud, "Master, master, they are come, they are come!" I jumped up, and, regardless of danger, I went out as soon as I could get my clothes on, through my little grove, which, by the way, was by this time grown to be a very thick wood; I went without my arms, which was not my custom to do: but I was surprised, when, turning my eyes to the sea, I presently saw a boat at about a league and a half distance, standing in for the shore, with a shoulder-of-mutton sail, and the wind blowing pretty fair. to bring them in: also I observed, presently, that they did not come from that side which the shore lay on, but from the southernmost end of the island.

Upon this I called Friday in, and bade him lie close, for these were not the people we looked for, and that we might not know yet whether they were friends or enemies. In the next place, I went in to fetch my perspective glass, to see what I could make of them; and, having taken the ladder out, I climbed to the top of the hill, as I used to do when I was apprehensive of anything, and to take my view the plainer, without being discovered. I had scarce set my foot upon the hill, when my eye plainly discovered a ship lying at an anchor, at about two leagues and a half distance from me, S.S.E., but not above a league and a half from the shore. By my observation, it appeared plainly to be an English ship, and the boat appeared to be an English long-boat.

I cannot express the confusion I was in, though the joy of seeing a ship, and one that I had reason to believe was manned by my own countrymen, and consequently friends, was such as I cannot describe; but yet I had some secret doubts hanging about me, bidding me keep upon my guard. In the first place, it occurred to me to consider what business an English ship could have in that part of the world, since it was not the way to or from any part of the world where the English had any traffic; and I knew there had been no storms to drive them in there, in distress; and that if they were really English, it was most probable that they were here upon no good design; and that I had better continue as I was, than fall into the hands of thieves and murderers.

Had I not been made cautious, I had been undone inevitably, and in a far worse condition than before, as you will see presently. I had not kept myself long in this posture, till I saw the boat draw near the shore, as if they looked for a creek to thrust in at, for the convenience of landing; however, as they did not come quite far enough they did not see the little inlet where I formerly landed my rafts, but run their boat on shore upon the beach, at about half a mile from me, which was very happy for me; for otherwise they would have landed just at my door, as I may say, and would soon have beaten me out of my castle, and perhaps have plundered me of all I had.

When they were on shore, I was fully satisfied they were English-men, at least most of them; one or two I thought were Dutch, but it did not prove so; there were in all eleven men, whereof three of them I found were unarmed, and, as I thought, bound; and when the first four or five of them jumped on shore, they took those three out of the boat, as prisoners: one of the three I could perceive, using the most passionate gestures of entreaty, affliction, and despair, even to a kind of extravagance; the other two, I could perceive, lifted up their hands sometimes, and appeared concerned, indeed, but not to such a degree as the first. I was perfectly confounded at the sight, and knew not what the meaning of it should be. Friday called out to me in English, as well as he could, "master! you see English mans eat prisoner as well as savage mans."

"Why, Friday," says I, "do you think they are going to eat them then ?"

"Yes," says Friday, "they will eat them."

"No, no," says I, "Friday; I am afraid they will murder them, indeed; but you may be sure they will not eat them."

All this while I had no thought of what the matter really was, but stood trembling with the horror of the sight, expecting every moment when the three prisoners should be killed; nay, once I saw one of the villains lift up his arms with a great cutlass, to strike one of the poor men; and I expected to see him fall every moment; at which all the blood in my body seemed to run chill in my veins. I wished heartily now for the Spaniard, and the savage that was gone with him, or that I had any way to have come undiscovered within shot of them, that I might have secured the three men, for I saw they had among them no firearms; but it fell out to my mind another way. After I had observed the outrageous usage of the three men by the insolent seamen, the fellows ran scattering about the island, as if they wanted to see the country. I observed that the three other men had liberty to go also where they pleased; but they sat down all three upon the ground, very pensive, and looked like men in despair.

It was just at high water when these people came on shore, and while they rambled about to see what kind of a place they were in,

162

they had carelessly staid till the tide was spent, and the water was ebbed considerably away, leaving their boat aground. They had left two men in the boat, who, as I found afterwards, having drunk a little too much brandy, fell asleep; however, one of them waking a little sooner than the other, and finding the boat too far aground for him to stir it, hallooed out for the rest, who were straggling about; upon which they all soon came to the boat: but it was past all their strength to launch her, being very heavy, and the shore on that side being a soft oozy sand, almost like a quicksand.

In this condition they gave it over, and away they strolled about the country again; and I heard one of them say aloud to another, calling them off from the boat, "Why, let her alone, Jack, can't you? she'll float next tide:" by which I was fully confirmed in the main inquiry of what countrymen they were. All this while I kept myself very close, not once daring to stir out of my castle, any farther than to my place of observation, near the top of the hill; and very glad I was to think how well it was fortified. I knew it was no less than ten hours before the boat could float again, and by that time it would be dark, and I might be at more liberty to see their motions, and to hear their discourse, if they had any. In the meantime, I fitted myself up for a battle, as before, though with more caution, knowing I had to do with another kind of enemy than I had at first. I ordered Friday also, whom I had made an excellent marksman with his gun, to load himself with arms. I took myself two fowling-pieces, and I gave him three muskets. My figure, indeed, was very fierce; I had my formidable goat-skin coat on, with the great cap I have mentioned, a naked sword by my side, two pistols in my belt, and a gun upon each shoulder.

It was my design, as I said above, not to have made any attempt till it was dark; but about two o'clock, being the heat of the day, I found that they were all gone straggling into the woods, and, as I thought, laid down to sleep. The three poor distressed men, too anxious for their condition to get any sleep, had, however, sat clown under the shelter of a great tree, at about a quarter of a mile from me, and, as I thought, out of sight of any of the rest. Upon this I resolved to discover myself to them, and learn something of their condition: immediately I marched, my man Friday at a good distance behind me, as formidable for his arms as I, but not making quite so staring a spectre-like figure as I did. I came as near them undiscovered as I could, and then, before any of them saw me, I called aloud to them in Spanish, "What are ye, gentlemen?" They started up at the noise, but were ten times more confounded when they saw me, and the uncouth figure that I made. They made no answer at all, but I thought I perceived them just going to fly from me, when I spoke to them in English. "Gentlemen," said I, "do not be surprised at me; perhaps you may have a friend near when you did not expect it."

"He must be sent directly from Heaven then," said one of them very gravely to me, and pulling off his hat at the same time to me; "for our condition is past the help of man."

"All help is from Heaven, sir," said I: "but can you put a stranger in the way to help you? for you seem to be in some great distress. I saw you when you landed; and when you seemed to make application to the brutes that came with you, I saw one of them lift up his sword to kill you."

The poor man, with tears running down his face, and trembling, looked like one astonished, returned, "Am I talking to God or man? Is it a real man or an angel?"

"Be in no fear about that, sir," said I; "if God had sent an angel to relieve you, he would have come better clothed, and armed after another manner than you see me. Pray lay aside your fears; I am a man, an Englishman, and disposed to assist you. You see I have one servant only; we have arms and ammunition: tell us freely, can we serve you? What is your case?"'

"Our case, sir," said he, "is too long to tell you, while our murderers are so near us; but, in short, sir, I was commander of that ship; my men have mutinied against me; they have been hardly prevailed on not to murder me, and, at last, have set me on shore in this desolate place, with these two men with me—one my mate, the other a passenger, where we expected to perish, believing the place to be uninhabited, and know not yet what to think of it."

"Where are these brutes, your enemies?" said I; "do you know where they are gone?"

"There they lie, sir," said he, pointing to a thicket of trees; "my heart trembles for fear they have seen us, and heard you speak; if they have, they will certainly murder us all."

"Have they any firearms?" said I.

He answered, "They had only two pieces, one of which they left in the boat."

"Well, then," said I, "leave the rest to me. I see they are all asleep; it is an easy thing to kill them all; but shall we rather take them prisoners?"

He told me there were two desperate villains among them that it was scarce safe to show any mercy to; but if they were secured, he believed all the rest would return to their duty. I asked him which they were? He told me he could not at that distance distinguish them, but he would obey my orders in anything I would direct. "Well," says I, "let us retreat out of their view or hearing, lest they awake, and we will resolve further." So they willingly went back with me, till the woods covered us from them.

"Look you, sir," said I, "if I venture upon your deliverance, are you willing to make two conditions with me?" He anticipated my proposals by telling me that both he and the ship, if recovered, should be wholly directed and commanded by me in everything; and if the ship was not recovered, he would live and die with me in what part of the world soever I would send him; and the two other men said the same. "Well," says I, "my conditions are but two; first,—that while you stay in this island with me, you will not pretend to any authority here; and if I put arms in your hands, you will, upon all occasions, give them up to me, and do no prejudice to me or mine upon this island, and in the meantime be governed by my orders; secondly,—that if the ship is recovered, you will carry me and my man to England passage free."

He gave me all the assurances that the invention or faith of man could devise that he would comply with these most reasonable demands, and besides would owe his life to me, and acknowledge it upon all occasions as long as he lived. "Well, then," said I, "here are three muskets for you, with powder and ball; tell me next what you think is proper to be done." He showed all the testimonies of his gratitude that he was able, but offered to be wholly guided by me. I told him I thought it was hard venturing anything; but the best method I could think of was to fire on them at once as they lay, and if any were not killed at the first volley, and offered to submit, we might save them, and so put it wholly upon God's providence to direct the shot. He said, very modestly, that he was loath to kill them, if he could help it; but that those two were incorrigible villains, and had been the authors of all the mutiny in the ship, and if they escaped, we should be undone still, for they would go on board and bring the whole ship's company, and destroy us all.

"Well, then," says I, "necessity legitimates my advice, for it is the only way to save our lives." However, seeing him still cautious of shedding blood, I told him they should go themselves, and manage as they found convenient.

In the middle of this discourse we heard some of them awake, and soon after we saw two of them on their feet. I asked him if either of them were the heads of the mutiny? He said, "No."

"Well, then," said I, "you may let them escape; and Providence seems to have awakened them on purpose to save themselves. Now," says I, "if the rest escape you, it is your fault." Animated with this, he took the musket I had given him in his hand, and a pistol in his belt, and his two comrades with him, with each a piece in his hand; the two men who were with him going first made some noise, at which one of the seamen, who was awake, turned about, and seeing them coming, cried out to the rest; but it was too late then, for the moment he cried out they fired—I mean the two men, the captain wisely reserving his own piece. They had so well aimed their shot at the men they knew, that one of them was killed on the spot, and the other very much wounded; but not being dead, he started up on his feet, and called eagerly for help to the other; but the captain, stepping to him, told him it was too late to cry for help, he should call upon God to forgive his villainy, and with that word knocked him down with the stock of his musket, so that he never spoke more: there were three more in the company, and one of them was slightly wounded.

By this time I was come; and when they saw their danger, and that it was in vain to resist, they begged for mercy. The captain told them he would spare their lives if they would give him an assurance of their abhorrence of the treachery they had been guilty of, and would swear to be faithful to him in recovering the ship, and afterwards in carrying her back to Jamaica, whence they came. They gave him all the protestations of their sincerity that could be desired: and he was willing to believe them, and spare their lives, which I was not against, only that I obliged him to keep them bound hand and foot while they were on the island.

While this was doing, I sent Friday with the captain's mate to the boat with orders to secure her, and bring away the oars and sails, which they did; and by-and-by three straggling men, that were (happily for them) parted from the rest, came back upon hearing the guns fired; and seeing the captain, who was before their prisoner, now their conqueror, they submitted to be bound also; and so our victory was complete.

It now remained that the captain and I should inquire into one another's circumstances. I began first, and told him my whole history, which he heard with an attention even to amazement,—and particularly at the wonderful manner of my being furnished with provisions and ammunition; and, indeed, as my story is a whole collection of wonders, it affected him deeply. But when he reflected from thence upon himself, and how I seemed to have been preserved there on purpose to save his life, the tears ran down his face, and he could not speak a word more. After this communication was at an end, I carried him and his two men into my apartment, leading them in just where I came out, *viz.*, at the top of the house, where I refreshed him with such provision as I had, and showed them all the contrivances I had made during my long, long inhabiting that place.

All I showed them, all I said to them, was perfectly amazing; but above all, the captain admired my fortification, and how perfectly I had concealed my retreat with a grove of trees, which, having been now planted near twenty years, and the trees growing much faster than in England, was become a little wood, so thick that it was impassable in any part of it but at that one side where I had reserved my little winding passage into it I told him this was my castle and my residence, but that I had a seat in the country, as most princes have, whither I could retreat upon occasion, and I would show him that too another time; but at present our business was to consider how to recover the ship.

He agreed with me as to that, but told me he was perfectly at a loss what measures to take, for that there were still six-and-twenty hands board, who, having entered into a cursed conspiracy, by which they had all forfeited their lives to the law, would be hardened in it now by desperation, and would carry it on, knowing that if they were subdued they would be brought to the gallows as soon as they came to England, or to any of the English colonies, and that therefore there would be no attacking them with so small a number as we were.

I mused for some time upon what he had said, and found it was a very rational conclusion, and that therefore something was to be resolved on speedily, as well to draw the men on board into some snare for their surprise, as to prevent their landing upon us, and destroying us. Upon this, it presently occurred to me that in a little while the ship's crew, wondering what was become of their comrades and of the boat, would certainly come on shore in their other boat to look for them, and that then perhaps they might come armed, and be too strong for us; this he allowed to be rational. Upon this, I told him the first thing we had to do was to stave the boat, which lay upon the beach, so that they might not carry her off, and taking everything out of her, leave her so far useless as not to be fit to swim; accordingly, we went on board, took the arms which were left on board out of her, and whatever else we found there,—which was a bottle of brandy, and another of rum, a few biscuit-cakes, a horn of powder, and a great lump of sugar in a piece of canvas, all which was very welcome to me, especially the brandy and sugar, of which I had had none left for many years.

When we had carried all these things on shore, we knocked a great hole in her bottom, that if they had come strong enough to master us, yet they could not carry off the boat. Indeed, it was not much in my thoughts that we could be able to recover the ship; but my view was, that if they went away without the boat, I did not much question to make her again fit to carry us to the Leeward Islands, and call upon our friends the Spaniards in my way, for I had them still in my thoughts.

While we were thus preparing our designs, and had first, by main strength, heaved the boat upon the beach, so high that the tide would not float her off at high water mark, and besides, had broke a hole in her bottom too big to be quickly stopped, and were set down musing what we should do, we heard the ship fire a gun, and make a waft with her ensign as a signal for the boat to come on board: but no boat stirred; and they fired several times, making other signals for the boat. At last, when all their signals and firing proved fruitless, and they found the boat did not stir, we saw them, by the help of my glasses, hoist another boat out, and row towards the shore; and we found, as they approached, that there were no less than ten men in her, and that they had firearms with them.

As the ship lay almost two leagues from the shore, we had a full view of them as they came, and a plain sight even of their faces; because the tide having set them a little to the east of the other boat, they rowed up under shore, to come to the same place where the other had landed, and where the boat lay; the captain knew the persons and characters of all the men in the boat, of whom, he said, there were three very honest fellows, who, he was sure, were led into this conspiracy by the rest, being overpowered and frightened; but that as for the boatswain, who it seems was the chief officer among them, and all the rest, they were as outrageous as any of the ship's crew, and were no doubt made desperate in their now enterprise; and terribly apprehensive he was that they would be too powerful for us. I smiled at him, and told him that men in our circumstances were past the operation of fear. I asked him what he thought of the circumstances of my life, and whether a deliverance were not worth venturing for? "And where, sir," said I, "is your belief of my being preserved here on purpose to save your life, which elevated you a little while ago? For my part," said I, "there seems to be but one thing amiss in all the prospect of it."

"What is that?" says he.

"Why," said I, "it is, that as you say there are three or four honest fellows among them, which should be spared, had they been all of the wicked part of the crew, I should have thought God's providence had singled them out to deliver them into your hands; for depend upon it every man that comes ashore is our own, and shall die or live as they behave to us." As I spoke this with a raised voice and cheerful countenance, I found it greatly encouraged him; so we set vigorously to our business.

We had, upon the first appearance of the boats coming from the ship, considered of separating our prisoners; and we had, indeed, secured them effectually. Two of them, of whom the captain was less assured, I sent with Friday, and one of the three delivered men, to my cave, where they were remote enough, and out of danger of being heard or discovered, or of finding their way out of the woods if they could have delivered themselves: here they left them bound, but gave them provisions; and promised them, if they continued there quietly, to give them their liberty in a day or two; but that if they attempted their escape, they should be put to death without mercy. They promised faithfully to bear their confinement with patience, and were very thankful that they had such good usage as to have provisions and light left them; for Friday gave them candles (such as we made ourselves) for their comfort; and they did not know but that he stood sentinel over them at the entrance.

The other prisoners had better usage; two of them were kept pinioned, because the captain was not able to trust them; but the two other were taken into my service, upon the captain's recommendation, and upon their solemnly engaging to live and die with us; so with them and the three honest men we were seven men, well armed; and I made no doubt we should be able to deal well enough with the ten that were coming, considering that the captain had said there were three or four honest men among them also. As soon as they got to the place where their other boat lay, they ran their boat into the beach and came all on shore, hauling the boat up after them, which I was glad to see, for I was afraid they would rather have left the boat at an anchor some distance from the shore, with some hands in her to guard her, and so we should not be able to seize the boat.

Being on shore, the first thing they did, they ran all to their other boat; and it was easy to see they were under a great surprise to find her stripped, as above, of all that was in her, and a great hole in her bottom. After they had mused awhile upon this, they set up two or three great shouts, hallooing with all their might, to try if they could make their companions hear; but all was to no purpose: then they came all close in a ring, and fired a volley of their small arms, which, indeed, we heard, and the echoes made the woods ring. They were so astonished at the surprise of this, that, as they told us afterwards, they resolved to go all on aboard again to their ship, and let them know that the men were all murdered, and the long-boat staved; accordingly, they immediately launched their boat again, and got all of them on board.

The captain was terribly amazed, and even confounded, at this, believing they would go on board the ship again, and set sail, giving their comrades over for lost, and so he should still lose the ship, which he was in hopes we should have recovered; but he was quickly as much frightened the other way.

They had not been long put off with the boat, when we perceived them all coming on shore again: but with this new measure in their conduct, which it seems they consulted together upon, viz., to leave three men in the boat, and the rest to go on shore, and go up into the country to look for their fellows. This was a great disappointment to us, for now we were at a loss what to do, as our seizing those seven men on shore would be no advantage to us if we let the boat escape; because they would row away to the ship, and then the rest of them would be sure to weigh and set sail, and so our recovering the ship would be lost. However, we had no remedy but to wait and see what the issue of things might present. The seven men came on shore, and the three who remained in the boat put her off to a good distance from the shore, and came to an anchor to wait for them; so that it was impossible for us to come at them in the boat.

Those that came on shore kept close together, marching towards the top of the little hill under which my habitation lay; and we could see them plainly, though they could not perceive us. We should have been very glad if they would have come nearer to us, so that we might have fired at them, or that they would have gone farther off, that we might come abroad. But when they were come to the brow of the hill, where they could see a great way into the valleys and woods, they shouted and hallooed till they were weary; and not caring, it seems, to venture far from the shore, nor far from one another, they sat down together under a tree to consider it.

The captain made a very just proposal to me upon this consultation of theirs—*viz.*, that perhaps they would all fire a volley again, to endeavour to make their fellows hear, and that we should all sally upon them just at the juncture when their pieces were all discharged, and they would certainly yield, and we should have them without bloodshed. I liked this proposal, provided it was done while we were near enough to come up to them before they could load their pieces again. But this event did not happen; and we lay still a long time, very irresolute what course to take.

At length, I told them there would be nothing done, in my opinion, till night; and then if they did not return to the boat, perhaps we might find a way to get between them and the shore, and so might use some stratagem with them in the boat to get them on shore. We waited a great while, though very impatient for their removing; and were very uneasy when, after long consultation, we saw them all start up, and march down towards the sea; it seems they had such dreadful apprehensions of the danger of the place, that they resolved to go on board again, give their companions over for lost, and so go on with their intended voyage with the ship.

As soon as I perceived them go towards the shore, I thought of a stratagem to fetch them back again, and which answered my end to a tittle. I ordered Friday and the captain's mate to go over the little creek westward, towards the place where the savages came on shore when Friday was rescued, and so soon as they came to a little rising ground, at about half a mile distance, I bade them halloo out, as loud as they could, and wait till they found the seamen heard them; that as soon as ever they heard the seamen answer them, they should return it again; and then, keeping out of sight, take a round, always answering when the others hallooed to draw them as far into the island, and among the woods as possible, and then wheel about again to me by such ways as I directed them.

They were just going into the boat when Friday and the mate hallooed: and they presently heard them, and, answering, ran along the shore westward, towards the voice they heard, when they were stopped by the creek, where, the water being up, they could not get over, and called for the boat to come up and set them over; as, indeed, I expected. When they had set themselves over, I observed that the boat, being gone a good way into the creek, they took one of the three men out of her to go along with them, and left only two in the boat, having fastened her to the stump of a little tree on the shore. This was what I wished for: and immediately leaving Friday and the captain's mate to their business, I took the rest with me, and crossing the creek out of their sight, we surprised the two men before they were aware; one of them lying on the shore and the other being in the boat. The fellow on shore was between sleeping and waking, and going to start up; the captain, who was foremost, ran in upon him and knocked him down; and then called out to him in the boat to yield, or he was a dead man.

There needed very few arguments to persuade a single man to yield, when he saw five men upon him, and his comrade knocked down: besides, this was, it seems, one of the three men who were not so hearty in the mutiny as the rest of the crew; and, therefore, was easily persuaded not only to yield, but afterwards to join very sincerely with us. In the meantime, Friday and the captain's mate so well managed their business with the rest, that they drew them, by hallooing and answering, from one hill to another, and from one wood to another, till they not only heartily tired them, but left them where they were very sure they could not reach back to the boat before it was dark; and, indeed, they were heartily tired themselves also, by the time they came back to us.

We had nothing now to do but to watch for them in the dark, and to fall upon them, so as to make sure, work with them. It was several hours after Friday came back to me before they came back to their boat; and we could hear the foremost of them, long before they came quite up, calling to those behind to come along; and could also hear them answer, and complain how lame and tired they were, and not able to come any faster: which was very welcome news to us. At length they came up to the boat: but it is impossible to express their confusion when they found the boat fast aground in the creek, the tide ebbed out, and their two men gone. We could hear them call to one another in a most lamentable manner, telling one another they were got into an enchanted island; that either there were inhabitants in it, and they should all be murdered, or else there were devils and spirits in it, and they should all be carried away and devoured. They hallooed again, and called their two comrades by their names a great many times, but no answer.

After some time, we could see them, by the little light there was, run about, wringing their hands like men in despair, and sometimes they would go and sit down in the boat to rest themselves: then come ashore again, and walk about, and so the same thing over again. My men would fain have had me give them leave to fall upon them at once in the dark; but I was willing to take them at some advantage, so as to spare them, and kill as few of them as I could; and especially I was unwilling to hazard the killing any of our men, knowing the others were very well armed. I resolved to wait, to see if they did not separate; and therefore, to make sure of them, I drew my ambuscade nearer, and ordered Friday and the captain to creep upon their hands and feet as close to the ground as they could, that they might not be discovered, and get as near them as they could possibly, before they offered to fire.

They had not been long in that posture, when the boatswain, who was the principal ringleader of the mutiny, and had now shown himself the most dejected and dispirited of all the rest, came walking towards them, with two more of the crew; the captain was so eager at having this principal rogue so much in his power, that he could hardly have patience to let him come so near as to be sure of him, for they only heard his tongue before: but when they came nearer, the captain and Friday, starting up on their feet, let fly at them. The boatswain was killed upon the spot: the next man was shot in the body, and fell just by him, though he did not die till an hour or two after; and the third ran for it. At the noise of the fire, I immediately advanced with my whole army, which was now eight men, *viz.*, myself, *generalissimo*; Friday, my lieutenant-general; the captain and his two men, and the three prisoners of war whom we had trusted with arms.

We came upon them, indeed, in the dark, so that they could not see our number; and I made the man they had left in the boat, who was now one of us, to call them by name, to try if I could bring them to a parley, and so perhaps might reduce them to terms; which fell out just as we desired: for indeed it was easy to think, as their condition then was, they would be very willing to capitulate. So he calls out as loud as he could to one of them, "Tom Smith! Tom Smith!"

Tom Smith answered immediately, "Is that Robinson?" for it seems he knew the voice.

The other answered, "Ay, ay; for God's sake, Tom Smith, throw down your arms and yield or you are all dead men this moment."

"Who must we yield to? Where are they?" says Smith again.

"Here they are," says he; "here's our captain and fifty men with him, have been hunting you these two hours; the boatswain is killed,

Will Fry is wounded, and I am a prisoner; and if you do not yield, you are all lost."

"Will they give us quarter then?" says Tom Smith, "and we will yield."

"I'll go and ask, if you promise to yield," said Robinson: so he asked the captain, and the captain himself then calls out, "You, Smith, you know my voice; if you lay down your arms immediately, and submit, you shall have your lives, all but Will Atkins."

Upon this, Will Atkins cried out, "For God's sake, captain, give me quarter; what have I done? They have all been as bad as I:" which, by the way, was not true; for, it seems, this Will Atkins was the first man that laid hold of the captain, when they first mutinied, and used him barbarously, in tying his hands, and giving him injurious language. However, the captain told him he must lay down his arms at discretion, and trust to the governor's mercy: by which he meant me, for they all called me governor. In a word, they all laid down their arms, and begged their lives; and I sent the man that had parleyed with them, and two more, who bound them all; and then my great army of fifty men, which, with those three, were in all but eight, came up and seized upon them, and upon their boat; only that I kept myself and one more out of sight for reasons, of state.

Our next work was to repair the boat, and think of seizing the ship: and as for the captain, now he had leisure to parley with them, he expostulated with them upon the villainy of their practices with him, and upon the further wickedness of their design, and how certainly it must bring them to misery and distress in the end, and perhaps to the gallows. They all appeared very penitent, and begged hard for their lives. As for that, he told them they were not his prisoners, but the commander's of the island; that they thought they had set him on shore in a barren uninhabited island; but it had pleased God so to direct them, that it was inhabited, and that the governor was an Englishman; that he might hang them all there, if he pleased; but as he had given them all quarter, he supposed he would send them to England, to be dealt with there as justice required, except Atkins, whom he was commanded by the governor to advise to prepare for death, for that he would be hanged in the morning.

Though this was all a fiction of his own, yet it had its desired effect; Atkins fell upon his knees, to beg the captain to intercede with the governor for his life; and all the rest begged of him, for God's sake, that they might not be sent to England.

It now occurred to me, that the time of our deliverance was come, and that it would be a most easy thing to bring these fellows in to be hearty in getting possession of the ship; so I retired in the dark from them, that they might not see what kind of a governor they had, and called the captain to me; when I called, at a good distance, one of the men was ordered to speak again, and say to the captain, "Captain, the commander calls for you;" and presently the captain replied, "Tell his Excellency I am just coming."

This more perfectly amazed them, and they all believed that the commander was just by, with his fifty men. Upon the captain coming to me, I told, him my project for seizing the ship, which he liked wonderfully well, and resolved to put it in execution the next morning. But, in order to execute it with more art, and to be secure of success, I told him we must divide the prisoners, and that he should go and take Atkins, and two more of the worst of them, and send them pinioned to the cave where the others lay. This was committed to Friday and the two men who came on shore with the captain. They conveyed them to the cave as to a prison: and it was, indeed, a dismal place, especially to men in their condition. The others I ordered to my bower; and as it was fenced in, and they pinioned, the place was secure enough, considering they were upon their behaviour.

To these in the morning I sent the captain, who was to enter into a parley with them—in a word, to try them, and tell me whether he thought they might be trusted or not to go on board and surprise the ship. He talked to them of the injury done him, of the condition they were brought to, and that though the governor had given them quarter for their lives as to the present action, yet that if they were sent to England, they would all be hanged in chains; but that if they would join in so just an attempt as to recover the ship, he would have the governor's engagement for their pardon.

Anyone may guess how readily such a proposal would be accepted by men in their condition: they fell down on their knees to the captain, and promised with the deepest imprecations, that they would be faithful to him to the last drop, and that they should owe their lives to him, and would go with him all over the world; that they would own him as a father to them as long as they lived.

"Well," says the captain, "I must go and tell the governor what you say, and see what I can do to bring him to consent to it." So he brought me an account of the temper he found them in, and that he verily believed they would be faithful. However, that we might be very secure, I told him he should go back again and choose out those five, and tell them, that they might see he did not want men, that he would take out those five to be his assistants, and that the governor would keep the other two, and the three that were sent prisoners to the castle (my cave), as hostages for the fidelity of those five; and that if they proved unfaithful in the execution, the five hostages should be hanged in chains alive on the shore. This looked severe, and convinced them that the governor was in earnest: however, they had no way left them but to accept it; and it was now the business of the prisoners, as much as of the captain, to persuade the other five to do their duty.

Our strength was now thus ordered for the expedition: first, the captain, his mate, and passenger: second, then the two prisoners of the first gang, to whom, having their character from the captain, I had given their liberty, and trusted them with arms: third, the other two that I had kept till now in my bower pinioned, but, on the captain's motion, had now released: fourth, these five released at last; so that they were twelve in all, besides five we kept prisoners in the cave for hostages.

I asked the captain if he was willing to venture with these hands on board the ship; but as for me and my man Friday, I did not think it was proper for us to stir, having seven men left behind; and it was employment enough for us to keep them asunder, and supply them with victuals. As to the five in the cave, I resolved to keep them fast, but Friday went in twice a day to them, to supply them with necessaries; and I made the other two carry provisions to a certain distance, where Friday was to take it.

When I showed myself to the two hostages, it was with the captain, who told them I was the person the governor had ordered to look after them; and that it was the governor's pleasure they should not stir anywhere but by my direction; that if they did, they would be fetched into the castle, and be laid in irons: so that as we never suffered them to see me as governor, I now appeared as another person, and spoke of the governor, the garrison, the castle, and the like, upon all occasions.

The captain now had no difficulty before him, but to furnish his two boats, stop the breach of one, and man them. He made his passenger captain of one, with four of the men; and himself, his mate, and five more, went in the other; and they contrived their business very well, for they came up to the ship about midnight. As soon as they came within call of the ship, he made Robinson hail them, and tell them they had brought off the men and the boat, but that it was a long time before they had found them, and the like; holding them in a chat till they came to the ship's side; when the captain and the mate entering first, with their arms, immediately knocked down the second mate and carpenter with the butt-end of their muskets, being very faithfully seconded by their men; they secured all the rest that were upon the main and quarter-decks, and began to fasten the hatches, to keep them down that were below; when the other boat and their men, entering at the fore-chains, secured the forecastle of the ship, and the scuttle which went down into the cook-room, making three men they found there prisoners.

When this was done, and all safe upon deck, the captain ordered the mate, with three men, to break into the round-house, where the new rebel captain lay, who, having taken the alarm, had got up, and with two men and a boy had got fire-arms in their hands; and when the mate, with a crow, split open the door, the new captain and his men fired boldly among them, and wounded the mate with a musket-ball, which broke his arm, and wounded two more of the men, but killed nobody. The mate calling for help, rushed, however, into the round-house, wounded as he was, and, with his pistol, shot the new captain through the head, the bullet entering at his mouth, and came out again behind one of his ears, so that he never spoke a word more: upon which the rest yielded, and the ship was taken effectually, without any more lives lost.

As soon as the ship was thus secured, the captain ordered seven guns to be fired, which was the signal agreed upon with me to give me notice of his success, which, you may be sure, I was very glad to hear, having sat watching upon the shore for it till near two o'clock in the morning. Having thus heard the signal plainly, I laid me down; and it having been a day of great fatigue to me, I slept very sound, till I was surprised with the noise of a gun; and presently starting up, I heard a man call me by the name of "Governor! Governor!" and presently I knew the captain's voice; when climbing up to the top of the hill, there he stood, and, pointing to the ship, he embraced me in his arms. "My dear friend and deliverer," says he, "there's your ship, for she is all yours, and so are we, and all that belong to her."

I cast my eyes to the ship, and there she rode, within little more than half a mile of the shore; for they had weighed her anchor as soon as they were masters of her, and, the weather being fair, had brought her to an anchor just against the mouth of the little creek; and, the tide being up, the captain had brought the pinnace in near the place where

I at first landed my rafts, and so landed just at my door. I was at first ready to sink down with the surprise; for I saw my deliverance, indeed, visibly put into my hands, all things easy, and a large ship just ready to carry me away whither I pleased to go. At first, for some time, I was not able to answer him one word; but as he had taken me in his arms, I held fast by him, or I should have fallen to the ground. He perceived the surprise, and immediately pulled a bottle out of his pocket, and gave me a dram of cordial, which he had brought on purpose for me.

After I had drank it, I sat down upon the ground; and though it brought me to myself, yet it was a good while before I could speak a word to him. All this time the poor man was in as great an ecstasy as I, only not under any surprise as I was; and he said a thousand kind, and tender things to me, to compose and bring me to myself: but such was the flood of joy in my breast, that it put all my spirits into confusion: at last it broke out into tears; and, in a little while after, I recovered my speech. I then took my turn, and embraced him as my deliverer, and we rejoiced together. I told him I looked upon him as a man sent from Heaven to deliver me, and that the whole transaction seemed to be a chain of wonders.

When we had talked a while, the captain told me he had brought me some little refreshment, such as the ship afforded, and such as the wretches that had been so long his masters had not plundered him of. Upon this, he called aloud to the boat, and bade his men bring the things ashore that were for the governor; and, indeed, it was a present as if I had been one that was not to be carried away with them, but as if I had been to dwell upon the island still. First, he had brought me a case of bottles full of excellent cordial waters, six large bottles of Madeira wine, two pounds of excellent good tobacco, twelve good pieces of the ship's beef, and six pieces of pork, with a bag of pease, and about a hundredweight of biscuit; he also brought me a box of sugar, a box of flour, a bag full of lemons, and two bottles of lime-juice, and abundance of other things.

But besides these, and what was a thousand times more useful to me, he brought me six new clean shirts, six very good neckcloths, two pair of gloves, one pair of shoes, a hat, and one pair of stockings, with a very good suit of clothes of his own: in a word, he clothed me from head to foot. It was a very kind and agreeable present, as anyone may imagine, to one in my circumstances; but never was anything in the world of that kind so unpleasant, awkward, and uneasy as it was to me to wear such clothes at first.

After these ceremonies were passed, and after all his good things were brought into my little apartment, we began to consult what was to be done with the prisoners we had. I told him that, if he desired it, I would undertake to bring the worst men he spoke of to make it their own request that he should leave them upon the island. "I should be very glad of that," says the captain, "with all my heart." So I caused Friday and the two hostages, for they were now discharged, to go to the cave, and bring up the five men, pinioned as they were, to the bower, and keep them there till I came.

After some time, I came thither dressed in my new habit; and now I was called governor again. Being all met, and the captain with me, I caused the men to be brought before me, and I told them I had got a full account of their villainous behaviour to the captain, but that Providence had ensnared them in their own ways, and that they had fallen into the pit which they had dug for others. I let them know that by my direction the ship had been seized; that she lay now in the road; and they might see, by-and-by, that their new captain had received the reward of his villainy, and that they would see him hanging at the yard-arm; that, as to them, I wanted to know what they had to say why I should not execute them as pirates, taken in the fact, as by my commission they could not doubt but I had authority so to do.

One of them answered in the name of the rest, that they had nothing to say but this, that when they were taken, the captain promised them their lives, and they humbly implored my mercy. But I told them I knew not what mercy to show them; for as for myself, I had resolved to quit the island with all my men, and had taken passage with the captain to go for England; and, as for the captain, he could not carry them to England, other than as prisoners, in irons, to be tried for mutiny, and running away with the ship; the consequence of which, they must needs know, would be the gallows; so that I could not tell what was best for them, unless they had a mind to take their fate in the island. If they desired that, as I had liberty to leave the island, I had some inebriation to give them their lives if they thought they could shift on shore. They seemed very thankful for it, and said they would much rather venture to stay there than be carried to England to be hanged. So I left it on that issue.

However, the captain seemed to make some difficulty of it, as if he durst not leave them there. Upon this, I seemed a little angry with the captain, and told him that they were my prisoners, not his; and, that seeing I had offered them so much favour, I would be as good as my word; and that if he did not think fit to consent to it, I would set them at liberty as I found them; and if he did not like it, he might take them again if he could catch them.

Upon this, they appeared very thankful, and I accordingly set them at liberty, and bade them retire into the woods, to the place whence they came, and I would leave them some firearms, some ammunition, and some directions how they should live very well if they thought fit. Upon this I prepared to go on board the ship; but told the captain I would stay that night to prepare my things, and desired him to go on board in the meantime, and keep all right in the ship, and send the boat on shore next day for me; ordering him, at all events, to cause the new captain, who was killed, to be hanged at the yard-arm, that these men might see him.

When the captain was gone, I sent for the men up to me to my apartment, and entered seriously into discourse with them on their circumstances. I told them I thought they had made a right choice; that if the captain had carried them away, they would certainly be hanged. I showed them the new captain hanging at the yard-arm of the ship, and told them they had nothing less to expect.

When they had all declared their willingness to stay, I then told them I would let them into the story of my living there, and put them into the way of making it easy to them. Accordingly, I gave them the whole history of the place, and of my coming to it; showed them my fortifications, the way I made my bread, planted my corn, cured my grapes; and, in a word, all that was necessary to make them easy. I told them the story also of the seventeen Spaniards that were to be expected, for whom I left a letter, and made them promise to treat them in common with themselves.

I left them my fire-arms—*viz.*, five muskets, three fowling-pieces, and three swords. I had above a barrel and a half of powder left. I gave them a description of the way I managed the goats, and directions to milk and fatten them, and to make both butter and cheese. In a word, I gave them every part of my own story; and told them I should prevail with the captain to leave them two barrels of gunpowder more, and some garden seeds, which I told them I would have been very glad of. Also, I gave them the bag of pease which the captain had brought me to eat, and bade them be sure to sow and increase them.

Having done all this, I left them the next day, and went on board the ship. We prepared immediately to sail, but did not weigh that night. The next morning early, two of the five men came swimming to the ship's side, and, making the most lamentable complaint of the other three, begged to be taken into the ship for God's sake, for they should be murdered, and begged the captain to take them on board, though he hanged them immediately. Upon this, the captain pretended to have no power without me; but, after some difficulty, and after their solemn promises of amendment, they were taken on board, and were, some time after, soundly whipped and pickled; after which they proved very honest and quiet fellows.

Some time after this, the boat was ordered on shore, the tide being up, with the things promised to the men; to which the captain, at my intercession, caused their chests and clothes to be added, which they took, and were very thankful for. I also encouraged them, by telling them, that if it lay in my power to send any vessel to take them in, I would not forget them.

When I took leave of this island, I carried on board, for relics, the great goat-skin cap I had made, my umbrella, und one of my parrots; also I forgot not to take the money I formerly mentioned, as also the money I found in the wreck of the Spanish ship. And thus I left the island, the 19th of December, as I found by the ship's account, in the year 1686, after I had been upon it eight-and-twenty years, two months, and nineteen days; being delivered from this second captivity the same day of the month that I first made my escape in the long-boat, from among the Moors of Sallee. In this vessel, after a long voyage, I arrived in England the 11th of June, in the year 1687, having been thirty-five years absent.

When I came to England I was as perfect a stranger to all the world as if I had never been known there. My benefactor and faithful steward, whom I had left my money in trust with, was alive, but had had great misfortunes in the world; was become a widow the second time, and very low in the world. I made her very easy as to what she owed me, assuring her I would give her no trouble; but, on the contrary, in gratitude for her former care and faithfulness to me, I relieved her as my little stock would afford; which at that time would, indeed, allow me to do but little: but I assured her I would never forget her former kindness to me; nor did I forget her when I had sufficient, as shall be observed in its proper place. I went down afterwards into Yorkshire; but my father was dead, and my mother and all the family extinct, except that I found two sisters, and two of the children of one of my brothers; and as I had been long ago given over for dead, there had been no provision made for me; so that I found nothing to relieve or assist me; and that the little money I had would not do much for me as to settling in the world.

I met with one piece of gratitude, which I did not expect; and this was, that the master of the ship, whom I had so happily delivered, and by the same means saved the ship and cargo, having given a very handsome account to the owners of the manner how I had saved the lives of the men and the ship, they invited me to meet them and some other merchants concerned, and all together made me a very handsome compliment upon the subject, and a present of almost £200 sterling.

But after making several reflections upon the circumstances of my life, and how little way this would go towards settling me in the world, I resolved to go to Lisbon, and see if I might not come at some information of the state of my plantation in the Brazils, and of what was become of my partner, who, I had reason to suppose, had some years past given me over for dead. With this view, I took shipping for Lisbon, where I arrived in April following; my man Friday accompanying me very honestly in all these ramblings, and proving a most faithful servant. When I came to Lisbon, I found out, by inquiry, and to my particular satisfaction, my old friend, the captain of the ship, who first took me up at sea off the shore of Africa. He was now grown old, and had left off going to sea, having put his son, who was far from a young man, into his ship, and who still used the Brazil trade. The old man did not know me; and indeed, I hardly knew him. But I soon brought him to my remembrance, and as soon brought myself to his remembrance, when I told him who I was.

After some passionate expressions of the old acquaintance between us, I inquired, you may be sure, after my plantation and my partner. The old man told me he had not been in the Brazils for about nine years; but that he could assure me, that when he came away my partner was living; but the trustees, whom I had joined with him to take cognizance of my part, were both dead: that, however, he believed I would have a very good account of the improvement of the plantation; for that, upon the general belief of my being cast away and drowned, my trustees had given in the account of the produce of my part of the plantation to the procurator-fiscal, who had appropriated it, in case I never came to claim it, one-third to the king, and two-thirds to the monastery of St. Augustine, to be expended for the benefit of the poor, and for the conversion of the Indians to the Catholic faith: but that, if I appeared, or any one for me, to claim the inheritance, it

182

would be restored; only that the improvement, or annual production, being distributed to charitable uses, could not be restored: but he assured me that the steward of the king's revenue from lands, and the *providore*, or steward of the monastery, had taken great care all along that my partner gave every year a faithful account of the produce, of which they had duly received my moiety.

I asked him if he knew to what height of improvement he had brought the plantation, and whether he thought it might be worth looking after; or whether, on my going thither, I should meet with any obstruction to my possessing my just right in the moiety. He told me he could not tell exactly to what degree the plantation was improved; but this he knew, that my partner was grown exceeding rich upon the enjoying his part of it; and that, to the best of his remembrance, he had heard that the king's third of my part, which was, it seems, granted away to some other monastery or religious house, amounted to above two hundred *moidores* a year: that as to my being restored to a quiet possession of it, there was no question to be made of that, my partner being alive to witness my title, and my name being also enrolled in the register of the country; also he told me that the survivors of my two trustees were very fair, honest people, and very wealthy; and he believed I would not only have their assistance for putting me in possession, but would find a very considerable sum of money in their hands for my account, being the produce of the farm while their fathers held the trust, and before it was given up, as above; which, as he remembered, was for about twelve years.

I showed myself a little concerned and uneasy at this account, and inquired of the old captain how it came to pass that the trustees should thus dispose of my effects, when he knew that I had made my will, and had made him, the Portuguese captain, my universal heir, &c.

He told me that was true; but that as there was no proof of my being dead, he could not act as executor, until some certain account should come of my death; and, besides, he was not willing to intermeddle with a thing so remote: that it was true he had registered my will, and put in his claim; and could he have given any account of my being dead or alive, he would have acted by procuration, and taken possession of the *ingenio* (so they call the sugar-house), and have given his son, who was now at the Brazils, orders to do it. "But," says the old man, "I have one piece of news to tell you, which perhaps may not be so acceptable to you as the rest; and that is, believing you were lost, and all the world believing so also, your partner and trustees did offer to account with me, in your name, for the first six or eight years' profits, which I received. There being at that time great disbursements for increasing the works, building an *ingenio*. and buying slaves, it did not amount to near so much as afterwards it produced: however," says the old man, "I shall give you a true account of what I have received in all, and how I have disposed of it."

After a few days' farther conference with this ancient friend, he brought me an account of the first six years' income of my plantation, signed by my partner and the merchant-trustees, being always delivered in goods; and I found by this account, that every year the income considerably increased; but the disbursements being large, the sum at first was small: however, the old man let me see that he was debtor to me four hundred and seventy *moidores* of gold, besides sixty chests of sugar, and fifteen double rolls of tobacco, which were lost in his ship: he having been shipwrecked coming home to Lisbon, about eleven years after my leaving the place. The good man then began to complain of his misfortunes, and how he had been obliged to make use of my money to recover his losses, and buy him a share in a new ship.

"However, my old friend," says he, "you shall not want a supply in your necessity; and as soon as my son returns, you shall be fully satisfied." Upon this he pulls out an old pouch, and gives me one hundred and sixty Portugal *moidores* in gold; and giving the writings of his title to the ship, which his son was gone to the Brazils in, of which he was quarter-part owner, and his son another, he puts them both into my hands for security of the rest.

I was too much moved with the honesty and kindness of the poor man to be able to bear this; and remembering what he had done for me, how he had taken me up at sea, and how generously he had used me on all occasions, and particularly how sincere a friend he was now to me, I could hardly refrain weeping at what he had said to me; therefore I asked him if his circumstances admitted him to spare so much money at that time, and if it would not straiten him? He told me he could not say but it might straiten him a little; but, however, it was my money, and I might want it more than he.

Everything the good man said was full of affection, and I could hardly refrain from tears while he spoke; in short, I took one hundred of the *moidores*, and called for a pen and ink to give him a receipt for them; then I returned him the rest, and told him if ever I had possession of the plantation I would return the other to him also (as, indeed, I afterwards did); and that as to the bill of sale of his part in his son's ship, I would not take it by any means; but that if I wanted the money, I found he was honest enough to pay me; and if I did not, but came to receive what he gave me reason to expect, I would never have a penny more from him.

When this was passed, the old man asked me if he should put me into a method to make my claim to my plantation.

I told him I thought to go over to it myself. He said I might do so if I pleased; but that, if I did not, there were ways enough to secure my right, and immediately to appropriate the profits to my use; and as there were ships in the river of Lisbon just ready to go away to Brazil, he made me enter my name in a public register, with his affidavit, affirming, upon oath, that I was alive, and that I was the same person who took up the land for the planting the said plantation at first. This being regularly attested by a notary, and a procuration affixed, he directed me to send it, with a letter of his writing, to a merchant of his acquaintance at the place; and then proposed my staying with him till an account came of the return.

Never was anything more honourable than the proceedings upon this procuration; for in less than seven months I received a large packet from the servitors of my trustees, the merchants, for whose account I went to sea, in which were the following particular letters and papers enclosed.

First, there was the account-current of the produce of my plantation, from the year when their fathers had balanced with my old Portugal captain, being for six years; the balance appeared to be one thousand one hundred and seventy-four *moidores* in my favour.

Secondly, there was the account of four years more, while they kept the effects in their hands, before the government claimed the administration, as being the effects of a person not to be found, which they called civil death; and the balance of this, the value of the plantation increasing, amounted to about three thousand two hundred and forty *moidores*.

Thirdly, there was the prior of St. Augustine's account, who had received the profits for above fourteen years; but not being to account for what was disposed of by the hospital, very honestly declared he had eight hundred and seventy-two *moidores* not distributed, which he acknowledged to my account: as to the king's part, that refunded nothing.

There was a letter of my partner's, congratulating me very affectionately upon my being alive, giving me an account how the estate was improved, and what it produced a year; with the particulars of the number of acres that it contained, how planted, how many slaves there were upon it; and making two-and-twenty crosses for blessings, told me he had said so many *Ave Marias* to thank the Blessed Virgin that I was alive; inviting me very passionately to come over and take possession of my own; and, in the meantime, to give him orders to whom he should deliver my effects, if I did not come myself; concluding with a hearty tender of his friendship, and that of his family; and sent me, as a present, seven fine leopards' skins, which he had, it seems, received from Africa, by some other ship that he had sent thither, and which, it seems, had made a better voyage than I. He sent me also five chests of excellent sweetmeats, and a hundred pieces of gold uncoined, not quite so large as *moidores*. By the same fleet, my two merchant-trustees shipped me one thousand two hundred chests of sugar, eight hundred rolls of tobacco, and the rest of the whole account in gold.

I might well say now, indeed, that the latter end of Job was better than the beginning. It is impossible to express the flutterings of my very heart when I found all my wealth about me; for as the Brazil ships come all in fleets, the same ships which brought my letters brought my goods: and the effects were safe in the river before my letters came to my hand.

I was now master, all on a sudden, of above five thousand pounds sterling in money, and had an estate, as I might well call it, in the Brazils, of above a thousand pounds a year, as sure as an estate in England: and, in a word, I was in a condition which I scarce knew how to understand, or how to compose myself for the enjoyment of it. The first thing I did was to recompense my original benefactor, my good old captain, who had been first charitable to me in my distress, kind to me in my beginning, and honest to me at the end. I showed him all that was sent to me; I told him that, next to the providence of Heaven, which disposed all things, it was owing to him; and that it now lay on me to reward him, which I would do a hundredfold: so I first returned to him the hundred *moidores* I had received of him; then I sent for a notary, and caused him to draw up a general release from the four hundred and seventy *moidores*, which he had acknowledged he owed me, in the fullest and firmest manner possible.

After which, I caused a procuration to be drawn, empowering him to be the receiver of the annual profits of my plantation; and appointing my partner to account with him, and make the returns, by the usual fleets, to him in my name; and by a clause in the end, made a grant of one hundred *moidores* a year to him during his life, out of the effects, and fifty *moidores* a year to his son after him, for his life: and thus I requited my old man.

I had now to consider which way to steer my course next, and what to do with the estate that Providence had thus put into my hands: and indeed, I had more care upon my head now than I had in my silent state of life in the island, where I wanted nothing but what I had, and had nothing but what I wanted; whereas I had now a great charge upon me, and my business was how to secure it. I had not a cave now to hide my money in, or a place where it might lie without lock or key, till it grew mouldy and tarnished before anybody would meddle with it; on the contrary, I knew not where to put it, or whom to trust with it. My old patron, the captain, indeed, was honest, and that was the only refuge I had. In the next place, my interest in the Brazils seemed to summon me thither; but now I could not tell how to think of going thither till I had settled my affairs, and left my effects in some safe hands behind me. At first I thought of my old friend the widow, who I knew was honest, and would be just to me; but then she was in years, and but poor, and, for aught I knew, might be in debt; so that, in a word, I had no way but to go back to England myself, and take my effects with me.

It was some months, however, before I resolved upon this; and, therefore, as I had rewarded the old captain fully, and to his satisfaction, who had been my former benefactor, so I began to think of the poor widow, whose husband had been my first benefactor, and she, while it was in her power, my faithful steward and instructor. So, the first thing I did, I got a merchant in Lisbon to write to his correspondent in London, not only to pay a bill, but to go find her out, and carry her, in money, a hundred pounds from me, and to talk with her, and comfort her in her poverty, by telling her she should, if I lived, have a farther supply: at the same time, I sent my two sisters in the country a hundred pounds each, they being, though not in want, yet not in very good circumstances; one having been married and left a widow; and the other having a husband not so kind to her as he should be. But, among all my relations or acquaintances, I could not yet pitch upon one to whom I durst commit the gross of my stock, that I might go away to the Brazils, and leave things safe behind me; and this greatly perplexed me.

I had once a mind to have gone to the Brazils, and have settled myself there, for I was, as it were, naturalised to the place; but I had some little scruple in my mind about religion, which insensibly drew me back. However, it was not religion that kept me from going there for the present; but that really I did not know with whom to leave my effects behind me; so I resolved at last to go to England, where, it I arrived, I concluded I should make some acquaintance, or find some relations, that would be faithful to me; and, accordingly, I prepared to go to England with all my wealth.

In order to prepare things for my going home, I first resolved to give answers suitable to the just and faithful account of things I had from thence; and, first, to the Prior of St. Augustine, I wrote a letter full of thanks for his just dealings, and the offer of the eight hundred and seventy-two *moidores* which were undisposed of, which I desired might be given, five hundred to the monastery, and three hundred and seventy-two to the poor, as the prior should direct; desiring the good padre's prayers for me, and the like. I wrote next a letter of thanks to my two trustees, with all the acknowledgment that so much justice and honesty called for: as for sending them any present, they were far above having any occasion for it.

Lastly, I wrote to my partner, acknowledging his industry in improving the plantation, and his integrity in increasing the stock of the works; giving him instructions for his future government of my part, according to the powers I had left with my old patron, to whom I desired him to send whatever became due to me, till he should hear from me more particularly; assuring him that it was my intention not only to come to him, but to settle myself there for the remainder of my life. To this I added a very handsome present of some Italian silks for his wife and two daughters, for such the captain's son informed me he had; with two pieces of fine English broad cloth, the best I could get in Lisbon, five pieces of black baize, and some Flanders lace of a good value.

Having thus settled my affairs, sold my cargo, and turned all my effects into good bills of exchange, my next difficulty was which way to go to England: I had been accustomed enough to the sea, and yet I had a strange aversion to go to England by sea at that time; and though I could give no reason for it, yet the difficulty increased upon me so much, that though I had once shipped my baggage in order to go, yet I altered my mind two or three times.

It is true, I had been very unfortunate by sea, and this might be one of the reasons; but let no man slight the strong impulses of his own thoughts in cases of such moment: two of the ships which I had singled out to go in, having put my things on board one of them, and in the other to have agreed with the captain, miscarried, one was taken by the Algerines, and the other was cast away on the Start, near Torbay, and all the people drowned, except three; so that in either of those vessels I had been made miserable.

Having been thus harassed in my thoughts, my old pilot, to whom I communicated everything, pressed me earnestly not to go by sea, but either to go by land to the Groyne, and cross over the Bay of Biscay to Rochelle, from whence it was but an easy and safe journey by land to Paris, and so to Calais and Dover; or to go up to Madrid, and so all the way by land through France. In a word, I was so prepossessed against my going by sea at all, except from Calais to Dover, that I resolved to travel all the way by land; which, as I was not in haste, and did not value the charge, was by much the pleasanter way: and to make it more so, my old captain brought an English gentleman, the son of a merchant in Lisbon, who was willing to travel with me; after which we picked up two more English merchants also, and two young Portuguese gentlemen, the last going to Paris only; so that, in all, there were six of us, and five servants; and as for me, I got an English sailor to travel with me as a servant, besides my man Friday, who was too much a stranger to be capable of supplying the place of a servant on the road.

In this manner I set out from Lisbon; and our company being very well mounted and armed, we made a little troop, whereof they did me the honour to call me captain, as well because I was the oldest man, as because I had two servants, and, indeed, was the origin of the whole journey.

As I have troubled you with none of my sea journals, so I shall trouble you now with none of my land journal; but some adventures that happened to us in this tedious and difficult journey I must not omit.

When we came to Madrid, we, being all of us strangers to Spain, were willing to stay some time to see the court of Spain, and what was worth observing; but, it being the latter part of the summer, we hastened away, and set out from Madrid about the middle of October; but when we came to the edge of Navarre, we were alarmed, at several towns on the way, with an account that so much snow was fallen on the French side of the mountains, that several travellers were obliged to come back to Pampeluna, after having attempted at an extreme hazard to pass on.

When we came to Pampeluna itself, we found it so indeed; and to me, that had always been used to a hot climate, and to countries where I could scarce bear any clothes on, the cold was insufferable: nor. indeed, was it more painful than surprising, to come but ten days before out of Old Castile, where the weather was not only warm, but very hot, and immediately to feel a wind from the Pyrenean mountains so very keen, so severely cold, as to be intolerable, and to endanger benumbing and perishing of our fingers and toes.

Poor Friday was really frightened when he saw the mountains all covered with snow, and felt cold weather, which he had never seen or felt before in his life. To mend the matter, when we came to Pampeluna, it continued snowing with so much violence and so long, that the people said winter was come before its time; and the roads, which were difficult before, were now quite impassable; for the snow lay in some places too thick for us to travel, and being not hard frozen, as is the case in the northern countries, there was no going without being in danger of being buried alive every step. We stayed no less than twenty days at Pampeluna; when (seeing the winter coming on, and no likelihood of its being better, for it was the severest winter all over Europe that had been known in the memory of man), I proposed that we should go away to Fontarabia, and there take shipping for Bordeaux, which was a very little voyage.

But, while I was considering this, there came in four French gentlemen, who, having been stopped on the French side of the passes, as we were on the Spanish, had found out a guide, who, traversing the country near the head of Languedoc, had brought them over the mountains by such ways that they were not much incommoded with the snow; for where they met with snow in any quantity, they said it was frozen hard enough to bear them and their horses. We sent for this guide, who told us he would undertake to carry us the same way, with no hazard from the snow, provided we were armed sufficiently to protect ourselves from wild beasts: for, he said, in these great snows, it was frequent for some wolves to show themselves at the foot of the mountains, being made ravenous for want of food, the ground being covered with snow.

We told him we were well enough prepared for such creatures as they were, if he would ensure us from a kind of two-legged wolves, which, we are told, we were in most danger from, especially on the French side of the mountains. He satisfied us that there was no danger of that kind in the way that we were to go; so we readily agreed to follow him, as did also twelve other gentlemen, with their servants, some French, some Spanish, who, as I said, had attempted to go, and were obliged to come back again.

Accordingly, we set out from Pampeluna with our guide, on the 10th of November; and I was surprised, when, instead of going forward, he came directly back with us on the same road that we came from Madrid, about twenty miles; when, having passed two rivers, and come into the plain country, we found ourselves in a warm climate again, where the country was pleasant, and no snow to be seen; but, on a sudden, turning to his left, he approached the mountains another way; and though it is true the hills and precipices looked dreadful, yet he made so many tours, such meanders, and led us by such winding ways, that we insensibly passed the height of the mountains without being much encumbered with the snow; and, all on a sudden, he showed us the pleasant and fruitful provinces of Languedoc and Gascony. all green and flourishing, though, indeed, at a great distance, and we had some rough way to pass still.

We were a little uneasy, however, when we found it snowed one whole day and a night so fast that we could not travel; but he bid us be easy; we should soon be past it all; we found, indeed, that we began to descend every day, and to come more north than before; and so, depending upon our guide, we went on.

It was about two hours before night, when, our guide being something before us, and not just in sight, out rushed three monstrous wolves, and after them a bear, from a hollow way adjoining to a thick wood: two of the wolves made at the guide, and, had he been far before us, he would have been devoured before we could have helped him as one of them had fastened upon his horse, and the other attacked the man with such violence, that he had not time or presence of mind enough to draw his pistol, but hallooed and cried out to us most lustily. My man Friday being next to me, I bade him ride up, and see what was the matter. As soon as Friday came in sight of the man, he hallooed out as loud as the other, "O master! O master!" but, like a bold fellow, rode directly up to the poor man, and with his pistol shot the wolf that attacked him in the head.

It was happy for the poor man that it was my man Friday; for, having been used to such creatures in his country, he had no fear upon him, but went close up to him and shot him; whereas any other of us would have fired at a farther distance, and have perhaps either missed the wolf, or endangered shooting the man.

But it was enough to have terrified a bolder man than I; and, indeed, it alarmed all our company, when, with the noise, of Friday's pistol, we heard on both sides the most dismal howling of wolves; and the noise, redoubled by the echo of the mountains, appeared to us as if there had been a prodigious number of them; and perhaps there was not such a few as that we had no cause of apprehension: however, as Friday had killed this wolf, the other that had fastened upon the horse left him immediately, and fled, without doing him any damage, having happily fastened upon his head, where the bosses of the bridle had stuck in his teeth. But the man was most hurt: for the raging creature had bit him twice, once in the arm, and the other time a little above his knee; and though he had made some defence, he was just tumbling down by the disorder of his horse, when Friday came up and shot the wolf.

It is easy to suppose that at the noise of Friday's pistol we all mended our pace, and rode up as fast as the way, which was very difficult, would give us leave, to see what was the matter. As soon as we came clear of the trees, which blinded us before, we saw clearly what had been the case, and how Friday had disengaged the poor guide, though we did not presently discern what kind of creature it was he had killed.

But never was a fight managed so hardily, and in such a surprising manner, as that which followed between Friday and the bear, which gave us all, though at first we were surprised and afraid for him, the greatest diversion imaginable. As the bear is a heavy, clumsy creature, and does not gallop as the wolf does, who is swift and light, so he has two particular qualities, which generally are the ride of his actions: first, as to men, who are not his proper prey, if you do not meddle with him, he will not meddle with you; but then you must take care to be very civil to him, and give him the road, for he is a very nice gentleman; he will not go a step out of his way for a prince; nay, if you are really afraid, your best way is to look another way and keep going on; for sometimes if you stop, and stand still, and look steadfastly at him, he takes it for an affront; but if you throw or toss anything at him, and it hits him, though it were but a bit of stick as big as your finger, he thinks himself abused, and sets all other business aside to pursue his revenge, and will have satisfaction in point of honour;—this is his first quality: the next is, if he be once affronted, he will never leave you, night or day, till he has his revenge, but follows at a good round rate until he overtakes you.

My man Friday had delivered our guide, and when we came up to him, he was helping him off his horse, for the man was both hurt and frightened, when on a sudden we espied the bear come out of the wood, and a monstrous one it was, the biggest by far that I ever saw. We were all a little surprised when we saw him; but when Friday saw him, it was easy to see joy and courage in the fellow's countenance: "O, O, O!" says Friday, three times, pointing to him: "O master! you give me to leave, me shakee te hand with him; me makee you good laugh."

I was surprised to see the fellow so well pleased: "You fool," says I, "he will eat you up."

"Eatee me up! eatee me up!" says Friday, twice over again; "me eatee him up; me make you good laugh; you all stay here, me show you good laugh." So down he sits, and gets off his boots in a moment and puts on a pair of pumps, gives my other servant his horse, and with his gun away he flew, swift like the wind.

The bear was walking softly on, and offered to meddle with nobody, till Friday coming pretty near, calls to him, as if the bear could understand him, "Hark ye, hark ye," says Friday, "me speakee with you." We followed at a distance, for now being come down on the Gascoigne side of the mountains, we were entered a vast forest, where the country was plain and pretty open, though it had many trees in it scattered here and there.

Friday who had, as we say, the heels of the bear, came up with him quickly, and took up a great stone, and threw it at him, and hit him just on the head, but did aim no more harm than if he had thrown it against a wall; but it answered Friday's end, for the rogue was so void of fear that he did it purely to make the bear follow him, and show us some laugh, as he called it. As soon as the bear felt the blow, and saw him, he turns about, and comes after him, taking very long strides, and shuffling on at a strange rate, as would have put a horse to a middling gallop: away runs Friday, and takes his course as if he ran towards us for help; so we all resolved to fire at once upon the bear, and deliver my man; though I was angry at him heartily for bringing the bear back upon us, when he was going about his own business another way: and especially I was angry that he had turned the bear upon us, and then run away; and I called out, "You dog! is this your making us laugh? Come away, and take your horse, that we may shoot the creature."

He heard me, and cried out, "No shoot, no shoot; stand still, and you get much laugh :" and as the nimble creature ran two feet for the bear's one, he turned on a sudden on one side of us, and seeing a great oak tree fit for his purpose, he beckoned us to follow; and doubling his pace, he got nimbly up the tree, laying his gun down upon the ground, at about five or six yards from the bottom of the tree. The bear soon came to the tree, and we followed at a distance: the first thing he did, he stopped at the gun, smelled at it, but let it be, and up he scrambles into the tree, climbing like a cat, though so monstrous heavy. I was amazed at the folly, as I thought it, of my man, and could not for my life see anything to laugh at yet, till seeing the bear get up the tree, we all rode near to him.

When we came to the tree, there was Friday got out to the small end of a large branch, and the bear got about halfway to him. As soon as the bear got out to that part where the limb of the tree was weaker,—"Ha !" says he to us, "now you see me teachee the bear dance:" so he began jumping and shaking the bough, at which the bear began to totter, but stood still, and began to look behind him, to see how he should get back; then, indeed, we did laugh heartily. But Friday had not done with him by a great deal: when seeing him stand still, he called out to him again, as if he had supposed the bear could speak English, "What, you come no farther? pray you come farther;" so he left jumping and shaking the tree; and the bear, just as if he understood what he said, did come a little farther; then he began jumping again, and the bear stopped again.

We thought now was a good time to knock him in the head, and called to Friday to stand still, and we would shoot the bear: but he cried out earnestly, "pray, pray! no shoot, me shoot by and then:" he would have said by-and-by. However, to shorten the story, Friday danced so much, and the bear stood so ticklish, that we had laughing enough, but still could not imagine what the fellow would do: for the first we thought he depended upon shaking the bear off; and we found the bear was too cunning for that too; for he would not go out far enough to be thrown down, but clung fast with his great broad claws and feet, so that we could not imagine what would be the end of it, and what the jest would be at last.

But Friday put us out of doubt quickly: for seeing the bear cling fast to the bough, and that he would not be persuaded to come any farther, "Well, well," says Friday, "you no come farther, me go; you no come to me, me come to you;" and upon this he went to the smaller end of the bough, where it would bend with his weight, and gently let himself down by it, sliding down the bough till he came near enough to jump down on his feet, and away he ran to his gun and took it up.

"Well," said I to him, "Friday, what will you do now? Why don't you shoot him?"

"No shoot," says Friday, "no yet; me shoot now, me no kill; me stay, give you one more laugh:" and, indeed, so he did; for when his enemy saw he was gone, he came back from the bough where he stood, but did it very cautiously, looking behind him every step, and coming backward till he got into the body of the tree; then, with the same hinder end foremost, he came down the tree, grasping it with his claws, and moving one foot at a time, very leisurely. At this juncture, and just before he could set his hind foot on the ground, Friday stepped up close to him, clapped the muzzle of his piece into his ear, and shot him dead. Then the rogue turned about to see if we did not laugh; and when he saw we were pleased, by our looks, he began to laugh very loud. "So we kill bear in my country," Says Friday.

"So you kill them?" says I; "why, you have no guns."

"No," says he, "no gun, but shoot great much long arrow." This was a good diversion to us; but we were still in a wild place, and our guide very much hurt, and what to do we hardly knew; the howling of wolves ran much in my head; and, indeed, except the noise I once heard on the shore of Africa, I never heard anything that filled me with so much horror.

These things, and the approach of night, called us off, or else, as Friday would have had us, we should certainly have taken the skin of this monstrous creature off, which was worth saving; but we had near three leagues to go, and our guide hastened us; so we left him, and went forward on our journey.

The ground was still covered with snow, though not so deep and dangerous as on the mountains; and the ravenous creatures, as we heard afterwards, were come down into the forest and plain country, pressed by hunger to seek for food, and had done a great deal of mischief in the villages, where they surprised the country people, killed a great many of their sheep and horses, and some people too. We had one dangerous place to pass, and our guide told us, if there were more wolves in the country we should find them there; and this was a small plain surrounded with woods on every side, and a long narrow defile, or lane, which we were to pass to get through the wood, and then we should come to the village where we were to lodge.

It was within half an hour of sunset when we entered the wood, and a little after sunset when we came into the plain: we met with nothing in the first wood, except that in a little plain within the wood, which was not above two furlongs over, we saw five great wolves cross the road, full speed, one after another, as if they had been in chase of some prey, and had it in view; they took no notice of us, and were gone out of sight in a few moments. Upon this, our guide, who by the way was but a faint-hearted fellow, bid us keep in a ready posture, for he believed there were more wolves a-coming. We kept our arms ready, and our eyes about us; but we saw no more wolves till we came through that wood, which was near half a league, and entered the plain.

As soon as we came into the plain, we had occasion enough to look about us: the first object we met with was a horse which the wolves had killed, and at least a dozen of them at work, we could not say eating him, but picking his bones rather; for they had eaten up all the flesh before. We did not think fit to disturb them at their feast, neither did they take much notice of us. Friday would have let fly at them, but I would not suffer him by any means; for I found we were like to have more business upon our hands than we were aware of. We had not gone half over the plain, when we began to hear the wolves howl in the wood on our left in a frightful manner, and presently after we saw about a hundred coming on directly towards us, all in a body, and most of them in a line, as regularly as an army drawn up by experienced officers.

I scarce knew in what manner to receive them, but found to draw ourselves in a close line was the only way; so we formed in a moment: but that we might not have too much interval, I ordered that only every other man should fire, and that the others, who had not fired, should stand ready to give them a second volley immediately, if they continued to advance upon us; and then that those who had fired at first, should not pretend to load their fusees again, but stand ready, every one with a pistol, for we were all armed with a fusee and a pair of pistols each man; so we were, by this method, able to fire six volleys, half of us at a time: however, at present we had no necessity; for, upon firing the first volley, the enemy made a full stop, being terrified as well with the noise as with the fire; four of them being shot in the head, dropped: several others were wounded, and went bleeding off, as we could see by the snow.

I found they stopped, but did not immediately retreat; whereupon, remembering that I had been told that the fiercest creatures were terrified at the voice of a man, I caused all the company to halloo as loud as we could; and I found the notion not altogether mistaken; for upon our shout they began to retire and turn about. I then ordered a second volley to be fired in their rear, which put them to the gallop, and away they went to the woods. This gave us leisure to charge our pieces again; and that we might lose no time, we kept going; but we had but little more than loaded our fusees, and put ourselves in readiness, when we heard a terrible noise in the same wood on our left, only that it was farther onward, the same way we were to go.

The night was coming on, and the light began to be dusky, which made it worse on our side; but the noise increasing, we could easily perceive that it was the howling and yelling of those hellish creatures; and on a sudden we perceived two or three troops of wolves, one on our left, one behind us, and one in our front, so that we seemed to be surrounded with them: however, as they did not fall upon us, we kept our way forward, as fast as we could make our horses go, which was only a good hard trot. In this manner, we came in view of the entrance of a wood, through which we were to pass, at the farther side of the plain; but we were greatly surprised. when coming nearer the lane or pass, we saw a confused number of wolves standing just at the entrance.

On a sudden, at another opening of the wood, we heard the noise of a gun, and looking that way, out rushed a horse, with a saddle and a bridle on him, flying like the wind, and sixteen or seventeen wolves after him full speed: the horse had the advantage of them; but as we supposed that he could not hold it at that rate, we doubted not but they would get up with him at last: no question but they did.

But here we had a most horrible sight; for riding up to the entrance where the horse came out, we found the carcasses of another horse and of two men, devoured by the ravenous creatures; and one of the men was no doubt the same whom we heard fire the gun, for there lay a gun just by him fired off; but as to the man, his head and the upper part of his body were eaten up. This filled us with horror, and we knew not what course to take; but the creatures resolved us soon, for they gathered about us presently, in hopes of prey; and I verily believe there were three hundred of them.

It happened, very much to our advantage, that at the entrance into the wood, but a little way from it, there lay some large timber trees, which had been cut down the summer before, and I suppose lay there for carriage. I drew my little troop in among those trees, and placing ourselves in a line behind one long tree, I advised them all to alight, and keeping that tree before us for a breastwork, to stand in a triangle, or three fronts, inclosing our horses in the centre. We did so, and it was well we did; for never was a more furious charge than the creatures made upon us in this place. They came on with a growling kind of noise, and mounted the piece of timber, which, as I said, was our breastwork, as if they were only rushing upon their prey; and this fury of theirs, it seems, was principally occasioned by their seeing our horses behind us I ordered our men to fire as before, every other man; and they took their aim so sure that they killed several of the wolves at the first volley; but there was a necessity to keep a continual firing, for they came on like devils, those behind pushing on those before.

When we had fired a second volley of our fusees, we thought they stopped a little, and I hoped they would have gone off, but it was but a moment, for others came forward again; so we fired two volleys of our pistols; and I believe in these four firings we had killed seventeen or eighteen of them, and lamed twice as many, yet they came on again. I was loath to spend our shot too hastily; so I called my servant, not my man Friday, for he was better employed, for, with the greatest dexterity imaginable, he had charged my fusee and his own while we were engaged,—but, as I said, I called my other man, and giving him a horn of powder, I bade him lay a train all along the piece of timber, and let it be a large train.

He did so, and had but just time to get away, when the wolves came up to it, and some got upon it, when I, snapping an uncharged pistol close to the powder, set it on fire; those that were upon the timber were scorched with it, and six or seven of them fell, or rather jumped in among us with the force and fright of the fire: we despatched these in an instant, and the rest were so frightened with the light, which the night—for it was now very near dark—made more terrible, that they drew back a little; upon which I ordered our last pistols to be fired off in one volley, and after that we gave a shout; upon this the wolves turned tail, and we sallied immediately upon near twenty lame ones that we found struggling on the ground, and fell to cutting them with our swords, which answered our expectation, for the crying and howling they made was better understood by their fellows; so that they all fled and left us.

We had, first and last, killed about three-score of them, and had it been daylight we had killed many more. The field of battle being thus cleared, we came forward again, for we had still near a league to go. We heard the ravenous creatures howl and yell in the woods as we went several times, and some times we fancied we saw some of them; but the snow dazzling our eyes, we were not certain. In about an hour more we came to the town where we were to lodge, which we found in a terrible fright, and all in arms; for, it seems, the night before the wolves and some bears had broke into the village, and put them in such terror, that they were obliged to keep guard night and day, but especially in the night, to preserve their cattle, and indeed their people.

The next morning our guide was so ill, and his limbs swelled so much with the rankling of his two wounds, that he could go no farther; so we were obliged to take a new guide here, and go to Thoulouse, where we found a warm climate, a fruitful, pleasant country, and no snow, no wolves, nor anything like them; but when we told our story at Thoulouse, they told us it was nothing but what was ordinary in the great forest at the foot of the mountains, especially when the snow lay on the ground; but they inquired much what kind of a guide we had got, who would venture to bring us that way in such a severe season, and told us it was surprising we were not all devoured.

When we told them how we placed ourselves and the horses in the middle, they blamed us exceedingly, and told us it was fifty to one but we had been all destroyed, for it was the sight of the horses which made the wolves so furious, seeing their prey, and that at other times they are really afraid of a gun; but being excessively hungry, and raging on that account, the eagerness to come at the horses had made them senseless of danger, and that if we had not by the continued fire, and at last by the stratagem of the train of powder, mastered them, it had been great odds but that we had been torn to pieces; whereas, had we been content to have sat still on horseback, and fired as horsemen, they would not have taken the horses so much for their own, when men were on their backs, as otherwise; and, withal, they told us that at last, if we had stood all together, and left our horses, they would have been so eager to have devoured them, that we might have come off safe, especially having our firearms in our hands, and being so many in number.

For my part, I was never so sensible of danger in my life, for, seeing above three hundred devils come roaring and open-mouthed to devour us, and having nothing to shelter us or retreat to, I gave myself over for lost; and, as it was, I believe I shall never care to cross those mountains again; I think I would much rather go a thousand leagues by sea, though I was sure to meet with a storm once a week.

I have nothing uncommon to take notice of in my passage through

France—nothing but what other travellers have given an account of with much more advantage than I can. I travelled from Thoulouse to Paris, and without any considerable stay came to Calais, and landed safe at Dover the 14th of January, after having a severe cold season to travel in.

I was now come to the centre of my travels, and had in a little time all my new-discovered estate safe about me, the bills of exchange which I brought with me having been very currently paid.

My principal guide and privy-counsellor was my good, ancient widow, who, in gratitude for the money I had sent her, thought no pains too much nor care too great to employ for me; and I trusted her so entirely with everything, that I was perfectly easy as to the security of my effects; and, indeed, I was very happy from the beginning, and now to the end, in the unspotted integrity of this good gentlewoman.

And now, having resolved to dispose of my plantation in the Brazils, I wrote to my old friend at Lisbon, who having offered it to the two merchants, the survivors of my trustees, who lived in the Brazils, they accepted the offer, and remitted thirty-three thousand pieces-of-eight to a correspondent of theirs at Lisbon to pay for it.

In return, I signed the instrument, of sale in the form which they sent from Lisbon, and sent it to my old man, who sent me the bills of exchange for thirty-two thousand eight hundred pieces-of-eight for the estate, reserving the payment of one hundred *moidores* a year to him (the old man) during his life, and fifty *moidores* afterwards to his son for his life, which I had promised them and which the plantation was to make good as a rent-charge. And thus I have given the first part of a life of fortune and adventure—a life of Providence's chequerwork, and of a variety which the world will seldom be able to show the like of—beginning foolishly, but closing much more happily than any part of it ever gave me leave so much as to hope for.

Anyone would think that in this state of complicated good fortune I was past running any more hazards, and so, indeed, I had been, if other circumstances had concurred; but I was inured to a wandering life, had no family, nor many relations; nor, however rich, had I contracted much acquaintance; and though I had sold my estate in the Brazils, yet I could not keep that country out of my head, and had a great mind to be upon the wing again; especially I could not resist the strong inclination I had to see my island, and to know if the poor Spaniards were in being there.

My true friend, the widow, earnestly dissuaded me from it, and so far prevailed with me, that for almost seven years she prevented my running abroad, during which time I took my two nephews, the children of one of my brothers, into my care: the eldest having something of his own, I bred up as a gentleman, and gave him a settlement of some addition to his estate after my decease. The other I placed with the captain of a ship; and after five years, finding him a sensible, bold, enterprising young fellow, I put him into a good ship, and sent him to sea; and this young fellow afterwards drew me in, as old as I was, to farther adventures myself.

In the meantime I in part settled myself here; for, first of all, I married, and that not either to my disadvantage or dissatisfaction, and had three children, two sons and one daughter; but my wife dying, and my nephew coming home with good success from a voyage to Spain, my inclination to go abroad and his importunity prevailed, and engaged me to go in his ship as a private trader to the East Indies; this was in the year 1694.

In this voyage I visited my new colony in the island—saw my successors the Spaniards—had the whole story of their lives, and of the villains I left there—how at first they insulted the poor Spaniards—how they afterwards agreed, disagreed, united, separated, and how at last the Spaniards were obliged to use violence with them—how they were subjected to the Spaniards—how honestly the Spaniards used them; a history, if it were entered into, as full of variety and wonderful accidents as my own part, particularly, also, as to their battles with the Caribbeans, who landed several times upon the island, and as to the improvement they made upon the island itself, and how five of them made an attempt upon the mainland, and brought away eleven men and five women prisoners, by which, at my coming, I found about twenty young children on the island.

Here I stayed about twenty days—left them supplies of all necessary things, and particularly of arms, powder, shot, clothes, tools, and two workmen, which I brought from England with me, *viz.*, a carpenter and a smith.

Besides this, I shared the lands into parts with them, reserved to myself the property of the whole, but gave them such parts respectively as they agreed on; and having settled all things with them, and engaged them not to leave the place, I left them there.

From thence I touched at the Brazils, from whence I sent a *bark*, which I bought there, with more people to the island; and in it, besides other supplies, I sent seven women, being such as I found proper for service, or for wives to such as would take thorn. As to the Englishmen, I promised them to send them some women from England, with a good cargo of necessaries, if they would apply themselves to planting, which I afterwards could not perform. The fellows proved very honest and diligent after they were mastered, and had their properties set apart for them. I sent them, also, from the Brazils five cows, three of them being big with calf, some sheep, and some hogs, which when I came again were considerably increased.

But all these things, with an account how three hundred Caribbees came and invaded them, and ruined their plantations, and how they fought with that whole number twice, and were at first defeated, and one of them killed; but, at last, a storm destroying their enemies' canoes, they famished or destroyed almost all the rest, and renewed and recovered the possession of their plantation, and still lived upon the island.

All these things, with some very surprising incidents in some new adventures of my own, for ten years more, I shall give a farther account of in the second part of my history.

PART 2

The Farther Adventures of Robinson Crusoe

That homely proverb, "*That what is bred in the bone will not go out of the flesh*," was never more verified than in the story of my life. Anyone would think that after thirty-five years' affliction, and a variety of unhappy circumstances, which few men, if any, ever went through before, and after near seven years of peace and enjoyment in the fullness of all things, grown old, and when, if ever, it might be allowed me to have had experience of every state of middle life, and to know which was most adapted to make a man completely happy; I say, after all this, any one would have thought that the native propensity to rambling, which I gave an account of in my first setting out in the world to have been so predominant in my thoughts, should be worn out, the volatile part be fully evacuated, or at least condensed, and I might, at sixty-one years of age, have been a little inclined to stay at home, and have done venturing life and fortune any more.

But when I came home, I was still as uneasy as I was before; I had no relish for the place, no employment in it, nothing to do but to saunter about like an idle person. This also was the thing which, of all circumstances of life, was the most my aversion, who had been all my days used to an active life.

It was now the beginning of the year 1693, when my nephew, whom I had brought up to the sea, and had made commander of a ship, was come home from a short voyage to Bilboa, being the first he had made. He came to me, and told me that some merchants of his acquaintance had been proposing to him to go a voyage for them to the East Indies and to China, as private traders. "And now, uncle," says he, "if you will go to sea with me, I will engage to land you upon your old habitation in the island; for we are to touch at the Brazils."

I was not long resolving; for, indeed, the importunities of my nephew joined so effectually with my inclination, that nothing could oppose me: on the other hand, my wife being dead, nobody concerned themselves so much for me as to persuade me to one way or the other, except my ancient good, friend the widow, who earnestly struggled with me to consider my years, my easy circumstances, and the needless hazards of a long voyage, and, above all, my young children. But it was all to no purpose. I had an irresistible desire for the voyage; and I told her I thought there was something so uncommon in the impressions I had upon my mind, that it would be a kind of resisting Providence if I should attempt to stay at home: after which she ceased her expostulations, and joined with me, not only in making provision for my voyage, but also in settling my family affairs for my absence, and providing for the education of my children.

In order to do this, I made my will, and settled the estate I had in such a manner for my children, and placed in such hands, that I was perfectly easy and satisfied they would have justice done them, whatever might befall me: and for their education, I left it wholly to the widow, with a sufficient maintenance to herself for her care—all which she richly deserved; for no mother could have taken more care in their education, or understood it better: and as she lived till I came home, I also lived to thank her for it.

My nephew was ready to sail about the beginning of January, 1694-5; and I, with my man Friday, went on board, in the Downs, the 8th; having besides a framed sloop, which was shipped in pieces, a very considerable cargo of all kinds of necessary things for my colony; which, if I did not find in good condition, I resolved to leave so.

First, I carried with me some servants, whom I purposed to place there as inhabitants, or at least to set on work there, upon my account, while I stayed, and either to leave them there or carry them forward, as they should appear willing ;. particularly I carried two carpenters, a smith, and a very handy, ingenious fellow, who was a cooper by trade, and was also a general mechanic; for he was dexterous at making wheels, and hand-mills to grind corn, was a good turner and a good pot-maker; he also made anything that was proper to make of earth or of wood; in a word, we called him our Jack-of-all-trades. With these I carried a tailor, who had offered himself to go a passenger to the East Indies with my nephew, but afterwards consented to stay on our new plantation; and who proved a most necessary, handy fellow, as could be desired, in many other businesses besides that of his. trade; for necessity arms us for all employments.

My cargo, as near as I can recollect, consisted of a sufficient quantity of linen, and some English thin stuffs, for clothing the Spaniards that I expected to find there; and enough as, by my calculation, might comfortably supply them for seven years. If I remember right, the materials I carried for clothing them amounted to above two hundred pounds; and near a hundred pounds more in iron-work, nails, tools of every kind, staples, hooks, hinges, and every necessary thing I could think of.

I carried also a hundred spare arms, muskets, and fusees; besides some pistols, a considerable quantity of shot of all sizes, three or four tons of lead, and two pieces of brass cannon; and, because I knew not what time and what extremities I was providing for, I carried a hundred barrels of powder, besides swords, cutlasses, and the iron part of some, pikes and halberts; so that, in short, we had a large magazine of all sorts of stores: and I made my nephew carry two small quarter-deck guns more than he wanted for his ship, to leave behind if there was occasion; that when we came there, we might build a fort, and man it against all sorts of enemies: and, indeed, I at first thought there would be need enough for all, and much more, if we hoped to maintain our possession of the island; as shall be seen in the course of the story.

We set out on the 5th of February from Ireland; and, to shorten my story, I came to my old habitation, the island, on the 10th of April, 1695.

As soon as I saw the place, I called for Friday, and asked him if he knew where he was? He looked about a little, and presently clapping his hands, cried, "O yes, O there, yes, O there !" pointing to our old habitation, and fell dancing and capering like a mad fellow; and I had much ado to keep him from jumping into the sea, to swim ashore to the place.

"Well, Friday," says I, "do you think we shall find anybody here or no? and do you think we shall see your father?"

The fellow stood mute as a stock a good while; but when I named his father, the poor affectionate creature looked dejected, and I could see the tears run down his face very plentifully.

"What is the matter, Friday ?" says I: "are you troubled because you may see your father?"

"No, no," says he, shaking his head, "no see him more; no, never more see him again."

"Why so," said I, "Friday? how do you know that?"

"O no, O no," says Friday; "he long ago die, long ago; he much old man."

"Well, well," says I, "Friday, you don't know: but shall we see any one else then?"

The fellow, it seems, had better eyes than I, and he points to the hill just above my old house; and though we lay half a league off, he cries out, "We see, we see, yes, yes, we see much man there, and there, and there."

I looked, but I saw nobody, no, not with a perspective-glass, which was, I suppose, because I could not hit the place; for the fellow was right, as I found upon inquiry the next day; and there were five or six men all together, who stood to look at the ship, not knowing what to think of us.

As soon as Friday told me he saw people, I caused the English ensign to be spread, and fired three guns, to give them notice we were friends; and in about half a quarter of an hour after, we perceived a smoke arise from the side of the creek: so I immediately ordered the boat out, taking Friday with me; and hanging out a white flag, I went directly on shore. We had about sixteen men well armed, if we had found any new guests there which we did not know of: but we had no need of weapons.

As we went on shore upon the flood tide, near high water, we rowed directly into the creek; and the first man I fixed my eye upon was the Spaniard whose life I had saved, and whom I knew by his face perfectly well. I ordered nobody to go on shore at first but myself; but there was no keeping Friday in the boat, for the affectionate creature had spied his father at a distance, a good way off the Spaniards, where, indeed, I saw nothing of him; and if they had not let him go ashore, he would have jumped into the sea. He was no sooner on shore, but he flew away to his father, like an arrow out of a bow. It would have made any man shed tears, to have seen the first transports of this poor fellow's joy when he came to his father: how he embraced him, kissed him, stroked his face, took him up in his arms, set him down upon a tree, and lay down by him; then stood and looked at him, as anyone would look at a strange picture, for a quarter of an hour together; then lay down on the ground, and stroked his legs, and kissed them, then got up again, and stared at him; one would have thought the fellow bewitched.

But it would have made a dog laugh the next day to see how his passion ran out another way: in the morning, he walked along the shore, with his father, several hours, always leading him by the hand, as if he had been a lady; and every now and then he would come to the boat to fetch something or other for him, either a lump of sugar, a dram, a biscuit, or something or other that was good. In the afternoon, his frolics ran another way; for then he would set the old man down upon the ground and dance about him, and make a thousand antic postures and gestures; and all the while he did this, he would be talking to him, and telling him one story or other of his travels, and of what had happened to him abroad, to divert him.

It would be needless to take notice of all the ceremonies and civilities that the Spaniards received me with. The first Spaniard, whose life I had saved, came towards the boat, attended by one more, carrying a flag of truce also; and he not only did not know me at first, but he had no thoughts, no notion of its being me that was come, till I spoke to him.

"*Seignior*," said I, in Portuguese, "do you not know me?" At which he spoke not a word, but giving his musket to the man that was with him, threw his arms abroad, saying something in Spanish that I did not perfectly hear, came forward and embraced me, telling me he was inexcusable not to know that face again that he had once seen as if an angel from Heaven, sent to save his life: he said abundance of very handsome things, and then beckoning to the person that attended him, bade him go and call out his comrades. He then asked me if I would walk to my old habitation, where he would give me possession of my own house again, and where I should see they had made but mean improvements: so I walked along with him; but, alas! I could no more find the place than if I had never been there; for they had planted so many trees, and placed them in such a position, so thick and close to one another, and in ten years' time they were grown so big, that in short, the place was inaccessible, except by such windings and blind ways as they themselves only, who made them, could find.

I asked them what put them upon all these fortifications: he told me I would say there was need enough of it, when they had given me an account how they had passed their time since their arriving in the island, especially after they had the misfortune to find that I was gone. He told me he could not but have some satisfaction in my good fortune, when he heard that I was gone in a good ship, and that he had oftentimes a strong persuasion that one time or other he should see me again: but nothing that ever befell him in his life, he said, was so surprising and afflicting to him at first, as the disappointment he was under when he came back to the island and found I was not there.

As to the three barbarians (so he called them) that were left behind, and of whom, he said, he had a long story to tell me, the Spaniards all thought themselves much better among the savages, only that their number was so small: "and," says he, "had they been strong enough, we had been all long ago in purgatory."

While I was thus saying this, the man came whom he had sent back, and with him eleven more. In the dress they were in, it was impossible to guess what nation they were of; but he made all clear, both to them and to me. First he turned to me, and pointing to them, said, "These, sir, are some of the gentlemen who owe their lives to you;" and then turning to them, and pointing to me, he let them know who I was; upon which they all came up, one by one, not as if they had been sailors, and ordinary fellows, and the like, but really as if they had been ambassadors or noblemen, and I a monarch or great conqueror: their behaviour was, to the last pegree, obliging and courteous, and yet mixed with a manly, majestic gravity, which very well became them; and in short, they had so much more manners than I, that I scarce knew how to receive their civilities, much less how to return them. in kind.

The history of their coming to, and conduct in, the island, after my going away, is so very remarkable, and has so many incidents, which the former part of my relation will help to understand, and which will, in most of the particulars, refer to the account I have already given, that I cannot but commit them, with great delight, to the reading of those that come after me.

I shall no longer trouble the story with a relation in the first person, which will put me to the expense of ten thousand "said I's," and "said he's," and "he told me's," and "I told him's," and the like; but I shall collect the facts historically, as near as I can gather them out of my memory, from what they related to me, and from what I met with in my conversing with them, and with the place.

In order to do this succinctly, and as intelligibly as I can, I must go back to the circumstances in which I left the island, and in which the persons were of whom I am to speak. And first, it is necessary to repeat that I had sent away Friday's father and the Spaniard to fetch over the Spaniard's companions that he left behind him.

And I desired the Spaniard would give me a particular account of his voyage back to his countrymen with the boat, when I sent him to fetch them over. He told me there was little variety in that part, for nothing remarkable happened to them on the way, having had very calm weather, and a smooth sea. As for his countrymen, it could not be doubted, he said, but that they were overjoyed to see him; that when he told them the story of his deliverance, and in what manner he was furnished for carrying them away, it was like a dream to them, and their astonishment, he said, was somewhat like that of Joseph's brethren, when he told them who he was, and the story of his exaltation in Pharaoh's court; but when he showed them the arms, the powder, the ball, and provisions, that he brought them for their voyage, they were restored to themselves, took a just share of the joy of their deliverance, and immediately prepared to come away with him.

Their first business was to get canoes: and in this they were obliged not to stick so much upon the honesty of it, but to trespass upon their friendly savages, and to borrow two large canoes, on pretence of going out a fishing, or for pleasure. In these they came away the next morning. It seems they wanted no time to get themselves ready; for they had no baggage, neither clothes, provisions, nor anything in the world but what they had on them, and a few roots to eat, of which they used to make their bread.

They were in all three weeks absent; and in that time, unluckily for them, I had the occasion offered for my escape, as I mentioned in the other part, and to get off from the island, leaving three of the most impudent, hardened, ungoverned, disagreeable villains behind me, that any man could desire to meet with; to the poor Spaniards' great grief and disappointment, you may be sure.

The only just things the rogues did was, that when the Spaniards came ashore, they gave my letter to them, and gave them provisions, and other relief, as I had ordered them to do; also they gave them the long paper of directions which I had left with them, containing the particular methods which I took for managing every part of my life there; nor did they refuse to accommodate the Spaniards with anything else, for they agreed very well for some time. They gave them an equal admission into the house, or cave, and they, began to live very sociably; and the head Spaniard, who had seen pretty much of my methods, and Friday's father together, managed all their affairs; but as for the Englishmen, they did nothing but ramble about the island, shoot parrots, and catch tortoises; and when they came home at night, the Spaniards provided their suppers for them.

The Spaniards would have been satisfied with this, had the others but let them alone; which, however, they could not find in their hearts to do long; but, like the dog in the manger, they would not eat themselves, neither would they let the others eat. The differences, nevertheless, were at first but trivial, and such as are not worth relating, but at last it broke out into open war: and it began with all the rudeness and insolence that can be imagined,—without reason or provocation, contrary to nature, and, indeed, to common sense: and though, it is true, the first relation of it came from the Spaniards themselves, whom I may call the accusers, yet when I came to examine the fellows, they could not deny a word of it.

But before I come to the particulars of this part, I must supply a defect in my former relation: and this was, I forgot to set down, among the rest, that just as we were weighing the anchor to set sail, there happened a little quarrel on board of our ship, which I was once afraid would have turned to a second mutiny; nor was it appeased till the captain, rousing up his courage, and taking us all to his assistance, parted them by force, and, making two of the most refractory fellows prisoners, he laid them in irons: and as they had been active in the former disorders, and let fall some dangerous words, the second time he threatened to carry them in irons to England, and have them hanged there for mutiny, and running away with the ship.

This, it seems, though the captain did not intend to do it, frightened some other men in the ship; and some of them had put it into the heads of the rest, that the captain only gave them good words for the present, till they should come to some English port, and that then they should be all put into gaol, and tried for their lives. The mate got intelligence of this, and acquainted us with it; upon which it was desired that I, who still passed for a great man among them, should go down with the mate, and satisfy the men, and tell them that they might be assured, if they behaved well the rest of the voyage, all they had done for the time past should be pardoned. So I went, and after passing my honour's word to them, they appeared easy, and the more so when I caused the two men that were in irons to be released and forgiven.

But this mutiny had brought us to an anchor for that night; the wind also falling cairn next morning, we found that our two men, who had been laid in irons, had stolen each of them a musket, and some other weapons (what powder or shot they had we knew not), and had taken the ship's pinnace, which was not yet hauled up, and ran away with her to their companions in roguery on shore. As soon as we found this, I ordered the long-boat on shore with twelve men and the mate, and away they went to seek the rogues; but they could neither find them or any of the rest, for they all fled into the woods when they saw the boat coming on shore. The mate was once resolved, in justice to their roguery, to have destroyed their plantations, burned all their household stuff and furniture, and left them to shift without it; but having no orders, he let it all alone, left everything as he found it, and, bringing the pinnace away, came on board without them. These two men made their number five; but the other three villains were so much more wicked than they, that after they had been two or three days together, they turned the two new comers out of doors to shift for themselves, and would have nothing to do with them; nor could they, for a good while, be persuaded to give them any food: as for the Spaniards, they were not yet come.

When the Spaniards came first on shore, the business began to go forward: the Spaniards would have persuaded the these English brutes to have taken in their countrymen again, that they might be all one family; but they would not hear of it: so the two poor fellows lived by themselves; and finding nothing but industry and application would make them live comfortably, they pitched their tents on the north shore of the island, but a little more to the west, to be out of danger of the savages, who always landed on the east parts of the island.

Here they built them two huts, one to lodge in, and the other to lay up their magazines and stores in; and the Spaniards having given them some corn for seed, and some of the pease which I had left them, they dug, planted, and enclosed, after the pattern I had set for them all, and began to live pretty well. Their first crop of corn was on the ground; and though it was but a little bit of land which they had dug up at first, having had but a little time, yet it was enough to relieve them, and find them with bread and other eatables; and one of the fellows being the cook's mate of the ship, was very ready at making soup, puddings, and such other preparations as the rice, and the milk, and such little flesh as they got, furnished him to do.

They were going on in this little thriving position when the three unnatural rogues—their own countrymen, too—in mere humour and to insult them, came and bullied them, and told them that the island was theirs: that the governor, meaning me, had given them the possession of it, and nobody else had any right to it; and that they should build no houses upon their ground, unless they would pay rent for them.

The two men, thinking they were jesting at first, asked them to come in and sit down, and see what fine houses they were that they had built, and to tell them what rent they demanded; and one of them merrily said, if they were the ground-landlords, he hoped, if they built tenements upon their land, and made improvements, they would, according to the custom of landlords, grant a long lease: and desired they would get a scrivener to draw the writings. One of the three, cursing and raging, told them they should see they were not in jest; and going to a little place at a distance, where the honest men had made a fire to dress their victuals, he takes a fire-brand, and claps it to the outside of their hut, and very fairly sets it on fire; and it would have been all burned down in a few minutes, if one of the two had not run to the fellow, thrust him away, and trod the fire out with his feet, and that not without some difficulty too.

The fellow was in such a rage at the honest man's thrusting him away, that he returned upon him, with a pole he had in his hand, and had not the man avoided the blow very nimbly, and run into the hut, he had ended his days at once. His comrade, seeing the danger they were both in, ran in after him, and immediately they came both out with their muskets, and the man that was first struck at with the pole, knocked the fellow down that began the quarrel, with the stock of his musket, and that before the other two could come to help him; and then seeing the rest come at them, they stood together, and presenting the other ends of their pieces to them, bade them stand off.

The others had fire-arms with them too; but one of the two honest men, bolder than his comrade, and made desperate by his danger, told them, if they offered to move hand or foot, they were dead men, and boldly commanded them to lay down their arms. They did not, indeed, lay down their arms, but seeing him so resolute, it brought them to a parley, and they consented to take their wounded man with them and be gone: and, indeed, it seems the fellow was wounded sufficiently with the blow. However, they were much in the wrong, since they had the advantage, that they did not disarm them effectually, as they might have done, and have gone immediately to the Spaniards, and given them an account how the rogues had treated them; for the three villains studied nothing but revenge, and every day gave them some intimation that they did so.

But not to crowd this part with an account of the lesser part of the rogueries, such as treading down their corn; shooting three young kids and a she-goat, which the poor men had got to breed up tame for their store; and plaguing them night and day in this manner; it forced the two men to such a desperation, that they resolved to fight them all three, the first time they had a fair opportunity. In order to do this, they resolved to go to the castle, as they called it (that was my old dwelling), where the three rogues and the Spaniards all lived together at that time, intending to have a fair battle, and the Spaniards should stand by to see fair play: so they got up in the morning before day, and came to the place, and called the Englishmen by their names, telling a Spaniard, that answered, that they wanted to speak with them.

It happened that the day before, two of the Spaniards, having been in the woods, had seen one of the two Englishmen, whom, for distinction, I called the honest men, and he had made a sad complaint to the Spaniards of the barbarous usage they had met with from their three countrymen, and how they had ruined their plantation, and destroyed their corn that they had laboured so hard to bring forward, and killed the milch-goat and their three kids, which was all they had provided for their sustenance; and that if he and his friends, meaning the Spaniards, did not assist them again, they should be starved. When the Spaniards came home at night, and they were all at supper, one of them took the freedom to reprove the three Englishmen, though in very gentle and mannerly terms, and asked them how they could be so cruel, they being harmless, inoffensive fellows: that they were putting themselves in a way to subsist by their labour, and that it had cost them a great deal of pains to bring things to such perfection as they were then in.

One of the Englishmen returned very briskly, "What had they to do there? that they came on shore without leave; and that they should not plant or build upon the island: it was none of their ground."

"Why," says the Spaniard very calmly, "*Seignior Inglese*, they must not starve."

The Englishman replied, like a rough-hewn tarpaulin, "They might starve, they should not plant nor build in that place."

"But what must they do, then, *seignior?*" said the Spaniard.

Another of the brutes returned, "Do? they should be servants, and work for them."

"But how can you expect that of them?" says the Spaniard: "they are not bought with your money: you have no right to make them servants."

The Englishman answered, "The island was theirs; the governor had given it to them, and no man had anything to do there but themselves;" and with that, swore by his Maker that they would go and burn all their new huts; they should build none upon their land.

"Why, *seignior*," says the Spaniard, "by the same rule, we must be your servants too."

"Aye," says the bold dog, "and so you shall, too, before we have done with you;" mixing two or three oaths in the proper intervals of his speech.

The Spaniard only smiled at that, and made him no answer. However, this little discourse had heated them; and starting up, one says to the other (I think it was he they called Will Atkins), "Come, Jack, let's go, and have t'other brush with them; we'll demolish their castle, I'll warrant you; they shall plant no colony in our dominions."

Upon this, they went all trooping away, with every man a gun, a pistol, and a sword, and muttered some insolent things among themselves, of what they would do to the Spaniards too, when opportunity offered; but the Spaniards, it seems, did not so perfectly understand them as to know all the particulars, only that, in general, they threatened them hard for taking the two Englishmen's part.

Whither they went, or how they bestowed their time that evening, the Spaniards said they did not know; but it seems they wandered about the country, part of the night, and then lying down in the place which I used to call my bower, they were weary, and overslept themselves. The case was this: they had resolved to stay till midnight, and so to take the two poor men when they were asleep, and, as they acknowledged afterwards, intended to set fire to their huts while they were in them, and either burn them there, or murder them as they came out. As malice seldom sleeps very sound, it was very strange they should not have been kept awake.

However, as the two men had also a design upon them, as I have said, though a much fairer one than that of burning and murdering, it happened, and very luckily for them all, that they were up and gone abroad, before the bloody-minded rogues came to their huts.

When they came there, and found the men gone, Atkins, who, it seems, was the forwarder man, called out to his comrade, "Ha, Jack, here's the nest, but the birds are flown."

They mused awhile, to think what should be the occasion of their being gone abroad so soon, and suggested presently that the Spaniards had given them notice of it; and with that they shook hands, and swore to one another that they would be revenged of the Spaniards. As soon as they had made this bloody bargain, they fell to work with the poor men's habitation; they did not set fire, indeed, to anything, but they pulled down both their houses, and pulled them so limb from limb that they left not the least stick standing, or scarce any sign on the ground where they stood; they tore all their little collected household stuff in pieces, and threw everything about in such a manner, that the poor men afterwards found some of their things a mile off their habitation. When they had done this, they pulled up all the young trees which the poor men had planted; pulled up an enclosure they had made to secure their cattle and their corn; and sacked and plundered everything as completely as a horde of Tartars would have done.

The two men were, at this juncture, gone to find them out, and had resolved to fight them wherever they had been, though they were but two to three; so that, had they met, there certainly would have been bloodshed among them; for they were all very stout, resolute fellows.

But Providence took more care to keep them asunder than they themselves could do to meet; for, as if they had dogged one another, when the three were gone thither, the two were here; and afterwards, when the two went back to find them, the three were come to the old habitation again: we shall see their different conduct presently. When the three came back like furious creatures, flushed with the rage which the work they had been about had put them into, they came up to the Spaniards, and told them what they had done, by way of scoff and bravado; and one of them stepping up to one of the Spaniards, as if they had been a couple of boys at play, takes hold of his hat as it was upon his head, and giving it a twirl about, fleering in his face, says to him, "And you, Seignior Jack Spaniard, shall have the same sauce if you do not mend your manners."

The Spaniard, who, though a quiet, civil man, was as brave a man as could be, and, withal, a strong, well-made man, looked at him for a good while, and then, having no weapon in his hand, stepped gravely up to him, and, with one blow of his fist, knocked him down, as an ox is felled with a pole-axe; at which one of the rogues, as insolent as the first, fired his pistol at the Spaniard immediately: he missed his body, indeed, for the bullets went through his hair, but one of them touched the tip of his ear, and he bled pretty much. The blood made the Spaniard believe he was more hurt than he really was, and that put him into some heat, for before he acted all in a perfect calm; but now resolving to go through with his work, he stooped, and took the fellow's musket whom he had knocked down, and was just going to shoot the man who had fired at him, when the rest of the Spaniards, being in the cave, came out, and calling to him not to shoot, they stepped in, secured the other two, and took their arms from them.

When they were thus disarmed, and found they had made all the Spaniards their enemies, as well as their own countrymen, they began to cool, and, giving the Spaniards better words, would have had their arms again; but the Spaniards, considering the feud that was between them and the other two Englishmen, and that it would be the best method they could take to keep them from killing one another, told them they would do them no harm; and if they would live peaceably, they would be very willing to assist and associate with them as they did before; but that they could not think of giving them their arms again, while they appeared so resolved to do mischief with them to their own countrymen, and had even threatened them all to make them their servants.

The rogues were now no more capable to hear reason than to act with reason; but being refused their arms, they went raving away, and raging like madmen, threatening what they would do, though they had no fire-arms. But the Spaniards, despising their threatening, told them they should take care how they offered any injury to their plantation or cattle, for if they did, they would shoot them as they would ravenous beasts, wherever they found them; and if they fell into their hands alive, they should certainly be hanged. However, this was far from cooling them, but away they went, raging and swearing like furies of hell. As soon as they were gone, the two men came back, in passion and rage enough also, though of another kind; for having been at their plantation, and finding it all demolished and destroyed, as above, it will easily be supposed they had provocation enough. They could scarce have room to tell their tale, the Spaniards were so eager to tell them theirs; and it was strange enough to find that three men should thus bully nineteen, and receive no punishment at all.

The Spaniards, indeed, despised them, and especially, having thus disarmed them, made light of their threatenings; but the two Englishmen resolved to have their remedy against them, what pains soever it cost to find them out. But the Spaniards interposed here too, and told them, that as they had disarmed them, they could not consent that they (the two) should pursue them with fire-arms, and perhaps kill them.

"But," said the grave Spaniard, who was their governor, "we will endeavour to make them do you justice, if you will leave it to us; for there is no doubt but they will come to us again, when their passion is over, being not able to subsist without our assistance: we promise you to make no peace with them, without having a full satisfaction for you; and, upon this condition, we hope you will promise to use no violence with them, other than in your own defence."

The two Englishmen yielded to this with great reluctance; but the Spaniards protested that they did it only to keep them from bloodshed, and to make them all easy at last.

In about five days' time, the three vagrants, tired with wandering, and almost starved with hunger, having chiefly lived on turtles' eggs all that while, came back to the grove; and finding my Spaniard, who, as I have said, was the governor, and two more with him, walking by the side of the creek, they came up in a very submissive, humble manner, and begged to be received again into the family. The Spaniards used them civilly, but told them they had acted so unnaturally to their countrymen, and so very grossly to them (the Spaniards), that they could not come to any conclusion without consulting the two Englishmen and the rest; but, however, they would go to them and discourse about it, and they should know in half an hour. It may be guessed that they were very hard put to it; for, it seems, as they were to wait this half-hour for an answer, they begged they would send them out some bread in the meantime, which they did; sending, at the same time, a large piece of goat's flesh, and a boiled parrot, which they ate very heartily, for they were hungry enough.

After half an hour's consultation, they were called in, and a long debate ensued; their two countrymen charging them with the ruin of all their labour, and a design to murder them; all which they owned before, and therefore could not deny now. Upon the whole, the Spaniards acted the moderators between them; and as they had obliged the two Englishmen not to hurt the three while they were naked and unarmed, so they now obliged the three to go and rebuild their fellows' two huts, one to be of the same, and the other of larger, dimensions than they were before; to fence their ground again where they had pulled up their fences, plant trees in the room of those pulled up, dig up the land again, for planting corn, where they had spoiled it, and to restore everything to the same state as they found it, as near as they could.

Well, they submitted to all this; and as they had plenty of provisions given them all the while, they grew very orderly, and the whole society began to live pleasantly and agreeably together again; only that these three fellows could never be persuaded to work for themselves, except now and then a little, just as they pleased. However, the Spaniards told them plainly, that if they would but live sociably and friendly together, and study the good of the whole plantation, they would be content to work for them, and let them walk about and be as idle as they pleased: and thus, having lived pretty well together for a month or two, the Spaniards gave them arms again, and gave them liberty to go abroad with them as before.

It was not above a week after they had these arms, and went abroad, before the ungrateful creatures began to be as insolent and troublesome as ever; but, however, an accident happened presently upon this, which endangered the safety of them all, and they were obliged to lay by all private resentments, and look to the preservation of their lives.

One night two of the Spaniards went out, to go up to the top of the hill, where I used to go; and were going round through the grove, unconcerned and unwary, when they were surprised with seeing a light of fire a as very little way off from them, and hearing the voices of men—not of one or two, but of a great number.

We need not doubt but that they were surprised with this sight, ran back immediately and raised their fellows, giving them an account of the imminent danger they were all in; but it was impossible to persuade them to stay close within where they were, but they must all run out to see how things stood.

The Spaniards were in no small consternation at this sight; and, as they found that the fellows ran straggling all over the shore, they made no doubt but, first or last, some of them would chop in upon their habitation, or upon some other place where they would see the token of inhabitants; and they were in great perplexity also for fear of their flock of goats, which would have been little less than starving them, if they should have been destroyed; so the first thing they resolved upon was to despatch three men away before it was light, to drive all the goats away to the great valley where the cave was, and, if need were, to drive them into the very cave itself. Could they have seen the savages altogether in one body, at a distance from their canoes, they resolved, if there had been a hundred of them, to have attacked them; but that could not be obtained; for they were some of them two miles off from the other; and, as it appeared afterwards, were of two different nations.

After having mused a great while on the course they should take, they resolved, at last, while it was still dark, to send Friday's father out as a spy, to learn, if possible, something concerning them, what they came for, what they intended to do, and the like. The old man readily undertook it; and stripping himself quite naked, as most of the savages were, away he went. After he had been gone an hour or two, he brings word that he had been among them undiscovered,—that he found they were two parties, and of two several nations, who had war with one another, and had a great battle in their own country; and that both sides having had several prisoners taken in the fight, they were, by mere chance, landed all on the same island, for the devouring their prisoners and making merry, but their coming so by chance to the same place had spoiled all their mirth,—that they were in a great rage at one another, and were so near, that he believed they would fight again as soon as daylight began to appear; but he did not perceive that they had any notion of anybody being on the island but themselves. He had hardly made an end of telling his story, when they could perceive, by the unusual noise they made, that the two little armies were engaged in a bloody fight.

Friday's father used all the arguments he could to persuade our people to lie close, and not be seen; he told them their safety consisted in it, and that they had nothing to do but lie still, and the savages would kill one another to their hands, and then the rest would go away; and it was so to a tittle. But it was impossible to prevail, especially upon the Englishmen; their curiosity was so importunate, that they must run out and see the battle; however, they used some caution, too; they did not go openly, just by their own dwelling, but went farther into the woods, and placed themselves to advantage, where they might securely see them manage the fight, and, as they thought, not be seen by them; but it seems the savages did see them, as we shall find hereafter

The battle was very fierce; and, if I might believe the Englishmen, one of them said he could perceive that some of them were men of great bravery, of invincible spirits, and of great policy in guiding the fight. The battle, they said, held two hours before they could guess which party would be beaten; but then that party which was nearest our people's habitation began to appear weakest, and after some time more some of them began to fly; and this put our men again into a great consternation, lest any one of those that fled should run into the grove before their dwelling for shelter, and thereby involuntarily discover the place; and that, by consequence, the pursuers would do the like in search of them.

Upon this, they resolved that they would stand armed within the wall, and whoever came into the grove, they resolved to sally out over the wall and kill them, so that, if possible, not one should return to give an account of it; they ordered also that it should be done with their swords, or by knocking them down with the stocks of their muskets, out not by shooting them, for fear of raising an alarm by the noise.

As they expected it fell out; three of the routed army fled for life, and crossing the creek, ran directly into the place, not in the least knowing whither they went, but running as into a thick wood for shelter. The scout they kept to look abroad gave notice of this within, with this addition, to that the conquerors had our men's great satisfaction—*viz.*, not pursued them, or seen which way they were gone; upon this, the Spaniard governor would not suffer them to kill the three fugitives, but sending three men out, ordered them to go round, come in behind them, and surprise and take them prisoners; which was done. The residue of the conquered people fled to their canoes, and got off to sea; the victors retired, made no pursuit, or very little, but drawing themselves into a body together, gave two great screaming shouts, which they supposed was by way of triumph—and so the fight ended; and the same day, about three o'clock in the afternoon, they also marched to their canoes. And thus the Spaniards had the island again free to themselves, their fright was over, and they saw no more savages for several years after.

After they were all gone, the Spaniards came out of their den, and viewing the field of battle, they found about two-and-thirty men dead on the spot; some were killed with great long arrows, some of which, were found sticking in their bodies; but most of them were killed with great wooden swords, sixteen or seventeen of which they found in the field of battle, and as many bows, with a great many arrows. These swords were strange, great unwieldy things, and they must be very strong men that used them: most of those men that were killed with them had their brains knocked out, and several their arms and legs broken; so that it is evident they fight with inexpressible rage and; fury;. We found not one man that was not stone dead:—for either they stay by their enemy till they have killed him, or they carry all the wounded men that are not quite dead away with them.

This deliverance tamed our Englishmen for a great while; the sight had filled them with horror, and the consequences appeared terrible to the last degree, especially upon supposing that some time or other they should fall into the hands of those creatures, who would not only kill them as enemies, but kill them for food, as we kill our cattle; and they professed to me that the thoughts of being eaten up like beef or mutton, though it was supposed it was not to be till they were dead, had something in it so horrible that it nauseated their very stomachs, made them sick when they thought of it, and filled their minds with such unusual terror, that they were not themselves for some weeks after. This, as I said, tamed even the three English brutes I have been speaking of; and for a great while after they were tractable, and went about the common business of the whole society well enough. But some time after this they fell into such simple measures again, as brought them into a great deal of trouble.

They had taken three prisoners, as I observed; and these three being lusty, stout young fellows, they made them servants, and taught them to work for them; and as slaves they did well enough; but they did not take their measures with them as I did by my man Friday— *viz.*, to begin with them upon the principle of having saved their lives, and then instruct them in the rational principles of life, much less of religion,—civilising and reducing them by kind usage and affectionate arguments; but as they gave them their food every day, so they gave them their work too, and kept them fully employed in drudgery enough; but they failed in this by it, that they never had them to assist them and fight for them as I had my man Friday, who was as true to me as the very flesh upon my bones.

But to come to the family part. Being all now good friends, for common danger, as I said above, had effectually reconciled them, they began to consider their general circumstances; and the first thing that came under consideration was whether, seeing the savages particularly haunted that side of the island, and that there were more remote and retired parts of it equally adapted to their way of living, and manifestly to their advantage, they should not rather move their habitation, and plant in some more proper place for their safety, and especially for the security of their cattle and corn.

Upon this, after long debate, it was concluded that they would not remove their habitation; because that, sometime or other, they thought they might hear from their governor again, meaning me; and if I should send any one to seek them, I should be sure to direct them to that side, where, if they should find the place demolished, they would conclude the savages had killed us all, and we were gone, and so our supply would go too. But as to their corn and cattle, they agreed to remove them into the valley where my cave was, where the land was as proper for both, and where, indeed, there was land enough; however, upon second thoughts, they altered one part of their resolution too, and resolved only to remove part of their cattle thither, and plant part of their corn there; and so, if one part was destroyed, the other might be saved. And one part of prudence they used, which it was very well they did—that they never trusted those three savages which they had made prisoners with knowing anything of the plantation they had made in that valley, or of any cattle they had there, much less of the cave there, which they kept, in case of necessity, as a safe retreat; and thither they carried also the two barrels of powder which I had sent them at my coming away.

But, however, they resolved not to change their habitation; yet they agreed, that as I had carefully covered it first with a wall or fortification, and then with a grove of trees, so seeing their safety consisted entirely in their being concealed, of which they were now fully convinced, they set to work to cover and conceal the place yet more effectually than before. For this purpose, as I planted trees, or rather thrust in stakes, which in time all grew up to be trees, for some good distance before the entrance into my apartments, they went on in the same manner, and filled up the rest of that whole space of ground from the trees I had set quite down to the side of the creek, where, as I said, I landed my floats, and even into the very ooze where the tide flowed, not so much as leaving any place to land, or any sign that there had been any landing thereabouts,—these stakes also being of a wood forward to grow, as I have noted formerly, they took care to have them generally much larger and taller than those which I had planted; and as they grew apace, so they planted them so very thick and close together, that when they had been three or four years grown, there was no piercing with the eye any considerable way into the plantation; and as for that part which I had planted, the trees were grown as thick as a man's thigh, and among them they placed so many other short ones, and so thick, that, in a word, it stood like a palisado a quarter of a mile thick, and it was next to impossible to penetrate it, but with a little army to cut it all down,—for a little dog could hardly get between the trees, they stood so close.

But this was not all; for they did the same by all the ground to the right hand and to the left, and round even to the side of the hill, leaving no way, not so much as for themselves, to come out but by the ladder placed up to the side of the hill, and then lifted up, and placed again from the first stage up to the top; and when the ladder was taken down, nothing but what had wings or witchcraft to assist it could come at them. This was excellently well contrived; nor was it less than what they afterwards found occasion for.

They lived two years after this in perfect retirement, and had no more visits from the savages. They had, indeed, an alarm given them one morning, which put them into a great consternation; for, some of the Spaniards being out early one morning on the west side, or rather end, of the island (which was that end where I never went, for fear of being discovered), they were surprised with seeing above twenty canoes of Indians just coming on shore. They made the best of their way home in hurry enough; and giving the alarm to their comrades, they kept close all that day and the next, going out only at night to make their observation; but they had the good luck to be mistaken; for wherever the savages went, they did not land that time on the island, but pursued some other design.

And now they had another broil with the three Englishmen; one of whom, a most turbulent fellow, being in a rage at one of the three slaves, whom I mentioned they had taken, because the fellow had not done something: right which he bid him do, and seemed a little untractable in his showing him, drew a hatchet out of a frog-belt, in which he wore it by his side, and fell upon the poor savage, not to correct him, but to kill him. One of the Spaniards, who was by, see-ing him give the fellow a barbarous cut with the hatchet, which he aimed at his head, but struck into his shoulder, so that he thought he had cut the poor creature's arm off, ran to him, and entreating him not to murder the poor man, placed himself between him and the savage to prevent the mischief. The fellow, being enraged the more at this, struck at the Spaniard with his hatchet, and swore he would serve him as he intended to serve the savage; which the Spaniard perceiv-ing, avoided the blow, and, with a shovel which he had in his hand, knocked the brute down.

Another of the Englishmen, running at the same time to help his comrade, knocked the Spaniard down; and then two Spaniards more came in to help their man, and a third Englishman fell in upon them. They had none of them any fire-arms or any other weapons but hatchets and other tools, except this third Englishman; he had one of my rusty cutlasses, with which he made at the two last Spaniards, and wounded them both. This fray set the whole family in an uproar, and more help coming in, they took the three Englishmen prisoners. The next question was, what should be done with them? They had been so often mutinous, and were so very furious, so desperate, and so idle withal, they knew not what course to take with them, for they were mischievous to the highest degree, and cared not what hurt they did to any man; so that, in short, it was not safe to live with them.

The Spaniard who was governor told them, in so many words, that if they had been of his own country, he would have hanged them; for all laws and all governors were to preserve society, and those who were dangerous to the society ought to be expelled out of it; but as they were Englishmen, and that it was to the generous kindness of an Englishman that they all owed their preservation and deliverance, he would use them with all possible lenity, and would leave them to the judgment of the other two Englishmen who were their countrymen:

One of the two honest Englishmen stood up, and said they desired it might not be left to them. "For," says he, "I am sure we ought to sentence them to the gallows;" and with that he gives an account how Will Atkins, one of the three, had proposed to have all the five Englishmen join together, and murder all the Spaniards when they were in their sleep.

When the Spanish governor heard this, he calls to Will Atkins, "How, Seignior Atkins, would you murder us all? What have you to say to that?"

The hardened villain was so far from denying it, that he said it was true, and swore they would do it still before they had done with them.

"Well, but Seignior Atkins," says the Spaniard, "what have we done to you that you will kill us? And what would you get by killing us? And what must we do to prevent your killing us? Must we kill you, or you kill us? Why will you put us to the necessity of this, Seignior Atkins?" says the Spaniard very calmly, and smiling.

Seignior Atkins was in such a rage at the Spaniard making a jest of it, that had he not been held by three men, and withal had no weapon near him, it was thought he would have attempted to have killed the Spaniard in the middle of all the company. This hair-brain carriage obliged them to consider seriously what was to be done; the two Englishmen, and the Spaniard who saved the poor savage, were of the opinion that they should hang one of the three, for an example to the rest, and that particularly it should be he that had twice attempted to commit murder with his hatchet. But the governor Spaniard still said no; it was an Englishman that had saved all their lives, and he would never consent to put an Englishman to death, though he had murdered half of them—nay, he said if he had been killed himself by an Englishman, and had time left to speak, it should be that they should pardon him.

This was so positively insisted on by the governor Spaniard, that there was no gainsaying it; and as merciful counsels are most apt to prevail, where they are so earnestly pressed, so they all came into it; but then it was to be considered what should be done to keep them from doing the mischief they designed; for all agreed that means were to be used for preserving the society from danger. After a long debate,' it was agreed, first, that they should be disarmed, and not permitted to have either gun, powder, shot, sword, or any weapon; and should be turned out of the society, and left to live where they would, and how they would by themselves: but that none of the rest, either Spaniards or English, should converse with them, speak with them, or have anything to do with them: that they should be forbid to come within a certain distance of the place where the rest dwelt; and if they offered to commit any disorder, so as to spoil, burn, kill, or destroy any of the corn, plantings, buildings, fences, or cattle, belonging to the society, they should die without mercy, and they would shoot them wherever they could find them.

The governor, a man of great humanity, musing upon the sentence, considered a little upon it; and turning to the two honest Englishmen, said, "Hold; you must reflect that it will be long ere they can raise corn and cattle of their own, and they must not starve; we must therefore allow them provisions." So he caused to be added, that they should have a proportion of corn given them to last them eight months, and for seed to sow, by which time they might be supposed to raise some of their own; that they should have six milch-goats, four he-goats, and six kids given them, as well for present subsistence as for a store; and that they should have tools given them for their work in the fields, such as six hatchets, an adze, a saw, and the like; but they should have none of these tools or provisions, unless they would swear solemnly that they would not hurt or injure any of the Spaniards with them, or of their fellow Englishmen.

Thus they dismissed them the society, and turned them out to shift for themselves. They went away sullen and refractory, as neither content to go away nor to stay; but, as there was no remedy, they went, pretending to go and choose a place where they would settle themselves; and some provisions were given them, but no weapons.

About four or five days after, they came again for some victuals, and gave the governor an account where they had pitched their tents, and marked themselves out a habitation and plantation; and it was a very convenient place, indeed, on the remotest part of the island, N.E., much about the place where I providentially landed in my first voyage, when I was driven out to sea, the Lord knows whither, in my foolish attempt to sail round the island.

Here they built themselves two handsome huts, and contrived them in a manner like my first habitation, being close under the side of a hill, having some trees growing already on three sides of it, so that by planting others, it would be very easily covered from the sight, unless narrowly searched for. They desired some dried goat-skins, for beds and covering, which were given them; and upon giving their words that they would not disturb the rest, or injure any of their plantations, they gave them hatchets, and what other tools they could spare; some pease, barley, and rice, for sowing; and anything they wanted, except arms and ammunition.

They lived in this separate condition about six months, and had got in their first harvest, though the quantity was but small, the parcel of land they had planted being but little; for having all their plantation to form, they had a great deal of work upon their hands; and when they came to make boards and pots, and such things, they were quite out of their element, and could make nothing of it: and when the rainy season came on, for want of a cave in the earth, they could not keep their grain dry, and it was in great danger of spoiling; and this humbled them much: so they came and begged the Spaniards to help them, which they very readily did; and in four days worked a great hole in the side of the hill for them, big enough to secure their corn and other things from the rain; but it was a poor place, at best, compared to mine, and especially as mine was then, for the Spaniards had greatly enlarged it, and made several new apartments in it.

About three quarters of a year after this separation, these rogues took a new frolic, which, together with the former villainy they had committed, brought mischief enough upon them, and had very near been the ruin of the whole colony. The three new associates began, it seems, to be weary of the laborious life they led, and that without hope of bettering their circumstances; and a whim took them that they would make a voyage to the continent, from whence the savages came, and would try if they could seize upon some prisoners among the natives there, and bring them home, so as to make them do the laborious part of the work for them.

The project was not so preposterous, if they had gone no farther. But they did nothing, and proposed nothing, but had either mischief in the design, or mischief in the event.

The three fellows came down to the Spaniards one morning, and in very humble terms desired to be admitted to speak with them. The Spaniards very readily heard what they had to say, which was this:— that they were tired of living in the manner they did: and that they were not handy enough to make the necessaries they wanted, and that having no help, they found they should be starved; but if the Spaniards would give them leave to take one of the canoes which they came over in, and give them arms and ammunition proportioned to their defence, they would go over to the main and seek their fortunes, and so deliver them from the trouble of supplying them with any other provisions.

The Spaniards were glad enough to get rid of them, but very honestly represented to them the certain destruction they were running into; told them they had suffered such hardships upon that very spot, they could, without any spirit of prophecy, tell them they would be starved or murdered; and bade them consider of it.

The men replied audaciously, they should be starved if they stayed here, for they could not and would not work, and they could but be starved abroad; and if they were murdered, there was an end of them; they had no wives or children to cry after them; and insisted importunately upon their demand; declaring they would go, whether they gave them any arms or no.

The Spaniards told them, with great kindness, that if they were resolved to go, they should not go like naked men, and be in no condition to defend themselves, and that though they could ill spare their fire-arms, having not enough for themselves, yet they would let them have two muskets, a pistol, and a cutlass, and each man a hatchet, which they thought was sufficient for them. They accepted the offer: and having baked bread enough to serve them a month, and given them as much goats' flesh as they could eat while it was sweet, with a great basket of dried grapes, a pot of fresh water, and a young kid alive, they boldly set out in the canoe for a voyage over the sea, where it was at least forty miles broad.

The boat was a large one, and would very well have carried fifteen or twenty men, and therefore was rather too big for them to manage; but as they had a fair breeze, and floodtide with them, they did well enough. They had made a mast of a long pole, and a sail of four large goat-skins dried, which they had sewed or laced together; and away they went merrily enough. The Spaniards called after them, "*Bon voyago*;" and no man ever thought of seeing them any more.

The Spaniards were often saying to one another, and to the two honest Englishmen who remained behind, how quietly and comfortably they lived, now these three turbulent fellows were gone. As for their coming again, that was the remotest thing from their thoughts that could be imagined; when, behold, after two-and-twenty days' absence, one of the Englishmen, being abroad upon his planting work, sees three strange men coming towards him from a distance, with guns upon their shoulders.

Away runs the Englishman, as if he was bewitched, comes frightened and amazed to the governor Spaniard, and tells him they were all undone, for there were strangers upon the island, but could not tell who they were. The Spaniard, pausing a while, says to him, "How do you mean, you cannot tell who? They are the savages, to be sure."

"No, no," says the Englishman; "they are men in clothes, with arms."

"Nay, then," says the Spaniard, "why are you so concerned? If they are not savages, they must be friends; for there is no Christian nation upon earth but will do us good rather than harm."

While they were debating thus, came the three Englishmen, and, standing without the wood, which was new planted, hallooed to them. They presently knew their voices, and so all the wonder ceased. But now the admiration was turned upon another question:—what could be the matter, and what made them come back again?

It was not long before they brought the men in, and inquiring where they had been, and what they had been doing, they gave them a full account of their voyage in a few words; that they reached the land in less than two days, but finding the people alarmed at their coming, and preparing with bows and arrows to fight them, they durst not go on shore, but sailed on to the northward six or seven hours, 'til they came to a great opening, by which they perceived that the land they saw from our island was not the main, but an island; upon entering that opening of the sea, they saw another island on the right hand, north, and several more west; and being resolved to land somewhere, they put over to one of the islands which lay west, and went boldly on shore: that they found the people very courteous and friendly to them; and that they gave several roots and some dried fish, and appeared very sociable; and the women, as well as the men, were very forward to supply them with anything they could get for them to eat, and brought it to them a great way upon their heads.

They continued here four days; and inquired, as well as they could of them, by signs, what nations were this way, and that way; and were told of several fierce and terrible people that lived almost every way, who, as they made known by signs to them, used to eat men; but as for themselves, they said, they never ate men or women, except only such as they took in the wars; and then, they owned, they made a great feast, and ate their prisoners.

The Englishmen seemed mighty desirous of seeing some of their prisoners; but the others mistaking them, thought they were desirous to have some of them to carry away for their own eating. So they beckoned to them, pointing to the setting of the sun, and then to the rising; which was to signify that the next morning at sunrising they would bring some for them; and, accordingly, the next morning they brought down five women and eleven men, and gave them to the Englishmen, to carry with them on their voyage, just as we would bring so many cows and oxen down to a seaport town to victual a ship.

As brutish and barbarous as these fellows were at home, their stomachs turned at this sight, and they did not know what to do. To refuse the prisoners would have been the highest affront to the savage gentry that could be offered them, and what to do with them they knew not. However, after some debate, they resolved to accept of them; and, in return, they gave the savages that brought them one of their hatchets, an old key, a knife, and six or seven of their bullets; which, though they did not understand their use, they seemed particularly pleased with; and then tying the poor creatures' hands behind them, they dragged the prisoners into the boat for our men.

In their voyage, they endeavoured to have some communication with their prisoners; but it was impossible to make them understand anything. Nothing they could say to them, or give them, or do for them, but was looked upon as going to murder them. They first of all unbound them; but the poor creatures screamed at that, especially the women, as if they had just felt the knife at their throats; for they immediately concluded they were unbound on purpose to be killed. If they gave them anything to eat, it was the same thing; they then concluded it was for fear they should sink in flesh, and so not be fat enough to kill. If they looked at one of them more particularly, the party presently concluded it was to see whether he or she was fattest, and fittest to kill first; nay, after they had brought them quite over, and began to use them kindly, and treat them well, they expected every day to make a dinner or supper for their captors.

When these three wanderers had given this unaccountable history of their voyage, the Spaniard asked them where their new family was; and being told that they had brought them on shore, and put them into one of their huts, and were come up to beg some victuals for them, the whole colony resolved to go all down to the place and see them; and did so, and Friday's father with them.

When they came into the hut, there they sat, all bound; for when they had brought them on shore, they bound their hands, that they might not take the boat and make their escape; there, I say, they sat, all of them stark naked. First, there were three men, lusty, comely fellows, well shaped, straight and fair limbs, about thirty to thirty-five years of age; and five women, whereof two might be from thirty to forty; two more not above four or five-and-twenty; and the fifth, a tall, comely maiden, about sixteen or seventeen. The women were well-favoured, agreeable persons, both in shape and features, only tawny; and two of them, had they been perfect white, would have passed for very handsome women, even in London itself, having pleasant, agreeable countenances, and of a very modest behaviour; especially when they came afterwards to be dressed, though that dress was very indifferent, it must be confessed.

The governor, who found that the having women among them would presently be attended with some inconvenience, and might occasion some strife, and perhaps blood, asked the three men what they intended to do with these women, and how they intended to use them, whether as servants or as wives? One of the Englishmen answered very boldly and readily, that they would use them as both; to which the governor said, "I am not going to restrain you from it; you are your own masters as to that; but this I think is but just, for avoiding disorders and quarrels among you, and I desire it of you for that reason only, *viz.*:—That you will all engage, that if any of you take any of these women as a wife, that he shall take but one; and that having taken one, none else shall touch her; for though we cannot marry any one of you, yet it is but reasonable that, while you stay here, the woman any of you takes shall be maintained by the man that takes her, and should be his wife; I mean," says he. "while he continues here, and that none else shall have anything to do with her." All this appeared so just, that every one agreed to it without any difficulty.

Then the Englishman asked the Spaniards if they designed to take any of them?

But every one of them answered "No:" some of them said they had wives in Spain, and the others did not like women that were not Christians; to be short, the five Englishmen took them every one a wife, and so they set up a new form of living: for the Spaniards and Friday's father lived in my old habitation, which they had enlarged exceedingly within. The three servants which were taken in the last battle of the savages lived with them: and these carried on the main part of the colony, supplied the rest with food, and assisted them in anything as they could, or as they found necessity required.

But the wonder of the story was, how five such refractory, ill-matched fellows should agree about these women, and that two of them should not choose the same woman, especially seeing two or three of them were, without comparison, more agreeable than the others: but they took a good way enough to prevent quarrelling among themselves; for they set the five women by themselves in one of their huts, and they went all into the other hut, and drew lots among them who should choose first.

He that drew to choose first went away by himself to the hut where the poor naked creatures were, and fetched out her he chose: and it was worth observing, that he that chose first took her that was reckoned the homeliest and oldest of the five, which made mirth enough among the rest; and even the Spaniards laughed at it: but the fellow considered better than any of them, that it was application and business they were to expect assistance in, as much as in anything else: and she proved the best wife of all the parcel.

When the poor women saw themselves set in a row thus, and fetched out one by one, the terrors of their condition returned upon them again, and they firmly believed they were now going to be devoured. Accordingly, when the English sailor came in and fetched out one of them, the rest set up a most lamentable cry, and hung about her, and took their leave of her with such agonies and affection as would have grieved the hardest heart in the world; nor was it possible for the Englishmen to satisfy them that they were not to be immediately murdered, till they fetched the old man, Friday's father, who immediately let them know that the five men, who were to fetch them out one by one, had chosen them for their wives.

When they had done, and the fright the women were in was a little over, the men went to work, and the Spaniards came and helped them;

and in a few hours they had built them every one a new hut or tent for their lodging apart; for those they had already were crowded with their tools, household stuff, and provisions. The three wicked ones had pitched farthest off, and the two honest ones nearer, but both on the north shore of the island, so that they continued separated as before: and thus my island was peopled in three places: and, as I might say, three towns were begun to be built.

But I now come to a scene different from all that had happened before, either to them or to me; and the origin of the story was this:— Early one morning, there came on shore five or six canoes of Indians, and there is no room to doubt they came upon the old errand of feeding upon their slaves; but that part was now so familiar to the Spaniards, and to our men too, that they did not concern themselves about it, as I did: but having been made sensible, by their experience, that their only business was to lie concealed, and that if they were not seen by any of the savages, they would go off again quietly, when their business was done, having, as yet, not the least notion of there being any inhabitants in the island; they had nothing to do but give notice to all the three plantations to keep within doors, and not show themselves, only placing a scout in a proper place, to give notice when the boats went to sea again.

This was, without doubt, very right; but a disaster spoiled all these measures, and made it known among the savages that there were inhabitants there; which was, in the end, the desolation of almost the whole colony. After the canoes with the savages had gone off, the Spaniards peeped abroad again; and some of them had the curiosity to go to the place where they had been, to see what they had been doing. Here, to their great surprise, they found three savages left behind, and lying fast asleep upon the ground.

The Spaniards were greatly surprised at this sight, and perfectly at a loss what to do. The Spanish governor, as it happened, was with them, and his advice was asked, but he professed he knew not what to do. As for slaves, they had enough already; and as to killing them, there were none of them inclined to do that. After some consultation, they resolved upon this; that they would lie still a while longer, till, if possible, these three men might be gone. But then the governor Spaniard recollected that the three savages had no boat; and if they were left to rove about the island, they would certainly discover that there were inhabitants in it; and so they would be undone that way. Upon this, they went back again, and there lay the fellows fast asleep still, and so they resolved to awaken them, and take them prisoners, and they did so. The poor fellows were strangely frightened when they were seized upon and bound; and afraid, like the women, that they should be murdered and eaten.

It was very happy for them that they did not carry them home to their castle; but they carried them first to the bower, and afterwards they carried them to the habitation of the two Englishmen.

Here they were set to work, though it was not much they had for them to do; and whether it was by negligence in guarding them, or that they thought the fellows could not mend themselves, I know not, but one of them ran away and taking to the woods, they could never hear of him any more.

They had good reason to believe he got home again soon after in some other canoes of savages who came on shore three or four weeks afterwards; and who, carrying on their revels as usual, went off in two days' time. This thought terrified them exceedingly: for they concluded, and that not without good cause indeed, that if this fellow got home safe among his comrades, he would certainly give them an account that there were people in the island, and also how few and weak they were; for this savage, as observed before, had never been told, and it was very happy he had not, how many there were, or where they lived; nor had he ever seen or heard the fire of any of their guns, much less had they shown him any of their other retired places; such as the cave in the valley, or the new retreat which the two Englishmen had made, and the like.

About two months after this, six canoes of savages, with about ten men in a canoe, came rowing along the north side of the island, where they never used to come before, and landed, about an hour after sunrise, at a convenient place, about a mile from the habitation of the two Englishmen, where this escaped man had been kept. As the Spaniard governor said, had they been all there, the damage would not have been so much, for not a man of them would have escaped: but the case differed now very much, for two men to fifty was too much odds. The two men had the happiness to discover them about a league off, so that it was above an hour before they landed; and as they landed a mile from their huts, it was some time before they could come at them. Now, having great reason to believe they were betrayed, the first thing they did was to bind the two slaves which were left, and cause two of the three men whom they brought with the women to lead them, with their two wives, and whatever they could carry away with them, to their retired places in the woods, and there to bind the two fellows hand and foot till they heard farther.

In the next place, seeing the savages were all come on shore, and that they had bent their course directly that way, they opened the fences where the milch-cows were kept, and drove them all out; leaving their goats to straggle in the woods, whither they pleased, that the savages might think they were all bred wild; but the rogue who came with them was too cunning for that, and he gave them an account of it all, for they went directly to the place.

When the two poor frightened men had secured their wives and goods, they sent the other slave they had of the three who came with the women, away to the Spaniards with all speed, to give them the alarm, and desire speedy help, and, in the meantime, they took their arms, and what ammunition they had, and retreated towards the place in the wood where their wives were sent; keeping at a distance, yet so that they might see, if possible, which way the savages took.

They had not gone far, but that from a rising ground they could see a little army of their enemies come on directly to their habitation, and, in a moment more, could see all their huts and household stuff flaming up together, to their great grief and mortification; for they had a very great loss, to them irretrievable, at least for some time. They kept their station for a while, till they found the savages, like wild beasts, spread themselves all over the place, rummaging every way, and every place they could think of, in search of prey; and in particular for the people, of whom, now, it plainly appeared they had intelligence.

The two Englishmen seeing this, thinking themselves not secure where they stood, because it was likely some of the wild people might come that way, and they might come too many together, thought it proper to make another retreat about half a mile farther; believing, as it afterwards happened, that the farther they strolled, the fewer would be together.

Their next halt was at the entrance into a very thick-grown part of the woods, and where an old trunk of a tree stood, which was hollow and vastly large; and in this tree they both took their standing, resolving to see there what might offer. They had not stood there long before two of the savages appeared running directly that way, as if they had already had notice where they stood, and were coming up to attack them; and a little way farther they espied three more coming after them, and five more beyond them, all coming the same way: besides which, they saw seven or eight more at a distance, running another way.

The poor men were now in great perplexity whether they should stand or fly; but, after a very short debate with themselves they considered, that if the savages ranged the country thus before help came, they might perhaps find out their retreat in the woods, and then all would be lost; so they resolved to stand them there; and if they were too many to deal with, then they would get up to the top of the tree, whence they doubted not to defend themselves, fire excepted, as long as their ammunition lasted, though all the savages that were landed, which was near fifty, were to attack them.

Having resolved upon this, they next considered whether they should fire at the first two, or wait for the three, and so take the middle party, by which the two and the five that followed would be separated; at length they resolved to let the first two pass by, unless they should spy them in the tree, and come to attack them. The first two savages confirmed them also in this regulation, by turning a little from them towards another part of the wood: but the three, and the five after them, came forward directly to the tree, as if they had known the Englishmen were there. Seeing them come so straight towards them, they resolved to take them in a line as they came: and as they resolved to fire but one at a time, perhaps the first shot might hit them all three; for which purpose the man who was to fire put three or four small bullets into his piece; and having a fair loop-hole, as it were, from a broken hole in the tree, he took a sure aim, without being seen, waiting till they were within about thirty yards of the tree, so that he could not miss.

While they were thus waiting, and the savages came on, they plainly saw that one of the three was the runaway savage that had escaped from them; and they both knew him distinctly, and resolved that, if possible, he should not escape, though they should both fire: so the other stood ready with his piece, that if he did not drop at the first shot, he should be sure to have a second. But the first was too good a marksman to miss his aim; for as the savages kept near one another, a little behind in a line, he fired, and hit two of them directly: the foremost was killed outright, being shot in the head; the second, which was the runaway Indian, was shot through the body and fell, but was not quite dead; and the third had a little scratch in the shoulder, perhaps by the same ball that went through the body of the second; and being dreadfully frightened, though not so much hurt, sat down upon the ground, screaming and yelling in a hideous manner.

The five that were behind, more frightened with the noise than sensible of the danger, stood still at first; for the woods made a sound a thousand times bigger than it really was.

However, all being silent again, and they not knowing what the matter was, came on unconcerned, till they came to the place where their companions lay in a condition miserable enough: and here the poor ignorant creatures, not sensible that they were within reach of the same mischief, stood all together over the wounded man, talking, and, as may be supposed, inquiring of him, how he came to be hurt: and who, it is very rational to believe, told them, that a flash of fire first, and immediately after that thunder from their gods, had killed those two and wounded him.

Our two men, though, as they confessed to me, it grieved them to be obliged to kill so many poor creatures, who, at the same time, had no notion of their danger; yet, having them all thus in their power, and the first having loaded his piece again, resolved to let fly both together among them; and singling out, by agreement, which to aim at, they shot together, and killed, or very much wounded, four of them; the fifth, frightened even to death, though not hurt, fell with the rest; so that our men, seeing them all fall together, thought they had killed them all.

The belief that the savages were all killed, made our two men come boldly out from the tree before they had charged their guns, which was a wrong step; and they were under some surprise when they came to the place, and found no less than four of them alive, and of them two very little hurt, and one not at all: this obliged them to fall upon them with the stocks of their muskets; and first they made sure of the runaway savage, that had been the cause of all the mischief, and of another that was hurt in the knee, and put them out of their pain: then the man that was not hurt at all, came and kneeled down to them, with his two hands held up, and made piteous moans to them, by gestures and signs, for his life, but could not say one word to them that they could understand.

However, they made signs to him to sit down at the foot of a tree hard by; and one of the Englishmen, with a piece of rope twined, which he had by great chance in his pocket, tied his two hands behind him, and there they left him; and with what speed they could, made after the other two, which were gone before, fearing they, or any more of them, should find the way to their covered place in the woods, where their wives, and the few goods they had left lay. They came once in sight of the two men, but it was at a great distance; however, they had the satisfaction to see them cross over a valley towards the sea, quite the contrary way from that which led to their retreat, which they were afraid of; and being satisfied with that, they went back to the tree where they left their prisoner, who, as they supposed, was delivered by his comrades, for he was gone, and the two pieces of rope-yarn, with which they had bound him, lay just at the foot of the tree.

They were now in as great concern as before, not knowing what course to take, or how near the enemy might be, or in what number; so they resolved to go away to the place where their wives were, to see if all was well there, and to make them easy, who were in fright enough to be sure; for though the savages were their own country-men, yet they were most terribly afraid of them, and perhaps the more for the knowledge they had of them.

When they came there, they found the savages had been in the wood, and very near that place, but had not found it; for it was indeed inaccessible, from the trees standing so thick, unless the persons seeking it had been directed by those that knew it, which these did not; they found, therefore, everything was safe, only the women in a terrible fright. While they were here, they had the comfort to have seven of the Spaniards come to their assistance; the other ten, with their servants, and old Friday (I mean Friday's father), were gone in a body to defend their bower, and the corn and cattle that was kept there, in case the savages should have roved over to that side of the country; but they did not spread so far. With the seven Spaniards came one of the three savages; and with them also came the savage whom the Englishman had left bound hand and foot at the tree; for it seems they came that way, saw the slaughter of the seven men, and unbound the eighth, and brought him along with them: where, however, they were obliged to bind him again, as they had the two others who were left when the third ran away.

The prisoners now began to be a burden to them; and they were so afraid of their escaping, that they were once resolving to kill them all, believing they were under an absolute necessity to do so for their own preservation. However, the Spaniard governor would not consent to it; but ordered, for the present, that they should be sent out of the way, to my old cave in the valley, and be kept there, with two Spaniards to guard them, and give them food for their subsistence, which was done; and they were bound there hand and foot for that night.

When the Spaniards came, the two Englishmen were so encouraged, that they could not satisfy themselves to stay any longer there; but taking five of the Spaniards and themselves, with four muskets and a pistol among them, and two stout quarter staves, away they went in quest of the savages. And first they came to the tree where the men lay that had been killed; but it was easy to see that some more of the savages had been there, for they had attempted to carry their dead men away, and had dragged two of them a good way, but had given it over.

Thence they advanced to the first rising ground, where they had stood and seen their camp destroyed, and where they had the mortification still to see some of the smoke; but neither could they here see any of the savages. They then resolved, though with all possible caution, to go forward towards their ruined plantation; but a little before they came thither, coming in sight of the seashore, they saw plainly the savages all embarked again in their canoes, in order to be gone. They seemed sorry at first, that there was no way to come at them, to give them a parting blow; but, upon the whole, they were very well satisfied to be rid of them.

The poor Englishmen being now twice ruined, and all their improvements destroyed, the rest all agreed to come and help them to rebuild, and assist them with needful supplies. Their three countrymen, who were not yet noted for having the least inclination to do any good, yet as soon as they heard of it, came and offered their help and assistance, and did, very friendly, work for some days to restore their habitation, and make necessaries for them. And thus, in a little time, they were set upon their legs again.

About two days after this, they had the farther satisfaction of seeing three of the savages' canoes come driving on shore, and, at some distance from them, two drowned men: by which they had reason to believe that they had met with a storm at sea, which had overset some of them; for it had blown very hard the night after they went off.

However, as some might miscarry, so, on the other hand, enough of them escaped to inform the rest, as well of what they had done as what had happened to them, and to whet them on to another enterprise of the same nature.

It was five or six months after this before they heard any more of the savages, in which time our men had hopes they had either forgot their former bad luck, or given over hopes of better; when, on a sudden, they were invaded with a most formidable fleet of no less than eight-and-twenty canoes, full of savages, armed with bows and arrows, great clubs, wooden swords, and such like engines of war; and they brought such numbers with them, that, in short, it put all our people into the utmost consternation.

As they came on shore in the evening, and at the easternmost side of the island, our men had that night to consult and consider what to do; and, in the first place, knowing that their being entirely concealed was their only safety before, and would be much more so now, while the number of their enemies would be so great, they therefore resolved, first of all, to take down the huts which were built for the two Englishmen, and drive away their goats to the old cave; because they supposed the savages would go directly thither, as soon as it was day, to play the old game over again, though they did not now land within two leagues of it. In the next place, they drove away all the flocks of goats they had at the old bower, as I called it, which belonged to the Spaniards; and, in short, left as little appearance of inhabitants anywhere as was possible: and the next morning early they posted themselves, with all their force, at the plantation of the two men, to wait for their coming.

As they guessed, so it happened. These new invaders, leaving their canoes at the east end of the island, came ranging along the shore, directly towards the place, to the number of two hundred and fifty, as near as our men could judge. Our army was but small, indeed; but that which was worse, they had not arms for all their number neither. The whole account, it seems stood thus: first, as to men, seventeen Spaniards, five Englishmen, Friday's father, the three slaves taken with the women, who proved very faithful, and three other slaves, who lived with the Spaniards. To arm these, they had eleven muskets, five pistols, eight fowling-pieces, two swords, and three old halberts.

To their slaves they did not give either musket or fusee, but they had each a halbert, or a long staff, like a quarter-staff, with a great spike of iron fastened into each end of it, and by his side a hatchet: also every one of our men had a hatchet. Two of the women could not be prevailed upon but they would come into the fight, and they had bows and arrows, which the Spaniards had taken from the savages when the first action happened, which I have spoken of, where the Indians fought with one another: and the women had hatchets too.

The Spaniard governor commanded the whole: and Will Atkins, who, though a dreadful fellow for wickedness, was a most daring fellow, commanded under him. The savages came forward like lions; and our men, which was the worse of their fate, had no advantage in their situation; only this Will Atkins, who now proved a most useful fellow, with six men, was planted just behind a small thicket of bushes, as an advanced guard, with orders to let the first of them pass by, and then fire into the middle of them, and, as soon as he had fired, to make his retreat as nimbly as he could round a part of the wood, and so come in behind the Spaniards, where they stood, having a thicket of trees before them.

When the savages came on, they ran straggling about every way in heaps, out of all manner of order, and Will Atkins let about fifty of them pass by him; then seeing the rest come in a very thick throng, he orders three of his men to fire having loaded their muskets with six or seven bullets a-piece about as big as large pistol bullets. How many they killed or wounded they knew not; but the consternation and surprise was inexpressible among the savages: they were frightened to the last degree to hear such a dreadful noise, and see their men killed, and others hurt, but see nobody that did it; when, in the middle of their fright, Will Atkins and his other three let fly again among the thickest of them and in less than a minute the first three being loaded again gave them a third volley.

Had Will Atkins and his men retired immediately, as soon as they had fired, as they were ordered to do, or had the rest of the body been at hand, to have poured in their shot continually, the savages had been effectually routed; for the terror that was among them came principally from this, that they were killed by the gods with thunder and lightning, and could see nobody that hurt them; but Will Atkins, staying to load again, discovered the cheat: some of the savages who were at a distance spying them, came upon them behind and though Atkins and his men fired at them also, two or three times, and killed above twenty, retiring as fast as they could, yet they wounded Atkins himself, and killed one of his fellow Englishmen with their arrows, as they did afterwards one Spaniard, and one of the Indian slaves who came with the women. This slave was a most gallant fellow, and fought most desperately, killing five of them with his own hand, having no weapon but one of the armed staves and a hatchet.

Our men being thus hard laid at, Atkins wounded, and two other men killed, retreated to a rising ground in the wood; and the Spaniards, after firing three volleys upon them, retreated also; for their number was so great, and they were so desperate, that though above fifty of them were killed, and more than as many wounded, yet they came on in the teeth of our men, fearless of danger, and shot their arrows like a cloud; and it was observed that their wounded men, who were not quite disabled, were made outrageous, and fought like madmen.

When our men retreated, they left the Spaniard and the Englishman that were killed behind them; and the savages, when they came up to them, killed them over again in a wretched manner, breaking their arms, legs, and heads, with their clubs and wooden swords, like true savages; but finding our men were gone, they did not seem to pursue them, but drew themselves up in a ring, which is, it seems, their custom, and shouted twice, in token of their victory; after which, they had the mortification to see several of their wounded men fall, dying with the mere loss of blood.

The Spaniard governor having drawn his little body up together upon a rising ground, Atkins, though he was wounded, would have had them march and charge again all together at once; but the Spaniard replied, "Seignior Atkins, you see how their wounded men fight; let them alone till morning; all the wounded men will be stiff and sore with their wounds, and faint with the loss of blood; and so we shall have the fewer to engage."

This advice was good: but Will Atkins replied merrily, "That is true, *Seignior*, and so shall I too; and that is the reason I would go on while I am warm."

"Well, Seignior Atkins," says the Spaniard, "you have behaved gallantly, and done your part; we will fight for you if you cannot come on; but I think it best to stay till morning;" so they waited.

But as it was a clear moonlight night, and they found the savages in great disorder about their dead and wounded men, and a great noise and hurry among them where they lay, they afterwards resolved to fall upon them in the night; especially if they could come to give them but one volley before they were discovered, which they had a fair opportunity to do: for one of the Englishmen in whose quarter it was where the fight began, led them round between the woods and the sea-side westward, and then turning short south, they came so near where the thickest of them lay, that, before they were seen or heard, eight of them fired in upon them, and did dreadful execution upon them; in half a minute more, eight others fired after them, pouring in their small shot in such a quantity, that abundance were killed and wounded; and all this while they were not able to see who hurt them, or which way to fly.

The Spaniards charged again with the utmost expedition, and then divided themselves into three bodies, and resolved to fall in among them all together. They had in each body eight persons, that is to say, twenty-two men, and the two women, who, by the way, fought desperately. They divided the fire-arms equally in each party, as well as the halberts and staves. They would have had the women kept back, but they said they were resolved to die with their husbands. Having thus formed their little army, they marched out from among the trees, and came up to the teeth of the enemy, shouting and hallooing as loud as they could: the savages stood all together, but were in the utmost confusion, hearing the noise of our men shouting from three quarters together: they would have fought if they had seen us; for as soon as we came near enough to be seen, some arrows were shot, and poor old Friday was wounded, though not dangerously; but our men gave them no time, but, running up to them, fired among them three ways, and then fell in with the butt-ends of their muskets, their swords, armed staves, and hatchets, and laid about them so well, that, in a word, they set up a dismal screaming and howling, flying to save their lives which way soever they could.

Our men were tired with the execution, and killed or mortally wounded in the two fights about one hundred and eighty of them; the rest, being frightened out of their wits, scoured through the woods and over the hills, with all the speed fear and nimble feet could help them to; and as we did not trouble ourselves much to pursue them, they got all together to the sea-side where they landed, and where their canoes lay. But their disaster was not at an end yet; for it blew a terrible storm of wind that evening from the sea, so that it was impossible for them to go off; nay, the storm continuing all night, when the tide came up, their canoes were most of them driven by the surge of the sea so high upon the shore that it required infinite toil to get them off; and some of them were even dashed to pieces against the beach, or against one another.

Our men, though glad of their victory, yet got little rest that night; but having refreshed themselves as well as they could, they resolved to march to that part of the island where the savages were fled, and see what posture they were in. This necessarily led them over the place where the fight had been, and where they found several of the poor creatures not quite dead, and yet past recovering life.

At length, they came in view of the place where the more miserable remains of the savages' army lay, where there appeared about a hundred still: their posture was generally sitting upon the ground, with their knees up towards their mouth, and the head put between the two hands, leaning down upon the knees.

When our men came within two musket-shots of them, the Spaniard governor ordered two muskets to be fired, without ball, to alarm them: this he did, that by their countenance he might know what to expect, whether they were still in heart to fight, or were so heartily beaten as to be dispirited and discouraged, and so he might manage accordingly. This stratagem took; for as soon as the savages heard the first gun, and saw the flash of the second, they started up upon their feet in the greatest consternation imaginable; and as our men advanced swiftly towards them, they all ran screaming and yelling away, with a kind of howling noise, which our men did not understand, and had never heard before; and thus they ran up the hills into the country.

At first our men had much rather the weather had been calm, and they had all gone away to sea; but they did not then consider that this might probably have been the occasion of their coming again in such multitudes as not to be resisted, or, at least, to come so many and so often, as would quite desolate the island, and starve them. Will Atkins, therefore, who, notwithstanding his wound, kept always with them, proved the best counsellor in this case: his advice was, to take the advantage that offered, and step in between them and their boats, and so deprive them of the capacity of ever returning any more to plague the island.

They consulted long about this; and some were against it for fear of making the wretches fly to the woods and live there desperate, and so they should have them to hunt like wild beasts, be afraid to stir out about their business, and have their plantations continually rifled, all their tame goats destroyed, and, in short, be reduced to a life of continual distress.

Will Atkins told them they had better have to do with a hundred men than with a hundred nations: that as they must destroy their boats, so they must destroy the men, or be all of them destroyed themselves. In a word, he showed them the necessity of it so plainly, that they all came into it; so they went to work immediately with the boats, and getting some dry wood together from an old tree, they tried to set some of them on fire, but they were so wet that they would not burn; however, the fire so burned the upper part, that it soon made them unfit for swimming in the sea as boats. When the Indians saw what they were about, some of them came running out of the woods, and coming as near as they could to our men, kneeled down and cried, "Oa, Oa, Waramoka," and some other words of their language, which none of the others understood anything of; but as they made pitiful gestures and strange noises, it was easy to understand they begged to have their boats spared, and that they would be gone, and never come there again.

But our men were now satisfied that they had no way to preserve themselves, or to save their colony, but effectually to prevent any of these people from ever going home again: depending upon this, that if even so much as one of them got back into their country to tell the story, the colony was undone; so that, letting them know that they should not have any mercy, they fell to work with their canoes, and destroyed every one that the storm had not destroyed before; at the sight of which the savages raised a hideous cry in the woods, which our people heard plain enough, after which they ran about the island like distracted men; so that, in a word, our men did not really know, at first, what to do with them.

Nor did the Spaniards, with all their prudence, consider that while they made those people thus desperate, they ought to have kept a good guard at the same time upon their plantations; for though it is true they had driven away their cattle, and the Indians did not find out their main retreat, I mean my old castle at the hill, nor the cave in the valley, yet they found out my plantation at the bower, and pulled it all to pieces, and all the fences and planting about it; trod all the corn under foot, tore up the vines and grapes, being just then almost ripe, and did our men an inestimable damage, though to themselves not one farthing's worth of service.

Though our men were able to fight them upon all occasions, yet they were in no condition to pursue them, or hunt them up and down: for as they were too nimble of foot for our men when they found them single, they durst not go abroad single, for fear of being surrounded with their numbers. The best was, they had no weapons; for though they had bows, they had no arrows left, nor any materials to make any; nor had they any edge-tool or weapon among them.

It was some while before any of them could be taken; but being weak and half-starved, one of them was at last surprised and made a prisoner. He was sullen at first, and would neither eat nor drink; but finding himself kindly used, and victuals given to him, and no violence offered him, he at last grew tractable and came to himself. They brought old Friday to him, who talked often with him, and told him how kind the others would be to them all; that they would not only save their lives, but give them part of the island to live in, provided they would give satisfaction that they would keep in their own bounds, and not come beyond it to injure or prejudice others; and that they should have corn given them to plant and make it grow for their bread, and some bread given them for their present subsistence: and old Friday bade the fellow go and talk with the rest of his countrymen, and see what they said to it; assuring them that, if they did not agree immediately, they should be all destroyed.

The poor wretches, thoroughly humbled, and reduced in number to about thirty-seven, closed with the proposal at the first offer, and begged to have some food given them; upon which, twelve Spaniards and two Englishmen, well armed, with three Indian slaves and old Friday, marched to the place where they were. The three Indian slaves carried them a large quantity of bread, some rice boiled up to cakes and dried in the sun, and three live goats; and they were ordered to go to the side of a hill, where they sat down, ate their provisions very thankfully, and were the most faithful fellows to their words that could be thought of; for, except when they came to beg victuals and directions, they never came out of their bounds; and there they lived when I came to the island, and I went to see them.

They had taught them both to plant corn, make bread, breed tame goats, and milk them: they wanted nothing but wives, and would soon have been a nation. They were confined to a neck of land, surrounded with high rocks behind them, and lying plain towards the sea before them, on the south-east corner of the island. They had land enough, and it was very good and fruitful; about a mile and a half broad, and three or four miles in length.

Our men taught them to make wooden spades, such as I made for myself, and gave among them twelve hatchets and three or four knives; and there they lived, the most subjected, innocent creatures that ever were heard of.

After this, the colony enjoyed a perfect tranquillity, with respect to the savages, till I came to revisit them, which was about two years after; not but that, now and then, some canoes of savages came on shore for their triumphal, unnatural feasts; but as they were of several nations, and perhaps had never heard of those that came before, or the reason of it, they did not make any search or inquiry after their countrymen; and if they had it would have been very hard to have found them out.

Having thus given a view of the state of things as I found them, I must relate the heads of what I did for these people, and the condition in which I left them.

We appointed a day to dine all together; and, indeed, we made a splendid feast. I caused the ship's cook and his mate to come on shore and dress our dinner, and the old cook's mate we had on shore assisted. We brought on shore six pieces of good beef, and four pieces of pork, out of the ship's provisions, with our punchbowl, and materials to fill it; and, in particular, I gave them ten bottles of French claret, and ten bottles of English beer: things that neither the Spaniards nor the English had tasted for many years, and which it may be supposed they were very glad of. The Spaniards added to our feast five whole kids, which the cooks roasted; and three of them were sent, covered up close, on board the ship to the seamen, that they might feast on fresh meat from on shore, as we did with their salt meat from on board.

After this feast, at which we were very innocently merry, I brought my cargo of goods; wherein, that there might be no dispute about dividing, I showed them that there was a sufficiency for them all, desiring that they might all take an equal quantity of the goods that were for wearing—that is to say, equal when made up. As, first I distributed linen sufficient to make every one of them four shirts, and, at the Spaniard's request, afterwards made them up six: these were exceeding comfortable to them, having been what they had long since forgot the use of. I allotted the thin English stuffs, which I mentioned before, to make every one a light coat, like a frock, which I judged fittest for the heat of the season, cool and loose; and ordered that whenever they decayed, they should make more, as they thought fit; the like for pumps, shoes, stockings, hats, etc.

I cannot express what pleasure and satisfaction sat upon the countenances of all these poor men, when they saw the care I had taken of them, and how well I had furnished them. They told me I was a father to them; and that having such a correspondent as I was in so remote a part of the world, it would make them forget that they were left in a desolate place; and they all voluntarily engaged to me not to leave the place without my consent.

Then I presented to them the people I had brought with me, particularly the tailor, the smith, and the two carpenters, all of them most necessary people; but, above all, my general artificer, than whom they could not name anything that was more useful: and the tailor, to show his concern for them, went to work immediately, and, with my leave, made them, every one, a shirt, the first thing he did; and, what was still more, he taught the women not only how to sew and stitch, and use the needle, but made them assist to make the shirts for their husbands, and for all the rest.

As to the carpenters, I scarce need mention useful they were; for they took to pieces all my clumsy, unhandy things, and made clever, convenient tables, stools, bedsteads, cupboards, lockers, shelves, and everything they wanted of that kind. But to let them see how nature made artificers at first, I carried the carpenters to see Will Atkins' basket-house, as I called it; and they both owned they never saw an instance of such natural ingenuity before, nor anything so regular and so handily built, at least of its kind; and one of them, when he saw it, after musing a good while, turning about to me, "I am sure," says he, "that man has no need of us; you need do nothing but give him tools."

Then I brought them out all my store of tools, and gave every man a digging spade, a shovel, and a rake, for we had no harrows or plough; and to every separate place a pickaxe, a crow, a broad axe, and a saw: always appointing, that as often as any were broken or worn out, they should be supplied, without grudging, out of the general stores that I left behind. Nails, staples, hinges, hammers, chisels, knives, scissors, and all sorts of iron-work, they bad without reserve, as they required; for no man would take more than he wanted, and he must be a fool that would waste or spoil them on any account whatever; and for the use of the smith, I left two tons of unwrought iron for a supply.

My magazine of powder and arms which I brought them was such, even to profusion, that they could not but rejoice at them; for now they could march as I used to do, with a musket upon each shoulder, if there was occasion; and were able to fight a thousand savages, if they had but some little advantages of situation, which also they could not miss, if they had occasion.

I carried on shore with me the young man whose mother was starved to death, and the maid also; she was a sober, well educated, religious young woman, and behaved so inoffensively that everyone gave her a good word; she had, indeed, an unhappy life with us, there being no woman in the ship but herself, but she bore it with patience. After a while, seeing things so well ordered, and in so fine a way of thriving upon my island, and considering that they had neither business nor acquaintance in the East Indies, or reason for taking so long a voyage, both of them came to me, and desired I would give them leave to remain on the island, and be entered among my family, as they called it. I agreed to this readily; and they had a little plot of ground allotted to them, where they had three tents or houses set up, surrounded with a basket-work, pallisadoed like Atkins's, adjoining to his plantation.

Their tents were contrived so that they had each of them a room apart to lodge in, and a middle tent like a great storehouse, to lay their goods in, and to eat and drink in. And now the other two Englishmen removed their habitation to the same place; and so the island was divided into three colonies, and no more, *viz.*, the Spaniards, with old Friday and the first servants, at my old habitation under the hill, which was, in a word, the capital city, and where they had so enlarged and extended their works, as well under as on the outside of the hill, that they lived, though perfectly concealed, yet full at large.

Never was there such a little city in a wood, and so hid, in any part of the world; for I verily believe that a thousand men might have ranged the island a month, and, if they had not known there was such a thing, and looked on purpose for it, they would not have found it; for the trees stood so thick and so close, and grew so fast woven one into another, that nothing but cutting them down first could discover the place, except the only two narrow entrances where they went in and out could be found, which was not very easy; one of them was close down at the water's edge, on the side of the creek, and it was afterwards above two hundred yards to the place: and the other was up a ladder at twice, as I have already described it; and they had also a large wood, thickly planted, on the top of the hill, containing above an acre, which grew apace, and concealed the place from all discovery there, with only one narrow place between two trees, not easily to be discovered, to enter on that side.

The only colony was that of Will Atkins, where there were four families of Englishmen, I mean those I had left there, with their wives and children: three savages that were slaves; the widow and the children of the Englishman that was killed; the young man and the maid; and, by the way, we made a wife of her before we went away. There was also the two carpenters and the tailor, whom I brought with me for them; also the smith, who was a very necessary man to them, especially as a gunsmith, to take care of their arms; and my other man, whom I called Jack-of-all-trades, who was in himself as good almost as twenty men; for he was not only a very ingenious fellow, but a very merry fellow; and before I went away we married him to the honest maid that came with the youth in the ship I mentioned before.

Having thus brought the affairs of the island to a narrow compass, I was preparing to go on board the ship, when the young man I had taken out of the famished ship's company came to me, and told me he understood I had a clergyman with me, and that I had caused the Englishmen to be married to the savages; that he had a match, too, which he desired might be finished before I went, between two Christians, which he hoped would not be disagreeable to me.

I knew this must be the young woman who was his mother's servant, for there was no other Christian woman on the island: so I began to persuade him not to do anything of that kind rashly, or because he found himself in this solitary circumstance. I represented to him that he had some considerable substance in the world, and good friends, as I understood by himself, and the maid also: that the maid was not only poor, and a servant, but was unequal to him, she being six or seven and twenty years old; and he not above seventeen or eighteen; that he might very probably, with my assistance, make a remove from this wilderness, and come into his own country again; and that then it would be a thousand to one but he would repent his choice, and the dislike of that circumstance might be disadvantageous to both.

I was going to say more, but he interrupted me, smiling, and told me, with a great deal of modesty, that I mistook in my guesses,—that he had nothing of that kind in his thoughts; and he was very glad to hear that I had an intent of putting them in a way to see their own country again; and nothing should have made him think of staying there, but that the voyage I was going was so exceeding long and hazardous, and would carry him quite out of the reach of all his friends; that he had nothing to desire of me, but that I would settle him in some little property in the island where he was, give him a servant or two, and some few necessaries, and he would live here like a planter, waiting the good time when, if ever I returned to England, I would redeem him; and hoped I would not be unmindful of him when I came to England: that he would give me some letters to his friends in London, to let them know how good I had been to him, and in what part of the world, and what circumstances I had left him in: and he promised me that whenever I redeemed him, the plantation, and all the improvements he had made upon it, let the value be what it would, should be wholly mine.

His discourse was very prettily delivered, considering his youth, and was the more agreeable to me, because he told me positively the match was not for himself. I gave him all possible assurances that if I lived to come safe to England, I would deliver his letters, and do his business effectually; and that he might depend I should never forget the circumstances I had left him in; but still I was impatient to know who was the person to be married: upon which he told me it was my Jack-of-all-trades and his maid Susan. I was most agreeably surprised when he named the match; for, indeed, I thought it very suitable. The character of that man I have given already; and as for the maid, she was a very honest, modest, sober, and religious young woman; had a very good share of sense, was agreeable enough in her person, spoke very handsomely and to the purpose, always with decency and good manners, and was neither too backward to speak when requisite, nor impertinently forward when it was not her business; very handy and housewifely, and an excellent manager; fit, indeed, to have been governess to the whole island; and she knew very well how to behave in every respect.

The match being proposed in this manner, we married them the same day; and as I was father at the altar, and gave her away, so I gave her a portion; for I appointed her and her husband a handsome large space of ground for their plantation; and, indeed, this match, and the proposal the young gentleman made to give him a small property in the island, put me upon parcelling it out amongst them, that they might not quarrel afterwards about their situation.

This sharing out the land to them I left to Will Atkins, who was now grown a sober, grave, managing fellow, perfectly reformed, exceedingly pious and religious; and, as far as I may be allowed to speak positively in such a case, I verily believe he was a true penitent. He divided things so justly, and so much to every one's satisfaction, that they only desired one general writing under my hand for the whole, which I caused to be drawn up, and signed and sealed, setting out the bounds and situation of every man's plantation, and testifying that I gave them thereby severally a right to the whole possession and inheritance of the respective plantations or farms, with their improvements, to them and their heirs, reserving all the rest of the island as my own property, and a certain rent for every particular plantation after eleven years, if I, or any one from me, or in my name, came to demand it, producing an attested copy of the same writing.

As to the government and laws among them, I told them I was not capable of giving them better rules than they were able to give themselves; only I made them promise me to live in love and good neighbourhood with one another; and so I prepared to leave them.

Having now done with the island, I left them all in good circumstances, and in a nourishing condition, and went on board my ship again on the 6th of May, having been about twenty-five days among them.

The next day, giving them a salute of five guns at parting, we set sail, and arrived at the bay of All Saints in the Brazils, in about twenty-two days, meeting nothing remarkable in our passage but this: that about three days after we had sailed, being becalmed, and the current setting strong to the E.N.E., into a bay or gulf on the land side, we were driven something out of our course, and once or twice our men cried out, "Land to the eastward!" but whether it was the continent or islands we could not tell by any means. But the third day, towards evening, the sea smooth, and the weather calm, we saw the sea covered, towards the land, with something very black; not being able to discover what it was, till, after some time, our chief mate going up the main-shrouds a little way, and looking at them with a perspective, cried out it was an army. I could not imagine what he meant by an army, and thwarted him a little hastily. "Nay, sir," says he, "don't be angry, for 'tis an army, and a fleet too; for I believe there are a thousand canoes, and you may see them paddle along, for they are coming towards us apace."

I was a little surprised then, indeed, and so was my nephew, the captain; for he had heard such terrible stories of them in the island, and having never been in those seas before, that he could not tell what to think of it, but said, two or three times, we should all be devoured. I must confess, considering we were becalmed, and the current set strong towards the shore, I liked it the worse; however, I bade them not be afraid, but bring the ship to an anchor as soon as we came so near as to know that we must engage them.

The weather continued calm, and they came on apace towards us; so I gave orders to come to an anchor, and furl all our sails; as for the savages, I told them they had nothing to fear but fire, and therefore they should get their boats out, and fasten them, one close by the head, and the other by the stern, and man them both well, and wait the issue in that posture: this I did, that the men in the boats might be ready with sheets and buckets to put out any fire these savages might endeavour to fix to the outside of the ship.

In this posture we lay by for them, and in a little while they came up with us; but never was such a horrid sight seen by Christians: though my mate was much mistaken in his calculation of their number, yet when they came up we reckoned about a hundred and twenty-six; some of them had sixteen or seventeen men in them, and some more, and the least six or seven.

When they came nearer to us, they seemed to be struck with wonder and astonishment, as at a sight which doubtless they had never seen before; nor could they at first, as we afterwards understood, know what to make of us; they came boldly up, however, very near to us, and seemed to go about to row round us: but we called to our men in the boats not to let them come too near them. This very order brought us to an engagement with them, without our designing it; for five or six of the large canoes came so near our long-boat, that our men beckoned with their hands to keep them back, which they understood very well, and went back; but at their retreat about fifty arrows came on board us from those boats, and one of our men in the long-boat was very much wounded. However, I called to them not to fire by any means; but we handed down some deal boards into the boat, and the carpenter presently set up a kind of fence, like waste boards, to cover them from the arrows of the savages, if they should shoot again.

About half an hour afterwards they all came up in a body astern of us, and so near that we could easily discern what they were, though we could not tell their design; and I found they were some of my old friends, the same sort of savages that I had been used to engage with; and in a short time more they rowed a little farther out to sea, till they came directly broadside with, us, and then rowed down straight upon us, till they came so near that they could hear us speak: upon this I ordered all my men to keep close, lest they should shoot any more arrows, and made all our guns ready; but being so near as to be within hearing, I made Friday go out upon the deck, and call aloud to them in his language, to know what they meant; which accordingly he did.

Whether they understood him I knew not: but as soon as he had called to them, six, who were in the foremost or nighest boat to us, turned their canoes from us, and stooping down, showed us their naked backs. Whether this was a defiance or challenge we knew not, or whether it was done in mere contempt, or as a signal to the rest; but immediately Friday cried out they were going to shoot, and, unhappily for him, poor fellow, they let fly about three hundred of their arrows, and, to my inexpressible grief, killed poor Friday, no other man being in their sight. The poor fellow was shot with no less than three arrows, and about three more fell very near him; such unlucky marksmen they were!

I was so enraged at the loss of my old trusty servant and companion, that I immediately ordered five guns to be loaded with small shot, and four with great, and gave them such a broadside as they had never heard in their lives before. They were not above half a cable's length off when we fired; and our gunners took their aim so well, that three or four of their canoes were overset, as we had reason to believe, by one shot only.

The ill manners of turning up their bare backs to us gave us no great offence; neither did I know for certain whether that which would pass for the greatest contempt among us might be understood so by them or not; therefore, in return, I had only resolved to have fired four or five guns at them with powder only, which I knew would frighten them sufficiently: but when they shot at us directly with all the fury they were capable of, and especially as they had killed my poor Friday, whom I so entirely loved and valued, and who, indeed, so well deserved it, I thought myself not only justifiable before God and man, but would have been very glad if I could have overset every canoe there, and drowned every one of them.

I cannot tell how many we killed nor now many we wounded at this broadside, but sure such a fright and hurry never were seen amongst such a multitude. There were thirteen or fourteen of their canoes split and overset in all, and the men set a-swimming: the rest, frightened out of their wits, scoured away as fast as they could, taking but little care to save those whose boats were split or spoiled with our shot; so I suppose that many of them were lost; and our men took up one poor fellow swimming for his life, above an hour after they were gone.

The small shot from our cannon must needs kill and wound a great many; but, in short, we never knew how it went with them, for they fled so fast that, in three hours or thereabouts, we could not see above three or four straggling canoes, nor did we ever see the rest any more; for a breeze of wind springing up the same evening, we weighed, and set sail for the Brazils.

We went away with a fair wind for Brazil; and in about twelve days' time we made land, in the latitude of five degrees south of the line, being the north-easternmost land of all that part of America. We kept on S. by E., in sight of the shore four days, when we made Cape St. Augustine, and came to an anchor off the Bay of All Saints, the old place of my deliverance, whence came both my good and evil fate.

Never came ship to this port that had less business than I had, and yet it was with great difficulty that we were admitted to hold the least correspondence on shore: not my partner himself, who was alive, and made a great figure among them, not my two merchant-trustees, not the fame of my wonderful preservation in the island, could obtain me that favour; but my partner, remembering that I had given five hundred *moidores* to the prior of the monastery of the Augustines, and two hundred and seventy-two to the poor, went to the monastery, and obliged the prior that then was to go to the governor, and get leave for me personally, with the captain and one more, besides eight seamen, to come on shore, and no more; and this upon condition that we should not offer to bad any goods out of the ship, or to carry any person away without license. They were so strict with us as to landing any goods, that it was with extreme difficulty that I got on shore three bales, such as fine broadcloths, stuffs, and some linen, which I had brought as a present to my partner.

He was a very generous, open-hearted man; though, like me, he began with little at first; and though he knew not that I had the least design of giving him anything, he sent me on board a present of fresh provisions, wine, and sweetmeats, worth above thirty *moidores*, including some tobacco, and three or four fine medals of gold: but I was even with him in my present, which, as I have said, consisted of fine broadcloth, English stuff, lace, and fine Hollands; also, I delivered him about the value of one hundred pounds sterling, in the same goods, for other uses; and I obliged him to set up the sloop, which I had brought with me from England, for the use of my colony, in order to send the refreshments I intended to my plantation.

Accordingly, he got hands, and finished the sloop in a very few days, for she was already framed; and I gave the master of her such instructions that he could not miss the place; nor did he, as I had an account from my partner afterwards. I got him soon loaded with the small cargo I sent them; and one of our seamen, that had been on shore with me there, offered to go with the sloop and settle there, upon my letter to the governor Spaniard, to allot him a sufficient quantity of land for a plantation, and giving him some clothes and tools for his planting work, which he said he understood, having been an old planter at Maryland, and a *buccaneer* into the bargain. I encouraged the fellow by granting all he desired; and, as an addition, I gave him the savage whom we had taken prisoner of war, to be his slave, and ordered the governor Spaniard to give him his share of everything he wanted with the rest.

When we came to fit this man out, my old partner told me there was a certain very honest fellow, a Brazil planter of his acquaintance who had fallen into the displeasure of the Church. "I know not what the matter is with him," says he, "but, on my conscience, I think he is a heretic in his heart, and he has been obliged to conceal himself for fear of the Inquisition;" that he would be very glad of such an opportunity to make his escape, with his wife and two daughters; and if I would let them go to my island, and allot them a plantation, he would give them a small stock to begin with—for the officers of the Inquisition had seized all his effects and estate, and he had nothing left but a little household stuff, and two slaves; "and," adds he, "though I hate his principles, yet I would not have him fall into their hands, for he will be assuredly burned alive if he does."

I granted this presently, and joined my Englishman with them; and we concealed the man, and his wife and "daughters, on board our ship, till the sloop put out to go to sea; and then, having put all their goods on board some time before, we put them on board after she was out of the bay.

Our seaman was mightily pleased with this new partner; and their stocks, indeed, were much alike, rich in tools, in preparations, and a farm—but nothing to begin with, except as above: however, they carried over with them, what was worth all the rest, some materials for planting sugar-canes, with some plants of canes, which he understood very well.

Among the rest of the supplies sent to my tenants in the island, I sent them by the sloop three milch cows and five calves, about twenty-two hogs among them, three sows big with pig, two mares, and a stone-horse. For my Spaniards, according to my promise, I engaged three Portugal women to go, and recommended it to them to marry them, and use them kindly. I could have procured more women, but I remembered that the poor prosecuted man had two daughters, and that there were but five of the Spaniards that wanted—the rest had wives of their own, though in another country.

All this cargo arrived safe, and, as you may easily suppose, was very welcome to my old inhabitants, who were now, with this addition, between sixty and seventy people, besides little children, of which there were a great many. I found letters at London from them all, by way of Lisbon, when I came back to England, of which I shall also take some notice immediately.

I have now done with the island, and all manner of discourse about it: and whoever reads the rest of my memorandums would do well to turn his thoughts entirely from it. and expect to read of the follies of an old man, not warned by his own harms, much less by those of other men, to beware; not cooled by almost forty years' miseries and disappointments—not satisfied with prosperity beyond expectation—nor made cautious by afflictions and distress beyond imitation.

I had no more business to go to the East Indies than a man at full liberty has to go to the turnkey at Newgate, and desire him to lock him up among the prisoners there, and starve him. Had I taken a small vessel from England, and gone directly to the island; had I loaded her, as I did the other vessel, with all the necessaries for the plantation, and for my people; taken a patent from the government here to have secured my property, in subjection only to that of England; had I carried over cannon and ammunition, servants and people to plant, and taken possession of the place, fortified and strengthened it in the name of England, and increased it with people, as I might easily have done; had I then settled myself there, and sent the ship back laden with good rice, as I might also have done in six months' time, and ordered my friends to have fitted her out again for our supply,—had I done this, and stayed there myself, I had at least acted like a man of common sense: but I was possessed of a wandering spirit, and scorned all advantages.

I pleased myself with being the patron of the people I placed there, and doing for them in a kind of haughty, majestic way, like an old patriarchal monarch, providing for them as if I had been father of the whole family, as well as of the plantation: but I never so much as pretended to plant in the name of any government or nation, or to acknowledge any prince, or to call my people subjects to any one nation more than another: nay, I never so much as gave the place a name, but left it as I found it, belonging to nobody, and the people under no discipline or government but my own; who, though I had influence over them as a father and benefactor, had no authority or power to act or command one way or other, farther than voluntary consent moved them to comply: yet even this, had I stayed there, would have done well enough; but as I rambled from them, and came there no more, the last letters I had from any of them were by my partner's means, who afterwards sent another sloop to the place, and who sent me word

Though I had not the letter till I got to London, several years after it was written, that they went on but poorly, were discontent with their long stay there: that Will Atkins was dead,—that five of the Spaniards were come away,— and though they had not been much molested by the savages, yet they had had some skirmishes with them; and that they begged of him to write to me to think of the promise I had made to fetch them away, that they might see their country again before they died.

But I was gone a wild-goose chase, indeed! and they that will have any more of me, must be content to follow me into a new variety of follies, hardships, and wild adventures, wherein the justice of Providence may be duly observed; and we may see how easily Heaven can gorge us with our own desires, make the strongest of our wishes be our affliction, and punish us most severely with those very things which we think it would be our utmost happiness to be allowed in. Whether I had business or no business, away I went: it is no time now to enlarge upon the reason or absurdity of my own conduct, but to come to the history,—I was embarked for the voyage, end the voyage I went.

Our ship was on a trading voyage, and had a supercargo on board, who has to direct all her motions after she arrived at the Cape, only being limited to a certain number of days for stay, by charter-party, at the several ports she was to go to.

We stayed at the Cape no longer than was needful to take in fresh water, but made the best of our way for the coast of Coromandel. We were, indeed, informed that a French man-of-war, of fifty guns, and two large merchant ships, were gone for the Indies; and as I knew we were at war with France, I had some apprehensions of them; but they went their own way, and we heard no more of them.

We touched first at the Island of Madagascar, where, though the people are fierce and treacherous, and very well armed with lances and bows, which they use with inconceivable dexterity, yet we fared very well with them a while; they treated us very civilly; and for some trifles which we gave them, such as knives, scissors, &c, they brought us eleven good fat bullocks, of a middling size, which we took in, partly for fresh provisions for our present spending, and the rest to salt for the ship's use.

We were obliged to stay here some time after we had furnished ourselves with provisions; and I, who was always too curious to look into every nook of the world wherever I came, went on shore as often as I could. It was on the east side of the island that we went on shore one evening: and the people, who, by the way, are very numerous, came thronging about us, and stood gazing at a distance: but as we had traded freely with them, and had been kindly used, we thought ourselves in no danger; but when we saw the people, we cut three boughs out of a tree, and stuck them up at a distance from us; which, it seems, is a mark in that country, not only of a truce and friendship, but when it is accepted, the other set side up three poles or boughs, which is a signal that they accept the truce too; but then this tree is a known condition of the truce, that you are not to pass beyond their three poles towards them, nor they to come past your three poles, or boughs, towards you; so that you are perfectly secure within the three poles, and all the space between your poles and theirs is allowed like a market for free converse, traffic, and commerce.

When you go there, you must not carry your weapons with you; and if they come into that space, they stick up their javelins and lances all at the first poles, and come on unarmed; but if any violence is offered them, and the truce thereby broken, away they run to the poles, and lay hold of their weapons, and the truce is at an end.

It happened one evening, when we went on shore, that a greater number of their people came down than usual, but all very friendly and civil; and they brought several kinds of provisions, for which we satisfied them with such toys as we had; the women also brought us milk and roots, and several things very acceptable to us, and all was quiet; and we made us a little tent or hut of some boughs or trees, and lay on shore all night.

I know not what was the occasion, but I was not so well satisfied to lie on shore as the rest; and the boat riding at an anchor at about a stone's cast from the land, with two men in her to take care of her, I made one of them come on shore; and getting some boughs of trees to cover us also in the boat, I spread the sail on the bottom of the boat, and lay under the cover of the branches of the trees in the boat.

About two o'clock in the morning, we heard one of our men make a terrible noise on the shore, calling out, for God's sake, to bring the boat in, and come and help them, for they were all like to be murdered; at the same time, I heard the fire of five muskets, which was the number of guns they had, and that three times over. All this while I knew not what was the matter, but rousing immediately from sleep with the noise, I caused the boat to be thrust in, and resolved, with three fusees we had on board, to land and assist our men.

We got the boat soon to the shore, but our men were in too much haste: for being come to the shore, they plunged into the water, to get to the boat with all the expedition they could, being pursued by between three and four hundred men. Our men were but nine in all, and only five of them had fusees with them; the rest had pistols and swords, indeed, but they were of small use to them.

We took up seven of our men, and with difficulty enough too, three of them being wounded; and that which was still worse was, that while we stood in the boat to take our men in, we were in as much danger as they were in on shore; for they poured their arrows in upon us so thick that we were glad to barricade the side of the boat up with the benches, and two or three loose boards, which, to our great satisfaction, we had by mere accident in the boat. And yet, had it been daylight, they are, it seems, such exact marksmen, that if they could have seen but the least part of any of us, they would have been sure of us. We had, by the light of the moon, a little sight of them, as they stood pelting us from the shore with darts and arrows; and having got ready our fire-arms, we gave them a volley, that we could hear, by the cries of some of them, had wounded several; however, they stood thus in battle array on the shore till break of day, which we supposed was that they might see the better to take their aim at us.

In this condition we lay, and could not tell how to weigh our anchor, or set up our sail, because we must needs stand up in the boat, and they were as sure to hit us as we were to hit a bird in a tree with small shot. We made signals of distress to the ship, and though she rode a league off, yet my nephew, the captain, hearing our firing, and by glasses perceiving the posture we lay in, and that we fired towards the shore, pretty well understood us: and weighing anchor with all speed, he stood as near the shore as he durst with the ship, and then sent another boat, with ten hands in her, to assist us; but we called to them not to come too near, telling them what condition we were in; however, they stood in near to us and one of the men taking the end of a tow-line in his hand and keeping one boat between him and the enemy, so that they could not perfectly see him, swam on board us, and made fast the line to the boat: upon which we slipped out a little cable, and leaving our anchor behind, they towed us out of reach of the arrows; we all the while lying close behind the *barricado* we had made.

As soon as we were got from between the ship and the shore, that we could lay her side to the shore, she ran along just by them, and poured in a broadside among them, loaded with pieces of iron and lead, small bullets, and such stuff, besides the great shot, which made a terrible havoc among them.

When we were got on board, and out of danger, we had time to examine into the occasion of this fray; and, indeed, our supercargo, who had been often in those parts, put me upon it; for he said he was sure the inhabitants would not have touched us after we had made a truce, if we had not done something to provoke them to it. At length, it came out that an old woman, who had come to sell us some milk, had brought it within our poles, and a young woman with her, who also brought some roots or herbs; and while the old woman was selling us the milk, one of our men offered some rudeness to the wench that was with her, at which the old woman made a great noise: however, the seaman would not quit his prize, but carried her out of the old woman's sight among the trees, it being almost dark: the old woman went away without her, and as we may suppose, made an outcry among the people she came from; who, upon notice, raised this great army upon us in three or four hours, and it was great odds but we had all been destroyed.

One of our men was killed with a lance thrown at him just at the beginning of the attack, as he sallied out of the tent they had made; the rest came off free, all but the fellow who was the occasion of all the mischief, who paid dear enough for his black mistress, for we could not hear what became of him for a great while. We lay upon the shore two days after, though the wind presented, and make signals for him, and made our boat sail up shore and down shore several leagues, but in vain, so we were obliged to give him over; and if he alone had suffered for it, the loss had been less.

I could not satisfy myself, however, without venturing on shore once more, to try if I could learn anything of him or them: it was the third night after the action that I had a great mind to learn what mischief we had done, and how the game stood on the Indians' side. I was careful to do it in the dark, lest we should be attacked again; but I ought, indeed, to have been sure that the men I went with had been under my command, before I engaged in a thing so hazardous and mischievous as I was brought into by it, without design.

We took twenty as stout fellows with us as any in the ship, besides the supercargo and myself, and we landed two hours before midnight, at the same place where the Indians stood drawn up in the evening before. I landed here, because my design, as I have said, was chiefly to see if they had quitted the field, and if they had left any marks behind them of the mischief we had done them: and I thought if we could surprise one or two of them, perhaps we might get our man again, by way of exchange.

We landed without any noise, and divided our men into two bodies, whereof the boatswain commanded one, and I the other. We neither saw nor heard anybody stir when we landed; and we marched up, one body at a distance from the other, to the place; but at first could see nothing, it being very dark; till by-and-by our boatswain, who led the first party, fell over a dead body. This made them halt a while, for knowing by the circumstances that they were at the place where the Indians had stood, they waited for my coming up there. We concluded to halt till the moon began to rise, which we knew would be in less than an hour, when we could easily discern the havoc we had made among them. We told thirty-two bodies upon the ground, whereof two were not quite dead; some had an arm, and some a leg shot off, and one his head: those that were wounded, we supposed, they had carried away.

When we had made, as I thought, a full discovery of all we could come to the knowledge of, I resolved on going on board; but the boatswain and his party sent me word that they were resolved to make a visit to the Indian town, where these dogs, as they called them, dwelt, and asked me to go along with them; and if they could find them, as they still fancied they should, they did not doubt of getting a good booty; and it might be they might find Tom Jeffry there: that was the man's name we had lost.

I positively refused, and rose up in order to go to the boat. One or two of the men began to importune me to go; and when I refused, began to grumble, and say they were not under my command, and they would go—in a word, they all left me but one, whom I persuaded to stay, and a boy left in the boat. So the supercargo and I, with the third man, went back to the boat, where we told them we would stay for them, and take care to take in as many of them as should be left; for I told them it was a mad thing they were going about, and supposed most of them would have the fate of Tom Jeffry.

They told me, like seamen, they would warrant it they would come again, and they would take care, &c.; so away they went, and though the attempt was desperate, and such as none but madmen would have gone about, yet, to give them their due, they went about it as warily as boldly: they were gallantly armed, for they had every man a fusee or musket, a bayonet, and a pistol; some of them had broad cutlasses, some of them had hangers, and the boatswain and two more had pole-axes: besides all which, they had among them thirteen hand grenades: bolder fellows, and better provided, never went about any wicked work in the world.

When they went out, their chief design was plunder, and they were in mighty hopes of finding gold there; but a circumstance which none of them were aware of set them on fire with revenge, and made devils of them all. When they came to the few Indian houses which they thought had been the town, which was not above half a mile off, they were under a great disappointment, for there were not above twelve or thirteen houses; and where the town was, or how big, they know not.

They consulted, therefore, what to do, and were some time before they could resolve; for if they fell upon these, they must cut all their throats, and it was ten to one but some of them might escape, it being in the night, though the moon was up; and if one escaped, he would run and raise all the town, so they should have a whole army upon them; again, on the other hand, if they went away and left these untouched, for the people were all asleep, they could not tell which way to look for the town: however, the last was the best advice, so they resolved to leave them, and look for the town as well as they could.

They went on for sometime, when three of them, who were a little before the rest, called aloud that they had found Tom Jeffry; they all ran up to the place, where they found the poor fellow hanging up naked by one arm, and his throat cut. There was an Indian house just by the tree, where they found sixteen or seventeen of the principal Indians, who had been concerned in the fray with us before, and two or three of them wounded with our shot; and our men found they were awake, and talking one to another in that house, but knew not their number.

The sight of their poor mangled comrade so enraged them, that they swore to one another they would be revenged, and that not an Indian that came into their hands should have any quarter; this barbarous resolution they carried into effect immediately, putting all the poor creatures to death that fell in their way, and setting fire to every hut in the village. Our men returned early the next morning without receiving any injury except that one had sprained his foot, and another had burned one of his hands.

The next day we set sail for the Gulf of Persia, and thence to the coast of Coromandel, only to touch at Surat; but the chief of the supercargo's design lay at the Bay of Bengal.

The first disaster that befell us was in the Gulf of Persia, where five of our men, venturing on shore on the Arabian side of the gulf, were surrounded and either killed or carried away into slavery; the rest of the boat's crew were not able to rescue them, and had but just time to get off their boat.

We were at this time in the road at Bengal; and being willing to see the place, I went on shore with the supercargo, in the ship's boat, to divert myself; and towards evening was preparing to go on board, when one of the men came to me, and told me he would not have me trouble myself to come down to the boat, for they had orders not to carry me on board any more. Anyone may guess what a surprise I was in at so insolent a message; and I asked the man, who bade him deliver that message to me? He told me the coxswain. I said no more to the fellow, but bade him let them know he had delivered his message, and that I had given him no answer to it.

I immediately went and found out the supercargo, and told him the story, adding, what I presently foresaw, that there would be a mutiny in the ship; and entreated him to go immediately on board the ship in an Indian boat, and acquaint the captain of it. But I might have spared this intelligence, for before I had spoken to him on shore, the matter was effected on board. The boatswain, the gunner, the carpenter, and all the inferior officers, as soon as I was gone off in the boat, came up, and desired to speak with the captain; and there the boatswain, making a long harangue, told the captain in a few words, that as I was now gone peaceably on shore, they were loath to use any violence with me, which, if I had not gone on shore, they would otherwise have done, to oblige me to have gone. They therefore thought fit to tell him, that as they shipped themselves to serve in the ship under his command, they would perform it well and faithfully; but if I would not quit the ship, or the captain oblige me to quit it, they would all leave, and sail no farther with him; and at that word all, he turned his face towards the mainmast, which was, it seems, the signal agreed on between them, at which, the seamen, being got together there, cried out, "One and all! one and all!"

My nephew, the captain, was a man of spirit, and of great presence of mind; and though he was surprised at the thing, yet he told them calmly that he would consider of the matter; but that he could do nothing in it till he had spoken to me. He used some arguments with them, to show the unreasonableness and injustice of the thing; but it was all in vain; they swore, and shook hands round before his face, that they would all go on shore, unless he would engage not to suffer me to come any more on board the ship.

This was hard upon him, who knew his obligation to me, and did not know how I might take it; so he began to talk smartly to them;

told them that I was a very considerable owner of the ship, and that, in justice, he could not put me out of my own house; that let them go into what ship they would, if ever they came to England again, it would cost them very dear; that the ship was mine, and that he could not put me out of it; and that he would rather lose the ship and the voyage too, than disoblige me so much; so they might do as they pleased. However, he would go on shore and talk with me, and invited the boatswain to go with him, and perhaps they might accommodate the matter with me. But they all rejected the proposal, and said they would have nothing to do with me any more; and if I came on board, they would all go on shore.

"Well," said the captain, "if you are all of this mind, let me go on shore and talk with him." So away he came to me with this account, a little after the message had been brought to me from the coxswain.

I was very glad to see my nephew, I must confess; for I was not without apprehensions that they would confine him by violence, set sail, and run away with the ship; and then I had been stripped naked in a remote country, having nothing to help myself. But they had not come to that length, it seems; and when my nephew told me what they had said to him, and how they had sworn and shook hands that they would, one and all, leave the ship, if I was suffered to come on board, I told him he should not be concerned at it at all, for I would stay on shore. I only desired he would take care and send me all my necessary things on shore, and leave me a sufficient sum of money, and I would find my way to England as well as I could.

This was a heavy piece of news to my nephew, but there was no way to help it; so, in short, he went on board the ship again, and satisfied the men that his uncle had yielded to their importunity, and had sent for his goods from on board the ship; so that the matter was over in a few hours, the men returned to their duty, and I began to consider what course I should steer.

I was now alone in the most remote part of the world, as I think I may call it, for I was near three thousand leagues by sea farther off from England, than I was at my island; only, it is true, I might travel here by land over the Great Mogul's country to Surat, might go from thence to Bassora by sea, up the Gulf of Persia, and take the way of the caravans, over the Desert of Arabia, to Aleppo and Scanderoon; thence by sea again to Italy, and so overland into France; and this put together, might at least be a full diameter of the globe or more.

I had another way before me, which was to wait for some English ships, which were coming to Bengal from Achin, on the Island of Sumatra, and get passage on board them for England. But as I came hither without any concern with the East-India Company, so it would be difficult to go hence without their license, unless with great favour of the captains of the ships, or the company's factors; and to both I was an titter stranger.

Here I had the mortification to see the ship set sail without me; however, my nephew left me two servants, or rather, one companion and one servant; the first was clerk to the purser, whom he engaged to go with me, and the other was his own servant. I took also a good lodging in the house of an Englishwoman, where several merchants lodged. Here I was handsomely enough entertained; and that I might not be said to run rashly upon anything, I stayed here above nine months, considering what course to take. I had some English goods with me of value, and a considerable sum of money; my nephew furnishing me with a thousand pieces-of-eight, and a letter of credit for more, if I had occasion, that I might not be straitened, whatever might happen.

I quickly disposed of my goods to advantage; and, as I originally intended, I bought here some very good diamonds, which, of all other things, were the most proper for me in my present circumstances, because I could always carry my whole estate about me.

After a long stay here, and many proposals made for my return to England, the English merchant who lodged with me, and whom I had contracted an intimate acquaintance with, came to me one morning: "Countryman," says he, "I have a project to communicate to you, which, as it suits, with my thoughts, may, for aught I know, suit with yours also, when you shall have thoroughly considered it. Here we are posted, you by accident, and I by choice, in a part of the world very remote from our own country; but it is in a country where, by us, who understand trade and business, a great deal of money is to be got. If you will put one thousand pounds to my one thousand pounds, we will hire a ship, the first we can get to our minds; you shall be captain, I'll be merchant, and we'll go a trading voyage to China; for what should we stand still for?"

I liked this proposal very well; and the more so because it seemed to be expressed with so much good will, and in so friendly a manner.

It was, however, some time before we could get a ship to our minds, and when we had got a vessel, it was not easy to get English sailors: that is to say, so many as were necessary to govern the voyage and manage the sailors which we should pick up there. After some time we got an English mate, a boatswain, and a gunner, a Dutch carpenter, and three foremast men. With these we found we could do well enough, having Indian seamen, such as they were, to make up.

We made the voyage to Achin, in the island of Sumatra, and thence to Siam, where we exchanged some of our wares for opium and arrack; we went up to Suskan, made a very good voyage, were eight months out, and returned to Bengal; and I was very well satisfied with my adventure.

I got so much money by my first adventure, and such an insight into the method of getting more, that had I been twenty years younger, I should have been tempted to have stayed here and sought no farther for making any fortune.

My friend, who was always upon the search for business, proposed another voyage to me among the Spice Islands, and to bring home a loading of cloves from the Manillas, or thereabouts; places, indeed, where the Dutch trade, but islands belonging partly to the Spaniards; though we went not so far, but to some other, where they have not the whole power, as they have at Batavia, Ceylon, etc.

We were not long in preparing for this voyage; the chief difficulty was in bringing me to come into it. However, at last, nothing else offering, and finding that really stirring about and trading, the profit being so great, had more pleasure in it, and more satisfaction to my mind, than sitting still, which, to me especially, was the unhappiest part of my life, I resolved on this voyage too, which we made very successfully, touching at Borneo, and several islands, and came home in about five months. We sold our spice, which was chiefly cloves and nutmegs, to the Persian merchants, who carried them away to the gulf; and making near five of one, we really got a great deal of money.

But, to be short with my speculations, a little while after this there came in a Dutch ship from Batavia. She was a coaster, not a European trader, of about two hundred tons burthen. The men, as they pretended, having been so sickly that the captain had not hands enough to go to sea with, he lay by at Bengal; and having, it seems, got money enough, or being willing, for other reasons, to go for Europe, he gave public notice he would sell his ship. This came to my ears before my new partner heard of it, and I had a great mind to buy it; so I went to him, and I told him of it. He considered awhile, for he was no rash man; but musing some time, he replied, "She is a little too big; but, however, we will have her."

Accordingly, we bought the ship, and agreeing with the master, we paid for her, and took possession. When we had done so, we resolved to engage the men, if we could, to join with those we had, for the pursuing our business; but, on a sudden, they having received not their wages, but their share of the money, as we afterwards learned, not one of them was to be found. We inquired much about them, and at length were told that they were all gone together by land to Agra, the city of the great Mogul's residence, and thence to travel to Surat, and go by the sea to the Gulf of Persia.

We picked up some English sailors here after this, and some Dutch; and now we resolved on a second voyage, for cloves, among the Philippine and Molucca Isles.

In this voyage, being by contrary winds obliged to beat up and down a great while in the Straits of Malacca, and among the islands, we were no sooner got clear of those difficult seas than we found our ship had sprung a leak, and we were not able, by all our industry, to find out where it was. This forced us to make some port, and my partner, who knew the country better than I did, directed the captain to put into the river of Cambodia. This river lies on the north side of the great bay or gulf which goes up to Siam. While we were here, and going often on shore for refreshment, there came to me one day an Englishman, a gunner's mate on board an English East India ship, which rode in the same river near the city of Cambodia. "Sir," says he, "you are a stranger to me, and I to you, but I have something to tell you that very nearly concerns you."

I looked steadfastly at him a good while, and thought at first I had known him, but I did not. "If it very nearly concerns me," said I, "and not yourself, what moves you to tell it to me?"

"I am moved," says he, "by the imminent danger you are in, and, for aught I see, you have no knowledge of it." He then went on to say, that we were supposed to be pirates; and that there were two large English and three Dutch ships lying up the river about live leagues, and that with the next tide they intended sending down all their large boats, and taking our vessel, and then hanging every one of us.

On hearing this, we immediately ordered the anchor to be got up; and though the tide was not quite down, yet a little land-breeze blowing, we stood out to sea. Before long, a seaman called out, that we were chased.

"Chased!" says I; "by what?"

"By five sloops, or boats," says the fellow, "full of men."

"Very well," said I, "then it is apparent there is something in it."

In the next place, I ordered all our men to be called up, and told them there was a design to seize the ship, and to take us for pirates, and asked them if they would stand by us, and by one another: the men answered cheerfully, one and all, that they would live and die with us. Then I asked the captain what way he thought best for us to manage a fight with them; for resist them I was resolved we would, and that to the last drop. He said readily, that the way was to keep them off with our great shot as long as we could, and then to fire at them with our small arms, to keep them from boarding us: but when neither of these would do any longer, we would retire to our close quarters; perhaps they had not materials to break open our bulk-heads, or get in upon us.

The gunner had, in the meantime, orders to bring two guns to bear fore and aft, out of the steerage, to clear the deck, and load them with musket-bullets and small pieces of old iron, and thus we made ready for fight; but all this while we kept out to sea, with wind enough, and could see the boats at a distance, being five large long boats, following us with all the sail they could make.

Two of these boats outsailed the rest, and endeavoured to come under our stern, so as to board us on our quarter; upon which, seeing they were resolute for mischief, and depended upon the strength that followed them, I ordered to bring the ship to, so that they lay upon our broadside; when immediately we fired five guns at them, one of which had been levelled so true as to carry away the stern of the hindermost boat, and bring them to the necessity of taking down their sail, and running all to the head of the boat, to keep her from sinking; but the others came up one after the other, but we succeeded in beating them off and disabling them all, for that they had to lay by to refit; we then crowded all the sail we could, and stood farther out to sea, and we found that they gave over their chase.

Being thus delivered from this danger, my partner told me he would put me in on the coast of Cochin China, intending afterwards to go to Macao. We sailed for a little port called Quinchang, where the fathers of the mission usually landed from Macao, and where no European ships ever put in, but did not come to it for five days. When I set my foot on shore, I resolved never to set one foot on board that unhappy vessel more. When we came on shore, the old pilot got us a lodging and a warehouse for our goods in that country.

The fair, or mart, usually kept in this place, had been over some time: however, we found that there were three or four *junks* in the river, and two ships from Japan, with goods which they had bought in China, and were not gone away, having some Japanese merchants on shore.

The first thing our old Portuguese pilot did for us was, to get us acquainted with three missionary Romish priests who were in the town. One of these was a Frenchman, whom they called Father Simon, who was courteous, easy in his manner, and very agreeable company; the other two were more reserved.

This French priest, Father Simon, was appointed to go up to Pekin, and waited only for another priest, who was ordered to come to him from Macao; and we scarce ever met together but he was inviting me to go the journey with him; and having, in course of time, disposed of our merchandise, and also the vessel to the Japanese merchant, I and my partner, with the old Portuguese pilot, set out with very good advantage, for we got leave to travel in the retinue of one of their mandarins.

He was respected as a king, surrounded always with his gentlemen, and attended in all his appearances with such pomp, that I saw little of him but at a distance. But this I observed, that there was not a horse in his retinue but that our carriers' packhorses in England seemed to me to look much better; though it was hard to judge rightly, for they were so covered with equipage, mantles, trappings, &c, that we could scarce see anything but their feet and their heads as they went along.

At length we arrived at Pekin. As for the Portuguese pilot, he being desirous to see the court, we bore his charges for his company, and to use him as an interpreter; indeed, this old man was most useful to us everywhere, for we had not been above a week at Pekin, when he came and told us there was a great caravan of Muscovite and Polish merchants in the city, preparing to set out on their journey by land to Muscovy, within four or five weeks, and he was sure we would take the opportunity to go with them, and leave him behind, to go back alone.

I confess I was greatly surprised with this good news. "How do you know this ?" said I: "are you sure it is true?"

"Yes," says he; "I met this morning in the street an old acquaintance of mine, an Armenian, who is among them. He came last from Astracan, is now going with the caravan to Moscow, and so down the River Wolga to Astracan."

"Well, *Seignior*," says I, "do not be uneasy about being left to go back alone; if this be a method for my return to England, it shall be your fault if you go back to Macao at all."

We then went to consult what was to be done; and we agreed that if our Portuguese pilot would go with us, we would bear his charges to Moscow, or to England, if he pleased; nor, indeed, were we to be esteemed over-generous in that either, if we had not rewarded him farther, the service he had done us being really worth more than that; for he had not only been a pilot to us at sea, but he had been like a broker for us on shore; and his procuring for us the Japan merchant was some hundreds of pounds in our pockets. So we consulted together about it, and being willing to gratify him, which was but doing him justice, and very willing also to have him with us besides, for he was a most necessary man on all occasions, we agreed to give him a quantity of coined gold, which, as I compute it, came to about one hundred and seventy-five pounds sterling, between us, and to bear all his charges, both for himself and horse, except only a horse to carry his goods. Having settled this, we called him to let him know what we had resolved.

I told him he had complained of our being willing to let him go back alone, and I was now about to tell him we were resolved he should not go back at all. That as we had resolved to go to Europe with the caravan, he also should go with us; and that we called him to know his mind. He shook his head, and said it was a long journey, and that he had no *pecune* to carry him thither, or to subsist himself when he came there. We told him we believed it was so, and therefore we had resolved to do something for him that should let him see how sensible we were of his services, and how agreeable he was to us; and then I told him what we had resolved to give him here, which he might lay out as we would do our own: and that as for his charges, if he would go with us we would set him safe on shore either in Muscovy or England, which he would, at our own charge, except only the carriage of his goods. He received the proposal like a man transported, and told us he would go with us over the whole world; and so we all prepared for our journey.

It was the beginning of February, our style, when we set out from Pekin. The company was very great, and, as near as I can remember, made between three and four hundred horse, and upwards of one hundred and twenty men, very well armed, and provided for all events; for as the eastern caravans are subject to be attacked by the Arabs, so are these by the Tartars; but they are not altogether so dangerous as the

Arabs, nor so barbarous when they prevail.

The company consisted of people of several nations; but there were above sixty of them merchants or inhabitants of Moscow, though some of them were Livonians; and to our particular satisfaction, five were Scots, who appeared also to be men of great experience in business, and of very good substance.

We travelled near a month still in the dominions of the Emperor of China, but lay for the most part in the villages, some of which were fortified, because of the incursions of the Tartars.

We wanted above two days' journey of the city of Naum, when messengers were sent express to every part of the road to tell all travellers and caravans to halt till they had a guard sent for them; for that an unusual body of Tartars, making ten thousand in all, had appeared in the way, about thirty miles beyond the city.

This was very bad news; however, it was carefully done of the governor, and we were very glad to hear we should have a guard. Accordingly, two days after, we had two hundred soldiers sent us from a garrison of the Chinese, on our left, and three hundred more from the city of Naum, and with these we advanced boldly; the three hundred soldiers from Naum marched in our front, the two hundred in our rear, and our men on each side of our camels, with our baggage, and the whole caravan in the centre; in this order, and well prepared for battle, we thought ourselves a match for the whole ten thousand Mogul Tartars, if they had appeared; but the next day, when they did appear, it was quite another thing.

It was early in the morning, when, marching from a well situated little town, called Changu, we had a river to pass, which we were obliged to ferry; and, had the Tartars had any intelligence, then had been the time to have attacked us, when the caravan being over, the rear guard was behind; but they did not appear there. About three hours after, when we were entered upon a desert of about fifteen or sixteen miles over, behold, by a cloud of dust they raised, we saw an enemy was at hand: and they were at hand indeed, for they came on upon the spur.

The Chinese, our guard in the front, who had talked so big the day before, began to stagger; and the soldiers frequently looked behind them, which is a certain sign in a soldier that he is just ready to run away. My old pilot was of my mind; and being near me, called out, "*Seignior Inglese,*" says he, "those fellows must be encouraged, or they will ruin us all; for if the Tartars come on they will never stand it."

"I am of your mind," said I; "but what must be done?"

"Done!" says he, "let fifty of our men advance, and flank them on each wing, and encourage them; and they will fight like brave fellows in brave company; but without this, they will every man turn his back."

Immediately, I rode up to our leader, and told him, who was exactly of our mind; and accordingly fifty of us marched to the right wing, and fifty to the left, and the rest made a line of rescue; and so we marched, leaving the last two hundred men to make a body by themselves, and to guard the camels; only that, if need were, they should send a hundred men to assist the last fifty.

In a word, the Tartars came on, and an innumerable company they were: how many we could not tell, but ten thousand, we thought, was the least; a party of them came on first and viewed our posture, traversing the ground in the front of our line: and, as we found them within gunshot, our leader ordered the two wings to advance swiftly, and give them a salvo on each wing with their shot, which was done; and they went off, I suppose, back, to give an account of the reception they were like to meet with; and, indeed, that salute cloyed their stomachs, for they immediately halted, stood awhile to consider of it, and wheeling off to the left, they gave over their design, and said no more to us for that time.

Two days after, we came to the city of Naum; we thanked the governor for his care of us, and collected to the value of a hundred crowns, or thereabouts, which we gave to the soldiers sent to guard us: and here we rested one day.

After this, we passed several great rivers, and two dreadful deserts; one of which we were sixteen days passing over, and which, as I said, was to be called no man's land; and, on the 13th of April, we came to the frontiers of the Muscovite dominions. I think the first town or fortress, whichever it may be called, that belonged to the Czar of Muscovy, was called Arguna, being on the west side of the River Arguna.

Some leagues to the north of this river, there are several considerable rivers, whose streams run as due north as the Yamour runs east, and these are all found to join their waters with the great River Tartarus, named so from the northernmost nations of the Mogul Tartars; who, as the Chinese say, were the first Tartars in the world; and who, as our geographers allege, are the Gog and Magog mentioned in sacred history. These rivers running all northward, as well as all the other rivers I am yet to speak of, make it evident that the northern ocean bounds the land also on that side; so that it does not seem rational in the least to think that the land can extend itself to join with America on that side, or that there is not a communication between the northern and eastern ocean: but of this I shall say no more; it was my observation at that time, and therefore I take notice of it in this place.

We now advanced from the River Arguna by easy and moderate journeys, and were very visibly obliged to the care the Czar of Muscovy has taken to have cities and towns built in as many places as it is possible to place them, where his soldiers keep garrison, something like the stationary soldiers placed by the Romans in the remotest countries of their empire; some of which I had read of were placed in Britain, for the security of commerce, and for the lodging travellers: and thus it was here; for wherever we came, though at these towns and stations the garrisons and governors were Russians and professed Christians, yet the inhabitants were mere pagans.

Our caravan rested three nights at the town called Nortriousky, in order to provide some horses, several having been lamed and jaded with the badness of the way and long march over the last desert.

From this city we had a frightful desert, which held us twenty-three days' march. "We furnished ourselves with some tents here, for the better accommodating ourselves in the night; and the leader of the caravan procured sixteen carriages or waggons of the country, for carrying our water or provisions; and these carriages were our defence, every night round our little camp: so that had the Tartars appeared, unless they had been very numerous indeed, they would not have been able to hurt us.

We may well be supposed to have wanted rest again after this long journey; for in this desert we neither saw house nor tree, and scarce a bush; though we saw abundance of the sable hunters, who are all Tartars of the Mogul Tartary, of which this country is a part; and they frequently attack small caravans, but we saw no numbers of them together.

After we had passed this desert, we came into a country pretty well inhabited; we found towns and castles, settled by the Czar of Muscovy, with garrisons of stationary soldiers, to protect the caravans, and defend the country against the Tartars, who would otherwise make it very dangerous travelling; and his *czarish* majesty has given such strict orders for the well guarding the caravans and merchants, that, if there are any Tartars heard of in the country, detachments of the garrison are always sent to see the travellers safe from station to station. And thus the governor of Adinskoy, whom I had an opportunity to make a visit to, by means of the Scots merchant, who was acquainted with him, offered us a guard of fifty men, if we thought there was any danger, to the next station.

I thought long before this, that as we came nearer to Europe, we should find the country better inhabited, and the people more civilized: but I found myself mistaken in both; for we had yet the nation of the Tongueses to pass through, where we saw the same tokens of paganism and barbarity.

If the Tartars had their Cham Chi-Thaungu for a whole village or country, these had idols in every hut and every cave: besides, they worship the stars, the sun, the water, the snow, and, in a word, everything they do not understand, and they understand but very little; so that every element, every uncommon thing, sets them sacrificing. I met with nothing peculiar myself in all this country, which I reckon was from the desert I spoke of last at least four hundred miles, half of it being another desert, which took us up twelve days' severe travelling, without house or tree; and we were obliged again to carry our own provisions, as well water as bread. After we were out of this desert, and had travelled two days, we came to Janezay, a Muscovite city or station on the great River Janezay, which, they told us there, parted Europe from Asia.

Here I observed ignorance and paganism still prevailed, except in the Muscovite garrisons; all the country between the River Oby and the River Janezay is as entirely pagan, and the people as barbarous, as the remotest of the Tartars; nay, as any nation, for aught I know, in Asia or America.

From this river to the great River Oby, we crossed a wild uncultivated country, barren of people and good management, otherwise it is in itself a most pleasant, fruitful, and agreeable country. What inhabitants we found in it are all pagans, except such as are sent among them from Russia: for this is the country—I mean on both sides the River Oby—whither the Muscovite criminals that are not put to death are banished, and from whence it is next to impossible they should ever get away.

I have nothing material to say of my particular affairs till I came to Tobolski, the capital city of Siberia, where I continued some time on the following account.

We had now been almost seven months on our journey, and winter began to come on apace; whereupon my partner and I called a

274

council about our particular affairs, in which we found it proper, as we were bound for England, and not for Moscow, to consider how to dispose of ourselves. They told us of sledges and reindeer to carry us over the snow in the winter time; and, indeed, they have such things that it would be incredible to relate the particulars of, by which means the Russians travel more in winter than they can in summer, as in these sledges they are able to run night and day; the snow, being frozen, is one universal covering to nature, by which the hills, vales, rivers, and lakes are all smooth and hard as a stone, and they run upon the surface, without any regard to what is underneath.

But I had no occasion to urge a winter journey of this kind; I was bound to England, not to Moscow, and my route lay two ways: either I must go on as the caravan went, till I came to Jaroslaw, and then go off west for Narva, and the Gulf of Finland, and so on to Dantzic, where I might possibly sell my China cargo to good advantage; or I must leave the caravan at a little town on the Dwina, from whence I had but six days by water to Archangel, and from thence might be sure of shipping either to England, Holland, or Hamburgh.

Now to go any of these journeys in the winter would have been preposterous; for as to Dantzic, the Baltic would have been frozen up, and I could not get passage; and to go by land in those countries was far less safe than among the Mogul Tartars; likewise, to go to Archangel in October, all the ships would be gone from thence, and even the merchants who dwell there in summer retire south to Moscow in the winter, when the ships are gone; so that I could have nothing but extremity of cold to encounter, with a scarcity of provisions, and must lie in an empty town all the winter; so that, upon the whole, I thought it much my better way to let the caravan go, and make provision to winter where I was, at Tobolski, in Siberia, in the latitude of about sixty degrees, where I was sure of three things to wear out a cold winter with, *viz.*, plenty of provisions, such as the country afforded, a warm house, with fuel enough, and excellent company.

I had been here eight months, and a dark, dreadful winter I thought it; the cold so intense that I could not so much as look abroad without being wrapped in furs, and a mask of fur before my face, or rather a hood, with only a hole for breath, and two for sight: the little daylight we had was, as we reckoned, for three months not above five hours a day, and six at most; only that the snow lying on the ground continually, and the weather being clear, it was never quite dark. Our horses were kept, or rather starved, under grounds; and as for our servants, whom we hired here to look after ourselves and horses, we had, every now and then, their fingers and toes to thaw and take care of, lest they should mortify and fall off.

It was now March, the days grown considerably longer, and the weather at least tolerable; so the other travellers began to prepare sledges to carry them over the snow, and to get things ready to be going; but my measures being fixed for Archangel, and not for Muscovy or the Baltic, I made no motion; knowing very well that the ships from the south do not set out for that part of the world till May or June, and that if I was there by the beginning of August, it would be as soon as any ships would be ready to go away; and therefore I made no haste to be gone, as others did: in a word, I saw all the travellers go away before me. It seems every year they go from thence to Muscovy for trade, to carry furs, and buy necessaries, which they bring back with them to furnish their shops: also others went on the same errand to Archangel; but then they all being to come back again above eight hundred miles, went out before me.

It was the beginning of June when I left this remote place; a city, I believe, little heard of in the world; and, indeed, it is so far out of the road of commerce, that I know not how it should be much talked of. We were now reduced to a very small caravan, having only thirty-two horses and camels. We had here the worst and the largest desert to pass over that we met with in our whole journey; I call it the worst, because the way was very deep in some places, and very uneven in others; the best we had to say for it was, that we thought we had no troops of Tartars or robbers to fear, and that they never came on this side the River Oby, or at least very seldom; but we found it otherwise.

We had just entered Europe, having passed the River Kama, which in these parts is the boundary between Europe and Asia, and the first city on the European side was called Soloy Kamskoi, which is as much as to say, the great city on the River Kama; and here we thought" to see some evident alteration in the people; but we were mistaken; for as we had a vast desert to pass, which is near seven hundred miles long in some places, but not above two hundred miles over where we passed it, so, till we came past that horrible place, we found very little difference between that country and the Mogul Tartary. The people are mostly pagans, and little better than the savages of America; their houses and towns full of idols, and their way of living wholly barbarous, except in the cities, and the villages near them, where they are Christians of the Greek Church.

A few days more we came to Veuslima upon the River Wirtzogda, and running into the Dwina. We were there, very happily, near the end of our travels by land, that river being navigable, in seven days' passage, to Archangel. From hence, we came to Lawrenskoy, the 3rd of July; and providing ourselves with two luggage boats, and a barge for our own convenience, we embarked the 7th, and arrived all safe at Archangel the 18th; having been a year, five months, and three days on the journey, including our stay of eight months at Tobolski. We were obliged to stay at this place six weeks for the arrival of the ships, and must have tarried longer, had not a Hamburgher come in above a month sooner than any of the English ships.

We then set sail from Archangel the 20th of August, the same year; and, after no extraordinary bad voyage, arrived safe in the Elbe the 18th of September.

To conclude, having stayed near four months in Hamburgh, I came thence by land to the Hague, where I embarked in the packet, and arrived in London the 10th of January, 1705, having been absent from England ten years and nine months. And here I resolved to prepare for a longer journey than all these, having lived a life of infinite variety seventy-two years, and learned sufficiently to know the value of retirement, and the blessings of ending my days in peace.

PART 3

Serious Reflections of Robinson Crusoe

ROBINSON CRUSOE'S PREFACE

As the design of everything is said to be first in the intention, and last in the execution, so I come now to acknowledge to my reader that the present work is not merely the product of the two first volumes, but the two first volumes may rather be called the product of this. The fable is always made for the moral, not the moral for the fable.

I have heard that the envious and ill-disposed part of the world have raised some objections against the two first volumes, on pretence, for want of a better reason, that (as they say) the story is feigned, that the names are borrowed, and that it is all a romance; that there never were any such man or place, or circumstances in any man's life; that it is all formed and embellished by invention to impose upon the world.

I, Robinson Crusoe, being at this time in perfect and sound mind and memory, thanks be to God therefore, do hereby declare their objection is an invention scandalous in design, and false in fact; and do affirm that the story, though allegorical, is also historical; and that it is the beautiful representation of a life of unexampled misfortunes, and of a variety not to be met with in the world, sincerely adapted to and intended for the common good of mankind, and designed at first, as it is now farther applied, to the most serious uses possible.

Farther, that there is a man alive, and well known too, the actions of whose life are the just subject of these volumes, and to whom all or most part of the story most directly alludes; this may be depended upon for truth, and to this I set my name.

The famous *History of Don Quixote*, a work which thousands read with pleasure, to one that knows the meaning of it, was an emblematic history of, and a just satire upon, the Duke de Medina Sidonia, a person very remarkable at that time in Spain. To those who knew the original, the figures were lively and easily discovered themselves, as they are also here, and the images were just; and therefore, when a malicious but foolish writer, in the abundance of his gall, spoke of the quixotism of R. Crusoe, as he called it, he showed, evidently, that he knew nothing of what he said; and perhaps will be a little startled when I shall tell him that what he meant for a satire was the greatest of panegyrics.

Without letting the reader into a nearer explication of the matter, I proceed to let him know, that the happy deductions I have employed myself to make, from all the circumstances of my story, will abundantly make him amends for his not having the emblem explained by the original; and that when in my observations and reflections of any kind in this volume I mention my solitudes and retirements, and allude to the circumstances of the former story, all those parts of the story are real facts in my history, whatever borrowed lights they may be repre- sented by. Thus the fright and fancies which succeeded the story of the print of a man's foot, and surprise of the old goat, and the thing rolling on my bed, and my jumping out in a fright, are all histories and real stories; as are likewise the dream of being taken by messengers, being arrested by officers, the manner of being driven on shore by the surge of the sea, the ship on fire, the description of starving, the story of my man Friday, and many more most material passages observed here, and on which any religious reflections are made, are all historical and true in fact. It is most real that I had a parrot and taught it to call me by my name; such a servant a savage, and afterwards a Christian, and that his name was called Friday, and that he was ravished from me by force, and died in the hands that took him, which I represent by being killed; this is all literally true, and should I enter into discoveries many alive can testify them. His other conduct and assistance to me also have just references in all their parts to the helps I had from that faithful savage in my real solitudes and disasters.

The story of the bear in the tree, and the fight with the wolves in the snow, is likewise matter of real history; and, in a word, the *Adven- tures of Robinson Crusoe* are one whole scheme of a real life of eight and twenty years, spent in the most wandering, desolate, and afflicting circumstances that ever man went through, and in which I have lived so long in a life of wonders, in continued storms, fought with the worst kind of savages and man-eaters; by unaccountable surprising in- cidents, fed by miracles greater than that of ravens; suffered all manner

279

of violences and oppressions, injurious reproaches, contempt of men, attacks of devils, corrections from Heaven, and oppositions on earth; have had innumerable ups and downs in matters of fortune, been in slavery worse than Turkish, escaped by an exquisite management, as that in the story of Xury, and the boat at Sallee; been taken up at sea in distress, raised again and depressed again, and that oftener perhaps in one man's life than ever was known before; shipwrecked often, though more by land than by sea. In a word, there is not a circumstance in the imaginary story but has its just allusion to a real story, and chimes part for part and step for step with the inimitable *Life of Robinson Crusoe.*

In like manner, when in these reflections I speak of the times and circumstances of particular actions done, or incidents which happened, in my solitude and island-life, an impartial reader will be so just to take it as it is, *viz.*, that it is spoken or intended of that part of the real story which the island-life is a just allusion to; and in this the story is not only illustrated, but the real part I think most justly approved. For example, in the latter part of this work called the *Vision*, I begin thus: "When I was in my island-kingdom I had abundance of strange notions of my seeing apparitions," &c. All these reflections are just history of a state of forced confinement, which in my real history is represented by a confined retreat in an island; and it is as reasonable to represent one kind of imprisonment by another, as it is to represent anything that really exists by that which exists not. The story of my fright with something on my bed was word for word a history of what happened, and indeed all those things received very little alteration, except what necessarily attends removing the scene from one place to another.

My observations upon solitude are the same; and I think I need say no more than that the same remark is to be made upon all the references made here to the transactions of the former volumes, and the reader is desired to allow for it as he goes on.

Besides all this, here is the just and only good end of all parable or allegoric history brought to pass, *viz.*, for moral and religious improvement. Here is invincible patience recommended under the worst of misery, indefatigable application and undaunted resolution under the greatest and most discouraging circumstances; I say, these are recommended as the only way to work through those miseries, and their success appears sufficient to support the most deadhearted creature in the world.

Had the common way of writing a man's private history been

taken, and I had given you the conduct or life of a man you knew, and whose misfortunes and infirmities perhaps you had sometimes unjustly triumphed over, all I could have said would have yielded no diversion, and perhaps scarce have obtained a reading, or at best no attention; the teacher, like a greater, having no honour in his own country. Facts that are formed to touch the mind must be done a great way off, and by somebody never heard of. Even the miracles of the blessed Saviour of the world suffered scorn and contempt, when it was reflected that they were done by the carpenter's son; one whose family and original they had a mean opinion of, and whose brothers and sisters were ordinary people like themselves.

There even yet remains a question whether the instruction of these things will take place, when you are supposing the scene, which is placed so far off, had its original so near home.

But I am far from being anxious about that, seeing, I am well assured, that if the obstinacy of our age should shut their ears against the just reflections made in this volume upon the transactions taken notice of in the former, there will come an age when the minds of men shall be more flexible, when the prejudices of their fathers shall have no place, and when the rules of virtue and religion, justly recommended, shall be more gratefully accepted than they may be now, that our children may rise up in judgment against their fathers, and one generation be edified by the same teaching which another generation had despised.

Rob. Crusoe.

INTRODUCTION

I must have made very little use of my solitary and wandering years if after such a scene of wonders, as my life may be justly called, I had nothing to say, and had made no observations which might be useful and instructing, as well as pleasant and diverting, to those that are to come after me.

CHAPTER ONE
OF SOLITUDE

How incapable to make us happy, and how unqualified to a Christian life.

I have frequently looked back, you may be sure, and that with different thoughts, upon the notions of a long tedious life of solitude, which I have represented to the world, and of which you must have formed some ideas, from the life of a man in an island. Sometimes I have wondered how it could be supported, especially for the first years, when the change was violent and imposed, and nature unacquainted with anything like it. Sometimes I have as much wondered why it should be any grievance or affliction, seeing upon the whole view of the stage of life which we act upon in this world it seems to me that life in general is, or ought to be, but one universal act of solitude; but I find it is natural to judge of happiness by its suiting or not suiting our own inclinations. Everything revolves in our minds by innumerable circular motions, all centring in ourselves. We judge of prosperity and of affliction, joy and sorrow, poverty, riches, and all the various scenes of life—I say, we judge of them by ourselves. Thither we bring them home, as meats touch the palate, by which we try them; the gay part of the world, or the heavy part; it is all one, they only call it pleasant or unpleasant, as they suit our taste.

The world, I say, is nothing to us but as it is more or less to our relish. All reflection is carried home, and our dear self is, in one respect, the end of living. Hence man may be properly said to be alone in the midst of the crowds and hurry of men and business. All the reflections which he makes are to himself; all that is pleasant he embraces for himself; all that is irksome and grievous is tasted but by his own palate.

What are the sorrows of other men to us, and what their joy? Something we may be touched indeed with by the power of sympathy, and a secret turn of the affections; but all the solid reflection is directed to ourselves. Our meditations are all solitude in perfection; our passions are all exercised in retirement; we love, we hate, we covet, we enjoy, all in privacy and solitude. All that we communicate of those things to any other is but for their assistance in the pursuit of our desires; the end is at home; the enjoyment, the contemplation, is all solitude and retirement; it is for ourselves we enjoy, and for ourselves we suffer.

What, then, is the silence of life? And how is it afflicting while a man has the voice of his soul to speak to God and to himself? That man can never want conversation who is company for himself, and he that cannot converse profitably with himself is not fit for any conversation at all. And yet there are many good reasons why a life of solitude, as solitude is now understood by the age, is not at all suited to the life of a Christian or of a wise man. Without inquiring, therefore, into the advantages of solitude, and how it is to be managed, I desire to be heard concerning what solitude really is; for I must confess I have different notions about it, far from those which are generally understood in the world, and far from all those notions upon which those people in the primitive times, and since that also, acted; who separated themselves into deserts and unfrequented places, or confined themselves to cells, monasteries, and the like, retired, as they call it, from the world. All which, I think, have nothing of the thing I call solitude in them, nor do they answer any of the true ends of solitude, much less those ends which are pretended to be sought after by those who have talked most of those retreats from the world.

As for confinement in an island, if the scene was placed there for this very end, it were not at all amiss. I must acknowledge there was confinement from the enjoyments of the world, and restraint from human society. But all that was no solitude; indeed no part of it was so, except that which, as in my story, I applied to the contemplation of sublime things, and that was but a very little, as my readers well know, compared to what a length of years my forced retreat lasted.

It is evident then that, as I see nothing but what is far from being retired in the forced retreat of an island, the thoughts being in no composure suitable to a retired condition—no, not for a great while; so I can affirm, that I enjoy much more solitude in the middle of the greatest collection of mankind in the world, I mean, at London, while I am writing this, than ever I could say I enjoyed in eight and twenty years' confinement to a desolate island.

I have heard of a man that, upon some extraordinary disgust which he took at the unsuitable conversation of some of his nearest relations, whose society he could not avoid, suddenly resolved never to speak any more. He kept his resolution most rigorously many years; not all the tears or entreaties of his friends—no, not of his wife and children—could prevail with him to break his silence. It seems it was their ill-behaviour to him, at first, that was the occasion of it; for they treated him with provoking language, which frequently put him into undecent passions, and urged him to rash replies; and he took this severe way to punish himself for being provoked, and to punish them for provoking him. But the severity was unjustifiable; it ruined his family, and broke up his house. His wife could not bear it, and after endeavouring, by all the ways possible, to alter his rigid silence, went first away from him, and afterwards away from herself, turning melancholy and distracted. His children separated, some one way and some another way; and only one daughter, who loved her father above all the rest, kept with him, tended him, talked to him by signs, and lived almost dumb like her father near twenty-nine years with him; till being very sick, and in a high fever, delirious as we call it, or light-headed, he broke his silence, not knowing when he did it, and spoke, though wildly at first. He recovered of the illness afterwards, and frequently talked with his daughter, but not much, and very seldom to anybody else.

Yet this man did not live a silent life with respect to himself; he read continually, and wrote down many excellent things, which deserved to have appeared in the world, and was often heard to pray to God in his solitudes very audibly and with great fervency; but the unjustice which his rash vow—if it was a vow—of silence was to his family, and the length he carried it, was so unjustifiable another way, that I cannot say his instructions could have much force in them.

Had he been a single man, had he wandered into a strange country or place where the circumstance of it had been no scandal, his vow of silence might have been as commendable and, as I think, much more than any of the primitive Christians' vows of solitude were, whose retreat into the wilderness, and giving themselves up to prayer and contemplation, shunning human society and the like, was so much esteemed by the primitive fathers; and from whence our religious houses and orders of religious people were first derived.

The Jews said John the Baptist had a devil because he affected solitude and retirement; and they took it from an old proverb they had in the world at that time, that "every solitary person must be an angel or a devil."

A man under a vow of perpetual silence, if but rigorously observed, would be, even on the Exchange of London, as perfectly retired from the world as a hermit in his cell, or a *solitaire* in the deserts of Arabia; and if he is able to observe it rigorously, may reap all the advantages of those solitudes without the unjustifiable part of such a life, and without the austerities of a life among brutes. For the soul of a man, under a due and regular conduct, is as capable of reserving itself, or separating itself from the rest of human society, in the midst of a throng, as it is when banished into a desolate island.

The truth is, that all those religious hermit-like solitudes, which men value themselves so much upon, are but an acknowledgment of the defect or imperfection of our resolutions, our incapacity to bind ourselves to needful restraints, or rigorously to observe the limitations we have vowed ourselves to observe. Or, take it thus, that the man first resolving that it would be his felicity to be entirely given up to conversing only with heaven and heavenly things, to be separated to prayer and good works, but being sensible how ill such a life will agree with flesh and blood, causes his soul to commit a rape upon his body, and to carry it by force, as it were, into a desert, or into a religious retirement, from whence it cannot return, and where it is impossible for it to have any converse with mankind, other than with such as are under the same vows and the same banishment. The folly of this is evident many ways.

I shall bring it home to the case in hand thus: Christians may, without doubt, come to enjoy all the desirable advantages of solitude by a strict retirement and exact government of their thoughts, without any of these formalities, rigours, and apparent mortifications, which I think I justly call a rape upon human nature, and consequently without the breach of Christian duties, which they necessarily carry with them, such as rejecting Christian communion, sacraments, ordinances, and the like.

There is no need of a wilderness to wander among wild beasts, no necessity of a cell on the top of a mountain, or a desolate island in the sea; if the mind be confined, if the soul be truly master of itself, all is safe; for it is certainly and effectually master of the body, and what signify retreats, especially a forced retreat as mine was? The anxiety of my circumstances there, I can assure you, was such for a time as was very unsuitable to heavenly meditations, and even when that was got over, the frequent alarms from the savages put the soul sometimes to such extremities of fear and horror, that all manner of temper was lost, and I was no more fit for religious exercises than a sick man is fit for labour.

Divine contemplations require a composure of soul, uninterrupted by any extraordinary motions or disorders of the passions; and this, I say, is much easier to be obtained and enjoyed in the ordinary course of life, than in monkish cells and forcible retreats.

The business is to get a retired soul, a frame of mind truly elevated above the world, and then we may be alone whenever we please, in the greatest apparent hurry of business or company. If the thoughts are free, and rightly unengaged, what imports the employment the body is engaged in? Does not the soul act by a differing agency, and is not the body the servant, nay, the slave of the soul? Has the body hands to act, or feet to walk, or tongue to speak, but by the agency of the understanding and will, which are the two deputies of the soul's power? Are not all the affections and all the passions, which so universally agitate, direct, and possess the body, are they not all seated in the soul? What have we to do then, more or less, but to get the soul into a superior direction and elevation? There is no need to prescribe the body to this or that situation; the hands, or feet, or tongue can no more disturb the retirement of the soul, than a man having money in his pocket can take it out, or pay it, or dispose of it by his hand, without his own knowledge.

It is the soul's being entangled by outward objects that interrupts its contemplation of Divine objects, which is the excuse for these solitudes, and makes the removing the body from those outward objects seemingly necessary; but what is there of religion in all this? For example, a vicious inclination removed from the object is still a vicious inclination, and contracts the same guilt as if the object were at hand; for if, as our Saviour says: *"He that looketh on a woman to lust after her"*— that is, to desire her unlawfully—has committed the adultery already, so it will be no inverting our Saviour's meaning to say that he that thinketh of a woman to desire her unlawfully has committed adultery with her already, though he has not looked on her, or has not seen her at that time. And how shall this thinking of her be removed by transporting the body? It must be removed by the change in the soul, by bringing the mind to be above the power or reach of the allurement, and to an absolute mastership over the wicked desire; otherwise the vicious desire remains, as the force remains in the gunpowder, and will exert itself whenever touched with the fire.

All motions to good or evil are in the soul. Outward objects are but second causes; and though, it is true, separating the man from the object is the way to make any act impossible to be committed, yet where the guilt does not lie in the act only, but in the intention or desire to commit it, that separation is nothing at all, and effects nothing at all. There may be as much adultery committed in a monastery, where a woman never comes, as in any other place, and perhaps is so. The abstaining from evil, therefore, depends not only and wholly upon limiting or confining the man's actions, but upon the man's limiting and confining his desires; seeing to desire to sin is to sin; and the fact which we would commit if we had opportunity is really committed, and must be answered for as such. What, then, is there of religion, I say, in forced retirements from the world, and vows of silence or solitude? They are all nothing. 'Tis a retired soul that alone is fit for contemplation, and it is the conquest of our desires to sin that is the only human preservative against sin.

It was a great while after I came into human society that I felt some regret at the loss of the solitary hours and retirements I had in the island; but when I came to reflect upon some ill-spent time, even in my solitudes, I found reason to see what I have said above—that a man may sin alone several ways, and find subject of repentance for his solitary crimes as well as he may in the midst of a populous city.

The excellency of any state of life consists in its freedom from crime; and it is evident to our experience that some society may be better adapted to a rectitude of life than a complete solitude and retirement. Some have said that next to no company, good company is best; but it is my opinion, that next to good company, no company is best; for as it is certain that no company is better than bad company, so 't is as certain that good company is much better than no company.

In solitude a man converses with himself, and as a wise man said, he is not always sure that he does not converse with his enemy; but he that is in good company is sure to be always among his friends.

The company of religious and good men is a constant restraint from evil, and an encouragement to a religious life. You have there the beauty of religion exemplified; you never want as well instruction in, as example for, all that is good; you have a contempt of evil things constantly recommended, and the affections moved to delight in what is good by hourly imitation. If we are alone we want all these, and are led right or led wrong, as the temper of the mind, which is sometimes too much the guide of our actions as well as thoughts, happens to be constituted at that time. Here we have no restraint upon our thoughts but from ourselves, no restraint upon our actions but from our own consciences, and nothing to assist us in our mortifications of our desires, or in directing our desires, but our own reflections, which, after all, may often err, often be prepossessed.

If you would retreat from the world, then be sure to retreat to good company, retreat to good books, and retreat to good thoughts; these will always assist one another, and always join to assist him that flies to them in his meditations, direct him to just reflections, and mutually encourage him against whatever may attack him from within him or without him; whereas to retreat from the world, as it is called, is to retreat from good men, who are our best friends. Besides, to retreat, as we call it, to an entire perfect solitude, is to retreat from the public worship of God, to forsake the assemblies, and, in a word, is unlawful, because it obliges us to abandon those things which we are commanded to do.

Solitude, therefore, as I understand by it, a retreat from human society, on a religious or philosophical account, is a mere cheat; it neither can answer the end it proposes, or qualify us for the duties of religion, which we are commanded to perform, and is therefore both irreligious in itself, and inconsistent with a Christian life many ways. Let the man that would reap the advantage of solitude, and that understands the meaning of the word, learn to retire into himself. Serious meditation is the essence of solitude; all the retreats into woods and deserts are short of this; and though a man that is perfectly master of this retirement may be a little in danger of quietism, that is to say, of an affectation of reservedness, yet it may be a slander upon him in the main, and he may make himself amends upon the world by the blessed calm of his soul, which they perhaps who appear more cheerful may have little of.

Retiring into deserts in the first days of religion, and into abbeys and monasteries since, what have they been, or what have they been able to do, towards purchasing the retirement I speak of? They have indeed been things to be reckoned among austerities and acts of mortification, and so far might be commendable; but I must insist upon it, that a retired soul is not affected with them any more than with the hurries of company and society. When the soul of a man is powerfully engaged in any particular subject, 't is like that of St. Paul, wrapt up, whether it be into the third heaven, or to any degree of lower exaltation. Such a man may well say with the apostle above, "Whether I was in the body, or out of the body, I cannot tell." It was in such a wrapt-up state, that I conceived what I call my vision of the angelical world, of which I have here subjoined a very little part.

Is it rational to believe, that a mind exalted so far above the state of things with which we ordinarily converse, should not be capable of a separation from them, which, in a word, is the utmost extent of solitude? Let such never afflict themselves that they cannot retreat from the world; let them learn to retreat in the world, and they shall enjoy a perfect solitude, as complete, to all intents and purposes, as if they were to live in the cupola of St. Paul's, or as if they were to live upon the top of Cheviot Hill in Northumberland.

They that cannot be retired in this manner must not only retire from the world, but out of the world, before they can arrive to any true solitude. Man is a creature so formed for society, that it may not only be said that it is not good for him to be alone, but 'tis really impossible he should be alone. We are so continually in need of one another, nay, in such absolute necessity of assistance from one another, that those who have pretended to give us the lives and manner of the *solitaires*, as they call them, who separated themselves from mankind, and wandered in the deserts of Arabia and Lybia, are frequently put to the trouble of bringing the angels down from heaven to do one drudgery or another for them, forming imaginary miracles to make the life of a true *solitaire* possible. Sometimes they have no bread, sometimes no water, for a long time together, and then a miracle is brought upon the stage, to make them live so long without food; at other times they have angels come to be their cooks, and bring them roast-meat; to be their physicians, to bring them physic, and the like.

If St. Hilary comes in his wanderings to the River Nile, an humble crocodile is brought to carry him over upon his back; though they do not tell us whether the crocodile asked him to ride, or he asked the crocodile, or by what means they came to be so familiar with one another. And what is all this to the retirement of the soul, with which it converses in heaven in the midst of infinite crowds of men, and to whom the nearest of other objects is nothing at all, any more than the objects of mountains and deserts, lions and leopards, and the like, were to those that banished themselves to Arabia?

Besides, in a state of life where circumstances are easy, and provision for the necessaries of life, which the best saint cannot support the want of, is quietly and plentifully made, has not the mind infinitely more room to withdraw from the world, than when at best it must wander for its daily food, though it were but the product of the field?

Let no man plead he wants retirement, that he loves solitude, but cannot enjoy it because of the embarrassment of the world; 't is all a delusion; if he loves it, if he desires it, he may have it when, where, and as often as he pleases, let his hurries, his labours, or his afflictions be what they will; it is not the want of an opportunity for solitude, but the want of a capacity of being solitary, that is the case in all the circumstances of life.

I knew a poor but good man, who, though he was a labourer, was a man of sense and religion, who, being hard at work with some other men removing a great quantity of earth to raise a bank against the side of a pond, was one day so out of himself, and wrapt up in a perfect application of his mind to a very serious subject, that the poor man drove himself and his wheelbarrow into the pond, and could not recover himself till help came to him. This man was certainly capable of a perfect solitude, and perhaps really enjoyed it, for, as I have often heard him say, he lived alone in the world:

(1) Had no family to embarrass his affections;

(2) his low circumstances placed him below the observation of the upper degrees of mankind;

(3) and his reserved meditations placed him above the wicked part, who were those in a sphere equal to himself, among whom, as he said, and is most true, it was very hard to find a sober man, much less a good man; so that he lived really alone in the world, applied himself to labour for his subsistence, had no other business with mankind but for necessaries of life, and conversed in heaven as effectually, and, I believe, every way as divinely, as St. Hilary did in the deserts of Lybia among the lions and crocodiles.

If this retirement, which they call solitude, consisted only of separating the person from the world—that is to say, from human society—it were itself a very mean thing, and would every way as well be supplied by removing from a place where a man is known to a place where he is not known, and there accustom himself to a retired life, making no new acquaintance, and only making the use of mankind which I have already spoken of, namely, for convenience and supply of necessary food; and I think of the two that such a man, or a man so retired, may have more opportunity to be an entire recluse, and may enjoy more real solitude than a man in a desert. For example:—

In the solitude I speak of, a man has no more to do for the necessaries of life than to receive them from the hands of those that are to furnish them, and pay them for so doing; whereas in the solitude of deserts and wandering lives, from whence all our monkish devotion springs, they had every day their food, such as it was, to seek, or the load of it to carry, and except where, as is said, they put Providence to the operation of a miracle to furnish it, they had frequently difficulties enough to sustain life; and if we may believe history, many of them were starved to death for mere hunger or thirst, and as often the latter as the former.

Those that had recourse to these solitudes merely as a mortification of their bodies, as I observed before, and delivering themselves from the temptations which society exposed them to, had more room for the pretence, indeed, than those who allege that they did it to give up themselves to prayer and meditation. The first might have some reason in nature for the fact, as men's tempers and constitutions might lead; some having an inordinate appetite to crime, some addicted by nature to one ill habit, some to another, though the Christian religion does not guide us to those methods of putting a force upon our bodies to subdue the violence of inordinate appetite. The blessed apostle St. Paul seems to have been in this circumstance when being assaulted with what is called in the text "*a thorn in the flesh;*" be it what it will that is meant there, it is not to my purpose, but he prayed to the Lord thrice; that was the first method the apostle took, and thereby set a pious example to all those who are assaulted by any temptation. He did not immediately fly to austerities and bodily modifications, separating himself from mankind, or flying into the desert to give himself up to fasting, and a retreat from the world, which is the object of all private snare, but he applied himself by serious prayer to Him who had taught us to pray, "*Lead us not into temptation.*" And the answer likewise is instructing in the case; he was not driven out as Nebuchadnezzar into the desert—he was not commanded to retire into the wilderness that he might be free from the temptation; nothing less; but the answer was, "*My grace is sufficient for thee*"—sufficient without the help of artificial mortification.

So that even in the case of these forcible mortifications they are not required, much less directed, for helps to meditation; for if meditation could not be practised beneficially, and to all the intents and purposes for which it wis ordained a duty, without flying from the face ol human society, the life of man would be very unhappy.

But doubtless the contrary is evident, and all the parts of a complete solitude are to be as effectually enjoyed, if we please, and sufficient grace assisting, even in the most populous cities, among the hurries of conversation and gallantry of a court, or the noise and business of a camp, as in the deserts of Arabia and Lybia, or in the desolate life of an uninhabited island.

CHAPTER TWO

AN ESSAY UPON HONESTY

When I first came home to my own country, and began to sit down and look back upon the past circumstances of my wandering state, as you will in charity suppose I could not but do very often, the very prosperity I enjoyed led me most naturally to reflect upon the particular steps by which I arrived to it. The condition I was in was very happy, speaking of human felicity; the former captivity I had suffered made my liberty sweeter to me; and to find myself jumped into easy circumstances at once, from a condition below the common rate of life, made it still sweeter.

One time as I was upon my inquiries into the happy concurrence of the causes which had brought the event of my prosperity to pass, as an effect, it occurred to my thoughts how much of it all depended, under the disposition of Providence, upon the principle of honesty which I met with in almost all the people whom it was my lot to be concerned with in my private and particular affairs; and I that had met with such extraordinary instances of the knavery and villainy of men's natures in other circumstances, could not but be something taken up with the miracles of honesty that I had met with among the several people I had had to do with, I mean, those whom I had more particularly to do with in the articles of my liberty, estate, or effects, which fell into their hands.

I began with my most trusty and faithful widow, the captain's wife with whom I first went to the coast of Africa, and to whom I entrusted £200, being the gain I had made in my first adventures to Guinea, as in the first book, appears.

She was left a widow, and in but indifferent circumstances; but when I sent to her so far off as the Brazils, where I was in such a condition as she might have reasonably believed I should never have been able to come myself, and if I had, might be in no condition to recover it of her, and having myself nothing to show under her hand for the trust, yet she was so just that she sent the full value of what I wrote for, being £100; and to show, as far as in her lay, her sincere honest concern for my good, put in among many necessary things which I did not write for, I say, put in two Bibles, besides other good books, for my reading and instruction, as she said afterwards, in Popish and heathen countries, where I might chance to fall. Honesty not only leads to discharge every debt and every trust to our neighbour, so far as it is justly to be demanded, but an honest man acknowledges himself debtor to all mankind, for so much good to be done for them, whether for soul or body, as Providence puts an opportunity into his hands to do. In order to discharge this debt, he studies continually for opportunity to do all the acts of kindness and beneficence that is possible for him to do; and though very few consider it, a man is not a completely honest man that does not do this.

Upon this consideration I question much whether a covetous, narrow, stingy man, as we call him, one who gives himself up to himself, as born for himself only, and who declines the advantages and opportunities of doing good, I mean extremely so—I say, I much question whether such a man can be an honest man; nay, I am satisfied he cannot be an honest man, for though he may pay every man his own, and be just, as he thinks it, to a farthing, yet this is part of the justice which, in the common phrase, is the greatest injustice. This is one meaning of that saying, *summum jus, summa injuria.*

To pay every man their own is the common law of honesty, but to do good to all mankind, as far as you are able, is the chancery law of honesty; and though, in common law or justice, as I call it, mankind can have no claim upon us if we do but just pay our debts, yet in heaven's chancery they will have relief against us, for they have a demand in equity of all the good to be done them that it is in our power to do, and this chancery court, or court of equity, is held in every man's breast—'tis a true court of conscience, and every man's conscience is a lord chancellor to him. If he has not performed, if he has not paid this debt, conscience wall decree him to pay it, on the penalty of declaring him a dishonest man, even in his own opinion; and if he still refuses to comply, will proceed by all the legal steps of a court of conscience process, till at last it will issue out a writ of rebellion against him, and proclaim him a rebel to nature and his own conscience.

But this is by the way, and is occasioned by the observations I have made of many people who think they are mighty honest if they pay their debts, and owe no man anything, as they call it; at the same time, like true misers, who lay up all for themselves, they think nothing of the debt of charity and beneficence which they owe to all mankind.

Rich men are their Maker's freeholders; they enjoy freely the estate He has given them possession of, with all the rents, profits, and emoluments, but charged with a fee-farm rent to the younger children of the family, namely, the poor; or if you will, you may call them God's copy-holders, paying a quit-rent to the lord of the manor, which quit-rent he has assigned for the use of the rest of mankind, to be paid in a constant discharge of all good offices, friendly, kind, and generous actions; and he that will not pay his rent cannot be an honest man, any more than he that would not pay his other just debts.

The Scripture concurs exactly with this notion of mine; the miser is called by the prophet Isaiah a vile person, one that works iniquity, and practises hypocrisy, and utters error before the Lord (Isaiah xxxii. 6). How does this appear? The very next words explain it. *"He makes empty the soul of the hungry, and he will cause the drink of the thirsty to fail."* But lest this should seem a strained text, let us read on, both before and after verse 5. "*The vile person shall no more be called liberal, nor the churl said to be bountiful.*" Here the opposite to a liberal man is called a vile person, and the opposite to a bountiful man is called a churl; and in the verse following, the same vile person, as opposed to the liberal man, is called a wicked man, and the liberal man is set up a pattern for us all, in opposition to the vile, churlish, • covetous wretch.—Vers. 7, 8. "*The instruments also of the churl are evil: he deviseth wicked devices to destroy the poor with lying words, even when the needy speaketh right; but the liberal deviseth liberal things, and by liberal things shall he stand.*"

In a word, I think my opinion justified by this text, that a churl, a morose, sour disposition, a covetous, avaricious, selfish-principled man, cannot be an honest man: he does not pay the common debt of mankind to one another, nor the fee-farm or quitrent of his estate to God, who is his great landlord or lord of the manor, and who has charged the debt upon him. I know the miser will laugh at this notion, but I speak my own opinion, let it go as far as reason will carry it.

I come back to the examples I was giving in my private case. As the widow was honest to me, so was my good Portuguese captain; and it is this man's original honesty that makes me speak of the honest man's debt to mankind. It was honesty, a generous honesty, that led the poor man to take me up at sea, which, if he had neglected, my boy Xury and I had perished together; it was no debt to me in particular, but a debt to mankind, that he paid in that action, and yet he could not have been an honest man without it. You will say, if he had gone away and left me, he had been barbarous and inhuman, and deserved to be left to perish himself in the like distress; but, I say, this is not all the case; custom and the nature of the thing leads us to say it would have been hard-hearted and inhuman, but conscience will tell any man that it was a debt, and he could not but be condemned by the court of conscience in his own breast if the had omitted it—nay, in the sight of Heaven he had tacitly killed us, and had been as guilty of our death as a murderer, for he that refuses to save a life thrown into his hands takes it away; and if there is a just retribution in a future state, if blood is at all required there, the blood of every man, woman, and child whom we could have saved, and did not, shall be reckoned to us at that day as spilt by our own hands; for leaving life in a posture in which it must inevitably perish, is without question causing it to perish, and will be called so then, by whatever gilded dressed-up words we may express and conceal it now.

But I go farther, for my good Portuguese went farther with me; he not only paid the debt he owed to Heaven in saving our lives, but he went farther—he took nothing of what I had, though, in the common right of the sea, it was all his due for salvage, as the sailors call it; but he gave me the value of everything, bought my boat, which he might have turned adrift, my boy Xury, who was not my slave by any right, or, if he had, became free from that time; and the life of Xury, which he had saved, as a servant, was his own, yet he bought everything of me for the full value, and took nothing of me, no, not for my passage.

Here was the liberal man devising liberal things, and the sequel made good the promissory text, for by these liberal things the honest liberal man might be truly said to stand. When I came to reward him at my coming to Lisbon to sell my plantation at Brazil, then he being poor and reduced, and not able to pay even what he owed me, I gave him a reward sufficient to make his circumstances easy all his life after.

The bounty of this man to me, when first he took me up out of the sea, was the highest and most complete act of honesty—a generous honesty, laying hold of an opportunity to do good to an object offered by the providence of Heaven, and thereby acknowledging the debt he had to pay to his Maker in the persons of His most distressed creatures.

And here also let me remind my readers of what, perhaps, they seldom much regard; it is not only a gift from Heaven to us to be put in a condition of doing good, but "'tis a gift, and a favour from Heaven, to have an opportunity of doing the good we are in a condition to do, and we ought to close with the opportunity, as a particular gift from above, and be as thankful for it, I say, as thankful for the occasion of doing good, as for the ability.

I might mention here the honesty of my fellow-planter in the Brazils, and of the two merchants and their sons, by whose integrity I had my share in the plantation preserved and taken care of; as also the honesty of the public treasurer for the church there, and the like; but I am carried off in my thoughts, to enlarge upon this noble principle, from the two examples I have already mentioned, *viz.*, the Guinea captain's widow and the Portuguese; and this in particular, because, since I came to England to reside, I have met with abundance of disputes about honesty, especially in cases where honest men come to be unhappy men, when they fall into such circumstances as they cannot be honest, or rather, cannot show the principle of honesty which is really at the bottom of all their actions, and which, but for those circumstances which entirely disable them, would certainly show itself in every branch of their lives; such men I have too often seen branded for knaves by those who, if they come into the same condition, would perhaps do the same things, or worse than they may have done.

Both my widow and my Portuguese captain fell into low circumstances, so that they could not make good to me my money that was in their hands; and yet both of them showed to me that they had not only a principle of justice, but of generous honesty too, when the opportunity was put into their hands to do so.

This put me upon inquiring and debating with myself what this subtle and imperceptible thing called honesty is, and how it might be described, setting down my thoughts at several times, as objects presented, that posterity, if they think them worth while, may find them both useful and diverting. And first, I thought it not improper to lay down the conditions upon which I am to enter upon that description, that I may not be mistaken, but be allowed to explain what I mean by honesty, before I undertake to enter upon any discourses or observations about it.

And to come directly to it, for I would make as few preambles as possible, I shall crave the liberty, in all the following discourse, to take the term honesty, as I think all English expressions ought to be taken, namely, honestly, in the common acceptation of the word, the general vulgar sense of it, without any circumlocutions or double-entendres whatsoever; for I desire to speak plainly and sincerely. Indeed, as I have no talent at hard words, so I have no great veneration for etymologies, especially in English, but since I am treating of honesty, I desire to do it, as I say above, honestly, according to the genuine signification of the thing.

Neither shall I examine whether honesty be a natural or an acquired virtue—whether a habit or a quality—whether inherent or accidental: all the philosophical part of it I choose to omit.

Neither shall I examine it as it extends to spirituals and looks towards religion; if we inquire about honesty towards God, I readily allow all men are born knaves, villains, thieves, and murderers, and nothing but the restraining power of Providence withholds us all from showing ourselves such on all occasions.

No man can be just to his Maker; if he could, all our creeds and confessions, litanies and supplications, were ridiculous contradictions and impertinences, inconsistent with themselves, and with the whole tenor of human life.

In all the ensuing discourse, therefore, I am to be understood of honesty, as it regards mankind among themselves, as it looks from one man to another, in those necessary parts of man's life, his conversation and negotiation, trusts, friendships, and all the incidents of human affairs.

The plainness I profess, both in style and method, seems to me to have some suitable analogy to the subject, honesty, and therefore is absolutely necessary to be strictly followed; and I must own, I am the better reconciled, on this very account, to a natural infirmity of homely plain writing, in that I think the plainness of expression, which I am condemned to, will give no disadvantage to my subject, since honesty shows the most beautiful, and the more like honesty, when artifice is dismissed, and she is honestly seen by her own light only; likewise the same sincerity is required in the reader, and he that reads this essay without honesty, will never understand it right; she must, I say, be viewed by her own light. If prejudice, partiality, or private opinions stand in the way, the man's a reading knave, he is not honest to the subject; and upon such an one all the labour is lost—this work is of no use to him, and, by my consent, the bookseller should give him his money again.

If any man, from his private ill-nature, takes exceptions at me, poor, wild, wicked Robinson Crusoe, for prating of such subjects as this is, and shall call either my sins or misfortunes to remembrance, in prejudice of what he reads, supposing me thereby unqualified to defend so noble a subject as this of honesty, or, at least, to handle it honestly, I take the freedom to tell such, that those very wild wicked doings and mistakes of mine render me the properest man alive to give warning to others, as the man that has been sick is half a physician. Besides, the confession which I all along make of my early errors, and which Providence, you see, found me leisure enough to repent of, and, I hope, gave me assistance to do it effectually, assists to qualify me for the present undertaking, as well to recommend that rectitude of soul which I call honesty to others, as to warn those who are subject to mistake it, either in themselves or others. Heaven itself receives those who sincerely repent into the same state of acceptance as if they had not sinned at all, and so should we also.

> They who repent, and their ill lives amend,
> Stand next to those who never did offend.

Nor do I think a man ought to be afraid or ashamed to own and acknowledge his follies and mistakes, but rather to think it a debt which honesty obliges him to pay; besides, our infirmities and errors, to which all men are equally subject, when recovered from, leave such impressions behind them on those who sincerely repent of them, that they are always the forwardest to accuse and reproach themselves. No man need advise them or lead them; and this gives the greatest discovery of the honesty of the man's heart, and sincerity of principles. Some people tell us they think they need not make any open acknowledgment of their follies, and 'tis a cruelty to exact it of them—that they could rather die than submit to it—that their spirits are too great for it—that they are more afraid to come to such public confessions and recognitions than they would be to meet a cannon bullet, or to face an enemy. But this is a poor mistaken piece of false bravery; all shame is cowardice, as an eminent poet tells us that all courage is fear; the bravest spirit is the best qualified for a penitent. 'Tis a strange thing that we should not be ashamed to offend, but should be ashamed to repent; not afraid to sin, but afraid to confess. This very thought extorted the following lines from a friend of mine, with whom I discoursed upon this head:—

Among the worst of cowards let him be named,
Who, having sinned, 's afraid to be ashamed;
And to mistaken courage he's betrayed,
Who, having sinned, 's ashamed to be afraid.

But to leave the point of courage and cowardice in our repenting of our offences, I bring it back to the very point I am upon, namely, that of honesty. A man cannot be truly an honest man without acknowledging the mistakes he has made, particularly without acknowledging the wrong done to his neighbour; and why, pray, is justice less required in his acknowledgment to his Maker? He, then, that will be honest must dare to confess he has been a knave; for, as above, speaking of our behaviour to God, we have been all knaves, and all dishonest; and if we come to speak strictly, perhaps it would hold in our behaviour to one another also, for where 's the man that is not chargeable by some or other of his neighbours, or by himself, with doing wrong, with some oppression or injury, either of the tongue or of the hands?

I might enlarge here upon the honesty of the tongue, a thing some people, who call themselves very honest men, keep a very slender guard upon, I mean, as to evil-speaking, and of all evil-speaking that worst kind of it, the speaking hard and unjust things of one another.

This is certainly intended by the command of God, which is so express and emphatic, Thou shalt not bear false witness against thy neighbour; at least that part which is what we call slander, raising an injurious and false charge upon the character and conduct of our neighbour, and spreading it for truth.

But this is not all; that honesty I am speaking of respects all detraction, all outrageous assaults of the tongue; reproach is as really a part of dishonesty as slander, and though not so aggravated in degree, yet 'tis the same in kind.

There is a kind of murder that may be committed with the tongue, that is in its nature as cruel as that of the hand. This can never be the practice of an honest man; nay, he that practises it cannot be an honest man.

But perhaps I may come to this again, but I must go back to explain myself upon the subject a little farther in the general, and then you shall hear more of me as to the particulars.

Of Honesty in General

I have always observed, that however few the real honest men are, yet every man thinks himself and proclaims himself an honest man. Honesty, like heaven, has all men's good word, and all men pretend to a share of it; so general is the claim, that like a jest which is spoiled by the repetition, 'tis grown of no value for a man to swear by his faith, which is, in its original meaning, by his honesty, and ought to be understood so.

Like heaven, too, 'tis little understood by those who pretend most to it; 'tis too often squared according to men's private interest, though at the same time the latitude which some men give themselves is inconsistent with its nature.

Honesty is a general probity of mind, an aptitude to act justly and honourably in all cases, religious and civil, and to all persons, superior or inferior; neither is ability or disability to act so any part of the thing itself in this sense.

It may be distinguished into justice and equity, or, if you will, into debt and honour, for both make up but one honesty.

Exact justice is a debt to all our fellow-creatures; and honourable, generous justice is derived from that golden rule, *Quod tibi fieri non vis alteri ne feceris*; and all this put together, makes up honesty; honour, indeed, is a higher word for it, but 'tis the same thing, and:

Differs from justice only in the name,

For honesty and honour are the same.

This honesty is of so qualifying a nature, that 'tis the most denominative of all possible virtues; an honest man is the best title can be given in the world; all other titles are empty and ridiculous without it, and no title can be really scandalous if this remain. 'Tis the capital letter, by which a man's character will be known, when private qualities and accomplishments are worm-eaten by time; without it a man can neither be a Christian or a gentleman. A man may be a poor honest man, an unfortunate honest man; but a Christian knave, or a gentleman knave, is a contradiction. A man forfeits his character and his family by knavery, and his escutcheon ought to have a particular blot, like that of bastardy. When a gentleman loses his honesty, he ceases to be a gentleman, commences rake from that minute, and ought to be used like one.

Honesty has such a general character in the minds of men, that the worst of men, who neither practise or pretend to any part of it, will yet value it in others; no man ever could be so out of love with it as to desire his posterity should be without it; nay, such is the veneration all men have for it, that the general blessing of a father to his son is, "Pray God make thee an honest man."

Indeed, so general is the value of it, and so well known, that it seems needless to say anything in behalf of it. So far as it is found upon earth, so much of the first rectitude of nature and of the image of God seems to be restored to mankind.

The greatest mischief which to me seems to attend this virtue, like the thorn about the rose, which pricks the finger of those who meddle with it, is pride; 'tis a hard thing for a man to be very honest, and not be proud of it; and though he who is really honest has, as we say, something to be proud of, yet I take this honesty to be in a great deal of danger who values himself too much upon it.

True honest honesty, if I may be allowed such an expression, has the least relation to pride of any view in the world; "'tis all simple, plain, genuine, and sincere; and if I hear a man boast of his honesty, I cannot help having some fears for him, at least, that 'tis sickly and languishing.

Honesty is a little tender plant, not known tp all who have skill in simples, thick sowed, as they say, and thin come up; 'tis nice of growth, it seldom thrives in a very fat soil, and yet a very poor ground, too, is apt to starve it, unless it has taken very good root. When it once takes to a piece of ground, it will never be quite destroyed; it may be choked with the weeds of prosperity, and sometimes 'tis so scorched up with the droughts of poverty and necessity, that it seems as if it were quite dead and gone; but it always revives upon the least mild weather, and if some showers of plenty fall, it makes full reparation for the loss the gardener had in his crop.

There is an ugly weed, called cunning, which is very pernicious to it, and which particularly injures it, by hiding it from our discovery, and making it hard to find. This is so like honesty, that many a man has been deceived with it, and has taken one for the other in the market; nay, I have heard of some who have planted this wild honesty, as we may call it, in their own ground, have made use of it in their friendships and dealings, and thought it had been the true plant, but they always lost credit by it. And that was not the worst neither, for they had the loss who dealt with them, and who chaffered for a counterfeit commodity; and we find many deceived so still, which is the occasion there is such an outcry about false friends, and about sharping and tricking in men's ordinary dealings in the world.

This true honesty, too, has some little difference in it, according to the soil or climate in which it grows, and your simplers have had some disputes about the sorts of it; nay, there have been great heats about the several kinds of this plant, which grows in different countries, and some call that honesty which others say is not; as, particularly, they say, there is a sort of honesty in my country, Yorkshire honesty, which differs very much from that which is found in these southern parts about London; then there is a sort of Scots honesty, which they say is a meaner sort than that of Yorkshire; and in New England I have heard they have a kind of honesty which is worse than the Scottish, and little better than the wild honesty called cunning, which I mentioned before. On the other hand, they tell us that in some parts of Asia, at Smyrna, and at Constantinople, the Turks have a better sort of honesty than any of us. I am sorry our Turkey Company have not imported some of it, that we might try whether it would thrive here or no. 'Tis a little odd to me it should grow to such a perfection in Turkey, because it has always been observed to thrive best where it is sowed with a sort of grain called religion; indeed, they never thrive in these parts of the world so well apart as they do together. And for this reason, I must own, I have found that Scots honesty, as above, to be of a very good kind. How it is in Turkey I know not, for, in all my travels, I never set my foot in the Grand Seignior's dominions.

But to waive allegories; disputes about what is or is not honesty are dangerous to honesty itself, for no case can be doubtful which does not border upon the frontiers of dishonesty; and he that resolves not to be drowned had best never come near the brink of the water.

That man who will do nothing but what is barely honest, is in great danger. It is certainly just for me to do everything the law justifies, but if I should only square my actions by what is literally lawful, I must throw every debtor, though he be poor, in prison, and never release him till he has paid the uttermost farthing; I must hang every malefactor without mercy; I must exact the penalty of every bond, and the forfeiture of every indenture. In short, I must be uneasy to all mankind, and make them so to me; and in a word, be a very knave too, as well as a tyrant, for cruelty is not honesty.

Therefore, the Sovereign Judge of every man's honesty has laid us down a general rule, to which all the particulars are resolved, *Quod tibi fieri non vis alteri ne feceris.* This is a part of that honesty I am treating of, and which indeed is the more essential of the two; this is the test of behaviour, and the grand article to have recourse to when laws are silent.

I have heard some men argue, that they are not bound to any such considerations of the indigence of persons as lead to concessions of time, or compositions with them for debts; that 't is all *ex gratia*, or the effects of policy, because circumstances lead them to judge it better to take what they can get than lose the whole.

Speaking of the letter of the law, I allow that they may be in the right.

On the other hand, a man who gives a bond for a debt, pleads he is answerable for no more than the law will force him to; that is, he may defend a suit, stand out to the last extremity, and at last keep out of the way, so as not to have judgment or execution served on him; he may secure his estate from the execution, as well as his person, and so never pay the debt at all, and yet in the eye of the law be an honest man; and this part of legal literal honesty is supported only by the other, namely, the cruel part; for really such a man, speaking in the sense of common justice, is a knave; he ought to act according to the true intent and meaning of his obligation, and in the right of a debtor to a creditor, which is to pay him his money when it became due, not stand out to the last, because he cannot be forced to it sooner.

The laws of the country indeed allow such actions as the laws of conscience can by no means allow, as in this case of the creditor suing for his debt, and the debtor not paying it till he is forced by law. The argument made use of to vindicate the morality of such a practice, stands thus:—

If a man trusts me with his money or goods upon my common credit, or upon my word, he then takes me for his money, and depends both upon my ability and my honesty; but if he comes and demands my bond, he quits his dependence upon my honesty, and takes the law for his security; so that the language of such an action is, he will have a bond, that it may be in his power to make me pay him whether I will or no; and as for my honesty, he'll have nothing to do with it; what relief, then, I can have against this bond by the same law to which the person refers himself, is as legal an action on my side as the other man's suing for his own is on his.

And thus the letter of the law will ruin the honesty of both debtor and creditor, and yet both shall be justified too.

But if I may give my opinion in this case, neither of these are the honest man I am speaking of; for honesty does not consist of negatives, and 't is not sufficient to do my neighbour no personal injury in the strict sense and letter of the law; but I am bound, where cases and circumstances make other measures reasonable, to have such regard to these cases and circumstances as reason requires. Thus, to begin with the creditor to the debtor, reason requires that where a man is reduced to extremities, he should not be destroyed for debt; and what is unreasonable cannot be honest.

Debt is no capital crime, nor ever was; and starving men in prison, a punishment worse than the gallows, seems to be a thing so severe as it ought not to be in the power of a creditor to inflict it. The laws of God never tolerated such a method of treating debtors as we have since thought proper, I won't say honest, to put in practice; but since the politics of the nation have left the debtor so much at mercy by the letter of the law, 'tis honest, with respect to the law, to proceed so; yet compassion is in this case thought reasonable—why shouldst thou take his bed from under him? says the text; which implies, 'tis unnatural and unreasonable.

I have heard some men insist upon it, that if a man be sued wrongfully at law, he ought rather to submit to the injury than oppose the wrong by the same law; and yet I never found those gentlemen so passive in matters of law, but they would sue a debtor at law if they could not otherwise obtain their right.

I confess I cannot blame them for the last, but I blame them for pretending to the first. I am not arguing against recovering a just debt by a just law, where the person is able but unwilling to be honest; but I think pursuing the debtor to all extremities, to the turning his wife and children into the street, expressed in the Scripture by taking his bed from under him, and by keeping the debtor in prison when really he is not able to pay it—there is something of cruelty in it, and the honest man I am speaking of can never do it.

But some may object, if I must serve all mankind as I would be served in like case, then I must relieve every beggar and release every poor debtor; for if I was a beggar I would be relieved, and if I was in prison I would be released; and so I must give away all I have. This is inverting the argument; for the meaning is in the negative still, do not to another anything, or put no hardship upon another, which you would not allow to be just if you were in their case.

Honesty is equity, every man is lord-chancellor to himself; and if he would consult that principle within him would find reason as fair an advocate for his neighbour as for himself. But I proceed.

OF THE TRIAL OF HONESTY

Necessity makes an honest man a knave; and if the world was to be the judge according to the common received notion, there would not be an honest poor man left alive.

A rich man is an honest man—no thanks to him; for he would be a double knave to cheat mankind when he had no need of it: he has no occasion to press upon his integrity, nor so much as touch upon the borders of dishonesty. Tell me of a man that is a very honest man, for he pays everybody punctually, runs into nobody's debt, does no man any wrong; very well—what circumstances is he in? Why, he has a good estate, a fine yearly income, and no business to do. The devil must have full possession of this man if he should be a knave, for no man commits evil for the sake of it; even the devil himself has some farther design in sinning than barely the wicked part of it. No man is so hardened in crimes as to commit them for the mere pleasure of the fact—there is always some vice gratified; ambition, pride, or avarice makes rich men knaves, and necessity the poor. But to go on with this rich honest man; his neighbour, a thriving merchant, and whose honesty had as untainted a character as he can pretend to, has a rich ship cast away, or a factor abroad broke in his debt, and his bills come back protested, and he fails—is fain to abscond and make a composition. Our rich honest man flies out upon him presently—he is a knave, a rogue, and don't pay people what he owes them; and we should have a law that he that runs into debt farther than he is able to pay should be hanged, and the like. If the poor man is laid hold on by some creditor, and put in prison—ay, there let him lie, he deserves it; 'twill be an example to keep others from the like. And now, when all is done, this broken merchant may be as honest a man as the other.

You say you are an honest man: how do you know it? Did you ever want bread, and had your neighbour's loaf in your keeping, and would starve rather than eat it? Was you ever arrested, and being not able by yourself or friends to make peace with your plaintiff, and at the same time having another man's money in your cash chest committed to your keeping, suffered yourself to be carried to gaol rather than break bulk and break in upon your trust? God Himself has declared that the power of extremity is irresistible, and that so, as to our integrity, that He has bid us not despise the thief that steals in such a case; not that the man is less a thief, or the fact less dishonest. But the text is most remarkably worded for instruction in this point; don't you despise the man, but remember, if you were driven to the same exigence, you would be the same man and do the same thing, though now you fancy your principle so good; therefore, whatever his crime may be as to God, don't reproach him with it here; but you that think you stand, take heed lest you fall.

I am of the opinion that I could state a circumstance in which there is not one man in the world would be honest. Necessity is above the power of human nature, and for Providence to suffer a man to fall into that necessity is to suffer him to sin, because nature is not furnished with power to defend itself, nor is grace itself able to fortify the mind against it.

What shall we say to five men in a boat at sea, without provision, calling a council together, and resolving to kill one of themselves for the others to feed on, and eat him? With what face could the four look up and crave a blessing on that meat? With what heart give thanks after it? And yet this has been done by honest men, and I believe the most honest man in the world might be forced to it; yet here is no manner of pretence, but necessity, to palliate the crime. If it be argued it was the loss of one man to save the four, it is answered, but what authority to make him die to save their lives? How came the man to owe them such a debt? 'Twas robbery and murder; 'twas robbing him of his life, which was his property, to preserve mine; 'tis murder, by taking away the life of an innocent man; and at best 'twas doing evil that good may come, which is expressly forbidden.

But there is a kind of equity pleaded in this case. Generally, when men are brought to such a pass, they cast lots who shall be the man, and the voluntary consent of the party makes it lawful (God Himself being supposed to determine who shall be the man), which I deny; for it is in no man's power legally to consent to such a lot; no man has a right to give away his own life; he may forfeit it to the law and lose it, but that 's a crime against himself, as well as against the law; and the four men might by our law have been tried and hanged for murder. All that can be said is, that necessity makes the highest crimes lawful, and things evil in their own nature are made practicable by it. From these extremes of necessity we come to lighter degrees of it, and so let us bring our honest man to some exigencies. He would not wrong any man of a farthing; he could not sleep if he should be in anybody's debt; and he cannot be an honest man that can.

That we may see now whether this man's honesty lies any deeper than his neighbour's, turn the scale of his fortune a little. His father left him a good estate; but here come some relations, and they trump up a title to his lands, and serve ejectments upon his tenants, and so the man gets into trouble, hurry of business, and the law. The extravagant charges of the law sink him of all his ready money, and, his rents being stopped, the first breach he makes upon his honesty (that is, by his former rules), he goes to a friend to borrow money, tells him this matter will be over, he hopes, quickly, and he shall have his rents to receive, and then he will pay him again; and really he intends to do so. But here comes a disappointment; the trial comes on, and he is cast, and his title to the estate proves defective; his father was cheated, and he not only loses the estate, but is called upon for the arrears of the rent he has received; and, in short, the man is undone, and has not a penny to buy bread or help himself, and, besides this, cannot pay the money he borrowed.

Now, turn to his neighbour the merchant, whom he had so loudly called knave for breaking in his trade; he by this time has made up with his creditors and got abroad again, and he meets him in the street in his dejected circumstances. "Well," says the merchant, "and why don't you pay my cousin, your old neighbour, the money you borrowed of him?"

"Truly," says he, "because I have lost all my estate, and can't pay; nay, I have nothing to live on."

"Well, but," returns the merchant, "wan't you a knave to borrow money, and now can't pay it?"

"Why, truly," says the gentleman, "when I borrowed it I really designed to be honest, and did not question but I should have my estate again, and then I had been able also, and would have paid him to a penny, but it has proved otherwise; and though I would pay him if I had it, yet I am not able."

"Well, but," says the merchant again, "did you not call me knave, though I lost my estate abroad by unavoidable disasters, as you have lost yours at home? Did you not upbraid me because I could not pay? I would have paid everybody, if I could, as well as you."

"Why, truly," says the gentleman, "I was a fool; I did not consider what it was to be brought to necessity; I ask your pardon."

Now, let's carry on this story. The merchant compounds with his creditors, and paying every one a just proportion as far as 'twill go, gets himself discharged; and being bred to business, and industrious, falls into trade again, and raises himself to good circumstances, and at last a lucky voyage or some hit of trade sets him above the world again. The man, remembering his former debts, and retaining his principle of honesty, calls his old creditors together, and though he was formerly discharged from them all, voluntarily pays them the remainder of their debts. The gentleman being bred to no business, and his fortune desperate, goes abroad and gets into the army, and behaving himself well, is made an officer, and, still rising by his merit, becomes a great man; but in his new condition troubles not his head with his former debts in his native country, but settles in the court and favour of the prince under whom he has made his fortunes, and there sets up for the same honest man he did before.

I think I need not ask which of these two is the. honest man, any more than which was the honest penitent, the Pharisee or the publican.

Honesty, like friendship, is tried in affliction; and he that cries out loudest against those who in the time of this trial are forced to give ground, would perhaps yield as far in the like shock of misfortune.

To be honest when peace and plenty flow upon our hands, is owing to the blessing of our parents; but to be honest when circumstances grow narrow, relations turbulent and quarrelsome, when poverty stares at us, and the world threatens, this blessing is from Heaven, and can only be supported from thence. God Almighty is very little beholding to them who will serve Him just as long as He feeds them. 'Twas a strong argument the devil used in that dialogue between Satan and his Maker about Job. "Yes, he is a mighty good man, and a mighty just man, and well he may while you give him everything he wants: I would serve you myself, and be as true to you as Job, if you would be as kind and as bountiful to me as you are to him: but now, do but lay your finger on him; do but stop your hand a little, and cut him short; strip him a little, and make him like one of those poor fellows that now bow to him, and you will quickly see your good man be like other men; nay, the passion he will be in at his losses will make him curse you to your face."

'Tis true the devil was mistaken in the man, but the argument had a great deal of probability in it, and the moral may be drawn, both from the argument and from the consequences:

1. That 'tis an easy thing to maintain the character of honesty and uprightness when a man has no business to be employed in, and no want to press him.

2. That when exigencies and distresses pinch a man, then is the time to prove the honesty of his principle.

The prosperous honest man can only by boasting tell the world he is honest, but the distressed and ruined honest man hears other people tell him he is honest.

In this case, therefore, since allowance must be made for human infirmities, we are to distinguish between an accident and a practice. I am not pleading to encourage any man to make no scruple of trespassing upon his honesty in time of necessity; but I cannot condemn every man for a knave who by unusual pressures, straits, difficulties, or other temptation, has been left to slip and do an ill action, as we call it, which perhaps this person would never have stooped to if the exigence had not been too great for his resolution. The Scripture says of David, "*He was a man after God's own heart;*" and yet we have several things recorded of him, which, according to the modern way of censuring people in this age, would have given him the character of a very ill man. But I conceive the testimony of David's uprightness, given us so authentically from the Scripture, is given from this very rule, that the inclination of his heart and the general bent of his practice were to serve and obey his great Sovereign Benefactor, however human frailty, backed with extremities of circumstances or powerful temptations, might betray him to commit actions which he would not otherwise have done

The falling into a crime will not denominate a man dishonest; for *humanum est errare.* The character of a man ought to be taken from the general tenor of his behaviour, and from his allowed practice. David took the shew-bread from the priests, which it was not lawful for him to eat. David knew that God, who commanded the shew-bread should not be eaten, had, however, commanded him by the law of Nature not to be starved, and therefore, pressed by his hunger, he ventures upon the commandment. And the Scripture is very remarkable in expressing it, "*David, when he was an hungry.*" And the occasion for which our blessed Lord Himself quoted this text is very remarkable, *viz.*, to prove that things otherwise unlawful may be made lawful by necessity.—Matt, xii. 4.

Another time, David in his passion resolves the destruction of Nabal and all his family, which, without doubt, was a great sin; and the principle which he went upon, to wit, revenge for his churlish and saucy answer to him, was still a greater sin; but the temptation, backed by the strength of his passion, had the better of him at that time; and this upright, honest man had murdered Nabal and all his house if God had not prevented him.

Many instances of like nature the Scripture has left upon record, giving testimony to the character of good men, from the general practice and bent of their hearts, without leaving any reproach upon them for particular failings, though those sins have been extraordinary provoking, and in their circumstances scandalous enough.

If any man would be so weak as from hence to draw encouragement to allow himself in easy trespasses upon his honesty, on the pretence of necessities, let him go on with me to the further end of this observation, and find room for it if he can.

If ever the honest man I speak of, by whatsoever exigence or weakness, thus slips from the principle of his integrity, he never fails to express his own dislike of it; he acknowledges upon all occasions, both to God and to man, his having been overcome, and been prevailed upon to do what he does not approve of; he is too much ashamed of his own infirmity to pretend to vindicate the action, and he certainly is restored to the first regulation of his principles as soon as the temptation is over. No man is fonder to accuse him than he is to accuse himself, and he has always upon him the sincere marks of a penitent.

'Tis plain from hence that the principle of the man's integrity is not destroyed, however he may have fallen, though seven times a day; and I must, while I live, reckon him for an honest man.

Nor am I going about to suppose that the extremities and exigencies which have pressed men of the best principles to do what at another time they would not do, make those actions become less sinful, either in their own nature or circumstances. The guilt of a crime with respect to its being a crime, *viz.*, an offence against God, is not removed by the circumstances of necessity. It is without doubt a sin for me to steal another man's food, though it was to supply starving nature; for how do I know whether he whose food I steal may not be in as much danger of starving for want of it as I? And if not, 't is taking to my own use what I have no right to, and taking it by force or fraud; and the question is not as to the right or wrong, whether I have a necessity to eat this man's bread or no, but whether it be his or my own? If it be his, and not my own, I cannot do it without a manifest contempt of God's law, and breaking the eighth article of it, "*Thou shalt not steal.*" Thus, as to God, the crime is evident, let the necessity be what it will.

But when we are considering human nature subjected, by the consequences of Adam's transgression, to frailty and infirmity, and regarding things from man to man, the exigencies and extremities of straitened circumstances seem to me to be most prevailing arguments why the denomination of a man's general character ought not by his fellow mortals (subject to the same infirmities) to be gathered from his mistakes, his errors, or failings; no, not from his being guilty of any extraordinary sin, but from the manner and method of his behaviour. Does he go on to commit frauds, and make a practice of his sin? Is it a distress? Is it a storm of affliction and poverty has driven him upon the lee-shore of temptation? Or is the sin the port he steered for? A ship may by stress of weather be driven upon sands and dangerous places, and the skill of the pilot not be blameable; but he that runs against the wind, and without any necessity, upon a shelf which he sees before him, must do it on purpose to destroy the vessel, and ruin the voyage.

In short, if no man can be called honest but he who is never overcome to fall into any breach of this rectitude of life, none but he who is sufficiently fortified against all possibility of being tempted by prospects, or driven by distress, to make any trespass upon his integrity— woe be unto me that write, and to most that read! where shall we find the honest man?

The Scripture is particularly expressive of this in the words, "*The righteous man falleth seven times a day, and riseth again.*" Why, this is very strange; if a man come to commit seven crimes in a day, that is, many, for the meaning is indefinite, can this be an honest man? What says the world of him? Hang him; he is a knave, a rascal, a dishonest fellow.

This is the judgment of men; but in the judgment of Scripture this may be a righteous man.

The main design of this head, and the proper application of it, is to tell us we ought not to be too hasty to brand our brother for his sins, his infirmities, or misfortunes, since he that is dishonest in your eyes, by a casual or other crime which he commits, may rise from that disaster by a sincere repentance, and be tomorrow an honester man than thyself in the eyes of his Maker.

But here I am assaulted with another censorious honest man. Here you talk of falling today, and rising again tomorrow; sinning and repenting; why, here is a fellow has cheated me of £500, and he comes canting to me of his repentance, tells me he hopes God has forgiven him, and it would be hard for me to call to remembrance what God has wiped out; he is heartily sorry for the fault, and the like, and begs my pardon, that is, begs my estate indeed. For what is all this to my money? Let him pay me, and I will forgive him too. God may forgive him the sin, but that's nothing to my debt.

Why, truly, in answer to this in part, you are in the right if the man be able to make you any satisfaction, and does not do it; for I question not, but every trespass of this nature requires restitution as well as repentance; restitution as far as the possible power of the party extends; and if the last be not found, the first is not likely to be sincere.

But if the man either is not able to make you any restitution at all, or does make you restitution to the utmost of his capacity, and then comes and says as before, then the poor man is in the right, and you in the wrong; for I make no question likewise to affirm, and could prove it by unanswerable arguments, he may be an honest man who cannot pay his debts, but he cannot be an honest man who can, and does not.

Innumerable accidents reduce men from plentiful fortunes to mean and low circumstances; some procured by their own vices and intemperance; some by infirmities, ignorance, and mere want of judgment to manage their affairs; some by the frauds and cheats of other men; some by mere casualty and unavoidable accidents, wherein the sovereignty of Providence shows us, that the race is not to the swift, or the battle to the strong, or riches to men of understanding.

First, some by vices and intemperance are reduced to poverty and distress. Our honest man cannot fall in the misfortunes of this class, because there the very poverty is a sin, being produced from a sinful cause. As it is far from being allowed as an excuse to a murderer to say he was in drink, because it is excusing a crime with a crime, so for a man to ruin his fortunes, as the prodigal in the Gospel, with riotous living, all the effects are wicked and dishonest, as they partake of the dishonesty of the cause from whence they proceed; for he cannot be an honest man who wants wherewith to pay his debts after having spent what should have discharged them in luxury and debauches.

Secondly, some by ignorance and want of judgment to manage their affairs are brought to poverty and distress. These may be honest men, notwithstanding their weakness, for I won't undertake that none of our honest men shall be fools. 'Tis true the good man is the wise man as to the main part of wisdom, which is included in his piety; but many a religious man, who would not do any wrong wilfully to his neighbour, is obliged at last to injure both his own family and other people's for want of discretion to guide him in his affairs, and to judge for himself; and therefore I dare not tax all our fools with being knaves, nor will I say but such a man may be honest. Some will say that such a man should not venture into business which he is not able to manage, and therefore 'twas the vice of his understanding, and, like the case in the first article, is excusing a fault with a fault.

I cannot allow this, for if I am asked why a fool ventures into trade, I answer, because he is a fool, not because he is a knave.

If fools could their own ignorance discern,
They'd be no longer fools, because they'd learn.

If you would convince a man that he wants discretion, you must give him discretion to be convinced; till then he cannot know he has it not, because he has it not. No man is answerable either to God or man for that which he never was master of. The most proper expression that ever I met with in this nature, was of a certain idiot or natural which a gentleman of my acquaintance kept in his family, who being on his deathbed, was observed to be very pensive and much concerned about dying. The gentleman sent a minister to him, who, as well as he could to his understanding, discoursed with him about death and judgment to come. The poor creature, who was hardly ever able to give a rational answer to a question before, after hearing him very attentively, broke out into tears with this expression—that he hoped God would not require anything of him that He had not given him judgment to understand. Whatever it may be as to the soul, I am positive, in the case of human affairs, no man is answerable to man for any more than his discretion. Events are not in our power; a man may be nicely honest in life, though he may be weak enough in judgment.

Thirdly, some are ruined, and are yet merely passive, being either defrauded and cheated by knaves, or plundered and rifled by thieves, or by immediate casualties, as fire, enemies, storms, floods, and the like; these are things which neither touch the man's honesty nor his discretion. Thus Job was, by God's permission and the agency of the devil, reduced in a moment from a plentiful estate to be as naked as he came out of his mother's womb. I would fain ask those who say no man can be an honest man if he does not pay his debts, who paid Job's debts if he owed any, and where was his dishonesty if he did not pay them? I still readily grant that he cannot be an honest man who does not pay his debts if he can; but if otherwise, then the words ought to be altered, and they should say, he cannot be an honest man who borrows any money, or buys anything upon his credit; and this cannot be true.

But since I have led myself into the argument, I cannot but make a small digression concerning people who fail in trade. I conceive the greatest error of such is their terror about breaking, by which they are tempted while their credit is good, though their bottom be naught, to push farther in, expecting, or at least hoping, by the profits of some happy voyage, or some lucky hit, as they call it, to retrieve their circumstances, and stand their ground.

I must confess I cannot vindicate the honesty of this; for he who, knowing his circumstances to be once naught, and his bottom worn out, ought not in justice to enter into any man's debt, for then he trades on their risk, not on his own, and yet trades for his own profits, not theirs. This is not fair, because he deceives the creditor, who ventures his estate on that bottom which he supposes to be good, and the other knows it not. Nay, though he really pays this creditor, he is not honest; for, in conscience, his former creditors had a right to all his effects in proportion to their debts; and if he really pays one all, and the rest but a share, 't is a wrong to the whole.

I would therefore advise all tradesmen who find their circumstances declining, as soon, at least, as they first discern themselves to be incapable of paying their debts, if not while yet they can pay every one all, make a full stop, and call all people together; if there is enough to pay them all, let them have it; if not let them have their just shares of it. By this means you will certainly have God's blessing, and the character of an honest man left to begin again with; and creditors are often prevailed with, in consideration of such a generous honesty, to throw back something to put such a man in a posture to live again, or by further voluntary credit and friendship to uphold him. This is much better also with respect to interest, as well as honesty, than to run on to all extremities, till the burden falls too heavy either for debtor or creditor to bear. This would prevent many of the extremities, which, I say, puts the honesty of a man to so extraordinary a trial.

An honest principle would certainly dictate to the man, if it were consulted with, that when he knows he is not able to pay, it is not lawful for him to borrow. Taking credit is a promise of payment: a promise of payment is tacitly understood, and he cannot be honest who promises what he knows he cannot perform, as I shall note more at large on another head. But if the man be paid, yet it was not an honest act; 'twas deceiving the man, and making him run a greater risk than he knew of, and such a risk as he would not have run had he known your circumstances and bottom as you do; so that here is deceit upon deceit.

This I know is a disputed point, and a thing which a great many practise who pass for very honest men in the world, but I like it not the better for that; I am very positive, that he who takes my good on the foot of his credit, when, if he should die the next day, he knows his estate will not pay me five shillings in the pound, though he should not die. but does pay me at the time appointed, is as much guilty of a fraud as if he actually robbed my house. Credit is a received opinion of a man's honesty and ability, his willingness to pay. and his having wherewith to pay; and he who wants either of these, his credit is lame. Men won't sell their goods to a litigious, quarrelsome man, though he be never so rich, nor to a needy man. though he be never so honest. Now if all the world believe that I am honest and able, and I know that I am not the last. I cannot be the first if I take their goods upon credit; 'tis vain to pretend men trade upon the general risk of men's appearance, and the credit of common fame, and all men have an equal hazard. I say no; men may venture their estates in the hands of a flourishing bankrupt, and he by virtue of his yet unshaken credit is trusted; but he cannot be honest that takes this credit, because he knows his circumstances are quite otherwise than they are supposed to be. that the man is deceived, and he is privy to the deceit.

This digression is not so remote from the purpose as I expected when I began it: the honesty that I am speaking of chiefly respects matters of commerce, of which credit and payment of debt are the most considerable branches.

There is another article in trade, which many very honest men have made familiar to themselves, which yet. I think, is in no case to be defended, and that is relating to counterfeit money. Custom, before the old money was suppressed in England, had prevailed so far upon honesty, that I have seen some men put all their brass money among their running cash, to be told over in every sum they paid, in order to have somebody or other take it; I have heard many people own they made no scruple of it, but I could never find them give one good reason to justify the honesty of it.

First, they say it comes for money, and it ought to go so: to which I answer, that is just as good a reason as this: A has cheated me, and therefore I may cheat B. If I have received a sum of money for good, and knowing not that any of it is otherwise offer it in payment to another, this is just and honest; but if, on this other man's telling it over, he returns me a piece of brass or counterfeit money which I change again, and afterwards, knowing this to be such, offer the same piece to another, I know no worse fraud in its degree in the world, and I doubt not to prove it so beyond contradiction.

If the first person did not take this piece of money, it was because, being both watchful and skilful, he could discover it; and if I offer it to another, 'tis with an expectation that he, being either less watchful or less skilful, shall overlook it, and so I shall make an advantage of my neighbour's ignorance, or want of care.

I'll put some parallel cases to this, to illustrate it. Suppose a blind man comes into a shop to buy goods of me, and giving me a guinea to change, I shall give him the remainder in bad money, would not everybody say 'twas a barbarous thing? Why, the other is all one, for if the person be ignorant of money, he is blind as to the point in hand; and nothing can be more unfair than to take the advantage.

Suppose, again, a young boy or a servant newly entered in trade is sent to buy goods, and by his master's order he asks for such a commodity; and you, presuming upon the rawness of the messenger, deliver a sort of a meaner quality, and take the full price of him; would you grudge to be used scurvily for such a trick? Why, no less or better is offering brass for silver, presuming only the want of care or skill in the receiver shall pass it unobserved.

"Ay, but," says a learned tradesman, who would be thought honester than ordinary, "I always change it again, if it be brought back." Yes, sir, so does a pickpocket give you your handkerchief again when you have fastened on him, and threatened him with the mob. The matter, in short, is this: if the man whom you have cheated can cheat nobody else, then no thanks to you; when he comes to you, and charges the fraud upon you, you'll make satisfaction, because, if you won't, the law will compel you to it.

But if the fraud may be carried on, as you are manifestly willing, consenting, and instrumental in it that it should, behold the consequence: your first sin against honesty is multiplied in all the hands through whom this piece of bad money knowingly so passes, till at last it happens to go single to a poor man that can't put it off, and the wrong and injury may issue where it was wanted to buy bread for a starving family.

All the excuses I could ever meet with could never satisfy me that it can consist with honesty to put brass or copper away for gold or silver, any more than it would to give a blind messenger sand instead of sugar, or brown bread instead of white.

Of Honesty in Promises

"*A man is known by his word, and an ox by his horns,*" says an old English proverb. If I understand the true meaning of it, 'tis that the honesty of a man is known by his punctually observing his word, as naturally and plainly as any creature is known by the most obvious distinction. 'Tis the peculiar quality of an honest man, the distinguishing mark to know him by. His word or promise is as sacred to him in all his affairs in the world as the strongest obligation which can be laid on him; nor is it a thing formed by him from settled resolutions, or measures of policy taken up of course to raise or fix his reputation, but it is the native produce of his honest principle; 'tis the consequence, and his honesty is the cause; he ceases to be honest when he ceases to preserve this solemn regard to his word.

If he gives his word, any man may depend upon it for the safety of his life or estate; he scorns to prevaricate or shift himself off from the punctual observance of it, though it be to his loss.

I can't abate an honest man an inch in the punctual observance of a promise made upon parole if it be in the man's possible power to perform it, because there seems to be something too base to consist with honesty in the very nature of a man that can go back from his word.

The reverence our ancestors paid to their promises, or word passed, I am of the opinion, gave that remarkable brand of infamy and scandal upon the affront of giving the lie. A gentleman, which is, in short, the modern term for an honest man, or a man of honour, cannot receive a greater reproach than to be told he lies; that is, that he forfeits his word, breaks his veracity; for the minute he does that he ungentlemans himself, disgraces the blood of his family, degenerates from his ancestors, and commences rake, scoundrel, and anything.

Some people, who have run their points of honour to the extremes, are of the opinion that this affront of the lie ought not to be given to anything they call a gentleman, or that calls himself so, till he has so far exposed himself to all other degrees of infamy as to bear kicking or caning, and the like; that after this, when he breaks his word, he may be told he lies, or anything else; but till then the very thing itself is so intolerable an abuse, that the person who ventures to trespass so foully on the rules of good manners deserves not the honour of fair play for his life; but as some beasts of prey are refused the fair law of the field, and are knocked down in every hedge, so these, like bullies and mere rakes, may be pistolled in the dark and stabbed at the corner of an alley; that is to say, any measure may be used with them to dismiss them from the society of mankind, as fellows not sufferable in the commonwealth of good manners.

I do not argue for these extremes; but I instance in this to testify the veneration all good men have for the word or promise of an honest man, and the esteem which the integrity of the mind, expressed by a zealous regard to the words of the mouth, has obtained in the world. The French, when they express themselves in vindication of their honour, always bring it about by this, *Je suis homme de parole,* I am an honest man, or a man of my word; that is, I am a man that may be trusted upon my parole, for I never break my word.

Such was the value put upon the promises of men in former time, that a promise of payment of money was recoverable in our courts by law, till the inconveniences proved so many that an Act was made on purpose to restrain it to a sum under ten pounds. But to this day if a man promises marriage to a woman, especially if she has granted him any favours upon that condition, the laws of the land, which therein have regard to the laws of honour, will oblige him to make it good, and allow it to be a sufficient plea to forbid his marrying with anybody else.

There are innumerable instances of the veneration all nations pay to the expressive article of human veracity. In the war you meet with frequent instances of prisoners dismissed by a generous enemy upon their parole, either to pay their ransom, or to procure such or such conditions, or come back and surrender themselves prisoners; and he that should forfeit this parole would be posted in the enemy's army, and hissed out of his own.

I know nothing a wise man would not choose to do rather than, by breaking his word, give the world such an undeniable testimony of his being a knave. This is that good name which Solomon says is better than life, and is a precious ointment, and which when a man has once lost he has nothing left worth keeping. A man may even hang himself out of the way, for no man that looks like a man will keep his company.

When a man has once come to breaking his word, no man that has any value for his reputation cares to be seen in his company; but all good men shun him, as if he were infected with the plague.

There are men, indeed, who will be exceeding punctual to their words and promises, who yet cannot be called honest men, because they have other vices and excursions that render them other ways wicked. These give their testimony to the beauty of honesty by choosing it as the best mask to put a gloss upon their actions, and conceal the other deformities of their lives; and so honesty, like religion, is made use of to disguise the hypocrite, and raise a reputation upon the shadow, by the advantage it takes of the real esteem the world has of the substance. I say of this counterfeit honesty, as is said of religion in like cases. If honesty was not the most excellent attainment, 't would not be made use of as the most specious pretence; nor is there a more exquisite way for a man to play the hypocrite, than to pretend an extraordinary zeal to the performance of his promises; because, when the opinion of any man's honesty that way has spread in the thoughts of men, there is nothing so great but they will trust him with, nor so hard but they will do it for him.

All men reverence an honest man: the knaves stand in awe of him, fools adore him, and wise men love him; and thus is virtue its own reward.

Honest men are in more danger from this one hypocrite than from twenty open knaves; for these have a mark placed upon them by their general character, as a buoy upon a rock to warn strangers from venturing upon it. But the hypocrites are like a pit covered over, like shoals under water, and danger concealed which cannot be seen. I must confess I have found these the most dangerous, and have too deeply suffered by throwing myself on their protestations of honesty. The esteem I always entertained of the most beautiful gift God has bestowed, or man could receive, has made me the easier to be deceived with the resemblance of it.

So much as I, or anyone else, by the viciousness of our own nature, or the prevailing force of accidents, snares, and temptations, have deviated from this shining principle, so far as we have been foolish as well as wicked, so much we have to repent of towards our Maker, and be ashamed of towards our neighbour.

For my part, I am never backward to own, let who will be the reader of these sheets, that to the dishonour of my Maker, and the just scandal of my own honesty, I have not paid that due regard to the rectitude of this principle which my own knowledge has owned to be its due; let those who have been juster to themselves, and to the Giver of it, rejoice in the happiness, rather than triumph over the infirmity.

But let them be sure they have been juster on their own parts; let them be positive that their own integrity is untainted, and would abide all the trials and racks that a ruined fortune, strong temptations, and deep distresses, could bring it into; let them not boast till these dangers are past, and they put their armour off; and if they can do it, then I will freely acknowledge they have less need of repentance than I.

Not that I pretend, as I noted before, and shall often repeat, that these circumstances render my failing, or any man's else, the less a sin, but they make the reason why we that have fallen should rather be pitied than reproached by those who think they stand, because, when the same assaults are made upon the chastity of their honour, it may be every jot as likely to be prostituted as their neighbour's.

And such is the folly of scandal, as well as the blindness of malice, that it seldom fixes reproach upon the right foot. I have seen so much of it, with respect to other people, as well as to myself, that it gives me a very scoundrel opinion of all those people whom I find forward to load their neighbours with reproach. Nothing is more frequent in this case than to run away with a piece of a man's character, in which they err, and do him wrong, and leave that part of him untouched which is really black, and would bear it; this makes me sometimes, when with the humblest and most abasing thoughts of myself I look up, and betwixt God and my own soul, cry out, "What a wretch am I!" at the same time smile at the hare-brained enemy, whose tongue, tipped with malice, runs ahead of his understanding, and missing the crimes for which I deserve more than he can inflict, reproaches me with those I never committed. Methinks I am ready to call him back, like the huntsman, when the dogs run upon the foil, and say, "Hold,

hold, you are wrong; take him here, and you have him."

I question not but 'tis the same with other people; for when malice is in the heart, reproach generally goes a mile before consideration, and where is the honesty of the man all this while? This is trampling upon my pride, *sed majori fastu*, but with greater pride; 'tis exposing my dishonesty, but with the highest knavery; 'tis a method no honest man will take, and when taken, no honest man regards; wherefore, let none of these sons of slander take satisfaction in the frequent acknowledgments I am always ready to make of my own failing, for that humility with which I always find cause to look into my own heart, where I see others worse, and more guilty of crimes than they can lay to my charge, yet makes me look back upon their weakness with the last contempt, who fix their impotent charges where there is not room to take hold, and run away with the air and shadow of crimes never committed.

I have instanced this, not at all on my own account, for 'tis not worth while, for if I am injured, what's that to troubling the world with when I am forgotten? But while I am examining the nicest article in the world, honesty, I cannot but lay down these three heads from the preceding observations:—

1. He who is forward to reproach the infirmities of other men's honesty, is very near a breach of his own.

2. He that hastily reproaches another without sufficient ground, cannot be an honest man.

3. Where there may be sufficient ground of reproach, yet an honest man is always tender of his neighbour's character from the sense of his own frailty.

But I return to honesty, as it affects a man's pledging his word, which is the counterpart of his principle, and this because, as I said, I should chiefly regard this honesty as it concerns human affairs, conversation, and negotiation.

And here I meet with a tradesman come just in from dunning one of his neighbours. "Well, I have been at a place for money," says he, "but I can get none. There's such an one, he passes for an honest man, but I am sure he is a great rogue to me, for he has promised me my money a long time, but puts me off still from time to time; he makes no more of breaking his word, than of drinking a glass of beer. I am sure he has told me forty lies already. This is one of your honest men; if all such honest men were hanged, we should have a better trade." And thus he runs on.

If all such honest men were hanged, they that were left might have a better trade; but how many of them would there be?

Now, though I shall in no way vindicate men's hasty promises absolutely to perform what is doubtful in the event, yet I cannot agree that every man who, having promised a payment, does not perform it to his time, is a knave or a liar. If it were so, the Lord have mercy upon three parts of the city.

Wherefore, to state this matter clearly, it must be taken a little to pieces, and the articles spoken to apart.

First. Without question, when a man makes a promise of payment to another on a set day, knowing in his own thoughts that it is not probable he should be capable to comply with it, or really designing not to comply with it, or not endeavouring to comply with it, 'tis a deceit put upon the party, 'tis a premeditated formal lie, the man that made it is a stranger to honesty; he is a knave, and everything that is base and bad. But,

Secondly. Promises ought to be understood, both by the person to whom and the person by whom they are made, as liable to those contingencies that all human affairs and persons are liable to, as death, accidents, disappointments, and disorder. Thus, if a man who ought to pay me today tells me, "Sir, I cannot comply with you today; but if you call for it next week, you shall have it; "if I may put this answer into plainer English, and I suppose the man to be an honest man, I cannot understand his meaning otherwise than thus:—

"Sir, I acknowledge your money is due. I have not cash enough by me to pay you today, but I have several running bills, and several persons who have promised me money, which I doubt not I shall receive against such a time; and if you call then, I make no question but I shall be able to do it; and if it is possible for me to pay you, I will do it at that time without fail.'"

I confess it were as well to express themselves thus at large in all the appointments people make for payment, and would the persons who make them consider it, they would do so; but custom has prevailed in our general way of speaking, whereby all things that are subject to the common known contingents of life, or visible in the circumstances of the case, are understood without being expressed. For example:—

I make an appointment of meeting a man positively at such a town, such a certain day or hour. If I were talking to a Turk or a pagan that knows nothing, or believes nothing of supreme Providence, I would say—If the Lord of heaven and earth, that governs all my actions, please to preserve and permit me. But when I am talking to a Christian, it should seem to be so universally supposed that every appointment is subjected and submits to the government of Providence, that the repetition would be needless; and that when a man promises positively to meet, 'tis with a general *sub-intelligitur*, a reserve as natural as Nature itself, to the Divine permission. All men know, that unless I am alive I cannot come there, or if I am taken sick, both which may easily happen, I shall disappoint him. And, therefore, if he should urge me again to come without fail, and I should reply, "I won't fail if I am alive and well," the man ought to take it for an affront, and ask me if I take him for a fool, to think if I am taken sick, I should come with my bed at my back, or if death should intervene, he had occasion to speak with my ghost.

In this sense, a tradesman who promises payment of money at a set time; first, 'tis supposed he has it not now in his hands, because he puts off the person demanding to a further day, and promises to comply with it then. This promise, therefore, can be understood no otherwise than that he expects to receive money by that time. Now, if this man, by the like disappointments from other men, or any other involuntary casualty, is really and *bonâ fide* unable to comply with the time of promised payment, I cannot see but this may befall an honest man, and he neither designing to fail when he promised, not being able to prevent the accident that obliged him to do it, nor in any way voluntary in the breach, is not, in my opinion, guilty of a lie, or breach of his honour, though he did not make those verbal reserves in the promises he had given.

If every man who cannot comply with promised payments should be thus branded with lying and dishonesty, then let him who is without the sin cast the stone, for nobody else ought to do it.

'Tis true, there is a difference between an accident and a practice; that is, in short, there is a difference between him who meets with a great many occasions thus to break his word, and he that meets with but few; but if it be a crime, he that commits it once is no more an honest man than he that commits it forty times; and if it be not a crime, he that does it forty times is as honest as he that has occasion to do it but once.

But let no man take encouragement from hence to be prodigal of his word, and slack in his performance; for this nice path is so near the edge of the pit of knavery, that the least slip lets you fall in.

These promises must have abundance of circumstances to bring the honest man out of the scandal.

As, first. The disappointments which occasioned this breach of his word must have been unforeseen and unexpected, otherwise the expectation of performing his promise was ill grounded, and then his honesty is answerable for the very making the promise, as well as the breaking it.

Second. No endeavours must be wanting to comply with the promise, otherwise 'tis wrong to say, "I am disappointed, and can't make good my word." The man ought to say, "Sir, I have disappointed myself by my negligence or wilfulness, and have obliged myself to break my word;" or, in English, "Sir, I am a knave; for though I made you a promise which I might have performed, I took no care about it, not valuing the forfeiture of my word."

If, then, the case is so nice, though, in the strictness of speaking, such a disappointment may oblige an honest man to break his word, yet every honest man, who would preserve that character to himself, ought to be the more wary, and industriously avoid making such absolute unconditional promises, because we are to avoid the circumstances of offence.

But as to the nature of the thing, 'tis plain to me that a man may in such cases be obliged to break his word unwillingly; and nothing can be a fraud or dishonest action in that case, which is not either voluntary in itself, or the occasion voluntarily procured.

Of Relative Honesty

As honesty is simple and plain, without gloss and pretence, so it is universal. He that may uphold an untainted reputation in one particular, may be justly branded with infamy in another. A man may be punctual in his dealings, and a knave in his relations; honest in his warehouse, and a knave at his fireside; he may be a saint in his company, a devil in his family; true to his word, and false to his friendship; but whosoever he be, he is no honest man. An honest man is all of a piece the whole contexture of his life; his general conduct is genuine, and squared according to the rules of honesty; he never runs into extremes and excesses on one hand or other.

I confess I find this thing which they call relative honesty very little thought of in the world, and that which is still worse, 'tis very little understood. I'll bring it down to but a few examples, some of which frequently happen among us, and will therefore be the more familiarly received.

There are relative obligations entailed on us in our family circumstances, which are just debts, and must be paid, and which, in a word, a man can no more be honest if he does not make conscience of discharging, than he can in the case of the most unquestionable debts between man and man.

The debts from children to parents, and from wives to their husbands, are in a manner relatively changed, and the obligation transferred into the order of religious duties. God, the guide and commander of all subordination, has, as it were, taken that part into His own hand. 'Tis rather called a duty to Him than a relative duty only. But if men take this for a discharge to them of all relative obligations to wives and to children, or that God had less required one than the other, they must act upon very wrong principles.

Nature, indeed, dictates in general a man's providing subsistence for his family, and he is declared to be so far from a Christian that he is worse than an infidel that neglects it. But there are other parts of our obligations which honesty calls upon us to perform.

A wife and children are creditors to the father of the family, and he cannot be an honest man that does not discharge his debt to them, any more than he could if he did not repay money borrowed to a stranger; and not to lead my reader on to intricate and disputed particulars, I instance principally in those that nobody can dispute, as, first, education. By this I mean, not only putting children to school, which some parents think is all they have to do with or for their children, and indeed with some is all that they know how to do, or are fit to do; I say, I do not mean this only, but several other additional cares, as: (1.) Directing what school, what parts of learning are proper for them, what improvements they are to be taught: (2.) studying the genius and capacities of their children in what they teach them. Some children will voluntarily learn one thing, and can never be forced to learn another, and for want of which observing the genius of children we have so many learned blockheads in the world, who are mere scholars, pedants, and no more. (3.) But the main part of this debt which relative honesty calls upon us to pay to our children, is the debt of instruction, the debt of government, the debt of example. He that neglects to pay any of these to his family is a relative knave, let him value himself upon his honesty in paying his other debts as much as he will.

'Tis a strange notion men have of honesty and of their being honest men, as if it related to nothing but tradesmen or men who borrow and lend, or that the title was obtained by an ordinary observance of right and wrong between man and man. 'Tis a great mistake; the name of an honest man is neither so easily gained, nor so soon lost as these men imagine. David was a very honest man, notwithstanding his passion and revenge in the case of Nabal, his murder in the case of Uriah, or his adultery in the case of Bathsheba. The intent and main design of his life was upright; and whenever he fell by the power of that temptation that overcame him, he rose again by repentance.

Let no vain men flatter themselves with the pride of their honesty in mere matters of debtor and creditor, though that is also absolutely necessary and essential to an honest man.

But trace this honest man home to his family. Is he a tyrant or a churl to his wife? Is he a stranger to the conduct and behaviour of his children? Is he an Eli to their vices? Are they uninstructed, uncorrected, unexhorted, ungoverned, or ill governed? That man is a knave, a relative knave; he neither does his duty to God, or pays the debt of a husband, or of a parent, to his wife or his family.

Secondly, after the debt of education, there is the debt of induction due from us to our children. The debt from a parent is far from ending when the children come from school, as the brutes who turn their young off from them when they are just able to pick for themselves. It is our business, doubtless, to introduce them into the world, and to do it in such a manner as suits the circumstances we are in, as to their supply, and the inclinations and capacities of our children. This is a debt the want of paying which makes many children too justly reproach their parents with neglecting them in their youth, and not giving them the necessary introduction into the world, as might have qualified them to struggle and shift for themselves.

Not to do this is to ruin our children negatively on one hand, as doing it without judgment and without regard to our family circumstances, and our children's capacities, is a positive ruining them on the other. I could very usefully run out this part into a long discourse on the necessity there is of consulting the inclinations and capacities of our children in our placing them out in the world. How many a martial spirit do we find damned to trade, while we spoil many a good porter, and convert the able limbs and bones of a blockhead into the figure of a long robe, or a gown and cassock?

How many awkward clumsy fellows do we breed to surgery or to music, whose fingers and joints Nature originally designed, and plainly showed it us by their size, were better suited for the blacksmith's sledge or the carpenter's axe, the waterman's oar or the carman's whip?

Whence comes it to pass that we have so many young men brought to the bar and to the pulpit with stammering tongues, hesitations and impediments in their speech, unmusical voices, and no common utterance; while, on the other hand, Nature's cripples—bow-legged, battle-hammed, and half-made creatures—are bred tumblers and dancing-masters?

I name these because they occur most in our common observation, and are all miserable examples, where the children curse the knavery of their fathers in not paying the debt they owed to them as parents, in putting them to employments that had been suitable to their capacities, and suitable to what Nature had cut them out for.

I came into a public-house once in London, where there was a black *mulatto*-looking man sitting, talking very warmly among some gentlemen, who, I observed, were listening very attentively to what he said, and I sat myself down and did the like. 'Twas with great pleasure I heard him discourse very handsomely on several weighty subjects. I found he was a very good scholar, had been very handsomely bred, and that learning and study were his delight; and, more than that, some of the best of science was at that time his employment. At length I took the freedom to ask him if he was born in England?

He replied with a great deal of good humour in the manner, but with an excess of resentment at his father, and with tears in his eyes, "Yes, yes, sir, I am a true-born Englishman; to my father's shame be it spoken, who, being an Englishman himself, could find it in his heart to join himself to a negro woman, though he must needs know the children he should beget would curse the memory of such an action, and abhor his very name for the sake of it. Yes, yes," says he, repeating it again, "I am an Englishman, and born in lawful wedlock; happy had it been for me, though my father had gone to the devil for whoredom, had he lain with a cookmaid, or produced me from the meanest beggarwoman in the street.

"My father might do the duty of nature to his black wife; but, God knows, he did no justice to his children. If it had not been for this damned black face of mine," says he, then smiling, "I had been bred to the law, or brought up in the study of divinity; but my father gave me learning to no manner of purpose, for he knew I should never be able to rise by it to anything but a learned *valet de chambre*. What he put me to school for I cannot imagine; he spoiled a good tarpaulin when he strove to make me a gentleman. When he had resolved to marry a slave and lie with a slave, he should have begot slaves, and let us have been bred as we were born; but he has twice ruined me—first, with getting me a frightful face, and then going to paint a gentleman upon me."

It was a most affecting discourse indeed, and as such I record it; and I found it ended in tears from the person, who was in himself the most deserving, modest, and judicious man that I ever met with under a negro countenance in my life.

After this story I persuaded myself I need say no more to this case; the education of our children, their instruction, and the introducing them into the world, is a part of honesty, a debt we owe to them; and he cannot be an honest man that does not, to the utmost of his ability and judgment, endeavour to pay it.

All the other relative obligations, which family circumstances call for the discharge of, allow the same method of arguing for, and are debts in their proportion, and must be paid upon the same principle of integrity. I have neither room nor is there any occasion to enlarge upon them.

CHAPTER THREE

OF THE IMMORALITY OF CONVERSATION, AND THE VULGAR ERRORS OF BEHAVIOUR

Conversation is the brightest and most beautiful part of life; 'tis an emblem of the enjoyment of a future state, for suitable society is a heavenly life; 'tis that part of life by which mankind are not only distinguished from the inanimate world, but by which they are distinguished from one another. Perhaps I may be more particularly sensible of the benefit and of the pleasure of it, having; been so effectually mortified with the want of it. But as I take it to be one of the peculiars of the rational life that man is a conversable creature, so it is his most complete blessing in life to be blessed with suitable persons about him to converse with. Bringing it down from generals to particulars, nothing can recommend a man more, nothing renders him more agreeable, nothing can be a better character to give of one man to another, next to that of his being an honest and religious man, than to say of him that he is very good company.

How delightful is it to see a man's face always covered with smiles, and his soul shining continually in the goodness of his temper; to see an air of humour and pleasantness sit ever upon his brow, and to find him on all occasions the same, ever agreeable to others and to himself—a steady calm of mind, a clear head, and serene thoughts always acting the mastership upon him. Such a man has something angelic in his very countenance; the life of such a man is one entire scene of composure; 'tis an anticipation of the future state, which we well represent by an eternal peace.

To such a man to be angry, is only to be just to himself, and to act as he ought to do; to be troubled or sad is only to act his reason, for as to being in a passion he knows nothing of it; passion is a storm in the mind, and this never happens to him; for all excesses, either of grief or of resentment, are foreigners, and have no habitation with him. He is the only man that can observe that Scripture heavenly dictate, "*be angry and sin not*;" and if ever he is very angry, 'tis with himself, for giving way to be angry with any one else.

This is the truly agreeable person, and the only one that can be called so in the world; his company is a charm, and is rather wondered at than imitated. 'Tis almost a virtue to envy such a man; and one is apt innocently to grieve at him, when we see what is so desirable in him, and cannot either find it or make it in ourselves.

But take this with you in the character of this happy man, namely, that he is always a good man, a religious man. 'Tis a gross error to imagine that a soul blackened with vice, loaded with crime, degenerated into immorality and folly, can be that man—can have this calm, serene soul, those clear thoughts, those constant smiles upon his brow, and the steady agreeableness and pleasantry in his temper, that I am speaking of; there must be intervals of darkness upon such a mind. Storms in the conscience will always lodge clouds upon the countenance, and where the weather is hazy within it can never be sunshine without; the smiles of a disturbed mind are all but feigned and forged; there may be a good disposition, but it will be too often and too evidently interrupted by the recoils of the mind, to leave the temper untouched and the humour free and unconcerned; when the drum beats an alarm within, it is impossible but the disturbance will be discovered without.

Mark the man of crime; sit close to him in company; at the end of the most exuberant excursion of his mirth, you will never fail to hear his reflecting faculty whisper a sigh to him; he will shake it off, you will see him check it and go on. Perhaps he sings it off, but at the end of every song, nay, perhaps of every *stanza*, it returns; a kind of involuntary sadness breaks upon all his joy; he perceives it, rouses, despises it, and goes on; but in the middle of a long laugh in drops a sigh; it will be, it can be no otherwise; and I never conversed closely with a man of levity in my life but I could perceive it most plainly; 'tis a kind of respiration natural to a stifled conviction—a hesitation that is the consequence of a captivated virtue, a little insurrection in the soul against the tyranny of profligate principles.

But in the good man the calm is complete—it is all nature, no counterfeit; he is always in humour, because he is always composed:

He's calm without, because he's clear within.

A stated composure of mind can really proceed from nothing but a fund of virtue; and this is the reason why it is my opinion that the common saying, that content of mind is happiness, is a vulgar mistake, unless it be granted that this content is first founded on such a basis as the mind ought to be contented with, for otherwise a lunatic in Bedlam is a completely happy man; he sings in his hutch, and dances in his chain, and is as contented as any man living. The possession or power which that vapour or delirium has upon his brain makes him fancy himself a prince, a monarch, a statesman, or just what he pleases to be; as a certain duchess is said to have believed herself to be an empress, has her footmen drawn up, with javelins, and dressed in antic habits, that she may see them through a window, and believe them to be her guards; is served upon the knee, called her majesty, imperial majesty, and the like; and with this splendour her distempered mind is deluded, forming ideas of things which are not, and at the same time her eyes are shut to the eternal captivity of her circumstances; in which she is made a property to other persons, her estate managed by guardianship, and she a poor demented creature to the last degree, an object of human compassion, and completely miserable.

The only contentment which entitles mankind to any felicity is that which is founded upon virtue and just principles, for contentment is nothing more or less than what we call peace; and what peace where crime possesses the mind, which is attended, as a natural consequence, with torment and disquiet? What peace where the harmony of the soul is broken by constant regret and self-reproaches? What peace in a mind under constant apprehensions and terrors of something yet attending to render them miserable; and all this is inseparable from a life of crime:

For where there's guilt, there always will be fear.

Peace of mind makes a halcyon upon the countenance, it gilds the face with a cheerful aspect, such as nothing else can procure; and which indeed, as above, it is impossible effectually to counterfeit.

> *Bow, mighty reason, to thy Maker's name,*
> *For God and Peace are just the same;*
> *Heaven is the emanation of His face,*
> *And want of peace makes hell in ev'ry place.*
> *Tell us, ye men of notion, tell us why*
> *You seek for bliss and wild prosperity*
> *In storms and tempests, feuds and war—*
> *Is happiness to be expected there?*
> *Tell us what sort of happiness*
> *Can men in want of peace possess?*
>
> *Blest charm of Peace, how sweet are all those hours*
> *We spend in thy society!*
> *Afflictions lose their acid powers,*
> *And turn to joys when join'd to thee.*
>
> *The darkest article of life with peace*
> *Is but the gate of happiness;*
> *Death in his blackest shapes can never fright,*
> *Thou can'st see day beyond his night;*
> *The smile of Peace can calm the frown of Fate,*
> *And, spite of death, can life anticipate,*
> *Nay, hell itself, could it admit of peace,*
> *Would change its nature, and its name would cease;*
> *The bright transforming blessing would destroy*
> *The life of death, and damn the place to joy;*
> *The metamorphosis would be so strange,*
> *'Twould fright the devils, and make them bless the change;*
> *Or else the brightness would be so intense*
> *They'd shun the light, and fly from thence.*
>
> *Let heav'n, that unknown happiness,*
> *Be what it will, 'tis best described by peace.*
> *No storms without, or storms within;*
> *No fear, no danger there, because no sin:*
> *'Tis bright essential happiness,*
> *Because He dwells within whose name is Peace.*
>
> *Who would not sacrifice for thee*
> *All that men call felicity?*
> *Since happiness is but an empty name,*

A vapour without heat or flame,
But what from thy original derives—
And dies with thee, by whom it lives.

But I return to the subject of conversation, from which this digression is made only to show that the fund of agreeable conversation is, and can only be, founded in virtue; this alone is the thing that keeps a man always in humour, and always agreeable.

They mistake much who think religion or a strict morality discomposes the temper, sours the mind, and unfits a man for conversation. 'Tis irrational to think a man can't be bright unless he is wicked; it may as well be said a man cannot be merry till he is mad, not agreeable till he is offensive, not in humour till he is out of himself. 'Tis clear to me no man can be truly merry but he that is truly virtuous; wit is as consistent with religion as religion is with good manners; nor is there anything in the limitations of virtue and religion, I mean the just restraints which religion and virtue lay upon us in conversation, that should abate the pleasure of it; on the contrary, they increase it. For example: restraints from vicious and indecent discourses; there's as little manners in those things as there is mirth in them, nor indeed does religion or virtue rob conversation of one grain of true mirth. On the contrary, the religious man is the only man fully qualified for mirth and good humour, with this advantage, that when the vicious and the virtuous man appears gay and merry, but differ, as they must do, in the subject of their mirth, you may always observe the virtuous man's mirth is superior to the other, more suitable to him as a man, as a gentleman, as a wise man, and as a good man; and, generally speaking, the other will acknowledge it, at least afterward, when his thoughts cool, and as his reflections come in.

But what shall we do to correct the vices of conversation? How shall we show men the picture of their own behaviour? There is not a greater undertaking in the world, or an attempt of more consequence to the good of mankind, than this; but 'tis as difficult also as it is useful, and at best I shall make but a little progress in it in this work: let others mend it.

Of Unfitting Ourselves for Conversation

Before I enter upon the thing which I call the immorality of conversation, let me say a little about the many weak and foolish ways by which men strive, as it were, to unfit themselves for conversation. Human infirmities furnish us with several things that help to make us unconversable; we need not study to increase the disadvantages we lie under on that score. Vice and intemperance, not as a crime only, that I should speak of by itself, but even as a distemper, unfit us for conversation; they help to make us cynical, morose, surly, and rude. Vicious people boast of their polite carriage and their nice behaviour, how gay, how good-humoured, how agreeable! For a while it may be so; but trace them as men of vice, follow them till they come to years, and observe, while you live, you never see the humour last, but they grow fiery, morose, positive, and petulant. An ancient drunkard is a thing indeed not often seen, because the vice has one good faculty with it, viz., that it seldom hands them on to old age; but an ancient and good-humoured drunkard I think I never knew.

It seems strange that men should affect unfitting themselves for society, and study to make themselves unconversable, whereas their being truly sociable as men is the thing which would most recommend them, and that to the best of men, and best answers to the highest felicity of life. Let no man value himself upon being morose and cynical, sour and unconversable—'tis the reverse of a good man; a truly religious man follows the rule of the apostle—"*Be affable, be courteous, be humble; in meekness esteeming every man better than ourselves;*" whereas conversation now is the reverse of the Christian rule; 'tis interrupted with conceitedness and affectation—a pride, esteeming ourselves better than every man; and that which is worse still, this happens generally when indeed the justice of the case is against us, for where is the man who, thus overruling himself, is not evidently inferior in merit to all about him? Nay, and frequently those who put most value upon themselves, have the least merit to support it. Self-conceit is the bane of human society, and, generally speaking, is the peculiar of those who have the least to recommend them: 'tis the ruin of conversation, and the destruction of all improvement; for how should any man receive any advantage from the conversation of others, who believes himself qualified to teach them, and not to have occasion to learn anything from them?

Nay, as the fool is generally the man that is conceited most of his own wit, so that very conceit is the ruin of him; it confirms him a fool all the days of his life, for he that thinks himself a wise man is a fool, and knows it not; nay, 'tis impossible he should continue to be a fool if he was but once convinced of his folly:

If fools could their own ignorance discern, They'd be no longer fools, because they'd learn.

It will be objected here, indeed, that folly and conceit may be hurtful to conversation, may rob men of the advantage of it, unfit one side for conversing, and make it unprofitable, as well as unpleasant to the other; but that this is nothing to the immorality of conversation; that ignorance and conceit may be an infirmity, but is not always a crime; that the mischief of men's being fools is generally their own, but the mischief of their being knaves is to other people; and this is very true. But certainly egregious folly merits one paragraph of rebuke; perhaps it may touch the senses of some weak brethren one time or other, and the labour may not be lost.

I never saw a more simple, or yet a more furious irreconcilable quarrel, than once between two of the most empty, conceited people that ever I knew in the world; and it was upon one calling the other fool, which, on both sides, was unhappily very true. They fought upon the spot, but were parted by the company; they challenged, and could not meet, their friends getting notice of it; in short, it ruined them both; they made new appointments, and at last deceived their friends and fought again; they were both wounded, and one died; the other fled the country, and never returned. The first owned he was a fool, which was indeed some diminution of his folly. I say he knew himself to be a fool, but could not bear the other to tell him so, who was more a fool than himself. The other boldly asserted his own capacities to be infinitely greater than they were, and despised the first to the last degree, who indeed, if he had not more wit, had more modesty than the other; but both, like fools, fought about nothing, for such, indeed, the question about their wit might very well have been called.

But it is true, after all, the want of a conversable temper, if from a want or defect of sense, may be an infirmity, not an immorality; that is to say, the cause is not so in itself, but it may be so in its consequences that way also, for the conversation of fools is vanity in the abstract. I might here, indeed, find subject for a large tract upon the infinite diversity of fools, and by consequence the wondrous beauty of their conversation. I have on this occasion reckoned up a list of about seven and thirty several sorts of fools, besides Solomon's fool, whom I take to be the wicked fool only; these I have diversified by their tempers and humours, and in the infinite variety of their follies of several sorts, in every one of which they rob themselves, and all that keep them company, of the felicity of conversation, there being nothing in them but emptiness, or a fullness of what is ridiculous, and only qualified to be laughed at or found fault with.

I have likewise described some of their conversation, their vain repetitions, their catchwords, their laughings and gestures, and adapted them to make the world merry. I have thoughts of running it on into foreign characters, and describe French, Spanish, Portuguese fools, and fools of Russia, China, and the East Indies; but as this is something remote from the design in hand, which is more serious, and done on a much better view, and likewise of an unmeasurable length, like the weighty subject it is upon (for folly is a large field), so I refer it to another opportunity.

The truth is, that part of conversation which I am now to speak of, or which I mean by what I have said upon this subject, is the weighty and serious part, and is not the mere common talk, or a conversation which fools are capable of; 'tis exercised in a solid and well-tempered, frame, and when regulated, as it ought to be, by virtue and good morals, is qualified to make mankind happy in the enjoyment of the best things and of the best company; and therefore the evils that creep into and corrupt this part of our conversation are of the more fatal quality, and worth our exposing, that people may see and shun them, and that conversation may be restored among us to what it should be.

1. Of the Immorality of Conversation in General.

Some may object against the term, the immorality of conversation, and think the word improper to the subject; but to save any critic the dearly beloved labour of cavilling in favour of ill manners and unbecoming behaviour, I shall explain myself before I go any farther.

I call conversation immoral where the discourse is indecent, where 'tis irreligious or profane, where 'tis immodest or scandalous, or where 'tis slanderous and abusive. In these and such cases, *loqui est agere*; thus talking lewdly, or talking profanely, is an immodest action. Such is the power of words, that mankind is able to act as much evil by their tongues as by their hands; the ideas that are formed in the mind from what we hear are most piercing and permanent, and the force of example in this case is not more powerful than the force of argument.

Some of the worst sins are not to be committed but by the tongue, as the sin of blasphemy, speaking treason against the majesty of God, cursings and imprecations among men, lies, slanders, and a vast variety of petty excursions, which are grown modish by custom, and seem too small to be reproved.

We are here in England, after many years' degeneracy, arrived to a time wherein vice is in general discountenanced by authority; God in mercy to the age has inspired our government with a resolution to discourage it; the king, now his wars are over, and his foreign enemies allow him some rest, will, we hope, declare war against this domestic enemy.

The late Queen Mary, of heavenly memory for her piety and blessed example, appeared in her time gallantly in the cause of virtue; magistrates were encouraged to punish vice, new laws made to restrain it, and justice seemed to be at work to reclaim it. But what can kings, or queens, or parliaments do? Laws and proclamations are weak and useless things, unless some secret influence can affect the practices of those whom no laws can reach.

To make laws against words would be as fruitless as to make a shelter against the lightning. There are so many inlets to the breach that the informers would be as numerous as the criminals, and the trespass as frequent as the minutes we live in.

Conversation has received a general taint, and the disease is become a charm. The way to cure it is not by forcible restraints on particulars, but by some general influence on the public practice. When a distemper becomes pleasant to a patient he is the harder to be cured; he has a sort of aversion to the remedy because he has none to the disease. Our modern people have such a passion for the mode, that if it be but the fashion to be lewd, they will scandalise their honour, debauch their bodies, and damn their souls to be genteel. If the *beaux* talk blasphemy, the rest will set up for atheists, and deny their Maker, to be counted witty in the defence of it; when our tradesmen would be thought wise, and make themselves appear nice and learned in their conversation, nothing will satisfy them but to criticise upon things sacred, run up to discuss the inscrutables of religion, search the arcana even of heaven itself. The divinity of the Son of God, the hypostatic union, the rational description of the state everlasting, nay, the demonstrations of undemonstrable things, are the common subject of their fancied affected capacities.

Hence come heresies and delusions. Men affecting to search into what is impossible they should clearly discover, learn to doubt because they cannot describe, and deny the existence because they cannot explain the manner of what they inquire after; as if a thorough impossibility of their acting by their sense upon objects beyond its reach was an evidence against their being. Thus, because the Trinity cannot appear to their reasoning, they oppose their reasoning to its reality; they will divest the Son of God of His divinity, and of the hypostatic union of the Godhead in the person of Christ, because they cannot distinguish between the actions done by Him in His mediatorial capacity, in virtue of His office, and those actions which He did in virtue of His omnipotence and Godhead.

This is not an immorality and error in conversation only, or not so much so as I think it is a judgment upon it, a blast from Heaven upon the arrogance of the tongue. When proud men give themselves a loose to talk blasphemously to be thought witty, their Maker gives them up to suggest damnable errors till they begin to believe them, and to broach their own wicked hints, till they by custom learn to espouse and defend them, as children tell feigned stories till they believe them to be true. If our town fopperies were visible only in the little excursions of dress and behaviour, it would be satisfaction enough for a wise man either to pity or laugh at them; but when wit is set on work, and invention racked to find out methods how they may be more than superlatively wicked, when all the endowments of the mind and helps of art, with the accomplishments of education, are ranged in battle against Heaven, and joined in confederacy to make mankind more wicked than ever the devil had the impudence to desire of them, this calls out aloud for the help of all the powers of government, and all the strength of wit and virtue, to detect and expose it.

Indeed I had some thoughts to leave upon record a melancholy kind of genealogy of this horrid perfection of vice, which so increases in our age, I mean as it respects this nation, in which 'tis too ancient, indeed, to trace it back to its original; yet since its visible increase has been within the reach of our own memory, and it is, as I may say, the adopted child of our age, we may judge of the extent of its influence, and may take a short view of it in miniature. None, indeed, can judge of the extent of its influence but such as have conversed with all sorts of people, from the court to the plough-tail, where you may too sadly see the effect of it in the general debauching both the principles and practice of all sorts and degrees of this nation; but it will be an ungrateful task; it would lead me to the characters of persons, and to write satires upon the times, as well those past as those present, which, indeed, is not my business in this work, and therefore I throw by some keen observations which I had made upon this subject, my business here, or at least my design, being rather to instruct the age than to reproach it; and as for the dead, they are gone to their place.

St. Augustine observes, *De civitate Dei*, that the ancients justified their liberty in all excesses of vice which they practised in those times from the patterns of their gods; that the stories of the rapes and incest of Jupiter, the lewdness of Venus and Mars, and the like, made those crimes appear less heinous, since people had them frequently in the histories of the deities they worshipped, and that they must of necessity be lawful, seeing they were practised by those famous persons whom they had placed above the skies, and thought fit to adore.

If modern times have received unhappy impressions from vicious courts, and princes have not taken the needful caution not to guide to evil by their example, instead of turning this into satire upon those that are past, I choose to give it another turn, which our kings, and people too, in time to come may make good use of, and I hope will not be offended at supposing that they will do so.

1. To kings or sovereigns in future reigns; for I am not in this intending the present reign: It may without offence be said, that they have a glorious advantage put into their hands to honour their Maker, and advantage their people, to the immortal glory of their own memory, by prompting virtue and discouraging vice by their happy examples; by removing the vicious habits of conversation from the court-modes, and making vice unfashionable as it is unseemly. Why may not the royal example go as far to reform a nation as it has formerly done to debauch and ruin it? But as this respects the heads [1] of the people, I desire to speak it with the deference of a subject, and close this discourse with only saying, that I pray and wish it may be so.

2. To the people, with more freedom, I apply it thus: Let past examples be what they will, the present reign encourages no crime; why then should our modern conversation receive this taint? Why should we be volunteers in the devil's service while the power we are under gives us neither precept or example? If we are guilty,'tis by mere choice; the crime is all our own, and we are patterns to ourselves.

2. Of Reforming the Errors of Conversation.

But I leave this part as less grateful, and perhaps not more significant than what I have yet to say upon this subject; 'tis not so absolutely material to inquire how his conversation came first to be corrupted, as how it shall be reformed or recovered. The question before us is, by what method to retrieve this miserable defection, and to bring back the nation to some tolerable degree of good manners, that morality at least may regain its authority, and virtue and sobriety be valued again as it ought to be. This, I say, is a difficult thing to direct.

---

1 This was all written in King William's reign, and refers to that time. (Defoe)

—Facilis descensus Averno:
Sed revocare gradum, . . .
Hoc opus, hie labor est.—Virg. Æneid, vi.

Englished thus:

It is easy into hell to fall,
But to get back from thence is all.

The method might be easier prescribed than practised, though it cannot be perfectly prescribed neither. Something may, however, be said by way of observation; perhaps other well-wishers may hereafter throw their mites into this treasury, and some zealous reformers may at last make the attempt upon these foundations.

1. A strict execution of the laws against vice. We have already and are every day making very good laws to reform the people; but the benefit of laws consists in the executive power, which if not vigorously put forth, laws become useless, and it were better they were not made at all. I was once going to have added here a treatise, intituled, *An Essay upon the Insignificancy of Laws and Acts of Parliament in England*; but upon second thoughts, resolving to mingle no satire with my serious observations, I omitted this also. The deficiency of our laws is chiefly in the want of laws to reform the lawmakers, that the wheel of executive justice might be kept going. Of what use else can laws be?

2. An exemplary behaviour in our gentry, after whose copy the poor people generally write; not but that I acknowledge it will be harder to reform a nation than it would be to debauch it, though virtue should obtain upon custom, and become the fashion, because inclination does not stand neuter; but it would be a great step to this reformation if we could all join to discourage immorality by example. That if a man will be drunk or lewd, he shall, as a thief robs a house, do it in the dark, and be ashamed of it. If these two heads were brought to pass, I question not but reformation would come to such an height, that if a poor man happened to be drunk he should come and desire the constable to set him in the stocks for fear of a worse punishment; and if a rich man swore an oath in his passion, he should send his footman to the next justice of the peace with his fine and get a discharge for fear of being informed against and exposed.

In order to the furthering this great work it would be very necessary, if possible, to draw the picture of our modern vices, to let mankind see by a true light what they are doing, and how ugly a phiz the mistress they court really appears with when inclination, which paints her in different colours, is taken off.

It will be impossible to bring vice out of fashion if we cannot bring men to an understanding of what it really is; but could we prevail upon a man to examine his vice, to dissect its parts, and view the anatomy of it; to see how disagreeable it is to him as a man, as a gentleman, or as a Christian; how despicable and contemptible in its highest fruition; how destructive to his senses, estate, and reputation; how dishonourable, and how beastly, in its public appearances: such a man would certainly be out of love with it; and be but mankind once out of love with vice, the reformation is half brought to pass.

I shall not pretend to invade the province of the learned, nor offer one argument from Scripture or Providence; for I am supposed to be talking to men that doubt or deny them both. Divinity is not my talent, nor ever like to be my profession; the charge of priestcraft and schoolmen would not lie against me; besides, it is not the way of talking that the world relishes at this time; in a word, talking Scripture is out of fashion. But I must crave leave to tell my reader that if there were no God or Providence, devil or future state, yet they ought not to be drunken and lewd, passionate, revengeful, or immoral; 'tis so unnatural, so unruly, so ungenteel, so foolish and foppish, that no wise man, as a man, can justify it so much as to his own reason or the memory of his ancestors.

I suppose myself talking to men that have nothing to do with God, and desire He should have nothing to do with them; and yet even to such a vicious conversation, looked on without the gust of inclination, would appear too brutish to be meddled with, if we will but choose like men, not to say like Christians. Virtue and morality is more agreeable to human nature, more manly than vice and intemperance; 't is more suitable to all the ends of life, to the being of society, to the public peace of families, as well as nations. Mankind would rather be virtuous than vicious, if they were to choose only for their own ease and convenience. Vice tends to oppression, war, and confusion; virtue is peaceable and honest; vice is a poison to society; no man is safe if men have neither sobriety nor honesty, for the innocent will be robbed by the thief, ravished by the lewd, and murdered by the drunkard.

It might not be a needless digression if I should examine here whether whoring and drunkenness be not the two mother sins of the times, the spring and original of all our fashionable vices. I distinguish this because other sins, as murders, thefts, rapes, and the like, are now come so much in vogue, we are content the laws should be executed for them, but should think it very hard a man should be hanged for whoring or transported for being drunk.

I would not have any of our gentlemen think that my laying the charge of our debauchery on the examples of the gods, has taken off anything of the blame from those who have industriously propagated the spreading evil among their tenants and neighbours, by their own vicious example; and I could turn the whole observation into a satire on the manners of our gentlemen, and describe with what easiness our magistrates let fall the reins of their authority, and connive at the practice of all manner of intemperance and excess among the people; with what eagerness the poor countrymen are called in to be made drunk upon every occasion; with what contempt any person is looked upon either in town or country, that either will not be drunk, or cannot bear an excessive quantity of wine; how our common mirth is filled with songs and poems, recommending drunkenness and lewdness; and rampant vice rides riot through the nation. But, as above, I avoid satire; I shall endeavour to treat this foul subject in as civil terms as the case will bear, and only examine general conversation in particular heads, with some vulgar errors of behaviour which are crept in, and which seem authorised by custom.

3. Of Atheistical and Profane Discourse.

God Almighty Himself is the least beholding to this age of any that ever was from the beginning of time; for that being arrived to a degree of knowledge superior to all that went before us, or at least fancying it to be so, whereby the greater glory might accrue to Himself, the Author of all wisdom, that every gift, the brightest of all the heavenly blessings, is made use of to put the greatest contempt upon His majesty that mankind is capable of—to deny His essence; such an affront that the devils themselves never had the impudence to suggest to the world till they found man arrived to a degree of hardness fit for something never done before. All the heathen nations in the world came short of this; the most refined philosophers owned a first cause of all things, and that something was superior, whose influence governed, and whose being was sacred and to be adored. The devil himself, who is allowed to be full of enmity against the Supreme Being, has often set up himself to be worshipped as a God, but never prompted the most barbarous nations to deny the being of a God; and 'tis thought that even the devil himself believed the notion was too absurd to be imposed upon the world. But our age is even with him for his folly, for since they cannot get him to join in the denial of a God they will deny his devilship too, and have neither one nor other.

'Tis worth observation, after the most convincing arguments that nature and reason can produce for the existence of a deity, what weak, foolish, ridiculous shifts the most refined of our atheistical disputants fly to in defence of their notion, with what senseless pains they labour to reason themselves into an opinion which their own constitution, nature, and way of living give the lie to every moment; with how little consistency they solve all the other phenomena of nature and creation; that when in all other points they are capable of arguing strenuously, and are not to be satisfied but with strength of reason and sound argument, here they admit sophisms, delusive suppositions, and miserable shams and pretences to prevail upon their own judgments. This is touched at in the following lines upon the system of Prometheus, which I could not omit upon this occasion, relating to the heathens' ignorance in the great doctrine of first causes:

> *The great Promethean artist, poets say,*
> *First made the model of a man in clay,*
> *Contrived the form of parts, and when he had done,*
> *Stole vital heat from the prolific sun;*
> *But not a poet tells us to this day*
> *Who made Prometheus first, and who the clay,*
> *Who gave the great prolific to the sun,*
> *And where the first productive work begun.*

Also Epicurus, his philosophy will satisfy some people, who fancy the world was made by a strange fortuitous conjunction of atoms, without any pre-existent influence, or without any immediate power, which Mr. Creech very well translates thus:

> *But some have dreamt of atoms strangely hurled*
> *Into the decent order of the world,*
> *And so by chance combined, from whence began*
> *The earth, the heaven, the sea, and beast, and man.*

To which I crave leave to subjoin one complement, by way of confutation of this folly:

> *Forgetting first that something must bestow*
> *Existence on those atoms that did so.*

The arguments for the existence of a deity are so many, so nicely handled, and so unanswerable, that 'tis needless to attempt anything that way; no man in his wits needs any further demonstration of it than what he may find within himself, nor is it any part of the work I am upon; I have only a few things to ask of our modern atheists.

1. Whether their more serious thoughts do not reflect upon them in the very act, and give the lie to their arguments. My Lord Rochester, who was arrived to an extraordinary pitch in this infernal learning, acknowledged it on his deathbed; the sense nature has upon her of the certainty of this great truth, will give some convulsions at so horrid an act.

> Nature pays homage with a trembling bow,
> And conscious men but faintly disallow;
> The secret trepidation racks the soul,
> And while he says, no God, replies, "Thou fool."

2. I would ask the most confident atheist, what assurance he has of the negative, and what a risk he runs if he should be mistaken? This we are sure of, if we want demonstration to prove the being of a God, they are much more at a loss for a demonstration to prove the negative. Now, no man can answer it to his prudence, to take the risk they run, upon an uncertain supposititious notion; for if there be such a thing as a First Cause, which we call God, they have very little reason to expect much from Him who have made it their business to affront Him by denying His existence. Nor have they acted in their denial like wise men, for they have not used so much as the caution of good manners; but as if they were as sure of His nonentity as of the strongest demonstration, they have been witty upon the thing, and made a jest of the supposition, turned all matters of faith into ridicule, burlesqued upon religion itself, and made ballads and songs on the Bible. Thus Rochester has left us a long lewd song, beginning thus:

> Religion's a politic cheat,
> Made up of many a fable;
> Ne'er trouble the wise or the great,
> But only amuses the rabble.

Now, I am not in this discourse entering into any of the arguments in these grand questions on one side or other—that would be to make this work a collection of polemics; nor am I casuist enough for such a work—but I am observing or remarking upon the wickedness of the treating these subjects with levity and ignorance in the common road of conversation.

Methinks these gentlemen act with more courage than discretion; for if it should happen at last that there should be a God, and that He has the power of rewards and punishments in His hand, as He must have or cease to be almighty, they are but in an ill case:

> *If it should so fall out, as who can tell,*
> *But there may be a God, a heaven, a hell,*
> *Mankind had best consider well for fear,*
> *'T should be too late when their mistakes appear.*

Nor do they, in my opinion, discover any great wit in it; there is, if I might pass for a judge, something flat, something that shocks the fancy, in all the satire upon religion that ever I saw; as if the muse were not so much an atheist as the poet, but baulks the hint, and could not favour a blasphemous flight with so much freedom and spirit that at other times it has shown; which is a notice that there is a tacit sense of the Deity, though they pretend to deny it, lodged in the understanding; that it is not stifled without some difficulty, and struggles hard with the fancy, when the party strives to be more than ordinarily insolent with his Maker.

In the next place, as 'tis one of the worst immoralities of conversation when it is profane, so blasphemy is the extreme of profaneness; you cannot come into company with an atheist but you have it in his common discourse; he is always putting some banter or foolish pun upon religion, affronting the invisible Power, or ridiculing his Maker; all his wit runs out into it, as all diseases run into the plague in a time of infection, and you must have patience to hear it or quarrel with him.

Below these we have a sort of people who will acknowledge a God, but he must be such a one as they please to make him; a fine, well-bred, good-natured, gentleman-like deity, that cannot have the heart to damn any of his creatures to an eternal punishment, nor could not be so weak as to let the Jews crucify his own son. These men expose religion, and all the doctrines of repentance, and faith in Christ, with all the means of a Christian salvation, as matter of banter and ridicule. The Bible, they say, is a good history in most parts, but the story of our Saviour they look upon as a mere novel, and the miracles of the New Testament as a legend of priestcraft.

Further, besides these, we have Arians and Socinians, the disciples of an ancient heretic who went out of the church always at the singing the *Gloria Patri*, that he might be out of the noise, and would sit down at the doxology of the prayers, to note his disowning the godhead of Jesus Christ.

These are iniquities, as Job said, should be punished by the judges (chap. xxii. ver. 20), and these are the things which have given such a stroke to the ruin of the nation's morals; for no method can be so direct to prepare people for all sorts of wickedness as to persuade them out of a belief of any Supreme Power to restrain them. Make a man once cease to believe a God, and he has nothing left to limit his appetite but mere philosophy; if there is no supreme judicature, he must be his own judge and his own law, and will be so; the notion of hell, devil, and infernal spirits are empty things, and have nothing of terror in them, if the belief of a Power superior to them be obliterated.

But to bring this particular case nearer to the point of conversation, the errors of which lie before me: though we live in an age where these horrid degrees of impiety are too much practised, yet we live in a place where religion is professed, the name of God owned and worshipped, religion and the doctrines of Christianity established; and as it is so, it ought as much to be preserved by the civil power from the horrid invasion of atheists, deists, and heretics, as the public peace ought to be defended against freebooters, thieves, and invaders.

'Tis very improbable any reformation of manners should be brought to pass, if the debauching the religious principles of the nation goes on with an unrestrained liberty. How incongruous is it to the decoration[2] of government, that a man shall be punished for drunkenness and set in the stocks for swearing, but shall have liberty to deny the God of heaven and dispute against the very sum and substance of the Christian doctrine, shall banter the Scripture and make ballads of the Pentateuch, turn all the principles of religion—the salvation of the soul, the death of our Saviour, and the revelation of the Gospel— into ridicule. And shall we pretend to reformation of manners and suppressing immoralities, while such as this is the general mixture of conversation? If a man talk against the government, or speak scurrilously of the king, he is had to the Old Bailey, and from thence to the pillory or whipping-post, and it is fit it should be so; but he may speak treason against the Majesty of heaven, deny the godhead of His Redeemer, and make a jest of the Holy Ghost—and thus affront the Power we all adore—and yet pass with impunity.

Perhaps some in the company may have courage enough to blame

---

2. Perhaps this is a misprint for "declaration."

him, and vindicate their religion with a "Why do you talk so?" but where is the man or the magistrate that ever vindicated the honour of his Maker with a resentment becoming the crime? If a man give the lie to a gentleman in company he takes it as an affront, flies into a passion, quarrels, fights, and perhaps murders him; nay, some have done it for an absent friend whom they have heard abused; but where is the gentleman that ever thought himself so much concerned in the quarrel of his Maker but that he could hear Him affronted, His being denied, the lie given to His divine authority, nay, to His divine being, and all His commands ridiculed and exposed, without any motion of spirit to punish the insolence of the party, and without drawing his sword in the quarrel, or letting him know he does not like it?

Methinks I need not make an apology for this, as if I meant that quarrelling and fighting were a proper practice in the case; the law does not admit it in any case, nor is it reasonable it should; and God Almighty is far from desiring us to run any risk in His service. But I choose to bring the cases into a parallel, to signify that I think it is a vulgar error in our behaviour not to show our resentment when we hear the honour and essence of God slighted and denied, His majesty abused, and religion bantered and ridiculed in common discourses. I think it would be very reasonable to tell a gentleman he wants manners when he talks reproachfully of his Maker, and to use him scurvily if he resented it. It would very well become a man of quality to cane a lewd fop, or kick him downstairs, when his insolence took a loose at religion in his company, else men may be bullied out of their Christianity and lampooned into profaneness, for fear of being counted fools.

Besides, it is in this as in all other like cases; he that will talk atheistically in my company, either believes me to be an atheist like himself, or ventures to impose upon me; and by imposing upon me, either accounts me a fool that cannot tell when I am put upon, or a coward that dare not resent it.

Upon which account, even in good manners, it ought to be avoided; for it cannot be introduced into any part of conversation where the company are not all alike, without the greatest affront upon the rest that can be offered them.

4. *Of Lewd and Immodest Discourse.*

Talking bawdy, that sodomy of the tongue, has the most of ill manners and the least of a gentleman in it of any part of common discourse. Sir George Mackenzie has very handsomely exposed it in its proper colours; but it may not be an intrenchment at all upon his province to say something to it in these observations.

This part is the peculiar practice of such persons as are hardened to a degree beyond other men, proficients in debauchery, whose lives are so continually devoted to lewdness, that their mouths cannot contain it; who can govern their tongues no better than their tails, and are willing to be thought what really they are. In these it is neither so strange nor so much a crime as in others; these are persons not to be reclaimed. This part of my observation is not designed for their use; they are not to be talked out of their vice; they must go on and run their length. Nothing but a gaol or an hospital ever brings them to a reformation; they repent sometimes in that emblem of hell, a fluxing house, and, under the surgeon's hands, wish a little they had been wiser; but they follow one sin with another, till their carcass stinks as bad as their discourse, and the body becomes too nasty for the soul to stay any longer in it. From these no discourse is to be expected but what is agreeable to the tenor of their lives; for then to talk otherwise would be strained and eccentric, and become them as little as it would be tedious to them; but for a gentleman, a man of seeming modesty and a man of behaviour, not arrived to that class in the devil's school, for such a one to mix his discourse with lewd and filthy expressions, has something in it of a figure which intends more than is expressed.

Either we must believe such a one to be very lewd in his practice, or else, that not being able yet to arrive to such a degree of wickedness as he desires, he would supply that defect with a cheat, and persuade you to believe he is really worse than he is.

Which of these two characters I would choose to wear I cannot tell, for he that desires to be worse than he thinks he is, is certainly as bad as he desires to be; and he that is so bad as to let fly the excrescences of it at his mouth, is as wicked as the devil can in reason desire of him.

But I descend from the wickedness to the indecency of the matter; its being a sin against God is not so much the present argument as its being unmannerly—a sin against breeding and society, a breach of behaviour, and a saucy, insolent affront to all the company.

I do not deny but that modesty, as it respects the covering our bodies, was at first an effect of the fall of our parents into crime, and is therefore said still to be the consequences of criminal nature, and no virtue in itself, because no part of the body had been unfit to be exposed if vice had not made the distinction necessary.

But from this very argument lewd discourse appears to be a sin against custom and decency; for why must the tongue industriously expose things and actions at which Nature blushes, and which custom, let the original be what it will, has dedicated to privacy and retirement? What if it be true that shame is the consequence of sin, and that modesty is not an original virtue; it cannot but be allowed that sin has thereby brought us to a necessity of making modesty be a virtue, and sin would have a double influence upon us if, after it had made us ashamed, it should make us not ashamed again.

'Tis, in my opinion, a mistake when we say sin was the immediate cause of shame; 't was sin indeed gave a nudity to our natures and actions; the innocence, which served as a glory and covering, being gone, then shame came in as the effect of the conscious sinner; so the text says, they knew that they were naked. Shame was the effect of nakedness, as nakedness was the effect of sin.

From hence, then, I argue, and this is the reason of my naming it, that to be ashamed of our nakedness is a token of our wisdom and a monument of our just sense of the first sin that made it so, and as much a duty now as any other part of our repentance.

To give the tongue then a liberty in that which there is so much reason to blush at, argues no sense of the original degeneracy. Where is the man that partakes not of Adam's fall, has no vicious contracted habit and nature conveyed to him from his grand predecessor? Let him come forth, let him go naked and live by himself, and let his posterity partake of his innocence; his tongue cannot offend, nothing can be indecent for him to say, nothing uncomely for him to see.

But if these gentlemen think it proper to cover their nakedness with their clothes, methinks they should not be always uncovering it again with their tongues; if there are some needful things which Nature requires to be done in secret, and which they by inclination choose to act in private, what reason can they give for speaking of them in public?

There is a strange incongruity in the behaviour of these people, that they fill their mouths with the foul repetition of actions and things which their own practising in private condemns them for, nay, which they would be ashamed to do in public; such men ought to act the common requirements of Nature in the most publickest places of the streets, bring their wives or whores to the exchange and to the market-places, and lie with them in the street, or else hold their tongues, and let their mouths have no more the stench of their vices in public than their actions.

And why, of all the rest of the parts of life, must the tongue take a peculiar licence to revel thus upon Nature, as if she had a mind to reproach her with the infirmities she labours under? The customs we are obliged to, though they are clogs upon Nature and a badge of original defection, yet neither is there anything so odious or so burdensome that these gentlemen should triumph over the nurse that brought them up.

Take the lewdest and most vicious wretch that ever gave his tongue a loose in this hateful practice, and turn him about to his mother, you shall hardly prevail upon him to talk his lewd language to her; there is something nauseous and surfeiting in that thought. This talking bawdy is like a man going to debauch his own mother; for it is raking into the arcana and exposing the nakedness of Nature, the common mother of us all.

If, as a famous man of wit pretended, lying with a woman was the homeliest thing that man can do,'tis much more true that talking of it is the homeliest thing that man can say.

Nor is there to me any jest in these things, any appearance of mirth. There may be some pleasure in wicked actions, as the world rates pleasure, but I must profess 'tis dull, and for want of other more regular tastes that there should be pleasure in the discourse. 'Ts a profaning of Nature, and bringing forth those things she has hallowed to secrecy and retirement to the scandalous indecency of public banter and jest.

But men, who have always something to say for their folly, tell us 't is custom only which has made any of these things uncommon, and there 's no sin in speaking that which there was no sin in doing.

Let us grant them that custom only has done this; but if custom has made these things uncommon, and concealed, or, at least, banished them from the voice of conversation, 't is a sin then against custom to expose them again. Lawful customs become allowed virtues, and ought to be preserved. Custom is a good reason in such concealments; if custom has locked them up, let them remain so, at least, till you can give a better reason for calling them abroad again than custom has given for restraining them. Custom has made these things uncommon, because that sin which first made Nature naked left her so captivated by some of her parts more than others, that she could not but blush at those where sin had taken up its peculiar residence. Now, as I noted before, no man can with any tolerable satisfaction expose the parts till he has first extracted and separated the sin which, having possessed them, covered them at first with shame. He that can do this may go naked and talk anything.

And, for the same reason, no man can justify talking lewdly but he that at the same time throws away his clothes, for to cover himself with his hands and uncover himself with his tongue are contradictions in their own nature, and one condemns the other.

He that scorns the decency of words should also scorn the decency of clothes, let his body be as bald as his discourse, and let him scorn the shame of one as well as the shame of the other.

It is no sin, they say, to talk of what it is no sin to do; and, I may add, it is no sin at all to show what it is no sin to describe. Why is the eye to be less offended than the ear, since both are but the common organs of the understanding?

But the weather and inconveniences of the climate are urged for clothing our bodies, and I urge decency and good manners for the government of our tongues; and let any one contend it with me that thinks he can prove that the obligation of the first is greater than the obligation of the last.

Much more might be said to this, but I make but an essay, and am unwilling to run out into a long discourse.

Of Talking Falsely

By talking falsely, I do not design to enter upon a long dissertation upon the sin of lying in general. I suppose all men that read me will acknowledge lying to be one of the most scandalous sins between man and man, a crime of a deep dye, and of an extensive nature, leading into innumerable sins, that is, as lying is practised to deceive, to injure, betray, rob, destroy, and the like. Lying in this sense, is the concealing of all other crimes; it is the sheep's clothing hung upon the wolf's back, it is the Pharisee's prayer, the whore's blush, the hypocrite's paint, the murderer's smile, the thief's cloak; 'tis Joab's embrace and Judas's kiss; in a word, it is mankind's darling sin and the devil's distinguishing character.

But this is not the case I am upon, this is not the talking falsely I am upon, but a strange liberty which (particularly in conversation) people take to talk falsely, without charging themselves with any offence in it either against God or man. This is to be considered in two or three parts, not but that it has many more.

1. The liberty of telling stories, a common vice in discourse. The main end of this extraordinary part of tittle-tattle is to divert the company and make them laugh; but we ought to consider whether that very empty satisfaction, either to ourselves or friends, is to be purchased at so great an expense as that of conscience and of a dishonour done to truth.

'Tis scarce fit to say how far some people go in this folly, to call it no worse, even till sometimes they bring the general credit of their conversation into decay, and people that are used to them learn to lay no stress upon anything they say.

For once, we will suppose a story to be in its substance true, yet to what monstrous a bulk doth it grow by that frequent addition put to it in the relation, till not only it comes to be improbable, but even impossible to be true; and the ignorant relater is so tickled with having made a good story of it, whatever it was when he found it, that he is blind to the absurdities and inconsistencies of fact in relation, and tells it with a full face even to those that are able to confute it by proving it to be impossible.

I once heard a man, who would have taken it very ill to be thought a liar, tell a story, the facts of which were impossible to be true, and yet assert it with so much assurance, and declare so positively that he had been an eye-witness of it himself, that there was nothing to do but, in respect to the man, let him alone and say nothing. A gentleman who sat by, and whose good breeding restrained his passion, turned to him and said, "Did you see this thing done, sir?"

"Yes, I did, sir," says the relater.

"Well, sir," replies the gentleman, "since you affirm that you did see it, I am bound in regard to you to believe it; but upon my word, 'tis such a thing, that if I had seen it myself, I would not have believed it." This broke the silence, set all the company a-laughing, and exposed the falsehood more than downright telling him it was a lie, which might, besides, have made a broil about it.

It is a strange thing that we cannot be content to tell a story as it is, but we must take from it on one side or add to it on another till the fact is lost among the addenda, and till in time even the man himself, remembering it only as he told it last, really forgets how it was originally. This being so generally practised now, nothing is more common than to have two men tell the same story quite differing one from another, yet both of them eyewitnesses to the fact related. These are that sort of people who, having once told a story falsely, tell it so often in the same or like manner, till they really believe it to be true.

This supplying a story by invention is certainly a most scandalous crime, and yet very little regarded in that part. It is a sort of lying that makes a great hole in the heart, at which by degrees a habit of lying enters in. Such a man comes quickly up to a total disregarding the truth of what he says, looking upon it as a trifle, a thing of no import, whether any story he tells be true or no, so it but commands the company, as they call it, that is to say, procures a laugh or a kind of amazement, things equally agreeable to these story-tellers, for the business is to affect the company; either startle them with something wonderful never heard of before, or made them laugh immoderately, as at something prodigiously taking, witty, and diverting.

It is hard to place this practice in a station equal to its folly; 't is a meanness below the dignity of common-sense. They that lie to gain, to deceive, to delude, to betray, as above, have some end in their wickedness; and though they cannot give the design for an excuse of their crime, yet it may be given as the reason and foundation of it; but to lie for sport, for fun, as the boys express it, is to play at shuttlecock with your soul, and load your conscience for the mere sake of being a fool, and the making a mere buffoonery of a story, the pleasure of what is below even madness itself.

And yet, how common is this folly? How is it the character of some men's conversation that they are made up of story! And how mean a figure is it they bear in company! Such men always betray their emptiness by this, and having only a certain number of tales in their budget, like a pedlar with his pack, they can only at every house show the same ware over again, tell the same story over and over, till the jest is quite worn out; and to convince us that much of it, if not all, is born of invention, they seldom tell it the same way twice, but vary it even in the most material facts; so that though it may be remembered that it was the same story, it ought never to be remembered that it was told by the same man.

With what temper should I speak of these people? What words can express the meanness and baseness of the mind that can do thus, that sin without design, and not only have no end in the view, but even no reflection in the act? The folly is grown up to a habit, and they not only mean no ill, but indeed mean nothing at all in it.

It is a strange length that some people run in this madness of life; and it is so odd, so unaccountable, that indeed 'tis difficult to describe the man, though not difficult to describe the fact. What idea can be formed in the mind of a man who does ill without meaning ill; that wrongs himself, affronts truth, and imposes upon his friends, and yet means no harm; or, to use his own words, means nothing; that if he thinks anything, it is to make the company pleasant? and what is this but making the circle a stage, and himself the Merry Andrew?

The best step such men can take is to lie on; and this shows the singularity of the crime. It is a strange expression, but I shall make it out. Their way is, I say, to lie on, till their character is completely known, and then they can lie no longer; for he whom nobody believes can deceive nobody, and then the essence of lying is removed; for the description of a lie is, that it is spoken to deceive, or 'tis a design to deceive. Now, he that nobody believes can never lie any more, because nobody can be deceived by him. Such a man's character is a bill upon his forehead, by which everybody knows, "Here dwells a lying tongue." When everybody knows what is to be had of him they know what to expect, and so nobody is deceived; if they believe him afterwards 'tis their fault as much as his.

There are a great many sorts of those people who make it their business to go about telling stories; it would be endless to enumerate them. Some tell formal stories forged in their own brain without any retrospect either on persons or things, I mean, as to any particular person or passage known or in being, and only with the ordinary introduction of "There was a man," or "There was a woman," and the like.

Others again, out of the same forge of invention, hammer out the very person, man or woman, and begin, "I knew the man," or, "I knew the woman," and these ordinarily vouch their story with more assurance than others, and vouch also that they knew the persons who were concerned in it.

The selling or writing a parable, or an illusive allegoric history, is quite a different case, and is always distinguished from this other jesting with truth, that it is designed and effectually turned for instructive and upright ends, and has its moral justly applied. Such are the historical parables in the Holy Scripture, such *The Pilgrim's Progress*, and such, in a word, the adventures of your fugitive friend, *Robinson Crusoe*.

Others make no scruple to relate real stories with innumerable omissions and additions; I mean, stories which have a real existence in fact, but which, by the barbarous way of relating, become as romantic and false as if they had no real original. These tales, like the old *Galley of Venice*, which had been so often new vamped, doubled, and redoubled, that there was not one piece of the first timber in her, have been told wrong so often, and so many ways, till there would not be one circumstance of the real story left in the relating.

There are many more kinds of these, such, namely, as are personal and malicious, full of slander and abuse; but these are not of the kinds I am speaking of; the present business is among a kind of white devils, who do no harm or injury to any but to themselves; they are like the grasshopper, that spends his time to divert the traveller, and does nothing but starve himself.

The conversation of these men is full of emptiness, their words are levity itself, and, according to the text, they not only tell untruths, but "the truth is not in them." There is not a settled awe or reverence of truth upon their minds; it is a thing of no value to them, it is not regarded in their discourse, and they give themselves a liberty to be perfectly unconcerned about the thing they say, or the story they tell, whether it be true or no.

This is a most abominable practice on another account, namely, that these men make a jest of their crime. They are a sort of people that sin laughing, that play upon their souls as a man plays upon a fiddle, to make other people dance and wear itself out; they may be said to make some sport indeed, but it is all at themselves—they are the hearers' comedy and their own tragedy, and, like a penitent jack-pudding, they will at last say, "I have made others merry, but I have been the fool."

I would be glad to shame men of common-sense out of this horrid piece of buffoonery; and one thing I would warn them of, namely, that their learning to lie so currently in story will insensibly bring them to a bold entrenching upon truth in the rest of their conversation. The Scripture command is, "*Let every man speak truth unto his neighbour.*" If we must tell stories, tell them as stories, and nothing wilfully to illustrate or set it forth in the relation. If you doubt the truth of it say so, and then every one will be at liberty to believe their share of it.

Besides, there is a spreading evil in telling a false story as true, namely, that you put it into the mouths of others, and it continues a brooding forgery to the end of time. It is a chimney-corner romance, and has in it this distinguishing article, that whereas parables and the inventions of men, published historically, are once for all related, and, the moral being drawn, the history remains allusive only as it was intended (as in several cases [3] may be instanced within our time [4] and

---

3. The *Pilgrim's Progress*. (Defoe.)
4 The *Family Instructor* and others. (Defoe.)

without), here the case alters; fraud goes unto the world's end, for story never dies; every relater vouches it for truth, though he knows nothing of the matter.

These men know not what foundations they are laying for handing on the sport of lying, for such they make of it to posterity, not only leaving the example, but dictating the very materials for the practice; like family lies handed on from father to son, till what begun in forgery ends in history, and we make our lies be told for truth by all our children that come after us.

If any man object here that the preceding volumes of this work seem to be hereby condemned, and the history which I have therein published of myself censured, I demand in justice such objector stay his censure till he sees the end of the scene, when all that mystery shall discover itself, and I doubt not but the work shall abundantly justify the design, and the design abundantly justify the work.

Chapter Four
An Essay on the Present State of Religion in the World

In that part of my work which may be called history, I have frequently mentioned the unconquerable impressions which dwelt upon my mind and filled up all my desires, immovably pressing me to a wandering, travelling life, and which pushed me continually on from one adventure to another, as you have heard.

There is an inconsiderate temper which reigns in our minds, that hurries us down the stream of our affections by a kind of involuntary agency, and makes us do a thousand things, in the doing of which we propose nothing to ourselves but an immediate subjection to our will, that is to say, our passion, even without the concurrence of our understandings, and of which we can give very little account after 'tis done.

You may now suppose me to be arrived, after a long course of infinite variety on the stage of the world, to the scene of life we call old age, and that I am writing these sheets in a season of my time when (if ever) a man may be supposed capable of making just reflections upon things past, a true judgment of things present, and tolerable conclusions of things to come.

In the beginning of this life of composure (for now, and not till now, I may say that I began to live, that is to say, a sedate and composed life), I inquired of myself very seriously one day what was the proper business of old age. The answer was very natural, and indeed returned quick upon me, namely, that two things were my present work, as above:

1. Reflection upon things past.
2. Serious application to things future. Having resolved the business of life into these heads, I began immediately with the first; and as sometimes I took my pen and ink to disburden my thoughts when the subject crowded in fast upon me, so I have here communicated some of my observations for the benefit of those that come after me.

About the time that I was upon these inquiries, being at a friend's house, and talking much of my long travels, as you know travellers are apt to do, I observed an ancient gentlewoman in the company listened with a great deal of attention, and, as I thought, with some pleasure, to what I was saying; and after I had done, "Pray, sir," says she, turning her speech to me, "give me leave to ask you a question or two."

"With all my heart, madam," said I; so we began the following short dialogue:—

Old Gent. Pray, sir, in all your travels, can you tell what is the world a-doing? What have you observed to be the principal business of mankind?

Rob. Cru. Truly, madam, 'tis very hard to answer such a question, the people being so differently employed, some one way, and some another; and particularly according to the several parts of the world through which our observations are to run, and according to the differing manners, customs, and circumstances of the people in every place.

Old. Gent. Alas! sir, that is no answer at all to me, because I am not a judge of the differing customs and manners of the people you speak of; but is there not one common end and design in the nature of men, which seems to run through all their actions, and to be formed by Nature as the main end of life, and by consequence is made the chief business of living? Pray, how do they spend their time?

R. C. Nay; now, madam, you have added a question to the rest of a different nature from what, if I take you right, you meant at first.

Old Gent. What question, sir?

R. C. Why, how mankind spend their time; for I cannot say that one-half of mankind spend their time in what they themselves may acknowledge to be the main end of life.

Old Gent. Pray, don't distinguish me out of my question; we may talk of what is the true end of life, as we understood it here in a Christian country, another time; but take my question as I offer it, what is mankind generally a-doing as their main business?

R. C. Truly, the main business that mankind seems to be doing is to eat and drink; that's their enjoyment, and to get food to eat is their employment, including a little their eating and devouring one another.

Old Gent. That's a description of them as brutes.

R. C. It is so in the first part, namely, their living to eat and drink; but in the last part they are worse than the brutes; for the brutes destroy not their own kind, but all prey upon a different species; and besides, they prey upon one another for necessity, to satisfy their hunger, and for food; but man for baser ends, such as avarice, envy, revenge, and the like, devours his own species, nay, his own flesh and blood, as my Lord Rochester very well expresses it:

> *But judge yourself, I'll bring it to the test,*
> *Which is the basest creature, man or beast?*
> *Birds feed on birds, beasts on each other prey,*
> *But savage man alone does man betray.*
> *Pressed by necessity, they kill for food,*
> *Man undoes man, to do himself no good.*
> *With teeth and claws, by Nature armed they hunt,*
> *Nature's allowance to supply their want:*
> *But man with smiles, embraces, friendship, praise,*
> *Inhumanly his fellow's life betrays.*
> *With voluntary pains works his distress,*
> *Not for necessity, but wantonness.*

Old Gent. All this I believe is true; but this does not reach my question yet. There is certainly something among them which is esteemed as more particularly the end of life and of living than the rest; to which they apply in common as the main business, and which is always esteemed to be their wisdom to be employed in. Is there not something that is apparently the great business of living?

R. C. Why, really, madam, I think not. For example: great part of the world, and a greater part by far than we imagine, is resolved into the lowest degeneracy of human nature, I mean, the savage life; where the chief end of life seems to be merely to eat and drink, that is to say, to get their food, just as the brutal life is employed, and indeed with very little difference between them; for except only speech and idolatry, I see nothing in the life of some whole nations of people, and for ought I know, containing millions of souls, in which the life of a lion or an elephant in the deserts of Arabia is not equal.

Old Gent. I could mention many things, sir, in which they might differ, but that is not the present thing I inquire about; but, pray, sir, is not religion the principal business of mankind in all the parts of the world? for I think you granted it when you named idolatry, which they, no doubt, call religion.

R. C. Really, madam, I cannot say it is; because, what with ignorance on one hand, and hypocrisy on the other, 'tis very hard to know where to find religion in the world.

Old Gent. You avoid my question too laboriously, sir; I have nothing to do either with the ignorance or hypocrisy of the people; whether they are blindly devout, or knavishly and designedly devout, is not the case; but whether religion is not apparently the main business of the world, the principal apparent end of life, and the employment of mankind.

R. C. What do you call religion?

Old Gent. By religion, I mean the worshipping and paying homage to some supreme being; some God, known or unknown is not to the case, so it be but to something counted supreme.

R. C. It is true, madam, there are scarce any nations in the world so stupid but they give testimony to the being of a God, and have some notion of a supreme power.

Old Gent. That I know also, but that is not the main part of my question; but my opinion is, that paying a Divine worship, acts of homage and adoration, and particularly that of praying to the Supreme Being which they acknowledge, is derived to mankind from the light of Nature with the notion or belief itself.

R. C. I suppose, madam, you mean by the question then, whether the notion or belief of a God in general, and the sense of worship in particular, are not one and the same natural principle.

Old Gent. I do so, if you and I do but agree about what we call worship.

R. C. By worship, I understand adoration.

Old Gent. But there you and I differ again a little; for by worship, I understand supplication.

R. C. Then you must take them both in together, for some part of the Indian savages only adore.

Old Gent. I confess there is much adoration, where there is little supplication.

R. C. You distinguish too nicely, madam.

Old Gent. No, no, I do not distinguish in what I call worship; I allege that all the adoration of those poor savages is mere supplication: you say they lift up their hands to their idols, for fear they should hurt them.

R. C. I do say so, and it is apparent.

Old Gent. Why, that is the same thing, for then they lift up their hands to him, that is to say, pray to him not to hurt them; for all the worship in the world, especially the outward performance, may be resolved into supplication.

R. C. I agree with you in that, if you mean the apparent end of worship.

Old Gent. Why, did not your man Friday and the savage woman you tell us of, talk of their old idol they called Benamuckee? And what did they do?

R. C. It is very true they did.

Old Gent. And did not Friday tell you they went up to the hills, and said "O" to him? Pray, what was the meaning of saying "O" to him, but "O do not hurt us; for thou art omnipotent, and canst kill us: O heal our distempers; for thou art infinite, and canst do all things: O give us what we want, for thou art bountiful: O spare us, for thou art merciful:" and so of all the other conceptions of a God?

R. C. Well, madam, I grant all this; pray what do you infer from it? What is the reason of your question?

Old Gent. O sir, I have many inferences to draw from it for my own observation; I do not set up to instruct you.

I thought this serious old lady would have entertained a farther discourse with me on so fruitful a subject, but she declined it, and left me to my own meditation, which, indeed, she had raised up to an unusual pitch; and the first thing that occurred to me, was to put me upon inquiring after that nice thing I ought to call religion in the world, seeing really I found reason to think that there was much more devotion than religion in the world; in a word, much more adoration than supplication; and I doubt, as I come nearer home, it will appear that there is much more hypocrisy than sincerity—of which I may speak by itself.

In my first inquiries, I looked back upon my own travels, and it afforded me but a melancholy reflection, that in all the voyages and travels which I have employed two volumes in giving a relation of, I never set my foot in a Christian country; no, not in circling three parts of the globe; for excepting the Brazils, where the Portuguese indeed profess the Roman Catholic principles, which, however, in distinction from paganism, I will call the Christian religion—I say, except the Brazils, where also I made little stay, I could not be said to set foot in a Christian country, or a country inhabited by Christians, from the bay of Larache, and the port of Sallee, by the Strait's mouth, where I escaped from slavery, through the Atlantic Ocean, the coasts of Africa on one side, and of Caribbee, on the American shore, on the other side; from thence to Madagascar, Malabar, and the bay and city of Bengal, the coast of Sumatra, Malacca, Siam, Cambodia, Cochin China, the empire and coast of China, the deserts of Karakathie, the Mongol Tartars, the Siberian, the Samoiede barbarians, and till I came within four or five days of Archangel in the Black Russia.

It is, I say, a melancholy reflection to think how all these parts of the world, and with infinite numbers of millions of people, furnished with the powers of reason and gifts of Nature, and many ways, if not every way, as capable of the reception of sublime things as we are, are yet abandoned to the grossest ignorance and depravity; and that not in religion only, but even in all the desirable parts of human knowledge, and especially science and acquired knowledge.

What the Divine wisdom has determined concerning the souls of so many millions, it is hard to conclude, nor is it my present design to inquire; but this I may be allowed here, as a remark: if they are received to mercy in a future state, according to the opinion of some, as having not sinned against saving light, then their ignorance and pagan darkness is not a curse, but a felicity; and there are no unhappy people in the world, but those lost among Christians, for their sins against revealed light; nay, then being born in the regions of Christian light, and under the revelation of the Gospel doctrines, is not so much a mercy to be acknowledged as some teach us, and it may in a negative manner be true that the Christian religion is an efficient in the condemnation of sinners, and loses more than it saves, which is impious but to imagine.

On the other hand, if all those nations are included under the sentence of eternal absence from God, which is hell in the abstract, then what becomes of all the sceptical doctrines of its being inconsistent with the mercy and goodness of an infinite and beneficent Being to condemn so great a part of the world, for not believing in Him of whom they never had any knowledge or instruction? But I desire not to be the promoter of unanswerable doubts in matters of religion;

much less would I promote cavils at the foundations of religion, either as to its profession or practice, and therefore I only name things. I return to my inquiry after religion as we generally understand the word.

And in this I confine myself in my present inquiries to the particular nations professing the Christian religion only; and I shall take notice afterward what influence the want of religion has upon the manners, the genius, and the capacities of the people, as to all the improvable parts of human knowledge.

The Moors of Barbary are Mahometans, and that of the most unpolished and degenerate sort, especially of that part of the world where they live; they are cruel as beasts, vicious, insolent, and inhuman as degenerated nature can make them: moral virtues have so little recommended themselves to any among them, that they are accounted no accomplishment, and are in no esteem; nor is a man at all respected for being grave, sober, judicious, or wise, or for being just in his dealings, or most easy in his conversation; but rapine and injury is the custom of the place, and it is to recommend a great man that he is rich, powerful in slaves, merciless in his government of them, and imperiously haughty in his whole household. Every man is a king within himself, and regards neither justice or mercy, humanity or civility, either to those above him or those below him, but just as his arbitrary passions guide him.

Religion here is confined to the *biram* and the *Ramadan*, the feast and the fast, to the mosque and the bath; reading the *Alcoran* on one hand, and performing the washings and purifications on the other, make up their religious exercises; and for the rest, conversation is eaten up with barbarisms and brutish customs; so that there is neither society, humanity, confidence in one another, or conversation with one another; but men live like the wild beasts, for every man here really would destroy and devour the other if he could.

This guided me to a just reflection, in honour of the Christian religion, which I have often since made use of, and which on this occasion I will make a digression to, *viz.*, that it is to be said for the reputation of the Christian religion in general, and by which it is justly distinguished from all other religions, that wherever Christianity has been planted or professed nationally in the world, even where it has not had a saving influence, it has yet had a civilising influence.

It has operated upon the manners, the morals, the politics, and even the tempers and dispositions of the people; it has reduced them to the practice of virtue, and to the true methods of living; has weaned them from the barbarous customs they had been used to, infusing a kind of humanity and softness of disposition into their very natures; civilising and softening them, teaching them to love a regularity of life, and filling them with principles of generous kindness and beneficence one to another; in a word, it has taught them to live like men, and act upon the foundations of clemency, humanity, love, and good neighbourhood, suitable to the nature and dignity of God's image, and to the rules of justice and equity, which it instructs them in.

Nay, farther, I must observe also, that as the Christian religion has worn out, or been removed from any country, and they have returned to heathenism and idolatry, so the barbarisms have returned, the customs of the heathen nations have been again restored, the very nature and temper of the people have been again lost, all their generous principles have forsaken them, the softness and goodness of their dispositions have worn out, and they have returned to cruelty, inhumanity, rapine, and blood.

It is true, and it may be named as an objection to this remark of mine, that the Romans though heathens, and the Grecians by the study of philosophy in particular persons, and by the excellency of their government in their general or national capacity, were filled with notions of virtue and honour, with most generous and just principles, and acted with an heroic mind on many occasions; practising the most sublime and exalted height of virtue, such as sacrificing their lives for their country with the utmost zeal; descending to great examples of humanity and beneficence, scorning to do base or vile actions, as unworthy the Roman name, to save their lives; and a great many most excellent examples of virtue and gallantry are found in the histories of the Roman Empire.

This does not oppose, or rather indeed illustrates, what I say; for with all the philosophy, all the humanity and generosity they practised, they had yet their remains of barbarity, were cruel and unmerciful in their natures, as appeared by the barbarity of their customs, such as throwing malefactors to wild beasts, the fightings of their gladiators, and the like; which were not only appointed as punishments and severities by the order of public justice, but to show it touched the very article I am upon, it was the subject of their sport and diversion, and these things were exhibited as shows to entertain the ladies; the cutting in pieces forty or fifty slaves, and the seeing twenty or thirty miserable creatures thrown to the lions and tigers, was no less pleasant to them than the going to see an opera, a masquerade, or a puppet-show is to us; so that I think the Romans were very far from a people civilised and softened in their natures by the influences of religion. And this is evident because that as the Christian religion came among them, all those cruel customs were abhorred by them, the famous theatres and circles for their public sports were overthrown, and the ruins of them testify the justice of my observation at this very day.

Nor will it be denied if I should carry this yet farther, and observe, that even among Christians, those who are reformed, and farther and farther Christianised, are still in proportion rendered more human, more soft and tender; and we do find, without being partial to ourselves, that even the Protestant countries are much distinguished in the humanity and softness of their tempers; the meek, merciful disposition extends more among Protestants than among the Papists, as I could very particularly demonstrate from history and experience.

But to return back to the Moors, where I left off; they are an instance of that cruelty of disposition which was anciently in their nature, and how in a country abandoned of the true Christian religion, after it has been first planted and professed among them, the return of heathenism or Mahometanism has brought back with it all the barbarisms of a nation void of religion and good nature.

I saw enough of these dreadful people to think them at this time the worst of all the nations of the world; a nation where no such thing as a generous spirit, or a temper with any compassion mixed with it, is to be found; among whom Nature appears stripped of all the additional glories which it derives from religion, and yet whereon a Christian flourishing church had stood several hundred years.

From these I went among the negroes of Africa; many of them I saw without any the least notion of a Deity among them, much less any form of worship; but I had not any occasion to converse with them on shore, other than I have done since by accident, but went away to the Brazils. Here I found the natives, and that even before the Portuguese came among them, and since also, had abundance of religion, such as it was; but it was all so bloody, so cruel, consisting of murders, human sacrifices, witchcrafts, sorceries, and conjurings, that I could not so much as call them honest pagans, as I do the negroes.

As for the cannibals, as I have observed in the discourse of them, on account of their landing on my island, I can say but very little of them. As to their eating human flesh, I take it to be a kind of martial rage rather than a civil practice, for it is evident they eat no human creatures but such as are taken prisoners in their battles, and, as I have observed in giving the account of those things, they do not esteem it murder, no, nor so much as unlawful. I must confess, saving its being a practice in itself unnatural, especially to us, I say, saving that part, I see little difference between that and our way, which in the war is frequent in heat of action, viz., refusing quarter; for as to the difference between eating and killing those that offer to yield, it matters not much. And this I observed at the same time, that in their other conduct those savages were as human, as mild, and gentle as most I have met with in the world, and as easily civilised.

From these sorts of people I come to the Indians; for as to the Madagascar men, I saw very little of them, but that they were a kind of negroes, much like those on the coast of Guinea, only a little more used and accustomed to the Europeans by their often landing among them.

The East Indians are generally pagans or Mahometans, and have such mixtures of savage customs with them, that even Mahometanism is there in its corruption; neither have they there the upright just dealing, in matters of right and wrong, which the Turks in Europe have, with whom 'tis generally very safe trading, but here they act all the parts of thieves and cheats, watching to deceive you, and proud of being thought able to do it.

The subjects of the Great Mogul have a seeming polite government, and the inhabitants of Ceylon are under very strict discipline, and yet what difficulty do we find to trade with them? Nay, their very economy renders them fraudulent, and in some places they cannot turn their thoughts to being honest.

China is famous for wisdom, that is to say, that they, having such a boundless conceit of their own wisdom, we are obliged to allow them more than they have; the truth is, they are justly said to be a wise nation among the foolish ones, and may as justly be called a nation of fools among the wise ones.

As to their religion, 'tis all summed up in Confucius's maxims, whose theology I take to be a rhapsody of moral conclusions; a foundation, or what we may call elements of polity, morality, and superstition, huddled together in a rhapsody of words, without consistency, and, indeed, with very little reasoning in it; then 'tis really not so much as a refined paganism, for there are, in my opinion, much more regular doings among some of the Indians that are pagans, in America, than there are in China; and if I may believe the account given of the government of Montezuma in Mexico, and of the Uncas of Cusco in Peru, their worship and religion, such as it was, was carried on with more regularity than these in China. As to the human ingenuity, as they call it, of the Chinese, I shall account for it by itself. The utmost discoveries of it to me appeared in the mechanics, and even in them infinitely short of what is found among the European nations.

But let us take these people to pieces a little, and examine into the great penetration they are so famed for. First of all, their knowledge has not led them that length in religious matters which the common notions of philosophy would have done, and to which they did lead the wise heathens of old among the Grecian and Roman Empires, for they, having not the knowledge of the true God, preserved, notwithstanding, the notion of a God to be something immortal, omnipotent, sublime; exalted above in place as well as authority, and therefore made heaven to be the seat of their gods, and the images by which they represented their gods and goddesses had always some perfections that were really to be admired as the attendants of their gods, as Jupiter was called the Thunderer for his power, father of gods and men, for his seniority; Venus, adored for her beauty; Mercury for swiftness; Apollo for wit, poetry, music; Mars for terror and gallantry in arms, and the like.

But when we come to these polite nations of China, which yet we cry up for sense and greatness of genius, we see them grovelling in the very sink and filth of idolatry; their idols are the most frightful monstrous shapes, not the form of any real creature, much less the images of virtue, of chastity, of literature, but horrid shapes, of their priests' invention; neither hellish or human monsters, composed of invented forms, with neither face or figure, but with the utmost distortions, formed neither to walk, stand, fly, or go, neither to hear, see, or speak, but merely to instil horrible ideas of something nauseous and abominable into the minds of men that adored them.

If I may be allowed to give my notions of worship, I mean as it relates to the objects of natural homage, where the name and nature of God is not revealed, as in the Christian religion, I must acknowledge the sun, the moon, the stars, the elements, as in the pagan and heathen nations of old; and above all these, the representations of superior virtues and excellences among men, such as valour, fortitude, chastity, patience, beauty, strength, love, learning, wisdom, and the like—the objects of worship in the Grecian and Roman times—were far more eligible and more rational objects of Divine rights than the idols of

China and Japan, where, with all the economy of their State maxims and rules of civil government, which we insist so much on as tests of their wisdom, their great capacities and understandings, their worship is the most brutish, and the objects of their worship the coarsest, the most unmanly, inconsistent with reason or the nature of religion, of any the world can show; bowing down to a mere hobgoblin, and doing their reverence not to the work of men's hands only, but the ugliest, basest, frightfullest things that man could make; images so far from being lovely and amiable, as in the nature of worship is implied, that they are the most detestable and nauseous, even to nature.

How is it possible these people can have any claim to the character of wise, ingenious, polite, that could suffer themselves to be overwhelmed in an idolatry repugnant to common-sense, even to nature, and be brought to choose to adore that which was in itself the most odious and contemptible to nature; not merely terrible, that so their worship might proceed from fear, but a complication of nature's aversions?

I cannot omit, that being in one of their temples, or rather in a kind of oratory or chapel, annexed to one part of the great palace at Peking, there appeared a mandarin with his attendants, or, as we may say, a great lord and his retinue, prostrate before the image, not of any one of God's creatures, but a creature of mere human forming, such as neither was alive, nor was like anything that had life, or had ever been seen or heard of in the world.

The like image, or something worse, if I could give it a true representation, may be found in a garden chapel, if not defaced by wiser heads, of a great Tartarian *mandarin*, at a small distance from Nanking, and to which the poor abandoned creatures pay their most blinded devotions.

It had a thing instead of a head, but no head; it had a mouth distorted out of all manner of shape, and not to be described for a mouth, being only an unshapen chasm, neither representing the mouth of a man, beast, fowl, or fish; the thing was neither any of the four, but an incongruous monster; it had feet, hands, fingers, claws, legs, arms, wings, ears, horns, everything mixed one among another, neither in the shape or place that Nature appointed, but blended together and fixed to a bulk, not a body, formed of no just parts, but a shapeless trunk or log, whether of wood or stone, I know not; a thing that might have stood with any side forward, or any side backward, any end upward, Or any end downward, that had as much veneration due to it on one side as on the other—a kind of celestial hedgehog, that was rolled up within itself, and was everything every way; that to a Christian could not have been worthy to have represented even the devil, and to men of common-sense must have been their very soul's aversion. In a word, if I have not represented their monstrous deities right, let imagination supply anything that can make a misshapen image horrid, frightful, and surprising; and you may with justice suppose those sagacious people called the Chinese, whom, forsooth, we must admire—I say, you may suppose them prostrate on the ground, with all their pomp and pageantry, which is in itself not a little, worshipping such a mangled, promiscuous-gendered creature.

Shall we call these a wise nation who represent God in such hideous, monstrous figures as these, and can prostrate themselves to things ten thousand times more disfigured than the devil? Had these images been contrived in the Romans' time, and been set up for the god of ugliness, as they had their god of beauty, they might, indeed, have been thought exquisite, but the Romans would have spurned such an image out of their temples.

Nothing can render a nation so completely foolish and simple as such an extravagance in matters of religious worship; for if gross ignorance in the notion of a God, which is so extremely natural, will not demonstrate a nation unpolished, foolish, and weak, even next to idiotism, I know nothing that will.

But let me trace this wise nation that we talk so much of, and who not only think themselves wise, but have drawn us in to pay a kind of homage to their low-prized wit.

Government and the mechanic arts are the two main things in which our people in England, who have admired them so much, pretend they excel. As to their government, which consists in an absolute tyranny, which, by the way, is the easiest way of ruling in the world where the people are disposed to obey as blindly as the mandarin commands or governs imperiously, what policy is required in governing a people of whom it is said, that if you command them to hang themselves, they will only cry a little, and then submit immediately? Their maxims of government may do well enough among themselves, but with us they would be all confusion. In their country it is not so, only because whatever the mandarin says is a law, and God Himself has no power or interest among them to contradict it, unless He pleases to execute it *brevi manu* from heaven.

Most of their laws consist in immediate judgment, swift executions, just retaliations, and fair protection from injuries. Their punishments are cruel and exorbitant, such as cutting the hands and the feet off for theft, at the same time releasing murders and other flagrant crimes.

Their *mandarins* are their judges in very many cases, like our justices of the peace; but then they judge by customs, oral tradition, or immediate opinion, and execute the sentence immediately, without room or time to reflect upon the justice of it, or to consider of mitigations, as in all Christian countries is practised, and as the sense of human frailty would direct.

But let me come to their mechanics, in which their ingenuity is so much cried up. I affirm there is little or nothing sufficient to build the mighty opinion we have of them upon, but what is founded upon the comparisons which we make between them and other pagan nations, or proceeds from the wonder which we make that they should have any knowledge of mechanic arts, because we find the remote inhabitants of Africa and America so grossly ignorant and so entirely destitute in such things; whereas we do not consider that the Chinese inhabit the continent of Asia, and though they are separated by deserts and wildernesses, yet they are a continuous continent of land with the parts of the world once inhabited by the politer Medes, Persians, and Grecians; that the first ideas of mechanic arts were probably received by them from the Persians, Assyrians, and the banished transplanted Israelites, who are said to be carried into the regions of Parthia and the borders of Karakathie, from whence they are also said to have communicated arts, and especially handicraft, in which the Israelites excelled, to the inhabitants of all those countries, and, consequently, in time to those beyond them.

But let them be received from whom they will, and how long ago so ever, let us but compare the improvement they have made with what others have made; and, except in things peculiar to themselves, by their climate, we shall find the utmost of their ingenuity amounts but to a very trifle, and that they are outdone even in the best of their works by our ordinary artists, whose imitations exceed their originals beyond all comparison.

For example, they have gunpowder and guns, whether they have learned to make them by direction of Europeans, which is most likely, or that they found it out by mere strength of invention, as some would advance, though without certainty, in their favour—be it which it will, as I say, it matters not much, their powder is of no strength for the needful operations of sieges, mines, batteries, no, nor for shooting of birds, as ours is, without great quantities put together; their guns are rather an ostentation than for execution, clumsy, heavy, and ill-made; neither have they arrived to any tolerable degree of knowledge in the art of gunnery or engineering. They have no bombs, carcasses, hand-grenades; their artificial fireworks are in no degree comparable or to be named with ours; nor have they arrived to anything in the military skill—in marshalling armies, handling arms, discipline, and the exercise in the field—as the Europeans have; all which is depending on the improvement of firearms, &c, in which, if they have had the use of gunpowder so many ages as some dream, they must be unaccountable blockheads that they have made no farther improvement; and if it is but lately, they are yet apparently dull enough in the managing of it, at least compared to what ought to be expected of an ingenious people, such as our people cry them up to be.

I might go from this to their navigation, in which it is true they outdo most of their neighbours; but what is all their skill in sailing compared to ours? Whither do they go? and how manage the little and foolish barks and junks they have? What would they do with them to traverse the great Indian, American, or Atlantic oceans? What ships, what sailors, what poor, awkward, and ignorant doings are there among them at sea! And when our people hire any of them, as sometimes they are obliged to do, how do our sailors kick them about, as a parcel of clumsy, ignorant, unhandy fellows!

Then for building of ships, what are they? and what are they able to do towards the glorious art of building a large man-of-war? It is out of doubt with me, that all the people of China could not build such a ship as the *Royal Sovereign* in a hundred years; no, not though she was there for them to look at and take pattern by.

I might go on to abundance more things, such as painting, making glasses, making clocks and watches, making bone-lace, framework knitting; all of which, except the two first, they know little or nothing; and of the two first nothing compared to what is done in Europe.

The height of their ingenuity, and for which we admire them with more colour of cause than in other things, is their porcelain or earthenware work, which, in a word, is more due to the excellent composition of the earth they make them of, and which is their peculiar, than to the workmanship; in which, if we had the same clay, we should soon outdo them as much as we do in other things. The next art is their manufacturing in fine silks, cotton, herbs, gold, and silver, in which they have nothing but what is in common with our ordinary poor weavers.

The next mechanic art is their lacquering, which is just, as in their China ware, a peculiar to their country, in the materials, not at all in the workmanship; and as for the cabinet-work of it they are manifestly outdone by us; and abundance is every year sent thither framed and made in England, and only lacquered in China, to be returned to us.

I might run the like parallel through most of the things these people excel in, which would all appear to be so deficient as would render all their famed wisdom and capacity most scandalously imperfect. But I am not so much upon their cunning in arts as upon their absurdity and ridiculous folly in religious matters, and in which I think the rudest barbarians outdo them.

From this wise nation we have a vast extent of ground, near two thousand miles in breadth, partly under the Chinese government, partly under the Muscovite, but inhabited by Tartars of Mongol Tartary, Karakathie, Siberian, and Samoiedes pagans, whose idols are almost as hideous as the Chinese's, and whose religion is all Nature—and not only so, but Nature under the greatest degeneracy, and next to brutal. Father le Comte gives us the pictures of some of their house idols, and an account of their worship; and this lasts, as I have observed, to within a few days of Archangel. So that, in a word, from the mouth of the Straits, that is to say, from Sallee over to Caribbee, from thence round Africa by the Cape of Good Hope, across the vast Indian Ocean, and upon all the coast of it, about by Malacca and Sumatra, through the straits of Singapore and the coast of Siam northwards to China, and through China by land over the deserts of the Grand Tartary to the river Dwina, being a circuit three times the diameter of the earth, and every jot as far as the whole circumference, the name of God is not heard of, except among a few of the Indians that are Mahometans; the Word of God is not known, or the Son of God spoken of.

Having some warmth in my search after religion, occasioned by this reflection, and so little of it appearing in all the parts which I had travelled, I resolved to travel over the rest of the world in books, for my wandering days are pretty well over; I say, I resolved to travel the rest in books; and sure, said I, there must appear abundance of serious religion in the rest of the world, or else I know nothing at all of where I shall find it.

But I find by my reading, just as I did in travelling, that all the customs of nations, as to religion, were much alike; that, one with another, they are more devout in their worship of something, whatever it be, than inquisitive after what it is they worship; and most of the altars of worship in the world might to this day be inscribed to the unknown God.

This may seem a strange thing; but that wonder may cease when further inquiry is made into the particular objects of worship which the several nations of the world bow down to, some of which are so horrid, so absurd, as one would think human nature could not sink so low as to do her homage in so irrational a manner.

And here, being to speak of religion as idolatrous, it occurs to me that it seemed strange that, except in Persia and some part of Tartary, I found none of the people look up for their gods, but down; by which it came into my mind that, even in idolatry itself, the world was something degenerated, and their reason was more hoodwinked than their ancestors 1 .

By looking up and looking down, I mean, they do not, as the Romans, look up among the stars for their idols, place their gods in the skies, and worship, as we might say, like men, but look down among the brutes, form idols to themselves out of the beasts, and figure things like monsters, to adore them for their ugliness and horrible deformity.

Of the two, the former, in my opinion, was much the more rational idolatry, as particularly the Persians worshipping the sun; and when I had a particular account of that of Bengal, it presently occurred to my thoughts that there was something awful, something glorious and godlike in the sun, that, in the ignorance of the true God, might rationally bespeak the homage of the creatures; and to whom it seemed reasonable, where reason was its own judge only, without the helps of Revelation, to pay an adoration as the parent of light, and the giver of life to all the vegetative world, and as in a visible manner enlivening and influencing the rational and sensitive life, and which might, for aught they knew, at first create, as it did since so plainly affect, all things round us.

This thought gave birth to the following excursion, with which I shall close this observation:

Hail! glorious lamp, the parent of the day,
Whose beams not only heat and life convey;
But may that heat and life, for aught we know,
On many, many distant worlds bestow.
Immense, amazing globe of heavenly fire,

To whom all flames ascend, in whom all lights expire,
Rolling in flames, emits eternal ray,
Yet self-sufficient suffers no decay.
Thy central vigour never, never dies,
But life the motion, motion life supplies,
When lesser bodies rob us of thy beams,
And intercept thy flowing, heavenly streams;
Fools by mistake eclipse thee from their sight,
When 'tis the eyes eclipsed, and not thy light.
Thy absence constitutes effectual night
When rolling earth deprives us of thy light;
And planets all opaque and beggarly,
Borrow thy beams, and strive to shine like thee;
In their mock, lifeless light we starve and freeze,
And wait the warmth of thy returning rays.
Thy distance leaves us all recline and sad,
And hoary winter governs in thy stead:
Swift thy returning vigour, warm and mild,
Salutes the earth, and gets the world with child.
Great soul of nature, from whose vital spring
Due heat and life diffused through everything:
Govern'st the moon and stars by different ray,
 She queen of night, thee monarch of the day,
The moon, and stars, and earth, and plants obey.
When darker nations see thee placed on high,
And feel thy warmth their genial heat supply;
How imperceptible thy influence
Slides through their veins, and touches every sense;
By glimmering nature led, they bow their knee,
Mistake their God, and sacrifice to thee,
Mourn thy declining steps, and hate the night,
But when in hope of thy approaching light,
Bless thy return, which brings the cheerful day,
And to thy wond'rous light false adorations pay.
Nor can we blame the justice of the thought,
In minds by erring reason only taught.
Nature, it seems, instructs a deity,
And reason says there's none so bright as thee.
Nor is thy influence so much a jest,
There's something shocks our nature in the rest:

To make a God, and then the tool adore,
And bow to that that worshipped us before.
The nonsense takes off all the reverence,
That can't be worshipping that is not sense.
But when the spring of Nature shows its face,
The glory of its rays, the swiftness of its race,
Stupendous height and majesty divine,
And with what awful splendour it can shine,
Who that no other news from heaven could hear,
Would think but this was God, would think and fear.
No other idol ever came so near.

Certain it is that the Persians, who thus paid their adoration to the sun, were at that time some of the wisest people in the world. Some tell us that the great image that Nebuchadnezzar set up for all his people to worship, was represented holding the sun in his right hand; and that it was to the representation of the sun that he commanded all nations and kindreds to bow and to worship. If so, then the Assyrians were worshippers also of the sun as well as the Persians, which is not at all improbable. We read also in the Scripture of those nations who worshipped all the host of heaven, a thing much more rational, and nearer of kin to worshipping the great God of heaven than worshipping the whole host of the earth, and worshipping the most abject and loathsome creatures, or but even the representations of those creatures, which was still worse than the other.

But what are all the absurdities of heathenism, which at last are resolved into the degeneracy of mankind, and their being fallen from the knowledge of the true God, which was once, as we have reason to believe, diffused to all mankind? I say, what are these? And how much ground for just reflection do they afford us, compared to the gross things in practice which we find every day among those nations who profess to have had the clear light of Gospel revelation?

How many self-contradicting principles do they hold? How contrary to their profession do they act? How does one side burn for what another side abhors? And how do Christians, taking that venerable name for a general appellation, doom one another to the devil for a few disagreeing clauses of the same religion, while all profess to worship the same Deity, and to expect the same salvation?

With what preposterous enthusiasms do some mingle their knowledge, and with as gross absurdities others their devotion? How blindly superstitious; how furious and raging in their zeal? How cruel, inexorable, and even inhuman and barbarous to one another, when they differ? as if religion divested us of humanity, and that in our worshipping a God of mercy, and in whose compassions alone it is that we have room to hope, we should, to please and serve Him, banish humanity from our nature, and show no compassion to those that fall into our hands.

In my travelling through Portugal, it was my lot to come to Lisbon while they held there one of their courts of justice called *Auto-de-fe*, that is to say, a court of justice of the Inquisition. It is a subject which has been handled by many writers, and indeed exposed by some of the best Catholics; and my present business is not to write a history, or engage in a dispute, but to relate a passage.

They carried in procession all their criminals to the great church, where eight of them appeared first, dressed up in gowns and caps of canvas, upon which were painted all that man could devise of hell's torments, devils broiling and roasting human bodies, and a thousand such frightful things, with flames and devils besides in every part of the dress.

Those I found were eight poor creatures condemned to be burnt, and for they scarce knew what, but for crimes against the Catholic faith, and against the blessed Virgin, and they were burnt. One of them, it was said, rejoiced that he was to be burnt, and being asked why, answered that he had much rather die than be carried back to the prison of the Inquisition, where their cruelties were worse than death. Of those eight, as I was told, some were Jews, whose greatest crime, as many there did not scruple to say, was that they were very rich; and some Christians were in the number at the same time, whose greatest misery was that they were very poor.

It was a sight that almost gave me a shock in my notion of Christianity itself, till I began to recollect that it might be possible that Inquisitors were scarce Christians, and that I knew many Catholic countries do not suffer this abominable judicature to be erected among them.

I have seen much, and read more, of the unhappy conduct, in matters of religion, among the other nations of the world professing the Christian religion; and upon my word I find some practices infinitely scandalous, some which are the common received customs of Christians, which would be the abhorrence of heathens; and it requires a strong attachment to the foundation, which is indeed the principal part in religion, to guard our minds against being offended even at the Christian religion itself, but I got over that part afterward.

Let it not offend the ears of any true lover of the Christian religion that I observe some of the follies of the professors of the Christian religion, assuring you 't is far from being my design to bring the least scandal upon the profession itself.

And here, therefore, let me give the words of a judicious person who travelled from Turkey through Italy. His words are these:—

"When I was in Italy I ranged over great part of the patrimony of St. Peter, where one would think, indeed, the face of religion would be plainest to be seen, and without any disguise; but, in short, I found there the face of religion, and no more.

"At Rome there was all the pomp and glory of religious habits: the Pope and the cardinals walked with a religious gravity, but lived in a religious luxury, kept up the pomp of religion and the dignity of religious titles; but, like our Lord's observation on the Pharisees, I found within they were all ravening wolves.

"The religious justice they do there is particularly remarkable, and very much recommends them. The Church protects murderers and assassins, and then delivers the civil magistrates over to Satan for doing justice. They interdict whole kingdoms, and shut up the churches for want of paying a few ecclesiastic dues, and so put a stop to religion for want of their money. I found the courtesans were the most constant creatures at the church, and the most certain place for an assignation with another man's wife was at prayers.

"The Court of Inquisition burnt two men for speaking dishonourably of the blessed Virgin, and the missionaries in China tolerated the worshipping the devil by their new convert. A Jew was likewise burnt for denying Christ, while the Jesuits joined the paganism of the heathen with the high mass, and sung anthems to the immortal idols of Tonquin.

"When I saw this I resolved to inquire no more after religion in Italy, till by accident meeting with a quietist, he gave me to understand that all religion was internal, that the duties of Christianity were summed up in reflection and ejaculation. He inveighed bitterly against the game of religion which he said was playing over the world by the clergy; and said Italy was a theatre, where religion was the grand opera, and the Popish clergy were the stage players. I liked him in many of his notions about other people's religion—; but when I came to talk with him a little closely about his own, it was so wrapped up in his internals, concealed in the cavities and dark parts of the soul, viz., meditation without worship, doctrine without practice, reflection without reformation, and zeal without knowledge, that I could come to no certainty with him but in this, that religion in Italy was really invisible."

This was very agreeable to my notions of Italian religion, and to what I had met with from other people that had travelled the country, but one observation of blindness and superstition I must give within my own knowledge, and nearer home. When passing through Flanders I found the people in a certain city there in a very great commotion. The case was this. A certain *scelerate* (so they call an abandoned wretch given up to all wickedness) had broken into a chapel in the city, and had stolen the *pix* or casket wherein the sacred host was deposited; which host, after rightly consecrated, they believe to be the real body of our blessed Saviour, being transubstantiated, as they call it, from the substance of bread.

The fact being discovered, the city, as I said above, was all up in a tumult; the gates were shut up, nobody suffered to go out, every house was searched, and the utmost diligence used; and at length, as it was next to impossibility he should escape, he was discovered.

His execution was not long deferred. But first he was examined, and I think by torture, what he had done with the sacred thing which was in the *pix*, which he had stolen? And at length he confessed that he had thrown it into a house of office, and was carried with a guard to show them the place.

As it was impossible to find a little piece of a wafer in such a place, though no pains were spared in a most filthy manner to search for it; but, as I say, it could not be found; immediately the place was judged consecrated *ipso facto*, turned into an oratory, and the devout people flocked to it to expiate, by their prayers, the dishonour done to the Lord God by throwing His precious body into so vile a place. It was determined by the wiser part that the body would not fall down into the place, but be snatched up by its inherent power, or by the holy angels, and not be suffered to touch the excrements in that place. However, the people continued their devotions for some time just in the place where it was, and afterwards a large chapel was built upon it, where the same prayers are continued, as I suppose, to this day.

I had a particular occasion to come at a very accurate account of Poland by a Polish gentleman, in whose company I travelled, and from whom I learned all that was worth inquiring of about religious affairs in Prussia on one side and Muscovy on the other.

As for Poland, he told me they were all confusion both in Church and in State; that notwithstanding their wars they were persecutors of the worst kind, that they let the Jews live among them undisturbed to such a degree, that in the country about Lemburg and Kiow there were reckoned above 30,000 Jews; that these had not toleration only but many privileges granted them, though they denied Christ to be the Messiah, or that the Messiah was come in the flesh, and blasphemed His name upon frequent occasions; and at the same time they persecuted the Protestants, and destroyed their churches, wherever they had power to do it.

On the other hand, when I came to inquire of those Protestants, and what kind of people they were who suffered so severely for their religion, I found they were generally a sort of Protestants called Socinians, and that Lelius Socinus had spread his errors so universally over this country that our Lord Jesus Christ was reduced here to little more than a good man sent from heaven to instruct the world, and far from capable of effecting by the influence of His Spirit and grace the glorious work of redeeming the world. As for the divinity of the Holy Ghost, they have no trouble about it.

Having given this account of knowledge and piety in the countries inhabited by Christians of the Roman Church, it seems natural to say something of the Greek Church.

There are in the Czar of Muscovy's dominions abundance of wooden churches, and had not the country been as full of wooden priests something might have been said for the religion of the Muscovites, for the people are wonderfully devout there; which would have been very well, if it had not been attended with the profoundest ignorance that was ever heard of in any country where the name of Christian was so much as talked of.

But when I came to inquire about their worship, I found our Lord Jesus Christ made so much a meaner figure among them than St. Nicholas that I concluded religion was swallowed up of superstition, and so indeed I found it was upon all occasions: as to the conduct of the people in religious matters, their ignorance is so established upon obstinacy, which is the Muscovite's national sin, that it would be really to no purpose to look any longer for a reformation among them.

In short, no man will, I believe, say of me that I do the Muscovites any wrong when I say they are the most ignorant and most obstinate people in the Christian world, when I tell the following story of them.

It was after the battle at Narva, where the late King of Sweden, Charles XII., defeated their great army, and after the victory extended his troops pretty far into their country, and perhaps plundered them a little as he advanced; when the Muscovites, we may be sure, being in the utmost distress and confusion, fell to their prayers. We read of nothing they had to say to God Almighty in that case; but to their patron saint they addressed this extraordinary prayer:

O thou, our perpetual comforter in all our adversities! thou infinitely powerful St. Nicholas, by what sin, and how have we highly offended thee in our sacrifices, genuflections, reverences, and actions of thanksgiving, that thou hast thus forsaken us? We had therefore sought to appease thee entirely, and we had implored thy presence and thy succour against the terrible, insolent, dreadful, enraged, and undaunted enemies and destroyers; when, like lions, bears, and other savage beasts that have lost their young ones, they attacked us after an insolent and terrible manner; and terrified and wounded, and killed us by thousands, us who are thy people. Now, as it is impossible that this should happen without witchcraft and enchantment, seeing the great care that we had taken to fortify ourselves, after an impregnable manner, for the defence and security of thy name, we beseech thee, O St. Nicholas, to be our champion, and the bearer of our standard, to be with us both in peace and in war, and in our necessities, and at the time of our death, to protect us against this horrible and tyrannical crew of sorcerers, and to drive them far enough off from our frontiers, with the recompense which they may deserve.

It may be hoped I may give a better account of religion among the Protestants than I have among the Roman and Grecian Churches; and I will, if in justice it is possible.

The next to the nations I have been mentioning, I mean in geographical order, are those reformed Christians called Lutherans; to say no worse of them, the face of religion indeed is altered much between these and the latter. But I scarce know what name to give it, at least as far as I have inquired into it, or what it is like.

It was Popery and no Popery; there was the *consub*, but not the *transub*. The service differed indeed from the mass, but the deficiency seemed to be made up very much with the trumpets, kettle-drums, fiddles, *hautboys*, &c, and all the merry part of the Popish devotion; upon which it occurred to me presently, that if there was no danger of Popery among the Lutherans, there was danger of superstition; and as for the pious part, I saw very little of it in either of them.

By religion, therefore, the reader is desired to understand here not the principles upon which the several nations denominate themselves, so much as the manner in which they discover themselves to be sincere in the profession which they make. I had no inclination here to enter into the inquiry after the creeds which every nation professed to believe, but the manner in which they practised that religion which they really professed; for what is religion to me without practice? And although it may be true that there can be no true religion where it is not professed upon right principles; yet, that which I observe here, and which to me is the greatest grievance among Christians, is the want of a religious practice even where there are right principles at bottom, and where there is a profession of the orthodox faith.

In brief, I am not hunting after the profession of religion, but the practice. The first I find almost in every nation—*nulla gens tam barbara*; but the last I am like to travel through the histories of all Christendom with my search, and perhaps may hardly be able, when I have done, to tell you where it is.

All the satire of this inquiry will look this way; for where God has not given a people the blessing of a true knowledge of Himself, it would call for our pity, not reproach. It would be a very dull satire indeed that a man should be witty upon the negroes in Africa for not knowing Christ, and not understanding the doctrine of a Saviour; but if turning to our modern Christians of Barbadoes and Jamaica for not teaching them, not instructing them, and for refusing to baptize them, there the satire would be pointed and seasonable, as we shall hear farther by-and-by.

But to return to the Lutherans, for there I am supposed to be at this time, I mean, among the courts and cities of Brandenburg, Saxony, &c,—I had opportunity here to view a court affecting gallantry, magnificence, and gay things, to such a height, and with such a passion, to exceed the whole world in that empty part of human felicity called show, that I thought it was impossible to pursue it with such an impetuous torrent of the affections without sacrificing all things to it which wise men esteem more valuable.

Nor was my notion wrong; for the first thing I found sacrificed, as I say, to this voluptuous humour was the liberties of the people, who being by constitution or custom rather under absolute government, and at the arbitrary will of the prince, are sure to pay, not all they can spare, but even all they have, to gratify the unbounded appetite of a court given up to pleasure and exorbitance.

By all I have read of the manner of living there, both court and people;, the latter are entirely given up to the former, not by necessity only, but by the consent of custom and the general way of management through the whole country; nay, this is carried to such a height that, as I have been told, the king's coffers are the general cesspool of the nations, whither all the money of the kingdoms flows, and only disperses again as that gives it out—whether by running over or running out at its proper vent, I do not inquire; so that as all the blood in the human body circulates in twenty-four hours through the ventricles of the heart, so all the money in the kingdom is said to pass once a year through the king's treasury.

How far poverty and misery may prompt piety and devotion among the poor inhabitants, I cannot say; but if luxury and gallantry, together with tyranny and oppression to support it, can subsist with true religion in the great men, then, for aught I know, the courts of Prussia and Dresden may be the best qualified in the world to produce this thing called religion, which, I have hitherto seen, is hard to be found.

It is true, that the magnificence of the wisest king in the world in Jerusalem was esteemed the felicity of his people; but it seems to be expressed very elegantly, not as a testimony of his glory only, but of the flourishing condition of his people at the same time, under the prosperous circumstances which his reign brought them to, *viz.*, that he made gold to be for plenty like the stones in the streets, amply expressing the flourishing condition of his people under him.

I have likewise read, indeed, and heard much of the same kind of the King of Prussia, and that even from his own subjects, who were always full of the generous and truly royal qualities of that prince; he was the first king of the country, which before was a dukedom or electorate only. The sum of their discourse is, that his majesty was so true a father of his country and of his people, that his whole care was the flourishing of their trade, establishing their manufactures, increasing their numbers, planting foreigners—French, Swiss, and other nations—among them to instruct and encourage them; and being no way accessory to any of their oppressions, but relieving and redressing all their grievances as often and as soon as they came to his knowledge; and, indeed, I could not but entertain a great regard to the character of so just and good a prince. But all I could infer from that was, that a government may be tyrannical, and yet the king not be a tyrant; but the grievances to the people are oftentimes much the same. And every administration, where the constitution is thus stated, as it seems to be in most, if not all of the northern courts, Protestant as well as others, seems inconsistent with the true ends of government; the thing we call government was certainly established for the prosperity of the people; whereas, on the contrary, in all those German courts, where I have made my observations, the magnificence of the court and the prosperity of the people stand like the two poles; what excess of light you see at one is exactly balanced by so much darkness at the other.

And where, pray, is the religion of all this? that a whole nation of people should appear miserable that their governors may appear gay; the people starve, that the prince may be fed; or rather, the people be lean, that their sovereign may be fat; the subjects sigh, that he may laugh; be empty, that he may be full; and all this for mere luxury, not for the needful defence of the government—resisting enemies, preserving the public peace, and the like, but for mere extravagance, luxury, and magnificence, as in Prussia; or for ambition, and pushing at crowns, and the lust of domination, as in Saxony.

But to come back to the religious transactions of these countries: how are the ecclesiastics, jealous of their hierarchy, afraid to reform farther lest, as they gave a mortal stab to the perquisites and vails of God Almighty's service in the Romish Church, modern reformation might give the like to them? For this reason they set a pale about their Church, and there, as well as in other places, they cry to their neighbours, "Stand off, I am holier than thou;" and with what persecution and invasion—persecuting for religion, and invading the principles of one another. If there was any peace among them, it was that only which passes all understanding. It presently occurred to me, what charity can here be where there is no peace? and what religion where there is no charity? And I began to fear I should find little of what I looked for in those odd climates.

I had travelled personally through the heart of France, where I had occasion to look round me often enough in my route from the foot of the Pyrenean mountains to Toulouse, from thence to Paris and Calais. Here I found the people so merry and yet so miserable, that I knew not where to make any judgment. The poverty of the poor was so great that it seemed to leave them no room to sigh for anything but their burdens, or to pray for anything but bread. But the temper of the people was so volatile, that I thought they went always dancing to church and came singing out of it.

I found a world of teachers here, but nobody taught. The streets were everywhere full of priests, and the churches full of women; but as for religion, I found most of the clergy were so far from having much of it, that few of them knew what it was. Never surely was a nation so full of truly blind guides; for nothing can be more grossly ignorant of religion than many of their clergy are, nothing more void of morals than many of those to whom other people go to confess their sins.

I made some inquiry about religion; and among the rest I happened to fall in company with a good honest Huguenot *incognito*; and he told me very honestly that the state of religion in France stood thus: First, that for some years ago it was put to the test by the king, and that was when the edicts came out to banish and ruin the Huguenots; "At which time," said he, "we thought there had been a great deal of religion in it; but really, when it came to the push," said he, "it was hard to tell where we should find it. The persecution, as it was thought at first, would be ungrateful to the more religious Roman Catholics, and that some would be found too good to do the drudgery of the devil. But we were mistaken; the best fell in with persecution when it was done by other hands and not their own, and those that would not do it acknowledged they rejoiced that it was done; which showed," said he, "that the Catholics either had no principle, or acted against principle, which is much as one. And as for us Huguenots," says he, "we have shown that we have no religion lost among us; for, first, some run away for their religion and yet left it behind them, and we that stayed behind did it at the price of our principles. For now," says he, "we are mere hypocrites, neither Papists nor Huguenots, for we go to mass with Protestant hearts; and while we call ourselves Protestants, we bow in the house of Rimmon."

"Where, then," said I, "is the religion once boasted of here to be found?"

"Indeed," said he, "it is hard to tell you, and except a little that is in the galleys, I can give you no good account of it."

This, indeed, was confining the remains of a flourishing church to about 350 confessors, who really suffered martyrdom for it—for it was no less. So I minuted down French religion tugging at the oar, and would have come away.

But it came into my thought to ask him what he meant by telling me that those who run away for their religion out of France left most of it behind them? He answered, I should judge of it better if I observed them when I came into my own country; where, if I found they lived better than other people, or showed anything of religion suitable to a people that suffered persecution for their profession, I should send word of it; for he had heard quite otherwise of them, which was the reason why he and thousands of others did not follow them.

It happened, while I was warm in my inquiries thus after religion, a proclamation came out in London for appointing a general thanksgiving for a great victory obtained by the English forces and their confederates over the French at (*Ramillies*). I care not to put names to the particular times of things.

I started at the noise when they cried it in the streets. "Ah!" said I, "then I have found it at last" and I rejoiced, in particular, that having looked so much abroad for religion I should find it out at home. Then I began to call myself a thousand fools, that I had not saved myself all this labour and looked at home first; though, by-the-bye, I had done no more in this than other travellers often or indeed generally do, *viz.*, go abroad to see the world and search into the curiosities of foreign countries, and know nothing of their own.

But to return to my observations. I was resolved to see the ceremonies of this pious piece of work; and as the preparations for it were prodigiously great, I inquired how it would be; but nobody could remember that the like had ever been in their time before. Everyone said it would be very fine, that the queen would be there herself, and all the nobility; and that the like had never been seen since Queen Elizabeth's time.

This pleased me exceedingly; and I began to form ideas in my mind of what had been in former times among religious nations; I could find nothing of what I was made to expect, unless it was Solomon's dedication of the temple, or Josiah's great feast of the reformation; and I expected God would have a most royal tribute of praise.

But it shocked me a little that the people said there had never been such a thanksgiving since Queen Elizabeth's time. What, thought I, can be the reason of that? and musing a little, O! says I to myself, now I have found it; I suppose nobody gives God thanks in our country but queens. But this looked a little harsh, and I rummaged our histories a little for my farther satisfaction, but could make nothing of it. At last, talking of it to a good old cavalier, that had been a soldier for King

Charles, "Oh," says he, "I can tell you the reason of it; they have never given thanks," says he, "because they have had nothing to give thanks for. Pray," says he, "when have they had any victories in England since Queen Elizabeth's time, except two or three in Ireland in King William's time? and then they were so busy, had so many losses with them abroad, that they were ashamed to give thanks for them."

This I found had too much truth in it, however bitter the jest of it; but still heightened my expectation, and made me look for some strange seriousness and religious thankfulness in the appearance that was to be on the occasion in hand; and accordingly I secured myself a place, both without and within the church, where I might be a witness to every part of the devotion and joy of the people.

But my expectations were wound up to a yet greater pitch when I saw the infinite crowds of people throng with so much zeal, as I, like a charitable coxcomb, thought it to be, to the place of the worship of God; and when I considered that it was to give God thanks for a great victory, I could think of nothing else than the joy of the Israelites, when they landed on the banks of the sea and saw Pharaoh's army, horses, and chariots, swallowed up; and I doubted not I should hear something like the song of Moses and the children of Israel on the occasion, and should hear it sung with the same elevation of soul.

But when I came to the point, the first thing I observed was that nine parts of ten of all the company came there only to see the queen and the show, and the other tenth part, I think, might be said to make the show.

When the queen came to the rails, and descended from her coach, the people, instead of crying out "Hosannah, blessed be the queen that cometh in the name of the Lord," I say, the people cried "Murder "and "Help, for God's sake," treading upon one another, and stifling one another at such a rate, that in the rear of the two lines or crowds of people through which the queen passed it looked something like a battle where the wounded were retired to die and to get surgeons to come to them; for there lay heaps of women and children dragged from among the feet of the crowd, and gasping for breath. I went among some of them, and asked them what made them go into such a crowd? and their answer was all the same, "O sir, I had a mind to see the queen, as the rest did."

Well, I had my answer here indeed; for in short, the whole business of the thanksgiving without doors was to see the queen, that was plain; so I went away to my stand, which, for no less than three guineas, I had secured in the church.

When I came there it was my fate to be placed between the seats where the men of God performed the service of His praise, and sung out the anthems and the *Te Deum*, which celebrated the religious triumph of the day.

As to the men themselves, I liked their office, their vestments, and their appearance; all looked awful and grave enough, suitable in some respects to the solemnity of a religious triumph; and I expected they would be as solemn in their performances as the Levites that blew the trumpets at Solomon's feast, when all the people shouted and praised God.

But I observed these grave people, in the intervals of their worshipping God, when it was not their turn to sing, or read, or pray, bestowed some of the rest of their time in taking snuff, adjusting their perukes, looking about at the fair ladies, whispering, and that not very softly neither, to one another, about this fine lady, that pretty woman, this fine duchess, and that great fortune, and not without some indecencies, as well of words as of gestures. Well, says I, you are none of the people I look for; where are they that give God thanks?

Immediately the organ struck up for the *Te Deum*, up starts all my gentlemen, as if inspired from above, and from their talking together, not overmodestly, fall to praising God with the utmost precipitation, singing the heavenly anthems with all the grace and music imaginable.

In the middle of all this music and these exalted things, when I thought my soul elevated with Divine melody, and began to be reconciled to all the rest, I saw a little rustling motion among the people, as if they had been disturbed or frighted. Some said it thundered, some said the church shook; the true business was, the *Te Deum* within was answered without by the thunder of a hundred pieces of cannon and the noise of drums, with the huzzas and shouts of great crowds of people in the streets. This I did not understand, so it did neither disturb nor concern me; I found indeed no great harmony in it; it bore no consort in the music, at least as I understood it; but it was over pretty soon, and so we went on.

When the anthem was sung, and the other services succeeded them, I, that had been a little disturbed with the lucid intervals of the choristers and the gentlemen that sat crowded in with them, turned my eyes to other places, in hopes I should find some saints among the crowd, whose souls were taken up with the exalted raptures of the day.

But, alas! it was all one, the ladies were busy singling out the men and the men the ladies. The star and garter of a fine young nobleman—beautiful in person, rich in habit, and sparkling in jewels, his blue ribbon intimating his character—drew the eyes of so many women off their prayer-books, that I think his grace ought to have been spoken to by the vergers to have withdrawn out of the church, that he might not injure the service, and rob God Almighty of the homage of the day.

As for the queen, her majesty was the star of the day, and infinitely more eyes were directed to her than were lifted up to heaven, though the last was the business of the whole procession.

"Well," said I," this is mighty fine, that's true; but where's the religion of all this? Heavens bless me," said I, out of this crowd, "and I'll never mock God any more here when the queen comes again. Cannot these people go and see the queen where the queen is to be seen, but must they come hither to profane the church with her, and make the queen an idol?" And in a great passion I was, both at the people and at the manner of the day, as you may easily see by what follows.

N.B.—I had made some other satirical reflections upon the conduct of the day; but as it looks too near home, I am not willing that poor Robinson Crusoe should disoblige anybody.

I confess, the close of the day was still more extravagant; for there the thanksgiving was adjourned from the church to the tavern, and to the street; and instead of the decency of a religious triumph, there was indeed a triumph of religious indecency; and the anthems, *Te Deum*, and thanksgiving of the day ended in the drunkenness, the bonfires, and the squibs and crackers of the street.

How far religion is concerned in all this, or whether God Almighty will accept of these noisy doings for thanksgivings, that I have nothing to do with; let those people consider of it that are concerned in it.

OF DIFFERENCES IN RELIGION

'Tis known alone to the Divine Wisdom why He has been pleased to suffer any part of religion, and the adoration paid to His majesty, the supplications made to Him, and the homage which His creatures owe to His glorious being, to be so doubtfully directed, or so differently understood by His creatures, as that there should be any mistakes or disagreements about them.

How comes it to pass, that the paying a reverence to the name and being of God should not be as incapable of being disputed in the manner of it as in the thing itself? That all the rules of worshipping, believing in, and serving the great God of heaven and earth, should be capable of being understood any more than one way? And that the infallible Spirit of God, who is our guide to heaven, should leave any one of its dictates in a state of being misunderstood?

Why have not the rules of religion, as well those of doctrine as of life, been laid down in terms so plain, and so impossible to be mistaken, that all men in the world, in every age, should have the same notions of them, and understand them, in every tittle of them, exactly alike? Then as heaven is but one blessed great port, at which all hope to arrive, there would have been but one road to travel the journey in; all men would have gone the same way, steered the same course; and brethren would no more have fallen out by the way.

God alone, for wise and righteous reasons, because He can do nothing but what is wise and righteous, has otherwise ordered it, and that is all we can say of it; as to the reason and justice of it, that is a thing of which, like as of the times and of the seasons, we may say, knoweth no man.

In the state of uncertainty we are now in, so it is; two men, believing in the same God, holding the same faith, the same Saviour, the same doctrine, and aiming at the same heaven, yet cannot agree to go to that heaven, or worship that God, or believe in that Saviour, the same way, or after the same manner; nay, they cannot know, or conceive of God, or of heaven, or of the Redeemer, or indeed of any one principle of the Christian religion, in the same manner, or form the same ideas of those things in their minds.

It is true, the different capacities and faculties of men are in part a reason for this, by which it is occasioned, that scarce two men together have the same notions and apprehensions even of one and the same thing, because their understandings are led by different guides, and they see by different lights.

But this is not all; they are not alike honest to the light they have. Three men read the same doctrinal article, say it be of the Trinity, or of any other, and they all examine the foundation of it in the Scripture; one thinks verily he has found out the mystery effectually, goes on with his inquiries, and brings every Scripture and every passage to correspond exactly with his first notion, and thus he confirms himself immovably in his opinion; and it is so clear to him, that he can not only never be argued out of it, but can entertain no good opinion of any man that conceives of it in any other way, but takes him for an enemy to the orthodox doctrine, and that he merits to be expelled out of Christ's Church, denied the Christian communion, and, in short, treats him with no respect, no, nor thinks of him with charity.

Another comes to the same Scripture, and in quest of the same doctrine, and he reads over the same texts and receives notions from them: he follows in his search through all the corroborating texts and is confirmed in his first opinion from them all: he grows as immoveable in his received construction

Could they differ with humility, they would differ with charity, but it is not to be in religion, whatever it may be in civil or politic affairs; for there is a thing called zeal, which men call a grace in religion, and esteem a duty, and this makes men fall out in religious matters with a more fatal warmth and more animosity than in other cases, according to Hudibras—

Zeal makes men fight, like mad or drunk,
For Dame Religion as for punk.

Nor is this the fate only of the Christian religion, though 'tis more so there than in any other, but 'tis the same in other cases, as between the Persians and the Turks about the successors of their prophet Mahomet. It was so of old between the heathen and the Jews; and the Assyrian monarch prepared a fiery furnace for those that would not fall down and worship the great image that he had set up.

In the primitive times of God's Church, the heathen did the like by the Christians, and *Christianos ad leones* was the common cry; but when the Church came to its halcyon days, Constantine the Great gave peace to the Christians, and it was but a little while that they enjoyed that peace before they fell out by the way. The Arian heresies rose up, and differing opinions rent the State into factions, the Church into schisms, and in the space of two reigns the Arians persecuted the orthodox, and the orthodox the Arians, almost with the same fury as the heathen had persecuted them both with before.

From thence to our time persecution has been the practice even of all parties, as they have been clothed with power, and as their differences have moved them; for example, in all the Christian countries, there is a mortal fend between Popish and the Protestant; and though, indeed, the former have carried their zeal farthest, yet the latter have not been able to say they have not persecuted in their turn, though not with fire and faggot.

What wars and bloodshed molested Europe on the account of religion in Germany! Especially till the general pacification of those troubles at the treaty of Westphalia, when the Protestants, having had the apparent advantage of the war, obtained the everlasting settlement of their religion as well as liberties through the whole empire.

Since those times, what persecution, in the same country, between the Lutheran and Calvinist churches, and how little charity is among them, insomuch that the Lutherans to this day will not allow the Reformed Evangelic churches, so the Calvinists are called, liberty to assemble for worship within the gates of their cities, or give them Christian burial.

I avoid looking too near home, or searching in Scotland and England, among the unhappy divisions of Episcopal and Presbyterian, Church of England and Dissenter, and this I do because it is at home; but it is too evident that all these come either from men's being negligent of right informations, or too tenacious when they have it; for it is evident, if all men would be honest to the light they have, and favourable to their neighbours, we might hope that, how many several ways so ever we chose to walk towards heaven, we should all meet there at last.

I look upon all the seeds of religious dissension as tares sowed by the devil among the wheat; and it may be observed, that though, as I have already said, the Assyrians persecuted the Jews, and the Romans the Christians, yet where the devil is immediately and personally worshipped, there we meet with little or no persecution; for Satan, having a kind of peaceable dominion there, offers them no disturbance; he desires no innovation for ever; he finds the sweetness of it, and lets it all alone.

But if once they talk of other gods before him, he is far less easy; there he is continually sowing strife and hatching divisions among them, for, like all other monarchs, the devil loves to reign alone.

It would be too long a task here to reckon up the several sorts of differences in religion even among us in England, where, if two happen to differ, presently, like St. Paul to St. Peter, they withstand one another to the face; that is to say, carry on the dispute to the utmost extremity.

But there is another question before me, and that is not only why there are such differences on the point of religion, and why are religious differences hotter and more irreconcilable than other breaches, but why are there more differences of this kind among us than among any other nation in the world?

Certainly this pushing on our religious broils to the extremity is the peculiar of this country of England, and is not the same thing in other places; and the variety is such here, that 't is said there are more several communions or communities of religious kinds in England than in all the other Protestant countries in the world.

The best and most charitable answer that I can think of to give for this is to compliment ourselves, and say, 'tis because we are the most religious nation in the world; that is to say, that we in general set more seriously to work to inquire into the substance and nature of religion; to examine principles, and weigh the reasons of things, than other people, being more concerned for and anxious about the affairs of God, of heaven, and our souls; that thinking, as we ought to do, that religion is of the utmost concern to us, and that it is of the last moment to us to be certain about it and well-grounded in the points before us, particularly whether we are rightly informed or not. This anxious concern makes us jealous of every opinion and tenacious of our own, breaks much in upon the custom of submitting our judgments to the clergy, as is the case in countries where people are more indifferent in their search after these things, and more unconcerned in the certainty or uncertainty of them.

I must acknowledge that I think the true and the only just reason that can be given for this matter, is not that we are more furious than other people, more censorious and rash in our judgment, that we have less charity, or less patience, in debating religious points than other people; but the truth is, that we have less indifference about them, and cannot sit down contented with a slight and overly inquiry, or a cursory or school answer to the doubts in question; but we make it a thing of absolute necessity to be fully informed of, and therefore, are earnest in the inquiry, and knowing the Scripture to be the great rule of faith, the standard for life and doctrine, we fly thither and search for ourselves, not having Popery enough to expect an infallible judge, not indifference enough to Acquiesce in the judgment of the clergy, and perhaps a little too tenacious of our own interpretation even in things we are uninstructed about.

This, indeed, I take to be the true reason why religious disputes increase so much here, and why there are such separations and schisms among us, more than there are in any other nation in the world.

I know much of it is laid to the door of the confusions they were all in here during the bloody intestine wars in the years 1640 to 1656, and the liberty given to all opinions to set up themselves at that time; but I waive that as a question that tends to more division. I believe the reason I have given for it stands as well grounded, and as likely to be approved, as any I can give, or as any that has been given in this case.

There is another difficult question which still remains before us, and that is, what remedy can we apply to this malady? And first, I must answer negatively, not to have us be less religious, that we might differ less about it, but to have us exercise more charity in our disputes, that we might differ more like men of temper, and more like Christians than we do. This is striking at the root of religious differences; for if they were carried on mildly, with a peaceable spirit, willing to be informed, a disposition to love as brethren, though in everything not like-minded—our variety of opinions would not then have the name of differences, we should not separate in communion and in charity, though we did not agree in everything we were to believe or not to believe about religion.

It is hard that we should say these differences are the consequences of a nation having more religion than their neighbours, since we have still this one part too little; and as I suppose us to have more religion, I must be obliged to grant we have not enough more; for if, as we have just so much more religion as is sufficient to make us quarrelsome in religious disputes, we had yet as much more as were sufficient to make us peaceable again after it, then we should be religious to purpose.

So that, in a word, our being so religious as above is only an unhappy middle composition between the inquiring and fully-informed Christian on one hand, and the careless, indifferent, unconcerned temper that takes up with anything on the other hand.

And this I take to be a just though short account of our differences in England about religion.

It might be a very useful question to start here, namely? where will all our unhappy differences end? I, that am not willing to give the worst-natured answer, where the best and kindest will hold water, am for the present disposed to answer in general, rather than descend to particulars, *viz.*, in heaven. There all our unkind, unchristian, unneighbourly, unbrotherly differences will end. We shall freely shake hands there with many a pardoned sinner that here we bid stand off; embrace many a publican that here we think it a dishonour to converse with; see many a heart that we have broken here, with censures, reproachings, and revilings, made whole again by the balm of the same Redeemer's blood.

There we shall see that there have been other flocks than those of our fold, other paths to heaven than those we shut men out from; that those we have excommunicated have been taken into that superior communion; and those we have placed at our left hand have been there summoned to the right hand; all separations will be there taken away, and the mind of every Christian be entirely reconciled to one another; no divisions, no differences, no charging sincere minds with hypocrisy, or embracing painted hypocrites for saints; everything to be seen and to be known as it really is, and by a clear light; none will desire to deceive, none be subject to be deceived.

There we shall look upon all we have done and said in prejudice of the character of our brethren with a just change, and sufficiently repair to one another all the injurious things we have said, or indeed but thought, of one another, by rejoicing in the common felicity and praising the Sovereign Glory that had received those we had foolishly rejected, and let those into the same heaven whom we had, in the abundance of our pride and the penury of our charity, shut out.

How many actions of men which we, seeing only their outside, have now censured, shall we find there by that penetration that cannot err, be accepted for their inside sincerity? How many an opinion that we condemn here shall we see then to be orthodox? In a word, how many contradicting notions and principles which we thought inconsistent with true religion shall we find then to be reconcilable to themselves, to one another, and to the fountain of truth?

All the difficulties in our conceptions of things invisible will then be explained; all the doctrines of the immutability of the Divine counsels will then be reconcilable to the changeable events of things, and to the varieties often happening in the world. The unchangeableness of the Eternal decrees will then appear; and yet the efficacy of praying to God to do this, or not do that, to pardon, forgive, spare, and forbear, which we now say is inconsistent with those unchangeable decrees, shall be reconcilable to that unchangeableness in a manner to us now inconceivable.

And this is the foundation of what I now advance, *viz.*, that in heaven all our differences in religion will be reconciled, and will be at an end. If any man ask me whether they cannot be ended before, I answer, if we were all thoroughly convinced that they would be reconciled then, we should certainly put an end to them before; but it is impossible to be done. Men's convictions of the greatest and most certain truths are not equal to one another, or equal to the weight and significancy of those truths; and therefore such a general effect of this affair cannot be expected on this side of time.

There is one very great reconciler of religious differences in this world, which has sometimes been made use of by Providence to heal the breaches in Christian charity among religious people, and it is, generally speaking, very effectual; but it is a bitter draught, a potion that goes down with great reluctance, and that is persecution. This generally reconciles the differences of Christians about the lesser matters in religion. The primitive churches, while under the Roman persecutions, had a much greater harmony among themselves, and very few schisms and divisions broke out among them. When they did differ in any particular points, they wrote healing epistles to one another, contended with modesty and with charity, and referred willingly their notions to be decided by one another. They did not separate communion, and excommunicate whole churches and nations, for a dispute about the celebration of Easter, or unchurch one another for the question of receiving and rebaptising of penitents, as was afterwards the case. The furnace of affliction burnt up all that dross, the fury of their persecutors kept their minds humble, their zeal for religion hot, and their affection for and charity to one another increased as their liberty and their number were lessened.

Thus Bishop Ridley and Bishop Hooper, the first a rigid Church of England bishop, the other almost a Presbyterian, or at least a Calvinist, like Peter and Paul, differed hotly, and withstood one another to the face in the very beginning of the Reformation; but when they came to burn for their religion, fire and faggot showed them the reconcilableness of all their disputes, convinced them that it was possible for both to hold fast the truth in sincerity and yet entertain differing notions of the rites and outsides of the Divine economy, and at the stake they ended all their disputes, wrote healing letters to one another, and became fellow-martyrs and confessors for that very profession which was so intermixed with censure and dislike before.

And let all that think of this remedy remember that whenever these quarrelsome Christians come, by persecution or any other incident, to be thus reconciled in their charity, they find always a great deal to ask pardon of one another for with respect to what is past; all their violence, heat of zeal, and much more heat of passion, all their breach of charity, their reproaches and censures and hard words, which have passed between them, will only then serve to bring them together with more affection, and to embrace more warmly; for, depend upon it, all the differences in religion among good men (for I do not mean essential, doctrinal, and fundamental differences), serve only to make them all ashamed of themselves at last.

OF THE WONDERFUL EXCELLENCY OF NEGATIVE RELIGION AND NEGATIVE VIRTUE

Negative virtue sets out like the Pharisee with "God, I thank thee;" it is a piece of religious pageantry, a jointed baby dressed up gay, but, stripped of its gewgaws, it appears a naked lump, fit only to please children and deceive fools. 'Tis the hope of the hypocrite, it is a cheat upon the neighbourhood, a dress for without doors, for 'tis of no use within; 'tis a mask put on for a character, and as generally it is used to cheat others, 'tis so ignorantly embraced that we cheat even ourselves with it.

In a word, negative virtue is positive vice, at least when it is made use of in any of the two last cases; namely, either as a mask to deceive others, or as a mist to deceive ourselves. If a man were to look back upon it to see in what part he could take up his nest, or lay a foundation of hope for the satisfaction of his mind as to future things, he would find it the most uncomfortable condition to go out of the world with that any man in the world can think.

The reason is plain; compare it with the publican, whom such a man despises.

"Here is my landlord a drunkard, one of my tenants is a thief, such a poor man is a swearer, such a rich man a blasphemer, such a tradesman is a cheat, such a justice of the peace is an atheist, such a rakish fellow is turned highwayman, such a *beau* is debauched; but I—I that am clothed in negatives, and walk in the light of my own vanity—I live a sober, regular, retired life, I am an honest man; I defraud nobody; no man ever heard me swear, or an ill word come out of my mouth; I never talk irreligiously or profanely, and I am never missed out of my seat at church. God, I thank thee! I am not debauched, I am no highwayman, no murderer," &c.

Now, what is the difference of all these? I must confess, speaking of all these together, and of what is usually the end of them, I think a man had better be any of them, nay, almost all of them together, than the man himself, and my reason is in a few words as follows.

All these know themselves to be wicked persons; conscience, though for a time oppressed and kept under, yet upon all occasions tells them plainly what their condition is, and oftentimes they repent.

'Tis true, sometimes they do not; God is pleased sometimes to treat them in the vindictive attribute, and they are cut off in their crimes, insensible and stupid, without a space or a heart to repent; and therefore let none take hope in their profligate living from what I am going to say.

Again, others, though they do repent, and God is pleased to give them the grace to return to Him as penitents, come to it very late, and sometimes under a severe hand, as perhaps on a deathbed, or under some disaster, and oftentimes at the gallows.

But still, I say, those men, though they sin, they do it as a crime, and when they come to be told of it often they are brought to repent. But the negative Christian I speak of is so full of himself, so persuaded that he is good enough, and religious enough already, that he has no thoughts of anything unless it be to pull off his hat to God Almighty now and then, and thank Him that he has no need of Him. This is the opiate that doses his soul even to the last gasp; and it is ten thousand to one but the lethargic dream shoots him through the gulf at once, and he never opens his eyes till he arrives in that light where all things are naked and open; where he sees too late that he has been a cheat to himself, and has been hurried by his own pride in a cloud of negatives into a state of positive destruction without remedy.

I am reading no particular man's fate; God forbid! I restrain it to no circumstances, I point out no persons; it is too solemn a thing to make it a satire; 'tis the state, not the man, I speak of. Let the guilty apply it to themselves, and the proud good man humble himself and avoid it.

I have observed that many fall into this case by the excessive vanity of being thought well of by their neighbours, obtaining a character, &c. It is a delusion very fatal to many; a good name is indeed a precious ointment, and in some cases is better than life. But with your pardon, Mr. Negative, it must be a good name for good deeds, or otherwise a good name upon a bad life is a painted whore, that has a gay countenance upon a rotten, diseased, corrupted carcass.

Much to be preferred is the general slander of a prejudiced age and a state of universal calumny, where the mind is free from the guilt they charge. Such a man, though the world spits upon and despises him, looks in with comfort, and looks up with hope.

———*Hic murus aëneus esto,*
Nil conscire sibi, nulla pallescere culpa.—Horace.

General contempt, universal reproach, is a life that requires a world of courage and steadiness of mind to support; but be this my portion in this world, with a heart that does not reproach me with the guilt, much rather than to be a man of negatives only, and who all the world caresses with their good wishes and good opinion, but is himself empty of real virtue, a hypocrite at bottom, a cheat, and under the delusion of it; whose portion is with hypocrites, and who can neither look in, or look up, with pleasure, but must look without himself, for all that can be called good, either by others or by himself.

As at the great and last day the secrets of all hearts shall be disclosed, so I am persuaded the opinion we have of one another here, will be one of the things which will be there, and perhaps not till then fully rectified; and we shall be there thoroughly enlightened, we shall find room to see that we have been much mistaken in our notions of virtue and vice, religion and irreligion, in the characters of our neighbours. And I am persuaded we shall see many of our acquaintances placed at the right hand of a righteous Judge, whose characters we have oppressed with slanders, and who we have censoriously placed at His left hand here; and many a painted hypocrite, who has insulted his neighbour with, "Stand off, I am holier than thou," or whom he has turned from with disdain, and with a "This publican!" placed at the left hand, who we made no doubt we should have seen at the right hand in triumph.

This is a support to the mind of a good man, even when his enemies, as David says, *"gnash upon him with their teeth, and have him in derision,"* that is to say, when he is run down by universal clamour, and damned by the tongues of men, even for this world and another.

> *Happy the man, who with exalted soul,*
> *Knows how to rate the great, the prosp'rous fool,*
> *Who can the insults of the street contemn,*
> *And values not the rage or tongues of men.*
> *He, like the sun, exists on his own flame,*
> *And, when he dies, is to himself a fame.*

But take this with you as you go, that as negative praise will build no man comfort, so negative virtue will not support the mind under universal contempt. Scandal is much worse than slander; for the first is founded upon real guilt, the other attacks innocence. Nothing is a scandal, but what is true; nothing is a slander, but what is false.

He that fortifies himself against reproach, must do it with a certain reserve of real and solid virtue and piety; it must be uprightness and integrity that must preserve him; nothing but a fund of what is good can support the mind under the reproach of being all that is bad; I do not mean neither that the man must be perfect, have no follies or failings, have made no excursions, have nothing to be laid to the charge of his character; for where then shall the man be found I am speaking of? And I may be said to be describing the black swan, a person that is not, and never was to be found; but the right way of judging men, and the way which alone can be just, is to judge of them by their general conduct; and so a man may in his own mind justly denominate himself: as every good action does not denominate me to be a good man, so neither does every failing, every folly, no, nor every scandalous action, denominate me a hypocrite, or a wicked man; otherwise some of the most eminent saints in Scripture, and of every age since the Scripture was written, are gone to the devil; and 'twill be hard to say there was ever a good man in the world.

But I return to my subject, the negative good man: and let me examine him a little in his just character, in his conduct, public and private. He is no drunkard, but is intoxicated with the pride of his own worth; he is a good neighbour, a common arbitrator and peacemaker in other families, but a cursed tyrant in his own; he appears in a public place of worship for a show, but never enters into his closet and shuts the door about him, to pray to Him that sees in secret; he is covered with the vainglorious and ostentatious part of charity, but does all his alms before men, to be seen of them; he is mighty eager in the duties of the second table, but regardless of the first; appearingly religious to be seen and taken notice of by men; but between God and his own soul no intercourse, no communication. What is this man? and what comfort is there of the life he lives? He knows little, or perhaps nothing, of faith, repentance, and a Christian mortified life; in a word, he is a man perfect in the circumstances of religion, and perfectly a stranger to the essential part of religion.

Take this man's conversation apart, enter into the private and retired part of it, what notions has he of misspent hours, and of the natural reflux of all our minutes, on to the great centre and gulf of life, eternity? Does he know how to put a right value upon time? Does he esteem it the life-blood of his soul, as it really is, and act in all the moments of it, as one that must account for them? Alas! this is of no weight with such a man; he is too full of himself to enter into any notions about an account, either for misspent time, or anything else misdone; but persuading himself that he never did anything amiss, entertains no notion of judgment to come, eternity, or anything in it.

What room has a man to expiate, in his thoughts upon so immense and inconceivable a subject as that of eternal duration, whose thoughts are all taken up, and swelled top-full with his own extraordinary self? It would be impossible for any man in the world to entertain one proud thought of himself, if he had but one right idea of a future state. Could such a man think that anything in him, or anything he could do, could purchase for him a felicity that was to last to eternity? What! that a man should be capable in one moment (for life is not that in length compared to eternity) to do anything for which he should deserve to be made happy to eternity?

If, then, you can form no equality between what he can do and what he shall receive, less can it be founded upon his negative virtue, or what he has forborne to do; and if neither his negative nor his positive piety can be equal to the reward, and to the eternity that reward is to last for, what then is become of the Pharisee? he must think no more of himself, for all his boasts; neither of his negatives nor his positives, but of a rich unbounded grace, that rewards according to itself, not according to what we can do; and that to be judged at the last day according to our works, if literally understood, would be to be undone; but we are to be judged by the sincerity of our repentance, to be rewarded according to the infinite grace of God, and purchase of Christ, with a state of blessedness to an endless eternity.

Indeed this eternity is not a meditation suitable to the man I am talking of; 'tis a sublime thought, which his bloated imagination has never descended to or engaged in; and when it comes he is like to have as little comfort of it as he has had thought about it.

This thought of eternity raises new ideas in my mind, and I cannot go forward without a digression upon so important a subject; if the reader approves the thought, he will not quarrel about its being a digression.

ETERNITY

Hail! mighty circle, unconceived abyss,
Centre of worlds to come, and grave of this;
Great gulf of Nature, in whose mighty womb,
Lies all that thing called Past, that nothing called To come.

Ever and never, both begun in thee,
The weak description of eternity,
Mere sounds which only can thy being confess;
For how should finite words thee infinite express?

Thou art duration's modern name,
To be, or to have been, in thee are all the same.

Thy circle holds the pre-existent state
Of all that's early, or that shall be late.
Thou know'st no past or future; all in thee,
Make up one point, Eternity:
And, if things mortal measure things sublime,
Are all one great ubiquity of time.

To end, begin, be born, and die,
The accidents of time and life,
Are nonsense in thy speech, Eternity
Swallows them all, in thee they end their strife.
In thee the ends of Nature form one line,
And generation with corruption join.

Ages of life describe thy state in vain,
Even death itself, in thee, lives o'er again.
Thy radiant, bright, unfaded face,
Shines over universal space.
All limits from thy vast extent must flee,
Old everlasting's but a point to thee.
Ten everlastings make not one Eternity.

To thee things past exist as things that are;
And things to come, as if they were;
Thou wast the first great when, while there was yet no where.
Even time itself's a little ball of space,
Borrowing a flame from thy illustrious face,
Which, wheeling round, in its own circle burns,
Rolls out from thy first spring, and into thee returns.

What we have been, and what we are,
The present and the time that's past,
We can resolve to nothing here,
But what we are to be in thee at last.

Deeds soon shall die, however nobly done,
And thoughts of men, like as themselves decay;
But time when to eternity roll'd on,
Shall never, never, never waste away.

Years, ages, months, weeks, days, and hours
Wear out, and words to number them shall fail,

One endless all the wild account devours,
And thy vast unit casts up all the tale.
Numbers as far as numbers run
Are all in thy account but one,
Or rather are thy reckoning just begun.

Thou art the life of immortality,
When time itself drowns and expires in thee.
All the great actions of aspiring men,
By which they build that trifling thing called fame,
In thy embrace lose all their where and when,
Reserving not so much as a mere empty name.

How vain are sorrows of a human state,
Why mourn th' afflicted at their fate?
One point, one moment's longer far
Than all their days of sorrow shall appear,
When wrapt in wonders we shall see,
And measure their extent by thee.

In vain are glorious monuments of fame,
Which fools erect t' immortalise a name,
Not half a moment when compared with thee,
Lives all their fancied immortality.

Start back, my soul! and with some horror view,
If with these eyes thou can'st look through,
Inquire what gives the pain of loss a sting,
Even hell itself's a hell, in no one other thing.

Then with a brightness on thy face,
An emanation from that glorious place,
A joy which no dark cloud can overcast,
And which Eternity itself cannot outlast,
Reflect, my soul! Duration dwells on high,
And heaven itself's made heaven, by blest Eternity.

But to the purpose in hand, for I have not done with this man of negatives yet. And now let us bring him more nearly and seriously to a converse with the invisible world. He looks into it with horror and dreadful apprehensions, as Felix, when St. Paul reasoned of temperance, righteousness, and of judgment to come. Felix was a moral heathen, that is to say, a man of negatives, like him I am speaking of. What was then the case? He trembled. Pray, what is it reasonable to think Felix trembled at? If I may give my opinion, who am but a very mean expositor of texts, it was this or something like it.

Felix was a philosopher as well as a man of power; and by his wisdom, as also by his reverence of the gods, which at that time was the sum of religion, had been a man of morals, a man that had practised temperance and righteousness, as the life which was unquestionably to be rewarded by the powers above with an Elysian felicity., that is to say, according to the Roman maxim, that the gods were the re warders of virtue.

But when the blessed Apostle came to reason with Felix how unlikely it was that these negatives should purchase our happiness hereafter, he showed him that the gods could not be in debt to us for the practice of virtue, which was indeed no more than living most suitable to our reason; that a life of virtue and temperance was its own reward, by giving a healthy body, a clear head, a composed life, &c, fitting the man for all other worldly enjoyments adequate to his reason and his present felicity as a man. But eternal happiness must come from another spring, namely, from the infinite, unbounded grace of a provoked God, who having erected a righteous tribunal, where every heart should be searched, and where every tongue would confess itself guilty, and stand self-condemned. Jesus Christ, whom Paul preached, would separate such as by faith and repentance He had brought home and united to Himself by the grace of adoption, and on the foot of His having laid down His life a ransom for them, had appointed them to salvation.

When poor negative Felix heard of this, and that all his philosophy, his temperance, and righteousness, if it had been ten thousand times as great, would weigh nothing and plead nothing for him at that judicature, and that he began to see the justice and reason of this, for Paul reasoned him into it; I say, when he saw this, he trembled indeed, as well he might, and as all negative people will.

What a strange idea must that Pharisee have of God, who went up with the publican to the temple to pray. 'Tis observable he went with a good stock of assurance in his face that could come to the altar as he did, not to offer any sacrifice; we do not find he carried any offering, or bespoke the priest to make any atonement; he wanted no priests to make any confession to. Good man, as he thought he was, he had no sins to confess; he rather came up to the altar to even accounts with heaven, and like the other man in the Gospel, tell God that he had fulfilled the whole law, and had done all those things that were commanded, even from his youth; so, as before, he only pulled off his hat to his God, and let Him know that there was nothing between them at present, and away he goes about his business.

But the poor wretch whom he despised, and whom he had left behind him, for he durst come no further, acted qui be another part. He had at first, indeed, in sense of his duty, resolved to go up to the temple; but when he saw the splendour and majesty of God represented by the glory of that elevated building, I say, when he saw that, though a great way off, and then looked into his own heart, all his negative confidences failing him, and a sense of miserable circumstances coming upon him, he stops short, and with a blow of reflection, and perfectly unmixed with any of the Pharisee's pride, he looks down in humility, but lifts up his heart in a penitential faith, with a "Lord, be merciful to me a sinner."

Here was faith, repentance, duty, and confession, all conjoined in one act, and the man's work was done at once, he went away justified. When the negative Pharisee went home, the self-same vain wretch that he came out, with "God, I thank thee," in his mouth, and a mass of pride in his heart, that nothing could convince.

In what glorious colours do the Scriptures upon all occasions represent those two hand-in-hand graces, faith and repentance! There is not one mention of faith in the whole Scripture but what is recommending some way or other to our admiration and to our practice; 'tis the foundation and the top-stone of all religion, the right hand to lead and the left hand to support, in the whole journey of a Christian, even through this world and into the next. In a word, 'tis the sum and substance of the Gospel foundation.

Religion seems to have been founded upon three establishments in the world, in all which the terms of life are laid down at the end of our acceptance of it.

The first establishment was with Adam in Paradise; the terms of which were, "*Forbear and live.*"

The second establishment was with the children of Israel, in the giving of the Law; the terms of which were, "*Do and live.*"

The third establishment is that of the Gospel of Jesus Christ; the terms of which are, "*Believe and live.*"

So that, in a word, faith is the substance and fulfilling of Gospel religion, the plan of righteousness, and the great efficient of eternal life. Let me break out here upon this glorious subject, and pardon the excursion, I entreat you.

FAITH

Hail! mystic, realising vision, hail!
Heaven's duplicate, eternity's entail;
God's representative to hand us on,
And for us claim a station near His throne.

Not the eternal battlements of brass,
Gates, a whole hell of devils could never pass;
Not angels, not the bright seraphic train,
Which drove out Adam from the sacred plain;
Not all the flaming swords Heaven ever drew,
Shall shut thee out, or intercept thy view.

Boldly thou scal'st the adamantine wall,
Where heaps of fainting suppliants fall,
Where doubt has thousands and ten thousands slain,
And hypocrites knock hard in vain.

Soaring above the dark abyss of fear,
Quite out of sight, behind thou leav'st despair,
Who fainting, and unable to keep pace,
Gives up the prize, gives out the race,
Faints by the way, and fainting cries,
I can't, and so for fear of dying, dies.

While thou, on air of hope, fanning thy wings,
With gentle gales of joy, from whence assurance springs,
Mount'st on, and passing all th'æthereal bounds,
Thy head with beatific rapture crowns.

Great pilot of the soul, who goes before
The dangers of the dreadful voyage t' explore,
Enters the very place, and when 'tis there,
Sends back expresses to support us here,
Negotiates peace, gains the great pledge of love,
And gets it ratified above.

With awful confidence at Heaven's high throne,
It rather humbly claims than merely prays.
Pleads, promises, and calls them all its own,
And trusts to have, even then, when Heaven denies.

On earth what wonders has it wrought!
Rather what wonders has it not?
It has parted rivers, dried up seas,

Made hills of those, and walls of these.
And if to this great mountain it should say
"Move off, O hill, and roll to yonder sea,"
The sea and mountain, too, must both obey.
If towards heaven it looks, 'tis ne'er in vain,
From thence 't has brought down fire, 't has brought down rain,
And thither it ascends in flame again.)

Its influence is so vigorous and intense,
It pierces all the negatives of sense.
Things quite invisible to sight it sees,
Things difficult performs with ease:
Things imperceptible to us it knows,
Things utterly impossible it does:
Things unintelligible it understands,
Things high (superior to itself) commands,
Things in themselves unnatural reconciles,
Weakness to strength, and to its sorrows smiles,
Hopes against hope, and in despair's resigned,
And spite of storms without, it calms the mind.

Say, unborn lamp, what feeds thy flame,
In all varieties the same?
What wonder-working hand thy power supplies?
Nature and reason's just surprise.

Nature and reason join thee hand in hand,
And to thy just dominion stoop the mind:
But neither can thy workings understand,
And in thy swifter pace thou leav'st them both behind.
'Twas from thy motion fortified by thee,
Peter asked leave to walk upon the sea,
When his great Lord said, "Come," and Faith said, "Go,"
What heart could fear? What coward tongue say, no?
Boldly he stept upon the flowing wave,
And might have marched through fire or through the grave,
While He stood by who had the power to save.

But soon as Peter lost his hold of thee,
He sunk like lead into the sea.
All thy magnetic power disperst and gone,
The heavenly charm was broke, and Peter quite undone;
And had not help been just at hand,

Peter had gone the nearest way to land.

Made up of wonders, and on wonders fixed,
Of contradicting qualities thou'rt mixed.
Small as a grain, yet as a mountain great,
A child in growth, yet as a giant strong;
A beggar, yet above a king in state:
Of birth but short, yet in duration long.
How shall we reconcile thee to our sense?
Here thou would'st pass for mere impertinence.
Thy teasing nature would thy end defeat,
So humble, and yet so importunate.

See the great test of faith, the greatest sure,
That Heaven e'er put a mortal to endure.
She cried, she begged, nay, she believed and prayed,
Yet long neglected, and as long denied;
At last, as if commanded to despair,
She 's almost told it was not in His power,
That she was out of His commission placed,
Shut out by Heaven, by race accurst.
Woman! I am not sent to thee!
Woman! thou hast no share in Me!
Was ever creature born, but this, could hear
Such words proclaimed from Heaven and not despair?

But still she prays, adheres, petitions, cries,
And on the Hand that thrusts her back relies: '
Till moved, as 'twere, with her impertinence,
He calls her dog, and challenges her sense,
To tell her whether such as she are fed,
With food appropriate, or the household bread.

But all was one; her faith so often tried,
Too strong to fail, too firm to be denied:
She follows still, allows her outcast state,
The more thrust off, the more importunate:
Every repulse she meets, revives her prayer.
And she builds hope because she's bid despair;
He call her dog, she calls herself so too,
But pleads as such the fragments that are due.
The case so doubtful, the repulse so long,
Her sex so weak, and yet her faith so strong,

Heaven yields! The victory of faith's obtained,
And all she asked, and all she sought for, gained.

Mysterious flame! tell us from whence
Thou draw'st that cleaving confidence,
That strange, that irresistible desire.
That with such magic force sets all the soul on fire;
By which thou can'st to Heaven itself apply,
In terms which Heaven itself cannot deny.

A power so great, an influence so sure,
Not Heaven itself the wrestlings can endure.
See how the struggling angel yields the day,
When Jacob's faith bids Jacob pray.
Let me alone, the heavenly vision cries.
No, no, says conquering faith, never without my prize.
Heaven yields! Victorious faith prevailed,
And all the blessings asked for he entailed.

Blest humble confidence, that finds the way
To know we shall be heard before we pray;
Heav'n's high insurance-office, where we give
The premium faith, and then the grant receive.

Stupendous gift! from what strange spring below,
Can such a supernatural product flow?
From Heaven, and Heaven alone it must derive;
For Heaven alone can keep its flame alive.

No spring below can send out such a stream,
No fire below emit so bright a flame,
Of nature and original divine,
It does all other gifts of Heaven outshine.

Thou art the touchstone of all other grace,
No counterfeits can keep thy pace.
The weighty standard of our best desires,
The true sublime, which every breast inspires,
By thee we rise to such a height of flame,
As neither thought can reach nor language name,
Such as St. Paul himself could hardly know,
Whether he really was alive or no:
When clothed in raptures lifted up by thee,
He saw by faith, what none without it see.

Just Heaven, that in thy violence delights,
And easily distinguishes thy flights
From the thin outside warmth of hypocrites,
Approves, accepts, rewards, and feeds thy flame,
And gives this glorious witness to thy fame,
That all our gifts are hallowed by thy name.

By thee our souls on wings of joy ascend,
Climb the third heaven, an entrance there demand,
As sure those gates to thee shall open wide,
As without thee we 're sure to be denied.
No bars, no bolts, no flaming swords appear,
To shock thy confidence, or move thy fear.

To thee the patent passage always free,
Peter himself received the keys from thee;
Or, which we may conceive with much more ease,
Thou art thyself the gate, thyself the keys.

Thine was the fiery chariot, thine the steeds,
That fetched Elijah from old Jordan's plains;
Such a long journey such a voiture needs,
And thou the steady coachman held the reins.

Thine was the wondrous mantle he threw down,
By which successive miracles were wrought;
For 'twas the prophet's faith, and not his gown,
Elisha so importunately sought.

Bright pole-star of the soul, for ever fixed,
The mind's sure guide, when anxious and perplexed;
When wandering in the abyss of thoughts and cares,
Where no way out and no way in appears;
When doubt and horror, the extremes of fear,
Surround the soul, and prompt her to despair.

Thou shin'st aloft, open'st a gleam of light,
And show'st all heaven to our sight;
Thou gild'st the soul with sudden smiles, and joy,
And peace, that hell itself can ne'er destroy.

If all this be to be said, and all indeed but a poetical trifle upon this
exalted subject, what is become of our negative Christian in all this?
There is not a word of negative religion in all the description of faith,
any more than there is of faith in all our negative religion.

Now let us follow this poor negative wretch to his deathbed; and there having very little other notion of religion—for 'tis the fate of those that trust to their negatives to have little else in their thoughts—if a good man come to talk with him, if he talks out of that way he puts him all into confusion; for if he cannot swim upon the bladders of his negatives he drowns immediately, or he buoys himself up above your reproofs, and goes on as before. He is a little like the Polish Captain Uratz, who was executed for the murder of Mr. Thynne, who, when they talked to him of repentance and of Jesus Christ, said he was of such and such a family, and he hoped God would have some respect to him as a gentleman.

But what must a poor minister do who, being filled with better principles, prays for this vainglorious man? Must he say, "Lord, accept this good man, for he has been no drunkard, no swearer, no debauched person; he has been a just, a charitable man, has done a great deal of good among his neighbours, and never wilfully wronged any man; he has not been so wicked as it is the custom of the times to be, nor has he shown bad examples to others; Lord, be merciful to this excellent good man?"

No, no, the poor sincere minister knows better things; and if he prays with him, he turns him quite inside out, represents him as a poor mistaken creature, who now sees that he is nothing, and has nothing in himself, but casts himself entirely, as a miserable lost sinner, into the arms of a most merciful Saviour, praying to be accepted on the merits of Jesus Christ, and no other; so that there is all his negative bottom unravelled at once; and if this is not his case it must be worse.

CHAPTER FIVE
OF LISTENING TO THE VOICE OF PROVIDENCE

We are naturally backward to inform ourselves of our duty to our Maker and to ourselves; it is a study we engage in with great reluctance, and it is but too agreeable to us, when we meet with any difficulty which we think gives us a just occasion to throw off any farther inquiries of that kind.

Hence I observe the wisest of men often run into mistakes about the things which, speaking of religion, we call duty, taking up slight notions of them, and believing they understand enough of them, by which they rob themselves of the advantages as well as comfort of a farther search; or, on the other hand, taking up with the general knowledge of religious principles, and the common duties of a Christian life, are satisfied with knowing what they say is sufficient to carry them to heaven, without inquiring into those things which are helpful and assistant to make that strait path easy and pleasant to themselves, and to make them useful to others by the way.

Solomon was quite of another opinion, when he bid us cry after knowledge, and lift up our voice for understanding—dig for her as for silver, and search for her as for hid treasure. It is certain here that he meant religious knowledge, and it is explained in the very next words, with an encouraging promise to those that shall enter upon the search, *viz.*, Then shalt thou understand the fear of the Lord, and find the knowledge of God.

I am of opinion that it is our unquestioned duty to inquire after everything in our journey to the eternal habitation which God has permitted us to know, and thus to raise difficulties in the way of our just search into Divine discoveries, is to act like Solomon's sluggard, who saith, "*There is a lion without, I shall be slain in the streets*" (Prov. xxii. 13). That is, he sits down in his ignorance, repulsed with imaginary difficulties, without making one step in the search after the knowledge which he ought to dig for as for hid treasure.

Let us, then, be encouraged to our duty; let us boldly inquire after everything that God has permitted us to know, I grant that secret things belong to God, and I shall labour to keep my due distance; but I firmly believe that there are no secret things belonging to God, and which as such we are forbidden to inquire into, but what also are so preserved in secrecy that by all our inquiries we cannot arrive at the knowledge of them; and it is a most merciful, as well as wise dispensation, that we are only forbid inquiring after those things which we cannot know, and that all those things are effectually locked up from our knowledge which we are forbidden to inquire into. The case is better with us than it was with Adam, We have not the tree of knowledge first planted in our view, as it were tempting us with its beauty, and within our reach, and then a prohibition upon pain of death; but blessed be God, we may eat of all the trees in the garden, and all those of which we are not allowed to take are placed both out of our sight and out of our reach.

I am making way here to one of the trees of sacred knowledge, which, though it may grow in the thickest of the wood, and be surrounded with some briars and thorns, so as to place it a little out of sight, yet I hope to prove that it is our duty to taste of it, and that the way to come at it is both practicable and plain.

But to waive the allegory, as I am entering into the nicest search of Divine things that perhaps the whole scheme of religion directs us to, it is absolutely necessary at our entrance, if possible, to remove every difficulty, explain every principle, and lay down every foundation so undeniably clear, that nothing may appear dark or mysterious in our first conceptions of things—no stumbling-block lie at the threshold, and the humble reader may meet with no repulse from his own apprehensions of not understanding what he is going to read.

Listening to the voice of Providence is my subject; I am willing to suppose, in the first place, that I am writing to those who acknowledge the two grand principles upon which all religion depends.

1. That there is a God, a first great moving cause of all things, an eternal Power, prior, and consequently superior, to all power and being.

2. That this eternal Power, which I call God, is the Creator and Governor of all things, *viz.*, of heaven and earth.

To avoid needless distinctions concerning which of the persons in the Godhead are exercised in the creating power, and which in the governing power, I offer that glorious text, Psalm xxxiii. 6, as a repulse to all such cavilling inquiries, where the whole Trinity is plainly entitled to the whole creating work:—"*By the Word (God the Son) of the Lord (God the Father) were the heavens made, and all the host of them by the breath (God the Holy Ghost) of His mouth.*"

Having thus presupposed the belief of the being and the creating work of God, and declared that I am writing to such only who are ready to own they believe that God is, and that He created the heaven and the earth, the sea and all that in them is, I think I need not make any preamble to introduce the following propositions, *viz.*:

1. That this eternal God guides by His providence the whole world, which He has created by His power.

2. That this Providence manifests a particular care over and concern in the governing and directing man, the best and last created creature on earth.

Natural religion proves the first, revealed religion proves the last of these beyond contradiction. Natural religion intimates the necessity of a Providence guiding and governing the world, from the consequence of the wisdom, justice, prescience, and goodness of the Creator.

It would be absurd to conceive of God exerting infinite power to create a world,. and not concerning His wisdom, which is His providence, in guiding the operations of Nature, so as to preserve the order of His creation, and the obedience and subordination of consequences and causes throughout the course of that nature, which is in part the inferior life of that creation.

Revealed religion has given such a light into the care and concern of this Providence, in an especial manner, in and over that part of the creation called man, that we must likewise deny principles if we enter into disputes about it.

For him the peace of the creation is preserved, the climates made habitable, the creatures subjected and made nourishing, all vegetative life made medicinal; so that indeed the whole creation seems to be entailed upon him as an inheritance, and given to him for a possession, subjected to his authority, and governed by him as viceroy to the King of all the earth; the management of it is given to him as tenant to the great Proprietor, who is Lord of the manor, or Landlord of the soil. And it cannot be conceived, without great inconsistency of thought, that this world is left entirely to man's conduct, without the supervising influence and the secret direction of the Creator.

This I call Providence, to which I give the whole power of guiding and directing of the creation, and managing of it, by man who is His deputy or substitute, and even the guiding, influencing, and overruling man himself also.

Let critical annotators enter into specific distinctions of Providence, and its way of acting, as they please, and as the formalities of the schoolmen direct; the short description I shall give of it is this, that it is that operation of the power, wisdom, justice, and goodness of God by which He influences, governs, and directs not only the means, but the events, of all things which concern us in this world.

I say it is that operation, let them call it what they will, which acts thus; I am no way concerned to show how it acts, or why it acts thus and thus in particular; we are to reverence its sovereignty, as it is the finger of God Himself, who is the Sovereign Director; and we are to observe its motions, obey its dictates, and listen to its voice, as it is, and because it is, particularly employed for our advantage.

It would be a very proper and useful observation here, and might take up much of this work, to illustrate the goodness of Providence, in that it is, as I say, particularly employed for the advantage of mankind. But as this is not the main design, and will come in naturally in every part of the work I am upon, I refer it to the common inferences, which are to be drawn from the particulars, as I go on.

It is, indeed, the most rational foundation of the whole design before me; it is therefore that we should listen to the voice of Providence, because it is principally determined, and determines all other things, for our advantage.

But I return to the main subject—the voice of Providence, the language or the meaning of Providence.

Nothing is more frequent than for us to mistake Providence, even in its most visible appearances; how easy, then, must it be to let its silent actings, which perhaps are the most pungent and significant, pass our observation.

I am aware of the error many fall into, who, determining the universal currency of events to Providence, and that not the minutest thing occurs in the course of life but by the particular destination of Heaven, by consequence entitle Providence to the efficiency of their own follies; as if a person presuming to smoke his pipe in a magazine of gunpowder should reproach Providence with blowing up the castle, for which indeed he ought to be hanged; or a man leaving his house or shop open in the night, should charge Providence with appointing him to be robbed, and the like. Nay, to carry it farther, every murderer or thief may allege Providence, that determines and directs everything, directed him to such wickedness; whereas Providence itself, notwithstanding the crimes of men, is actively concerned in no evil.

But I pass all these things; the subject I am treating upon is of another nature. The design here is to instruct us in some particular things relating to Providence and its government of men in the world, which it will be worth our while to observe, without inquiring how far it does or does not act in other methods.

There is, it is true, a difficulty to shake off all the wry steps which people take to amuse themselves about Providence, and for this reason I take so much pains at first to avoid them. Many men entitle Providence to things which it is not concerned about, speaking abstractedly; but, which is a much worse error, many also take no notice of those things which Providence particularly, and even in a very remarkable manner, distinguishes itself by its concern in.

If Providence guides the world, and directs the issues and events of things; if it commands causes and forms the connection of circumstances in the world, as no man that owns the principles mentioned above will deny; and, above all, if the general scope of Providence, and of the government of the world by its influence, be for our advantage, then it follows, necessarily, that it is our business and our interest to listen to its voice.

By listening to the voice of Providence, I mean to study its meaning in every circumstance of life, in every event; to learn to understand the end and design of Providence in everything that happens, what is the design of Providence in it respecting ourselves, and what our duty to do upon the particular occasion that offers. If a man were in danger of drowning in a shipwrecked vessel, and Providence presented a boat coming towards him, he would scarce want to be told that it was his business to make signals of distress, that the people in the said boat might not pass by ignorant of his condition, and give him no assistance; if he did, and omitted it, he would have little cause to concern Providence in his ruin.

There is certainly a rebellion against Providence, which Heaven itself will not always concern itself to overrule; and he that throws himself into a river to drown himself, he that hangs himself up to a beam, he that shoots himself into the head with a pistol, shall die in spite of all the notions of decree, destiny, fate, or whatever we weakly call Providence; in such cases, Providence will not always concern itself to prevent it; and yet it is no impeachment of the sovereignty of Heaven in directing, decreeing, and governing all events in the world.

Providence decrees that events shall attend upon causes in a direct chain, and by an evident necessity, and has doubtless left many powers of good and evil seemingly to ourselves, and, as it were, in our hands, as the natural product of such causes and consequences, which we are not to limit and cannot expressly determine about, but which we are accountable for the good or evil application of; otherwise we were in vain exhorted and commanded to do any good thing, or to avoid any wicked one. Rewards and punishments would be incongruous with sovereign justice, and promises and threatenings be perfectly unmeaning, useless things—mankind being no free agent to himself, or intrusted with the necessary powers which those promises and threatenings imply.

But all these things are out of my present inquiry. I am for freely and entirely submitting all events to Providence; but not to be supinely and unconcernedly passive, as if there was nothing warning, instructing, or directing in the premonitions of God's providence, and which He expected we should take notice of, and take warning by. The "prudent man foreseeth the evil, and hideth himself." How does he foresee it, since it is not in man to direct himself? There are intimations given us, by which a prudent man may sometimes foresee evil and hide himself; and I must take these all out of the devil's hands if possible, and place Providence at the head of the invisible world, as well as at the helm of this world; and though I abhor superstitious and sceptical notions of the world of spirits, of which I purpose to speak hereafter, either in this work or in some other by itself—I say, though I am not at all a sceptic, yet I cannot doubt but that the invisible hand of Providence, which guides and governs this world, does with a secret power likewise influence the world, and may, and I believe does, direct from thence silent messengers on many occasions—whether sleeping or waking, whether directly or indirectly, whether by hints, impulses, allegories, mysteries, or otherwise, we know not; and does think fit to give us such alarms, such previous and particular knowledge of things that, if listened to, might many ways be useful to the prudent man to foresee the evil, and hide himself.

The only objection, and which I can see no method to give a reason for and no answer to, is, why, if it be the work of Providence, those things should be so imperfect, so broken, so irregular, that men may either never be able to pass any right judgment of them, as is sometimes the case, or make a perfect judgment of them, which is often the case, and so the end of the intimation be entirely defeated, without any fault, neglect, or omission of the man.

This we can no more account for than we can for the handwriting upon the wall at the great feast of Belshazzar, *viz.*, why it was written in a character which none could understand; and which, if the prophet had not been found, had perhaps never been known, or at least not till the king's fate, which was even then irretrievable, had been over.

This, indeed, we cannot account for, and can only say it is our duty to study these things, to listen to the voice of them and obey their secret dictates, as far as reason directs, without an over-superstitious regard to them any more than a total neglect, leaving the reason of Providence's acting thus to be better understood hereafter.

But to describe a little what I mean by listening to the voice of Providence: it is the reverse of the supine stupid man, whose character I shall come to by-and-by. The man I would recommend lives, first, in a general belief that Providence has the supreme direction of all his affairs, even of his in particular, as well as those of the world; that 'tis his mercy that it is so, that 'tis the effect of an infinitely wise and gracious disposition from above that he subsists; and that it is not below the dignity any more than 'tis remote from the power of an infinite, wise, and good Being to take cognisance of the least thing concerning him.

This, in the consequence, obliges him to all I say; for to him who firmly believes that Providence stoops to concern itself for him, and to order the least article of his affairs, it necessarily follows that he should concern himself in everything that Providence does which comes within his reach, that he may know whether he be interested in it or not.

If he neglects this, he neglects himself—he abandons all concern about himself; since he does not know but that the very next particular act of Providence, which comes within his reach to distinguish, may be interested in him and he in it.

It is not for me to dictate here to any man what particular things relating to him Providence is concerned in, or what not, or how far any incident of life is or is not the particular act and deed of the government of Providence. But as it is the received opinion of every good man that nothing befalls us without the active or passive concern of Providence in it, so it is impossible this good man can be unconcerned in whatever that Providence determines concerning him.

If it be true, as our Saviour Himself says, that not a hair falls from our heads without the will of our heavenly Father, then not a hair ought to fall from our heads without our having our eyes up to our heavenly Father in it.

I take the text in its due latitude, namely, that not the minutest incident of life befalls us without the active will of our Father directing it, or the passive will of our Father suffering it; so I take the deduction from it in the same latitude, that nothing, of how mean a nature so ever, can befall us, but what we ought to have our eyes up to our heavenly Father in it, be resigned to Him in the event, and subjected to Him in the means; and he that neglects this lives in contempt of Providence, and that in the most provoking manner possible.

I am not answerable for any extremes these things may lead weak people into; I know some are apt to entitle the hand of God to the common and most ridiculous trifles in Nature; as a religious creature I knew, seeing a bottle of beer being over ripe burst out, the cork fly up against the ceiling, and the froth follow it like an engine, cried out, "O! the wonders of omnipotent Power!" But I am representing how a Christian with an awful regard to the government of Providence in the world, and particularly in all his own affairs, subjects his mind to a constant obedience to the dictates of that Providence, gives an humble preference to it in all his conclusions, waits the issues of it with a cheerful resignation, and, in a word, listens carefully to the voice of

414

Providence, that he may be always obedient to the heavenly vision.

Whether this Divine emanation has any concern in the notices, omens, dreams, voices, hints, forebodings, impulses, &c, which seem to be a kind of communication with the invisible world, and a converse between the spirits embodied and those unembodied, and how far, without prejudice to the honour and our reverence of Providence, and without danger of scepticism and a kind of radicated infidelity, those things may be regarded, is a nice and difficult thing to resolve, and I shall treat of it by itself.

It has been the opinion of good men of all ages that such things are not to be totally disregarded; to say how far they are to be depended upon, I am not to take upon me.[1] How far they may or may not be concerned in the influence of Providence, I also dare not say. But as the verity of astronomy is evidenced by the calculation of eclipses, so the certainty of this communication of spirits is established by the concurrence of events with the notices they sometimes give; and if it be true, as I must believe, that the divine Providence takes cognisance of all things belonging to us, I dare not exclude it from having some concern, how much I do not say, in these things also. But of this in its place.

Whenever Providence discovers anything of this Arcanum I desire to listen to the voice of it, and this is one of the things I recommend to others. Indeed, I would be very cautious how I listen to any other voices from that country than such as I am sure are conveyed to me from Heaven for my better understanding the whole mystery.

If, then, we are to listen to the voice of Nature, and to the voices of creatures, viz., to the voice of the invisible agents of the world of spirits, as above, much more are we to listen to the voice of God.

I have already hinted that He that made the world we are sure guides it, and His providence is equally wonderful as His power. But nothing in the whole course of His providence is more worthy our regard, especially as it concerns us His creatures, than the silent voice, if it may be allowed me to call it so, of His managing events and causes. He that listens to the Providence of God listens to the voice of God, as He is seen in the wonders of His government, and as He is seen in the wonders of His omnipotence.

If, then, the events of things are His, as well as the causes, it is certainly well worth our notice, when the sympathy or relation between

---

1. I have here transposed some words which seem to have got out of their proper place.

events of things and their causes most eminently appears; and how can any man who has the least inclination to observe what is remarkable in the world, shut his eyes to the visible discovery which there is in the events of Providence of a supreme Hand guiding them? For example, when visible punishments follow visible crimes, who can refrain confessing the apparent direction of supreme justice? When concurrence of circumstances directs to the cause, men that take no notice of such remarkable pointings of Providence openly contemn Heaven, and frequently stand in the light of their own advantages.

The concurrence of events is a light to their causes, and the methods of Heaven, in some things, are a happy guide to us to make a judgment in others; he that is deaf to these things shuts his ears to instruction, and, like Solomon's fool, hates knowledge.

The dispositions of Heaven to approve or condemn our actions are, many of them, discovered by observation; and it is easy to know when that hand of Providence opens the door for, or shuts it against, our measures, if we will bring causes together, and compare former things with present, making our judgment by the ordinary rules of Heaven's dealing with men.

How, and from what hand, come the frequent instances of severe judgment following rash and hellish imprecations, when men call for God's judgment, and Providence, or justice rather, obeys the summons, and comes at their call? A man calls God to witness to an untruth, and wishes himself struck dumb, blind, or dead, if it is not true, and is struck dumb, blind, or dead. Is not this a voice? does not Heaven, with the stroke, cry, *Castigo te*—be it to thee as thou hast said? He must be deaf who cannot hear it, and worse than deaf that does not heed it; such executions from Heaven are *in terrorem*, as offenders among men are punished as well for example to others as to prevent their doing the like again.

Innumerable ways the merciful disposition of Providence takes to discover to us what He expects we should do in difficult cases; and doubtless, then, it expects at the same time we should take notice of those directions.

We are short-sighted creatures at best, and can see but a little way before us—I mean, as to the events of things. We ought, therefore, to make use of all the lights and helps we can get; these, if nicely regarded, would be some of the most considerable to guide us in many difficult cases.

Would we carefully listen to the concurrence of Providence in the several parts of our lives, we should stand less in need of the more dangerous helps of visions, dreams, and voices from less certain intelligences.

A gentleman of my acquaintance, being to go a journey into the north, was twice taken very ill the day he had appointed to begin his journey, and so was obliged to put off going. This he took for a direction from Heaven that he should not go at all; and in very few days after his wife was taken sick and died, which made it absolutely necessary for him to be at home to look after his affairs; and had he gone away before, must certainly have been obliged to come back again.

The Romans had certainly the foundation of this principle in their prudent observations of days and circumstances of days, nor is Scripture itself void of the like, but rather points out to the observation, particularly that of the children of Israel, who, after 430 years were expired from their coming into Egypt, "*Even in the selfsame day departed they thence*" Exod. xii. 41, 42). This is the day, that remarkable day; several other Scriptures mention periodical times, dies infaustus—the prudent shall keep silence in that time, for it is an evil time.

We find Providence stoops to restrain not the actions of men only, but even its own actions to days and times; doubtless for our observation, and in some things for our instruction. I do not so much refer to the revolutions of things and families on particular days, which are therefore by some people called lucky and unlucky days, as I do to the observing how Providence causes the revolutions of days to form a concurrence between the actions of men, which it does not approve, or does approve, and the reward of these actions in this world, by which men may, if they think fit to distinguish and observe right upon them, see the crime or merit of those actions in the Divine resentment, may read the sin in the punishment, and may learn conviction from the revolution of circumstances in the appointment of Heaven.

I have seen several collections of such things made by private hands, some relating to family circumstances, some to public; also, in the unnatural wars in England, between the King and the Parliament, I have heard many such things have been observed. For example, the same day of the year and month that Sir John Hotham kept out Hull against King Charles the First, and refused him entrance, was the same Sir John Hotham put to death by the very Parliament that he did that exploit for; that King Charles himself was sentenced to die by the High Court of Justice, as it was then called, the same day of the month that he signed the warrant for the execution of the Earl of Strafford, which, as it was then said by some of his friends, was cutting off his own right hand. The same day that King James the Second came to the crown, against the design of the Bill of Exclusion, the same day he was voted abdicated by Parliament, and the throne filled by the Prince of Orange and his princess.

These, or such as these, seem to be a kind of silent sentence of Providence upon such actions, animadverting upon them in a judicial manner, and intimating plainly, that the animadversion had a retrospect to what was passed, and those that listen to the voice of Providence in such things should at least lay them up in their hearts.

Eminent deliverances in sudden dangers are of the most significant kind of providences, and which, accordingly, have a loud voice in them, calling upon us to be thankful to that blessed Hand that has been pleased to spare and protect us. The voice of such signal deliverances is frequently a just call upon us to repentance, and looks directly that way; often 'tis a caution against falling into the like dangers we were exposed to, from which nothing but so much goodness could deliver us again. In how many occasions of life, if God's providence had no greater share in our safety than our own prudence, should we plunge and precipitate ourselves into all manner of misery and distress? And how often, for want of listening to those providences, do we miscarry?

Innumerable instances present themselves to us every day, in which the providence of God speaks to us in things relating to ourselves; in deliverances to excite our thankfulness; in views of danger to awaken our caution, and to make us walk wisely and circumspectly in every step we take; those that are awake to these things, and have their ears open to the voice of them, many times reap the benefit of their instruction by being protected, while those who neglect them are of the number of the simple, who pass on and are punished.

To be utterly careless of ourselves in such cases, and talk of trusting Providence, is a lethargy of the worst nature; for as we are to trust Providence with our estates, but to use, at the same time, all diligence in our callings, so we are to trust Providence with our safety, but with our eyes open to all its necessary cautions, warnings, and instructions, many of which Providence is pleased to give us in the course of life for the direction of our conduct, and which we should ill place to the account of Providence without acknowledging that they ought to be regarded, and a due reverence paid to them upon all occasions.

I take a general neglect of these things to be a kind of practical atheism, or at least a living in a kind of contempt of Heaven, regardless of all that share which His invisible hand has in the things that befall us.

Such a man receives good at the hand of his Maker, but unconcerned at the very nature or original of it, looks not at all to the Benefactor; again, he receives evil, but has no sense of it, as a judicial dispensing of punishment from Heaven; but, insensible of one or other, he is neither thankful for one, nor humble under the other, but stupid in both, as if he was out of God's care, and God Himself out of his thoughts; this is just the reverse of the temper I am recommending, and let the picture recommend itself to any according to its merits.

When Prince Vandemont commanded the confederate army in Flanders, the same campaign that King William was besieging Namur, some troops were ordered to march into the flat country towards Nieuport, in order to make a diversion, and draw down the Count de Montal, who commanded a flying body about Menin, and to keep him from joining the Duke de Villeroy, who commanded the main body of the French army.

The soldiers were ordered, upon pain of death, not to stir from their camp, or to plunder any of the country people; the reason was evident, because provisions being somewhat scarce, if the boors were not protected they would have fled from their houses, and the army would have been put to great straits, being just entered into the enemy's country.

It happened that five English soldiers, straggling beyond their bounds, were fallen upon, near a farmhouse, by some of the country people (for indeed the boors were oftentimes too unmerciful to the soldiers), as if they had plundered them, when, indeed, they had not; the soldiers defended themselves, got the better, and killed two of the boors, and being, as they thought, justly provoked by being first attacked, they broke into the house, and then used them roughly enough indeed.

They found in the house a great quantity of apples; the people being fled had left them in possession, and they made no haste to go away, but fell to work with the apples, and heating the oven put a great quantity of apples into the oven to roast. In the meantime the boors, who knew their number to be but five, and had got more help on their side, came down upon them again, attacked the house, forced their way in, mastered the Englishmen, killed two, and took a third and barbarously put him into the oven, which he had heated, where he was smothered to death; it seems it was not hot enough to burn him.

The other two escaped, but in coming back to the camp they were immediately apprehended by the provosts, and brought to a court-martial, where they were sentenced, not for plundering, for that did not appear, but for being out of the bounds appointed by the general order, as above.

When the sentence came to be executed, the general was prevailed upon to spare one of them, and to order them to cast lots for their lives. This, as it is known, is usually done by throwing dice upon a drum-head, and he that throws highest or lowest, as is appointed before, is to die; at this time he that threw lowest was to live.

When the fellows were brought out to throw, the first threw two sixes, and fell immediately to wringing his hands, crying he was a dead man, but was as much surprised with joy when his comrade throwing, there came up two sixes also.

The officer appointed to see the execution was a little doubtful what to do, but his orders being positive, he commanded them to throw again; they did so, and each of them threw two fives; the soldiers that stood round shouted, and said neither of them was to die. The officer, being a sober thinking man, said it was strange, and looked like something from heaven, and he would not proceed without acquainting the council of war, which was then sitting; they considered a while, and at last ordered them to take other dice and to throw again, which was done, and both the soldiers threw two fours.

The officer goes back to the council of war, who were surprised very much, and looking on it as the voice of Heaven, respited the execution till the general was acquainted with it.

The general sends for the men, and examines them strictly, who telling him the whole story, he pardoned them, with this expression to those about him: "I love," says he, "in such extraordinary cases to listen to the voice of Providence."

While we are in this uninformed state, where we know so little of the invisible world, it would be greatly our advantage if we knew rightly, and without the bondage of enthusiasm and superstition, how to make use of the hints given us from above for our direction in matters of the greatest importance.

It has pleased God very much to straighten the special and particular directions which He gives to men immediately from Himself; but I dare not say they are quite ceased. We read of many examples in

Scripture, how God spake to men by voice immediately from heaven, by appearance of angels, or by dreams and visions of the night, and by all these, not in public and more extraordinary cases only, but in private, personal, and family concerns.

Thus God is said to have appeared to Abraham, to Lot, and to Jacob; angels also have appeared in many other cases, and to many several persons, as to Manoah and his wife, to Zachariah, to the Virgin Mary, and to the Apostles; others have been warned in a dream, as King Abimelech, the false prophet Balaam, Pontius Pilate's wife, Herod, Joseph, the Apostles also, and many others.

We cannot say but these and all the miraculous voices, the prophetic messages prefaced boldly by the ancients with "*thus saith the Lord*," are ceased, and as we have a more sure word of prophecy handed to us by the mission of Gospel ministers, to which the Scripture says, "*We do well that we take heed;*" and to whom our blessed Lord has said, "*Lo, I am with you to the end of the world;*" I say, as we have this Gospel backed with the Spirit and presence of God, we are no losers if we observe the rule laid down, *viz.*, that we be obedient to the heavenly vision, for such it is, as well as that of the Apostle Peter's dream of the sheet let down from heaven.

I mention this to pay a due reverence to the sufficiency of Gospel revelation, and to the guiding of the Spirit of God, who in spiritual things is given to lead us into all truth; nor would I have anything which I am going to say tend to lessen these great efficients of our eternal salvation.

But I am chiefly upon our conduct in the inferior life, as I may call it; and in this, I think, the voice of God, even His immediate voice from heaven, is not entirely ceased from us, though it may have changed the mediums of communication.

I have heard the divines tell us by way of distinction, that there is a voice of God in His word, and a voice of God in His work; the latter I take to be a subject very awful and very instructing.

This voice of God in His works, is either heard in His works which are already wrought, such as of creation, which fill us with wonder and astonishment, admiration and adoration; "*When I view the heavens, the work of Thy hands, the moon and the stars which Thou hast made, then I say, what is man?*" &c. Or (2.) His works of government and providence, in which the infinite variety affords a pleasing and instructing contemplation; and it is without question our wisdom and advantage to study and know them, and to listen to the voice of God in them; for

421

this listening to the voice of Providence is a thing so hard to direct, and so little understood, that I find the very thought of it is treated with contempt, even by many pious and good people, as leading to superstition, to enthusiasm, and vain fancies tainted with melancholy, and amusing the mind with the vapours of the head.

It is true, an ill use may be made of these things, and to tie people too strictly down to a rule, where their own observation is to be the judge, endangers the running into many foolish extremes, entitling a distempered brain too much to the exposition of the sublimest things, and tacking the awful name of Providence to every fancy of their own.

From hence, I think, too much proceeds the extraordinary (note, I say extraordinary) homage paid to omens, flying of birds, voices, noises, predictions, and a thousand foolish things, in which I shall endeavour to state the case fairly between the devil and mankind; but at present I need say no more here, than that they have nothing to do with the subject I am now upon, or the subject I am upon with them.

But as my design is serious, and I hope pious, I shall keep strictly to the exposition I give of my own meaning, and meddle with no other.

By the voice of Providence, therefore, I shall confine myself to the particular circumstances, incident, and accident, which every man's life is full of, and which are, in a more extraordinary manner, said to be peculiar to himself or to his family.

By listening to them, I mean, making such due application of them to his own circumstances as becomes a Christian, for caution in his conduct, and all manner of instruction, receiving all the hints as from Heaven, returning all the praise to, making all the improvement for, and reverencing the sovereignty of his Maker in everything, not disputing or reproaching the justice of Providence; and, which is the main thing I aim at, taking such notice of the several providences that happen in the course of our lives, as by one circumstance to learn how to behave in another.

For example, supposing from my own story, when a young fellow broke from his friends, trampled upon all the wise advices and most affectionate persuasions of his father, and even the tears and entreaties of a tender mother, and would go away to sea, but is checked in his first excursions by being shipwrecked, and in the utmost distress saved by the assistance of another ship's boat, seeing the ship he was in soon after sink to the bottom;—ought not such a young man to have listened to the voice of this providence, and have taken it for a summons to him, that when he was on shore he should stay on shore, and go back to the arms of his friends, hearken to their counsel, and not precipitate himself into farther mischiefs? what happiness might such a prudent step have procured, what miseries and mischiefs would it have prevented in the rest of his unfortunate life!

An acquaintance of mine, who had several such circumstances befall him, as those which I am inclined to call warnings, but entirely neglected them, and laughed at those that did otherwise, suffered deeply for his disregard of omens. He took lodgings in a village near the city of London, and in a house where either he sought bad company, or, at best, could meet, with little that was good. Providence, that seemed to animadvert upon his conduct, so ordered it that something or other mischievous always happened to him there, or as he went thither; several times he was robbed on the highway going thither, once or twice taken very ill, at other times his affairs in the world went ill, while he diverted himself there. Several of his friends cautioned him of it, and told him he ought to consider that some superior Hand seemed to hint to him that he should come there no more; he slighted the hint, or at least neglected it after some time, and went to the same place again, but was so terrified with a most dreadful tempest of thunder and lightning, which fell as it were more particularly upon that part of the country than upon others, that he took it as a warning from Heaven, and resolved not to go there again, and some time after a fire destroyed that house, very few escaping that were in it.

It would be an ill account we should give of the government of divine Providence in the world, if we should argue that its events are so unavoidable, and every circumstance so determined, that nothing can be altered, and that therefore these warnings of Providence are inconsistent with the nature of it. This, besides that I think it would take from the sovereignty of Providence, and deny even God Himself the privilege of being a free agent, it would also so contradict the experience of every man living, in the varieties of his respective life, that he should be unable to give any account for what end many things which Providence directs in the world are directed, and why so many things happen which do happen. Why are evils attending us so evidently foretold, that by those foretellings they are avoided, if it was not determined before they should be avoided and should not befall us?

People that tie up all to events and causes, strip the providence of God which guides the world of all its superintendency, and leave it no room to act as a wise disposer of things.

It seems to me that the immutable wisdom and power of the Creator, and the notion of it in the minds of men, is as dutifully preserved, and is as legible to our understanding, though there be a hand left at liberty to direct the course of natural causes and events. 'Tis sufficient to the honour of an immutable Deity, that, for the common incidents of life, they be left to the disposition of a daily agitator, namely, divine Providence, to order and direct them, as it shall see good, within the natural limits of cause and consequence.

This seems to me a much more rational system than that of tying up the hands of the Supreme Power to a road of things, so that none can be acted or permitted but such as was so appointed before to be acted and permitted.

But what if, after all, we were to sit down and acknowledge that the immutability of God's being and the unchangeableness of His actings are not easy to be comprehended by us, or that we may say we are not able to reconcile them with the infinite variation of His Providence, which in all its actings seems to us to be at full liberty to determine anew and give events a turn this way or that way, as its sovereignty and wisdom shall direct; does it follow that these things are not reconcilable because we cannot reconcile them? Why should we not as well say nothing of God is to be understood, because we cannot understand it? or that nothing in Nature is intelligible but what we can understand?

Who can understand the reason, and much less the manner, of the needle tending to the pole by being touched with the loadstone, and by what operation the magnetic virtue is conveyed with a touch? Why that virtue is not communicable to other metals—such as gold, silver, or copper—but to iron only? What sympathetic influence is there between the stone and the star, or the pole? Why tending to that point in the whole arch and not to any other? And why face about to the south pole as soon as it has passed the equinox? Yet we see all these things in their operations and events; we know they must be reconcilable in nature, though we cannot reconcile them; and intelligible in nature, though we cannot understand them. Sure it is as highly reasonable then for us to believe that the various actings of Providence, which to us appear changeable—one decree, as it were, reversing another, and one action superseding another—may be as reconcilable to the immutability of God and to the unchangeableness of His purposes, though we cannot understand how it is brought to pass, as it is to believe that there is a reason to be given for the agreement and sympathetic correspondence between the magnet and the pole, though at present the manner of it is not discovered and cannot be understood.

If, then, the hand of divine Providence has a spontaneous power of acting, and directed by its own sovereignty proceeds by such methods as it thinks fit, and as we see daily in the course of human things, our business is to converse with the acting part of Providence, with which we more immediately have to do, and not confound our judgment with things which we cannot fully comprehend, such as the why, to what end, and the how, in what manner it acts so and so.

As we are then conversant with the immediate actions of divine Providence, it is our business to study it as much as may be in that part of its actings wherein it is to be known; and this includes the silent actings of. Providence, as well as those which are more loud, and which, being declared, speak in public.

There are several silent steps which Providence takes in the world which summon our attention; and he that will not listen to them shall deprive himself of much of the caution and counsel, as well as comfort, which he might otherwise have in his passage through this life; particularly by thus listening to the voice, as I call it, of Providence, we have the comfort of seeing that really an invisible and powerful Hand is employed in, and concerned for, our preservation and prosperity in the world. And who can look upon the manifest deliverances which he meets with in the infinite variety of life, without being convinced that they are wrought for him without his own assistance by the wise and merciful dispositions of an invisible and friendly Power?

The bringing good events to pass by the most threatening causes, as it testifies a Power that has the government of causes and effects in its hand, so it gives a very convincing evidence of that Power being on good terms with us; as on the contrary, when the like Providence declares against us, we ought to make a suitable use of it another way, that is to say, take the just alarm, and apply to the necessary duties of humiliation and repentance.

These things may be jested with by the men of fashion, but I am supposing myself talking to men that have a sense of a future state, and of the economy of an invisible world upon them, and neither to atheists, sceptics, or persons indifferent, who are, indeed, near of kin to them both.

As there are just reflections to be made upon the various conduct of Providence in the several passages of man's life, so there are infinite circumstances in which we may furnish ourselves with directions in the course of life, and in the most sudden incidents, as well to obtain good as avoid evil.

Much of the honour due to the goodness of Providence is unjustly taken away from it by men that give themselves a loose in a general neglect of these things; but that which is still more absurd to me is, that some men are [so] obstinately resolved against paying the homage of their deliverances to their Maker, or paying the reverence due to His terrors in anything that befalls them ill, where it ought to be paid, that they will give all that honour to another. If it was well, they tell you they know not how. but so it happened, or it was so by good chance, and the like. This is a sort of language I cannot understand; it seems to be a felonious thought in its very design, robbing Heaven of the honour due to it, and listing ourselves in the regiment of the ungrateful.

But this is not all, for one crime leads on to another; if this part is felony or robbery, the next is treason, for resolving first to deny the homage of good or evil events to God, from whose hands they come, they go on and pay it to the devil, the enemy of His praise, and rival of His power.

Two of these wretches travelled a little journey with me some years ago, and in their return, some time after I was gone from them, they met with a different adventure, and telling me the story, they expressed themselves thus: They were riding from Huntingdon towards London, and in some lanes betwixt Huntingdon and Caxton. one happened, by a slip of his horse's foot, which lamed him a little, to stay about half a mile behind the other, was set upon by some highwaymen, who robbed him, and abused him very much; the other went on to Caxton, not taking care of his companion, thinking he had staved on some particular occasion, and escaped the thieves, they making off across the country towards Cambridge.

"Well." says I to the first, "how came you to escape?"

"I don't know, not I." says he; "I happened not to look behind me when his horse stumbled, and I went forward, and by good luck," adds he again, "I heard nothing of the matter." Here was, "it happened," and "by good luck," but not the least sense of the government of Providence in this affair, or its disposition for his good, but an empty idol of air, or rather an imaginary, nonsensical nothing, an image more inconsistent than those I mentioned among the Chinese; not a monster, indeed, of a frightful shape and ugly figure, loathsome and frightful, but a mere phantasm, an idea, a nonentity—a name without being, a miscalled, unborn, nothing, hap, luck, chance; that is to say, a name put upon the medium, which they set up in their imagination for want of a will to acknowledge their Maker, and recognise the goodness which had particularly preserved him. This was the most ungrateful piece of folly, or, to speak more properly, the maddest and most foolish piece of ingratitude, that ever I met with.

Well, if this was foolish and preposterous, the other was as wicked and detestable; for when the first had told his tale I turned to the other, and asked him what was the matter. "Why, how came this to pass?" said I; "why has this disaster fallen all upon you? How was it?"

"Nay," says he, "I do not know; I was a little behind, and my horse chanced to slip and lame himself, and he went forward and left me; and as the devil would have it, these fellows came across the country and chopped upon me," &c.

Here was first chance, the same mock goddess as before, lamed his horse, and next, the devil ordered the highwaymen to chop upon him that moment. Now, though it may be true that the highwaymen were, even by their employment, doing the devil's office of going to and fro, seeking whom they may plunder, yet 'twas a higher Hand than Satan's that delivered this poor blind fellow into their power.

We have a plain guide for this in Scripture language, in the law of manslaughter, or death, as we call it foolishly enough, by misadventure; it is in Exod. xxi. 13, in the case of casual killing a man; it is expressed thus: "*If a man lie not in wait, but God deliver him into his hand.*" This was not to be accounted murder, but the slayer was to fly to the city of refuge.

Here it is evident that God takes all these misadventures into His own hand; and a man killed by accident is a man whom God has delivered up, for what end in His providence is known only to Himself, to be killed in that manner, perhaps vindictively, perhaps not.

With what face can any man say, this was as the devil would have it, or as bad luck would have it, or it happened, or chanced, or fell out? all which are our simple and empty ways of talking of things that are ordered by the immediate hand or direction of God's providence.

The words last quoted from the Scripture, of God's delivering a man into another man's hand to be killed unwillingly, are fully explained in another place, Deut. xix. 5. "*As when a man goeth into the wood with his neighbour to hew wood, and his hand fetcheth a stroke with the axe to cut down the tree, and the head slippeth from the helve, and lighteth upon his neighbour, that he die, he shall flee unto one of these cities and live."*

The wicked thoughtless creature I have just mentioned, whose horse fell lame, and stopped his travelling till he might come just in the way of those thieves, who, it seems, were crossing the country, perhaps upon some other exploit, ought to have reflected that Providence, to chastise him, and bring him to a sense of his dependence upon and being subjected to His power, had directed him to be separated from his companion, that he might fall into the hands that robbed and abused him; and the other had no less obligation to give thanks for his deliverance; but how contrary they acted in both cases you have heard.

We have had abundance of collections, in my remembrance, of remarkable providences, as they are called, and many people are forward to call them so, but this does not come up to the case in hand.

Though contemning Providence, and giving the homage due to it, as above, to the devil, or to chance, fate, and I know not what embryos of the fancy, are impious; yet every one that avoids this evil does not come up to the particular point I am speaking of, for there is a manifest difference between acknowledging the being and operations of Providence and listening to its voice, as many people acknowledge a God that obey none of His commands, and concern themselves in nothing of their duty to Him.

To listen to the voice of Providence, is to take strict notice of all the remarkable steps of Providence which relate to us in particular, to observe if there is nothing in them instructing to our conduct, no warning to us for avoiding some danger, no direction for the taking some particular steps for our safety or advantage, no hint to remind us of such and such things omitted, no conviction of something committed, no vindictive step, by way of retaliation, marking out the crime in the punishment. You may easily observe the differences between the directions and warnings of Providence, when duly listened to, and the notices of spirits from an invisible world, *viz.*, that these are dark hints of evil, with very little direction to avoid it; but those notices, which are to be taken from the proceedings of Providence, though the voice be a kind of silent or soft whisper, yet 'tis generally attended with an offer of the means for escaping the evil, nay, very often leads by the hand to the very proper steps to be taken, and even obliges us, by a strong conviction of the reason of it, to take those steps.

It is in vain for me to run into a collection of stories; for example, where the variety is infinite, and things vary as every particular man's circumstances vary; but as every event in the world is managed by the superintendency of Providence, so every providence has in it something instructing, something that calls upon us to look up, or look out, or look in.

Every one of those heads is big with particular explanations, but my business is not preaching, I am making observations and reflections, let those make enlargements who read it; in a word, there is scarce any particular providence attends our lives, but we shall find, if we give due weight to it, that it calls upon us, either—

1. To look up, and acknowledge the goodness of God in sparing us, the bounty of God in providing for us, the power of God in delivering and protecting us; not forgetting to look up, and acknowledge, and be humble under the justice of God in being angry with and afflicting us.

2. Or to look out, and take the needful caution and warning given of evil approaching, and prepare either to meet or avoid it.

3. Or to look in, and reflect upon what we find Heaven animadverting upon, and afflicting us for taking notice of the summons to repent and reform.

And this is, in a word, what I mean by listening to the voice of Providence.

Chapter Six
Of the Proportion Between the Christian and Pagan World

I have said something of this already in my inquiry after the state of religion in the world, but upon some reflections which fell in my way since, I think it may offer further thoughts, very improving, as well as diverting. When we view the world geographically, take the plane of the globe, and measure it by line, and cut it out into latitude and longitude, degrees, leagues, and miles, we may see, indeed, that a pretty large spot of the whole is at present under the government of Christian powers and princes, or under the influence of their power and commerce, by arms, navies, colonies, and plantations, or their factories, missionaries, residences, &c.

But I am loath to say we should take this for a fulfilling the promise made to the Messiah, that His kingdom should be exalted above all nations, and the Gospel be heard to the end of the earth; I was going to say, and yet without any profaneness, that we hope God will not put us off so. I must acknowledge I expect, in the fulfilling of these promises, that the time will come when the knowledge of God shall cover the earth as the waters cover the sea, that the Church of God shall be set open to the four winds, that the mountain of the Lord's house shall be exalted above the tops of the mountains, and all the nations shall flow into it (Isaiah ii. 2); that is to say, that the Christian religion, or the profession of the doctrine of the Messiah, shall be made national over the whole globe, according to those words (Matt. xxiv. 14; Mark xiii. 13; Luke xxiv. 17). But this may be a little too apocalyptical or visionary for the times; and it is no business of mine to enter upon the interpretation of Scripture difficulties, whatever I may understand or believe myself about them, but rather to make my observations, as I have begun, upon things which now are, and which we have seen and know; let what is to come be as He pleases who has ordered things past, and knows what is to follow.

The present case is to speak of the mathematical proportion that there is now to be observed upon the plane of the globe, and observe how small a part of the world it is where the Christian religion has really prevailed and is nationally professed—I speak of the Christian religion where it is, as I call it, national, that is, in its utmost latitude; and I do so that I may give the utmost advantage, even against myself, in what I am going to say; and therefore, when I come to make deductions for the mixtures of barbarous nations, I shall do it fairly also.

I have nothing to do with the distinctions of Christians: I hope none will object against calling the Roman Church a Christian Church in this respect, and the professors of the Popish Church Christians; neither do I scruple to call the Greek Church Christian, though in some places so blended with superstition and barbarous customs, as in Georgia, Armenia, and the borders of Persia and Tartary, likewise in many parts of the Czar of Muscovy's dominions, that, as before, the name of Christ is little more than just spoken of, and literally known, without any material knowledge of His person, nature, and dignity, or of the homage due to Him as the Redeemer of the world.

The nations of the world, then, where Christ is acknowledged, and the Christian religion is professed nationally, be it Romish Church or Greek Church, or even the Protestant Church, including all the several subdivisions and denominations of Protestants, take them all as Christians, I say, these nations are as follow:—

1. In Europe: Germany, France, Spain, Italy, Great

Britain, Denmark, Sweden, Muscovy, Poland, Hungary, Transylvania, Moldavia, and Wallachia.

2. In Asia: Georgia and Armenia.

3. In Africa: no place at all, the few factories of European merchants only excepted.

4. In America: The colonies of Europeans only, as follow:—

1. The Spaniards in Mexico and Peru, the coasts of Chili, Carthagena, and St. Martha, and a small colony at Buenos Ayres on the Rio de la Plata.

2. The Portuguese in the Brazils.

3. The British on the coast of America, from the Gulf of Florida to Cape Breton, on the mouth of the Gulf of St. Lawrence, or the great river of Canada, also a little in Newfoundland and Hudson's Bay.

4. The French in the river of Canada and the great river of Mississippi.

5. The English, French, and Dutch on the islands called the Caribbees, &c.

The chief seat of the Christian religion is at present in Europe. But if we measure the quarter of the world we call Europe upon the plan of the globe, and cast up the northern, frozen, and indeed uninhabitable part of it, such as Laponia, Petzora, Candora, Obdora, and the Samoiedes, with part Siberia, they are all pagans, with the eastern unpeopled deserts bordering on Asia, on the way to China, and the vast extent of land on that side, which, though nominally under the dominion of Muscovy, is yet all pagan, even nationally so—under no real government, but of their own pagan customs.

If we go from thence to the south, and take out of it the European Tartars, *viz.*, of Circassia, the Crimea, and Budziack—if you go on, and draw a line from the Crim Tartary to the Danube, and from thence to the Adriatic Gulf, and cut off all the Grand Seignior's European dominions—I say, take this extent of land out of Europe, and the remainder does not measure full two-thirds of land in Europe under the Christian government, much of which is also desert and uninhabited, or at least by such as cannot be called Christians and do not concern themselves about it, as, particularly, the Swedish and Norwegian Lapland, the more eastern and southern Muscovy, beyond the Volga, even to Karakathie, and to the borders of Asia, on the side of India—I say, taking in this part, not above one-half of Europe is really inhabited by Christians.

The Czar of Muscovy, of the religion of whose subjects I have said enough, is lord of a vast extended country; and those who have measured it critically say his dominions are larger than all the rest of

Europe, that is to say, that he possesses a full half as much as Europe; and in those dominions he is master of abundance of nations that are pagan or Mahomedan, as, in particular, Circassia, being conquered by him, the Circassian Tartars, who are all Mahometans, or the most of them, are his subjects.

However, since a Christian monarch governs them, we must, upon the plan I laid down, call this a Christian country; and that alone obliges me to give two-thirds of Europe to the Christians.

But this will bring another account upon my hands to balance it, *viz.*, that excepting this two thirds, there will not come one Christian to be accounted for in any of the other three parts of the world, except Georgia and Armenia. As for Africa, there is nothing to be mentioned on that side, all the Christians that are on the continent of Africa consisting only of a few merchants residing at the coast towns in the Mediterranean, as at Alexandria, Grand Cairo, Tunis, Tripoli, Algiers, &c.; the factories of the English and Dutch on the coast of Guinea, the Gold Coast, the coast of Angola, and at the Cape of Good Hope; all which put together, as I have calculated them, and as they are calculated by a better judgment than mine, will not amount to 5000 people, excepting Christian slaves in Sallee, Algiers, Tunis, Tripoli, &c, which are not so many more.

America is thronged with Christians, God wot, such as they are; for I must confess the European inhabitants of some of the colonies there, as well French and English as Spanish and Dutch, very ill merit that name.

Some part of America is entirely under the dominion and government of the European nations; and having indeed destroyed the natives, and made desolate the country, they may be said to be Christian countries in the sense as above.

But what numbers do these amount to compared to the inhabitants of so great a part of the world as that of America, which at least is three times as big as Europe, and in which are still vast extended countries, infinite numbers of people, of nations unknown and even unheard of, which neither the English, French, Spanish, or Portuguese have ever seen? Witness the populous cities and innumerable nations which Sir Walter Raleigh met with in his voyage up the great River Oronooque, in one of which they talk of two millions of people; witness the nations, infinitely populous, spread on both sides the river Amazon, and all the country between these two prodigious rivers, being a country above 400 miles in breadth and 1600 miles in length, besides its extent south, even to the Rio Paraguay, and S.E. to the Brazils, a rich, fruitful, and populous country; and in which, by the accounts given, there must be more people inhabiting at this time than in all the Christian part of Europe put together, being the chief if not the only part of America into which the Spaniards never came, and whither the frighted people fled from them, being so fortified with rivers and impassable bays and rapid currents, and so inaccessible by the number of inhabitants, the heat of the climate, and the mountains, waterfalls, and such other obstructions, that the Spaniards durst never attempt to penetrate the way.

What are the numbers of Christians in America, put them all together, to the inhabitants of these parts of America, besides the northern parts of America, not inquired into?

But we are not calculating of people yet, but the extent of land that the Christians possess; the British colonies in the north are by far the most populous, even more than the Spaniards themselves, though the latter extend themselves over more land.

The British colonies in the north of America are supposed to contain three hundred thousand souls, including Nova Scotia, New England, New York, New Jersey, East and West Pennsylvania, Maryland, Virginia, and Carolina; and these lie extended upon the coast from the latitude of 32 degrees to 47, or thereabouts, being about 750 miles in length; but then much of this is very thinly peopled, and the breadth they lie west into the country is little or nothing, 50 or 60 miles is in many places the most. And except some plantations in Virginia, in Rappahanock, and James River in Virginia, occasioned by the great inlet of the bay there, and of the rivers that fall into it, we can see nothing a hundred miles within that land but waste and woods, whose inhabitants seem to be fled farther up into the country, from the face of their enemies the Christians.

So that all this planting, though considerable, amounts to no more, compared to the country itself, than a long narrow slip of land upon the sea-coast, there being very few English inhabitants planted anywhere above twenty miles from the sea, or from some navigable river, and even that sea-coast itself very thinly inhabited, and particularly from New England to New York, from New England north to Annapolis, from Virginia to Carolina; so that all this great colony or collection of colonies—nay, though we include the French at Canada—are but a point, a handful, compared to the vast extent of land lying west and north-west from them, even to the South Sea, an extent of continent full of innumerable nations of people unknown, undiscovered, never searched into, or indeed heard of but from one another, much greater in its extent than all Europe.

If we take the north part of America, exclusive of all the country which the Spaniards possess, and which they call the empire of Mexico, and exclusive too of what the English and French possess on the coast and in the two rivers of Canada and Mississippi as above, which indeed are but trifles, the rest of that country, which, as far as it has been travelled into, is found exceeding populous, is a great deal larger than all Europe, though we have not reckoned the most northern, frozen, and almost uninhabitable part of it, where no end can be found, and where it is there can be no doubt but there is a contiguous continent with the northern part of Asia, or so near joining it as to be only parted by a narrow gulf or strait of sea, easily passed over both by man and beast, or else it would be hard to give an account how man or beast came into that part of the world—I say this vast continent, full of people, and no doubt inhabited by many millions of souls, is all wrapt up in idolatry and paganism, given up to ignorance and blindness, worshipping the sun, the moon, the fire, the hills their fathers, and, in a word, the devil.

As to the thing we call religion, or the knowledge of the true God, much less the doctrine of the Messiah and the name of Christ, they not only have not, but never had the least intimation of it on earth, or revelation of it from heaven, till the Spaniards came among them; nay, and now Christians are come among them, it is hard to say whether the paganism is much abated except by the infinite ravages the Spaniards made where they came, who rooted out idolatry by destroying the idolaters, not by converting them; having cruelly cut off, as their own writers affirm, above seventy millions of people, and left the country naked of its inhabitants for many hundred miles together.

But what need we come to calculations for the present time with respect to America? Let us but be at the trouble to look back a little more than a hundred years, which is as nothing at all in the argument; how had the whole continent of America, extended almost from pole to pole, with all the islands round it, and peopled with such innumerable multitudes of people, been as it were entirely abandoned to the devil's government, even from the beginning of time, or at least from the second peopling the world by Noah to the sixteenth century, when Ferdinando Cortez, general for the famous Charles the Fifth, first landed in the Gulf of Mexico.

We have heard much of the cruelty of the Spaniards in destroying such multitudes of the inhabitants there, and of cutting off whole nations by fire and sword; but as I am for giving up all the actions of men to the government of Providence, it seems to me that Heaven had determined such an act of vengeance should be executed, and of which the Spaniards were instruments, to destroy those people, who were come up (by the influence of the devil, no doubt) to such a dreadful height, in that abhorred custom of human sacrifices, that the innocent blood cried for it, and it seemed to be time to put a stop to that crime, lest the very race of people should at last be extinct by their own butcheries.

The magnitude of this may be guessed at by the temple consecrated to the great idol of Vistlipustli, in the city of Mexico, where, at the command of Montezuma, the pagan monarch, twenty thousand men were sacrificed in a year, and the wall hung a foot thick with clotted blood, dashed in ceremony against the side of that place on those occasions.

This abomination God in His providence put an end to by destroying those nations from the face of the earth, bringing a race of bearded strangers upon them, cutting in pieces man, woman, and child, destroying their idols, and even the idolatry itself by the Spaniards, who, however wicked in themselves, yet were in this to be esteemed instruments in the hand of Heaven to execute the Divine justice on nations whose crimes were come up to a full height, and that called for vengeance.

I make no doubt (to carry on this digression a little farther) that when God cast out the heathen, so the Scripture calls it, from before the Israelites, and the iniquity of the people of the land was full, Joshua, Moses, and the Israelites were taxed with as much cruelty and inhumanity in destroying the cities, killing man, woman, and child, nay, even destroying the very cattle, and trees, and fruits of the earth, as ever the Spaniards were charged with in the conquest of Mexico.

This is apparent by the terror that was spread upon the minds of the people round about them, whereof thousands fled to other parts of the world. History tells us that the first builders of the city of Carthage, long before the Roman times, or before the fable of Queen Dido, were some Phoenicians, that is to say, Canaanites, who, flying for their lives, got ships and went away to sea, planting themselves on the coast of Africa as the first place of safety they arrived at; and to prove this a pillar of stone was found not far from Tripoli, on which was cut, in Phoenician characters, these words: "We are of those who fled from the face of Joshua the robber."

The cruelties of the Israelites, in destroying the nations of the land of Canaan, was commanded from heaven, and therein Joshua was justified in what was done. The cruelties of the Spaniards, however abhorred by us, was doubtless an appointment of God for the destruction of the most wicked and abominable people upon earth.

But this is all a digression; I come to my calculation. It is true that the Spaniards, whom I allow to be Christians, have possessed the empires of Mexico and Peru; but after all the havoc they made, and the millions of souls they dismissed out of life there, yet the natives are infinitely the majority of the inhabitants; and though many of them are Christianised, they are little more than subjected; and take all the Spaniards, Christians, and all the Portuguese in the Brazils, all the English and French in the north, and, in a word, all the Christians in America, and put them together, they will not balance one part of the pagans or Mahometans in Europe; for example, take the Crim Tartars of Europe, who inhabit the banks of the Euxine Sea, they are more in number than all the Christians in America; so that setting one nation against the other, and you may reckon that there is not one Christian, or as if there were not one Christian, in those three parts of the world, Asia, Africa, and America, except the Greeks of Asia.

This is a just but a very sad account of the small extent of Christian knowledge in the world; and were it considered as it ought, would put the most powerful princes of Europe upon thinking of some methods, at least, to open a way for the spreading Christian knowledge. I am not much of the opinion, indeed, that religion should be planted by the sword; but as the Christian princes of Europe, however few in number, are yet so superior to all the rest of the world in martial experience and the art of war, nothing is more certain than that, if they could unite their interest, they are able to beat paganism out of the world. Nothing is more certain than this, that would the Christian princes unite their powers and act in concert, they might destroy the Turkish Empire and the Persian kingdom, and beat the very name of Mahomet out of the world.

It is no boast to say that, were there no intestine broils among us, the Christian soldiery is so evidently superior to the Turkish at this time, that had they all joined after the late battle at Belgrade to have sent 80,000 veteran soldiers to have joined Prince Eugene, and supplied him with money and provisions by the ports of the Adriatic Gulf and the Archipelago, that prince would in two or three campaigns have driven the Mahomedans out of Europe, taken Constantinople, and have overturned the Turkish Empire.

After such a conquest, whither might not the Christian religion have spread? The King of Spain with the same ease would reduce the Moors of Barbary, and dispossess those sons of hell, the Algerines, Tripolines, Tunizens, and all the Mahomedan pirates of that coast, and plant again the ancient churches of Africa, the sees of Tertullian, St. Cyprian, &c.

Nay, even the Czar of Muscovy, an enterprising and glorious prince, well assisted and supported by his neighbours, the northern powers, who together are masters of the best soldiery in the world, would not find it impossible to march an army of 36,000 foot and 16,000 horse, in spite of waste and inhospitable deserts, even to attack the Chinese Empire, who, notwithstanding their infinite numbers, pretended policy, and great skill in war, would sink in the operation; and such an army of disciplined European soldiers would beat all the forces of that vast empire with the same or greater ease as Alexander with 30,000 Macedonians destroyed the army of Darius, which consisted of 680,000 men.

And let no man ridicule this project on account of the march, which I know they will call 3000 miles, and more. While there is no obstruction but the length of the way, it is not so difficult as some may imagine; 'tis far from impossible to furnish sufficient provisions for the march, which is indeed the only difficulty that carries any terror in it.

Such a prince as the Czar of Muscovy cannot want the assistance of innumerable hands for the amassing, or carriage for conveying, to proper magazines sufficient stores of provisions for the maintaining a select chosen body of men to march over the deserts, for in the grand march no useless mouths should be found to feed.

Why, then, should not the Christian princes think it a deed of compassion to the souls of men, as well as an humble agency to the work of Providence, and to the fulfilling the promises of their Saviour, by a moderate and, as far as in them lies, a bloodless conquest, to reduce the whole world to the government of Christian power, and so plant the name and knowledge of Christ Jesus among the heathens and Mahomedans? I am not supposing that they can plant real religion in this manner; the business of power is to open the way to the gospel of peace; the servants of the king of the earth are to fight, that the servants of the King of Heaven may preach.

Let but an open door be made for the preaching of the word of God, and the ministers of Christ be admitted, if they do not spread Christian knowledge over the face of the earth the fault will be theirs. Let but the military power reduce the pagan world, and banish the devil and Mahomet from the face of the earth, the knowledge of God be diligently spread, the word of God duly preached, and the people meekly and faithfully instructed in the Christian religion, the world would soon receive the truth, and the knowledge of Divine things would be the study and delight of mankind.

I know some nice and difficult people would object here, How are the present body of Christians, as you call them, qualified to convert the pagan and Mahomedan world, when they are not able to settle the main point, *viz.*, What the Christian religion is, or what they would convert them to? That Christianity is subdivided into so many parts and particular principles, the people so divided in their opinion; and, that which is still worse, there is so little charity among the several sorts, that some of them would sooner side with Mahomet against their neighbours than assist to propagate that particular doctrine in religion which they condemn. Thus the members of the Protestant faith would make it a point of principle not to support or propagate the interest of Popery in such a conquest as this; and again, the Catholics would as much make it a duty on them to root out heresy—so they call the Protestant doctrine—as they would to root out paganism and the worship of devils.

I would not answer for some Protestants that they would not be of the same mind, as to particular divisions among Protestants. The difference among some opinions is such, and their want of charity one to another sets them at such variance, that if they do not censure one another for devil-worshippers, yet we know they frequently call some of the opposite principles doctrines of devils, and persecute one another with as much fury as ever the heathen persecuted the primitive churches.

Witness the violences which have reigned between the Episcopal and Presbyterian parties in the north of Ireland and in Scotland, which has so often broken out into a flame of war, and that flame been always quenched with blood.

Witness the frequent persecutions, wars, massacres, and other cruel and unnatural doings, which have been in these parts of the world among Christians the effect of a mistaken zeal for the Christian religion; which, as it was not planted by blood and violence, so much less can Christians justify the endeavours to erect this or that opinion in it by the ruin and blood of their brethren.

But this is far from being a reason why we should not think it our duty to subdue the barbarous and idolatrous nations of the world in order to suppress the worshipping the devil, who is the enemy not only of God and of all true religion in the world, but who is the great destroyer and enemy of mankind, and of his future or present felicity; and whose business is always, to the utmost of his power, to involve or retain them either in ignorance or in error.

I distinguish between forcing religion upon people, or forcing them to entertain this or that opinion of religion—I say, I distinguish between that and opening the door for religion to come among them. The former is a violence, indeed, inconsistent with the nature of religion itself, whose energy prevails and forces its way into the minds of men by another sort of power; whereas the latter is removing a force unjustly put already upon the minds of men, by the artifice of the devil, to keep the Christian religion out of the world; so that, indeed, I propose a war not with men, but with the devil—a war to depose Satan's infernal tyranny in the world and set open the doors to religion, that it may enter if men will receive it; if they will not receive it, be that to themselves.

In a word, to unchain the wills of men, set their inclinations free, that their reason may be at liberty to influence their understandings, and that they may have the faith of Christ preached to them, whether they will hear or forbear, I say, as above, is no part of the question; let the Christian doctrine and its spiritual enemies alone to struggle about that. I am for dealing with the temporalities of the devil, and deposing that human power which is armed in the behalf of obstinate ignorance, and resolute to keep out the light of religion from the mind.

I think this is a lawful and just war, and, in the end, kind both to them and their posterity: let me bring the case home to ourselves.

Suppose neither Julius Caesar or any of the Roman generals or emperors had cast their eyes towards Britain for some ages, or till the Christian religion had spread over the whole Roman Empire: 't is true the Britons might at last have received the Christian faith in common with the rest of the northern world, but they had yet lain above three hundred years longer in ignorance and paganism than they did; and some hundred thousands of people who proved zealous Christians, nay, even martyrs for the Christian doctrine, would have died in the professed paganism of the Britons.

Now 'tis evident the invasion of the Romans was an unjust, bloody, tyrannical assault upon the poor Britons, against all right and property, against justice and neighbourhood, and merely carried on for conquest and dominion. Nor, indeed, had the Romans any just pretence of war; yet God was pleased to make this violence be the kindest thing that could have befallen the British nation, since it brought in the knowledge of God among the Britons, and was a means of reducing a heathen and barbarous nation to the faith of Christ, and to embrace the Messias.

Thus Heaven serves itself of men's worst designs, and the avarice, ambition, and rage of men have been made use of to bring to pass the glorious ends of Providence, without the least knowledge or design of the actors. Why, then, may not the great undertakings of the princes of Europe, if they could be brought to act in concert, with a good design to bring all the world to open their doors to the Christian religion, and by consequence their ears—I say, why may not such an attempt be blessed from heaven with so much success, at least as to make way for bringing in nominal Christianity among the nations? For as to obliging the people to be of this or that opinion afterward, that is another case.

There is a great pother made in the world among the several denominations of Christians about coercion, erecting a church, and compelling men to come in; that is to say, one sort of Christians persecuting another sort of Christians to make them worship Christ their way, as if Christ had no sheep but one fold.

I distinguish much between using force to reduce heathens and savages to Christianity, and using force to reduce those that are already Christians to be of this or that opinion; I will not say but a war might be very just, and the cause be righteous, to reduce the worshippers of the pagodas of India to the knowledge and obedience of Christianity, when it would be a horrible injustice to commence a like war to reduce even a Popish nation to be Protestant.

But my proposed war does not reach so far as that neither; for though I would have a nation of pagans conquered that their idols and temples might be destroyed, and their idol worship be abolished, yet I would be very far from punishing and persecuting the people for not believing in Christ; for if we believe that faith, as the Scripture says, is the gift of God, how can we, upon any Christian foundation, punish or persecute the man for not exercising that which God had not given him? Hence, compelling men to conform to this or that particular profession of the Christian religion, is to me impious and unchristian.

And shall I speak a word here of the unhappy custom among Christians of reviling one another with words on account of differing opinions in religion? It was a part of apocryphal scripture, taken from one of the traditional sayings of the *rabbis*, "*Thou shalt not mock at the gods of the heathens;*" but ribaldry, satire, and sarcasms are the usage we give one another every day on the subject of religion, as if slander and the severities of the tongue were not the worst kind of violence in matters of the Christian religion.

In a word, I must acknowledge, if I am to speak of reproach in general, I know no worse persecution than that of the tongue. Solomon says, "*There are that speak like the piercing of a sword;*" and King David was so sensible of the bitterness of the tongue, that he is full of exclamations upon the subject; among the rest, he says of his enemies, "*They have compassed me about with words of hatred. . . . He clothed himself with cursing like as with his garment*" (Psalm cix. 3, 18).

It is indeed remote from the subject I am upon to talk of this kind of uncharitable dealing, but as just observations are never out of season, it may have its uses; let no man slight the hint, though it were meant for religion only, for that, indeed, is my present subject: there is doubtless as severe a persecution by the tongue as that of fire and faggot, and some think "'t is as hard to be borne.

I have never met with so much of this anywhere in all my travels as in England, where the mouths of the several sects and opinions are so effectually open against one another, that, albeit common charity commands us to talk the best of particular persons in their failings and infirmities, yet here, censuring, condemning, and reproaching one another on account of opinions is carried on with such a gust, that lets every one see nothing but death and destruction can follow, and no reconciliation can be expected.

I have lived to see men of the best light be mistaken, as well in party as in principles, as well in politics as in religion, and find not only occasion, but even a necessity, to change hands or sides in both; I have seen them sometimes run into contrary extremes, beyond their first intention, and even without design; nay, in those unhappy changes I have seen them driven into lengths they never designed, by the fiery resentment of those whom they seemed to have left, and whom they differed from. I have lived to see those men acknowledge, even publicly and openly, they were wrong and mistaken, and express their regret for being misled very sincerely; but I cannot say I have lived to see the people they have desired to return to forgive or receive them. Perhaps the age I have lived in has not been a proper season for charity; I hope futurity will be furnished with better Christians; or perhaps 't is appointed so to illustrate the Divine mercy, and let mankind see that they are the only creatures that never forgive. I have seen a man in the case I speak of, offer the most sincere acknowledgments of his having been mistaken, and this not in matters essential either to the person's morals or Christianity, but only in matters of party, and with the most moving expressions desire his old friends to forgive what has been passed, and have seen their return be mocking him with what they called a baseness of spirit, and a mean submission; I have seen him expostulate with them, why they should not act upon the same terms with a penitent, as God Himself not only prescribed, but yields to; and have seen them in return tell him God might forgive him if He pleased, but they would never, and then expose all those offers to the first comer in banter and ridicule: but take me right too, I have seen at the same time, that to wiser men it has been always thought to be an exposing themselves, and an honour to the person.

I speak this too feelingly, and therefore say no more; there is a way by patience, to conquer even the universal contempt of mankind; and though two drams of that drug be a vomit for a dog, it is, in my experience, the only method; there is a secret peace in it, and in time the rage of men will abate. A constant steady adhering to virtue and honesty, and showing the world that whatever mistakes he might be led into, supposing them to be mistakes, that yet the main intention and design of his life was sincere and upright: He that governs the actions of men by an unbiassed hand, will never suffer such a man to sink under the weight of universal prejudice and clamour.

I, Robinson Crusoe, grown old in affliction, borne down by calumny and reproach, but supported from within, boldly prescribe this remedy against universal clamours and contempt of mankind: patience, a steady life of virtue and sobriety, and a comforting dependence on the justice of Providence, will first or last restore the patient to the opinion of his friends, and justify him in the face of his enemies; and in the meantime will support him comfortably in despising those who want manners and charity, and leave them to be cursed from Heaven with their own passions and rage.

This very thought made me long ago claim a kind of property in some good old lines of the famous George Withers, Esq., made in prison in the Tower. He was a poetical gentleman who had, in the time of the civil wars in England, been unhappy in changing sides too often, and had been put into the Tower by every side in their turn; once by the king, once by the Parliament, once by the army, then by the rump, and at last again, I think, by General Monk; in a word, whatever side got up, he had the disaster to be down. The lines are thus:

The world and I may well agree,
As most that are offended;
For I slight her, and she slights me,
And there's our quarrel ended.
For service done and love expressed,
Though very few regard it,
My country owes me bread at least;
But if I am debarred it,
Good conscience is a daily feast,
And sorrow never marred it.

But this article of verbal persecution has hurried me from my subject, which I must return to.

I have spoken of a project for the Czar of Muscovy, worthy of a monarch who is lord of so vast an extent of country as the Russian Empire reaches to, which is in effect, as I have said, much more than half Europe, and consequently an eighth part of the world. I have given my thoughts how a war to open a door for the Christian religion may be justifiable, and that it has not the least tincture of persecution in it. If the Christian princes of the world, who now spend their force so much to an ill purpose in real persecution, would join in an universal war against paganism and devil-worship, the savage part of mankind would, in one age, be brought to bow their knees to the God of Truth, and would bless the enterprise itself in the end of it, as the best thing that ever befell them; nor could such an attempt fail of success, unless Heaven in justice had determined to shut up the world longer in darkness, and the cup of their abominations was not yet full. But I may venture to say there would be much more ground for such Christian princes to hope and expect the concurrence of Heaven in such an undertaking, than in sheathing their swords in the bowels of their brethren, and making an effusion of Christian blood upon every slight pretence, as we see has been the case in Europe for above thirty years past.

I had intended to remark here that, as the country possessed by Christians is but a spot of the globe compared to the heathen, pagan, and Mahometan world, so the number of real Christians among the nations professing the Christian name is yet a more disproportioned part, a mere trifle, and hardly to be compared with the infinite numbers of those who, though they call themselves Christians, yet know as little of God and religion as can be imagined to be known where the word Christian is spoken of, and neither seek or desire to know more; in a word, who know but little of God or Jesus Christ, heaven or hell, and regard none of them.

This is a large field, and being thoroughly searched into, would, I doubt not, reduce the real faithful subjects of the kingdom of Jesus Christ to a much fewer number than those of Mahomet; nay, than those of the monarch of Germany, and make our Lord appear a weaker prince, speaking in the sense of kingdoms, than many of the kings of the earth. And if it be true that the old king of France should say, that he had more loyal subjects than King Jesus, I do not know but, in the sense his most Christian majesty meant it, the thing might be very true.

But this observation is something out of my present road, and merits to be spoken of by itself.

The number of true Christians will never be known on this side the great bar, where they shall be critically separated. No political arithmetic can make a calculation of the number of true Christians while they live blended with the false ones, since it is not only hard, but impossible, to know them one from another in this world.

We shall perhaps be surprised at the last day to see some people at the right hand of the righteous Judge whom we have condemned with the utmost zeal in our opinions, while we were contemporary with them in life; for charity, as it is generally practised in this world, and mixed with our human infirmities, such as pride, self-opinion, and personal prejudice, is strangely misguided, and makes us entertain notions of things and people quite different from what they really deserve; and there is hardly any rule to prescribe ourselves, except it be of the text—"*In meekness, every one esteeming others better than themselves*," which, by the way, is difficult to do.

But though we shall thus see at the great audit a transposition of persons from the station they held in our charity, we shall only thereby see that our judgment was wrong; that God judgeth not as man judgeth, and that we too rashly condemn whom He has thought fit to justify and accept.

Let, then, the number of Christians be more or less, as He that makes them Christians determines, this is not for us to enter into; and this brings me back to what I said before, that though we cannot make Christians, we both can and may, and indeed ought, to open the door to Christianity, that the preaching of God's word, which is the ordinary means of bringing mankind to the knowledge of religion, may be spread over the whole world.

With what vigour do we consult, and how do the labouring heads of the world club together, to form projects, and to raise subscriptions to extend the general commerce of nations into every corner of the world! But 't would pass for a bubble of all bubbles, and a whimsy that none would engage in, if ten millions should be asked to be subscribed for sending a strong fleet and army to conquer heathenism and idolatry, and protect a mission of Christians, to be employed in preaching the Gospel to the poor heathens, say it were on the coast of Coromandel, the island of Ceylon, and country of Malabar, or any of the dominions of the Great Mogul; and yet such an attempt would not only be just, but infinitely advantageous to the people who should undertake it, and to the people of the country on whom the operation should be wrought.

In the occasional discourses I had on this subject, in conversation with men of good judgment and principles, I have been often asked in what manner I would propose to carry on such a conquest as I speak of, and how it should answer the end; and that I may not be supposed to suggest a thing impracticable in itself, or for which no rational scheme might be proposed, I shall make a brief essay, at the manner, in which the conquest I speak of should be, or ought to be, carried on; and if it be considered seriously, the difficulties and perhaps all the reasonable objections might vanish in an instant. I will therefore, first, for the purpose only, suppose that an attempt was made by a Christian nation to conquer and subdue some heathen or Mahometan people at a distance from them, place the conquest where and among whom we will; for example, suppose it was the great island of Madagascar, or that of Ceylon, Borneo in the Indies, or those of Japan, or any other where you please.

I would first suppose the place to be infinitely populous, as any of those countries, though they are islands, are said to be; and because the Japanese are said to be a most sensible, sagacious people, under

445

excellent forms of government, and capable more than ordinarily of receiving impressions, supported by the argument and example of a virtuous and religious conqueror.

For this purpose you must grant me, that the island or islands of Japan were in a situation proper for the undertaking, and that a powerful European army, being landed upon them, had in a great battle, or in divers battles, overthrown all their military force, and had entirely reduced the whole nation to their power; as, to go back to examples, the Venetians had done by the Turks in the Morea in a former war, or as the Turks did in the isles in Candia, Cyprus, and the like. The short scheme for establishing the government in those countries should be this:—

First, as the war is pointed chiefly against the kingdom of the devil in behalf of the Christian worship, so no quarter should be given to Satan's administration; and as nothing else should willingly be treated with violence, so, indeed, no part of the devil's economy should have any favour, but all the idols should be immediately destroyed and publicly burnt, all the pagodas and temples burnt, and the very face and form of paganism, and the worship attending it, be utterly defaced and destroyed.

Secondly, the priests and dedicated persons of every kind, by whatsoever names or titles known or distinguished, should be at least removed, if not destroyed.

Thirdly, all the exercise of profane and idolatrous rites, ceremonies, worship, festivals, and customs should be abolished entirely, so as by time to be forgotten, and clean wiped out of the minds as well as out of the practice of the people.

This is all the coercion I propose, and less than this cannot be proposed; because, though we may not by arms and force compel men to be religious—because if we do we cannot make them sincere, and so by persecution we only create hypocrites—yet I insist that we may by force, and that with the greatest justice possible, suppress paganism, and the worship of God's enemy the devil, and banish it out of the world; nay, that we ought to do it to the utmost of our power. But I return to the conquest.

The country being thus entirely reduced under Christian government, the inhabitants, if they submit quietly, ought to be used with humanity and justice, no cruelty, no rigour. They should suffer no oppression, injury, or injustice, that they may not receive evil impressions of the people that are come among them; lest, entertaining an abhorrence of Christians from their evil conduct, cruelty, and injustice, they should entertain an abhorrence of the Christian religion for their sakes; as the poor wretches the Indians in America, who, when they were talked to of the future state, the resurrection of the dead, eternal felicity in heaven, and the like, inquired where the Spaniards went after death, and if any of them went to heaven; and being answered in the affirmative, shook their heads, and desired they might go to hell then, for that they were afraid to think of being in heaven if the Spaniards were there.

A just and generous behaviour to the natives, or at least to such of them as should show themselves willing to submit, would certainly engage them in their interest, and accordingly would in a little while bring them to embrace that truth which dictated such just principles to those who espoused it.

Thus prejudices being removed, the way to instruction would be made the more plain, and then would be the time for Gospel labourers to enter upon the harvest; ministers should be instructed to teach them our language, to exhort them to seek the blessings of religion and of the true God, and so gradually to introduce right principles among them at their own request.

From hence they should proceed to teach all the young children the language spoken by them, who would then be their benefactors rather than conquerors; and a few years wearing the old generation out, the posterity of them and of their conquerors would be all one nation.

In case any rejected the instruction of religious men and adhered obstinately to his idolatry, and would not be reclaimed by gentle and Christian usage, suitable methods are to be taken with such, that they might not make a religious faction in the country and gain others to side with them in order to recover their liberty, as they might call it, to serve their own gods, that is to say, idols; for it must be for ever as just not to permit them to go back to idolatry by force as it was to pull them from it by force.

By this kind of conquest the Christian religion would be most effectually propagated among innumerable nations of savages and idolaters, and as many people be brought to worship the true God as may be said to do it at this time in the whole Christian world.

This is my *crusado*; and it would be a war as justifiable on many accounts as any that was ever undertaken in the world, a war that would bring eternal honour to the conquerors and an eternal blessing to the people conquered.

It were easy now to cut out enterprises of this nature for other of the princes of the world than the Czar of Muscovy; and I could lay very rational schemes for such undertakings, and the schemes that could, if thoroughly pursued, never fail of success. For example, an expedition against the Moors of Africa by the French, Spanish, and Italian princes, who daily suffer so much by them, and the last of whom are at perpetual war with them; how easy would it be to those powers to join in a Christian confederacy to plant the Christian religion again in the Numidian and Mauritanian kingdoms—where was once the famous church of Carthage, and from whence thousands of Christians have gone to heaven—the harvest of the primitive labours of St. Cyprian, Xertullian, and many more, whose posterity now bow their knees to that latest and worst of all impostors, Mahomet.

But unchristian strife was always a bar against the propagation of the Christian religion, and unnatural wars, carried on among the nations I speak of, are made so much the business of the Christian world, that I do not expect in our time to see the advantages taken hold of that the nature of the thing offers. But I am persuaded, and leave it upon record as my settled opinion, that one time or other the Christian powers of Europe shall be inspired from Heaven for such a work, and then the easiness of subduing the kingdom of Africa to the Christian power shall shame the generations past, who had the opportunity so often in their hands, but made no use of it.

Note.—In this part of the subject I am upon, I must acknowledge there is a double argument for a war: (1.) In point of the interfering interests, Europe ought to take possession of those shores, without which it is manifest her commerce is not secured; and indeed, while that part of Africa bordering on the sea is in the hands of robbers, pirates cannot be secured. Now, this is a point of undisputed right, for a war-trade claims the protection of the powers to whom it belongs, and we make no scruple to make war upon one another for the protection of our trade, and it is allowed to be a good reason why we should do so. Why, then, is it not a good reason to make war upon thieves and robbers? If one nation take the ships belonging to another, we immediately reclaim the prize from the captors, and require of the prince that justice be done against the aggressor, who is a breaker of the peace; and if this is refused we make war.

But shall we do thus to Christians, and scruple to make an universal war for the rooting out a race of pirates and rovers, who live by rapine, and are continually employed, like the lions and tigers of their own Lybia, in devouring their neighbours? This, I say, makes such a war not only just on a religious account, but both just and necessary upon a civil account.

The war, then, being thus proved to be just on other accounts, why should not (2.) the extirpation of idolatry, paganism, and devil-worship be the consequence of the victory? If God be allowed to be the giver of victory, how can it be answered to Him that the victory should not be made use of for the interest and glory of the God of war, from whom it proceeds? But these things are not to be offered to the world till higher principles work in the minds of men in their making war and peace than yet seems to take up their minds.

I was tempted upon this occasion to make an excursion here upon the subject of the very light occasions princes and powers, states and statesmen, make use of for the engaging in war and blood one against another; one for being ill satisfied with the other, and another for preserving the balance of power; this for nothing at all, and that for something next to nothing; and how little concern the blood that is necessarily spilt in these wars produces among them. But this is not a case that will so well bear to be entered upon in a public manner at this time.

All I can add is, I doubt no such zeal for the Christian religion will be found in our days, or perhaps in any age of the world, till Heaven beats the drums itself, and the glorious legions from above come down on purpose to propagate the work, and to reduce the whole world to the obedience of King Jesus—a time which some tell us is not far off, but of which I heard nothing in all my travels and illuminations, no, not one word.

A VISION OF THE ANGELIC WORLD

They must be much taken up with the satisfaction of what they are already, that never spare their thoughts upon the subject of what they shall be. The place, the company, the employment which we expect to know so much of hereafter, must certainly be well worth our while to inquire after here.

I believe the main interruptions which have been given to these inquiries, and perhaps the reason why those that have entered into them have given them up, and those who have not entered into them have satisfied themselves in the utter neglect, have been the wild chimeric notions, enthusiastic dreams, and unsatisfying ideas, which most of the conceptions of men have led them into about these things.

As I endeavour to conceive justly of these things, I shall likewise endeavour to reason upon them clearly, and, if possible, convey some such ideas of the invisible world to the thoughts of men as may not be confused and indigested, and so leave them darker than I find them.

The locality of heaven or hell is no part of my search; there is doubtless a place reserved for the reception of our souls after death; as there is a state of being for material substances, so there must be a place; if we are to be, we must have a where; the Scripture supports reason in it—Judas is gone to his place; Dives in hell lifted up his eyes, and saw Lazarus in Abraham's bosom: the locality of bliss and misery seems to be positively asserted in both cases.

But there is not so clear a view of the company as of the place; it is not so easy to inquire into the world of spirits, as it is evident that there are such spirits and such a world. We find the locality of it is natural, but who the inhabitants are is a search of still a sublimer nature, liable to more exception, encumbered with more difficulties, and exposed to much more uncertainty.

I shall endeavour to clear up as much of it as I can, and intimate most willingly how much I rejoice in the expectation that some other inquirers may go farther, till at last all that Providence has thought fit to discover of that part may be perfectly known.

The discoveries in the Scripture which lead to this are innumerable, but the positive declaration of it seems to be declined. When our Saviour walking on the sea frighted His disciples, and they cried out, what do we find terrified them? Truly they thought they had seen a spirit. One would have thought such men as they, who had the vision of God manifest in the flesh, should not have been so much surprised if they had seen a spirit, that is to say, seen an apparition, for to see a spirit seems to be an allusion, not an expression to be used literally, a spirit being not visible by the organ of human sight.

But what if it had been a spirit? If it had been a good spirit, what had they to fear? And if a bad spirit, what would crying out have assisted them? When people cry out in such cases, it is either for help, and then they cry to others; or for mercy, and then they cry to the subject of their terror to spare them. Either way it was either the foolishest or the wickedest thing that ever was done by such grave men as the apostles; for if it was a good spirit as before, they had no need to cry out; and if it was a bad one, who did they cry to? for 't is evident they did not pray to God, or cross and bless themselves, as was afterwards the fashion; but they cried out, that is to say, they either cried out for help, which was great nonsense to call to man for help against the devil; or they cried to the spirit they saw, that it might not hurt them, which was, in short, neither less nor more than praying to the devil.

This put me in mind of the poor savages in many of the countries of America and Africa, who, really instructed by their fear, that is to say, by mere nature, worship the devil that he may not hurt them.

Here I must digress a little, and make a transition from the story of the spirit to the strange absurdities of men's notions at that time, and particularly of those upon whom the first impressions of Christ's preachings were wrought; and if it be looked narrowly into, one cannot but wonder what strange ignorant people even the disciples themselves were at first; and indeed their ignorance continued a great while, even to after the death of Christ Himself—witness the foolish talk of the two disciples going to Emmaus. It is true they were wiser afterwards when they were better taught; but the Scripture is full of the discoveries of their ignorance, as in the notions of sitting at His right hand and His left in His kingdom, asked for by Zebedee's children; no doubt but the good woman their mother thought one of her sons should be lord treasurer there, and the other lord chancellor, and she could not but think those places their due when she saw them in such favour with Him here. Just so in their notion of seeing a spirit here, which put them into such a fright, and indeed they might be said, according to our dull way of thinking, to be frighted out of their wits; for had their senses been in exercise, they would either have rejoiced in the appearance of a good angel, and stood still to hear his message as from Heaven, or prayed to God to deliver them out of the hands of the devil on their supposing it, as above, to be a vision from hell.

But I come to the subject. It is evident that the notion of spirits, and their intermeddling with the affairs of men, and even of their appearing to men, prevailed so universally in those ages of the world, that even God's own people, who were instructed from Himself, believed it, nor is there anything in all the New Testament institution to contradict it, though many things to confirm it; such particularly as the law against what is called a familiar spirit, which was esteemed n better or worse than a conversing with the devil, that is to say, with some of the evil spirits of the world I speak of.

The witch of Endor, and the story of an apparition of an old man personating Samuel, which is so plainly asserted in Scripture, and which the learned opposers of these notions have spent so much weak pains to disturb our imaginations about, yet assure us that such apparitions are not inconsistent with Nature or with religion; nay, the Scripture allows this woman to *paw waw*, as the Indians in America call it, and conjure for the raising this spectre, and when it is come, allows it to speak a great prophetic truth, foretelling the king, in all its terrible particulars, what was to happen to him, and what did befall him the very next day.

Either this appearance must be a good spirit or a bad; if it was a good spirit it was an angel, as it is expressed in another place of the Apostle Peter, when he knocked at the good people's door in Jerusalem (Acts xii. 15); and then it supports my opinion of the spirits unembodied conversing with and taking care of the spirits embodied; if it was an evil spirit, then they must grant God to be making a prophet of the devil, and making him personate Samuel to foretell things to come; permitting Satan to speak in the first person of God's own prophet, and indeed to preach the justice of God's dealing with Saul for rejecting His prophet Samuel; which, in short, is not a little odd, putting the spirit of God into the mouth of the devil, and making Satan a preacher of righteousness.

When I was in my retirement I had abundance of strange notions of my seeing apparitions there, and especially when I happened to be abroad by moonshine, when every bush looked like a man, and every tree like a man on horseback; and I so prepossessed myself with it that I scarce durst look behind me for a good while, and after that durst not go abroad at all at night; nay, it grew upon me to such a degree at last, that I as firmly believed I saw several times real shapes and appearances, as I do now really believe and am assured that it was all hypochondriac delusion.

But, however, that the reader may see how far the power of imagination may go, and judge for me whether I showed any more folly and simplicity than other men might do, I'll repeat some little passages, which for a while gave me very great disturbances, and everyone shall judge for me whether they might not have been deluded in the like circumstances as well as I.

The first case was, when I crept into the dark cave in the valley, where the old goat lay just expiring, which, wherever it happened, is a true history, I assure you.

When first I was stopped by the noise of this poor dying creature, you are to observe that the voice was not only like the voice of a man, but even articulate, only that I could not form any words from it; and what did that amount to more or less than this, namely, that it spoke, but only it was in a language that I did not understand. If it was possible to describe the surprise of my spirits on that occasion, I would do it here, how all my blood run, or rather stood still, chilled in my veins, how a cold dew of sweat sat on my forehead, how my joints, like Belshazzar's knees, shook one against another, and how, as I said, my hair would have lifted off my hat if I had had one on my head.

But this is not all. After the first noise of the creature, which was a faint, dying kind of imperfect bleating, not unusual, as I found afterward; I say, after this he fetched two or three deep sighs, as lively, and as like human, as it is possible to imagine, as I have also said.

These were so many confirmations of my surprise, besides the sight of his two glaring eyes, and carried it up to the extreme of fright and amazement; how I afterwards conquered this childish beginning, and mustered up courage enough to go into the place with a firebrand for light, and how I was presently satisfied with seeing the creature whose condition made all the little accidental noises appear rational, I have already said.

But I must acknowledge that this real surprise left some relics or remains behind it that did not wear quite off a great while, though I struggled hard with them; the vapours that were raised at first were never so laid but that on every trifling occasion they returned; and I saw, nay, I felt apparitions as plainly and distinctly as ever I felt or saw any real substance in my life.

The like was the case with me before that, when I first found the print of a man's foot upon the sand, by the seaside, on the north part of the island.

And these, I say, having left my fancy a little peevish and wayward, I had frequently some returns of these vapours, on differing occasions, and sometimes even without occasion; nothing but mere hypochondriac whimsies, fluttering of the blood, and rising of vapours, which nobody could give any account of but myself.

For example, it was one night, after my having seen some odd appearances in the air, of no great significance, that coming home, and being in bed, but not asleep, I felt a pain in one of my feet, after which it came to a kind of numbness in my foot, which a little surprised me, and after that a kind of tingling in my blood, as if it had been some distemper running up my leg.

On a sudden I felt, as it were, something alive lie upon me, as if it had been a dog lying upon my bed, from my knee downwards, about half way up my leg, and immediately afterwards I felt it heavier, and felt it as plainly roll itself upon me upwards upon my thigh, for I lay on one side, I say, as if it had been a creature lying upon me with all his weight, and turning his body upon me.

It was so lively and sensible to me, and I remember it so perfectly well, though it is now many years ago, that my blood chills and flutters about my heart at the very writing it. I immediately flung myself out of my bed and flew to my musket, which stood always ready at my hand, and naked as I was, laid about me upon the bed in the dark, and everywhere else that I could think of where anybody might stand or lie, but could find nothing. "Lord deliver me from an evil spirit," said I, "what can this be?" And being tired with groping about, and having broke two or three of my earthen pots with making blows here and there to no purpose, I went to light my candle, for my lamp which I used to burn in the night either had not been lighted, or was gone out.

When I lighted a candle, I could easily see there was no living creature in the place with me but the poor parrot, who was waked and frighted, and cried out, "Hold your tongue," and "What's the matter with you?" Which words he learned of me, from my frequent saying so to him, when he used to make his ordinary wild noise and scream-ing that I did not like.

The more I was satisfied that there was nothing in the room, at least to be seen, the more another concern came upon me. "Lord!" says I aloud, "this is the devil!"

"Hold your tongue," says Poll. I was so mad at the bird, though the creature knew nothing of the matter, that if he had hung near me, I believe I should have killed him.

I put my clothes on, and sat me down, for I could not find in my heart to go to bed again, and as I sat down, "I am terribly frighted," said I.

"What's the matter with you?" says Poll.

"You toad," said I, "I'd knock your brains out if you were here."

"Hold your tongue," says he again, and then fell to chattering "Robin Crusoe," and "Poor Robin Crusoe," as he used to do.

Had I been in any reach of a good temper, it had been enough to have composed me, but I was quite gone; I was fully possessed with a belief that it was the devil, and I prayed most heartily to God to be delivered from the power of the evil spirit.

After some time I composed myself a little, and went to bed again, and lying just in the posture as I was in before, I felt a little of the tingling in my blood which I felt before, and I resolved to lie still, let it be what it would; it came up as high as my knee, as before, but no higher; and now I began to see plainly that it was all a distemper, that it was something paralytic, and that affected the nerves; but I had not either experience of such a thing, or knowledge of diseases enough to be fully satisfied of the nature of them, and whether anything natural, any numbness or dead palsy affecting one part of the thigh, could feel as that did, till some months after that I felt something of the very same again at my first lying down in my bed for three or four nights together, which at first gave me a little concern as a distemper, but at last gave me such satisfaction, that the first was nothing but the same thing in a higher degree; that the pleasure of knowing it was only a disease was far beyond the concern at the danger of it, though a dead palsy to one in my condition might reasonably have been one of the most frightful things in Nature, since, having nobody to help me, I must have inevitably perished for mere want of food, not being able to go from place to place to fetch it.

But to go back to the case in hand, and to the apprehension I had been in all the several months that passed between the first of this and the last, I went about with a melancholy, heavy heart, fully satisfied that the devil had been in my room, and lay upon my bed.

Sometimes I would try to argue myself a little out of it, asking my-self whether it was reasonable to imagine the devil had nothing else to do than to come thither, and only lie down upon me, and go away about his business, and say not one word to me; what end it could answer; and whether I thought the devil was really busied about such trifles; or whether he had not employment enough of a higher nature, so that such a thing as that could be worth his while.

But still, then, I was answered with my own thoughts returning thus—What could it be? Or, if it was not a devil, what was it? This I could not answer by any means at all; and so I still sunk under the belief that it was the devil, and nothing but the devil.

You may be sure, while I had this fancy in my head, I was of course overrun with the vapours, and had all the hypochondriac fancies that ever any melancholy head could entertain; and what with ruminating on the print of a foot upon the sand, and the weight of the devil upon me in my bed, I made no difficulty to conclude that the old gentleman really visited the place; and, in a word, it had been easy to have possessed me, if I had continued so much longer, that it was an enchanted island, that there were a million of evil spirits in it, and that the devil was lord of the manor.

I scarce heard the least noise, near or far off, but I started, and expected to see a devil; every distant bush upon a hill, if I did not particularly remember it before, was a man, and every stump an apparition; and I scarce went twenty yards together, by night or by day, without looking behind me.

Sometimes, indeed, I took a little heart, and would say, "Well, let it be the devil if it will! God is master of the devil, and he can do me no hurt unless he is permitted; he can be nowhere but He that made him is there too;"and, as I said afterwards, when I was frighted with the old goat in a cave, "He is not fit to live all alone in such an island for twenty years that would be afraid to see the devil."

But all these things lasted but a short while, and the vapours that were raised at first were not to be so easily laid; for, in a word, it was not mere imagination, but it was the imagination raised up to disease; nor did it ever quite wear off till I got my man Friday with me, of whom I have said so much; and then, having company to talk to, the hypo wore off, and I did not see any more devils after that.

Before I leave this part, I cannot but give a caution to all vapourish, melancholy people, whose imaginations run this way; I mean about seeing the devil, apparitions, and the like; namely, that they should never look behind them, and over their shoulders, as they go upstairs, or look into the corners and holes of rooms with a candle in their hands, or turn about to see who may be behind them in any walks or dark fields, lanes, or the like; for let such know, they will see the devil whether he be there or no; nay, they will be so persuaded that they do see him, that their very imagination will be a devil to them wherever they go.

But after all this is said, let nobody suggest that because the brain-sick fancy, the vapourish hypochondriac imagination represents spectres and spirits to us, and makes apparitions for us, that therefore there are no such things as spirits, both good and evil, any more than we should conceive that there is no devil, because we do not see him.

The devil has witnesses of his being and nature, just as God Himself has of His; they are not indeed so visible or so numerous, but we are all able to bring evidence of the existence of the devil from our own frailties, as we are to bring evidence of the existence of God from the faculties of our souls, and from the contexture of our bodies.

As our propensity to evil rather than good is a testimony of the original depravity of human nature, so the harmony between the inclination and the occasion is a testimony which leaves the presence of the evil spirit with us out of question.

Not that the devil is always the agent in our temptations, for though the devil is a very diligent fellow, and always appears ready to fall in with the allurement, yet the Scripture clears him, and we must do so too, of being the main tempter; 't is our own corrupt, debauched inclination, which is the first moving agent; and therefore the Scripture says, "A man is tempted when he is drawn away of his own lusts, and enticed." The devil, who, as I said, is a very diligent fellow in the infernal work, and is always ready to forward the mischief, is also a very cunning fellow, and knows how most dexterously to suit alluring objects to the allurable dispositions; to procure ensnaring things, and lay them in the way of the man whom he finds so easily to be ensnared; and he never fails to prompt all the mischief he can, full of stratagem and art, to ensnare us by the help of our corrupt affections, and these are called "Satan's devices."

But having charged Satan home in that part, I must do the devil that justice as to own that he is the most slandered, most abused creature alive; thousands of crimes we lay to his charge that he is not guilty of; thousands of our own infirmities we load him with which he has no hand in; and thousands of our sins, which, as bad as he is, he knows nothing of; calling him our tempter, and pretending we did so and so as the devil would have it, when on the contrary the devil had no share in it, and we were only led away of our own lusts, and enticed.

But now, having made this digression in the devil's defence, I return to the main question, that of the being of the devil, and of evil spirits; this I believe, there is no room to doubt of; but this, as I have observed, is not the thing; these are not the spirits I am speaking of, but I shall come directly to what I mean, and speak plain without any possibility of being misunderstood.

I make no question but that there is not only a world of spirits, but that there is a certain knowledge of it, though to us impossible as to the manner of it; there is a certain converse between the world of spirits, and the spirits in this world; that is to say, between spirits uncased or unembodied and souls of men embodied or cased up in flesh and blood, as we all are on this side death.

It is true that we cannot describe this converse of spirits, as to the way of it, the manner of the communication, or how things are mutually conveyed from one to another. How intelligences are given or received, we know not; we know but little of their being conveyed this way from the spirits unembodied to ours that are in life; and of their being conveyed that way, namely, from us to them—of that we know nothing. The latter certainly is done without the help of the organ, the former is conveyed by the understanding, and the retired faculties of the soul, of which we can give very little account.

For spirits, without the help of voice, converse.

Let me, however, give, as reasons for my opinion, some account of the consequences of this converse of spirits; I mean, such as are quite remote from what we call apparition or appearance of spirits; and I omit these, because I know they are objected much against, and they bear much scandal from the frequent impositions of our fancies and imaginations upon our judgments and understandings, as above.

But the more particular discoveries of this converse of spirits, and which to me are undeniable, are such as follows, namely,—

Dreams	Impulses	Involuntary sadness, &c.
Voices	Hints	
Noises	Apprehensions	

Dreams are dangerous things to talk of; and we have such dreaming about them, that indeed the least encouragement to lay any weight upon them is presently carried away by a sort of people that dream waking, and that run into such wild extremes about them, that indeed we ought to be very cautious what we say of them.

It is certain dreams of old were the ways by which God Himself was pleased to warn men, as well what to do, as what not to do; what services to perform, what evils to shun. Joseph, the husband of the blessed Virgin Mary, was appeared to in both these (Matt. ii. 13, 19). He was directed of God, in a dream, to go into Egypt; and he was bid return out of Egypt in a dream; and in the same chapter, the wise men of the East were warned of God in a dream to depart into their own country another way to avoid the fury of Herod.

Now as this, and innumerable instances through the whole Scripture, confirm that God did once make use of this manner to convey knowledge and instruction to men, I wish I could have this question well answered, *viz.*, Why are we now to direct people to take no notice of their dreams?

But farther; it appears that this was not only the method God Himself took by His immediate power, but it is evident He made use of it by the ministry of spirits; the Scripture says in both the cases of

Joseph above named, that the "angel of the Lord appeared to Joseph in a dream." Now every unembodied spirit is an angel of the Lord in some sense; and as angels and spirits may be the same thing in respect of this influence upon us in dreams, so it is still; and when any notice for good, or warning against evil, is given us in a dream, I think 'tis no arrogance at all for us to say the angel of the Lord appeared to us in a dream; or to say some good spirit gave me warning of this in a dream;—take this which way you will.

That I may support this with such undeniable arguments, drawn from examples of the fact, as no man will, or reasonably can oppose, I first appeal to the experience of observing people; I mean, such people as observe these things without a superstitious dependence upon the signification of them, that look upon dreams but with such a moderate regard to them as may direct to a right use of them. The question I would ask of such is, whether they have never found any remarkable event of their lives so evidently foretold them by a dream, as that it must of necessity be true that some invisible being foresaw the event, and gave them notice of it? And that, had that notice been listened to, and the natural prudence used which would have been used if it had been certainly discovered, that evil event might have been prevented?

I would ask others whether they have not, by dreams, been so warned of evil really approaching, as that, taking the hint, and making use of the caution given in those dreams, the evil has been avoided? If I may speak my own experience, I must take leave to say, that I never had any capital mischief befall me in my life but I have had notice of it by a dream; and if I had not been that thoughtless, unbelieving creature, which I now would caution other people against, I might have taken many a warning, and avoided many of the evils that I afterwards fell into merely by a total obstinate neglect of those dreams.

In like manner I have in some of the greatest distresses of my life been encouraged to believe firmly and fully that I should one time or other be delivered; and I must acknowledge, that in my greatest and most hopeless banishment I had such frequent dreams of my deliverance, that I always entertained a firm and satisfying belief that my last days would be better than my first; all which has effectually come to pass.

From which I cannot determine, as I know some do, that all dreams are mere dozings of a delirious head, delusions of a waking devil, and relics of the day's thoughts and perplexities, or pleasures. Nor do I see any period of time fixed between the two opposite circumstances—namely, when dreams were to be esteemed the voice of God and when the delusion of the devil.

I know some have struggled hard to fix that particular article, and to settle it as a thing going hand in hand with the Jewish institutions; as if the oracle ceasing in the temple with the consummation of the typical law, all the methods which Heaven was pleased to take in the former times for revealing His will to men were to cease also at the same time, and the Gospel revelation being fully and effectually supplied by the mission of the Holy Spirit, dreams and all the uses and significations of dreams were at an end, and the esteem and regard to the warnings and instructions of dreams was to expire also.

But the Scripture is point-blank against this in the history of fact relating to Ananias and the conversion of St. Paul, and in the story of St. Peter and Cornelius, the devout centurion at Antioch; both of them eminent instances of God's giving notice of His pleasure to men by the interposition or medium of a dream. The first of these is in Acts ix. 10: "*There was a certain disciple at Damascus named Ananias. To him said the Lord in a vision,*" &c.; the words spoken in this vision to Ananias, directing to go to seek out one Saul of Tarsus, go on thus (ver. 12), "*and hath seen in a vision a man named Ananias coming in.*"

The other passage is of St. Peter and Cornelius the centurion (Acts x. vers. 3, 10, 11). In the third verse it is said, Cornelius, fasting and praying, saw a vision, which afterwards, in the 22nd verse, is called an holy angel warning him; in the 30th verse it is said, "*a man stood before me in bright clothing;*" at the same time (ver. 10) it is said, St. Peter was praying and fell into a trance—this we all agreed to be a possession of sleep, or a deep sleep—and in this trance it is said he saw heaven opened; that is to say, he dreamed that he saw heaven opened; it could be nothing else, for no interpreters will offer to insist that heaven was really opened; also, the hearing a voice (vers. 13, 15) must be in a dream. Thus 'tis apparent the will of God concerning what we are to do or not to do, what is or is not to befall us, is and has been thus conveyed by vision or dream since the expiration of the Levitical dispensation, and since the mission of the Holy Ghost.

When, then, did it cease? And if we do not know when it ceased, how then are we sure it is at all ceased, and what authority have we now to reject all dreams or visions of the night, as they are called, more than formerly?

I will not say but there may be more nocturnal delusions now in

460

the world than there were in those times; and perhaps the devil may have gained more upon mankind in these days than he had then, though we are not let into those things enough to know whether it is so or not; nor do we know that there were not as many unsignifying dreams in those days as now, and perhaps as much to be said against depending upon them; though I think there is not one word in Scripture said to take off the regard men might give to dreams, or to lessen the weight which they might lay on them.

The only text that I think looks like it is the flout Joseph's brethren put upon him, or threw out at him, when they were speaking of him with contempt (Gen. xxxvii. 19), *"Behold, this dreamer cometh;"* and again (ver. 20), *"Let us slay him and cast him into some pit, and we shall see what will become of his dreams."*

This, indeed, looks a little like the present language against dreams; but even this is sufficiently rebuked in the consequences, for those dreams of Joseph did come all to pass, and proving the superior influence such things have upon the affairs of men, in spite of all the contempt they can cast upon them.

The maxim I have laid down to myself for my conduct in this affair is, in few words, that we should not lay too great stress upon dreams, and yet not wholly neglect them.

I remember I was once present where a long dispute was warmly carried on between two persons of my acquaintance upon this very subject, the one a layman, the other a clergyman, but both very pious and religious persons. The first thought there was no heed at all to be given to dreams, that they could have no justifiable original, that they were delusions and no more, that it was atheistical to lay any stress upon them, and that he could give such objections against them as that no man of good principles could avoid being convinced by; that as to their being a communication from the invisible to the visible world 't was a chimera, and that he saw no foundation for believing any reality in such a thing, unless I would set up for a Popish *limbus*, or purgatory, which had no foundation in the Scripture.

(1.) He said, if dreams were from the agency of any prescient being, the notices would be more direct and the discoveries clear—not by allegories and emblematic fancies, expressing things imperfect and dark. For to what purpose should spirits unembodied sport with mankind, warning him of approaching mischiefs by the most ridiculous enigmas, figures, &c, leaving the wretch to guess what awaited him, though of the utmost consequence, and to perish if he mistook the meaning of it; and leaving him sometimes perfectly at a loss to know whether he was right or wrong, and without any rule or guide to walk by in the most difficult cases?

(2.) He objected, that with the notice of evil, suppose it to be rightly understood, there was not given a power to avoid it, and therefore it could not be alleged that the notice was any way kind, and that it was not likely to proceed from a beneficent spirit, but merely fortuitous, and of no significancy.

(3.) He objected, that if such notices as those were of such weight, why were they not constant, but that sometimes they were given and sometimes omitted, though cases were equally important? and that, therefore, they did not seem to proceed from any agent whose actions were to be fairly accounted for.

(4.) He said, that oftentimes we had very distinct and formal dreams, without any signification at all, that we could neither know anything probable or anything rational of them; and that it would be profane to suggest that to come from heaven which was too apparently foolish and inconsistent.

(5.) As men were not always thus warned, or supplied with notices of good or evil, so all men were not alike supplied with them; and what reason could we give why one man or one woman should not have the same hints as another?

The clergyman gave distinct answers to all these objections, and to me, I confess, very satisfactory; whether they may be so to those that read them, is no concern of mine; let every one judge for himself.

(1.) He said, that as to the signification of dreams, and the objections against them, because dark and doubtful, that they are expressed generally by hieroglyphical representations, similes, allusions, and figurative emblematic ways of expressing things, was true, and that by this means, for want of interpretation, the thing was not understood, and consequently the evil not shunned. This, he said, was the only difficulty that remained to him in the case, but that he could see nothing in it against the signification of them, because thus it was before, for dreams were often allegoric and allusive when they were evidently from God, and what the end and design of Providence in that was, we could not pretend to inquire.

(2.) To the second he said, we charged God foolishly, to say He had given the notice of evil without the power to avoid it, which he denied, and affirmed that, if any one had not power to avoid the evil, it was no notice to him that it was want of giving due heed to that notice, not for want of the notice being sufficient that any evil followed, and that men first neglected themselves, and then charged the Judge of all the earth with not doing right.

(3.) Likewise he said, the complaint that these notices were not constant, was unjust, for he doubted not but they were so, but our discerning was crazed and clouded by our negligence in not taking due notice of it; that we hookwinked our understanding by pretending dreams were not to be regarded; and the voice really spoke, but we refused to hear, being negligent of our own good.

(4.) In the same sense he answered the fourth, and said it was a mistake to say that sometimes dreams had no import at all; he said it was only to be said, none that we could perceive the reason of, which was owing to our blindness and supine negligence, to be secure at one time, and our heads too much alarmed at another, so that the spirit which we might be said to be conversing with in a dream was constantly and equally kind and careful; but our powers not always in the same state of action, nor equally attentive to or retentive of the hints that were given, or things might be rendered more or less intelligible to us, as the powers of our soul were more or less dozed or somniated with the oppression of vapours from the body, which occasions sleep; for though the soul cannot be said to sleep itself, yet how far its operations may be limited, and the understanding prescribed by the sleepiness of the body, says he, I will not undertake; let the anatomist judge of it who can account for the contexture of the parts, and for their operations, which I cannot answer to.

(5.) As to the last question, why people are not equally supplied with such warnings, he said, this seemed to be no question at all in the case, for Providence itself might have some share in the direction of it, and then that Providence might perhaps be limited by some superior direction, the same that guides all the solemn dispositions of Nature, and was a wind blowing where it listeth; that as to the converse of spirits, though he allowed the thing itself, yet he did not tie it up to a stated course of conversing, that it should be the same always, and to all people, and on all occasions, but that it seemed to be spontaneous, and consequently arbitrary, as if the spirits unembodied had it left to them to converse as they thought fit, how, where, and with whom they would; that all he answered for in that discourse was for the thing itself, that such a thing there was, but why there was so much of it, or why no more, was none of his business, and he believed a discovery was not yet made to mankind of that part.

I thought it would be much to the purpose to remark this opinion of another man, because it corresponded so exactly with my own; but I have not done with my friend, for he led me into another inquiry, which, indeed, I had not taken so much notice of before, and this was introduced by the following question:—

"You seem," says he, "to be very inquisitive about dreams, and to doubt—though I think you have no reason for it—of the reality of the world of spirits, which dreams are such an evidence of. Pray," says he, "what think you of waking dreams, trances, visions, noises, voices, hints, impulses, and all these waking testimonies of an invisible world, and of the communication that there is between us and them, which are generally entertained with our eyes open?"

This led me into many reflections upon past things, which I had been witness to as well in myself as in other people, and particularly in my former solitudes, when I had many occasions to mark such things as these, and I could not but entertain a free conversation with my friend upon this subject as often as I had opportunity, of which I must give some account.

I had one day been conversing so long with him upon the common received notions of the planets being habitable, and of a diversity of worlds, that I think verily I was for some days like a man transported into these regions myself. Whether my imagination is more addicted to realising the things I talk of, as if they were in view, I know not, or whether by the power of the converse of spirits I speak of I was at that time enabled to entertain clearer ideas of the invisible world, I really cannot tell, but I certainly made a journey to all those supposed habitable bodies in my imagination, and I know not but it may be very useful to tell you what I met with in my way, and what the wiser I am for the discovery; whether you will be the wiser for the relation at second hand, I cannot answer for that.

I could make a long discourse here of the power of imagination, and how bright the ideas of distant things may be found in the mind when the soul is more than ordinarily agitated. It is certain the extraordinary intelligence conveyed in this manner is not always regular; sometimes it is exceeding confused, and the brain being not able to digest it, turns round too fast; this tends to lunacy and distraction, and the swiftness of the motion these ideas come in with occasions a commotion in Nature; the understanding is mobbed with them, disturbed, runs from one thing to another, and digests nothing; this is well expressed in our common way of talking of a madman, namely, that his head is turned. Indeed, I can liken it to nothing so well as to the wheels of a windmill, which, if the sails or wings are set, and the wind blow a storm, run round so fast, that they will set all on fire if a skilful hand be not ready to direct and manage it.

But not to enter upon this whimsical description of lunacy, which, perhaps, may be nobody's opinion but my own, I proceed thus, that when the head is strong, and capable of the impressions, when the understanding is empowered to digest the infinite variety of ideas which present to it from the extended fancy, then, I say, the soul of man is capable to act strangely upon the invisibles in Nature, and upon futurity, realising everything to itself in such a lively manner, that what it thus thinks of it really sees, speaks to, hears, converses with, &c, as lively as if the substance was really before his face; and this is what I mean by those that dream waking, by visions, trances, or what you please to call them, for it is not necessary to this part that the man should be asleep.

I return to my share of these things. It was after my conversing with my learned friend about the heavenly bodies, the motion, the distances, and the bulk of the planets, their situation, and the orbits they move in; the share of light, heat, and moisture which they enjoy; their respect to the sun; their influences upon us; and, at last, the possibility of their being habitable, with all the arcana of the skies; it was on this occasion, I say, that my imagination, always given to wander, took a flight of its own, and as I have told you that I had an invincible inclination to travel, so I think I travelled as sensibly, to my understanding, over all the mazes and wastes of infinite space, in quest of those things, as ever I did over the deserts of Karakathie, and the uninhabited wastes of Tartary, and perhaps may give as useful an account of my journey.

When first my fancy raised me up in the confines of this vast abyss, and having now travelled through the misty regions of the atmosphere could look down as I mounted, and see the world below me, it is scarcely possible to imagine how little, how mean, how despicable everything looked. Let any man but try this experiment of himself, and he shall certainly find the same thing; let him but fix his thoughts so intensely upon what is and must necessarily be seen in a stage or two higher than where we now live, removed from the particular converse with the world, as to realise to his imagination what he can suppose to be there, he shall find all that is below him, as distant objects always do, lessen in his mind as they do in his sight.

Could a man subsist without a supply of food, and live but one mile in perpendicular height from the surface, he would despise life and the world at such a rate that he would hardly come down to have it be all his own; the soul of man is capable of being continually elevated above the very thoughts of human things—is capable of travelling up to the highest and most distant regions of light, but when it does, as it rises above the earthly globe, so the things of this globe sink to him.

When I was at first lifted up in my imaginary travels, this was the first thing of moment I remarked, namely, how little the world and everything about it seemed to me. I am not given to preach, or drawing long corollaries, as the learned call them, but I recommend it to my friends to observe that, could we always look upon the things of life with the same eyes as we shall do when we come to the edge of time, when one eye can as it were look back on the world, and the other look forward into eternity, we should save ourselves the trouble of much repentance, and should scorn to touch many of those things in which we now fancy our chief felicity is laid up; believe me, we shall see more with half an eye then, and judge better at first glance, than we can now, with all our pretended wisdom and penetration. In a word, all the passions and affections suffer a general change upon such a view, and what we desire before, we contemn them with abhorrence.

Having begun to soar, the world was soon out of sight, unless that as I rose higher, and could look at her in a due position as to the sun, I could see her turned into a moon, and shine by reflection. "Ay, shine on," said I, "with thy borrowed rays, for thou hast but very few of thy own."

When my fancy had mounted me thus beyond the vestiges of the earth, and leaving the atmosphere behind me, I had set my firm foot upon the verge of infinite, when I drew no breath, but subsisted upon pure ether, it is not possible to express fully the vision of the place. First, you are to conceive of sight as un confined, and you see here at least the whole solar system at one view. Nor is your sight bounded by the narrow circumference of one sun and its attendants of planets, whose orbits are appropriated to its proper system, but above and beyond, and on every side, you see innumerable suns, and, attending on them, planets, satellites, and inferior lights, proper to their respective systems, and all these moving in their subordinate circumstances, without the least confusion, with glorious light and splendour inconceivable.

In this first discovery 'tis most natural to observe how plainly it is to be seen that the reason of the creation of such immense bodies as the sun, stars, planets, and moons, in the great circle of the lower heaven, is far from being to be found in the study of Nature on the surface of our earth, but he that will see thoroughly why God has formed the heavens, the work of His hands, and the moon and the stars which He has made, must soar up higher, and then, as he will see with other eyes than he did before, so he will see the God of Nature has formed an infinite variety which we know nothing of, and that all the creatures are a reason to one another for their creation.

I could not forget myself, however, when I was got up thus high; I say, I could not but look back upon the state of man in this life, how confined from these discoveries, how vilely employed in biting and devouring, envying and maligning one another, and all for the vilest trifles that can be conceived.

But I was above it all here, and all those things which appeared so afflicting before gave me not the least concern now; for the soul being gone of this errand had quite different notions of the whole state of life, and was neither influenced by passions or affections, as it was before.

Here I saw into many things by the help of a sedate inquiry, that we can entertain little or no notion of in a state of common superficial life, and I desire to leave a few remarks of this imaginary journey, as I did of my ordinary travels.

When I came, I say, to look into the solar system as I have hinted, I saw perfectly the emptiness of our modern notions that the planets were habitable worlds, and shall give a brief description of the case, that others may see it too, without the necessity of taking so long a journey.

And first for the word habitable: I understand the meaning of it to be, that the place it is spoken of is qualified for the subsistence and existence of man and beast, and to preserve the vegetative and sensitive life, and you may depend upon it that none of the planets, except the moon, are in this sense habitable; and the moon, a poor, little, watery, damp thing, not above as big as Yorkshire, neither worth being called a world, nor capable of rendering life comfortable to mankind, if indeed supportable; and if you will believe one's mind capable of seeing at so great a distance, I assure you I did not see man, woman, or child there in all my contemplative voyage to it: my meaning is, I did not see the least reason to believe there was or could be any there. As to the rest of the planets, I will take them in their order. Saturn (the remotest from the sun, which is in the centre of the system) is a vast extended globe, of a substance cold and moist; its greatest degree of light is never so much as our greatest darkness may be said to be in clear weather, and its cold insufferable; and if it were a body composed of the same elements as our earth, its sea would be all brass, and its earth all iron; that is to say, both would be continually frozen, as the north pole in the winter solstice. What man or men, and of what nature, could inhabit this frigid planet, unless the Creator must be supposed to have created animal creatures for the climate, not the climate for the creatures? All the notions of Saturn's being a habitable world are contrary to nature, and incongruous with sense; for Saturn is at so infinite a distance from the sun, that it has not above one ninetieth part of the light and heat that we enjoy on our earth; so that the light there may be said to be much less than our starlight, and the cold ninety times greater than the coldest day in our winter.

Jupiter is in the same predicament; his constitution, however, in its degree much milder than Saturn, yet certainly is not qualified for human bodies to subsist, having only one twenty-seventh part of the light and heat that we enjoy here; consequently its light is at best as dim as our twilight, and its heat so little in the summer of its situation as to be as far from comfortable as it is in its winter situation insupportable.

Mars, if you will believe our ancient philosophers, is a fiery planet in the very disposition of its influence, as well as by the course of its motion; and yet even here the light is not above one-half, and its heat one-third of ours. And on the other hand, as Saturn is cold and moist, so this planet is hot and dry, and would admit no habitation of man, through the manifest intemperance of the air, as well as want of light to make it comfortable, and moisture to make it fruitful; for by the nature of the planet, as well as by clear-sighted observation, there is never any rain, vapour, fog, or dew in that planet.

Venus and Mercury are in the extreme the other way, and would destroy nature by their heat and dazzling light, as the other would by their darkness and cold; so that you may depend upon it I could see very clearly that all these bodies were neither inhabited or habitable; and the earth only, as we call it, being seated between these intemperances, appeared habitable, surrounded with an atmosphere to defend it from the invasion of the inconsistent ether, in which perspiration could not be performed by the lungs, and by which the needful vapour it sends forth is preserved from dissipating into the waste and abyss, and is condensed, and timely returns in showers of rain to moisten, cool, and nourish the exhausted earth.

It is true the way I went was no common road, yet I found abundance of passengers going to and fro here, and particularly innumerable armies of good and evil spirits, who all seemed busily employed, and continually upon the wing, as if some expresses passed between the earth, which in this part of my travels I place below me, and some country infinitely beyond all that I could reach the sight of; for, by the way, though I take upon me in this sublime journey to see a great deal of the invisible world, yet I was not arrived to a length to see into any part of the world of light beyond it all. That vision is beyond all, and I pretend to say nothing of it here, except this only, that a clear view of this part with optics unclouded is a great step to prepare the mind for a look into the other.

But to return to my station in the highest created world; flatter not yourselves that those regions are uninhabited because the planets appear to be so. No, no; I assure you this is that world of spirits, or at least is a world of spirits.

Here I saw a clear demonstration of Satan being the prince of the power of the air; 't is in this boundless waste he is confined, whether it be his busy restless inclination has posted him here, that he may affront God in His government of the world, and do injury to mankind in mere envy to his happiness, as the famed Mr. Milton says it, or whether it is that by the eternal decree of Providence he is appointed to be man's continual disturber for Divine ends, to us unknown; this I had not wandered far enough to be informed of, those secrets being lodged much higher than imagination itself ever travelled.

But here, I say, I found Satan keeping his court, or camp we may call it, which we please. The innumerable legions that attended his immediate service were such that it is not at all to be wondered that he supplied every angle of this world, and had his work going forward, not in every country only, but even in every individual inhabitant of it, with all the dexterity and application imaginable.

This sight gave me a just idea of the devil as a tempter, but really let me into a secret which I did not so well know before, or at least did not consider, namely, that the devil is not capable of doing half the mischief in the world that we lay to his charge. That he works by engines and agents, stratagems and art, is true, and a great deal is owing to his vigilance and application, for he is a very diligent fellow in his calling. But 'tis plain his power is not so great as we imagine; he can only prompt to the crime—he cannot force us to commit it; so that if we sin it is all our own, the devil has only to be charged with the art of insinuation. Just as he began with Eve, he goes on with us; in short, he reasons us out of our resolutions to do well, and wheedles us to an agreement to do ill, working us up to an opinion, that what evil we are about to do is no sin, or not so great a sin as we feared, and so draws us by art into the crime we had resolved against. This, indeed, the Scripture intimates when it speaks of Satan's devices, the subtlety of the wicked one, his lying in wait, &c. But to charge the devil with forcing us to offend, is doing the devil a great deal of wrong; our doing evil is from the native propensity of our wills: *humanum est peccare.* I will not enter here into the dispute about original corruption in nature, which I know many good and learned men dispute; but that there is a secret aptness to offend, and a secret backwardness to what is good, which, if it is not born with us, we can give no account how we came by, this I think every man will grant; and that this is the devil that tempts us the Scripture plainly tells us, when it says, "*Every man is tempted when he is drawn away of his own lust and enticed.*"

There is a secret love of folly and vanity in the mind, and mankind are hurried down the stream of their own affections into crime; 't is agreeable to them to do this, and 't is a force upon nature not to do it.

Vice is downhill, and when we do offend,
'Tis nature all, we act as we intend.
Virtue's uphill, and all against the grain,
Resolved reluctant, and pursued with pain.

But to return to the devil: his power not extending to creation, and being not able to force the world into an open rebellion against Heaven, as doubtless he would do if he could, he is left to the exercise of his skill; and, in a word, we may say of him, that he lives by his wits, that is to say, maintains his kingdom by subtlety and most exquisite cunning; and if my vision of his politics is not a new discovery, I am very much mistaken.

His innumerable *legions*, as I hinted above, like *aides-de-camp* to a general, are continually employed to carry his orders and execute his commissions in all parts of the world, and in every individual to oppose the authority of God and the felicity of man to the utmost of his power.

The first and greatest part of his government is over those savage nations where he has obtained to set himself up as God, and to be worshipped instead of God; and I observed that though, having full possession of these people, even by whole nations at a time, that is the easiest part of his government; yet he is far from neglecting his interest there, but is exceeding vigilant to keep up his authority among those people. This he does by sending messengers into those parts to answer the *pawawings* or conjurings even of the most ignorant old wizard, raising storms and making noises, and shrieks in the air, flashes of infernal fire, and anything but to fright the people, that they may not forget him, and that they may have no other gods but him.

He has his peculiar agents for this work, which he makes detachments of, as his occasions require, some to one part of the world, some to another, as to the North America, even as far as to the frozen provinces of Greenland; to the north of Europe, to the Laplanders, Samoiedes, and Mongol Tartars; also to the Gog and Magog of Asia, and to the devilmakers of China and Japan; again to the southern parts of Asia, to the isles of the Indian and South Seas, and to the south part of America and Africa.

Through all these parts he has an uncontrolled power, and is either worshipped in person or by his representatives, the idols and monsters which the poor people bow down to, and Satan has very little trouble with them.

He employs, indeed, some millions of his missionaries into those countries, who labour *ad propaganda fid.*, and fail not to return and bring him an account of their success, and I doubt not but some of them were at my hand in my island when the savages appeared there; for if the devil had not been in them, they would hardly have come straggling over the sea so far to devour one another.

In all these countries the brutality, the cruelty, and ravenous bloody dispositions of the people, is to me a certain testimony that the devil has full possession of them.

But to return to my observations in the exalted state of my fancy; I must tell you that though the devil carried on his schemes of government in those blinded parts of the world with great ease and all things went to his mind, I found he had more difficulty in the northern parts of the temperate zone; I mean, our climate and the rest of Christendom, and consequently he did not act here by whole squadrons and by generals, but was obliged to carry on his business among us by particular solicitations, to act by particular agents upon particular persons, attacking the personal conduct of men in a manner peculiar

471

to himself. But so far was this difficulty from being any advantage to the world, or disadvantage to the devil, that it only obliged him to make use of the more engines; and as he had no want of numbers, I observed that his whole clan seemed busy on this side, the number of which consists of innumerable millions; so that, in short, there was not a devil wanting, no, not to manage every individual man, woman, and child in the world.

How, and in what manner, evil angels attend us, what their business, how far their power extends, and how far it is restrained, and by whom, were all made plain to me at one view in this state of *eclaircissement* that I stood in now, and I will describe it if I can in a few heads of fact; you may enlarge upon them as experience guides.

And first, the limitations of the devil's power are necessary to be understood, and how directed. For example, you must know, that though the numbers of these evil spirits, which are thus diligently employed in mischief, are so infinitely great, yet the numbers of good angels or good spirits which are employed by a superior authority, and from a place infinitely distant and high above the devil's bounds, is not only equal, I say equal at least, in number, but infinitely superior in power, and it is this particular which makes it plain that all the devil does, or that his agents can do, is by continual subtlety, extreme vigilance and application, under infinite checks, rebukes, and callings off by the attendant spirits, who have power to correct and restrain him upon all occasions, just as a man does a dog or a thief when he is discovered.

On this account it is first plain, I say, that the devil can do nothing by force; he cannot kill, maim, hurt, or destroy; if he could, mankind would have but a very precarious state of life in the world; nay the devil cannot blast the fruits of the earth, cause dearth, droughts, famine, or scarcity; neither can he spread noxious fumes in the air to infect the world; if any of those things were in his power, he would soon unpeople God's creation, and put his Maker to the necessity of a new fiat, or of having no more human creatures to worship and honour Him.

You will ask me how I came to know all this? I say, ask me no questions till the elevation of your fancy carries you up to the outer edge of the atmosphere, as I tell you mine did. There you will see the prince of the air in his full state, managing his universal empire with the most exquisite art; but if ever you can come to a clear view of his person, do but look narrowly, and you will see a great clog at his foot, in token of his limited power; and though he himself is immense in bulk, and moves like a fiery meteor in the air, yet you always see a hand with a thunderbolt impending just over his head; the arm coming out of a fiery cloud, which is a token of the sentence he is under, that at the end of his appointed time that cloud shall break, and that hand strike him with the thunder represented, down, down, for ever, into a place prepared for him.

But all this does not hinder him, who is prompted by infernal rage against the kingdom of God and the welfare of man, from pushing mankind, as above, upon all the methods of their own ruin and destruction, by alluring baits, cunning artifice, night whispers, infusing wicked desires, and fanning the flames of men's lusts, pride, avarice, ambition, revenge, and all the wicked excursions of corrupt nature.

It would take up a long tract by itself to form a system of the devil's politics, and to lay down a body of his philosophy. I observed, however, that some of his general rules are such as these:—

(1.) To infuse notions of liberty into the minds of men; that it is hard they should be born into the world with inclinations, and then be forbidden to gratify them; that such and such pleasure should be prepared in the nature of things, made suitable and proper to the senses and faculties, which on the other hand are prepared in mere constitution, and placed in his soul, and that then he should be forbidden, under the penalty of a curse, to taste them; that to place an appetite in the man, and a strong powerful gust to these delights, and then declare them fatal to him, would be laying a snare to mankind in his very constitution, and making his brightest faculties be the betrayers of his soul to misery, which would not consist with justice, much less with the goodness of a creator.

(2.) To persuade from hence, that the notions of future punishments are fables and amusements, that it is not rational to think a just God would prepare infinite and eternal punishments for finite and trivial offences; that God does not take notice of the minute acts of life, and lay every slip to our charge, but that the merciful dispositions of God, who so bountifully directs the whole world to be assistant to the profit and delight of mankind, has certainly given him leave to enjoy it at will, and take the comfort of it without fear.

(3.) Of late, indeed, the devil has learned—for devils may improve as well as men in the arts of doing ill—at last, I say, he has learned to infuse a wild notion into the heads of some people, who are first fitted for it by having reasoned themselves in favour of their loose desires up to a pitch, that there is no such thing as a God or a future state at all.

Now, as at first the devil was not fool enough to attempt to put this jest upon man, his own antiquity and eternity being a contradiction to it; so I found among my new discoveries that the devil took this absurdity from man himself, and that it went among Satan's people for a new invention. I found also that there was a black party employed upon this new subtlety; these were a sort of devils, for Satan never wants instruments, who were called insinuators, and who were formerly employed to prompt men to crimes by dreams; and here I shall observe, that I learned a way how to make any man dream of what I please. For example: suppose one to be sound asleep, or, as we say, in a deep sleep or dead sleep, let another lay his mouth close to his ear and whisper anything to him so softly as not to awaken him, the sleeping man shall certainly dream of what was so whispered to him.

Let no man despise this hint: nothing is more sure than that many of our dreams are the whispers of the devil, who, by his insinuators, whispers into our heads what wicked things he would have our thoughts entertain and work upon; and take this with you as you go, those insinuating devils can do this as well when we are awake as when we are asleep. And this will bring me to what I call impulses upon the mind, which are certainly whispers in the ear and no other, and come either from good angels attending us, or from the devil's insinuators, which are always at hand, and may be judged of according as the subject our thoughts are prompted to work upon is good or evil.

From whence but from these insinuators come our causeless passions, our involuntary wickedness, sinning in desire as effectually as by actual committing the crime we desire to commit?

Whence comes imagination to work upon wicked and vicious objects when the person is fast asleep, and when he had not been under the preparation of wicked discourse or wicked thoughts previous to those imaginations? Who forms ideas in the mind of man? who presents beautiful or terrible figures to his fancy, when his eyes are closed with sleep? who but these insinuating devils, who invisibly approach the man, sleeping or waking, and whisper all manner of lewd, abominable things into his mind.

Mr. Milton, whose imagination was carried up to a greater height than I am now, went farther into the abyss of Satan's empire a great way, especially when he formed Satan's palace of pandemonium; I say, he was exactly of this opinion when he represented the devil tempting our mother Eve in the shape of a toad lying just at her ear, when she lay fast asleep in her bower, where he whispered to her ear all the wicked things which she entertained notions of by night, and which prompted her the next day to break the great command, which was the rule of her life; and, accordingly, he brings in Eve, telling Adam what an uneasy nights rest she had, and relating her dream to him.

This thought, however laid down in a kind of jest, is very seriously intended, and would, if well digested, direct us very clearly in our judgment of dreams, *viz.*, not to suggest them to be always things of mere chance; but that sometimes they are to be heeded as useful warnings of evil or good by the agency of good spirits, as at other times they are the artful insinuations of the devil to inject wicked thoughts and abhorred abominable ideas into the mind; which we ought not only as much as possible to guard against, but even to repent of so far as the mind may have entertained and acted upon them.

From this general vision of the devil's management of his affairs, which I must own I have had with my eyes wide open, I find a great many useful observations to be made; and first, it can be no longer strange that, while the commerce of evil spirits is so free and the intercourse between this world and that is thus open, I say, it can be no longer strange that there are so many silent ways of spirits conversing; I mean, spirits of all kinds.

For, as I have observed already, there is a residence of good spirits, but they are placed infinitely higher, out of the reach and out of the sight of this lower orbit of Satan's kingdom; as those pass and repass invisible, I confess I have yet had no ideas of them but those which I have received from my first view of the infernal region. If I should have any superior elevations, and should be able to see the economy of Heaven in His disposition of things on earth, I shall be as careful to convey them to posterity as they come in.

However, the transactions of good spirits with man are certainly the same; for as God has, for a protection and safeguard to mankind, limited the devil from affrighting him by visible appearances in his native and hellish deformity, and the horrid shape he would necessarily bear; so, for man's felicity, even the glorious angels of heaven are very seldom allowed, at least not lately, to appear in the glorious forms they formerly took, or, indeed, in any form, or with a voice; the restraint of our souls in the case of flesh and blood we now wear not admitting it, and not being able to familiarise those things to us; man being by no means, in his incorporated state, qualified for an open and easy conversation with unembodied spirit.

Moreover, this would be breaking into the limits which the wisdom and goodness of God has put to our present state, I mean as to futurity, our ignorance in which is the greatest felicity of human life; and without which necessary blindness man could not support life, for nature is no way able to support a view into futurity; I mean, not into that part of futurity which concerns us in our state of life in this world.

I have often been myself among the number of those fools that would be their own fortune-tellers; but when I look thus beyond the atmosphere, and see a little speculatively into invisibles, I could easily perceive that it is our happiness that we are shortsighted creatures, and can see but a very little before us. For example, were we to have the eyes of our souls opened through the eyes of our bodies, we should see this very immediate region of air which we breathe in thronged with spirits, to us, blessed be God, now invisible, and which would otherwise be most frightful; we should see into the secret transactions of those messengers who are employed when the passing soul takes its leave of the reluctant body, and perhaps see things nature would shrink back from with the utmost terror and amazement. In a word, the curtain of Providence for the disposition of things here, and the curtain of judgment for the determination of the state of souls hereafter, would be alike drawn back; and what heart could support here its future state in life, much less that of its future state after life, even good or bad?

It is, then, our felicity that the converse of spirits and the visions of futurity are silent, emblematic, and done by hints, dreams, and impulses, and not by clear vision and open discovery. They that desire a fuller and plainer sight of these things ask they know not what; and it was a good answer of a gipsy, when a lady of my acquaintance asked her to tell her fortune, "Do not ask me, lady," said the gipsy, "to tell you what you dare not hear." The woman was a little honester than her profession intimated, and freely confessed it was all a cheat, and that they knew nothing of fortunes, but had a course or round of doubtful expressions, to amuse ignorant people and get a little money.

Even the devil's oracles—for such, no doubt, they were at Delphos and at other places, though the devil seemed at that time to have some liberties granted him which it is evident have since been denied him—were allowed to be given only in doubtful expressions, double entendres, echoes of words, and such like. For example: a man going to sea, and inquiring of the oracle thus—

"Have I just cause the seas and storms to fear?

"Echo—"Fear."

Another.

"Shall we the Parthian boatmen fight, or fly?
"Echo—"Fly."

Such dark replies, and other words doubtful and enigmatic, were frequently given and taken for answers, by which the deluded world were kept in doubt of that futurity they hunted after. But Satan, even then, was not permitted to speak plain, or mankind to see what awaited them behind the dark veil of futurity; nor was it proper, on any account whatsoever, that it should be otherwise.

But before I come to this let me put some limits to the elevations and visions I have mentioned before; for as I am far from enthusiastic in my notions of things, so I would not lead any one to fancy themselves farther enlightened than is meet, or to see things invisible, as St. Paul heard things unutterable.

And, therefore, let me add here, that the highest raptures, trances, and elevations of the soul are bounded by the eternal decree of Heaven, and let men pretend to what visions they please, it is all romance; all beyond what I have talked of above is fabulous and absurd, and it will for ever be true, as the Scripture says, not only those things are hid from the eye, but even from the conception.

Upon this occasion, I must own that I think it is criminal to attempt to form ideas either of hell or of heaven in the mind, other than as the Scripture has described them, by the state rather than the place. We are told, in plain words, it hath not entered into the heart of man to conceive either of what is prepared for the future state of the happy or miserable; 't is enough for us to entertain the general notion—the favour of God is heaven, and the loss of it the most dreadful of all, hell.

A heaven of joy must in His presence dwell,
And in His absence every place is hell.

My meaning is this; all visions, or propounded visions, either of heaven or hell, are mere delusions of the mind, and generally are fictions of a waking bewildered head; and you may see the folly of them in the meanest of the descriptions, which generally end in showing some glorious place, fine walks, noble illustrious palaces, gardens of gold, and people of shining forms and the like. Alas! these are all so short that they are unworthy the thoughts of a mind elevated two degrees above darkness and dirt. All these things amount to no more than Mahomet's *Alcoran* and the glorious state of things represented by him to his believers. In short, all this makes only a heaven of sense, but comes so infinitely short of what alone must or can be a heaven to an exalted glorified spirit, that I as much want words to express how contemptible the best of these descriptions are as to a true description of heaven as I do to express a true idea or description of heaven myself.

And how should this be done? We can form no idea of anything that we know not and have not seen but in the form of something that we have seen. How, then, can we form an idea of God or heaven in any form but of something which we have seen or known? By what image in the mind can we judge of spirits? By what idea conceive of eternal glory? Let us cease to imagine concerning it; 'tis impossible to attain, it is criminal to attempt it.

Let me, therefore, hint here, that supposing myself, as before, in the orbit of the sun, take it in its immense distance as our astronomers conceive of it, or on the edge only of the atmosphere with a clear view of the whole solar system, the region of Satan's empire all in view, and the world of spirits laid open to me:

Yet let me give you this for a check to your imagination, that even here the space between finite and infinite is as impenetrable as on earth, and will for ever be so till our spirits, being uncased, shall take their flight to the centre of glory, where everything shall be seen as it is; and therefore you must not be surprised if I am come down again from the verge of the world of spirits the same short-sighted wretch as to futurity and things belonging to heaven and hell as I went up; for elevations of this kind are meant only to give us a clearer view of what we are, not of what we shall be, and 'tis an advantage worth travelling for too. All this I thought necessary to prevent the whimsical building of erroneous structures on my foundation, and fancying themselves carried farther than they are able to go.

I come, therefore, back to talk of things familiar, and particularly to mention in the next place some of those other ways by which we have notice given of this converse of spirits which I have been speaking of; for the whispers and insinuators I have mentioned go sometimes farther than ordinary.

One of those other methods is, when, by strong impulses of the mind, as we call them, we are directed to do or not to do this or that particular thing that we have before us to do, or are under a consultation about. I am a witness to many of these things, as well in my own life as in my observation of others.

I know a man, who being at some distance from London, not above six or seven miles, a friend that came to visit and dine with him urged him to go to London. "What for?" says his friend; "is there any business wants me?"

"Nay, nothing,!" says the other, "but for your company; I do not know of anything wants you; "and so gave over importuning him. But as his friend had given it over a strong impulse of mind seized him and followed him, like a voice, with this—Go to London, go to London. He put it by several times, but it went on still—Go to London, go to London, and nothing else could come upon his thoughts but Go to London. He came back to his friend, "Hark ye," says he, "tell me sincerely, is all well at London? Am I wanted there? Did you ask me to go to London with you on any particular account?"

"Not I," says his friend, "in the least; I saw all your family, and all is very well there; nor did they say they had any particular occasion for you to return; I only ask it, as I told you, for the sake of your company." So he put off going again, but could have no quiet, for it still followed him, and no doubt a good spirit communicated it—Go to London; and at length he resolved he would go, and did so; and when he came there he found a letter, and messengers had been at his house to seek him and to tell him of a particular business, which was, first and last, worth above a thousand pounds to him, and which, if he had not been found that very night, would have been in danger of being lost.

I seriously advise all sober-thinking persons not to disregard those powerful impulses of the mind in things otherwise indifferent or doubtful, but believe them to be whispers from some kind spirit, which sees something that we cannot see, and knows something that we cannot know.

Besides, unless infinite Power should take off the silence that is imposed upon the inhabitants of the invisible world, and allow them to speak audibly, nothing can be a plainer voice; they are words spoken to the mind, though not to the ear, and they are a certain intelligence of things unseen, because they are given by persons unseen, and the event confirms it beyond all dispute.

I know a man who made it his rule always to obey these silent hints, and he has often declared to me that when he obeyed them he never miscarried; and if he neglected them, or went on contrary to them, he never succeeded; and gave me a particular case of his own, among a great many others, wherein he was thus directed. He had a particular case befallen him, wherein he was under the displeasure of the Government, and was prosecuted for a misdemeanour, and brought to a trial in the King's Bench Court, where a verdict was brought against him, and he was cast; and times running very hard at that time against the party he was of, he was afraid to stand the hazard of a sentence, and absconded, taking care to make due provision for his bail, and to pay them whatever they might suffer. In this circumstance he was in very great distress, and no way presented unto him but to fly out of the kingdom, which, being to leave his family, children, and employment, was very bitter to him, and he knew not what to do; all his friends advising him not to put himself into the hands of the law, which, though the offence was not capital, yet, in his circumstances, seemed to threaten his utter ruin. In this extremity he felt one morning—just as he awaked, and the thoughts of his misfortune began to return upon him—I say, he felt a strong impulse darting into his mind thus, Write a letter to them. It spoke so distinctly to him, and as it were forcibly, that, as he has often said since, he can scarce persuade himself not to believe but that he heard it; but he grants that he really did not hear it too.

However, it repeated the words daily and hourly to him, till at length, walking about in his chamber, where he was hidden, very pensive and sad, it jogged him again, and he answered aloud to it, as if it had been a voice, Who shall I write to? It returned immediately, Write to the judge. This pursued him again for several days, till at length he took his pen, ink, and paper, and sat down to write, but knew not one word of what he should say; but, *dabitur in hac hora,* he wanted not words. It was immediately impressed on his mind, and the words flowed upon his pen in a manner that even charmed himself, and filled him with expectations of success.

The letter was so strenuous in argument, so pathetic in its eloquence, and so moving and persuasive, that as soon as the judge read it he sent him word he should be easy, for he would endeavour to make that matter light to him; and, in a word, never left till he obtained to stop prosecution, and restore him to his liberty and to his family.

These hints, I say, are of a nature too significant to be neglected; whence they come is the next inquiry. I answer, they are the whispers of some subsisting spirit communicated to the soul without the help of the organ, without the assistance of a particular sound, and without any other communication; but, take it as you go, not without the merciful disposition of that Power that governs that world, as well as this that we are sensible of. How near those spirits are to us, who thus foresee what concerns us, and how they convey these hints into our minds as well waking as sleeping, or how they are directed, that I could not discover, nor can yet resolve, no, not in the highest of my imaginary elevation, any more than in what manner they are limited and restrained.

I have been asked by some, to whom I have talked freely of my frequent applications to these things, if I knew anything by those observations of the manner of the disposition of the human soul after its departure out of the body, I mean, as to its middle state, and whether, as some, it has a wandering existence in the upper part of the waste or abyss near to, but not in, a present state of felicity? Whether it is still confined within the atmosphere of the earth, according to others, as in a *limbus*, or purgatory; or in the circle of the sun, as others say? Whether I knew or perceived anything of our Saviour's being ascended into the body of the sun only, and not into the highest heaven, receiving His redeemed souls to Himself, and into an incorporation with His glory there, till the restitution of all things? Whether I perceived anything of Satan being possessed of the reprobate souls as they departed; and of his substitutes, as executioners, being empowered and employed to torment them according to the received notions of the wise contemplators of such things?

I answered, as I do now, that not only nothing of all this appears, but, on the contrary, such serious contemplations as mine give a great and abundant reason to be satisfied that there is nothing in it all but mere dream and enthusiastic conjecture. I own that the agents I mentioned make use of all those things to terrify and affright poor ignorant people out of their senses, and to drive them often into desperation, and after to restore them by a cure that is worse than the distemper, namely, by a hardness and coldness of temper, rejecting entirely all the notions of eternity and futurity, and so fitting them to go out of the world as they lived in it, *viz.*, without troubling themselves with what is to come after it.

But I return to the article of impulses of the mind, for I lay a greater weight upon these than upon any of the other discoveries of the invisible world, because they have something in them relating to what we are about, something directing, something to guide us in avoiding the evils that attend us, and to accepting, or rather embracing, opportunities of doing ourselves good when they present, which many times, for want of the knowledge of our way, we irrecoverably let slip.

Voices, apparitions, noises, and all the other affrighting things which unavoidably follow the neighbourhood of spirits in the air we breathe in, seem to have much less signification, as to us, than these seasonable kind whispers to our souls, which, it is plain, are directed for the advantage of life.

It seems hard that mankind should be so open to the secret insinuators, the whispering devils I have been speaking of, who are night and day, sleeping and waking, working upon his senses by the arts and subtleties of hell, to fill his imagination with a thousand devilish contrivances to gratify his vanity and lust; and that our thoughts should be always ready to receive the impressions they make, pressed to follow the infernal counsel, be awake to listen to all his directions, but should be deaf to the instructions of any kind spirits that would influence us for our advantage, and insensible to those impressions which are made upon us for our immediate good by an agent good in itself, and acting from a principle, whatever it be, of good to us.

We have a foolish saying, though taken from something that is more significant than we imagine, when any danger has surprised us—Well, my mind misgave me when I was going about it; well, I knew some mischief would come of it. Did you so? And why then did you do it? Why did you go on? Why, when your mind misgave you, did you not obey the friendly caution? Whence do you think your mind received the speaking, though silent impression? Why did you not listen to it as to a voice? For such a one it was, no doubt; and let all those unthinking people who go on in anything they are upon, contrary to those secret, silent impressions upon their minds, I say, let them know and observe it, they will very seldom fail of meeting some mischief in the way. They will very seldom fail of miscarrying in the way. I say very seldom, because I would not take upon me to prescribe things positively, which the reader will take me up short in, and say, how do I know it? But I will take the liberty to say, I durst be positive in it, relating to myself, and I durst be positive from the nature and reason of the thing.

As to my own experience, I waive saying much of it, but that in general I never slighted these impulses but to my great misfortune; I never listened to and obeyed them, but to my great advantage; but I choose to argue from the reason of them, rather than from my own experience.

As they are evident warnings of what is to come, and are testified daily and hourly by the things coming to pass afterwards, so they are undeniable testimonies that they proceed from some being, intelligent of those things that are at hand, while they are yet to come. If, then, I am satisfied that it is a notice given from a something, be it what it will, which is fully informed of what is attending me, though concealed from me, why should I slight the hint given me from anything that knows what I know not, and especially, for example, for avoiding evils to come?

I know a person, who had so strong an impression upon her mind that the house she was in would be burnt that very night, that she could not go to sleep; the impulse she had upon her mind pressed her not to go to bed, which, however, she resisted and went to bed, but was so terrified with the thought, which, as she called it, run in her mind, that the house would be burnt, that she could not go to sleep.

She had made so much discovery of her apprehensions in the family, that they were all in a fright, and applied themselves to search from the top of the house to the bottom, and to see every fire and every candle safe out, so that, as they all said, it was impossible anything could happen in the house, and they sent to the neighbours on both sides to do the like. Thus far they did well, but had she obeyed the hint, which pressed upon her strangely not to go to bed, she had done much better, for the fire was actually kindled at that very time, though not broken out.

In about an hour after the whole family was in bed, the house just over the way, directly opposite, was all in a flame, and the wind, which was very high, blowing the flame upon the house this gentlewoman lived in, so filled it with smoke and fire in a few moments, the street being narrow, that they had not air to breathe, or time to do anything but jump out of their beds and save their lives. Had she obeyed the hint given, and not gone to bed, she might have saved several things of value which she lost; but as she neglected that, and would go to bed, the moments she had spared to her were but just sufficient to get out of bed, get some clothes on, and get downstairs, for the house was on fire in half a quarter of an hour.

It might be asked here, why could not the same kind spirit have intimated by the same whispers where the danger lay, and from what quarter it was to be expected; in what manner the fire would attack them, and that it would come from the other side of the street, the wind blowing it directly upon them?

To this I answer, that it is our business the more vigilantly to observe and listen to the hints which are given, seeing the intimations are not so particular as we might wish, without inquiring into the reasons why they are given no plainer. We have a great deal of reason to believe the kind spirit that gives these intimations and whispers thus to us, gives us all the light it is permitted to give, and whispers as much, either as it knows, or as it is allowed to communicate; otherwise, why does it give any intimations at all? But, on the other hand, it may be alleged that enough is intimated to suffice for our safety, if we will obey the intimation; and it would be a much more reasonable question to ask why we slight and disobey the impression that we acknowledge to have received, rather than why the intimation was no plainer.

A person of my acquaintance being to go to New England by sea, two ships presented, and the masters earnestly solicited to take him as a passenger; he asked my advice, professing that as well the ships as the captains were perfectly indifferent to him, both the men being equally agreeable to him, and the vessels equally good. I had my eye upon this notion of impulses, and pressed upon him to observe strictly if he had not some secret motion of his mind to one ship rather than another, and he said he had not.

After some time he accidentally met one of the captains, and falling into terms with him, agreed for his passage, and accordingly prepared to go on board; but from the very time that he made the agreement, nay, even while he was making the bargain, he had a strong impression on his mind that he should not go in that ship.

It was some days after this that he told me of these impressions, which increased on him every day; upon which I pressed him earnestly not to go, but to take passage with the other. After he had resolved upon this, he came to me, and told me, that he had with some difficulty and some loss put off the first ship, but now he had the same, or rather stronger aversion to going in the second ship, and had a strong impression on his mind that if he went in the second ship he should be drowned. I bid him consider it a little, and tell me if he had any further intimations of it; and he continued to tell me that he had no rest about his going in either of those ships, and yet his affairs lay so that he was under a necessity of going, and there was no other ship put up upon the Exchange for going.

I pressed him, however, not to venture by any means; I convinced him that those impulses of his mind were the whispers of some kind spirit, that saw things farther than he could, and were certainly given him as cautions to save him from some mischief which he might not foresee; that it could be no evil spirit, because the keeping him back could be no injury to him of such a nature as would gratify the devil in any part of his usual desires; it must therefore be something for his good, and he ought to be very cautious how he slighted the silent admonition. In a word, I prepossessed him so much in aid of the secret impulses of his own mind, that he resolved not to go that year, and he saw clearly afterwards that the secret intimation was from a good hand, for both the ships miscarried; the first being taken by the Turks, and the latter cast away and all the men lost, the ship foundering at sea, as was supposed, for she was never heard of.

I could fill this tract with accounts of this nature, but the reason of the case is stronger than the example; for as it is an intimation of something future, and that is to come to pass, it is certain there is a state in which what is future and must come to pass is known, and why should we not believe the news, if it comes from the place where the certainty of it is known?

Some give all this to a prescience peculiar to the soul itself, and of kin to that we call the second sight; but I see no ground for this but mere presumption. Others call it an afflatus, which they think is a distemper of the brain. Others call it a sympathetic power in the soul, foreboding its own disasters. But all this is short of the thing, for here is not a foreboding only, which indeed is often felt, but is expressed another way; but here is a direct intelligence, a plain intimation of the evil, and warning to avoid it: this must be more than an afflatus, more than a sympathy; this must be from a certain knowledge of a thing that exists not, by a something that does exist; and must be communicated by a converse of spirits unembodied, with the spirit embodied, for its good; unless you will call it Divine revelation, which I see no ground for.

All these reasonings make it abundantly our concern to regard these things, as what we are greatly concerned in; however, that is not the chief use I make of them here, but (1.) they abundantly explain the nature of the world of spirits, and the certainty of an existence after death; (2.) they confirm that the disposition of Providence concerning man, and the event of things, are not so much hidden from the inhabitants of that world as they are from us; as also (3.) that spirits unembodied see with a sight differing from us, and are capable of knowing what attends us, when we know nothing of it ourselves.

This offered many useful reflections to my mind, which, however, 'tis impossible for me to communicate with the same vivacity, or to express with the same life, that the impression they make on my own thoughts came with.

The knowledge of there being a world of spirits, may be many ways useful to us, and especially that of their seeing into futurity, so as to be able to communicate to us, by what means so ever they do it, what we shall or shall not do, or what shall or shall not befall us; to communicate dangers before us so as they may be avoided, and mischiefs awaiting us, so as they may be prevented, and even death itself, so as we may prepare for it; for we may certainly, if we would attend to these things, increase our acquaintance with them, and that very much to our advantage.

I would be far from prompting the crazy imaginations of hypochondriac distempered heads, which run men out to so many extravagancies, and which, in fixing their thoughts upon the real world of spirits, make this an imaginary world of spirits to them; who think they are talked to from the invisible world by the howling of every dog, or the screeching of every owl. I believe it was much of this vapourish dreaming fancy by which the augurs of the Romans determined events from the flying of birds, and the entrails of beasts.

It will be hard for me to be prevailed on to suppose that even those intelligent spirits which I speak of, who are able by such easy ways, as the impulses of our minds, dreams, and the like, to convey the knowledge of things to us, can be put to the necessity, or find reason to make use of the agency of dogs and birds, to convey their notices by; this would be to suppose them to be much more confined in their converse with us, than we evidently find they are; and, on the other hand, would suppose the inanimate world to have more knowledge of the invisible than we have, whereas, on the other hand, we know they have nothing at all to do with it.

There is only this to be said for it, namely, that those inanimate creatures do it involuntarily, and, as it were, under the power of a possession.

I will not affirm but that the invisible inhabitants I have been speaking of may have power to act upon the brute creatures, so as to employ them, or make use of their agency, in the warnings and notices which they give to us of things to come; but that the brutes have otherwise any farther sight of things than we have, I can see nothing at all of that. It is true Balaam's ass saw the angel with the flaming sword standing in the road when the prophet did not, but the reason is plainly expressed; the angel was really there, and actually presenting terror to them with a flaming sword in his hand, only the prophet's eyes were miraculously withheld that he could not see him.

I shall unriddle this mystery of the agency of beasts and birds as far as reason dictates; and it seems to be easy upon the scheme of the nearness of the spirits I am speaking of to us, and their concern to convey intelligence to us. They may, I say, have power to terrify the brutes by horrible apparitions to them, so as to force those howlings and screechings we have been told of, and to do this in such places, and at such times, as shall suit with the circumstances of the family or person concerned, and so far their said extraordinary howlings and screechings may be significant; but that the brutes can either, by sense or by extraordinary sight, have any foreknowledge of things in futurity relating to us, or to themselves, this has no foundation in reason or philosophy, any more than it has in religion. Matter may act upon material objects, and so the understanding or sense of a brute may act upon visible objects, but matter cannot act upon immaterial things, and so the eye of a beast cannot see a spirit, or the mind of a brute act upon futurity, eternity, and the sublime things of a state to come.

What use, then, the spirits we speak of, inhabiting the invisible world, can make of the inanimate world to direct them, as missionaries to us, I do not see, neither did I in all my altitudes perceive they employed any such agents.

It is from the misunderstanding of these things that we place abundance of incidents, merely fortuitous, to the devil's account, which he knows nothing of. Many a storm blows that is none of his raising; many a midnight noise happens that is none of his making. If Satan or his instruments had one tenth part of the power, either of the air, or in the air, or over the elements, that we give them in our imaginations, we should have our houses burnt every night, hurricanes raised in the air, floods made in the country, and, in a word, the world would not be habitable; but you remember I told you, as powerful as he is, he is chained, he has a great clog at his foot, and he can do nothing by violence, or without permission.

I might hint here at abundance of idle, ridiculous devils, that we are daily told of, that come and only make game among us, put out our candles, throw chairs and stools about the house, break glasses, make a smoke, a stink of brimstone, &c, whereas, after all, the devil has no more sulphur about him than other folks, and I can answer for it that Satan is not disposed for mirth; all the frolics and gambols we ascribe to him, I dare say, are antics of our own brain. I heard of a house in Essex which they told me was haunted, and that every night the devil or a spirit, call it which you will, came into such a room, and made a most terrible knocking, as if it had a hammer or a mallet, and this for two or three hours together. At length, upon looking about in an empty closet in that room, there was found an old mallet, and this was presently concluded to be the mallet which the devil made such a noise with, so it was taken away; but the next night they said the devil made such a racket for want of the mallet, that they were much more disturbed than before, so they were obliged to leave the mallet there again, and every night the devil would come and knock in the window, for two or three hours together, with that mallet. I have seen the room and the mallet, in neither of which was anything extraordinary, but never heard the noise, though I sat up to wait for it, nor after causing the mallet to be taken away was there any noise; belike the mannerly spirit would not disturb us who were strangers.

This passed for a most eminent piece of walking or haunting, and all the difficulty was to inquire to what purpose all this disturbance was made, seeing there was no end answered in it, and I always thought the devil was too full of business to spend his time to no manner of purpose.

At last all the cheat was discovered, *viz.*, that a monkey, kept in a house three or four houses from it, had found the way into that room, and came every night almost about midnight, and diverted himself with the frolic, and then went home again.

If these things were not frequently detected, it would be a great scandal upon the devil that he had nothing to employ himself in more significant than rapping all night with a hammer to fright and disturb the neighbours, making noises, putting out candles, and the like. When we come into the invisible state, of which we now know so little, we shall be easily convinced that the devil is otherwise employed, and has business of much more importance upon his hands.

It would be very insignificant to have us so frequently warned against Satan's devices, to have us be cautioned to be sober and vigilant, knowing that our adversary, the devil, goes about like a roaring lion, seeking, &c. All these things import that he is diligent in attacking us, watching all advantages, hunting as down, circumventing, waiting, and constantly plying us with snares that he may trepan and devour us. This admits not any of those simple, ludicrous, and senseless digressions which we set him to work upon in our imaginations.

Perhaps it may be expected I should enter here upon the subject of apparitions, and discourse with equal certainty of that undecided question concerning the reality of apparitions, and whether departed souls can revisit the place of their former existence, take up shapes, bodies, and visible and apparent beings, assume voices, and concern themselves with the affairs of life, of families, persons, and even of estates, and the like, as many have affirmed they have been witnesses to.

I must be allowed to leave this where I find it. There are some difficulties which I am not yet got over in it, nor have I been elevated high enough to determine that point, and shall not venture to decide it without more certainty than I am yet arrived to.

I would warn all people not to suffer their imagination to form shapes and appearances where there are none; and I may take upon me to say that the devil himself does not appear half so often as some people think they see him: fancy governs many people, and a sick brain forms strange things to itself; but it does not follow from thence that nothing can appear because nothing does at that time.

However, as my design is to instruct, not amuse, so, I say, I forbear to enter upon a subject which I must leave as doubtful as I find it, and consequently talk of to no purpose.

I have heard of a man that would allow the reality of apparitions, but would have it be nothing but the devil; that the souls of men departed or good spirits never appeared. It happened that to this very man something appeared, as he said, and insisted upon it to the last. He said he saw the shape of an ancient man pass by him in the dusk of the evening, who, holding up his hand as it were in a threatening posture, said aloud, "O wicked creature! repent, repent." He was exceedingly terrified, and consulted several people about it, who all advised him seriously to take the advice, for his life made it well known, it seems, that he stood in need of it; but being seriously debating about it, one of his friends asked what he thought of the apparition, and whether it was any of the devil's business to bid him repent. This puzzled his thoughts, and, in a word, he grew a very sober man; but, after all, it was a real man, and no apparition, that spoke to him, though his frighted fancy made him affirm that he vanished out of his sight, which he did not; and the person who did it, being a grave and pious gentleman, met him by mere accident, without any design, and spoke as he did, from the knowledge he had of his being indeed a most wretched wicked fellow. By the way, the gentleman had the opportunity to hear the use that was made of it, and to hear himself mistaken for an apparition of the devil, but he was so prudent as not to discover it to the man, lest the reformation, which was the consequence of the fright, should wear off, when he should know that there was nothing in the thing but what was common.

If we would always make the like good use of Satan's real appearances, I do not know but it would go a great way to banish him from the visible world; for I am well assured he would very seldom visit us, if he thought his coming would do us any good; at least, he would never come but when he was sent, he would never come willingly; for he is so absolutely at the Divine disposal, that if Heaven commands he must go, though it were to do the good he abhors. Not that I believe Heaven ever thinks fit to employ him in doing good; if ever he is let loose, 't is to act in judgment as an instrument of vengeance, and some are of opinion he is often employed as a destroying angel, though I do not grant that; I can hardly think the justice of God would gratify Satan's gust of doing evil so far as to suffer him to be even so much as an executioner; but that is by the way.

I have another turn to give this part of my observations, which though, perhaps, some may not think so much to the purpose as entering into a critical inquiry after the devil's particular mission in these cases, yet I think otherwise.

I have observed that some desperate people make a very ill use of the general notion, that there are no apparitions, nor spirits at all; and really, the use they make of it is worse than the extreme of those who, as I said, make visions and devils of everything they see or hear. For these men persuade themselves there are no spirits at all, either in the visible or invisible world, and, carrying it on farther, they next annihilate the devil, and believe nothing about him, either of one kind or another.

This would not be of so much bad consequence if it was not always followed by a worse, namely, that when they have prevailed with themselves to believe there is no devil, the next thing is, and they soon come to it, that there is no God, and so atheism takes its rise in the same sink, with a carelessness about futurity.

I have no mind to enter upon an argument to prove the being of our Maker, and to illustrate His power by words, who has so many undeniable testimonies in the breasts of every rational being to prove His existence. But I have a mind to conclude this work with a short history of some atheists, which I met with many years ago, and whether the facts are testified or not, may be equally useful in the application, if you do not think them a little too religious for you.

Some years ago there was a young gentleman, a scholar at the university, eminent for learning and virtue, of prompt parts and great proficiency, insomuch that he was taken great notice of by the masters and fellows, and every one promised fair in their thoughts for him, that he would be a great man. It happened, whether from his earnest desire of more knowledge, or the opinion of his own great capacity, I know not which, that this gentleman, falling upon the study of divinity, grew so opinionative, so very positive and dogmatic in his notions in religious things, that by degrees it came to this height, that his tutor saw plainly that he had little more than notions in all his religious pretences to knowledge, and concluded he would either grow enthusiastic or obstinately profane and atheistic.

He had three chums, or companions, in his studies, and they all fell into the same error, as well by the consequence of a great deal of wit and little grace, as by the example and leading of this other young gentleman, who was, indeed, their oracle almost in everything.

As his tutor, who was a very good man, feared for him, so it came to pass with him and all the rest; for they ran up their superficial notions in divinity to such a height that, instead of reasoning themselves into good principles of religion, they really reasoned themselves out of all religion whatsoever, running on to expunge every right idea from their minds; pretending those things really were not, of which they could not define both how and what they were, they proceeded to deny the existence of their Maker, the certainty of a future state, a resurrection, a judgment, a heaven, or a hell.

They were not contented to satisfy themselves with these impious foundations, but they set up to dispute in private societies against all revealed religion, thereby bringing on themselves the curse denounced in Scripture against those that do evil and teach men so to do; in a little time they grew so public that more company came in, and, which was worse, many joined with them in principle, or, as I should rather have said, in casting off all principles, and they began to be famous in the place, though to the offence of all good men, and were called "The Atheistical Club."

They soon began to see sober, religious people shun them, and in some time, upon information given, they were obliged, by authority, to separate for fear of punishment, so that they could not hold their public disputations as they began to do, yet they abated nothing of their wicked custom; and this dreadful creature, who set up at the head of the rest, began to be so open in his blasphemies that he was at length obliged to fly from the university.

However, he went a great while before it came to that; and though he had been often admonished, yet, instead of reclaiming, he grew the more impious, making the most sacred things his jest and the subject of his ridicule. He gave out that he could frame a new gospel, and a much better system of religion than that which they called Christian; and that if he would trouble himself to go about it, he would not fail to draw in as great a part of the world to run after him as had been after any other. I care not to repeat any of his blasphemous words; it is not to be supposed there can be any blasphemous abominable thing that this set of wicked wretched young men did not run into, neither any wickedness of that kind within their reach which they did not commit.

It would be too long to enter into the particular history of these men, and how it pleased God to dispose of them; they might be in number, before they separated, about twenty-two in all; I shall tell you of some of them, however, who did not run such lengths as the rest. There was a young man who frequented their society, though, as he afterwards said, he was rather persuaded to be among them than to be one of them; he had, however, too much yielded to their delusions; and though they made him very much their jest, because they found he still retained some little sense of a God and of a future state in his mind, yet he had yielded dreadfully to them, and began to do so more and more every day.

It happened one day this young man was going to their hellish society, and not minding the weather, the clouds gathered over his head, and he was stopped by a sudden shower of rain in the street. It rained so very hard that it obliged him to stand up in the gateway of an inn for some time; while he was standing here a great flash of lightning more than ordinarily surprised him; it seems the fire came so directly in his face that he felt the very warmth of it, and was exceedingly startled; in the same moment almost, as is natural in the case, followed such a clap of thunder that perfectly astonished him. The rain continuing kept him in the gateway, as I said, for a good while, till he had time for such reflections as these: "Where am I going? What am I going about? Who is it has stopped me thus? Why are these thunders, these rains, and this lightning thus terrible? and whence are they?" And with the rest came in this thought, warm and swift as the lightning which had terrified him before, "What if there should be a God! what will become of me then?" Terrified with these things he starts

492

out of the gateway into the street, notwithstanding the wet, and runs back through the rain, saying to himself as he went, "I will go among them no more!"

When he came home to his chambers he fell into dreadful agonies of mind, and at length broke out thus: "What have I been doing! have I been denying the Power that made me? despising that God whose fire flashed just now in my face; and which, had not that mercy I have abused interposed, might have burnt me to death? What kind of creature am I?" While he was thus giving vent to his reflections a near relation of his—a pious, good man, who had often used to speak very plainly to him of the horrid sin he was guilty of—happened to come to visit him.

The young man had thrown himself upon his bed, and had, with the deepest sense of his madness and most serious reproaches of himself for his horrid life, been expressing himself to his friend, and he had been comforting him in the best manner he could, when, after a while, he desired his friend to retire that he might be a little alone and might give vent to his thoughts with the more freedom; and his friend taking a book in his hand stayed in the outer room.

In this interval came another scholar to the door, who was one of the wicked company I mentioned just now. He came not to visit this first gentleman, but to call him to go with him to the usual meeting of their dreadful society; and knocking at his chamber door, this gentleman who was left in the chamber stepped to the door, and, looking through a little grate, not only knew the person, but knew him to be one of the wicked company I have been speaking of. Now, as he was very loath his friend should have such an interruption to the good disposition he was then in, so, above all, he was loath he should be persuaded to go any more among that miserable gang; wherefore he opened the door a little way, so as he was not very distinctly seen, and spoke aloud in the person of his friend thus: "O sir, beseech them all to repent; for, depend upon it, there is a God; tell them I say so;" and with that he shut the door upon him violently, giving him no time to reply, and, going back into his friend's room, took no notice of anybody having been at the door at all.

The person who knocked at the door you may suppose was one of the leaders of the company, a young scholar of good parts and sense, but debauched by that horrid crew, and one that had made himself eminent for his declared opposition to all the common notions of religion; a complete atheist, and publicly so, without God or the desire of God in the world. However, as he afterwards confessed, the repulse he met with at the door, and which he thought came from his friend, gave him a strange shock at first and filled him with horror. He went down the college stairs in the greatest confusion imaginable, and went musing along a good way, not knowing where he was or whither he went, and in that embarrassment of thought went a whole street out of the way. The words had made an unusual impression upon his mind, but he had his other surprises too; for he thought his friend, for he believed firmly that it was he that had spoken to him, had treated him very rudely.

Sometimes he resented it, and reflected upon it as an affront, and once or twice was upon the point of going back again to him to know the reason of his using him so, and to demand satisfaction; but still the words, "There is a God," dwelt upon his mind. "And what if it should be so?" says he, "what then?" Upon this question to himself, the answer immediately occurred to his mind. "What then? Why, then, I am undone! For, have not I declared war against the very notion, defied all the pretenders to it as mere enthusiasts and men of whimsy?" However, after these thoughts his mind cooled a little again, and it offered to him, no doubt injected by an evil spirit, that he should not trouble himself with inquiring into it one way or another, but be easy.

This pacified him for a little while, and he shook off the surprise he was in; the hardened temper seemed to return, and he kept on his way towards the hellish society that he was going to before. But still the words returned upon him, "There is a God," and began to bring some terror with it upon his mind; and the last words of his friend came into his mind often, "tell them I say so." This filled him with a curiosity which he could not withstand, *viz.*, of going back to his friend and inquiring of him what discoveries he had made of this kind? How he came to have changed his mind so suddenly? And, especially, how he was arrived to a certainty of the thing?

I told you that there had been a great shower of rain, which had stopped the first young gentleman in his way out; it seems the day was still showery, and a little rain happening to fall again as this gentleman went by a bookseller's shop, he stops at the door to stand up a little out of the wet.

There happened to be sitting in the shop reading a book a gentleman of his acquaintance, though far differing from him in his principles, being a very sober, studious, religious young man, a student in divinity of the same college, who, looking up, called him in, and after a few common salutes he whispers in his ear.

Student. I was looking in an old book here just now, and began the following short dialogue; and I found four lines written on the back of the title-page which put me in mind of you.

Atheist. Me! why did they put you in mind of me?

Stud. I'll tell you presently; come hither. [He retires into a back room, and calls the other after him.]

Ath. Well, now tell me.

Stud. Because I think they are very fit for such an atheistical wretch as you to read.

Ath. You are very civil.

Stud. You know you deserve it.

Ath. Come, let me see them, however.

Stud. Let me look in your face all the while, then.

Ath. No, you shan't.

Stud. Then you shan't see them.

Ath. Well, let it alone, then.

Stud. Come, give me your hand; you shall see them if you will promise to read them over three times.

Ath. There's my hand, I'll read them out to you.

Stud. I'll hold your hand all the while, because I'll be sure of your performance.

Ath. I'll warrant you I'll read them. [He reads.]

But if it should fall out, as who can tell,
That there may be a God, a heaven, and hell, ★
Had I not best consider well, for fear
'T should be too late when my mistakes appear?

[★ He held him by the hand till that word, and then let it go, pressing gently one of his fingers.]

Stud. Well, what do you say to them?

Ath. I'll tell you my thoughts farther by-and-by, but first tell me, what did you press my hand for when you let it go?

Stud. Did you feel no motion within you when you read those words, "*there may be a God*"?

Ath. What motion? What do you talk of?

Stud. Come, do not deny it, for I am a witness against you.

Ath. Witness, for what? I have killed nobody, I have robbed nobody; if you would turn informer, I value not your evidence.

Stud. No, no, I shall not turn informer of that kind, but I am a witness in your Maker's behalf.

Ath. What can you witness?

Stud. I'll tell you what I can witness; I can testify that your own conscience is against you in your impious denying the existence of that God that gave you life; you could not conceal it; I tell you I felt it.

Ath. How do you pretend to know what my conscience dictates to me, or what the result of secret reflections may be in the mind? You may be mistaken; have a care, you know you are not to bear false witness.

Stud. 'T is in vain to struggle with it—' is not to be concealed; you betrayed yourself, I tell you.

Ath. How betrayed myself? you are mighty dark in your expressions.

Stud. Did I not tell you I would look in your face all the while you read? Did I not see into the distraction of your soul? Did you not turn pale at the very words, when your tongue said, "there may be a God"? Was there not a visible horror in your countenance when you read the word heaven? a horror which signified a sense of your having no share in it, or hope about it? And did I not feel a trembling in your very joints, as I held you by the hand, when you read the word hell?

Ath. And was that it you held me by the hand for?

Stud. Indeed it was; I was persuaded I should find it, for I could never believe that an atheist had always a hell within him, even while he braved it out against a hell without him.

Ath. You speak enough to fright one; how can you say so positively a thing which you cannot be sure of?

Stud. Never add sin to sin; 't is in vain to deny it.

Ath. Well, well, it's none of your business; who made you my father confessor? [He is a little angry.]

Stud. Nay, do not be angry with your friend; and though you are, do but take the hint, and be as angry as you will.

Ath. What hint? What is it you aim at? Your hints are all so general, I can make nothing of them.

Stud. I aim at nothing but your eternal felicity; I thought those lines very apposite to your case, and was wishing you had them before I happened to see you. I thought that such a reflection in the case of atheism, so natural, so plain, especially blessed from Him whose secret voice can effectually reach the mind, might be some means to open your eyes.

Ath. Open my eyes!—to what?

Stud. To something that I am persuaded you see already in part, though I find you struggle hard against your own convictions.

Ath. What is this something you speak of?

Stud. I mean in a few words what the lines you have read mean, *viz.*, that perhaps there may be a God, a heaven, and hell.

Ath. I don't know but there may. [He observes tears stand in his eyes.]

Stud. Well, I see it begins to touch you; if you are uncertain, that is a step to conviction; and the rest of the words you have read are a most natural inference in your case.

You'd best consider well, for fear
'T should be too late when your mistakes appear.

Ath. What would you have me consider?

Stud. I am not able to enter into that part now; the first thing is to persuade you to look in; listen to the voice of conscience; I am satisfied you stand convicted at that bar; you cannot plead not guilty there.

Ath. Convicted of what?

Stud. Of having acted contrary to the light of nature, of reason, and indeed of common-sense; most impiously denied the God whose air you breathe in, whose earth you tread on, whose food you eat, whose clothes you wear, who is your life, and will be your Judge.

Ath. I do not absolutely deny; I tell you I don't know but there may be a God.

Stud. Don't you know but there may! O sir, I beseech you, repent; for certainly there is a God, depend upon it; I say so.

Ath. You fright me. [He starts and looks surprised.]

Stud. Indeed I think it may well fright you.

Ath. But you fright me upon a quite different account from what you imagine; I am indeed very much surprised, and so would you too, if you knew the circumstance.

Stud. What circumstance?

Ath. Pray did you bear those words spoken anywhere to-day before you spoke them?

Stud. No, not I.

Ath. Was you at Mr. ——'s chamber about half-an-hour ago?

Stud. I have not been there this month past; I have given over visiting him, and all such as he is, long ago.

Ath. Have you seen him to-day, or when did you last see him?—

did he speak those words to you, or you to him?

Stud. I have not seen him since I saw him with you about fourteen days ago, when your discourse (even both of you) was so blasphemous and so atheistical as made my very heart tremble, and I resolved never to come into company with either of you again, and it was that very discourse that made me think of you when I found those lines in this book. I should think it an evident discovery of God, and what I might hope should best forward your conviction, if His providence should have sent you to this door at that minute to receive the hint on this occasion.

Ath. There is something more than common in everything that has happened to me today.

Stud. If you would explain yourself a little I might say more; but you know very well I cannot make the least guess at what you mean.

Ath. Ask me no more questions; there must be a God or a devil in being. [He looks wildly and amazed.]

Stud. Dear friend, there are both, depend upon it; but I beseech you, compose your mind, and do not receive the conviction with horror, but with comfort and hope.

Ath. One or other of them has been concerned in what has happened to me today; it has been a strange day with me.

Stud. If it relates only to these things, perhaps it may be of use to you to communicate the particulars, at least it may give some vent to the oppression of thought which you seem to be under; you cannot open your mind to one that has more earnest desires to do you good, though perhaps not sufficiently furnished to advise you.

Ath. I must tell it or burst. [Here he gave him the whole story of his going to his friend's chamber in order to take him with him to the wicked club they had kept; and how he had met him at the door, and said the same words to him that the Student had repeated, and when he had done, says he to his friend]—And who now do you think must dictate the same words to him, and afterwards to you, to say to me on the same occasion?

Stud. Who do I think? Nay, who do you think?

Ath. Who? the devil, if there is a devil.

Stud. Why, do you think the devil preaches repentance? [He stands stock still, and says not a word, which the other perceiving, goes on]— Pray think seriously, for I see it does a little touch your reason. Is it likely the devil should bid either of us, or both of us, entreat you to repent? Is it the devil, think you, that would pronounce the certainty of the great truth I speak of? Is it his business to convince you that there is a God?

Ath. That's very true.

Stud. One thing, however, I'll say in Satan's behalf, and that is, that he never came up to your height of sinning. The devil has frequently set up himself, and persuaded poor deluded people to worship him as a God; but, to do him justice, he never had the impudence to deny the being of a God; that 's a sin purely human, and even among men very modern too, the invention of witty men, as they call themselves—a way they have lately found out to cherish superlative wickedness, and flatter themselves that they shall have no audit of their accounts in a future state; of whom it may indeed be said in that particular, they have outsinned the devil.

Ath. Indeed I think we have.

Stud. I wish you would consider a little farther of it.

Ath. What can men consider that have gone that length?

Stud. Yes, yes; remember what St. Peter said to Simon the sorcerer.

Ath. What was that?

Stud. Read Acts viii. 22; "Repent, therefore, of this thy wickedness, and pray God, if perhaps the thought of thine heart may be forgiven thee."

Ath. No, no; the last of your verses is against me there most directly.

It's all too late, now my mistakes appear.

Stud. No, no; remember what you said, that it must be a God or a devil.

Ath. What is that to the purpose?

Stud. Why, you seemed satisfied that it could not be from the devil.

Ath. But what the better am I for that, if the other is my enemy?

Stud. Much the better if it was from God, if the words you heard were from God, and that two unconcerned persons so eminently concurred in speaking to you; you cannot believe God would bid you repent if it was too late, or if He were your irreconcilable enemy; on the contrary, if you believe it to be the voice of His providence, you ought to listen to and obey it.

Ath. You have a strange power of persuasion, there is no resisting your argument.

Stud. It is not in me to persuade, but Heaven may make use of me to convince.

Ath. To convince is to persuade; I am convinced that I have been a dreadful wretch.

Stud. I am persuaded you were convinced of that before.

Ath. I cannot deny but my heart always struck me—a kind of chill horror ran through my veins, when I have uttered the blasphemous opinions that I have been drawn into; my very blood stagnated at the thought of it, and I look back on it with astonishment.

Stud. I tell you, I felt a tremor even in your flesh when you read the words, a God, a heaven, a hell.

Ath. I confess to you my very heart sunk within me at the words *who can tell*; my soul answered that I could tell myself that it both is and must be so.

Stud. Conscience is a faithful and never-failing evidence in his Maker's behalf.

Ath. It is a very terrible evidence against me, and where will it end?

Stud. I hope it will end where it began, I mean in a heavenly call to you to repentance.

Ath. That is not always the consequence of conviction.

Stud. You must therefore distinguish again of what proceeds from heaven, what from hell, the voice of God, and the voice of the devil; the first calls upon you to repent, the last prompts you to despair.

Ath. Despair seems to be the natural consequence of denying God, for it shuts out the power that can alone restore the mind.

Stud. The greater is that love which refuses to be shut out, that sends such a heavenly summons to you to repent, and in so eminent a manner; it is not your having been an enemy, a blasphemer, a denier of God; Peter denied Christ three times, nay, the third time he even abjured Him, and yet, mark the words—the Lord looked on him, and immediately he repented.

Ath. My case is worse than Peter's.

Stud. And yet you see you are called on to repent.

Ath. I think you are called to make me repent; there's no answering you.

Stud. Amen; may I have the blessing of being an instrument to so good a work; there seems to be something extraordinary in it all.

Ath. It's all a surprise to me how came I hither.

Stud. Nay, how came I hither?—How came this book here?—Who writ the lines in the frontispiece?—How came I to read them?—'Tis all a dream to me!

Ath. How came you to think of me upon the reading them? And how came I here just at the moment, and out of my way too?

[He lifts up his hands and cries out, "There is a God, certainly there is; I am convinced of it; it must be so."]

Stud. Nothing more certain; nor is there any doubt but all these things are of Him.

Ath. But there are yet greater things behind; I wish you would go with me to my friend Mr. ——'s chamber; I am persuaded something yet more extraordinary must have befallen him.

Stud. With all my heart.

[They both go to the first gentleman's chamber; and find him at home, very much out of order, but willing enough to discourse with them.]

Ath. Well, friend of mine, I hope you are better disposed to your friends than when I saw you last.

Gent. Truly, when I saw you last, I was disposed of by the devil, and so, I doubt, were you; I hope I shall never come into that horrid place again.

Ath. What horrid place?

Gent. You know where I mean; I tremble at the very thoughts of the place, and much more of the company; I wish I could prevail upon you to come no more among them too; I assure you, if I know myself, and if God would assist me to do it, I would much rather go to a stake to be burnt.

Stud. I rejoice in such an alteration, sir, upon you, and I hope our friend here is of the same mind; long may it continue in you both.

Ath. Well, pray tell us something of the occasion of this happy alteration, for it will seem still more strange how you came to be instrumental to my change, if I know nothing of the means that brought about your own.

Gent. Mine! I assure you it was all from heaven; not the light that shone about St. Paul was more immediately from heaven than the stroke that touched my soul; it is true I had no voice without, but a voice has spoken (I hope) effectually to my understanding; I had voice enough to tell me how I was in the hands of that Power, that Majesty, that God, whom I had wickedly, and with a hardness not to be expressed, disowned and denied.

Stud. Pray, sir, if you care to have it known, give us some account of the particulars of this wonderful thing.

Gent. Sir, I shall do it freely; I think I ought not to conceal it.

[Here he gives an account of the surprise he was in by the lightning, how he was stopped in his way to his wicked company, and went back to his chamber.]

Ath. Well, now I will no more wonder at the salutation you gave me when I came to call you, but thank you for it.

Gent. What salutation?

Ath. Why, when I was at your chamber about two hours ago.

Gent. You at my chamber!

Ath. Nay, you need not conceal it, for I have told our friend here all the story.

Gent. I know nothing of what you talk of, much less what you mean.

Ath. Nay, what need you go about to conceal it? I tell you I do not take it ill; I hope I may have reason to be thankful for what you said to me, and look upon it as spoken from Heaven; for I assure you, it has been an introduction to that light in my thoughts which I hope shall never be extinguished.

Gent. Dear friend, as I believe you are serious, so I hope you believe I am so; I profess I know nothing of all you talk about.

Ath. Why, was I not at your door this afternoon a little after the great shower of rain?

Gent. Not that I know of.

Ath. Why, did not I knock at your chamber door, and you come to the door yourself and speak to me?

Gent. Not today, I am very sure of it.

Ath. Am I awake? Are you Mr——? am I sure we are all alive, and know what we are saying, and to whom?

Gent. I beseech you unriddle yourself, for I am surprised.

Ath. Why, about three o'clock this afternoon I came to this chamber-door; I knocked; you came and opened the door; I began to speak, you interrupted me, and——

[Here he repeats the passage at large, and his own thoughts and resentment, as before.]

Gent. Depend upon it, was some voice from heaven, it was nothing of mine; I have not been at the door since two of the clock, when I came first in, but have been on the bed, or in my study ever since, wholly taken up with my own thoughts, and very much indisposed.

[The young man turns pale, and falls into a swoon.]

There was a great deal more belonging to this story, but it is too long for the present purpose; I have related this part on several accounts, and it hits the purpose I am upon many ways.

(1.) Here is a visible evidence of God, and of His being and nature, fixed so in the mind, that not the most hardened atheist can deny it; nature recoils at every endeavour to suppress it, and the very pulsation of his blood shall discover and acknowledge it.

(2.) Yet even in this we see how the power of imagination may be worked up by the secret agency of an unknown hand, how many things concurred to make this man believe he had seen an apparition, and heard a voice; and yet there was nothing in it but the voice of a man unseen and mistaken. The young man was so surprised at his friend's declaring that he knew nothing of his coming there, that he concluded it had been all a vision or apparition that opened the door, and that it was a voice that had spoken to him, of what kind he knew not; and the reflection upon this surprised him so much as threw him into a swoon, and yet here was neither vision or voice, but that of an ordinary person, and one who meant well and said well.

It is not to be doubted but that many an apparition related with a great deal of certainty in the world, and of which good ends have followed, has been no more than such a serious mistake as this.

But before I leave it, let me observe that this should not at all hinder us from making a very good use of such things; for many a voice may be directed from heaven that is not immediately spoken from thence; as when the children cried Hosannah to our Saviour, they fulfilled the Scripture, which said, "*Out of the mouths of babes and sucklings Thou hast ordained praise;*" so doubtless He that made all things and created all things, may appoint instruction to be given by fortuitous accidents, and may direct concurring circumstances to touch and affect the mind as much and as effectually as if they had been immediate and miraculous.

Thus was the two persons happening to say the same words to the atheist, the strange reading of those lines when the person came into the bookseller's shop, the incident of his running into the shop for shelter, and many the like things of the same nature, and ordered in the same manner as the cock crowing when Peter denied Christ, which, though wonderfully concurrent with what his blessed Master had foretold, yet was no extraordinary thing in a cock, who naturally crows at such a time of the morning.

In a word, all these things serve to convince us of a great superintendency of divine Providence in the minutest affairs of this world, of a manifest existence of the invisible world, of the reality of spirits, and of the intelligence between us and them. I hope I have said nothing of it to misguide anybody, or to assist them to delude themselves, having spoken of it with the utmost seriousness in my design, and with a sincere desire for a general good.

APPENDIX 1

CAPTAIN WOODES ROGERS'S ACCOUNT OF THE RESCUE OF ALEXANDER SELKIRK. *A CRUISING VOYAGE ROUND THE WORLD.*

At seven this morning (Jan. 31, 1709) we made the island of Juan Fernandez. . . . In the afternoon we hoisted our pinnace out; Captain Dover, with the boat's crew, went in her to go ashore, though we could not be less than four leagues off. As soon as the pinnace was gone, I vent on board the *Duchess*, who admired our boat attempting going ashore at that distance from land. 'Twas against my inclination, but to oblige Captain Dover I consented to let her go. As soon as it was dark we saw a light ashore. Our boat was then about a league from the island, and bore away for the ships as soon as she saw the lights. We put our lights abroad for the boat, though some were of opinion the lights we saw were our boat's lights; but as night came on, it appeared too large for that. We fired our quarterdeck gun and several muskets, showing lights in our mizen and fore shrouds, that our boat might find us whilst we plied in the lee of the island. About two in the morning our boat came on board, having been two hours on board the *Duchess*, that took them up astern of us; we were glad they got well off, because it began to blow. We are all convinced the light is on the shore, and design to make our ships ready to engage, believing them to be French ships at anchor, and we must either fight them or want water. We stood on the back side along the south end of the island, in order to lay in with the first southerly wind, which Captain Dampier told us generally blows there all day long. In the morning, being past the island, we tacked to lay it in close aboard the land, and about ten o'clock opened the south end of the island, and ran close aboard the land that begins to make the north-east side.

The flaws came heavy off the shore, and we were forced to reef our topsails when we opened the middle bay, where we expected to find our enemy, but saw all clear, and no ships in that nor the other bay next the north-west end. These two bays are all that ships ride in which recruit on this island; but the middle bay is by much the best. We guessed there had been ships there, but that they were gone on sight of us. We sent our yawl ashore about noon, with Captain Dover,

Mr. Fry, and six men, all armed. Meanwhile we and the *Duchess* kept turning to get in, and such heavy flaws came off the land, that we were forced to let go our topsail sheet, keeping all hands to stand by our sails, for fear of the wind's carrying them away; but when the flaws were gone we had little or no wind. These flaws proceeded from the land, which is very high in the middle of the island. Our boat did not return; so we sent our pinnace, with the men armed, to see what was the occasion of the yawl's stay, for we were afraid that the Spaniards had a garrison there, and might have seized them. We put out a signal for our boat, and the *Duchess* showed a French ensign. Immediately our pinnace returned from the shore, and brought abundance of cray-fish, with a man clothed in goat's skins, who looked wilder than the first owners of them.

He had been on the island four years and four months, being left there by Captain Stradling in the *Cinque Ports*; his name was Alexander Selkirk, a Scotchman, who had been master of the *Cinque Ports*, a ship that came here last with Captain Dampier, who told me that this was the best man in her; so I immediately agreed with him to be a mate on board our ship. 'Twas he that made the fire last night when he saw our ships, which he judged to be English. During his stay here he saw several ships pass by, but only two came to anchor. As he went to view them, he found them to be Spaniards, and retired from them, upon which they shot at him. Had they been French, he would have submitted, but chose to risk his dying alone on the island rather than fall into the hands of the Spaniards in these parts; because he apprehended they would murder him, or make a slave of him in the mines, for he feared they would spare no stranger that might be capable of discovering the South Seas.

The Spaniards had landed before he knew what they were, and they came so near him that he had much ado to escape; for they not only shot at him, but pursued him to the woods, where he climbed to the top of a tree, at the foot of which they made water, and killed several goats just by, but went off without discovering him. He told us that he was born at Largo, in the county of Fife, in Scotland, and was bred a sailor from his youth. The reason of his being left here was a difference betwixt him and his captain; which, together with the ship's being leaky, made him willing rather to stay here than go along with him at first; and when he was at last willing, the captain would not receive him. He had been in the island before to wood and water, when two of the ship's company were left upon it for six months till the ship returned, being chased thence by two French South Sea ships.

He had with him his clothes and bedding, with a firelock, some powder, bullets, and tobacco, a hatchet, a knife, a kettle, a Bible, some practical pieces, and his mathematical instruments and books. He diverted and provided for himself as well as he could, but for the first eight months had much ado to bear up against melancholy, and the terror of being left alone in such a desolate place. He built two huts with pimento trees, covered them with long grass, and lined them with the skins of goats, which he killed with his gun as he wanted, so long as his powder lasted, which was but a pound; and that being almost spent, he got fire by rubbing two sticks of pimento wood together upon his knee. In the lesser hut, at some distance from the other, he dressed his victuals; and in the larger he slept and employed himself in reading, singing psalms, and praying; so that he said he was a better Christian while in this solitude than ever he was before, or than, he was afraid, he should ever be again.

At first he never ate anything till hunger constrained him, partly for grief, and partly for want of bread and salt. Nor did he go to bed till he could watch no longer; the pimento wood, which burnt very clear, served him both for firing and candle, and refreshed him with its fragrant smell. He might have had fish enough, but could not eat them for want of salt, because they occasioned a looseness; except crayfish, which are there as large as lobsters, and very good. These he sometimes boiled, and at other times broiled, as he did his goats' flesh, of which he made very good broth, for they are not so rank as ours. He kept an account of 500 that he killed while there, and caught as many more, which he marked on the ear, and let go. When his powder failed, he took them by speed of feet; for his way of living and continual exercise of walking and running cleared him of all gross humours; so that he ran with wonderful swiftness through the woods, and up the rocks and hills, as we perceived when we employed him to catch goats for us. We had a bulldog, which we sent, with several of our nimblest runners, to help him in catching goats; but he distanced and tired both the dog and the men, catched the goats, and brought them to us on his back.

He told us that his agility in pursuing a goat had once like to have cost him his life: he pursued it with so much eagerness that he catched hold of it on the brink of a precipice, of which he was not aware, the bushes hiding it from him; so that he fell with the goat down the said precipice, a great height, and was so stunned and bruised with the fall that he narrowly escaped with his life; and when he came to his senses, found the goat dead under him. He lay there about twenty-four hours, and was scarce able to crawl to his hut, which was about a mile distant, or to stir abroad again for ten days.

He came at last to relish his meat well enough without salt or bread; and in the season had plenty of good turnips, which had been sowed there by Captain Dampier's men, and have now overspread some acres of ground. He had enough of good cabbage from the cabbage trees, and seasoned his meat with the fruit of the pimento trees, which is the same as Jamaica pepper, and smells deliciously. He found also a black pepper called *malageta*, which was very good to expel wind, and against griping in the guts.

He soon wore out all his shoes and clothes by running through the woods; and at last, being forced to shift without them, his feet became so hard that he ran everywhere without difficulty, and it was some time before he could wear shoes after we found him; for, not being used to any so long, his feet swelled when he came first to wear them again.

After he had conquered his melancholy, he diverted himself sometimes by cutting his name on the trees, and the time of his being left, and continuance there. He was at first much pestered with cats and rats, that bred in great numbers from some of each species which had got ashore from ships that put in there to wood and water. The rats gnawed his feet and clothes whilst asleep, which obliged him to cherish the cats with his goats' flesh, by which many of them became so tame, that they would lie about him in hundreds, and soon delivered him from the rats. He likewise tamed some kids, and to divert himself would, now and then, sing and dance with them and his cats; so that, by the care of Providence, and vigour of his youth, being now about thirty years old, he came at last to conquer all the inconveniences of his solitude, and to be very easy.

When his clothes wore out, he made himself a coat and a cap of goat's skins, which he stitched together with little thongs of the same, that he cut with his knife. He had no other needle but a nail; and when his knife was wore to the back, he made others, as well as he could, of some iron hoops that were left ashore, which he beat thin and ground upon stones. Having some linen cloth by him, he sewed himself shirts with a nail, and stitched them with the worsted of his old stockings, which he pulled out on purpose. He had his last shirt on when we found him on the island.

At his first coming on board us, he had so much forgot his language, for want of use, that we could scarce understand him, for he seemed to speak his words by halves. We offered him a dram, but he would not touch it, having drank nothing but water since his being there; and 'twas some time before he could relish our victuals.

He could give us an account of no other product of the island than what we have mentioned, except small black plums, which are very good, but hard to come at, the trees which bear them growing on high mountains and rocks. Pimento trees are plenty here, and we saw some of sixty feet high, and about two yards thick, and cotton trees higher, and more than four fathom round in the stock.

The climate is so good that the trees and grass are verdant all the year. The winter lasts no longer than June and July, and is not then severe, there being only a small frost and a little hail, but sometimes great rains. The heat of the summer is equally moderate, and there 's not much thunder or tempestuous weather of any sort. We saw no venomous or savage creature on the island, nor any other sort of beast, but goats, &c, as above mentioned, the first of which had been put ashore here on purpose for a breed by Juan Fernandez, a Spaniard, who settled there with some families for a time, till the continent of Chili began to submit to the Spaniards; which, being more profitable, tempted them to quit this island, which is capable of maintaining a good number of people, and of being made so strong that they could not be easily dislodged.

Rengrose, in his account of Captain Sharpens voyage, and other buccaneers, mentions one who had escaped ashore here, out of a ship which was cast away with all the rest of the company, and says he lived five years alone, before he had the opportunity of another ship to carry him off. Captain Dampier talks of a Mosquito Indian that belonged to Captain Watlin, who, being a-hunting in the woods when the captain left the island, lived there three years alone, and shifted much in the same manner as Mr. Selkirk did, till Captain Dampier came hither in 1684 and carried him off. The first that went ashore was one of his countrymen, and they saluted one another, first, by prostrating themselves by turns on the ground, and then embracing. But whatever there is in these stories, this of Mr. Selkirk I know to be true; and his behaviour afterwards gives me reason to believe the account he gave me how he spent his time, and bore up under such an affliction, in which nothing but the Divine Providence could have supported any man.

Appendix 2

Steele's Account of Selkirk ([*The Englishman*, December 1-3, 1713)

Under the title of this paper, I do not think it foreign to my design to speak of a man born in Her Majesty's dominions, and relate an adventure in his life so uncommon, that it is doubtful whether the like has happened to any other of the human race. The person I speak of is Alexander Selkirk, whose name is familiar to men of curiosity, from the fame of his having lived four years and four months alone in the island of Juan Fernandez. I had the pleasure, frequently, to converse with the man soon after his arrival in England in the year 1711. It was matter of great curiosity to hear him, as he is a man of good sense, give an account of the different revolutions in his own mind in that long solitude. When we consider how painful absence from company, for the space of but one evening, is to the generality of mankind, we may have a sense how painful this necessary and constant solitude was to a man bred a sailor, and ever accustomed to enjoy and suffer, eat, drink, and sleep, and perform all offices of life, in fellowship and company.

He was put ashore from a leaky vessel, with the captain of which he had had an irreconcilable difference; and he chose rather to take his fate in this place than in a crazy vessel, under a disagreeable commander. His portion was a sea-chest, his wearing clothes and bedding, a firelock, a pound of gunpowder, a large quantity of bullets, a flint and steel, a few pounds of tobacco, a hatchet, a knife, a kettle, a Bible, and other books of devotion; together with pieces that concerned navigation, and his mathematical instruments. Resentment against his officer, who had ill-used him, made him look forward on this change of life as the more eligible one, till the instant in which he saw the vessel put off; at which moment his heart yearned within him, and melted at the parting with his comrades and all human society at once. He had in provisions for the sustenance of life but the quantity of two meals, the island abounding only with wild goats, cats, and rats.

He judged it most probable that he should find more immediate and easy relief by finding shell-fish on the shore than seeking game with his gun. He accordingly found great quantities of turtles, whose flesh is extremely delicious, and of which he frequently ate very plentifully on his first arrival, till it grew disagreeable to his stomach, except in jellies. The necessities of hunger and thirst were his greatest diversion from the reflections on his lonely condition. When those appetites were satisfied, the desire of society was as strong a call upon him, and he appeared to himself least necessitous when he wanted everything; for the supports of his body were easily attained, but the eager longings for seeing again the face of man, during the interval of craving bodily appetites, were hardly supportable.

He grew dejected, languid, and melancholy, scarce able to refrain from doing himself violence, till by degrees, by the force of reason and frequent reading the Scriptures, and turning his thoughts upon the study of navigation, after the space of eighteen months he grew thoroughly reconciled to his condition. When he had made this conquest, the vigour of his health, disengagement from the world, a constant cheerful, serene sky and a temperate air, made his life one continual feast, and his being much more joyful than it had before been irksome. He now, taking delight in everything, made the hut in which he lay, by ornaments which he cut down from a spacious wood on the side of which it was situated, the most delicious bower, fanned with continual breezes and gentle aspirations of wind, that made his repose after the chase equal to the most sensual pleasures.

I forgot to observe, that during the time of his dissatisfaction monsters of the deep, which frequently lay on the shore, added to the terrors of his solitude; the dreadful howlings and voices seemed too terrible to be made for human ears; but upon the recovery of his temper he could with pleasure not only hear their voices, but approach the monsters themselves with great intrepidity. He speaks of sea-lions, whose jaws and tails were capable of seizing or breaking the limbs of a man if he approached them. But at that time his spirits and life were so high, that he could act so regularly and unconcerned, that merely from being unruffled in himself he killed them with the greatest ease imaginable; for observing that though their jaws and tails were so terrible, yet the animals being mighty slow in working themselves round, he had nothing to do but place himself exactly opposite to their middle, and as close to them as possible, and he despatched them with his hatchet at will.

The precautions which he took, against want, in case of sickness, was to lame kids when very young, so as that they might recover their health, but never be capable of speed. These he had in great numbers about his hut; and as he was himself in full vigour, he could take at full speed the swiftest goat running on a promontory, and never failed of catching them, but on a descent.

His habitation was extremely pestered with rats, which gnawed his clothes and feet when sleeping. To defend himself against them he fed and tamed numbers of young kitlings, who lay about his bed and preserved him from the enemy. When his clothes were quite worn out he dried and tacked together the skins of goats, with which he clothed himself, and was inured to pass through woods, bushes, and brambles with as much carelessness and precipitance as any other animal. It happened once to him that running on the summit of a hill he made a stretch to seize a goat, with which under him he fell down a precipice and lay senseless for the space of three days, the length of which he measured by the moon's growth since his last observation. This manner of life grew so exquisitely pleasant, that he never had a moment heavy upon his hands; his nights were untroubled and his days joyous, from the practice of temperance and exercise. It was his manner to use stated hours and places for exercises of devotion, which he performed aloud, in order to keep up the faculties of speech, and to utter himself with greater energy.

When I first saw him I thought if I had not been let into his character and story I could have discerned that he had been much separated from company from his aspect and gesture; there was a strong but cheerful seriousness in his look, and a certain disregard to the ordinary things about him, as if he had been sunk in thought. When the ship which brought him off the island came in, he received them with the greatest indifference with relation to the prospect of going off with them, but with great satisfaction in an opportunity to refresh and help them. The man frequently bewailed his return to the world, which could not, he said, with all its enjoyments, restore him to the tranquillity of his solitude. Though I had frequently conversed with him, after a few months' absence he met me in the street, and though he spoke to me, I could not recollect that I had seen him; familiar discourse in this town had taken off the loneliness of his aspect, and quite altered the air of his face.

This plain man's story is a memorable example that he is happiest who confines his want to natural necessities; and he that goes further in his desires, increases his want in proportion to his acquisitions; or, to use his own expression, "*I am now worth eight hundred pounds, but shall never be so happy as when I was not worth a farthing.*"

The Story of Alexander Selkirk

Contents

CHAPTER 1

He Resolves to Go to Sea

I suppose all my little readers know the story of *Robinson Crusoe*. It is very interesting, but it is not true. The fact is that a famous man by the name of De Foe, made up the story from the adventures of Alexander Selkirk, which I am now going to relate.

Alexander Selkirk, the hero of the following little narrative, was born in Largo, in the county of Fife, Scotland, in the year 1676. His father, an honest fisherman, like most of his fellow villagers, thought no course of life more honourable, or better for his two sons, than the one he had himself pursued, in imitation of his own parent.

He, therefore, adopted the maxim of the wise penman; and, in choosing a profession for his boys, and beginning to bring them up in the way which he thought they ought to go, that when they were old they might not depart from it, he designed that their lives should be spent with the fish-line and the net. He viewed the former as the most profitable *line* of business, and the latter, to use a term of his own, most likely to bring them in "good hauls."

But Mr. Selkirk was not actuated altogether by mercenary feelings and worldly wisdom, in making this choice. He knew that the line would hold his boys to the water at times when they might otherwise be in danger from vicious associates on land; and that the net would confine their attention, and keep them secure from many a snare to which the feet of youth are liable, when not under the eye of a paternal guardian.

Besides, he probably had in view the simple lives and humble occupation of the fishermen so celebrated in Scripture, and felt very willing to see his sons in the same rank of life and kind of employment, provided that they might also deserve the name of followers of Him who was " meek and lowly," and lay up for themselves the treasures that perish not in the using.

But his plans and his kind intentions were, like those of many an affectionate father, frustrated by the waywardness of his child.

In naming his son Alexander, report saith not, whether Mr. Selkirk yielded to a momentary fit of ambition, and did it in honour of Alexander of Macedon, the ancient monarch of the world; or in commemoration of some honourable fisherman ancestor. But, it is certain, that, Alexander, son of Philip, wishing to lay the plan, and mark out the boundaries of his great city, having nothing else to do it with, marked it out by scattering flour, which was immediately picked up by large flocks of birds, had not the plan of his city more completely destroyed, than Mr. Selkirk had, the one he had formed for his youngest son.

Alexander of Macedon, when quite a boy, tamed, by his skilful management and gentle usage, a wild, fiery horse, which neither his father nor any one else could subject to the bridle. But Alexander of Largo, was himself wild and fiery in his nature, and had not learned to restrain the violence of his own passions.

He was not malicious, or unkind in his disposition, but, he was so quick-tempered, and so hasty in showing his resentment, that he often occasioned great uneasiness in the house, and brought himself into many difficulties, that might have been avoided by a little gentleness and forbearance.

The picture of a child angry with his parents, is too sad a one to be drawn, and the reader shall be spared the pain of seeing it here, as it shall not be stated how the young Selkirk would manifest his anger when either of his parents displeased him. But, if his brother, his sister, or any of his equals touched his sensitive spirit, up came his little hand for a blow, or to hurl a stone, or some other thing that chanced to be first in its way.

This irritability, though combined with a great deal that was noble in his nature, brought him into the quarrel that was finally the cause of his first leaving the house in which he was born. This was a small, one-storey building with a garret, which is still standing on the north side of the principal street of Largo, after this long lapse of years. It has been continued to this day in possession of the descendants of the family of the noted Selkirk, one of which is its present occupant.

The last quarrel which the young Alexander had in it, began thus. Having come some distance one evening, after a hard day's work, and feeling very thirsty, as he entered the house, where his brother was sitting in the chimney corner, he hastily took up a pipkin of water that stood near, and began to drink. Having taken one swallow, he set down the pipkin with an exclamation and a look of great disgust, for he found it was salt water that he had taken.

His brother, highly amused at his wry faces, began to joke him, and to laugh at his eagerness and disappointment. To take this, after his salt draught, was more than the high-spirited young hero would brook. He flew at his brother, and gave him a blow; his brother returned it, and closing in with him, a hard squabble ensued.

Their father, seeing that Alexander had got the better in the struggle, and was taking his revenge, attempted to interpose; but the paternal command was unheeded in the heat of the affray. One member of the family after another interfered, till finally, the whole house was filled with noise and uproar.

At length the neighbours began to gather round—some upholding one brother, and some the other, till the strife formed parties, and the quarrel became so public throughout the whole village, that it was deemed proper for the kirk session to take the aggressor in hand.

He was brought before the venerable body of old women, and condemned, according to their custom in such cases of offence, to stand, a certain number of Sundays, in the aisle of the church, to be rebuked as a culprit, by the clergyman, in presence of the congregation, before whom he must stand as a penitent.

At first, Alexander declared that nothing should make him submit to such humiliation; and he stood out very stoutly about it, for a good while. But, his anger having subsided, his better feelings were touched by the entreaties of his friends, who feared that higher powers might be appealed to, and severer punishment inflicted, if he resisted in this instance.

He submitted at last to the sentence; and went through the mortifying trial to which his rashness had exposed him; but this public expiation of his fault, and public exhibition of penitence, so affected his spirits, that he was filled with a sort of disgust and discontent towards his native town; and he determined to quit it, and go to sea.

And now do we behold the young adventurer about to take leave of his native village, his father's house, his friends and early companions, to cast himself upon a world to which he is a stranger, in consequence of a sudden burst of angry passion, in an unguarded moment, which he would give all that he has, and all his hopes of future success, to recall.

If the consequences of anger were as soon got over as the anger itself, it would not be such an enemy to the peace of the *human heart*.

But, like the tempest that soon passes off, we often see it laying waste many fair things, whose ruins are a sad witness to its fury, long after the sun shines out, and the clouds have all been scattered.

Many a one, if he had them at command, would give empires with all their riches, for the power of undoing some rash deed that he has done in a fit of anger.

He who cherishes a quick and violent temper, is not only troublesome to all connected with him, and within the reach of its smoke and flame, but he carries a foe about in his own bosom. He keeps there, some of the sparks of that fire that inflamed Cain, and caused him to lift his hand against his brother.

But, while this impetuosity was so conspicuous a trait in the character of Selkirk, it must not be forgotten that he had many redeeming qualities. He was naturally generous, kind-hearted and warm in his affections; and he bore within his young breast, a great and noble spirit, that ever taught him to despise and shun a dishonest, or mean action.

CHAPTER 2

Selkirk Sails

When all was ready for Alexander's departure, and he found himself on the deck of the ship, where everyone was busy, pulling here, and pulling there, till she fairly cleared the land, and there was no way for him to step on shore, he began to feel heavy at the heart, and to wish he had never formed the resolution of going from home.

He thought of his father's kindness, of his mother's tender care, of the endearments of brother, sister and playmate, and of the scenes of his childhood—all of which seemed sacrificed to the unholy fire of his angry feelings in a moment when he did not try for that profitable victory, the victory over *self*. His bosom was burdened with self-reproach, and regret, and it began to swell and to heave, long before the heaving of the ship and the swelling of the sea made his condition more pitiable, by a sickness of another kind than that of the heart.

But, by and by, the ship began to roll and to toss, and Alexander's stomach began to roll, too. He staggered, and pitched, first against one thing, and then against another; but the ship would not keep steady long enough for him to get a firm footing, and down he went at full length, on the deck.

Every sailor that passed him, would either touch him with his toe, and laugh at his pale face, or twitch him by the arm, and ask him how he happened to take so much grog; if he would not like to go to sea in a ship that could stop and be tied to a tree every night; or some question equally tantalising to one, who like him, had the stomach full of sickness, and the heart full of sorrow, so that he feared to open his lips lest they should expose the secret concerns of both.

He had shipped as a sailor boy, and when his call to duty came, he sighed and wished it could come in his kind father's voice. The whole, restless, awful ocean now lay before him, like an eternal remembrance of his draught of salt water from the pipkin; and he felt as if he would gladly drink up a whole wave, for the opportunity of undoing all that had occurred since that memorable swallow.

His brother's playfulness and laugh he would gladly have borne, and he thought it a slight thing to incur his jest, when he felt the keen raillery of his messmates. He had not been many hours out on his first voyage, when the sky began to blacken, and a hard thunderstorm came up from somewhere under the great deep, as it seemed to him; for, where else the clouds arose from, he could not tell.

The sailors ran to and fro, pulling at the ropes and taking in the sails, while the canvass puffed out, and flapped back again, and the cordage rattled in the squall, till it seemed as if confusion and disorder had taken command of the ship.

Soon it began to rain; and then, *rattle, rattle, rattle,* came the hail-stones on the deck. The captain's loud voice was heard, crying to one to do this thing, another to do that, and trying to be obeyed, while the noise of the vessel, and the wind and thunder, mingled with the fall of the hail, drowned half his words.

Alexander did not understand what was to be done, nor know the meaning of the sea-phrases addressed to him. While looking about to find out what part he was told to perform, he stood in the way, where one would push him this side, and another that, till the hail rolled under his feet, that had just begun to keep the motion of the vessel a little, and down he went upon his face.

The hail scratched his cheek and cut his chin, and the red drops came forth. This a sailor saw, and with a laughing look that cut him more than the hailstones, told him he saw there *was* blood in his face notwithstanding its pale looks.

But when the storm had subsided, and the first dreadful night, which was a sleepless one to our hero, had passed away, he began to feel somewhat at home in the ship, and to make his way about much better than he had done the first day.

His appetite had not quite returned, but he thought the sea had got over some of its frolic, and grown more even and steady, and he found that the ship was not to be blown or beaten to pieces quite so easily as he had thought she might be. He could now stand firmly and look at the dolphin that jumped up out of the water, and the porpoises that huddled together in shoals, as thick as the company of a fashionable party, or the locusts that came in swarms like clouds, to bring terror to the Egyptians. He saw, also, something which he took to be a floating island; for, to tell the truth, it seemed to Alexander, as if every thing was now afloat. "What is that?" said he, to one of the hands. "'Tis the fish that swallowed Jonah," answered the sailor; and as it drew near the vessel, Alexander was filled with wonder at the enormous size of the whale, and its power to throw up water from its spiracles, till it came down like showers of rain.

The next night he slept soundly, and dreamed of home,—of the scene in the church, of the kirk session, of the prophet Jonah, of St. Paul's voyage and shipwreck, of the barbarians that he went among, on the island of Melita—of the viper that twined round his hand till he shook it into the fire; and, besides many other things, he fancied that he was in the bowels of the whale, and rocked in a living cradle, as long as his father's whole humble habitation.

He felt pent up and suffocated, and talked in his sleep; and moving to get breath, raised himself till his head went bump against the top of his berth.

The blow brought him to his senses, and relieved him of the nightmare; and of course, ejected him from the mouth of his imaginary whale. So, he awoke to find that he was not so much of a prophet as he had thought himself; and that, the smell of tar, and other odours peculiar to a vessel, together with the want of air in his confined sleeping-place, was not the effluvia of the liver or any other internal organ of the mighty fish.

His was not the sweet *Sailor Boy's Dream*, that the poet, Dimond, so beautifully describes, where,

Memory turned sidewise, half covered with flowers,
Presenting the rose, but concealing the thorn.

He felt as if the rose was shattered by his own rashness, and he had only the thorns left to torture him.

But Alexander Selkirk, the boy of Nether Largo, had now set out for himself; and if, like the "ploughman turned sailor," "he didn't like the rocking about," he found, like him also, that there was no door, where in danger he might "creep out" of the ship. He therefore resolved on making the best of his condition, and on doing his duty faithfully, according to his ability.

As day after day, and week after week passed off, he became familiarized with the habits of a seafaring life; and when the ship arrived at her place of destination, the scenes of a foreign city, and what was to his young eyes, a new world, amused him, and kept him busy, when he was not employed at the vessel, till his spirits regained their cheerfulness, and he cared less and less about the unpleasant affair at his native village.

He made up his mind to follow the seas, till he should outlive the recollection of the quarrel, or, at least, get above caring about it, by making his fortune, and establishing himself at home as a rich and benevolent man.

He even began to count on what he would do when he should rise to be captain of a fine ship; and then, to lay plans for the after years which he intended to spend as a *nabob*, in ease and independence, among his early associates.

There were many things that he meant to do in Largo, when he should make money enough; for, notwithstanding the temporary disaffection which he had entertained towards the place, and many of its inhabitants, he still loved it, as the scene of his nativity and all his childish enjoyments.

He was not so thoughtless, or so ignoble in spirit as to lose his attachment to his birthplace; nor so destitute of natural and filial affection, as not to blend with his many schemes, the good which he intended to do to his father and family.

For one thing, he thought he should like to build them a new house, and enable his father to live better and more at his ease in the decline of his life, than he had thus far been able to do; and to purchase for his mother and other members of the family, not only the comfortable things of life, but many that comfort did not actually require, but which it would please his ambitious eye to see them possess.

When the ship returned to England, after a long and pleasant voyage, Selkirk did not go home, for he had resolved not to see Largo again, till he was promoted in rank and had a purse full of money.

He shipped again and went another voyage; and, proving a good seaman, he rose in the estimation of his employers, till, as years rolled over his head, and he went one voyage after another, he was promoted in rank; and when about twenty-seven years old he went out as sailing-master in an armed vessel called the *Cinque-Ports* galley, that sailed in the year 1703, with about sixteen guns and sixty-three men, under the command of Captain Charles Pickering.

CHAPTER 3

The 'Cinque Ports' on a Cruise

In September of the same year, the vessel sailed from Cork, in Ireland, in company with a larger one, a ship of twenty-six guns, and a hundred and twenty men, commanded by the far-famed navigator. Captain William Dampier. This ship was called the *St. George*.

The object of the two vessels, in undertaking this expedition, was, to cruise among the Spaniards in the South Sea, along the coast of Brazil.

While on this coast, Captain Pickering died, and his lieutenant, whose name was Thomas Stradling, was his successor in command. Whether the name of Stradling had anything to do with his character, or not, is not recorded; but certain it was, that his strides in his newly-acquired authority seemed rather too long, to please our hero, Alexander, who had never liked the man, and who now felt indignant at many of his imperious airs.

This growing dislike began at first to break out in little bickerings and murmurings, and finally ripened into an open quarrel between the commander and his sailing-master.

The vessels made their wav round Cape Horn, and proceeded to the Island of Juan Fernandez, for the purpose of replenishing their stores of wood and water.

While at this island, they were alarmed by the sudden appearance of two French armed ships; and fearing a capture, they put hastily to sea; and scudding away in their fright left five of Capt. Stradling's men on the uninhabited island.

The situation of these forsaken men, seemed sad and forlorn indeed, left, as they were, where all was wild and unimpressed with the work of a human hand, or the print of the foot of a brother man. They knew not how they were to obtain the next food to satisfy their hunger; or what wild beast might spring upon them from the forests, to make his nocturnal feast on their unsheltered and unprotected persons.

They also had much uneasiness, lest their paths might be infested with some deadly foe, in the form of poisonous serpents and stinging insects. Their imaginations began to torment them with many fearful forms of the death that they might die, and conjecture was busy with the inquiry who should go first, and who should be left till the last, to bury his only remaining companion, and have none in his turn to give his lonely body, a covering of earth to conceal it from the birds of prey, or to save it from the melancholy fate of consuming in the open air, and the glaring light of day.

But their fears on these grounds were soon ended by the French ships which came to the island, and took them off, when they had surrendered themselves as voluntary prisoners, to avoid what they thought a still worse condition, imprisonment on a wild spot of earth, that was shut out from all intercourse with the world, by the wild and restless waters that encompassed it.

As these men are now safe off the island, and gone where they give us no farther account of their fate, we will follow up our two English vessels a little while longer.

They made their way to the coast of South America, where they had not remained together long, before Capt. Dampier, sympathizing with Selkirk in his dislike for Stradling, fell out with him; and their quarrel ended in their finally separating, each to steer his vessel his own way.

This separation took place on the 19th of May, 1704. In the September following, Stradling came again to Juan Fernandez. While here, another difficulty arose between Selkirk and his unamiable commander, and the vessel at the same time, proving leaky, and as Alexander thought, unsafe, he began to have serious thoughts of remaining alone on the island, and letting the vessel depart without him.

It is not likely that the condition of the vessel alone would have induced him to quit her; and it is very probable that some of the old embers of his temperament which kindled the fire at Largo, had now been uncovered and fanned into a hasty fire by the provoking treatment of Stradling, though Alexander had had many years in which to subdue his passions, and the ocean, to quench the violence of their fire.

He at length went so far as to remove his chest, his gun and his bed from the vessel to the shore; and he told Stradling that rather than be *straddled* over by him any longer, he would remain and take his chance alone.

The captain was at first loath to lose so valuable a member of his crew; but as Selkirk persisted in his determination, he made all things ready to depart without him.

When Selkirk had taken more time to reflect on the rashness of his step, and to cast the eye of his mind forward on the cheerless prospect that lay before him, and the probability of having even a worse fate than that of being under a disagreeable commander, he began to relent.

His comrades were taking leave of him, one after another, and the vessel about to depart, when he made out to conquer his spirit so far, as to request the captain to take him again on board. But Stradling's stern heart was not to be easily softened, and he refused to receive the repentant Selkirk into the vessel.

Our hero had now the sorrow to see every face depart, and to watch the vessel till she grew smaller and smaller, and finally, after becoming a little speck against the distant horizon, disappeared from the view of his lonely and weary eye.

But, inhumanity and wrong do not escape the eye of the Judge of all the earth, nor go unrequited, by Him who says, "*Vengeance is mine and I will repay.*" A few months after this cruel act of Stradling, he had the misfortune to get the *Cinque Ports* aground, where she was seized by the Spaniards against whom she had come out, and her captain and men made prisoners.

They were slaves to new and unmerciful masters, and underwent much cruel treatment and hard labour. So, it eventually turned out, that the five men whom they had first left, and Selkirk, were not so badly off as if they had remained in the vessel to share the unhappy fate of the rest of her men.

If people of all ages and conditions, who find causes of complaint and resentment against each other, when they are thrown together by the circumstances of their lives, would only stop to think how these causes will diminish and sink into nothingness, when the boiling and bubbling of their feelings are allayed by the lapse of a little time, how differently would they treat each other, even if they pretended not to act upon Christian principles, but only on those of common sense and self-interest.

But, this important person, *self*, is a great busy body, standing foremost in every thing; and of course often getting severely wounded when a little modesty might have spared her the pain and mortification of the cuts and bruises.

Selkirk, when left alone with no companions but his own thoughts; and with no human face to behold, except, as his own appeared in the water, that he bent over, felt, no doubt, how much wiser it would have been in him to have put up with a little wrong, in silence, than to be left in his present solitary state,

Stradling, on the other hand, would probably have consented to treat Alexander with kindness and forbearance, for the opportunity of escaping from his tyrannical masters the Spaniards; and he felt that one must begin by doing to others as he would wish others to do to him, if he would turn out well in the end.

A reproachful conscience is a terrible companion for one under any circumstances—but to a man in slavery among a cruel enemy, it must be tormenting beyond expression.

CHAPTER 4

Discovery of the Island

Selkirk kept up his spirits very well till the vessel sailed, and the faces of his companions were gone from his sight. Then his heart sunk; and he said to himself, for he had no one else to hear him, "I never heard a sound so dismal as their parting oars."

The island of which he was now left sole monarch, lies to the west of South America, about three hundred miles from the coast of Chili.

Its name is derived from its discoverer, Juan Fernandez, a Spanish pilot, who, about the year 1653, made the first bold experiment of standing to a distance from the south-western coast of South America, and of scudding about at a risk which no other navigator had dared to run, till he beheld what he at first thought to be two clouds that hung on the distant horizon.

On drawing nearer, he found the clouds assumed the solidity of earth in the form of two islands. The one nearest the coast took his own name, and the other, that of Mas-a-fuera, which signifies *more without*. Juan Fernandez, afterwards became a sort of rendezvous for the *buccaneers* who infested the South Seas, on account of its remote and unfrequented situation.

The pirates against whom that noted one, Captain Kidd, was sent out, made this island a resort, and used it as a convenient stopping place for wood and water; and it is even probable that Kidd himself might have buried some of the treasures here, that he had obtained by the shedding of blood, and wasting the lives of his fellow men.

The name of Robert Kidd is familiar to most American ears, though, many among the youthful of the present generation may not be acquainted with his history.

He was a skilful seaman and a bold officer in the navy, in the reign of King William III, and, having distinguished himself in the service of his king, was appointed to the command of an armed ship, to go out for the suppression of the pirates who, at this time, overran the South Seas.

Kidd had a wife and family whom he left in New York, when he went forth on this bold enterprise.

Having cruised about a long time without success, and finding that he was not going in this way to make his fortune very soon,—(for, he took no prizes, as he had expected to do,)—he conceived the evil plan of turning pirate himself, as a shorter road to the temple of fortune.

He therefore began cautiously to sound the minds of his men, and finding them willing to league with him in his desperate purpose, he set up as a pirate, and became a true Ishmaelite, inasmuch as his hand was "against every man, and every man's hand against him." He committed many terrible murders, and destroyed a great number of vessels, after having plundered them of all that was valuable.

The gold, silver and other treasurer which he thus obtained by crime and a waste of human life, he buried here and there, on the islands or unfrequented tracts of coast where he could, with the least fear of observation, put in, and conceal them, so as not to have them found upon him, in case of an encounter, till a convenient time for him to come and remove them, and take his ill-gotten wealth to his possession again.

Having gone on long in this guilty career, and taken a great many rich prizes, he came boldly into Boston, intending to return to his family in New York.

But, here he was arrested, and with several of his murderous crew, was put in irons and sent to England for trial.

There, with six of his men, he died on the gibbet at Execution Dock. Their bodies were afterwards removed to the river-side and hung up in chains, at a little distance from each other, where they remained several years as a beacon to warn others to avoid the guilty course that had brought them to so terrible an end.

The treasures which they had buried were never found. Many people employed themselves from time to time in seeking for the places and digging in the earth where they supposed they might be concealed; but all to no purpose.

The earth, as if indignant at the crimes of which the gold that had originally sprung from her bosom, had been the cause, never yielded it up again to circulate through the hands of man.

A great many stories were made up, and flew about among the

superstitious, concerning the sudden tempests that would arise, or the strange sights and sounds that were seen and heard, just as the treasure seekers had come so near the object of their search, as to feel their spades strike upon the metal vessels in which the gold was buried; and to hear the sound, in a ringing noise, as the blow fell; when they were obliged to leave all, and flee away.

But these were, probably, the offspring of the imagination; and occasioned by its being filled with the scenes of horror and death which had occurred when the wealth was obtained by its last human possessor; or, more properly, its *inhuman* one.

Such is the story of the pirate, Kidd, and the wealth for which he sold his mortal life, if not his rest beyond the bounds of time.

In him we have a specimen of those desperate men who made Juan Fernandez their place of resort and accommodation, long before Alexander Selkirk was left there; and who were now gone to meet those whom they had slain, in the presence of Him whose eye is every where, "beholding the evil and the good."

But whoever or whatever might have been formerly on the island, it had never been the permanent abode, nor held the human habitation or anyone before the arrival of our Scottish hero upon it; and he found there, no trace of man or his works to remind him that he belonged to a human family; and he probably said to himself of the beasts and birds, as Cowper has since supposed him to have done—

They are so unacquainted with man.
That their tameness is shocking to me.

The first night of his solitude was the most solemn one that ever had come down upon Alexander. No darkness since his eyes first opened upon the world, in his forsaken Largo, had seemed like that which now shrouded his homeless, houseless form, concealing it even from his own sight.

His whole worldly wealth, which had no shelter but the overhanging rocks by which it was deposited, consisted of his bed and bedding, his chest of clothing, his books, mathematical and nautical instruments, a hatchet, a knife, a kettle, a gunpowder and balls. With these he had some tobacco, and a few other small articles contained in his chest.

When the night had passed heavily away, and the light of morning dawned, he bethought himself of the one great source of consolation that he had still, in his Bible; and he began the day by reading it.

The stillness of the scene made him feel his loneliness so powerfully that he opened his lips and read aloud—but the sound of his voice vibrating among the rocks thrilled through his whole frame—and he shut the book, and took a walk upon his new heritage to see what he could discover, and what means it might afford of bettering his condition.

He struck a fire, and broiled a fish that he took from the water, and, on this, with a draught from a little brook that ran sparkling along, close by where his effects were lodged, he made his first breakfast, as lord of Juan Fernandez.

The island he found to be a romantic spot with much beautiful scenery about it. Here high hills and wild crags would meet his eye, and there, green vales, bright streams and shadowy woods diversified the prospect.

Several bays surrounded it, but still the island was of very difficult and dangerous access to navigators; and this was the cause of its having been so little frequented, except by those who had wished to shun the observation of their fellow men.

It produced a great many beautiful flowers, and was the abode of a variety of gay birds. It was also thickly peopled with wild goats that were seen leaping from crag to crag and bounding about in every direction. These had sprung from a few goats that Juan Fernandez left on the island when he first went there, and they constituted the greatest part of the animal life which it possessed.

Thus, our hero found himself placed over a kingdom of goats; and he soon set about bringing them under his control so far as making them serviceable to his necessities was concerned.

The first few days of his solitude he spent chiefly in making discoveries,—in meditating on his new condition—in thinking of all from which he was now shut out—in reading his Bible—and in trying to make himself as comfortable as he could, till night came.

Then he kindled a fire to keep him company, and laid down on his bed beneath the shelving rock.

His food he obtained either by fishing or hunting, and cooked it over a brisk fire of the pimento, or pepper tree, which burnt very freely, and served, when night came, both for fire and candles, as it made a lively flame and a cheering light.

He found some turnips and other vegetables growing wild, from seeds which had probably been scattered by the Spaniards, or some others that had put into the island, afterwards, for wood and water.

There was also a great abundance of the cabbage tree, the top of which when boiled with the flesh of the goat and seasoned with the pimento, which is the same as the Jamaica pepper, tasted very much like the common cabbage. This dish lacked only salt and the accompaniment of bread to render it very palatable to the simple taste of its lonely proprietor.

CHAPTER 5

He Builds Two Houses

With the prospect of passing the rest of his life on the island, our hero now began to cast about, and call up his inventive and mechanic powers, to see what could be done by way of erecting a habitation; and in this useful work, himself and his hatchet were the chief agents, till his gun was afterwards made instrumental in its completion.

He had not, like the ancients, a tent to pitch, nor, like the North American Indians, some one to help him in hacking down trees for the pillars of a bark-covered hovel; neither had he any one to consult, in selecting the spot for a dwelling.

He looked around, and, fixing on one place which, more than any other, within the scope of his eye, he thought would be convenient and agreeable, he marked it out as the chosen one for his home; and removed all the little stock of his worldly wealth to it, as a sort of dedication.

Having done this, he took his hatchet and went into the wood to fell such small trees as he wanted to begin his building with. The sound of the strokes of the hatchet, as it pealed in echoes through the wood and among the rocks, was new music to the startled goats.

They looked at each other as if they only wanted speech to inquire what it meant; and when the crash of the falling tree came, they leaped away, and bounding over the crag and into the dell, gave, by the swiftness of their feet, a *speedy* proof of their intention not to fall in the same way.

When they had first beheld the form of man in the person of Selkirk, they paid little heed to the new shape that had come among them, and only noticed him with a look of curiosity, without recognising him as "lord of the fowl and the brute." But when his gun was levelled at them, and took down one of their number after another, though the shot was so quick as hardly to convince them that it had come from him, they grew suspicious, and began to think him a more terrible animal than had ever before entered the borders of their territory.

And, seeing, now, that even the trees could not stand before him, they thought it was some awful power that had come embodied in "such a questionable shape," and it was imperiously demanded by the wisdom of a goat, and the sound principle of self-preservation, that they should keep clear of him so far as their nimble limbs would enable them to do it.

But, with all their fleetness, a ball from the muzzle of Selkirk's gun would fly faster than their feet could carry them; and whenever he wanted a new supply of fresh meat, he sent his leaden messenger by the force of powder, to make known his purpose. The flesh of the animal, which he dressed with the aid of his knife, he used as food, cooked either by boiling, roasting or broiling.

The skin he dried, and appropriated in a way that will, in due time, be mentioned.

The birds too, began to be filled with consternation at him who had come among them. They had never before seen their companions drop as he dropped them, nor heard such a sudden noise as preceded their fall, whenever Selkirk's taste required a more delicate bit of flesh, than that of the goat, upon his table of stone.

When they saw that the very boughs from which they sent forth their sweet music, and on which their nests were built were not spared, they flew away affrighted, and mourned in the distance, the loss of their homes and their helpless little ones that must perish in the ruins.

But Selkirk thought more about the home that he had forsaken, and the one he must now provide for himself, than of that of any bird; and he busied himself in cutting down trees and dragging them to his chosen spot, till he got enough together to form a palisade for the walls of his house.

While thus busily employed, the exercise gave him a good appetite during the day, and the fatigue made him sleep soundly at night. He made it a rule never to lie down to rest, or rise up to work, without reading a portion of the word of God, and communing with Him by prayer and meditation.

By this he strengthened his mind for the solitary business of the day; and during the solemnity of the night, it made him feel that he had still for his friend and watchman. Him whose eye never sleepeth.

The pimento tree was the one which he had selected as the chief material in building. It was the most manageable one, and most easily brought into his service, as well as being possessed of a spicy and delicious odour, which rendered it a very pleasant thing to have about him.

He sharpened the ends of the small bodies of the trees which he had collected together on his premises, when he had made them of a length sufficient for the height of his house, which he only sought to make such as to accommodate his own height; and then set them down in the earth at short distances, round the spot which was to be the interior of his dwelling.

On the upper ends of his pillars he had left in the place where the tree branched out, a short fork on which to lay sticks to support the materials of which tile roof was to be formed.

When these sticks were laid across the top of the walls from side to side, he covered them with a thick coat of long grass, twigs, and bark, so as to make quite a secure shelter from the rain, as well as the sun; for, he took care to form the roof with a slant so as to let the water slide off as fast as it fell.

To enclose the sides of his house, he hung up the skins of the goats that he killed for food, and stretched them out, fastening them on the posts, as he took them from time to time, till the whole inside of his habitation had at length a complete lining of hair.

When his house was done, his next object was to furnish it. For a bedstead he collected a heap of small sticks, which he laid carefully together, and filled up the crevices with grass. Then he laid a coat of grass over them, and covered the whole with goat skins; and on this mass he deposited his bed, and found it just high enough from the ground, to feel comfortable.

His chest, his gun, kettle, &c. he then put within his house, and began to feel as if he had a home. But he had not yet brought his feeling into such a state as to enable him to sing "*Sweet Home,*" to this humble centre from which all his walks radiated, in the morning, and to which they pointed at night.

When his first building was erected, he began to feel the want, not only of more room, but of employment, also: for he was of industrious habits, and never could feel contented in idleness.

He now thought he should like a place to build his fire, and to do his cooking in; and for such other purposes as he did not like to use his bedroom for, or to accomplish without a shelter. His next business, therefore, was to set about building another little hut close by the first one.

He was now engaged again in felling trees and dragging them home, and no beaver ever worked more diligently than he did till his second house was done, and he was the owner of a *kitchen*.

From the shell of a cocoa-nut, he formed a cup by cutting a round piece out of one end, and fastening it with a peg, in the other, bringing the edge downward so as to make a bottom on which it could stand firm and even. This he used for a drinking-cup.

He found along the shore some iron hoops that had been thrown out from the vessel; and these he picked up and carefully saved in his house to serve him in some way at a future day. He also found a few nails of which he took equal care, thinking he should have nil opportunity to turn them to some use in the course of time.

His houses, it was true, had gone up without the sound of a hammer, but the nails were a precious treasure to him; and the use to which he put them very different from that for which they were originally designed, as will be seen hereafter.

Selkirk could now lay himself down to rest under his own roof; but a new source of trouble arose to deprive him of the uninterrupted enjoyment of sleep.

This was a troop of nocturnal visitors that came about him in the form of rats. They bit his toes, his ears, and other parts of his body, so as to make him feel afraid to lie down at night, lest they should come and open a vein that would let out more blood than he felt disposed or able to lose.

This numerous host of small animals, but great foes, had originated in a few of their species that had come ashore from vessels which had in other days put into the island for wood and water. They were not natives and children of the soil. At least, their *ancestors* were foreigners, as well as Alexander.

There were also a great many wild cats that had probably multiplied on the island from some that had come to it in the same way. These were likewise somewhat troublesome to our hero. The only way that seemed open to him, to rid himself of such unwelcome guests, seemed to be to make friends with one race of his foes, and enter into a league with them against the other enemy.

He, therefore, allured the cats to him, by throwing out fish, goat's flesh, birds, &c. which drew them towards him more and more, till they began to look on him only as their benefactor, and became so attached to his person as to follow him, in the day; and to sleep round his bed by night.

Thus, the tamed cats formed a sort of social circle, of which he was the centre, while awake; and during his slumber, he had in them a faithful guard against the attacks of his other disagreeable company, between which and his now friendly allies, nature has established an unconquerable enmity.

He had, therefore, no longer any fear of losing his toes or his blood by the operations of the teeth of these four-footed pilferers and phlebotomists.

CHAPTER 6

A Fight

Having formed this companionship with his cats, Selkirk felt less lonely, and more cheerful than before; and he could now sing, and talk to them, as a substitute for more understanding auditors.

He was one night waked from his slumber by a terrible sound, like the roaring of a lion. What could be coming he could not imagine; but he thought it must be some powerful foe, against which he had no protection.

For, if the monster should prove as formidable in appearance as it seemed, by its voice, he thought it might easily overcome all his courage; and if the strength of it was equal to its noise, it might tear both him and his house in pieces.

The longer he listened, the more loud and terrible the cries grew—and the nearer they seemed to come. The cats jumped up and began to caper about, and their master thought he would get up, too. He put forth his head from his little cabin—the moon shone bright and clear—all the rocks, hills and woods were distinctly defined; but nothing of animal life could be seen.

He found the sound came from the quarter in which the ocean lay; and he mustered courage to bend his steps a little way in the direction in which the water was nearest.

As he drew nearer the water-side, he heard a great sousing about among the waves, and discovered that the noise came from something that was either an inhabitant of the ocean, or was enjoying the night in a salt-water bath.

By and by, voice answered to voice from out the deep and along the shore, till it was evident that there was a number of huge animals concerned in the riot, or the serenade, whichsoever it might please the solitary judge to call their nocturnal amusement. Upon farther observation, he found that what had been the cause of his disturbance and his fright, was a company of sea-lions, that were holding a revel by dashing about near the shore in foamy brine. These animals, as was afterwards ascertained, were as large as common oxen. Their roaring was loud and terrible. Seamen who have since traversed those waters, have taken them for their oil, and found their fat nearly a foot in thickness.

But our hero had in the process of time an opportunity of becoming better acquainted with their character and habits, as they sometimes came on shore and fed on the grass by the seaside, being amphibious in their nature.

He observed that they were somewhat like the sea-calf in appearance, but much larger. They were covered with a coat of short, dark brown hair; were web-footed, with each toe terminating with a sharp claw.

In their motions they were very heavy and clumsy. Their teeth seemed to be their only weapon of attack or defence when on the land; but, how they managed to fight their battles, or to secure their prey, when in the unstable element of the great deep, Selkirk could not, of course, follow them to ascertain.

Their voices were various in their intonations, making sometimes a grunting hoarse sound, like swine, and at others, loud, shrill cries.

They often came on the muddy soil, where they enjoyed a nap in the mire, some being set as sentinels, to watch by those who slept; and they, in their turn, would take their repose, while the others acted as guardians of their slumbers, the whole race being of a drowsy make, and very fond of a soft dormitory.

Those who have engaged in encountering a sea-lion, say that it has taken six men, hard at work a whole hour to kill one; and two barrels of blood have been drawn from a single animal, the blubber of which has yielded upwards of ninety gallons of oil.

The seal lion is not a native of the sea. They are all born on the land, and commonly, during the winter season, leave the water where they have passed the summer, and winter on the shore.

The mother usually has twins, and never more, at a birth; these she nourishes as the cow or the sheep does her offspring. The young sea-lion is as large as a hog of the full size.

When Commodore Byron was among the Falkland Isles he was attacked by an animal of this tribe, and came very near being a victim to the terrible power of its teeth.

The commodore's men had quite a battle with his infuriated foe, which tore a fine mastiff-dog in pieces by one bite, before they could overcome his strength, and succeed in killing him.

But Selkirk never had any skirmishes with an enemy of this kind; and after he became a little familiarized to the sound of their voices, it ceased to disturb him.

But he could not help thinking that he should like more company than he had in his tribe of cats, to share with him the joys of home.

Though we cannot trace an exact analogy between his house and *"the house that Jack built,"*

yet there may be found some little similarity in the two establishments and their population.

Alexander sought a goat, to give him milk, to feed the cat, that killed the rat, that gnawed the toes of him who slept, on the bed, that lay in the house, that *he* built.

The way our hero devised to tame some goats, was this. He aimed his musket charged with small shot, at the legs of a kid, which lamed it so much that he could take it. He brought it to his home; and the mother followed. As the kid could not run away, the dam staid by, till both, at length became so tame as to look on their master as their friend, and finally to form such an alliance as not to feel any disposition to leave him.

This method he pursued, till he had a large flock of goats to keep him company, when at home, and to follow him about in his rambles. The mother goats would stand and let him milk them, into his cocoa-nut cup; and their milk furnished a delicious beverage for him, as well as for his kittens. He often took enough, not only to satisfy himself, but also, a portion for them, which he would pour into the hollow of a rock, and amuse himself by watching them in the enjoyment of their sweet meal, till they had lapped it all up.

The goats either came into the house, and laid down with the cats, beside their master's bed, by night, or enjoyed their repose just without the cabin, on the grass that carpeted the earth around it. Selkirk read his Bible constantly, aloud, and cheered himself by singing hymns and psalms. He was constant in his devotions, and became a more pious man than he had ever before been.

Sometimes he amused himself by talking, or singing and dancing to his cats and goats. Though he felt that in this way, he had begun to *enjoy society*, he could not, for a long time, overcome the depression and melancholy, brought on by his isolated situation; and it was more than a year before he could subdue his discontent, and become reconciled to his lot. He kept a regular account of the days, weeks and months, by making notches in the trees which he selected for this purpose.

When the winter season came round, he found that he had been cast in a latitude where the winter was scarcely felt, and where the trees and the grass were green all the year round. He often passed away the weary hours in fishing; and found the streams on the island abundant in a great many kinds of fish.

When tired with one kind of employment, he would seek another. Chasing the wild goats was a favourite sport with him; and his temperate way of living, together with his roving, active habits, gave him a nimbleness of limb, and a speed of foot that enabled him often to overtake them, when he had no other desire than just to see which could run the fastest.

When he could catch one by outstripping it in this way, if he did not need it for food, he contented himself with cutting a slit in its ear, and letting it go. This he did so as to know when he caught a new one, and to help him to ascertain the number that he had overtaken, which proved to be very great in the end. He counted at least one thousand whose ears had felt the knife.

When tired of chasing the goats, he would pass off the hours by reading, or amuse himself in carving his name, with the time of his being left on the island, on the trees; or, in some other way that kept him busy.

By running constantly about among the woods and rocks, he found that his shoes grew the worse for their owner's activity; and this sort of exercise proved not so healthful for them, as for their master. They gave way, and let his feet come to the ground, long before he could find a shoemaker to supply him with another pair.

But this failure did not put a stop to the motion of the feet of the man of Juan Fernandez. On the contrary, they felt the lighter for being unshod; and in process of time, their soles became so hardened, that he could run over rocks and sands, and all the rough surface of the soil, without minding it, or suffering from it, any more than the goats that fled before him, did, when they scampered from crag to crag.

CHAPTER 7

Spaniards Land and Pursue Him

Selkirk found that not only his shoes must be cast aside, but that, time and a wild life, conspired to turn the rest of his clothing into tatters. He had no needle or thread to mend them; but, he found out a way to tack his rags together so as to make them hang on him a little longer; and thereby proved that necessity is indeed "*the mother of invention.*"

He drew out some of the worsted from the remains of his old stockings, and fastening it to one of the nails he had saved, used it as a needle to mend his clothes as long as he could make them last by such repairs. He had in his chest a piece of linen, from which he pulled out threads which he doubled and twisted, and used for the purpose of sewing a shirt which, with his knife, he cut from the linen.

He managed to get it together so as to make him a covering; and when his upper garments failed entirely, he made him a coat and trowsers of goats' skins which he sewed together with fine thongs cut from the skins, and the nail for a needle. He also made him a cap of the same material.

The goats, seeing their master thus habited, felt more strongly attached to him than ever. They did not, of course, consider that his dress had cost the lives of some of their own species; and the hairy coat made them feel that he was more akin to them than they before took him to be.

As he had been long enough on the island, to feel confident that no venomous reptile inhabited it; and to find that no wild beast but the inoffensive goat was among its woods and hills, he often laid himself down by the side of some beautiful stream that was bordered with verdure and flowers, and falling asleep, forgot his solitude in some sweet dream of home, and of the society of man.

The fatigue of running as he was accustomed to do, combined with the murmur of the waters and the songs of the birds conspired to bring sleep easily upon him, during the long and warm days of summer; while his temperate habits and constant exercise rendered it refreshing, and full of pleasant visions. These were the more delightful as his melancholy gave way to resignation to his lot, and he felt a serenity and a cheerfulness of spirits, which, at first, he could not bring to his aid. What it was hard for him to adopt, even as use, in the beginning of his solitude, had now become a kind of second nature, and calling both religion and philosophy to his assistance, he became a better and a happier man than he had ever before been.

He felt assured by the former, that he was under the protection of Him who knows what is best for man, and the chastening that he often needs to bring him to an entire dependence on the only sure foundation of happiness.

From the latter, he reasoned, that man has a great many artificial and unnecessary wants; and that, failing in the attainment of his desires causes the greatest disquietude and trouble that he usually suffers— that he who limits his desires to the actual needs of nature, is the wisest and the richest of his race, and the surest of having all his wishes gratified.

When he took his mid-day nap, beside the brook, or under the verdant hill, the tame goats would lie down by him, or feed near him, so that whenever he awoke he found himself surrounded by his faithful, hairy associates.

His cats, that had now multiplied to hundreds, would follow him and lie down by him, whenever he did not drive them back to keep house while he was abroad.

His knife, by constant usage, and by serving so many purposes for which it was not originally designed, grew short and narrow, and finally became so worn up, that he had to study how to make one to supply its place.

And now, the iron hoops came m requisition. He broke a piece from one, and sharpened it on a stone till he made a blade, and then, with the help of its own edge, made a wooden handle; and these being put together, made quite a convenient knife. He had enough of the hoops left to make more knives in this way, as occasion might require.

It has already been remarked that Selkirk found the winter on Juan Fernandez very mild. He found it brought but little frost, and some slight hailstorms and long rains. During these, he made himself a good brisk fire of the pimento wood, boiled his kettle with such food as he was able to command, and, clothed in his hairy covering, made himself sociable with his four-footed companions, and passed off the stormy weather in a very comfortable manner.

He had been on the island more than two years before he saw a vessel pass. To the first that he saw, he did not dare to make any signal, but kept where he could not be seen from it, fearing it might be a Spanish crew that would take him for a slave to work in the mines of South America. To such a fate, he preferred the lonely isle, and the company of his tame quadrupeds.

But it happened one day, that a Spanish ship made for the island, and her men came on shore so near him, that he could not escape their observation. They took him for some strange animal, and pursued him; but his fleetness of foot enabled him to outstrip both them, and their dogs.

He ran, and they fired after him, without getting near enough to hit their firing mark. He lost himself in the woods, and eluded their sight. He then climbed up into the top of a large tree, and hid himself among the thick leaves and branches.

The Spaniards came to the tree, and stopped under it long enough to kill and dress a goat, but did not see him where he had perched; while he had a full view of all their motions, till they withdrew, and returned to their vessel.

It will be easy to conceive of the joy he felt when he saw the sails of their ship lessening in the distance, as he looked from his green observatory over the wide expanse of water, across which his troublesome visitors were making their way.

"Good breezes to them!" said he, as he descended from his roost, to return to his hut. He felt that he had now escaped a more serious enemy, than he had thought about to assail him, on the night of his alarm from the sea-lions.

In the woods where he took his rambles, he found pimento trees of an immense size, the fruit of which seasoned his dishes; cotton trees, and many others, besides his friendly cabbage tree, that yielded him tender cabbage whenever he chose to cook it.

As the small stock of powder which he had, failed, he had to use his wits in the invention of a way to get fire, which he had till now, obtained by striking it with his gun. He, therefore, after studying on the subject awhile, took a couple of sticks of the pimento wood, and placing one on his lap, rubbed them together till they grew so heated by the friction as to take fire.

The wood, being very dry and light, soon insured his success, and he thenceforth adopted this kind of tinder-box whenever his fire went out, a thing which he took good care to have but seldom occur.

In one of his excursions, he made a very pleasant discovery of a kind of black plum that was sweet and delicious. This fruit grew on trees that were so situated on the high mountains and crags, as to render it difficult to be obtained; but when he was able to come at it, he thought it paid him for all his trouble.

He made a little bag, or basket, with goat-skin strained over a small hoop, and used it for various purposes, one of which was to bring home the plums that he gathered. For, as they grew at a distance from his establishment, he could not always go to pick them, when he felt as if he should like to eat some.

CHAPTER 8

Need of a Companion

One day, when Selkirk was out in chase of the wild goats, he pursued one that fled to the brink of a precipice, the edge of which was concealed by the thick bushes. He seized the goat at the very place and moment when he was about to take the fearful leap, but knew not what was before him, till down they both went, headlong together.

The fall stunned him, and he lay senseless till nearly the same hour the next day, as well as he could judge by the sun. When he came to himself he found the goat dead and stiff under him, and himself so lame and weak, that it was with great difficulty that he made out to reach his house.

But when he did arrive at home, full of pain and bruises, he found little there to relieve the suffering of one in his condition, except the balm which he drew from his bible, for the mind. There was none there for the body, and no nurse, physician or friend to attend him, or administer to the necessities of his aching frame.

The cats and goats, it was true, greeted him with kindness, and welcomed their master back, by every expression of joy which they could make, but this was all. The lonely man drank a little milk from his cup, and then lay down on his bed to rest, moving as little as possible, till his bruised limbs and body got so much better as to bear some exercise. He was hardly able to move for ten days.

Never before, since he had been in his hermitage, had he felt the need of a human companion, as he now did; while his heart was at the same time filled with gratitude towards his omnipresent Friend, who had spared him yet alive, and without broken bones, in this dangerous fall. But as time advanced, he got over his injuries, and resumed his former habits of active life.

To give an account of him, as day after day, week after week, and month after month sped by, would only be to tell the same thing over and over again, as there was little change of scene after he first established himself on the island, and very little variety in his solitary life, except what may be supposed, from the things already related.

When he had been a resident of Juan Fernandez about four years, and four or five months, living in his huts and in the manner described, the time of his removal came.

On the second day of February, 1709, as he cast his eye over the wide waters, where it had so often looked out in vain, for a sail belonging to his own nation, he descried, much to his astonishment, two ships that he knew to be English. He immediately lighted a large fire, for a signal that he wished them to approach the island.

The fire was seen, and the vessels made all speed towards him. They were the *Duke*, commanded by Captain Woodes Rogers,[1] and the *Duchess*, Captain Courtney, two privateers from Bristol. Captain Rogers sent his pinnace ashore, and when it returned it brought a great many fishes of various kinds, but what surprised Captain Rogers most, was the odd figure of a man clothed in goat-skins from head to foot, with a long beard, shaggy hair, and a face tanned as black as a savage.

He looked altogether wild, and, as Captain Rogers said, wilder than the goats, that first wore the skins which now clothed him, could have looked. He had been so long without human society that he could but with difficulty express himself in words to tell his story.

Having invited the men of the ships to go on shore to his humble home, he found that one of them was Captain Dampier, the shipmaster who disagreed with Stradling, and left him to go his way alone, before Selkirk had his falling out with him.

These men were overjoyed to meet each other after so long a separation, and under such circumstances. Captain Dampier, who was now pilot of the *Duke*, told Captain Rogers that he knew Selkirk to be the best man on board the Cinque Ports, when he was in company with her.

Selkirk killed some goats, and roasted them for his guests, and boiled some fine cabbage, which was a very acceptable entertainment; for they had been a great while at sea, and put to severe trials on account of their first being long confined to salt provisions, which brought on the scurvy; and afterwards having their stores fail.

The milk of the goats, as well as their other fresh food, they found

---

1. *Life Aboard a British Privateer* by Robert C. Leslie & Woodes Rogers (the man who rescued 'Robinson Crusoe') also published by Leonaur.

very grateful After remaining long enough on the island to get well refreshed, and to have their curiosity gratified by being shown all the hermit's haunts, they took a good store of goat's flesh, fish, wood, water and other things that they found, and prepared to depart.

Captain Rogers appointed the wild-looking man, master's mate on board his ship; and when the few articles of worldly goods which Selkirk possessed, were removed from his humble little houses, he cast a farewell look on them, and his family of cats and goats, and passed into the ship.

Providential as he considered this opportunity of escape from the solitary spot where he had so long been, it was really a trying hour to the heart of our hero, when he was to take leave of all those objects which were now so familiar; and knew it was for ever.

Nature in this solitude had been kind and pleasant to him and nothing had aimed to hurt or annoy him, except the little quadrupeds that had easily been put to flight by some of a larger kind , and in the one instance when the Spaniards shot after him. No accident had befallen him here, but the one that threw him from the crag; he had conversed with God, with nature, and with his own heart; he had escaped many temptations, and become a more reflective, pious man than he ever was before.

In short, he had learnt wisdom, and he felt a strong attachment to the scene where it had been taught him, and many yearnings of heart did he feel as he turned his back for ever on his now beloved Juan Fernandez, to return to a busy, bustling world.

His habits had been such, that he could with difficulty bring himself to fall in with those of the men on board the ship; and he showed great disgust when they offered him some ardent spirits to drink; neither could he take tea, coffee, &;c. without showing that they were unpleasant to him. His odd ways made much amusement for the seamen; and when he arrived in England, he was an object of general interest and curiosity.

He returned to Largo, where he found great changes wrought among persons and things, daring the years that he had been absent. Some had left their places for ever, and they had been filled by others. The young, ardent and buoyant spirit with which he quitted the village, had been subdued by misfortune, and cooled and balanced by years. He had not realized any of the plans for wealth and grandeur, which had filled his young imagination: but he had stored his mind with that wisdom which "cometh down from above;" and he had laid up for himself a treasure that the "moth could not corrupt," nor the hand of time destroy.

The villagers of Largo thronged round him to hear the wonderful account of his adventures, and his name became celebrated throughout the world. He remained only nine months at home with his family. He then went to sea again, and was never afterwards heard of; so that, from that time to this, none has ever known how he came to his end, or where he spent his last days.

Some imagined that the love of solitude, and his attachment to his island, had become so strong in his bosom as to induce him to seek out some way to return to his hermitage, and his goats and cats.

Others supposed, and without doubt, correctly, that the vessel in which he sailed was lost, and that the hero of the Island had a watery grave.

As it has before been stated, the house in which he was born, and where he first tasted of the salt water, is still standing. In the year 1824, its owner, John Selkirk, grandson of the brother with whom Alexander had his quarrel, died, and left it to his daughter, Mrs. Catharine Selkirk Gellies, who is its present occupant, (as at time of first publication).

Mrs. Gellies still possesses the cocoanut cup, and the chest that served her renowned relation on the island; and she has called one of her sons, Alexander, to honour his memory, and to perpetuate the name in the family.

The cup has been recently mounted with silver at the expense of a Mr. Constable, a celebrated bookseller in Scotland. The chest is of common size; it is made of very fine wood, and joined in a peculiar manner so as to render it exceedingly strong—it has a convex top, and is a curious piece of workmanship. Mrs. Gellies takes great pleasure in showing these articles to strangers, and giving them some little particulars of this story.

The gun with which the hero killed his game and struck his fire, has passed out of the hands of the family, and is in possession of Major Lumsdale of Lethallan.

The reader has now the history of one of the most noted men the world has produced, in this little volume, which embodies the chief of what ever has been, or ever will be known, of the renowned Alexander Selkirk!